BRIAN LUMLEY'S
MYTHOS OMNIBUS
Volume II

Spawn of the Winds
In the Moons of Borea
Elysia

THE ULTRA-HUMAN EVIL
FROM BEYOND THE STARS

It was no natural cold, but an awful condition brought about through the will of Ithaqua . . . frost thickened in the interior of the plane, blanketing it in white crystals that glittered like evil eyes in the glow from the colored panel lights. Finally, completely exhausted of physical strength and drained of emotion, Tracy lay down beside me and crept under the parka . . . hugging my cold form to her. And one by one the glass instruments of the plane's control panel commenced to crack and splinter with gunshot explosions as the temperature fell still further . . .

BRIAN LUMLEY'S
MYTHOS OMNIBUS

Volume II

Spawn of the Winds
In the Moons of Borea
Elysia

BRIAN LUMLEY

HarperCollins*Publishers*

HarperCollins*Publishers*
1 London Bridge Street, London SE1 9GF

This paperback edition 1997

First published in Great Britain in three volumes:

Spawn of the Winds published by Grafton 1992
Copyright © Brian Lumley 1978

In the Moons of Borea published by Grafton 1992
Copyright © Brian Lumley 1979

Elysia published by Grafton 1993
Copyright © Brian Lumley 1989

This one-volume edition copyright © Brian Lumley 1997

The Author asserts the moral right to
be identified as the author of this work

ISBN 978-0-00-649938-1

Set in Times

Contents

In the Moons of Borea

Elysia

SPAWN OF
THE WINDS

For Gail

Introduction

by Professor Wingate Peaslee of Miskatonic University, Director of the Wilmarth Foundation

In 1966 the Wilmarth Foundation recruited a telepath of exceptional talent, a man who could tune his mind to the aberrant sendings of the CCD, the Cthulhu Cycle Deities, and make a sort of sense out of what he 'heard'. Hank Silberhutte was the man: a tall, tow-headed Texan of daring and adventurous, albeit hasty and often hot-headed, inclinations.

Several years prior to his joining the Foundation, Silberhutte had lost a cousin in the cold wastes of Canada. The circumstances had been mysterious; following an unexpected cold snap of especial ferocity the party of six, engaged on government survey work, was suddenly missing, 'lost from all contact with the civilized world.' He joined in the Foundation. Having learned something of the CCD, it dawned on Silberhutte that his cousin's disappearance had coincided with strange undercurrents of unrest in the Canadian trail towns and logging camps, and with the peculiarly feverish culmination of a five-year cycle of esoteric religious festivities as practised by certain local Indians and, farther north, Eskimos.

In short, he became interested in Ithaqua, that fearful air-elemental of the CCD. It was this fascination of Silberhutte's – one might almost say obsession – which, following the very successful part he had played in a major Foundation project, prompted me to offer him the job of researching, compiling and correlating a working file or dossier on this mythical being of the Arctic snows; further, of carrying out his own survey work in Canada

11

on the periphery of the Wind-Walker's domain, and over the line of the Arctic Circle into the interior of that frozen territory itself.

Silberhutte immediately jumped at the chance I offered and in very short order produced an almost Fortean file of related incidents and occurrences, all of them showing definite connections with that monstrous manifestation known as Ithaqua, 'the Thing that walks on the wind.' I was amazed that any single man could have accumulated so vast an amount of lore in such a short time – much of which had previously been overlooked, had gone unnoticed, or was quite frankly unknown to the Foundation archives – until I recalled that the Wind-Walker had a very special attraction for him.

Genial and affable though Hank Silberhutte invariably was, at the merest mention of elementals of the air, Eskimo legend, or cycles of morbid CCD influence, his face would harden and his eyes narrow. He was a Texan and was as proud of that fact as any man of his race, and his cousin had died in the white wastes of Ithaqua's Arctic domain. Enough said.

Perhaps in retrospect, knowing what I knew of him, I should have thought twice about giving Silberhutte the job of tracking down the Snow Thing. One needs a cool head when dealing with such horrors, and the Texan could fly off the handle in as little time as it takes to tell. But the man's physical strength and keen intelligence, his dedication and great telepathic talent, more than balanced the odds and qualified him for the tasks he might need to perform. Or so I thought.

It came about that at a time when I myself was in Denizli, directing the commencement of certain operations in Turkey, Silberhutte was making preparations for an aerial reconnaissance of the Arctic Circle, or rather of its rim, from the Bering Strait to Baffin Island. His reason for this survey, in his own words, was to allow him 'to get the feel of it; to look down on the ice-wastes from on high and see them as a great bird might see them – or as a Thing that Walks on the Wind!'

But of course there was more to his planned survey than that. There would be a strenuous series of treks to follow it, commencing before the thaws set in, for which he intended to prepare detailed routes from the air. Of these treks, one would be across the Brooks Range northwest of Fort Yukon on the Arctic Circle; another would cover a large area north of the Great Bear Lake; yet another should prove to be particularly gruelling and would take the Texan's team along the Mackenzie Mountains Trail to Aklavik.

Tough groundwork of this nature was to be a period of acclimatization for the team rather than an actual frontal attack on the Snow Thing. Those regions where Ithaqua had made his awesome presence known in the past – and where doubtless he would make it known again in the future – were to receive the team's attention at a later date, when its members had been made more able to survive by these 'toughening-up' exercises of Silberhutte's.

Finally, the third and possibly most important of all reasons for this aerial survey: he intended to put his telepathic talents to the test in a series of attempts to search out from the air the massed mental sendings of local religious cults and sects. Strangers of many lands with no easily discernible purposes were massing northward; rumours of a 'Great Coming' were legion among the barely civilized inhabitants of the whole vast region, and whispers were already filtering back to Miskatonic through strategically placed Foundation agents.

This, in the main, formed the core of my knowledge of Hank Silberhutte's initial plan of campaign against Ithaqua. Busy as I was in Denizli, he was now completely in charge of Project Wind-Walker, free to get on with it in his own way. All that I asked of him was that I be kept notified of the operation's progress.

And here I find I must insert something about Juanita Alvarez. Silberhutte was on vacation in Mexico prior to being offered Project Wind-Walker. He found Juanita in Monterrey working as an interpreter with an international firm. She was young and single, very well educated, extremely independent, she spoke four languages without a trace of accent in any of them – and she was telepathic! And here is an exceedingly strange thing; Juanita's talent was in a way as unique as Silberhutte's, for she was only telepathic with him. In exhaustive tests later carried out at Miskatonic, this proved to be an enigma that baffled all the experts. Only Hank Silberhutte could receive her mind-sendings; she in turn could only receive his. It was as if, at their first accidental meeting in Monterrey, Hank had sparked off something in her mind, something that had found and formed a unique empathy with his own extraordinary talent. They had seen one another – and they had *known*. It was as simple as that.

And of course Hank had known that this would be a major breakthrough for the Foundation, because very few members of its telepathic fraternity were actually capable of communicating with one another; those who could were usually only able to receive very vague and ill-defined mental pictures. It was not their purpose to talk telepathically with *people*, but to use their talents to detect the machinations of the lurking, alien CCD and their minions; in Hank Silberhutte and Juanita Alvarez, however, the perfect link of mental communication had been forged.

So it was to the utter despair of the theorists and telepathic technicians at Miskatonic when Hank accepted his new job, and even more so when after some months he left Arkham to travel up to Edmonton with his team, there to form a Foundation detachment for the duration of the project. In his absence they would have to temporarily suspend their attempts to discover what made Hank and Juanita tick. As Hank himself pointed out, he would not be completely out of touch; they could contact him any time they so desired – through Juanita. Still, the professors would have preferred the telepathic 'twins' together in the laboratory, in a controlled environment.

However they might have wanted it, the girl stayed on while her alter ego (that was how they had come to think of one another, even though there was absolutely nothing else between them; there was no romantic connection) was off to Canada at the start of the greatest adventure of his life. In the days that followed, try as they might, the Foundation's experts in mental telepathy could get nothing out of the girl. To all intents and purposes, except for her ability instantly to contact the Texan whenever she felt inclined or obliged to do so, she was telepathically deaf, dumb and blind.

That was how things stood when, on January 22, I received word from Miskatonic that Hank's plane was missing somewhere over the Mackenzie Mountains. Had there been an accident? A long letter from Juanita Alvarez, doubling as a report and confirming the disaster, followed. The following excerpt is part of what Hank Silberhutte's devastated alter ego had to say of the matter:

His call was like an alarm clock, waking me from nightmares that I could not quite remember – but the reality was worse than any dream. It was about 9:15 A.M. and I had slept late. Immediately I was wide awake, knowing that he had called out to me, feeling for him with my mind.

'Hank,' I answered him, speaking it out loud as well as with my mind, 'what is it?'

'Juanita!' he answered. 'Get all of this – don't miss a thing!' And then he simply opened up all his senses to me and let me see it all, everything that was happening . . .

15

. . . The plane was low, skimming the undersides of boiling black clouds as the pilot tried to keep his craft below the weather but above the white peaks of mountains that rushed madly by on both sides. Weaving and bucking, riding the wind wildly and whirling in mad currents of air, the plane fought its pilot like a wild animal, and through all this Hank started to tell me the story:

'We spotted him, Juanita – Ithaqua, the Wind-Walker – and our very first time out at that. It was no coincidence; we were looking for him, certainly, but he was just as surely looking for us. Or at least he was looking for me, and he certainly picked me up easily enough. We were at about N. 63°, W. 127° when we first felt it – that fantastic pull!

'. . . What a bloody fool I am, to go chasing the Snow Thing in the sky, his own element! We can forget whatever remains of that old fallacy about Ithaqua being restricted to the Arctic Circle. To the Far North, yes, but we have ample evidence that he's ventured as far south as North Manitoba, and so he could certainly –'

Abruptly he stopped consciously sending to let me see more clearly through his eyes. Only a few miles ahead of the rushing plane the white peaks reached up to the turbulent clouds. The pilot was wrestling with the controls, trying to pull the plane's nose up into the swirling cauldron above, but the wind seemed actually to be blowing now from on high, blowing *down* on the wings of the straining plane and driving it toward the harsh ice-peaks of the mountains.

Hank could see what was going to happen – what *must* happen – and now his mental transmissions became a frenzied gabble as he tried to tell me all before – before –

'We must have been somewhere between Dawson and Norman Wells when we saw him a great blot in the sky like smoke solidifying taking on a vaguely manlike but gigantic shape a beast exactly as described in the Lawton Manuscript but a description is one thing while actually to see him is –

'Then the skies darkened over in what seemed like only a few seconds and the black clouds boiled up out of nowhere and he walked up the wind on his great splayed feet and disappeared into the clouds. But before he went completely his awful face came out of the clouds to look at us through flickering carmine stars that were like the very pits of hell!

'Juanita – look!'

And again Hank's mind opened up to show me the scene he himself saw at that exact moment of time, allowing me to participate visually in his experience. It was a favour I might well have done without; the Thing that Walks on the Wind had returned.

I had read something about Ithaqua, and Hank had told me a lot more. There is one part of the legend that warns of an unholy curse; to see the Snow Thing is to be doomed, for having seen him is to know that you must become his victim – sooner or later. With me it is sooner. I can no longer close my eyes without that hideous vision of Ithaqua being there, lurking in my mind, behind my eyelids, etched on my memory's retina. Professor Peaslee, Ithaqua is a monster, indeed a 'Prime Evil', a being that never was spawned on this world and could never be accepted in any sane universe.

He – *it* – was there, perched atop that mountain peak directly ahead of the crazily lurching plane, a black bulk against the white snow and blue ice, filling the space between frozen peak and tortured sky and radiating his alienness more tangibly than the sun radiates light. To look at the sun for too long would burn one's eyes out, but to gaze into those carmine pits that Ithaqua wears for eyes – that is to scar one's very mind!

Oh, I can well believe that Ithaqua's curse might work. Out there in the snowy wastes, it must be a very strange and lonely world. A weak person, perhaps even a strong one, having seen the Wind-Walker, might easily be drawn to go in search of him, simply to prove that the nightmare he had suffered was only a nightmare. Then again, perhaps it is the being's mind that draws its victims back again, as in posthypnotic commands.

It could be so, Professor, I know it. Why, I can almost hear his command in my own mind at this very moment! But I am strong and I understand what this hellish attraction is. I can fight it.

There he was, that monster, stretching out his great arms to snatch with massive hands at the plane before it could crash into the peak, drawing it to him until the metallic grey of its wings and fuselage glowed a flickering pink and red in the reflection from the twin stars that burned in his face.

I had seen all this with Hank's own eyes, until the last moment when he deliberately shut the vision out. But even so I could still read what was in his mind. I saw the cold despair and bleak but useless anger and hatred there. So powerfully was he transmitting that I could actually feel the machine gun in my own hands as Hank put a flaming stream of tracers across the snarling dark visage of the Wind-Walker, tracers that seemed to pass right through the horror's face and into the furious clouds above.

Then Hank sought out an eye, and his shells found its centre to pour into it like a swarm of angry bees – only to burst from the back of the darkly massive head as a shower of drifting sparks! And that monstrous being threw back his head and laughed, shaking with hellish glee; but his shaking turned instantly into the hideously aberrant, spastic twitchings of indescribable madness, and this in turn gave way just as abruptly to anger and then to megalomaniac rage as finally . . . I *heard* him!

For until that last moment of time the Wind-Walker had been a creature of silence; indeed, I believe he is vocally dumb, inarticulate – but mentally . . .?

I have been told, Professor, that telepathy is telepathy and thought is thought, and there are theories and theories of which the majority agree that one telepathic being sends thoughts which must be at least partially understandable to any other. It is not so. The minority which has it that truly alien thoughts would be incomprehensible are right. *Nothing* is more alien than the Wind-Walker, despite his anthropomorphism – nothing that I can imagine anyway – and his thoughts are . . . they are terrible things.

I *think* that it was an alien mixture of glee and murderous rage I heard, an obscene flux reflecting telepathically from Hank's mind like images from a cracked mirror, but the thoughts of Hank himself came to me clear as crystal in the final moment. He knew what must happen, you see, and I anticipated his shutting me out.

And I fought him because I wanted to be there, to help if I could. Oh, Hank won, but even as he drove me from his thoughts and back to my bedroom at Miskatonic, still I received impressions of the terrific acceleration he felt as Ithaqua lifted the plane high, high in his hands, even reaching up through the clouds – as a child lifts up a stone to skim across the water, or a ball to bounce.

And at the very end Hank said, '*Juanita, tell them –*'

And that was all, he was gone. There was nothing in my mind at all; it was a vacuum into which the Miskatonic morning flooded as if all the doors and windows had been opened together. And though I screamed for Hank to come back, to talk to me, all the while searching desperately for even the faintest echo of his telepathic voice, I knew that it was over.

There is one other thing, Professor. I believe that Hank's sister, Tracy Silberhutte, was on board the plane. I do not know why; she was not part of his team (in fact I do not think that she knew anything of his work with the Wilmarth Foundation), but she was certainly on board. His mind was full of her, worrying about her . . .

And Juanita was right; Tracy Silberhutte was on board Hank's plane. Later we were to discover how she came to be there, but not for a period of some four months. In the meantime Juanita, no longer of any telepathic value and having no desire to become an agent of the Wilmarth Foundation, went back to Monterrey. Search parties, both aerial and on foot, scoured the area north of Hank's last known position but found nothing; it was as if the plane had been lifted from the face of the Earth.

Then, late in May, when I was busy organizing my expedition to the Great Sandy Desert of Western Australia, Juanita returned to Miskatonic. Her arrival was as unexpected as her personal appearance was changed. She looked as though she had not had a wink of sleep in a week. She was distraught, haggard; when she saw me she threw herself into my arms and began babbling hysterically and incoherently. Plainly she had received a terrific shock.

I immediately ordered that a sedative be administered and that she be put to bed. Even under sedation, however, she rambled on about Hank, about his being alive somewhere, and about the terrible winds that blow between the worlds and the thing that walks those winds, often carrying its victims with it out of this place and time into alien voids.

When the effects of the sedative wore off, experts at the University verified that she was indeed in contact with someone; but while they were able to detect the phenomenon of telepathic communication, they were completely at a loss as to whom *exactly* she was talking to. There was only one thing to do and that was to accept what she said as truth.

It was at this point, too, that one of my 'hunchmen' – a member of a team of psychically aware specialists, the scientifically enlightened counterparts of medieval mediums and spiritualists – asked me a rather strange question. Quite casually, he stopped me to ask if Hank Silberhutte had ever been an astronaut.

I might normally have laughed but was in no mood. Instead I told him curtly that no, Silberhutte had never been an astronaut – what was this, some sort of macabre riddle? He answered in these words, which I will always remember:

'No riddle, Professor, and no offence intended – but after all I am a hunchman. And I'll tell you something: I'd bet a month's salary that it *is* Hank Silberhutte who's trying to contact Miss Alvarez. And one other thing – wherever he's transmitting from, it's no part of this Earth!'

On the morning of June 3 Juanita began picking up a very clear telepathic transmission. The following narrative, relayed through her mind from incredible and unknown voids of space and time, was recorded exactly as she received it.

1
Winds of the Void

(Recorded through the Medium of Juanita Alvarez)

I'm sorry about that, Juanita. I realize now that it must have given you a terrific jolt to receive what must have seemed like messages from a dead man. But I've been trying to reach you ever since we got here three months ago, and –

You say it's been *four* months? Well, that tells me something; it took us a month to get here. And during that month we were all dead to the world except for Tracy, who had the stone, and of course poor Dick Selway, the pilot. He was just . . . dead. I'm not being callous, Juanita, but it's been three pretty hellish months for us, one way or another, and we've seen enough of death in that time to –

We? Yes, Tracy, Jimmy Franklin, Paul White and myself. All right, I'll go right back to square one for you, Juanita – back to where I cut you off when I thought that Ithaqua was going to flatten the plane against that mountain . . .

Oh, I knew we were done for, no doubt about it. And that damned . . . *Thing!* He was massive enough when we first spotted him – shapeless, writhing like disturbed smoke, big as a building – but when he has a mind to he can simply, well, *expand*. He was just starting to puff himself up when he caught hold of the plane with a hand black as night, five-fingered but like a bird's claw, with talons instead of fingers, and his strength was unbelievable.

I thought he intended to crush us; I actually saw the inner wall of the fuselage starting to buckle as he tightened his grip. But then he lifted us up into the sky, way up above those clouds, and for an instant he paused in that position. Juanita, I admit that when he did that I just closed my eyes, gritted my teeth and prayed. And I'm not a man that prays too often.

That was when Tracy grabbed me. Scared to death, all tears and snuffles, just like when she was a little kid sister. She threw her arms around my neck, and I felt the star-stone pressed between us.

I hadn't realized it but the thing outside the plane must have been listening and watching inside my head. He pounced on the picture of that star-stone right there in my mind, stared for a split second – then threw it straight back, withdrawing his mind from mine completely. Only after he had gone was I sure he'd ever been there.

Now, I suppose you caught his thoughts when he was – laughing? – just before he grabbed the plane? Well, I've since learned that his mind-talk can only be picked up when he's really angry or, yes, frightened. Even then, though, his thoughts can't positively be interpreted. But still I somehow knew that when the great beast saw the star-stone in my mind it had shocked him rigid, frightened him. And it had made him angry!

He was snarling and mewling in a frenzy of frustration and rage. I guessed right away then that he couldn't hurt us, not directly at any rate, and for the first time since I joined the Foundation I really appreciated the power of the five-pointed stars. Think of it – a thing that can walk on the wind, an alien monster from God only knows what infinities of space and time – and a little star-shaped stone from Miskatonic's kilns rendered him powerless to harm us. Almost.

No, he couldn't directly hurt us any worse than he had already, but he certainly didn't intend to let us off lightly.

By then I think Dick Selway was already dead. He'd cracked his head against the control panel and there was blood everywhere; he just hung limp, trapped in the pilot's seat. Still, even with Dick gone, if Ithaqua had let go of the plane right then – which I thought he was going to for a second – I think that perhaps I could have landed her. And I believe the horror outside picked *that* little fact right out of my head, too. Only he had worked it out differently.

After being hoisted up to the sky, I had fallen back away from the gun in the nose; now Paul White, hunchman and photographer, made it up there hand over hand and checked Dick Selway's pulse. Whitey cursed softly and pushed Dick's body over to one side, then wedged himself against the gun. He had taken all the pictures he wanted; now he wanted something else.

Jimmy Franklin was still on the radio but getting nowhere; the aerial must have been ripped away. And so Whitey started hammering away with the tracers, hitting the Wind-Walker almost point-blank right in those eyes of his. And all he got for his pains was a shower of harmless sparks from somewhere at the back of Ithaqua's head.

Then the creature was off with us, loping across the Arctic skies in lengthening strides that took us even farther north and farther – *up*! The ice-wastes fell away beneath the plane as we rose into the sky ever faster; the acceleration was tremendous and I was slammed against the buckled wall of the fuselage with Tracy still in my arms.

Whitey, shaken loose from the gun, whirled by us and fell down into the tail section as the whole plane suddenly tilted. Before I blacked out I managed to clear the frost from one of the windows. Looking out I saw a black sky, and away and below I could plainly make out the curve of the Earth.

Yes, frost on the windows, Juanita. That started the moment Ithaqua grabbed us; ice formed on the inside as well as the outside of the plane, but without making us feel any normal sort of chill. Oh, yes, it was a strange cold.

Not merely the subzero temperatures of Arctic climes but an iciness unique in Ithaqua and the weird ways he treads. It was the bitter chill of the winds that blow between the worlds.

From then on until we touched down on the littered plains of Borea – beneath vast, pitted triplet moons that hung low over the plateau on the horizon, eternally frozen in a starless sky – Whitey, Jimmy and I were unconscious. Yes, for a whole month, it seems. Some sort of deep-frozen suspended animation, I suppose. But not Tracy.

Oh, she passed out initially, but later she regained consciousness while we were still en route. She didn't know that right off, though, for there was no sensation of movement or acceleration. She believed that we were down somewhere in the mountains; coming from outside was an eerie whine or hum, like the thin winds of high peaks. The inside of the plane was all white with frost; the windows were completely iced over and opaque; she could detect no sign of life in any of us and our bodies were heavily rimed with frost. Poor kid, she could hardly be blamed for thinking that we were all dead.

Yet in a way she was lucky, too, because the door of the plane was frozen shut, and though she put everything she could into getting it open it simply wouldn't budge. God knows what might have happened if she *had* opened that door!

It was when she realized that she couldn't get out of the plane that Tracy panicked and tried to smash one of the windows in the nose. Well, she could make no impression on the window either, but she did manage to clear the frost and ice away from an area of the glass. And so she looked out.

Picture it for yourself, Juanita: to be in a plane full of icy corpses, like the interior of some weirdo outsize freezer, listening to a strange rushing hum, like a distant wind blowing through a thousand telegraph wires. To know the nightmare of being lost and alone, trapped in an ice-tomb high in mountain fastnesses. And then to peep out and discover that as bad as your plight might have seemed a moment ago, its terrors could never have equalled the horror facing you now. For staring right back at her, with the plane held at arm's length in front of him as he flew through the star-voids, was Ithaqua, the Thing that Walks on the Wind!

Strange starlanes – a hyperspace dimension where inconceivable currents rush and roar in interstellar spaces – and a being of utterly alien energies who knows the ways between the spheres as an eel knows the derelict and weed-strewn deeps of the dark Sargasso. But it wasn't only this sudden inundating flood of revelation that caused Tracy to faint away on the frosted floor of the plane. Neither that nor the sight of strange stars shooting dizzyingly by – like summer showers of meteorites magnified a thousand times – as Ithaqua hurtled through the void. No, it was the *look* on the Wind-Walker's face. It was those eyes, seeming to peel away the metal hull of the plane like tinsel to stare into Tracy's very soul. For she knew that those eyes saw her even as they narrowed in that inhuman face – and she knew, too, that they had filled suddenly with all the lusts of hell.

Thinking back to what Tracy told me when I came out of the freeze on Borea, I'm inclined to believe that time must be different for Ithaqua when he glides along the star winds, and for anything he carries with him. Not slowed down, as might be expected, but accelerated somehow. According to our calculations we've been on Borea for three months, and we left Earth four months ago, but Tracy reckons she slept only three or four times during the whole trip. As for myself, I wouldn't know one way or the other. I do remember dreams – of Tracy's head on my cold chest and her hands on my face, and her voice, crying out to me about the horror outside the plane.

But that's jumping things a bit. I'll tell it as Tracy told it to me.

When she came to after her faint it was dark; she'd accidentally knocked off the cabin lights when she slipped down the wall. The control-panel lights were still on though, and she could see well enough in their glow. Deciding to leave the main lights off to conserve the batteries, she set about making herself a sandwich and some coffee.

That was when she first noticed that despite the ice and frost everywhere she herself was not unbearably cold. And the star-stone about her neck was warm.

She felt a lot better after a bite to eat and a cup of hot coffee; but she kept well away from the windows and refused even to think about what was outside. And through all this there was no sensation of free-falling, none of the physiological phenomena of spaceflight at all; which leads me to believe that in fact Ithaqua was moving *between* dimensions.

Then Tracy noticed another queer thing. She had moved over to sit beside me on the cabin floor, and as she sipped the last of her coffee she saw that my right arm had moved; it had left a clear space in the frost on the rubberized surface of the deck. She caught her breath. I couldn't be alive, could I? No, not possibly. There I was, white as a snowflake and looking stiff as mutton in a freezer. But putting her ear to my chest Tracy listened breathlessly until she heard a heartbeat. Just one, and then several seconds later, another.

From then on, except during those periods when she was sleeping, Tracy spent her time frantically trying to rouse me from my strange, frozen sleep; not only me but Whitey and Jimmy, too. Jimmy Franklin lost the skin off his lower lip through Tracy's ministrations with hot coffee! But for all this she was out of luck and had to be satisfied with the knowledge that at least we were alive when by rights we ought to have been dead.

The answer, of course, lay in the star-stones of ancient Mnar, but she didn't know that. Besides the stone she wore about her neck there was one other aboard the plane – in the first-aid cabinet, of all places. That was Paul White's stone. If it weren't for those stones we really would have been dead by then, all of us. Only their presence in the plane had forced the Wind-Walker to exercise restraint. The ancient magic of the Elder Gods was still at work.

Like myself, this was for Whitey his first really active stint with the Wilmarth Foundation, and he had made the same mistake as I had. I had always sort of scorned the star-stones, in the way a greenhorn soldier might scorn a bulletproof vest before he's seen the terrible mess a bullet can make of a man's chest – or in my case, before I really knew the kind of horror a Thing that Walks on the Wind might wreak. Whitey, a do-it-by-the-book man, had brought his stone along all right but felt stupid wearing it, so he'd placed it in the plane's first-aid cabinet out of the way. Dick Selway and Jimmy Franklin, greener in the ways of the CCD even than Whitey and I, hadn't bothered with their stones at all! And all Tracy knew of these things, of the star-stones, was that the one she wore about her neck, which by then she'd forgotten was there at all, had been my good luck charm, my rabbit's foot.

In fact that star-stone was Tracy's reason for being on the plane in the first place. It was pure coincidence that she had been staying with friends in Edmonton for a few days while I was starting out on Project Wind-Walker. The night before we started the flying programme I attended a party at the home of her friends. I had a few drinks and must have mentioned something of my preparatory work at the airfield. The next morning when Paul White picked me up, I forgot my star-stone and left it in the room where

29

I had bunked down. Tracy found it. Since she intended to start the long trip back down to our home in Texas that same morning, she decided to go via the airfield and return the stone to me. Driving out to the field, she worked out a little prank to play on me.

For some time Tracy and my father had been speculating on my work with 'The Government', and now finally her curiosity had gotten the better of her. She saw this situation as a chance to find out what it was all about.

The Foundation had secured for my team an outlying area of the airport; a fenced-off, run-down, dusty area with its own rather worse-for-wear landing strip. But it was good enough for us and anyway, our plane was no luxury airliner. We had also been supplied with a full-time guard for the gated entrance, though I have to admit that I didn't brief him well. I was hardly expecting trouble, certainly not Tracy's sort. She arrived at the gates, told the guard who she was and showed him my star-stone. She said I had forgotten it and she knew I wouldn't want to go off without it.

Well, Tracy's a damned good-looking girl. She probably turned on the charm. And since the guard could have no idea just what she intended to do, I don't suppose he could really be blamed for letting her in. . . .

Delighted with herself that her plan was working out, Tracy parked her car behind a hangar and sneaked over to our plane. She couldn't mistake it. It was the only one, standing out on the runway close to the hangar. The door was open; she climbed in and tucked herself away in the tail, and that was that.

Some time later, together with the three legitimate members of my team, I left our headquarters shack at the other side of the field and slung my gear into our jeep. We drove to the plane and boarded. Tracy didn't show herself until we were airborne and well to the north. And like a fool, after first blowing my stack, I decided to let her stay. To head back then would have been to slow the work down for a whole day, and the team was anxious to get on with the job. In any case, there wouldn't be a great deal for Tracy to see, would there?

So that was how she came to be on board, and looking back now I suppose it's just as well for the rest of us that she was. God only knows what our fate might have been without her. But I've been straying a bit, I think.

After her third or fourth period of sleep, Tracy woke to an unsettling, irritable and unaccustomed feeling quite different from any emotional disturbance she might have expected to suffer in her present circumstances. She felt drawn somehow to the frosted windows, and even began to clear a large area of one of them before she realized what she was doing, but not before the huge form of the horror hurtling through the void outside began to take on an ominous shape through the glass.

Then Tracy knew that the compulsion she felt and the inner voice she heard in her head insistently demanding that she warm the glass of the window until it cleared to its normal transparency, was not her own but the hypnotically telepathic voice of the being who now rushed with the plane on an unguessable course. And recognizing the fact that she knew him, Ithaqua grew angry. He doubled, then redoubled his mental effort to control her.

She saw his alien lust clearly in her mind even as she stepped closer to the window, reaching out her warm, trembling zombie hands to the task imposed by the Wind-Walker's will. And she knew too, his purpose; to bend her mind, body and soul, completely and everlastingly to his will through those evilly flaring eyes of his, which loomed dully behind an all-too-thin layer of frosted glass.

And instinctively, impelled by horror alone, Tracy's hands flew to her breast, finding my star-shaped talisman there and unconsciously pressing that sigil of the Elder Gods to her heart. Instantly the Wind-Walker

31

withdrew from her mind, recoiling and shrivelling before that abhorred symbol of the power of Good as a feather before a candle's flame. And Tracy did not know why, suddenly, the magnet pull on her mind was at an end, leaving her stumbling, numb, almost completely drained of strength. She only knew that beyond the semi-opaque window those eyes blazed more hideously yet, and that the plane now shook like a toy in the fist of a demented giant as Ithaqua's rage brought on a massive trembling.

She moved away from the window on unsteady legs and gradually the shaking of the plane subsided. For a spell she moved dazedly about the aircraft, listening to the maddeningly slow beatings of our hearts and doing what she could to improve our comfort until, feeling hunger stir, she turned herself again to making coffee and preparing something to eat. And as she was about that task, the temperature began to drop in the aircraft, plunging in the space of only a minute or so from its previously frozen chill into sub-zero temperatures. A sheet of deep white stretched itself over the windows of the nose and fuselage, completely obscuring once more the horror sailing on the winds of the void outside. Icy fingers spread over the metal walls, rubber floor coverings, equipment and motionless men.

It was no natural cold, but an awful condition brought about through the will of Ithaqua. As such it could not affect Tracy, unknowingly protected as she was by the star-shaped symbol of Eld that she wore about her neck; instead it speeded her to the task of throwing extra blankets over our all but inanimate forms where they lay about the floor, to insulate us as much as possible from the incredible cold.

Having done what she could for us and astonished and frightened that she herself should feel nothing of the effects of the plummeting temperature, Tracy turned once more to her coffee, only to discover that though the electricity still freely flowed, nevertheless the water had frozen solid in the kettle. Only then, briefly, did she think of giving in, bursting into tears and crying unashamedly as she tried once more, futilely, to shake me awake.

The depth of frost thickened in the interior of the plane, blanketing it in white crystals that glittered in the glow from coloured panel lights. Finally, completely exhausted of physical strength and drained of emotion, Tracy lay down beside me and crept under the parka that covered me, hugging my cold form to her. And one by one the glass instruments of the pilot's control panel cracked and splintered as the temperature fell still lower.

2

World of the Winds

(Recorded through the Medium of Juanita Alvarez)

When Tracy next awakened it was to find her body a mass of bruises and aching bones. The interior of the plane was in complete disorder but – miracle of miracles! – her three 'corpses' were all stirring, and we were groaning almost with one voice. I can vouch for that last. I most certainly was groaning! My entire body felt swollen and inflamed.

We had obviously been tossed down hard. The door was hanging open on snapped safety bolts; one of the windows had been shattered outward, I guessed by a box of ammunition flying against it; the broken box and a number of ammunition belts were strewn across the narrow deck. Snow was hissing softly in through the open door and broken window, settling in small drifts on the tilted floor. The nose of the plane was down, tail up, at an angle of between fifteen and twenty degrees. I remember thinking as I climbed stiffly, painfully to my feet that I ought to feel terribly cold, so high up in the mountains of the far North. . . .

Then it was a matter of fighting Tracy off. She was hysterical with relief, going from me to Whitey, then to Jimmy, finally back to me, crying and kissing us and babbling out her story, which I gradually began to take in. It took me a few moments to get oriented. I seemed to be more or less whole – nothing broken at any rate, despite the multiple aches and pains – and Whitey seemed fine, too, just a little shaken up. But Jimmy had a nasty bump on his head and he hadn't quite managed to get to his feet yet.

Since it was plain we weren't about to die or stiffen up on her again, Tracy soon calmed down enough to make coffee. She was shivering like a leaf in a gale, which I believed was probably just as much the result of shaken nerves as physical coldness. I managed to get the door shut and fixed up a blanket over the broken window. That would keep some of the cold out, at least. Even though I didn't feel any real discomfort myself, there was no telling what shock might do to the others. One glance out of the door as I closed it had been sufficient to confirm at least part of Tracy's story; we certainly weren't down in any mountains. Outside, under lowering clouds, a vast white plain stretched away, with strangely shaped hummocks of snow dotting it at intervals. In the distance I could just make out what looked like – but then the snow blew up like an opaque white curtain. It was a relief, though, to note that if Tracy's story should prove to be one hundred per cent fact and not fifty per cent fancy, fever or nightmare, then at least there was no sign of the Wind-Walker for the moment. Wherever he had gone, I hoped he would stay there.

But why wasn't I cold? Already the blanket at the open window had frozen stiff as a board, and Tracy was still shivering as if she would shake herself to pieces. I noticed that like myself, Whitey and Jimmy didn't seem uncomfortable, and immediately something began tugging at the back of my memory, something I had read of Ithaqua. The Wind-Walker was able to bring about alterations in the body temperatures of those he contaminated. Were we then contaminated? I suspected that my sister was not.

Breaking into my thoughts, Tracy passed me a steaming cup of coffee. Her hands were white and they shook. I looked at the cup for a moment, then passed it right back. 'You drink it, Tracy. I think you need it more than I do.'

I shrugged out of my outsize parka and wrapped it around her shoulders over the one she wore already, zipping it up the front. Then I moved past Jimmy, on his feet now, and opened up the first aid cabinet. The kit inside was all tumbled about but I found a clinical thermometer and put it under my tongue. I also found Whitey's star-stone.

I lifted the thing out of the debris of bandages and bottles, turning to the other three. 'Who does this belong –' I started to mumble around the thermometer – then dropped the star-stone. It was hot as hell! A tiny puff of steam or smoke rose up from my stinging fingers; the skin of my palm was cracked where I had held the five-pointed star.

'That's mine,' Whitey said, sipping his coffee and starting to look a lot more human. He was frowning, plainly wondering why I had dropped the star-stone. 'What's up?'

Tracy hurried over and took hold of my damaged hand, staring in astonishment at the redly blistering flesh, then at me, finally stooping to pick up the star-stone. I started to stop her until I saw that she plainly couldn't feel the thing's heat. But was it really hot?

I took the thermometer out of my mouth and squinted at it. The scale started at 35° Centigrade, its lowest point – useful if someone were suffering from extreme hypothermia or exposure – but the mercury wasn't showing at that level. It had shrunk back into a silver blob at the frozen end of the scale. I was dead, or should be!

I knew then that Whitey and Jimmy would be the same. Wherever we were, well it could get as cold as it damn well wanted to; *we* weren't going to freeze to death. But Tracy was something else again.

Obviously the star-stone she wore had saved her from this effect of close proximity to the Wind-Walker, but it had also left her as vulnerable to normal low temperatures as she had been before, as any normal person always is. Now I could see why Ithaqua had placed this weird stricture upon us, why Whitey, Jimmy and I had suffered this incredible change. This way Ithaqua wouldn't have to worry about our threatening him with our star-stones. We wouldn't be able to touch the damned things.

I looked at the others and saw a little of the panic hidden in their eyes, the grim fears hiding behind the white masks of their faces. The telepathic impressions I was getting were nervous, disorganized, bordering on the hysterical. Things needed sorting out right now, before matters got worse.

'Tracy,' I said, 'you'd better put that second stone around your neck along with the other. We can hardly afford to lose them, and you're the only one who can handle them.' I brought out my metal security box from where it was stowed beneath a seat and unlocked it, taking out a duplicate copy of my complete file on Project Wind-Walker.

'You'd better read this, too,' I said, passing her the heavy file of papers and documents. 'Then you'll know what you've gotten yourself into.'

While I was busy dealing with Tracy's education, Whitey took a small electric heater from among the items in his personal kit, a tiny Japanese model with its own adapter. He plugged it into a battery-fed outlet. In a matter of only a minute or so warm air began to pour from the grill, driven by a hidden fan. Whitey directed the stream of warmth at Tracy where she sat turning the pages of my file and sipping her coffee.

'All right,' I said to the two men, inclining my head toward the back of the fuselage. We moved into a rather cramped huddle.

'Boys,' I started, 'I think we're in a pretty bad mess, and I admit that I'm mainly to blame. Things happened a lot too fast for me; but that's no excuse, or at best a lame one. Up to now this has been a pretty messed-up job. And again, well, I suppose the fault is mine; I *know* it's mine. So if you're starting to feel that it's high time we voted in a new chief, then –'

'You're joking, Hank!' Whitey's naturally mournful voice cut me off in mid-sentence, his eyebrows seeming to droop from the centre where they met over his nose as he frowned.

'No way,' Jimmy agreed with Whitey, shaking his head, dark eyes bright in his bronze face. 'You got us into this, you get us out.'

37

They were both smiling now, albeit lopsidedly. Whitey continued, 'I'm a hunchman, Hank, and it's my bet that you'll boss this show no matter what anyone else decides. Anyway, we're all equally to blame for what's happened.'

'All right,' I told them, relieved that they were still with me, 'but that's something else we need to decide; just exactly what *has* happened. I don't know if you were listening to Tracy while she was going on about all she saw, her experiences since the Big Fellow grabbed us?'

'I was listening,' Whitey answered, his eyebrows drooping again.

Jimmy nodded grimly. 'Sounded to me like Tracy believes we're no longer on Earth.'

'Yes, that's what it sounded like,' I agreed. 'But we'll talk about that in a minute. First I want to clear up this thing with the star-stones.'

'Confession,' Jimmy sheepishly offered. 'I forgot to bring mine.'

'I wouldn't feel too bad about it,' I told him. 'I forgot mine, too. If it weren't for Tracy we'd only have the one – Whitey's. And I have a feeling that we didn't simply "forget" them, either. No, it wasn't bravado but something else. The Wind-Walker is telepathic; if anyone knows that I do. If I'm right, then it's an even bet he's known about us all along, probably right from the moment Peaslee decided we should have a go at him. I think he's been applying subtle telepathic pressures that have gone completely undetected. I can show you evidence for what I say. Here's Whitey, a strong-willed man. He brings along his stone but then doesn't wear it. Then I conveniently "forget" my stone. You, Jimmy, and poor Dick – you don't bother with your stones at all! Oh, yes, I guess we can be truly thankful for Tracy. She's thrown one hell of a monkeywrench right in Ithaqua's works.'

'And my star-stone really burned you?' Whitey asked, confirming more than questioning the fact.

'Would you like to go and ask Tracy to let you have it back?' I said. 'Perhaps wear it round your neck?' I showed him my blistered hand.

'I'll take your word for it. But how?'

Here Jimmy cut in. 'I think I know. When Ithaqua grabbed the plane we were unprotected, all of us except Tracy. I must have read everything you ever put together, Hank, on Ithaqua. Don't know of a single case where he was involved when there wasn't some mention of this tremendous drop in body temperature. He – he *changes* people!'

'Right,' I put in. 'He brings them under his influence, subtly alters them, imbues them, I believe, with something of his own aura, which he radiates as intense cold.'

Jimmy chewed his lip. 'Isn't that a whole lot of guesswork, Hank?'

'Not really,' I answered. 'The star-stone burned me, didn't it? Just like I was Ithaqua myself, or one of his minions.'

'Are you saying that we are – his?'

'Not necessarily. You've read the case histories. There was that woman, Lucille Bridgeman. She certainly didn't knuckle under to him, and she suffered the same fate. In fact I think we may soon be glad we're immune to the cold. Wherever we are, it seems a pretty grim place. *We* should be all right, but we'll have to look after Tracy. She's more than just my sister; she's the only one who can handle the star-stones. As long as she can do that we're "untouchable" – I hope.'

'Maybe,' Whitey interrupted, 'maybe we *have* to be immune to the cold simply to live here.'

'I know what you mean. You think that Ithaqua has acclimatized us, right?'

'Something like that, yes,' he answered.

'Which brings us back to an earlier question,' Jimmy put in. 'Just where *is* this place? Where the hell are we?'

'That's something that will have to wait, for now,' I told him. 'There are other things we have to do. We ought to take inventory, see what we've got that we can use, decide what should be done immediately, and work out plans to cover as many eventualities as we can think of. That last should be a good one for you, Whitey, although at the moment it's the least important of the lot. Survival is the main thing, but we don't know until the snow clears just exactly what our position is. Or how to improve it.'

'Obviously we can't stay in the plane,' Jimmy said. 'Not for any great length of time. But if we are going to move on, we'll need to take as much of our kit with us as we can carry.'

'The door will lift right off its hinges,' Whitey said. 'It ought to make a good sledge.'

'And of course we have our guns,' Jimmy butted in. 'There's a rifle in Dick's kit, and a couple of pistols. He was looking after the weapons side of it, but now –' He let it tail off, his eyes straying to the nose of the plane where a frozen shape lay wrapped in blankets.

'Yes,' I nodded, 'and we'll need to take care of Dick, too.'

Whitey added, 'If we're going to leave the plane anyway, I think perhaps Dick would be just as happy if he stayed right here. Captain of his ship, so to speak.'

I nodded. 'Maybe you're right. Right now I suggest we see what we can pack away. We'll carry the weapons openly, of course. Jimmy, you can start –'

'Hank!' Tracy suddenly shouted, her voice somehow managing to rise hysterically in the space of that single exclamation.

I half-leaped, half-skidded down the frosted floor of the tilted fuselage to where she stood at a window. She had cleared the frost from one corner of the glass. Outside the snow had stopped. The great plain with its strange snow hummocks stood out stark against a dull grey sky. In the

40

distance a pyramidal structure stood up from the snow. At its apex – a shape. And that shape was unmistakable.

'Ithaqua!' I heard myself say, the name hissing off my tongue.

The two men joined me as Tracy moved shakily away from the window, her hand to her throat. Clearing the frost from a larger area of the glass, I asked, 'How far, do you think?'

'Mile and a half, two miles,' Jimmy answered, producing a pair of binoculars. He put them to his eyes. 'God, look at that – *horror!*'

I took the binoculars from him, put them to my eyes, and the distant scene sprang up large as life. Indeed, the Wind-Walker was larger than life; a fantastic, towering shape, black as a starless night, with gaping eyes that glowered and burned in his awful face. He straddled the apex of the pyramid on massive legs, gesticulating with his threatening arms.

Gesticulating, threatening what? Whom?

I increased the magnification of the binoculars and followed the outline of the pyramid down to its base. People, a crowd of them, on their knees, heads down in supplication – worshippers.

Their faces were indistinct, blurred, but I could see that they were a squat, dark people, most of them. Of Eskimo or Mongol origins, perhaps.

At the front of this prone assembly stood two men, whites, long-haired and dressed in black robes. Priests or spokesmen. Managing to get the magnification just right at last, I focused upon the nearer of the two. European, at a guess; his gaunt face seemed full of fanatic fervour. I turned my attention to the pyramid, Ithaqua's 'altar'. I judged the thing to be all of eighty, maybe ninety feet in height.

'That pyramid is like a damned junk-pile!' I gasped. 'A heap of scrap sheathed in ice. Near the base there's what looks like a small airplane. Yes, I can see the cockpit clearly, and part of one wing. Halfway up there's some sort of tracked vehicle, and a bit higher something that looks like the gondola of a balloon. And, by God, I believe there's a heavy-duty truck in there as well! Other stuff, too, things I can't quite identify. All encased in ice, frozen solid.'

I went on to describe the worshippers at the base of the conglomerate cone, then did a slow sweep of the plain in its immediate vicinity. 'There are totems. Huge carved totems circling the pyramid; Eskimo, I'm sure of it, and crowned with effigies of Ithaqua. These are his worshippers, all right, and this is their place of worship.'

I looked again at the thing standing splay-footed atop its altar, with one great misshapen foot resting upon what looked like the jutting bonnet of an automobile, the other gripping a second projection on the opposite side of the ice pyramid. As I did so I saw him fling out an arm in my direction, the hand pointing.

His black face with its alien contours and flaring eyes convulsed briefly, then turned to stare in the direction of the pointing hand, towards the plane. His other hand lifted high to the leaden sky and the great fist clenched. He struck himself in the chest with a downward-sweeping, imperious blow.

By that time Whitey had found a second pair of binoculars. He too had seen these last actions of the Wind-Walker. 'He's giving orders,' Whitey said. 'Can you get to him telepathically, Hank?'

'I daren't,' I answered. 'Not right now. For the moment he holds all the aces. Later, if the situation improves – then, maybe –'

'In that case I'll voice a hunch; a pretty safe one, too, I think.'

'Let me take a guess at it,' I said, thinking about what I had just seen. 'You think we've been sent for – that Ithaqua has told his boys to come and get us, right?'

Whitey frowned, his eyebrows drooping ominously. He handed his binoculars to Jimmy, then looked around to make sure Tracy was out of the way. She had moved up close to the tiny heater and had her nose stuck deep in my file again, seemingly absorbed in it. 'Not necessarily *us*,' Whitey quietly corrected me. 'I don't think Ithaqua gives a hoot for us.' He grimaced. 'Except perhaps for our entertainment value. But,' he nodded in Tracy's direction, 'your sister –'

At that same moment she looked up, meeting our gaze. She had been listening in on us after all. 'I've just been reading all about him,' she said, her face ashen. 'About his appetites. You don't need to whisper.'

'Forget it, Tracy,' I told her, anger roughening my voice. 'No harm will come to you. I'll see to that, no matter what.'

She tried to smile, failed to make it all the way and settled for a tragicomic pose with her hands held up before her against an unseen menace. 'A fate worse than death!' she shrilled, much too shrilly.

'You just hang onto those star-stones, Tracy,' Jimmy Franklin told her from the nose of the plane. He had taken the gun off its mountings and now dragged it into position in front of the closed door. 'Old Windy will hardly dare to bother you while you have those hanging round your neck.' He sat behind the gun and traversed it left to right and back again on its swivel, squinting down the sights. 'Just let us worry about the rest of it, all right?'

3

Children of the Winds

(Recorded through the Medium of Juanita Alvarez)

From that time on our salvage work went ahead full speed, with one brief break when Tracy called us over to look out of a window she had cleared of frost on that side of the plane away from the altar of the Snow-Thing. And if we had needed convincing that indeed we were stranded on a world other than our own Earth, now we were convinced.

Tracy had started on the job of clearing the windows when she saw how quickly the steady increase in temperature in the plane was breaking up the ice and frost. Obviously we were now subject to a 'natural' cold as opposed to the preternatural iciness generated by the Wind-Walker. The plane's batteries were quickly failing, true, but Whitey's heater had sent the temperature in the plane soaring, however temporarily. That the frost inside the aircraft and the ice on its wings and fuselage were formed initially through the presence of Ithaqua seemed undeniable, but obviously in the Wind-Walker's absence the frozen inorganic residuum of his passing became subject once more to mundane laws and conditions.

Unfortunately the same was not true for my crew. Tracy appreciated the warmth, of course. That was obvious from the way she had thrown off her parkas. We three men, however, remained in that same cold condition to which we had awakened. Not that we *felt* physically cold in ourselves; no, though our body temperatures were such as would not normally support human life, we suffered no abnormal discomfort whatever. To further complicate matters our circulatory and respiratory systems, in fact almost the entire scale of our physiological functions, seemed somehow contracted, slowed down. But not, mercifully, the speed of our mental and physical reactions and responses.

A very ironic situation to say the least: Tracy was affected quite normally by low temperatures of natural sources, but protected from the monstrous machineries of the Wind-Walker while the rest of us were impervious to subzero temperatures but incapable of handling the only real weapons we had against our awesome enemy.

But there I go, straying from the point again.

Let me show you the scene as we viewed it once the windows of our aircraft were back to their normal state of transparency. To one side of us, sloping almost imperceptibly down and away from our crippled machine, stretched a great white expanse that reached to a distant and grey horizon, an expanse dotted here and there with strange piles of snow whose often fascinatingly familiar shapes kept drawing my eyes to them more and more frequently as time passed.

To the other side, topping a very gradually rising slope, a vast, sheer-sided hump of rock sat at a distance of some four to five miles. This solitary feature in the otherwise featureless white expanse was a relief to the eyes, though I admit we speculated rather morbidly about the black tunnel entrances that could be seen in the base of the massive, plateau-like formation. There was life there too, showing especially in an increasing amount of activity about the mouths of the tunnels and behind turrets cut into the icy roof of the ominous stone face, but our binoculars were not strong enough to show just who or what was responsible for this activity, or to what end it was directed.

And how did all of this tell us that we were no longer on Mother Earth? Couldn't we have been somewhere in Canada, in Greenland or Baffin Island, or maybe even Siberia? Well, perhaps we could have been – but not with those three great moons hanging in the sky behind the plateau!

All grey and green, those moons, completely awe-inspiring in the grandeur they lent the otherwise desolate scene. These were the Moons of Borea, though we were not to know what this place was called until later; and those moons moved across the heavens not at all but hung immobile and unchanging always over the horizon. Even the most distant of the three orbs, its disc three-quarters hidden by that of the second, was bigger than the moon of Earth as we had known it.

And it was as I stood there in awe of this scene that Tracy, whose fearful interest was firmly and not surprisingly centred in Ithaqua rather than in this alien planet and its moons, called out to me from the other side of the plane. Two short strides took me to her side; Jimmy and Whitey crowded a second window.

For the better part of an hour while we had worked in the plane the Wind-Walker had simply stood, arms folded across his chest, atop the distant pyramid. His worshippers had remained kneeling during that period, while their lord and master stared out through partly lidded eyes over their heads and across the white plains. Now, however, he was expanding, raising his arms up to the skies, growing upward and outward faster and faster until, billowing skyward like some djinn from an Arabian bottle, he bent his legs and thrust himself up.

Then his great webbed feet spread wide and he walked the wind that suddenly came rushing out of nowhere. Rising up and up, he turned, headed towards the Moons of Borea and, passing high over our plane in an instant, finally seemed to dwindle to a dot and vanish over the distant horizon. Only once did he pause; that was when he passed over the plateau. Then his gravity-defying steps seemed to falter momentarily and his great head inclined toward the world below. His eyes turned almost sulphurous as he gazed intently down; his great arms seemed to reach toward the plateau, about which no single sign of life could now be seen. But then he checked himself and was off again, striding into the heavens. From the time he left his position atop the pyramid, he passed completely out of sight in less than twenty seconds.

That strange wind the Snow-Thing had called up carried now to the plane, flurrying the loose snow in white wind-devils and bringing with it the cries and ululations of Ithaqua's worshippers as they voiced their songs of praise. Eerily they reached out to us on the lessening squalls that shook the frozen blanket where I had fastened it up, filling the plane with an ominous foreboding.

'Batteries are nearly dead,' Whitey said, cocking an ear at the dying whir of the heater.

'Yes, I think it's pretty near time we were leaving,' I told him. 'Tracy, you'd better get back into your parka. Wrap yourself up as much as you can.'

Standing at the window as before, with a pair of binoculars lifted to her eyes, she answered, 'His worshippers are leaving the altar. They – they seem to be – disappearing!'

Again I moved to her side, taking the binoculars from her. For half a minute I gazed. 'They're leaving, yes, but not disappearing. They have white cloaks or pelts; when they use them to cover their bodies they seem to vanish against the snow.' Then I repeated my words of a few seconds earlier, this time with more urgency. 'I think we'd better be getting on our way.'

'All right,' Jimmy Franklin said, standing up as he finished securing his load of packs and equipment. 'I'm all ready.'

'Me too,' Whitey agreed, heading for the door. 'I'll get down outside. You two can lift the door off its hinges and pass it down to me, or simply let it fall. Then you can toss down the extra supplies and I'll stow them on our sledge. With three of us to do the hauling, Tracy might like to ride.'

'Oh, no!' she cried. 'I'm not going to be an extra weight for you three. Besides, I would probably freeze to death sitting still. I'll walk. And I'll do my share of the carrying. Which way are we going?'

Before I could answer her Whitey said, 'Toward the plateau.' He managed a grin and his eyebrows lifted momentarily from their accustomed droop. 'Sorry to anticipate you Hank, but we are heading for the plateau, aren't we?'

I nodded. 'Yes, there's something there that Ithaqua doesn't like, and what's bad for him is good enough for me!'

Whitey unbolted and threw open the damaged door of the aircraft, making as if to jump down – then froze as he stared out at our immediate surroundings. An instant later he stepped back and slammed the door shut behind him. I, too, had seen what waited for us outside, and suddenly the flesh crawled on my back with a life of its own. Obviously not all of Ithaqua's followers had stayed to see the end of his ceremonies, to watch him take his departure. They were waiting on the frozen snows of the plain outside even now, encircling the aircraft in a single row, having approached unnoticed in their white robes.

It was as I had suspected when I saw them through the binoculars; they were of an ancient Eskimo breed, the majority of them, although here and there in the surrounding circle I had seen white faces, too. But it was not the sight of these squat, flat-featured men that filled me with dread and set my flesh to creeping – they were, after all, only men. No, it was their mounts.

Wolves! Great white wolves as big as ponies, fanged and fire-eyed, pawed the snow with heavy pads, tongues lolling redly and hot breath condensing as it left flaring nostrils. And their silent riders sat these lupine mounts surely and with authority, arrogantly. Well, we would see about their arrogance; despite the initial dread that had filled me, we were not without weapons.

'Whitey, get the gun set up again in front of the door here,' I snapped. 'Jimmy, you're a good shot. Get into the nose with the rifle. Pull down that blanket so you can see what you're doing. Tracy, you'd better keep out of sight in the tail of the plane.'

I carefully shot out a window in the wall opposite the door, then knocked the remaining fragments of laminated glass loose from the frame. For a minute or so there was frantic activity in the confines of the plane, then an unnerving quiet. Our breathing began to form plumes, especially Tracy's, and of course she was the only one to actually suffer from the falling temperature. We waited, not wanting to precipitate matters.

From the door, which he had opened just a fraction, Whitey suddenly called out to me, 'Hank, one of the white men is making his way to the plane on foot. He's holding his hands up in the air. Doesn't appear to be armed. I think he wants to talk.'

'Let him in,' I answered. 'But watch him closely.'

Whitey swung the door open, pivoting his gun in an arc that covered a quarter of the surrounding circle. In the centre of his arc a thin-featured white man stepped forward. He was dressed in a snowy pelt that covered him head to toe. He was tall. He moved right up to the door and his head and shoulders came level with the lower sill. I kept him covered while Whitey stood up to slide the metal steps into position.

The stranger climbed the steps, lowering his head to enter, then threw back the hood of his robe and shook loose his hair. It was long and white, complementing the glacial paleness of his face in which, in complete contrast, huge dark eyes blazed with mad fervour. This was that priest I had seen at the foot of Ithaqua's altar.

As Whitey slid the steps back into their recess, closing the door again to its previous crack of an opening, I asked the stranger, 'Do you speak English?'

'I speak it,' he answered, in what I recognized as a Russian accent. 'I used to teach it, at the College of Cultural Sciences at Kiev. I also speak the languages of the Canadian Indians and the Eskimos. I am versed, too, in the tongues of Greenland, Sweden, Finland, Norway and Iceland – in all of the tongues of the lands that encroach upon the Wind-Walker's domain on Earth. Besides all these, I speak Ithaqua's tongue, which is not a tongue at all. The Snow-Thing knew this when he called me to Igarka. There I went, ostensibly to ski in the mountains, and there Ithaqua found me. Now I am the most powerful of all his priests!'

'You're a telepath, then,' I said, making it more a statement of fact than a question.

He turned to face me more fully and raised one white eyebrow. 'What would you know of telepathy?' he asked, in a voice which told me that my own talents were less than important. 'What I am – who I am – is of no consequence.' He looked round the interior of the plane. In profile, the hook of his nose gave him the look of some strange white bird of prey. His eyes became slits staring at Tracy where she huddled down in the narrow tail section. 'What I have been sent to do, however,' he continued, 'is all important!'

He pointed imperiously at Tracy: 'You, girl. You are to come with me – now!'

Before I could deny him, before I could even recover from the shock of his words, which had choked me with astonishment and rage, he turned again to me. 'You are

50

the leader here, yes? I see that it is so. The rest of your party – the three of you – all are invited to join the Brotherhood of Ithaqua.'

His black eyes seemed to burn into mine as he scrutinized me intently; then they narrowed. 'The Wind-Walker is particularly interested in your welfare. We are his people here on Borea, the Children of the Winds, and I am his messenger. You will have a short time to think about his offer. Consider it carefully; the alternative is terrible. Now I will take the girl, whom Ithaqua has found fair, and then I will return for your answer. You have three hours.'

He turned back to Tracy, a devilish smile twisting the line of his cold mouth. 'Come, girl. We go to prepare you for Ithaqua!'

Moving closer to him, I jammed my pistol into the hollow under his chin. 'What's your name, you dog?' I choked, no longer fully able to control my voice.

He drew himself up to his full height, an inch or two greater even than my own, and his eyes were like dark marbles as he answered: 'My name *was* Boris Zchakow, which is meaningless. Now I am High Priest of Ithaqua, who is not to be denied. Do you refuse to let the girl accompany me?'

'Listen, Boris Zchakow,' I answered, my mind seething with murderous thoughts. 'This girl is my sister. Neither you nor any other man – or monster – may take her where she will not go. Not while I live. You came here unarmed, so I won't kill you, not now. But if we ever meet again –'

'Then the pleasure will be mine!' he cut me off.

For a moment longer we stood face to face, then with a contemptuous gesture he turned once more to Tracy. 'Well, girl, do you want to see your brother and his friends dead, and perhaps yourself with them? Or would you not prefer to be one with Ithaqua, bride of the Snow-Thing, and live in wonder and glory forever?' His black eyes blazed insanely.

Tracy had come forward. Before I could make a move to stop her she reached out a trembling hand to the Russian, a peculiar, half-amazed, bemused expression on her face. He took her hand in his own pale claw – then threw back his head and screamed as though pierced through with a white-hot spike!

For a long moment his outstretched arm seemed to vibrate, as if he had taken hold of a naked high-tension cable; then he snatched back his hand and, cradling it, fell to his knees. His eyes were no longer imperious and huge but sunken black holes in a dead white face. As Tracy stepped nearer still he held up his hands before him, cringing away from her like a whipped dog. And then I understood, for the hand with which he had taken hold on her was black as pitch; the flesh curled crisply from the little finger, exposing white bone!

Tracy's face, too, had changed. Gone the bemused, hypnotized look that had fooled me, her own brother, no less than it had fooled the Russian. She again held out her hand, this time palm up, to show him one of the star-stones. Then she dangled it at the end of its chain, swinging it before Zchakow's contorted face.

'You tell Ithaqua that if he wants Tracy Silberhutte, he'll have to take these, too!' she said.

Gasping, sobbing in his pain, terror and rage, with the madness in his eyes beginning to shine out as blackly as before, the Russian slowly climbed to his feet. He held his roasted hand close to him, averting his mad eyes from the star-stone, seeking only Tracy's face as he backed toward the door.

'You –' he choked out the word. 'You *will* be·Ithaqua's, I promise you!' His voice rose, bubbling with insane rage. 'And when he's done with you, if I have to wait a lifetime, then –'

'Out!' I told him. 'Now – before I kill you out of hand!'

I motioned to Whitey. He opened the door – then threw his weight against the Russian's back. With a gurgled cry of astonishment Zchakow hurtled out and down. Moments later he staggered into view on the snow and without looking back made his way to a wolf mount. He was helped onto its back and took a fistful of white mane, yanking the animal about face. He kicked the wolf's flanks, driving it in the direction of the pyramid.

Hunched over his mount's back like some nightmare hag, Zchakow threw up his head to utter a weird, ululant cry that rang loud in frozen air. As its echoes died away there came the sharp crack of Jimmy's rifle from the nose of the plane.

'Here they come!' Whitey yelled, crouching down quickly behind his machine gun. I moved to my window. And then all hell broke loose.

4

Battle on Borea

(Recorded through the Medium of Juanita Alvarez)

Out there on the plains of snow behind the advancing single rank of wolf-warriors, six white-robed priests threw up their arms to the skies and repeated the departing Russian's eerie cry. We heard that concerted wail even as we opened fire on the charging warriors – heard it and saw its result.

As the first of the advancing riders went down beneath our bullets, the grey skies of Borea began to darken over. Black clouds piled up out of nowhere and a rushing wind filled the air with loose snow. Through this whirling white screen the wolf-warriors reached the plane, dividing into two main groups, one battering at the windows of the nose while the other gathered about the door. Whitey's target was a mass of snarling wolf-masks and inscrutable, flat leathery faces. Riders stood up on the backs of their mounts, ready to leap in at us through the open door, only to find a deadly hail of lead spraying out at them from that opening. The snow of the plain in a wide area about the door began to turn red with spouting blood, animal and human alike, spilling out like scarlet pearls on a vast white feather bed. On and on the machine gun chattered its mad message of death, hot barrel swinging in a wide arc.

In the nose of the aircraft Jimmy constantly changed his position, now firing to the left, now right, and the sharp crack of his rifle was accompanied by a steady piling up of white-robed bodies and huge carcasses. In my own position, I was able to lean out of the window and pick

54

off riders as they circled the plane trying to find vulnerable spots in our defences. But seeing that the fuselage windows were too small to admit our attackers, I quickly moved down into the plane's nose to put a shot through a window on that side away from Jimmy. Then we sat back to back. He blazed away with his rifle; I rested my pistol across my forearm as I carefully picked off my targets one by one.

It was a sickening, bloody massacre – there could be no thrill in this wholesale taking of life. And no sooner had this thought occurred to me than the wolf-warriors broke off their attack, drawing back to their previous positions away from the plane and becoming lost in the madly blowing snow. Many riderless wolves trotted after the surviving party of mounted animals.

'Hold your fire!' I cried. 'No point in wasting ammunition.' I looked around the interior of the aircraft. 'Anyone hurt?'

Grim faces turned in my direction. Thumbs up from Whitey; a cheerless grin from Jimmy. Tracy came to me and took hold of my arm. It suddenly dawned on me how cold the plane must be now – how cold Tracy must be.

'Tracy, I –'

'It's all right, Hank,' she hushed me. 'I'm fine.'

'You're sure?'

She nodded. 'I was frightened at first – of the Russian, of those wolf-things – but now I'm fine. Just a bit cold.' She blew on her hands and thrust them deep into parka pockets. 'Didn't Jimmy say that there were two pistols?'

Before I could answer her, Whitey called to me from the door. 'Hank, they're up to something. Come and have a look.'

I went to the door and peered over his shoulder. The wind still moaned like a thousand demons in pain, like all the ghosts of the spaces between the spheres, rushing here and there and flinging up the snow in our faces. Between flurries I saw that Whitey was right; the Children of the Winds were definitely up to something. Having lost about twenty per cent of their number, several of the remaining riders had now dismounted. I saw one of them call over a pair of riderless animals ·and pull their great heads close – and in the next instant I understood.

'They're going to send in the wolves alone!' I yelled. The words were barely out of my mouth when a great white shape came leaping up out of the flurrying snow to slam head and forelegs in through the open door. The huge wolf hung there for a moment, yellow eyes wild above snarling gnashing fangs, scrabbling at the rubber of the floor with massive paws before falling back outside. The sight of the thing had so petrified me that I hadn't managed to get off a shot. Now I pulled myself together.

Whitey had been thrown back from his position, the machine gun too, and as he struggled to get his weapon back into place a second wolf flew at the door. I almost had the door shut when the beast landed; its wild rush and weight jammed the door wide open on bent hinges, throwing me back.

Yet another wolf leaped, sending the gun flying for a second time. The beast found a purchase with three of its great paws before I could start forward, ram my pistol in its ear and pull the trigger. The convulsing body fell back outside.

Now Jimmy had come out of the nose to help Whitey with the big gun, at the same time firing his rifle with one hand, as if it were a pistol. A snarling mask with yellow eyes appeared, framed momentarily in the opening as forepaws gripped the lower sill – then one of the eyes turned red as I fired point-blank into that grinning wolf-face. Again the door was clear, and now there came a brief lull in which I quickly reloaded my spare magazines.

But the lull was far too brief, for as Whitey finally got the machine gun back into position yet another wolf crashed into the opening of the door, scrabbling and snarling hideously as it fought to get inside. Both Jimmy and I fired simultaneously, and again a great white body toppled out of sight.

Tracy suddenly yelled and Jimmy dived past me to pump off three rapid shots at a massive white head that was tearing with slavering jaws at the frame of the broken window in the nose. As the wolf howled and jerked back its bloodied head, so the machine gun coughed back into life. With a wild glad cry Whitey traversed left and right, hurling a deadly stream of lead out into the teeth of the wind.

For several moments he fired until, realizing that this second attack had stopped as quickly as it had begun, I yelled, 'Save your shots!'

The lunatic chatter of the machine gun died away, and with it the howling of the wind seemed also to retreat, crying with a distant voice as the whirling snowflakes fell once more to the frozen plain.

'Save it,' I said yet again, unnecessarily. 'I think we've won the first round. Let's keep something for later.'

Within the space of only a few more minutes the frozen plain outside our aircraft was as still as a winter scene on a postcard. The remainder of the wolf-warriors and their mounts, and a fair number, too, of riderless wolves, stood well back and out of effective range.

And it was then, when even the smallest of the swirling snow devils had subsided, that I saw for the first time the true composition of those previously noted anomalous humps out on the great white plain. Unwilling at first to credit the evidence of my own eyes, I focused on the nearest mass with a pair of binoculars. That unnatural wind called up by Ithaqua's priests had blown much of the surface snow from the queer shape, revealing much more of its basic outline. Half of it, at least, was completely clear of the shrouding snow.

It was a ship. As a boy ships had always fascinated me. British by the style of her, there she lay on the snow, keeled over on one side like some vast, stranded whale. A vessel of heavy steel plates with powerful propellers and a reinforced steering system. At a guess, an ice-breaker of the late '20s, fashioned perhaps in the shipyards of the Wear or the Tyne and long since paid for by Lloyds of London; 'lost with all hands, somewhere inside the Arctic Circle.' Little they knew of it . . .

Again I swept the plain with my binoculars until I found another shape I recognized. And again it was the shape of a ship – a Viking dragonship!

Proudly that ancient sea-serpent prow lifted yet from the sea – albeit a sea of snow – and still a number of round, painted shields adorned the sweeping line of the hull. A *big* dragon, this ship, like Fafnir risen from deeps of frozen ocean, but the great mast was broken and the decks were awash in ice. It seemed to me as I gazed that the songs of old Norse ghosts came whispering to me across the bitter wastes, and a voice that called on Odin and screamed for red revenge.

When Jimmy Franklin's hand fell on my shoulder I started violently. 'What the –?'

'Easy, Hank,' he calmed me. 'It's just me, Jimmy. I've been using the glasses too, and I too have felt it, the aching and the loneliness. The Snow-Thing has a lot to pay for.'

I nodded. 'Yes, he has.'

'See over there,' Jimmy pointed across the gleaming plain at what looked like a large outcrop of rock jutting up through the snow and ice. 'Part of Earth's heritage, stolen by Ithaqua like a magpie might steal a bright button. What do you make of it?'

I turned my binoculars in that direction, focusing on the monolith. The view I got was not as distinct as I would have liked, but nevertheless the outlines of that tremendous *menhir* showed up clear enough to suggest the origins of the primitive but colossal artists whose work it was. Eskimo, very probably, though of no really definite ethnic lineage that I could pinpoint – that mansion-sized block of carved black basalt reeked of age.

Vague images stirred behind my mind's eye – of the gauntly gigantic carvings of Easter Island and the Temple of Ramses the Great at Abu Simbel, which would be dwarfed beside this monumental work – but I guessed, I *knew*, that it was older by far than these. Lost Mu and legendary Lomar might have raised vaguely similar colossi in those ages when the forebears of Khem and Babylon were wandering desert tribes, but this vast sculpture predated even such lost or drowned monuments as these.

Cut into many of the monolith's flat facets were larger-than-life pictures of mighty mammoths, shown mainly in attitudes of frenzied fear, flight, stampede! And beside the carved pachyderms ran men, squat aborigines carrying axes and spears, and also sabertooth tigers, massive reindeer and bison, wolves, bears and foxes. A primitive, Paleolithic panorama, wherein all the characters fled in terror of one universal enemy. And that enemy stood out suddenly in the upper areas of the massive block as finally I corrected the magnification of the binoculars until the hitherto blurred pictures came up fine and sharply etched.

Ithaqua! A crude representation, true, but no less obscene for that, the Thing that Walks on the Wind, a being known and dreaded and worshipped by the very earliest of man's forebears. Alien the Snow-Thing most certainly was, but his *conceit* was almost human. The primitives of Earth had sculpted a vast monument to his might, and he had brought it here with him to this world of snow and winds.

'I think I can understand why he wanted to bring *that* here,' Jimmy said, perhaps reading what was in my mind. 'But why the ships, why *people*? What sort of creature is Ithaqua really, and why does he, well, *migrate* between worlds, between dimensions? I've read just about all you ever collected on the Wind-Walker, Hank, but sometimes I really think that we all must be missing something somewhere.'

'I don't think we've missed much, Jimmy,' I told him. 'But there are certain things that haven't been written down yet – ideas Peaslee has been toying with, odd bits and pieces of information that the Wilmarth Foundation hasn't yet categorized, probabilities that the hunchmen have come up with – stuff like that. And since I've had to coordinate all this, well, I have ideas of my own.'

I put down the binoculars and looked to see how the others were making out. Whitey had made himself comfortable behind the machine gun. A cigarette drooped from his mouth and he appeared to be completely relaxed. His finger lay alongside his weapon's triggerguard, however, and his partly hooded eyes were sharply alert as they moved slowly over the thinned ranks of the seemingly impassive wolf-warriors. Tracy was merely a green and brown bulk in her camouflaged parka, calmly watchful where she half-reclined in a leather bucket-seat in the nose of the plane. I couldn't see her face for she had the hood of the inner parka up over her head, but her breathing made small regular plumes in the icy air.

Jimmy looked at me expectantly. 'Go on, I'm still listening,' he reminded me.

I paused for a moment to sort out my thoughts, then began to talk. 'All right, let's see if I can tell you something you don't already know.' It seemed a good idea at that, to chat about it, pass a little time until – until whatever was going to happen, happened.

'Ithaqua,' I began, 'is a horror come down the ages from the very mists of myth. He was known to the Ptetholites and his image may be found on Auderic cromlechs. The ancient peoples of all the lands adjacent to the Arctic Circle have left evidence of his being, and as recently as the early nineteenth century certain North American and Canadian Indian tribes have fashioned likenesses of him on their totems. Just such as we've seen on the totems of his worshippers here on Borea.'

'Speak up, big brother,' Tracy's voice interrupted, coming to me from the front of the plane. She inclined her head slightly in my direction. 'I'm not quite in on all of this yet, so if there's anything else I should know I'll gladly listen in.'

I nodded, pleased with her plucky acceptance of everything, and raised my voice. 'Among many other names, Ithaqua has been called "God of the Great White Silence", "the Snow-Thing", "God of the Winds", "the Death-Walker", "the Thing that Walks on the Wind", "the Strider in Strange Spaces", "the Wind-Walker" and "Lord of the Winds". Such is his fascination, his morbid attraction for various popular writers that they have created remarkably good fictions based upon the ancient legends. Algernon Blackwood, a British author of world-wide repute, no doubt fashioned his "Wendigo" on Ithaqua; and August Derleth, whose home was in Wisconsin and not so very far removed from the far northern territories, was the author of a number of extremely original and remarkable accurate stories about Ithaqua's incursions.

'He is the original air-elemental, in which every other Earthly myth and legend having regard to beings of the air has its source. The prototype of Gaoh, Chastri–Shahl, Quetzalcoatl, Negafok, Hotura, Tha'thka and Enlil, Ithaqua is given mention in the most ancient and most forbidden works known to man; and his winged totem-symbol is carved upon Geph's broken columns and crumbling stelae along with the insignia of the rest of the loathsome Cthulhu Cycle Deities. For of course Ithaqua is of the CCD, a prime elemental whose true origin is as dim and conjectural as that of the Universe itself.

'The Wilmarth Foundation believes that in forgotten prehistoric times, in ages predating Earthly life as we know and recognize it in its mundane forms, there was a battle. Earth and the Solar System formed the battle-ground. Beings of whom little is now known – super scientists named in those same forbidden books I have already mentioned as "the Elder Gods" – won the interplanetary war. The CCD, defeated but still threatening, were banished to prison environments. Mental and genetic blocks were planted upon them, imprinted *within* them, just as modern criminals are made to wear handcuffs or shackles. These blocks were designed to repeat through heredity, so that any offspring of the CCD would be imprisoned by those same restrictions no less than their forebears.

'Ithaqua was perhaps the least penalized of all the Cthulhu Cycle Deities in that he was banished to the alien star-winds which he still walks and, on Earth, to the windswept ice-wastes of the Arctic Circle and lands adjacent. In this he is the fulcrum upon which the futures of all his alien "cousins" of the cycle balance. Compara-tively free of the restrictions of the Elder Gods, he is the hope of the CCD; he is the one to whom all of the others look for eventual release from their immemorial impris-onment. And that is not his only ambition.

'Ithaqua is miscegenetic, with a taste for strong, beau-tiful white women. In this respect as in all others he is completely unscrupulous, sating his lusts whenever the mood takes him and with whatever woman is unfortunate enough to be to hand. He has already foisted children upon mankind – mated with "the daughters of Adam" – but of his progeny there are no known survivors. Three children there were that we know of, all of them born to white women; and all of them, mercifully, too alien to live. There may have been others that we don't know of, but that seems unlikely.

'Certainly, though, there have been other women out in the snows; women who have known Ithaqua's attentions without being strong enough, either physically or mentally, to suffer them and live knowing what they knew. Why, there's evidence to show that the Wind-Walker has had whole communities of worshippers in Canada, and that human sacrifices are still periodically made to him. Nearly always young, attractive women. As to why he desires children —'

'It's a terribly lonely existence,' Whitey cut in, 'walking the spaces between the spheres.'

I nodded. 'Yes, that's probably it in a nutshell.'

'That – *thing* – lonely?' Jimmy Franklin frowned. 'But loneliness is a human emotion, surely?'

'What about a swan that loses its mate?' Tracy argued, 'or a dog when his master dies? Surely that is loneliness?'

Whitey half nodded his head, half shook it in a curiously self-denying gesture. 'He *is* lonely,' he said, 'but it's a loneliness that's different from anything we could ever conceive of. And it's more than just loneliness, too. He has a definite purpose.'

'Whitey's right,' I agreed, 'I'm sure of it. It all goes back to the monster's ultimate purpose, that of freeing his hellish kith and kin. Think about it; there's only one Ithaqua, one Wind-Walker, and his ambition is to turn all of his alien, hideous cousins loose from their many prisons. Cthulhu from sunken R'lyeh, Hastur from the Lake of Hali, Yog-Sothoth from some dark dimension – oh, all of them.

'But if there were *two* such as Ithaqua, two "Things that Walk on the Winds", why, then the task would be that much easier. And if there were three – four?

'The mercy is that he is not invincible. There are weapons which work against him. We have such weapons in the star-stones from forgotten Mnar.' I looked at my hand, at the large blisters that covered my palm, and I laughed ruefully. 'True, only Tracy can handle the things, but that's a lot better than –'

'Hank!' Whitey called. I looked at him in time to see his eyebrows shoot up, then lower again quickly as he squinted down the sights of his machine gun. 'Reinforcements,' he grunted.

I jerked the binoculars up to my eyes and scanned the white plain in the direction of the pyramid altar.

Reinforcements, yes! Led by the Russian priest they came, gathering out of the ice-shrouded bases of the plain's weird hummocks. For those relics of Ithaqua's visits to Earth over eon-embracing ages were nothing less than the artificial wigwams and igloos of these Children of the Winds, provided for them by their Lord and Master, Ithaqua of the Snows. Wolf-warriors in their hundreds, and in their midst a large sledge, and upon that sledge –

'What do you make of that, Jimmy?' I asked.

'I would say it was a totem,' he answered. 'A heavy pole, lashed to the sledge and carved with faces and figures.'

'Yes,' Whitey snorted derisively, 'it would need to be a heavy pole. It *has* to be.' He looked at me and his eyebrows drooped ominously. 'It's a battering-ram!'

5
Ships of the Snow

(Recorded through the Medium of Juanita Alvarez)

As the great sledge bearing the battering-ram totem drew closer, the wolf-warriors formed a circle round our crippled airplane as before, only now they were three and four ranks deep. There must have been twelve hundred men and beasts surrounding us, and I doubted that we had enough ammunition to fire more than one shot at each of them. Even then, if every single round we fired found its target, we would still be swamped, inundated by sheer numbers.

The battering-ram was all of fifty feet long. Drawn by a dozen massive wolves in harness, with the leading pair bearing riders, it bumped roughly over the snow, jerking at the lashings that held it to the straining sledge. Cut from some giant pine the thing must have been, though as yet I had seen no tree growing on Borea, carved in designs of gods and devils, its head shaped into a blunt likeness of Ithaqua. That heavy head now pointed toward the plane, and as the wolf-warriors gave way to let the totem through their ranks its purpose suddenly became obvious. The nose of our craft was mainly of laminated glass and comparatively thin metal frames; the ram was directed straight at that fragile bubble.

'Whitey,' I said, knowing that the battle must break at any moment, 'whatever else you do, try to bring down those wolves pulling the totem. Same goes for you, Jimmy. Tracy, you give Jimmy cover; I'll cover Whitey from the door. Make all your shots count.'

Now, as the circle of wolf-warriors tightened and beasts and riders drew closer to the plane, a contingent of them gathered around the totem-bearing sledge, making the animals that pulled it much more difficult targets. Closer the sea of faces came – flat faces and copper faces, slant-eyed and straight, Eskimo, Indian and white – faces and pointed muzzles.

'If we don't cut loose soon,' Whitey breathed, 'we'll never thin them down.'

Even as he spoke the closing ranks began to move faster, human heels digging into animal flanks in a concerted spurring. From behind the wolf-warriors an eerie cry rang out in the frozen air: the wailing of the Priests of Ithaqua, begging the Wind-Walker to look favourably upon his warriors in battle.

'Here they come,' I yelled. 'Now . . . *let them have it!*'

The words were hardly out of my mouth before they were drowned by the stuttering rattle of the machine gun and the rapidly repeating crack of the rifle. Down went a dozen of the warriors escorting the battering-ram, one of them vanishing with a scream beneath the runners of the great sledge, and Whitey's roaring battle cry rang out triumphant – only to turn to a yelp of surprise as the first of the mounted Eskimos and Indians reached the plane.

A mass of white fur flashed by the jammed door; simultaneously a squat figure hurtled into the plane over the top of Whitey's deadly arc of fire. My single shot, striking the Eskimo in the chest, threw him sideways, dead before he hit the floor. Down he crashed, his fur-clad feet flopping across the barrel of the machine gun. The gun's chattering stilled at once and shapes swiftly gathered at the door. I fired point-blank into dark and light faces and slavering, snarling muzzles alike until my pistol was empty – but by that time Whitey had freed the gun.

Now he traversed the weapon, triggering it back into deadly life. But though the gun was alive its harshly uttered message was death. Death flew out through the open door in an arc, slicing into the wolf-warriors milling on the bloody snow. Whitey's attention, however, had been successfully drawn from the battering-ram; in the next instant we knew that the first stroke of that wolf-drawn totem was a telling one.

Still firing rapidly, Jimmy Franklin gave a sudden yell of warning as there came a tremendous crash from the nose of the plane. In the same second, caught unawares and in the act of reloading, I was thrown off my feet as the entire aircraft jerked violently. Whitey, firing the machine gun with one hand, somehow managed to hang on until the rocking of the plane subsided. Then the firing-pin of the machine gun fell on an empty chamber; the ammunition belt was exhausted.

I grabbed up another belt and threw it towards Whitey, kicking as I did so at a flat, oval-eyed face that appeared suddenly over the lower sill of the door. Then I was sent hurtling backward, knocked off my feet by a huge furry shape that shot in through the door with outstretched paws and bared fangs. Sprawling on my back I threw up my pistol against the pony-sized wolf crouching over me. I looked straight into the eyes of death as the beast's hideous muzzle descended. Then my bullet went in through his dripping jaws to blow out the back of his skull, lifting him from me with the shock of its impact. I rolled out of the way as the toppling, shuddering carcass collapsed with a crash where I had lain.

Through all of this it dawned on me that I had not heard the crack of Jimmy Franklin's rifle since the jarring crash when the totem struck the plane. Similarly the spitting sounds of Tracy's pistol had been absent. Now, as I leaped to my feet, the machine gun began to snarl once more to the accompaniment of Whitey's whooping. Mercifully, when the great wolf had leaped at me, it had done little more than pass over Whitey's head, causing him

67

to duck down and momentarily lose control of his weapon.

I saw this and barely had time to breath a sigh of relief before a gasp from Tracy swung me in her direction. She was spreadeagled against the curving wall of the plane, moving slowly away from the shattered nose section, staring back hypnotized at a squat white figure that moved after her with outstretched arms. She pointed her empty pistol at the Eskimo warrior, repeatedly, uselessly pulling at the trigger. Over and over she gasped my name.

At Tracy's stumbling feet, stretched on his back with a great bruise shining on his forehead, Jimmy Franklin lay, his rifle inches from hands that were limp and motionless. Faster the Eskimo moved after Tracy, black eyes glittering as he grabbed at her. In that same moment the head and shoulders of a second wolf-warrior appeared at the gaping hole where half the plane's nose had been caved in.

I aimed my pistol as carefully as my shaking hand would allow, pulled the trigger, aimed and fired again. My first shot went high, but was nonetheless effective for that. It seemed that the face of Tracy's attacker had barely flown apart, his corpse slamming backward into the nose section like a felled tree, before the second Eskimo was flying out through the gaping hole in the nose of the plane. As he went his arms flapped loosely, nervelessly, while the white furs on his upper body turned red in a sudden spouting.

I dropped to one knee beside Jimmy, snatched up his rifle and pumped off one quick shot into the wreckage of the nose section where I thought I saw a movement beyond the shattered windows. Then I slapped the downed man's face until he opened his eyes. Groggily he lifted his head from the floor and tried to get up; he was not seriously hurt.

'What happened?' he asked.

'You got a knock on the head,' I told him. 'Here, take your rifle.'

As I began to busy myself, swiftly reloading magazines for Tracy's and my own weapon, suddenly the lunatic chatter of the machine gun died. There came an abrupt, unbelievable silence; then, filling that silence, springing up all around the aircraft, came the moaning of vast winds.

Listening to that wind I felt the hair of my neck rise. I knew that it was unnatural, this wind, but I was equally sure that its source was *not* Ithaqua. This wind was – different. I felt not chill in my heart, my soul, listening to the blowing of this wind – only a sense of awe, of wonder.

'Whitey, what is it?' I cried. 'Why have you stopped firing?'

'Gun jammed,' he hoarsely answered, his hands tearing ineffectually at the breech-block mechanism of his weapon. 'Can't be fixed this side of – of Earth!'

'But what's happening?' Jimmy Franklin asked, staggering to a window.

Whitey's eyes went wide and his black eyebrows lifted. He peered out through the door and across the white wastes. The moaning of the wind grew louder, intermingled now with strange low cries of – fear? – from the horde outside. Snow blew into the shattered nose section, whirling along the inside of the plane and settling on our parkas. The wind howled more mournfully yet.

I went to the door, stood there beside Whitey and gazed out onto the plains of Borea. The wolf-warriors were lining up, reforming their ranks parallel to our battered aircraft, but their faces were turned away from the plane and they gazed as one toward the enigmatic plateau. Though the bodies of hundreds of their erstwhile fellows littered the snow, they had momentarily forgotten us and their attention was centred upon something else.

Then, from the direction of the pyramid altar, two more sledges rushed forward toward the lines of warriors. They were hauled by howling wolves that answered to the crack of Eskimo whips, and they were laden with weapons; large, tomahawk-like axes, harpoons and spears.

'I wondered where all their weaponry was,' Jimmy Franklin said. 'It looked for a while as though we were supposed to be taken alive. But now – now it looks like we're really in for it!'

Whitey studied the scene out on the snows a moment longer and his eyebrows knitted as his frown deepened. 'No, no. Those weapons are not intended for use on us.'

'What do you mean?' I questioned.

He grinned in answer, then pulled me over to the opposite window. Louder and louder howled the eerie wind, blowing now quite perceptibly from the direction of the plateau, bringing with it the sound of – *slapping sails and creaking rigging!*

'It's my hunch we're about to be rescued,' Whitey grinned again. 'Look, here comes the cavalry!'

I looked, and at first could not believe my eyes.

Down the gradual slope from the plateau they sailed, majestic and awesome on huge skis, with billowing triangular sails reaching high into whistling air – platforms with shallow hulls, upon whose decks crouched half-naked warriors amid what at first appeared to be great heaps of furs – ships, a dozen of them, sailing the snows! I snatched my binoculars up to my eyes incredulously, cursed the flurries of snow blown up by the phantom wind to obscure my vision, then finally managed to focus on one of the snow-ships.

Triple skis each perhaps forty feet long and six wide, one fore and two aft, supported the structure of the snow-ship's deck; the high mast was secured fore and aft, port and starboard with heavy lines. Crouching behind narrow gunwales were the warriors, wiry white bodies and squat brown ones together, gleaming with oils, eyes eager and staring straight ahead. And those piles of furs I had seen – now I could make them out more clearly. Piles of fur they were indeed, but more fearsome furs a man never saw.

Suddenly one of them *stood up*, a great white mass that pawed the air and stretched itself, dwarfing its human master. Then the warrior jumped up to throw an arm about the animal's neck and pull it down again to the deck. But I had seen it, and could only gape in amazement.

A bear! They were all bears, those vast furry heaps, huge white Polar bears almost twice as big as any I ever saw in the zoos of Earth.

'The – the cavalry.' I lamely echoed Whitey's words.

'Right,' he nodded, turning to step back to the door, 'and just look at those so-called "priests" run!'

The two sledges were flying back across the snows now, back toward the pyramid altar. Emptied of their weapon loads, now they carried the priests of Ithaqua three to a sledge. Like rats from a sinking ship. 'No fighters, those priests,' Whitey muttered.

'Jimmy,' I swung about, an idea forming in my mind. 'How do you feel?'

'I think I'm all right,' he answered, gingerly fingering his bruise. 'An almighty headache, that's all.'

'And you, Tracy?'

'Fine, Hank,' her voice began to tremble, then steadied. 'But what's on your mind?'

'Whitey reckons that these ships and their crews are here to dig us out of this mess we're in. I say let's make their job a bit easier. We can perhaps leave the plane and fight our way over to the men of the ships. If they are here to pull us out of the fire, they'll be able to disengage that much earlier and take us back to the plateau. Who's for it?'

All three nodded as one person; then Whitey reminded, 'We have only three guns among us.'

71

'We'll keep Tracy in the middle,' I answered. 'Form a triangle around her. Jimmy keeps his rifle; you and I, Whitey, have the pistols.'

'And all these supplies of ours, that we planned to take with us?' Jimmy asked.

'They may still come in handy,' I told him. 'We'll take them.'

The three of us tugged and wrestled at the door while Tracy urged us on. Finally we forced it from bent hinges, letting it fall onto the reddened snow outside. We quickly threw down our belongings and equipment, then jumped down ourselves. Tracy came last, dropping into Jimmy's arms.

Now we could clearly hear the swish of the great skis and the crack of snapping sails. Hurrying around under the tail of our crippled aircraft, loaded down with equipment and hauling a sledge heaped high with bundles, we caught our first glimpse of the two factions as they faced up to one another.

The snow-ships were still now, twelve of them in a line, sails already half-furled and decks half-cleared; and the gleaming warriors who had crowded those decks were mounting massive bears on the plain and moving their mounts into a tight formation. Men and bears; a fearful army, a fantastic sight!

In their right hands the fighting men of the ships carried lances, and swinging from their leather waist-belts were picklike weapons, polished bright. The bears, of course, required neither arms nor armour; their furs were thick and their hides tough, and their terrible claws were the most lethal weapons for hand-to-hand fighting that I had ever seen. The two armies of warriors, both double-ranked now, moved toward each other. Fur-clad Eskimo, Indian and white man, spurring on their huge wolves; face to face with men of similar origins but different ideals and creeds, mounted on massive Polar bears. The armies moved closer, seemed to poise for an instant of time on the white plains of Borea, then rushed together in the clash and roar of terrible battle!

In a moment the double line of wolf-warriors broke and the bears surged through the gap, tearing all apart that stood in their way. But for all their giant strength and determined ferocity, not all of them won through. I saw one bear go down, hamstrung by the slashing claws of a great wolf; but even as the Eskimo rider of the bear fell, so he hurled his weapon at a mounted, copper-coloured wolf-warrior. Such was the force of the Eskimo's hurled lance that even striking its target a glancing blow it lifted the Indian from his wolf's back. In another second the two unseated men were hand-to-hand, and in the next the squat man of the snow-ships had driven his bright picklike weapon through the proud hawk face of the redskin wolf-warrior. Then the battle surged over that gory, heroic scene and it was lost to me.

We ran as best we could toward the break in the ranks of the Children of the Winds, hauling our sledge behind us, keeping close together and forming a knot around Tracy. As we went we fired our weapons at the closest of the wolf-warriors and their mounts. We had been spotted as we left the plane and this closest group of our previous attackers was already fighting its way desperately toward us; the wolf-warriors did not intend to let us go so easily. Then additional orders were given by someone behind us, from the direction of the distant pyramid.

A strange, drawn-out ululation sounded, and it caused a greater contingent of the fighting wolf-warriors to wheel about face and come racing back toward us!

Cursing the utterer of that cry out loud, glancing back as I urged the other three on to the spitting song of the pistols and the cracking tune of Jimmy Franklin's rifle, I saw a sleek sledge knifing over the plain. The crusty snow flew in a white sleeting as bright runners cut through it, crushed it, hurled it aside. Six massive wolves hauled the sledge at a loping run, labouring under the whip of an Eskimo driver, and holding to the skimming vehicle's chariotlike prow crouched a half-dozen of the fiercest, largest men I have ever seen. Giants all, only three of these prime warriors were Eskimo; two others were copper-skinned Indians, the last a white man.

Ah, yes. And behind them crouched the utterer of that ululant alarm: Boris Zchakow, the fanatic, wind-maddened Russian. Ithaqua's number one priest. Behind Zchakow's sledge sped two others recently fled, returning again with their complement of lesser priests; and bringing up the very rear, at a distance of about a mile, as many wolf-warriors again as I had yet seen.

Twelve, no fifteen hundred of them. All armed and hurtling pell-mell in a strong, wedge-shaped formation, harpoons and spears tilted forward – and then, even as we threw ourselves to one side to sprawl on the frozen snow, the runners of the leading sledge hurled ice in our faces as it careened past. The six great warriors leaped from it to rush upon us. Now I could see that they carried metal shields – and huge metal tomahawks!

Crouching low, advancing with their weapons held high, they closed in a circle backed by a dozen wolves and their riders. From my prone position I could see the Russian priest's face. His eyes were triumphantly ablaze as, behind the advancing warriors, he peered over the prow of the now stationary sledge.

'Zchakow, you dog!' I yelled, firing one quick shot in his direction. I saw splinters fly from the sledge's woodwork near his face, then was forced to turn my weapon to more immediate work. Almost upon us, at point-blank range, was a furclad giant, then a second. My first shot clanged harmlessly off metal, the second took its target full in the throat above the giant's shield. This was the white man,

74

towering at least seventy-eight inches and broad-bodied, screaming bubblingly and clawing at his scarlet throat as he went down in a welter of blood. Far from deterring the remaining five warriors, my shots seemed to spur them on. They leaped forward –

Jimmy Franklin's weapon had more penetrating power than the two pistols; crouching, he now slammed round after round into whichever target presented itself. Two of the huge Eskimos and an Indian fell, gaping holes showing in both shields and bodies. A pair of the wolf-warriors, too, reeling bloodily from their mounts. My own and Whitey's weapon both were taking their toll in support of the rifle, but they were simply not enough. Spears flew; the warriors rushed in; tomahawks flashed –

Knocked down, I rolled, and hearing a shrill scream from Tracy bounded back to my feet. Whitey was down, struggling with the shaft of a spear where it pinned his thigh to the snow. A great arm had snatched my sister aloft to throw her across a broad, fur-draped shoulder. I fired a bullet straight into the heart of the hawkfaced redskin who held her struggling form, heard his scream as he toppled.

Tracy fell beside me, winded and sobbing. Whitey had passed out flat on the snow. Jimmy Franklin's hoarse cry rang out, bringing me whirling about in a crouch to seek a new target. None was near. Some way off stood the single remaining giant Eskimo. I aimed at him carefully and pulled the trigger. The hammer fell on an empty chamber.

Now I saw that Jimmy deliberately held his fire, noticed that the special force of wolf-warriors had fallen back along with the sole surviving giant. And yet still the Russian priest roared with rage from the safety of the sledge. Without understanding a single word of the language he spoke I knew that he goaded them on, calling them cowards and heaping all kinds of insults upon them. But they were not listening to him, and though they were suddenly

75

fearful I knew that it was neither fear of my pitifully small party nor of our marvellous weapons that stayed them.

They stared at something behind us, *above* us – stared open-mouthed, wide-eyed – fearfully! They lowered their weapons and backed still farther away from us, a lone foot-soldier springing into the saddle of a riderless wolf; and all the time they stared, yes, and they *listened*.

In another second the mad Russian's roaring stopped abruptly as he, too, looked beyond and above us, stared and listened. Now there was an amazing hush as the armies froze in the midst of bloody battle. Slowly we turned our heads, Tracy, Jimmy and I. We looked in the direction of the plateau.

PART TWO

1
Woman of the Winds

(Recorded through the Medium of Juanita Alvarez)

Staring at the sky above the low, ominous outcropping of the plateau, I thought: *One of two things: either these people have especially sensitive hearing, or they are accustomed to listening for things that I would not normally expect to hear.*

But then I did hear it; a whirling of high winds, a great tumult in the heavens of Borea whose physical effects could not for the moment be felt on the plain where I stood. Then, slowly but surely, the whirling became a rushing, a roaring as of a swollen river.

Since the battle on the plain first began the skies had been piling up with cloud. Over the plateau the air was dark and writhing, pulsating as if alive; and now, in the centre of this chaos, there formed a circle of madly spinning black cloud like a slice cut through the upper stem of a tornado.

Weirdly that disc of frenzied vapour tilted toward us and with quickening pace, independent of all other atmospheric formations, sped across the lowering skies. Such was its independence that all other clouds, large and small, fled to clear a grey path for it that led straight across the heavens! Strangely, seeing that clearing of the sky-path, the stricken wolf-warriors were mortally afraid, while I personally felt great awe but no fear. Neither did the men of the snow-ships nor my own small team, although judging by the gasps of amazement from the latter they were as much in awe of this fantastic sight as I was.

Tilting my head up higher, I followed the flight of the disc of whirling cloud along the sky-path until it slowed and stopped almost immediately overhead. And now a vast and gasping sigh, composed of a mass moaning from the wolf-warriors and a concerted, ecstatic exhalation from the rest, went up from the hypnotized tableau on the plain. In the next moment, as if a spell had been lifted by that sighing murmur of the armies, the battle resumed.

But now there was a difference, for from the instant of resumption the battle progressed clearly in favour of the men of the snow-ships. The wolf-warriors fought as they retreated, true, but their lines were bending like grass before a breeze as they milled back from the swaggering bears and their jubilant riders, and to a man they seemed to keep one eye on the sky overhead – on the sky, and on the ominous black disc that whirled and roared above us.

Seeing that the battle was rejoined and having clipped a fresh magazine into my pistol, I prepared to defend myself once more. I crouched beside Tracy where she huddled over Whitey's still form, trying to free the spear that pinned his leg to the frozen surface. Whitey's pistol, flown from his hand when he fell, was nowhere to be seen.

Jimmy Franklin, out of ammunition, had reversed his rifle and now gripped the barrel with both hands like a club. For a moment we stared at each other, Jimmy and I, and then he said, 'Hank, it looks to me like these people here are scared to death – almost as scared as I am. This could be our chance to make a break for the snow-ships.'

He was right. The circling wolf-warriors had pulled farther back from us; much closer were the advancing lines of fighting bears, cutting off our attackers from the rest of the wolf-warrior pack. I handed Tracy my pistol, put both hands to the shaft of the spear (mercifully a true spear and not a barbed harpoon) that fastened Whitey down, and pulled it free as smoothly and gently as I could.

Whitey moaned and trembled on the frozen ground. Tracy handed the pistol back to me and sat down to cradle Whitey's head, wiping his brow with snow.

Jimmy Franklin threw down his useless rifle and reached for the bloodied spear. 'All right,' I told him, 'we'll make a break for it. I'll carry Whitey; Tracy will have to stay between us.'

Then, before we could make our move – even above the crazed rushing and roaring of the whirling black disc hanging above us, over the clash of battle and the screams of dying men and beasts – again the mad Russian priest's scornful voice rang out, lashing our ring of attackers into activity.

But no, despite the fact that they obviously feared this wild-eyed white man, the warriors would have none of it. True, they made a half-hearted show of rushing upon us, but as soon as my pistol resumed its vicious spitting they spurred their wolves to a hurried retreat. And now they were gathering into a group, no longer ringing us, backing away in the direction of the distant pyramid altar and prepared at any moment to turn and flee.

It could have been that their reluctance was due to the fact that the men of the snow-ships were now breaking through the disordered wolf-warrior lines in a dozen different places, but I was sure that it was much more than this, that it still had a lot to do with the whirling disc in the maddened sky. But now, however hesitantly, indecisively, massive wolf-warrior reinforcements were arriving to bolster the faltering morale of their bat-' tered brothers. Well over a thousand of them, these were the men of that wedge-shaped formation I had seen bringing up the rear behind the three sledges of the priests. They paused momentarily before entering the battle.

It was at that moment that the insane Russian, wearied now of trying to goad his men to the attack, grabbed the Eskimo driver of his sledge by the arm and screamed a harsh command into his ear. Immediately the squat driver leaned forward to crack his whip across the backs of the six harnessed wolves.

Round in a semicircle the heavy sledge skidded, while Zchakow clung like a great white leech to its prow. Now, as the team of wolves hurtled straight toward us, I saw that it was the Russian's intention simply to run us down. I yanked Tracy to her feet and thrust her away, slipping and stumbling over the snow.

The sledge of the high priest hissed down upon us, and again he screamed a harsh command. In answer to that urgent cry, spurring his wolf forward out of a milling, snarling crush of human and animal bodies, rode that massive Eskimo survivor of the six warriors Zchakow had sent against.us. Straight for Tracy the giant guided his massive mount, leaning out to reach for her with avid, grasping hands.

'Tracy!' I yelled. 'Tracy – *look out!*'

And at that precise instant of time, simultaneous with my cry, came a fantastic intervention. Twin, deafening reports sounded from the sky, a double-barrelled blast like that of some cosmic shotgun.

High in the heavens, emanating from the centre of the whirling disc of cloud, two great dazzling bands of fire reached out, curling over and down, swaying above the plain like twin serpent heads before leaping earthward to flash unerringly to their targets. Magnificent, awesome, fearfully *sentient* they were – thunderbolts that crashed down with pin-point accuracy upon those who would destroy us!

When they were almost upon us, suddenly the wolves that hauled Zchakow's sledge were enveloped in crackling white flame that reached from the sky. One second they were there, caught in that awful holocaust of electrical energies, and the next second that pillar of fire was gone and they were ashes through which the sledge, its prow blazing, careened to spill onto its side.

Two figures were thrown like rag dolls onto the snow: the Russian and his Eskimo driver. The latter got to his knees – just in time to catch a stray spear full in the back. The shaft ran him through, knocking him face down and stone dead upon the frozen ground. It was just as well for him that he died that way. He had been screaming hideously even before the spear hit him, and I had seen that his arms ended in steaming, redly dripping stumps at the elbows. Reaching over the prow of the sledge, those arms of his must have been caught in that same pillar of flame that incinerated the wolves.

But what of Zchakow? Where was he now? Then I saw him, mounting a riderless wolf, in a hurry to make good his escape. I lifted my weapon and had him fairly in my sights when a stumbling figure fell against me, deflecting my aim. It was Tracy, weakly calling my name, half-fainting with shock and terror.

'Oh, Hank, Hank – it was *terrible*!' she cried. I tried to clasp her to me but she pulled free to point shudderingly at a pile of smouldering fur and grey ashes on the snow: the remains of the giant Eskimo warrior and his mount. 'That fire – that awful fire from the sky!'

'Come on!' Jimmy Franklin suddenly cried. 'Now we can make it!'

I saw that he was right; the tide of battle had washed by us. Apart from a narrow strip of frozen plain littered with dead and dying men and animals, nothing now stood between us and the line of motionless snow-ships.

I threw Whitey across my shoulders and Jimmy picked up Tracy. As we stumbled toward the snow-ships a quartet of massive bears lumbered forward, their riders holding out brawny arms to us. Tracy was taken from Jimmy by a black-haired, hawkfaced man who could only be of pure Indian stock, possibly Tlingit or Chinook. She clung to him grimly as his huge mount turned about. Ten or eleven feet tall, a second bear approached me. At the command of its Eskimo rider, this moving mountain of fur lifted Whitey from my back to tuck him under a massive limb. Yet another rider reached down a hand to me, and as I swung up beside him I saw the fourth pick up Jimmy. Then we were off at a lumbering run for the nearest ship of the snow.

As we reached the ship, willing hands reached down to lift us aboard from the backs of the bears. The deck was of rough planking, along which we were hurried to the upward-sweeping prow. Whitey was borne away to the rear of the ship; I assumed that his wound was to be given immediate attention.

Tracy was on her own feet again by then, and as we gathered at the rail of the bird-beaked prow to watch the battle from this point of higher elevation, so Jimmy Franklin struck up a conversation with the stern-faced brave whose arms had lifted my sister from him. They spoke slowly at first, Jimmy finding his way with the Koluscha-Tlingit tongue, but soon the conversation became an excited babble. Shortly Jimmy held up his hand to still the tongue of his new friend; he turned to me.

'He says that we showed great courage in defying Ithaqua, and that we have done the people of the Plateau a great service in ridding Borea of so many of Ithaqua's people. He welcomes us aboard the ship of Northan the Warlord, where we await the coming of Armandra, the Woman of the Winds.'

'Hold on, Jimmy,' I told him. 'Let's take it slowly. Is your friend here this, er, Northan the Warlord? And who is Armandra?'

Again they engaged in the obscure Indian dialect, then, 'No, this is not Northan; his name is Kota'na, and he is the

Keeper of the Bears. Northan is a man like you – and yet not like you. He has your height and your blue eyes, but he is darker skinned and his hair is jet.'

'And Armandra?' Tracy asked him.

Jimmy lifted his eyes to stare out over the battle that still raged on the white plain, then turned them skyward to that enigmatic disc of madly spinning darkness. 'He says that Armandra is Priestess of the Plateau, the Woman of the Winds.' He paused, then lifted an unsteady hand to point at the whirling disc. 'And he says that Armandra is – *there*!'

'Look!' Tracy cried. 'Hank, what's happening?'

Decimated, the ranks of wolf-warriors had drawn back to form triple lines of perhaps four hundred and fifty men mounted, and another two hundred or so riderless wolves. Behind them, spaced out along the line they formed, Ithaqua's six lesser priests leaped and cavorted on the snow, their cries reaching us on the wings of a wind that suddenly rose up to blow from the distant altar into the faces of the warriors of the snow-ships. Behind the six priests, raised high atop a human pyramid of white-robed warriors, Boris Zchakow held up his arms to the skies and offered up a cry the like of which I was sure civilized man never heard before from throat of man.

Close about us pressed a dozen or so of the half-naked men of the ships, murmuring excitedly, expectantly, staring out across the plain. Jimmy Franklin asked a further guttural question of Kota'na and on receipt of the answer again turned to me.

'He says that Ithaqua's priests are fools; that while their master is undisputed "First Lord of the Winds", Armandra's powers are second only to his, and that any forces the priests can call up will be child's play for the Woman of the Winds. And such tomfoolery, he says, will only anger her. Look!'

As he spoke he flung out an arm to point across the battlefield. About two hundred yards of death-littered plain separated the two armies. Now, between them and growing up out of the frozen ground in front of the ranks of wolf-warriors, six towering tornadoes reached skyward. Thin spirals at their bases, thickening at their tops to about one hundred feet in diameter, they whirled like spinning tops, gathering up all of the loose surface rime of the plain and rapidly becoming almost solid cones of snow and ice.

Then, with almost military precision, these evocations of an alien science began to move forward toward the opposing army. As they crossed the open space the bodies of fallen men and beasts – Eskimo, Indian, Mongol and European, and the carcasses of wolves and bears alike – were swept up into their funnels to whirl madly in the tumult of frozen debris.

Now those six priests also moved forward, advancing between the wolf-warriors, urging their fantastic, inhuman charges on with cries and crazed cavortings. All of this I saw through the binoculars which I still wore round my neck, but soon I could no longer hear the cries of those priests for they were utterly drowned out in the torrent of sound that washed outward from the awesome scene on the plain.

Staunchly stood the men and bears of the ships, un-faltering in a whipping wind that threatened to blow them all away like leaves in a gale, facing the whirligigs of doom that rushed upon them. And then a gasp went up from the figures that crowded me in the prow of the snow-ship. In the sky above the armies, something was happening.

Dead centre in the whirling disc of black cloud an opening had appeared, and down through this opening a shape now lowered – a human shape. No, perhaps not human, for how could any person of flesh and blood be up there, walking down the wind beneath that enormous aerial Catherine-wheel? And yet, unless my own eyes played games with me, that figure was indeed human – the gorgeous shape of a woman whose flesh was as white as the snow of the plain – a woman garbed in white fur boots and a short fur smock, who fell in a swift but *controlled* motion down through the air with her arms held wide and parallel to the ground, forming a living cross. Her hair was billowing above her, long and flaming red, rippling as she fell like the tail of some fiery meteorite of flesh.

Down she came, slowing to a gradual halt, still as a hawk on the wind, level with and facing the flat caps of the viciously spinning tornadoes. She stood in thin air, surveying the scene before and beneath her with lowered head. Her back was toward us and her face hidden, but nevertheless I knew she must be beautiful. Beautiful and regal – and powerful.

Now she moved her arms out toward the six white titans that threatened her with their spinning, nodding heads, palms flat against them, denying them – and they paused in their forward motion as if suddenly come up against an invisible wall. Trembling and swaying wildly, fighting to move forward against the will of that Woman of the Winds, the great spinning tops strove to obey the ecstasies of the priests behind them. But her will was stronger than theirs, stronger than the combined wills of all the priests of Ithaqua together.

Faster the tornadoes whirled, frenziedly battering themselves against the invisible wall of Armandra's will, gyrating erratically and losing all of that precision with which they had marched across the plain. Their end was quick; unable to move forward they began to sway from side to side, falling one against the next like dominoes tumbling in a row, and since they could not tumble forward they fell back the way they had come.

And that was a sight to remember, the tumbling and crashing of those nearly solid inverted cones of snow and ice. An avalanche from the sky, the collapsing columns smashed down to raise a thick haze of ice-dust that momentarily obscured the panic gripping the wolf-warrior army. How the Priests of Ithaqua escaped with their lives in that shattering deluge I could never say, but escape they did, for when the white haze began to settle they were already aboard their sledges, and Boris Zchakow with them, rushing back across the white waste toward the distantly towering pyramid altar.

With my binoculars I found the mad Russian, saw him turn to glare, eyes bulging, at the figure of the woman in the sky, mouthing some unheard obscenity and shaking a fist at her in lunatic fury.

Ah, the fool – for Armandra saw him too!

The flaming hair of that fantastic figure billowed up on her head and seemed to glow with an unnatural light, turning her whole body and the simple garment she wore a peculiar copper colour, like frozen gold. Slowly, deliberately, she reached up one slender arm above her head and the chill copper glow extended from her pointing hand to spiral upward to the great disc of black cloud that yet whirled and roared above her, a primal watchdog guarding its mistress.

She began to rotate her arm, the circle rapidly growing wider as if she twirled the rope of some enormous lasso. And the cloud-disc, the loop of that lasso, spun with her arm, speeding up until its edges became a wispy blur laced with flickering traceries of electrical fire.

Now the wolf-warrior army was in full flight, hurtling away down the slight slope toward the distant circle of totems and its central altar. Totally disarrayed, chaotic, theirs was a panic flight which, like a stampede, would not be checked until men and beasts had run themselves out. They were done with fighting for this day, hurrying home to lick their wounds and count their dead; and riding with them in their midst went Boris Zchakow, head and shoulders taller than the three men who rode his sledge with him.

From this fleeing rabble back to the Woman of the Winds my binoculars flew, and now I could almost feel the anger radiating from her where she stood in coppery splendour atop the very air. *'Zchakow,'* I told the distant madman under my breath, *'Russian – if you think you have an enemy in me, you don't know the half of it. Human enemies you can possibly afford, but not such as this Woman of the Winds!'*

And oh, I was right.

Now the figure in the sky seemed to swell outward, burning bronze to match the billowing tresses that crowned her – and for a moment I thought I knew where I had seen a similar *expansion* before. But then, in another moment, the shape was human again, only human.

Human? I laughed at myself derisively. There must be that in this being which was human, yes, but there was more, much more than that to her. There was this power of hers over the elements – and there was her anger.

Now she lowered that slender arm of hers to a horizontal position, and the great disc above her head tilted forward, dipped, slid down the wind, rushed like some gigantic discus thrown by a god in the Games of Heaven – or a demon in hell's chaos. Levelling out over the white waste, it rushed after the fleeing army of wolf-warriors.

Tracy clutched my arm, her breath pluming faster as she watched that incredible scene. 'Oh, Hank – how *could* she?'

It was one thing to be engaged in a fight for one's life with fallible, mortal enemies, but another thing entirely to see this Woman of the Winds, this being who fought with weapons fashioned of the forces of nature, ruthlessly, cold-bloodedly destroy a small army.

And surely that army, or what was left of it, would be destroyed if the whirling juggernaut Armandra had unleashed upon it were allowed to run amuck through its scattered, fleeing ranks.

'I – I don't know,' finally I answered Tracy's question, surprised to find that my throat was dry and my voice cracked.

'They are terrible people,' Tracy continued, 'but they *are* people!' Then she closed her eyes and turned her face to me as the great disc caught up with the hindmost of the fleeing wolf-warriors.

Unable to tear my eyes away from the scene, I felt my lips draw back in a gasp of horror as the disc struck, tearing into and ripping through men and beasts as the blade of a circular saw rips wood, flinging the debris of its passing hundreds of feet into the icy air and across the white waste. And then, even as I watched, the disc paused, hesitated.

With shaking hands I focused yet again upon the Woman of the Winds. Now she had thrown up an arm before her eyes, her other hand thrust out before her as if to ward off some unseen horror – the horror of her own inhuman anger unleashed. In the next instant she shook her head, sending her magnificent red tresses billowing, then waved her arms outward in a sharp, clear sign of dismissal.

And suddenly there was a tremendous roaring from the plain, such as a tidal wave might make breaking on some unsuspecting promontory. The weapon she had hurled at the fleeing army flew apart, disintegrated, returned in the space of a few seconds to its elemental form, lay as inert over the plain as a grey cloud! A cloud that settled to a ground haze, revealing at last the hundred or so remaining wolf-warriors racing frenziedly on beyond its drifting, curling tendrils.

Faintly, breaking the sudden silence, reaching us on a mournful wind that sprang up in the wake of all that had

passed, came a distant rumbling and hysterical screaming from the spared, fleeing wolf-warriors. For certainly
Armandra had spared them, and I knew now that there
was more of the human in her than I had suspected.

'She let them go!' breathed Tracy.

'Let them go!' Jimmy Franklin gasped, echoing her, his
voice clearly displaying relief.

'Yes she did,' said another well known voice, edged now
with pain, from behind us.

It was Whitey, hobbling on one leg, his arm around the
fat neck of a grinning Eskimo. 'She did, so there's hope
for her yet,' he finished.

'Whitey, what do you mean?' I asked.

He nodded grimly in answer, eyebrows lowering, staring
at the figure of the woman in the sky. 'See for yourself,'
he said.

As a tremendous accolade of cheering, whooping, and
the rattling of hundreds of weapons on shields went up
from the victorious army of the snow-ships, I looked up
and saw – and understood. I understood this woman's
power over the elements of the air, her ability to walk
on the wind, her inhuman anger and her all-too-human
anguish.

For now she had turned to face her people, and hearing
their wildly clamorous applause she held out her slender
arms to them. Her marvellous hair swirled above her and
her eyes shone momentarily as a great queen's to the
ringing cheers of her subjects.

Her eyes shone, then for the space of a single instant
blazed bright carmine, twin stars in her regal face!

Whitey nodded again, then said, 'The safest hunch I
ever had in my life, Hank. That woman is without doubt
a child of Ithaqua, and we must thank our lucky stars that
she appears to have broken away from her monstrous
father!'

2

On the Ship of Northan

(Recorded through the Medium of Juanita Alvarez)

Half an hour later, during which time the ski-borne ships were brought about and the great bears paraded up onto their decks to be chained to individual rings, the last few wounded men and animals were being brought aboard when Armandra herself took her place at the prow of this ship of her warlord.

During that interval we had also met Northan the War-lord, if it could be called a meeting. A big man, tall as myself and muscled about his arms and shoulders like one of the bears, he had paused momentarily in the issuing of multilingual commands to stride to the prow of the ship and look us over. He literally did that; looked us over, and the frown of disdain that grew on his darkly handsome face told me that he hardly considered us worth the effort.

I immediately, irrationally, took a dislike to him. Blue-eyed with light brown skin and long dark hair, his face and form seemed to me to hold elements of many races, a powerful lineage.

My dislike increased by leaps and bounds when he casually chucked Tracy under the chin, lifted her head and grunted grudgingly. Before I could say or do anything he had strode away again, but from then on I watched him more closely; not because I believed that Tracy needed a watchdog, but simply because I don't like being held in any sort of contempt. The man who does that to me or mine must then live up to it.

I was still thinking dark and as yet unjustified thoughts when finally Armandra came aboard. Her arrival at the prow of the snow-ship was as awe-inspiring as anything we had seen of her yet, for of course she walked down the wind to step aboard the vessel from an invisible platform of air that buoyed her up as if she were a bubble.

Watching Northan as he strode the deck issuing his orders and pointing here and there with the stock of a short whip, I turned only in time to see her take the last step that brought her aboard – from a position some fifteen to twenty feet above the frozen surface of the plain! – and I would have missed even that last step but for the sudden gasp that went up from the vessel's crew. That and the fact that all around me men were falling to their knees, heads bowed in absolute reverence. Kota'na went down instantly, dragging Jimmy Franklin with him unprotesting; even Whitey knelt, though it brought a moan of pain to his lips to have to bend his wounded leg. I couldn't see Tracy for she stood slightly to my rear, but I later learned that even she had humbly lowered her head; Tracy, as proud a girl as ever walked.

Without any shadow of doubt this Woman of the Winds had magic; a magic which, while my body must ever stay rooted to earth, was nevertheless powerful enough to send my soul walking on air. Oh, yes, she was beautiful, this Armandra.

Draped as she was in a white fur smock, still her long full body was a wonder of half-real, half-imagined curves that grew out of the perfect pillars of her white thighs. Her neck, framed now in the red silk of her tresses, was long and slender, adorned with a large golden medallion.

I have never been much of a poet, and no less could do justice to her face. It was the face of an angel; oval and beautifully moulded, white as snow. In it great green eyes – mercifully green where once I had seen them glow red – stared out from beneath fine golden eyebrows that lay straight and horizontal beneath a high brow. Her nose was straight, too, but delicate and rounded at its tip, while her mouth was curved in a perfect, if a fraction too ample, cupid's bow.

Hair red as fire and eyes green as the deep northern seas of Earth, and a skin as white and smooth as the snowy marble of quarries of dream; this was Armandra's face. And as I gazed at that face I saw one eyebrow lift a little, wonderingly, and the smallest of smiles beginning to –

– And then I was knocked from my feet by a charging blow to my shoulder that would have brought down an ox! I went flying, to crash jarringly against the rail of the prow where I fell to my knees. The next moment Northan appeared over me, legs spread wide and eyes blazing.

I knew immediately that the warlord's anger sprang from my apparently irreverent attitude toward the Woman of the Winds, in which he could not in fact be more mistaken. Indeed, I already revered this woman, but not as any religious worshipper. Snarling and blustering the bully raised his whip, and as I came to my feet he snapped the thing to send its single metal-tipped thong flying in my face. How easily he might have caught my eye, but instead the metal cut me high on the cheek – and higher still on my pride. Pride goes before a fall they say, but be that as it may this time it would be Northan's fall. On that I was determined.

I reached up a hand to my face to feel a thin trickle of blood, and I felt my eyes widen and the skin about my mouth tighten involuntarily. Northan's arm went back again – and immediately a chiming voice rang out. Too late that golden voice of imperial command, for already the whip was snapping, and I was moving forward inside its wicked radius.

As the metal-tipped thong flew harmlessly over my shoulder I turned slightly to one side and drove my elbow deep into Northan's body below his ribcage. He bent over, almost double, and as he expelled air in a great gasp of surprise, so my cupped hands, clenched into a hard knot, rose up to strike his descending brow.

Most men would have died there and then, of a fractured skull or broken neck, but not Northan the Warlord. His neck was like that of a bull. The shock of the blow I had delivered nearly broke my arms as my opponent's body lifted clear from the planking, flew across the narrow prow and smashed through the opposite rail. He spun out of sight and fell to earth. The fact that I had not killed him was all too obvious from the cry of disbelieving rage that swelled up a moment later from below, and in the outraged bellow that followed as the warlord came limping up the wide gangplank amidships his dark face working and a picklike weapon gleaming in his fist.

But again Armandra's bell-like tones rang out, and this time she spoke in English. 'Stop this now, Northan! You should be ashamed of yourself, thus to treat a man who has fought so well against Ithaqua's wolf-warriors. And you –' she turned her now wrathful eyes on me, 'to attack the man whose army has saved all of your lives!'

'I only returned his blows,' I answered, neither liking this chastisement nor yet quite knowing how to answer it.

'My brother allows no man to strike him.' Tracy's sweet, angry voice came from beside me as Northan swung himself up onto the raised platform. 'The warlord must consider himself lucky to be alive!'

I had to grin at my sister's pluck and her faith in me; and I saw now that Armandra also smiled at Tracy, that her smile widened noticeably as she said, 'Your brother? I had thought perhaps that –'

'You, man, stand and fight!' came Northan's rage-filled, guttural voice. He crouched before me on the raised deck, eyes red with fury, picklike weapon grasped tightly in a massive, bloodless hand.

'Northan!' the Woman of the Winds gasped. 'I have told you that –'

'But Armandra, he refused to kneel before you, and struck me with his naked hands when I would have punished him! The dog must –'

'He struck fair blows when you should have expected them, and they were telling blows,' she taunted him. 'And where you used a weapon, he did not, though his weapon,' she indicated the pistol at my waist, 'could have killed you instantly.'

For a moment longer we stood there, the three of us, in some sort of confrontation. Then, 'Enough,' the Woman of the Winds cried. 'It is done now, finished. We are wasting time and no one knows when Ithaqua might return to Borea.' She fingered the medallion she wore about her neck, seeming suddenly nervous. 'It is time we were away. I will call a wind to blow us home to the plateau.'

The dark frown stayed on Northan's face, but as Armandra spoke he lifted his head and sniffed the air. 'It's much too quiet,' he finally rumbled in agreement. 'Can you not see, Armandra, what Ithaqua's devils are up to?'

'No, not now,' she shook her head. 'I need my strength to call the wind. Today's work was hard.'

So saying, she stepped into the very point of the prow, lifting up her arms until she resembled some perfectly carved figurehead. As she assumed that posture her red tresses eerily floated up over her head, while tiny gusts of wind sprang up from nowhere to play with the fur collar of her smock. A moment later the great, loosely hanging sails began to fill out. Behind us, far back across the death-strewn white waste, a hundred snow-devils grew up from the frozen ground to race toward us, lifting into the air and swirling themselves into nothingness.

And then the wind came, moaning in tune to the sudden groaning of the rigging and the creaking of straining timbers, and we were off with a lurch and a slither and a hissing of huge skis, riding the snow-ship of Northan the Warlord back to its berth in the base of the plateau. Gracefully the great ships slid into an arrowhead formation, and the wind Armandra had called blew us steadily away from the scene of the recent battle.

Oh, there were sights to be seen and thrills to be experienced during that short, strange voyage, no doubt about that; but for me – I could not take my eyes off the figure of the not-quite-human woman-creature who stood so proudly in the prow with her hair floating weirdly over her head and her slender arms held up to feel the loving caress of currents of air. And I envied those gentle currents whose soft fingers caressed her. The others – Tracy, Whitey and Jimmy – they could watch the sailors of the snow-ship about their tasks, speculate on the origins of the many tongues they heard, thrill to the sway of the deck and the strange odours of men and beasts. For my eyes there was only Armandra.

After a while she must have felt my eyes upon her for she turned her head slightly in my direction. Can snow blush? I believe I saw the slightest tinge of red blossoming on her cheeks, or was it only the reflection of that red halo of hair she wore? Whichever it was, she immediately lifted her head higher and looked straight ahead, but I saw that now her great green eyes twinkled with something that had not been there before.

I was just wondering if I dared attempt to touch her telepathically, if that were at all possible, when suddenly, without looking at me, she said, 'Why do you stare at me so?'

I was taken unawares. 'Why – because – because you are a fascinating woman. You have strange powers,' I lamely answered.

'And is that all?' Still she stared straight ahead, but I sensed disappointment in her tone.

95

Encouraged, I told her, 'No, that's not all. You are very beautiful. In my world women are seldom so beautiful.'

'In your world,' she dreamily answered. 'In the Mother-world. And are they also fascinating, these women of the Motherworld?'

'Not like you.'

'Northan would whip you for your boldness. He would have Kota'na set his bears on you.' Her warning was offered in grave tones, but there was colour in her cheeks.

'Is the fervour of Northan's loyalty really so great, or does he lay claim to you as a woman, Armandra?' Having uttered these words I could have bitten my tongue clean through. Her eyebrows lifted and her smile disappeared in a twinkling. She half-lowered her arms and tossed her head angrily, setting her red tresses in motion. Most of her humanity was gone in as much time as it takes to tell. She was now the Woman of the Winds again, a chill priestess of powers unknown.

'Am I a spear or axe or piece of fine fur that a man shall *claim* me?' her voice cracked as sharply as had Northan's whip. 'Northan? He has hopes, the warlord, and he is a strong man and a brave warrior. But a *claim*? No man has any *claim* over Armandra – no man! What mere man could ever hope to hold me, when the winds themselves want me for their bride?'

Finally she turned to me, anger and frustration bubbling up from oceanic depths of eyes, flaming tresses alive upon her head. 'I have promised my people that soon I will take a man, and it will be so. But no man *claims* Armandra. I will have a mate, yes, and bear his children as my duty to the plateau. But he will not be my lover on his terms, nor my "husband" on any terms. His task may give him pleasure but it will only give me children. Children to walk the winds like their mother, and do mortal battle with their unutterable grandfather!'

96

Now she leaped up – or did she float? – nimbly to the rail of the prow, poising for a moment before diving head-long to breast the air, to spiral up, up to the skies, borne aloft in a cauldron of rushing wind that almost bowled me from my position. She disappeared over the rim of the now looming plateau.

As suddenly as she was gone Northan was at my side. He had plainly been close at hand, had seen the anger in Armandra's face. His own face was not so dark now; blue eyes glittered slyly as he said, 'Perhaps I should have warned you, man of the Motherworld. Men do not speak to Armandra as they do to other women. She is no pretty toy but a princess of the gods.'

He turned as if to leave me, then looked back. 'One other thing; when Armandra takes a mate it will be Northan the Warlord. Others want her, true, and they may challenge my right if they dare. Make sure that *you* do not challenge it. You have yet to pay for shaming me today, in which you were exceedingly lucky and though Armandra has forbidden it I would dearly love to crush you like a snowflake. Do not give me the oppor-tunity.'

'If I loved a woman enough, then I might fight for her, Northan,' I told him. 'But Armandra? She is like the great glacier whose chill wears away even the mountain. Can you warm her, Northan? I doubt it. And take heed; Armandra is no snowflake to be crushed in your hand, and neither am I.'

Now the wind that filled our sails quickly fell away and the twelve ships turned to run parallel with the base of the plateau in single file, gradually slowing upon their polished skis until they were all brought to a halt by use of a system of spiked brakes. Then the great bears were paraded down the gangplanks and chained up in teams fifty strong to haul the snow-ships to anchorage in entrances at the base of the plateau.

As the men and bears finished their various tasks and went off along tunnels that pointed directly into the heart of the vast, flat-topped outcropping, my small party and I began to feel more and more out of things. Ignored and feeling inconsequential, not knowing what else to do, we simply stood idle aboard the snow-ship watching as the members of her crew and their mounts gradually dispersed. Jimmy Franklin tried to catch Kota'na's eye, but the Indian was busy organizing the bears into groups to be led away. Northan had long since gone off with a party of his men.

When it seemed that we were to be left to our own devices, as we descended the steep gangplank to the frozen floor of this rock-walled harbour, a young girl ran out from one of the cavelike entrances to approach us, bowing and curtsying as she came. She was an Indian, and spoke a very broken, pleasantly quaint English.

'She is a Blackfoot!' Jimmy excitedly, laughingly exclaimed. 'A pureblood Blackfoot, not diluted like me through contact with you palefaces.' Then he delighted the girl by speaking in her native tongue. As they conversed, the rest of us kept a polite silence, taking note of how pretty the girl was and the pride of her bearing. She was dressed as richly as an Indian princess, the daughter of a chief, and this opulence was finally explained as Jimmy told us:

'Oontawa is handmaiden and companion to the Woman of the Winds. She has been sent to look after us until we go before the Council of Elders, the "government" of the People of the Plateau. First, though, we are to be shown our quarters. Oontawa will stay with us while we eat. After sleeping, we will see the Council of Elders. They will decide what's to be done with us. Also, there's to be a guided tour of this place. Apparently the plateau is honeycombed with caves and corridors, a multi-level labyrinth like some super beehive!'

'Well, then,' Tracy answered him, 'you'd better tell Oontawa to lead on. I don't know about you boys, but I could do with a bite to eat.'

As we trooped along behind Jimmy Franklin and the Indian girl, with Whitey hobbling along with one arm about Tracy's shoulders and the other around my neck, my sister added, 'Oh, and Jimmy, if I'm going for an interview,' she sniffed disdainfully at the heavy parkas that wrapped her slim girl's figure, 'perhaps Oontawa has a spare fur or two for me? Do be a sweetheart and ask her for me, will you?'

3

In the Hall of the Elders

(Recorded through the Medium of Juanita Alvarez)

After a distance of some forty yards or so, the tunnel we followed into the basalt bowels of the plateau opened into a gallery from which many more tunnels led off. Each of these shafts had its own symbol carved into the rock above it, and Oontawa pointed out the symbol we were to follow to our quarters, a long, inverted heart or arrowhead shape. Once these many symbols were memorized it would not be difficult to find one's way about the cave-system.

The shafts were lighted by flambeaux formed of stone bowls of oil supported upon wooden brackets fixed to the walls at intervals of about fifty feet. The smell of their burning was like a pungent but not overly unpleasant incense. As we went I dipped a finger into one of the bowls, sniffed at the greasy fuel and gingerly tasted it. Mineral oil, with some sweet, sticky additive. I was surprised. Animal fats would have been far more likely. Where would the plateau's people get oil?

On our way we saw single members and groups of the plateau's inhabitants going about their various businesses. They all paid us what passed for compliments as they met us in the corridors. Though they were mainly of Eskimo and Indian extraction, many other elements were also present, including Mongol, white European and white American. Whenever we met up with a group of them they would politely stand aside for us. Oontawa explained that news of my run-in with Northan had already spread and that it had been greeted in many quarters with no uncertain delight. Plainly the warlord's bullying ways were not generally appreciated.

Passing through at least three more galleries and crossing as many major tunnel systems, we finally arrived at a gallery larger than any we had seen so far. Here, cut into the walls between tunnel mouths, rock-hewn steps ascended to higher levels. Climbing a wide stairway and entering a shaft two levels higher, I noted that we seemed to have turned at right angles to our original course, that now we were moving back towards the outer wall of the plateau, which fronted on the white wastes of the frozen plain and the distant scene of the recent battle.

When I mentioned this to Jimmy Franklin, he replied, 'Yes, our apartments are right on the outer wall. Oontawa tells me that we are particularly fortunate; our rooms are comfortable, light and airy, and they command a view overlooking the entire front of the plateau. She says that Tracy's room is really something; all furs and fancy carvings. It seems that Armandra is quite taken with you, Tracy.'

'How much farther are these rooms of ours?' Whitey painfully asked. 'This leg's giving me hell.'

'Almost there,' Jimmy answered.

As he spoke there came the smell of good, hot food from somewhere ahead. Suddenly I was very hungry. 'Jimmy,' I said, 'ask Oontawa what kind of food her people eat, will you? It strikes me that they're bound to be short on vegetables. In fact from what we've seen of this world so far I'd say they only eat meat. But surely they couldn't make out on a diet of meat alone?'

'Sure they could,' he answered. 'The Eskimos of good old Mother Earth have always been meat eaters – *just* meat – and raw at that! In fact that's what the word Eskimo means: "eater of raw meat". And all of the northern Indian tribes lived mainly on meat. They had their berries and fruits, yes, but their diet was ninety per cent flesh, and they did pretty well on it, too.'

Whitey sniffed the air. 'You've convinced me, Jimmy, at least,' he said. 'If that's our meal I can smell – well, I only hope it tastes as good, that's all.'

We rounded a slight bend in the tunnel and natural light suddenly flooded the shaft, showing curtained entrance-ways to caves on both sides. Here, too, the tunnel ended, and we saw that the light came in through square windows cut into the shaft's terminal wall. Oontawa beckoned us forward to these windows, indicating that we should look out.

We were at a height of some seventy feet above the white waste that gently, almost unnoticeably sloped away down to the distant, ominous pyramid whose hazy outline, even at this distance, marred the view. The very sight of the evil altar filled me with the same shuddery feeling I might get from the sight of a black, triangular fin cutting the surface of inviting blue waters . . .

'Rooms with a view,' said Tracy. 'But where's this meal?'

Oontawa led us in through one of the curtained entrances to a large cave beyond. Since this cave stood away from the outer wall, here the light was from candles in stone holders that stood upon a large ornamental stone table. The weak light of these candles was supplemented by a flickering of flames that leaped up from a metal grille, set in the floor of the farthest corner, to disappear with a quiet, controlled murmur through a similar grille in the ceiling.

While I could feel no change in the temperature (my own flesh remained as chill as Ithaqua's influence had left it), Tracy was obviously delighted with the cave's warmth; she immediately threw off her parkas and stretched herself luxuriously. 'Hey,' she asked Jimmy, 'do all of these people live like this?'

For in this cave the austerity of the tunnels and passage-ways ended. Here the walls were hung with sumptuous drapes of an American Indian weave; the floors were thick with soft furs; wherever naked rock might have shown unadorned it was carved with ethnic designs so intermingled that their ancient origins were no longer easily discernible.

Oontawa was plainly pleased that we were impressed. She sat down to eat with us. The still steaming meats, of appetizing cuts, were in stone bowls; and I was surprised to note that there were also two types of vegetable prep-arations upon the table, not counting the mushrooms that decorated the central dish, a splendid joint of meat not unlike a leg of pork. Each place of the five at the table was set with a large, slightly hollowed slab of agate and a goblet of the same exotic material.

Jimmy and Oontawa conversed while we ate, but I had little time for talking. I have never enjoyed food so much in my entire life. When at last we were done we washed down the meal with cool sweet water from the goblets. Then Jimmy told us of his conversation with Oontawa.

'I asked her about the fire in the corner there,' he nodded at the flickering column of flame. 'Told her I saw no point in warming the plateau when no one seems to appreciate or need heat. Apparently all of the plateau's outer caves are heated, not for the comfort of their dwellers but simply to stop them from freezing over and filling with ice! Apparently the weather is quite mild at the moment.

'She also tells me that the interiors of all the dwelling-caves are done up in pretty much the same way as this one. She'll show us our personal caves in a moment. I asked her how many people there are in the plateau. She says there are some twenty thousand, and –'

'Twenty thousand!' I cut him off. 'But where did they all come from? They can't be indigenous to Borea?'

Jimmy cocked his head at me. 'They are *now*, I suppose, but certainly their forebears came from Earth, the Motherworld. They were brought here by Ithaqua, just like us. Their history goes back thousands of years, before the races of Earth had writing, but their numbers have been kept down through warring with the Children of the Winds, Ithaqua's own people. It is only recently, since Armandra grew to womanhood, that the People of the Plateau have started to win out over the Wind-Walker's worshippers.

'Now there are twenty thousand of them in the plateau, and room for ten times that number. It is a spare-time task of each family unit or military group to prepare dwelling-caves, barrack halls and stables for future families and armies, future generations. In this way the plateau's many natural tunnel systems have been supplemented over the centuries, or extended and improved. The entire outer wall of the plateau, its face, a fortress, with hundreds of observation posts and hidden exits from which the warriors and their bears can go out to battle in times of siege.'

'Times of siege?' Whitey repeated him. 'You mean when Ithaqua and his lads are about?'

Oontawa nodded, speaking now for herself. 'Yes, when Ithaqua leads Children of Winds against us, then we must stay within walls of plateau or die. Only bravest of our warriors go out to defend outer tunnels and snow-ship harbours.'

'And Armandra?' I asked. 'Does she fight with the warriors, as we saw her fighting today?'

The girl's almond eyes widened and her hand flew to her breast. 'No, lord, not when Ithaqua rides wind, for it is only to trap her and take her back that he wages war against plateau's people. She is his daughter, but she rebels against her father's tyranny, defying him.'

As she finished speaking I saw that my question had disturbed her deeply; the thought of losing Armandra to

104

Ithaqua and the Children of the Winds was too dreadful to contemplate. Now Oontawa stood up.

'Come, I show you your rooms and bathing place. And you –' she turned to Whitey, 'I tend to your leg. Then you all sleep before going to Council of Elders.'

And sleep we did, but not before bathing.

I bathed quickly, along with the other two men, in the hot waters of a cave with a scooped out rock floor. Tracy had a smaller, private bath, a hypocaust affair, in the quite large and sumptuous cave that was her apartment. The water of these baths was constantly changing itself; melting and dripping down from higher, outer ramparts of the plateau, heated by the oil-fire systems of the outer caves and channelled to the baths, finally overflowing to spill away down stone sluices into the plateau's heart, there to turn the wheels of the work-shops.

My own small room was as richly appointed as the others and had a deep square window that looked out over the white wastes. There, stretched out on my back on a pile of furs a foot thick, I quickly fell into a deep, dreamless sleep, one of complete exhaustion and oblivion.

And I came even more quickly awake at the urgent touch of Oontawa's hand. I felt refreshed, reborn, a new man from the moment she shook me awake, and I knew that my sleep must have been a long one.

'Up, up,' Oontawa was saying. 'You are summoned to Council of Elders. Armandra is there. She prepares to see – to see –' She stumbled over her words, searching for an expression. 'She looks over long distances. I do not know, in your tongue, how –'

'Tell me, Oontawa,' said Jimmy Franklin from the door. 'Tell me in your own tongue.'

They conversed rapidly while I put on fur boots, then Jimmy said: 'It appears that Armandra is, well, a seer, I suppose you could call her. She can see things at a distance, with her mind, things that are happening here on

105

Borea. But she can only do this when – when her father himself is personally concerned.'

Snapping shut the heavy buckle of my fur belt, I turned to Oontawa. 'You mean Ithaqua is back on Borea?'

She nodded. 'He is at his temple. Armandra desires that you should know your enemy better. When she is finished with her seeing, then you speak with Council of Elders. But hurry, they are waiting.'

We went out into the tunnel where Tracy soon joined us. She was dressed in fur trousers, fur boots and a splendid fur jacket with a high collar. She seemed to glow. Whitey appeared last, and it amazed me that his limp was barely noticeable. Whatever ointments these people used, they were certainly effective.

Then, with Oontawa leading, this time following a rock-carved symbol we all recognized well, a five-pointed star! – we proceeded to the Hall of the Elders. The way must have been half a mile, on a course that saw us climbing massive flights of stone stairs and passing through at least a dozen of the great galleries. Finally we approached the end of a wide tunnel that terminated in a smooth stone face of rock through which a great doorway had been cut. Above this entrance a huge five-pointed star was deeply carved in the rock. The Hall of the Elders.

Some fifty feet ahead of us, passing through the entrance in something of a hurry, went three Indians dressed in what looked to me like full ceremonial regalia. Jimmy stared after them and gasped. 'Blackfoot, Chinook and Nootka, chiefs of the most northerly of the Northwest Tribes, just as they were two hundred years ago! Ithaqua doesn't seem to have strayed off limits very far south of the Canadian border.'

'Come,' Oontawa whispered, leading the way through the door. 'We are last to enter, but not too late.'

We followed her into a vast cave or chamber lit by huge, brightly flaring flambeaux. The first thing that caught my eye was a carved throne in the dead centre of the chamber. Decked in furs and standing upon a raised section of the floor with stone steps leading up to it, the thing was massively ornate. Seated upon it with her white hands curved over its stone arms, her head upright and her eyes closed, was Armandra. Her breast moved slowly beneath the beautiful jacket of fox fur that she wore.

She was in a deep trancelike state; before her face, hanging motionless from a golden chain suspended from the top of the high throne's back where it curved forward over her head, was the medallion she had previously worn about her neck. Motionless? Perhaps not. The medallion was not distinct to my eyes; its disc seemed blurred. Slowly, very slowly, it turned on its golden chain.

The second most noticeable thing in the Hall of the Elders was the silence. Though the descending tiers of stone benches that circled the amphitheatre-like chamber were filled almost to capacity, not a single whisper stirred the assembly. Or was I mistaken in this also? Mistaken I was, for now I heard a distinct sound, a humming as of winds blowing far away, and it issued from that slowly turning, *vibrating* medallion!

The medallion hummed and vibrated, echoing however faintly the hum and roar of weird winds blowing out beyond the rim of the universe. It hung before Armandra's face and she heard it, and I knew instinctively that its voice formed pictures for her – sounds transmuted into visions – so that what she heard she also saw.

But now Oontawa was standing on tiptoe, whispering something urgently into my ear and tugging at my hand, indicating that my party should take seats. A space had been cleared for us; the occupants of the lowest tiers of seats had moved silently along to make room. I blinked my eyes and shook my head. I had been very nearly hypnotized by the sight of Armandra in her trance.

As I followed Tracy and my friends to our places, every eye in the Hall of the Elders was upon me. At a guess some four thousand eyes frowned at me, the latecomer. While we sat down Oontawa moved quickly to the raised dais, climbing its steps to stand at the left hand of Armandra. For a moment she leaned forward to peer anxiously into Armandra's white face, at the closed eyes and drawn, regal features. Then she kneeled and bowed her head, this handmaiden to a goddess.

The silence in the Hall of the Elders seemed to deepen, or perhaps it was simply that the humming and roaring of the suspended medallion increased. Whichever, soon it was as though a torrent of whispering ghost-winds rushed through the chamber. And ghost-winds they must have been, for despite the fact that the distant tumult rapidly increased, not a single breath of disturbed air touched us and the fires of the flambeaux burned as steadily as before. And now I sensed that the rushing of air was only an illusion, like the crash of waves heard in a shell, an illusion magnified by the absolute silence of the assembly.

So the shock of Armandra's voice, clear, golden and bell-like, breaking that ghost-ridden whisper of weird winds, was electric! I felt the hair of my neck prickle as she spoke, and instantly all heads turned once more in the direction of my party. The Woman of the Winds was speaking in English, plainly for our benefit, and in the eyes of all present our importance had immediately trebled.

'Ithaqua stands atop his altar,' Armandra intoned in a voice which, except for its singular golden ring, was so void of modulation or emotion that it might have been the voice of Death himself. 'He is returned from dark meditations in the moons of Borea and now awaits his tribute – of which there is none, for we have snatched the girl he lusted after and the men whose souls he wanted from the very jaws of his wolf-warriors!

108

'There he stands.' Her hand, alabaster in motion, trembling slightly, pointed eerily across the hall at nothing. Her eyes remained closed; her hair, living fire, stirred strangely and began to rise up over her head. 'There he stands atop his pedestal of ice, my *father*!' The last word fell like a golden icicle from her lips, seeming to splinter into shards of ice in the air of the great cave.

Her hand fell back to rest upon the carved arm of her throne while her hair continued its coppery swirling above her head. 'They gather, his priests, cowering about the foot of his altar: whipped wolf puppies that snarl at each other, eager to give the blame, grovelling within the circle of totems. Outside the totem ring the Children of the Winds wait. Ithaqua has called them forth from far across the white wastes to see his justice. And he *is* just, for he commanded and his commands went unanswered, his hunger unappeased. And how shall a god correct such deliberate contempt?

'But see, there are only six of them within the totem ring. The High Priest is not there . . .

'Ah, *now* I see him!' She leaned forward slightly, her fingers tightening upon the arms of her throne. 'I see the dog, fighting and screaming, dragged from his hiding place and thrown before the altar of his master. He grovels, begs, pleads – this so-called priest who dared to threaten, to curse me – and Ithaqua stands over him, dark atop the pyramid of ice. Now the groveller rages at the lesser priests and they cower, fearing the Wind-Walker's wrath. But the Wind-Walker is cold and still.

'Now the High Priest bows himself down, kneels and cries out his innocence to Ithaqua, giving the six lesser priests the blame. Ah, but they stand united now, those six, ringing him about and pointing their accusation.

'See! The game is up! He tries to run! . . . They bring him down! . . . And now – *now Ithaqua takes a hand!*'

It became obvious to me then that the entire audience understood at least the rudiments of the English language; almost every head in that great cave, my own included, must have moved forward in unison as Armandra spoke those words. I sensed the concerted movement all about me; the rapt attention of every one of us was full upon Armandra. And we all saw and gasped together at the change that stole swiftly over her face.

A ruddy light seemed to burn upon her cheeks, upon her high brow and closed eyes, subtly complementing the flaming copper of her hair. The medallion upon its chain glittered brightly as its gyrations grew more visibly erratic, its humming and roaring forming a definite presence in the great chamber.

Armandra leaned forward further yet until her face almost touched the spinning disc. Her fingers gripped the arms of her throne like claws. Gone now was the calm, deathlike mask she had worn. In its place a feral skull snarled beneath wildly swaying masses of burning hair.

This was the moment I had waited for, my chance to attempt a penetration of Armandra's mind. Oh, I entertained no real doubt that her trance was genuine – nor did I doubt that she was indeed the daughter of Ithaqua – but if the latter were true then she was only half human, spawn of a demon or god of the Cthulhu Cycle of Myth, in which event I should at least be able to gauge the power and direction of her mental emissions.

As to *why* I wanted to do this thing: I found in this woman-creature a vast enigma, a great challenge. Not once did I think of myself as an intruder. If her concentration was as great as it appeared to be, then she would not even notice my presence. When I think now of my audacity . . .

Tentatively I reached out my mind to her, and instantly I was *enveloped*!

She was a whirlpool of concentrated mental energy that sucked me in like a spider flushed down a drain. I could neither fight nor withdraw. I became part of her, hearing what she heard, seeing what she saw. And so superior was her power that my own puny energies were not even perceptible in the mental vortex.

Physically I sat there on that stone bench between Tracy and Jimmy Franklin, but mentally I was a mote in the cosmos of Armandra's psyche. I whirled away with her on the wings of strange winds and stared down with her upon a distant scene . . .

4

'Bring this Man to Me!'

(Recorded through the Medium of Juanita Alvarez)

'Now Ithaqua takes a hand!'

The words seemed to repeat over and over, receding into vast distances and returning to reverberate in my mind. Then abruptly, there was only the wind; a wind that blew mournfully across the white wastes, bringing with it the distant howling of frightened wolves. And perhaps those wolves sensed that which would frighten any living creature: Ithaqua, the Thing that Walks on the Wind!

For now I saw him, bloated with anger where he stood at the apex of his pyramid altar, and I saw the six priests scatter like cockroaches as the monster stepped down onto the frozen surface within the totem ring. Ah, but those were no human feet with which the Wind-Walker strode the crushed snow. They were huge and webbed, out of all proportion even to the towering size he had attained, which now lifted him head and shoulders above his own altar.

Doomed, Zchakow the Russian fled, feet flying, arms reaching, eyes bulging and fear foaming from between his champing jaws. He fled before the tread of his monstrous master.

With a thrill of pure horror I suddenly found myself lusting for the Russian's blood, eager to see him struck down and destroyed! It dawned on me that this was not Hank Silberhutte but Armandra. I was now part of Armandra, influenced by her emotions, her desires, which were stronger than mine. And yet, paradoxically, human compassion was not absent in her; indeed it was strong. I could feel it like the pulse of a powerful heart. Ah, but that compassion was fighting a losing battle with her inhuman side, the incalculably alien and abhorrent cruelty inherited from her father. And Zchakow was her enemy.

Now I moved closer to the terrible drama being enacted down on the frozen plain. Out between the carved totems raced Boris Zchakow, his face twisted with hideous fear. He was, or had been, Ithaqua's High Priest, with power of life and death over the Children of the Winds. He *knew* his master; he recognized his fate. And perhaps it was this knowledge of that ultimate fate of all of Ithaqua's followers that robbed the Russian of his senses. When I saw what that fate was, I thought that I too might easily go mad confronted with it.

But even transfixed with horror, feeling empathy with the madman with every psychic nerve I possessed, nevertheless I also thrilled to the chase. For Armandra was Hank Silberhutte, and he was only a tiny part of Armandra, and both were lost now to a raging vortex of bloodlust!

I remembered her face as I had last seen it: a skull-like mask surmounted by living, flaming hair; lips drawn back from gleaming white teeth; the whole burning with hell's own fires. And now I saw that face again, only her eyes were no longer closed.

Carmine pits blazed where only depths of submarine green had opened before, eyes that burned with the energies of alien suns, and somewhere, like subdued background music to a conversation, I heard again a concerted gasping from two thousand throats.

The Hall of the Elders! Struggling still to free myself from Armandra's magnet mind, I had almost made it back to that great cave deep in the bowels of the plateau, only to be snatched back again to my mental vantage point above the Temple of Ithaqua.

In that same instant, as if my mind were not already more than sufficiently whirling, I sensed that something was different, wrong – terribly wrong! I was no longer merely a part of the Woman of the Winds but of something far greater, something utterly alien.

Ithaqua-Armandra – I brushed aside massive totems, smashing them like matchsticks, reached to snatch the gibbering lunatic from the frozen ground and hold him high aloft. He – we tossed him into the sky, limbs thrashing like a crippled bird, catching him before he could crash to earth.

Then we laughed, Ithaqua-Armandra and I – laughed in a maelstrom of mirth that I knew could only be subdued, could only end in an act of the cruellest horror.

I fought against the unholy glee that filled me, fought to be free of its hold as it moved toward livid, lunatic rage. But I might as well have tried to beat down the winds with my bare fists. And Armandra fought too, bravely, but uselessly, as the human side of her nature strove harder than ever to turn her back from her monstrous sire's dread attraction.

Physically I was Hank Silberhutte, a man sitting between his sister and a friend in the Hall of the Elders; mentally I was a telepathic observer, an unseen intruder, a part of Armandra's psyche. But since she in turn had been drawn into the Ithaqua id, then I was also part of Him. Part of the ultimate horror. He had planned for Boris Zchakow.

The Wind-Walker, Armandra and I stared through avid carmine orbs, shrinking ocean depths of green, flinching blue slits, as he-she-we lifted Zchakow up to his-her-my face, where he screamed and frothed as Ithaqua-Armandra-I scrutinized him minutely.

Then, in another instant, it was over. We threw back our hideous head and lifted the shrieking figure of the mad, wildly kicking Russian up, up into the air. A sudden moan of horror, rising to rival the mournfully moaning wind, came up from the assembled thousands of Ithaqua's people, held captive audience. But no, they could not watch, they had seen this before. To a man they turned and fled, even those six lesser priests whose accusations had brought Zchakow to this – to the very gates of hell! Yes, the gates of hell, in the shape of Ithaqua's eyes – *into one of which he-she-I now dropped the wriggling form of the mad Russian!*

A bubbling scream, shrill and rising, cut off in a shower of carmine sparks that burst upwards from the flickering rim of that seething crater eye like lava bombs from a volcano – and Zchakow was gone.

And I had felt something. Something which I cannot, *must* not attempt to describe in detail, except to say that perhaps it was an overflow of Ithaqua's hideous *satisfaction* . . .

Now for a moment the Wind-Walker grimly surveyed the fleeing hordes of his people, then turned to stride up a staircase of air back to his position at the summit of the pyramid altar. There he stood, arms akimbo, great feet gripping the sides of the ice mountain, and as his rage subsided I found myself freed of the tremendous attraction of his id. I began to withdraw, to retreat along with Armandra from the mental maw of the Wind-Walker.

– And at that very moment he saw us!

No, he saw *her*, only Armandra, for my own feeble essence was insignificant. I call it essence because I realize now that it was no simple mind-web that had enmeshed me, and therefore that I had not been trapped telepathically. After all, I had looked into Ithaqua's mind before without any of this. But the power Armandra had which enabled her to visit and observe scenes afar was more than merely telepathic; it was more truly psychic, the essential power of the id itself. Her *Ka* had been part of her awesome father for a few brief moments of time, hers and mine too; and now, when we had almost managed to break free –

Quickly the scene of the monster atop his pyramid of ice shrank as I fled with Armandra back toward the plateau, and quickly Ithaqua turned his head to stare after us, realization growing in the flickering of his flaring eyes. He reached out bestial psychic arms after Armandra, again casting that net whose meshes she had managed to escape before he even knew she was there. Ah, but now he *did* know she was there, and again she was caught.

Armandra was caught and so was I, and it seemed as good a time as any to make my presence known, this time telepathically, as I had intended in the first place.

'*Armandra!*' I cried with my mind. '*Fight him. You have to fight him. I'm here to help you. Together we can beat him!*'

'*What?*' Armandra's mind reached out unbelievingly to mine. '*Who is it that offers aid, and how did –*' but that was all.

At last Ithaqua had seen me too, but too late. Something that seethed like acid touched my mind, touched Armandra, too, then burned through to the Being of Ithaqua himself. He staggered atop his pyramid. He snatched back those greedily reaching mental and physical arms of his and slammed down the shutters of his alien id, his psyche, his mind, cutting us free of him. No, cutting *himself* free of us! We fled back to our bodies in the Hall of the Elders.

I was stretched out full length on the stone floor. Tracy and Jimmy were trying to get me to my feet. I shook my head and stood up, noting that the chamber was now empty of all but a group of magnificently robed old men, my own party, Oontawa, and –

I started forward when I saw Armandra being helped down the dais steps to Oontawa. The Indian girl's eyes flashed a warning, saying that this was not the time to approach the Woman of the Winds. But perhaps she was wrong.

Armandra's beautiful face was drawn, strained. As she passed close to me she held up a trembling hand and turned my way. 'What is your name, man of the Motherworld?'

'Hank,' I told her. 'Hank Silberhutte.'

'And it was you that –?'

I nodded. 'Yes.'

She leaned toward me, searching my face. 'At the end there – what was it that came to sting my mind, burning Ithaqua and making him release me?'

'Was it this?' Tracy asked, holding up one of the five-pointed star-stones from her neck, where the fur of her jacket had kept it and its twin hidden. 'When you cried out, Hank, when you shouted to Armandra that she must fight her father, I sort of instinctively held the stone up before your eyes. Then you leaped up and fell to the floor, and Armandra almost toppled from her throne.'

Tracy stopped talking, gazed nervously about as the elders all around her stepped quickly back, away from the star-stone sigil, and I stepped back with them. Armandra's eyes grew huge and round. She pointed a trembling hand at the powerful symbol of old gods spinning at the end of the chain Tracy held. Then she fell back weakly, leaning on Oontawa.

The group of elders, ten of them, now clustered closer, and one of them stretched out a finger before I could offer a warning. Briefly he touched the star-stone – and instantly snatched his finger back, the skin of its tip scorched and blackened. For a moment anguish showed on his face, then he turned to his colleagues.

'The stone is genuine – and yet,' he stared fascinated at Tracy, 'the girl is unhurt!'

'Elders, I go now,' Armandra broke in, stronger now, commanding everyone's attention. 'But there are things I

117

would know. See to the strangers and ask what questions you will, but do not keep these people here too long. They are to be our special guests until I decide on the best way to employ their talents.' She turned to move on, paused.

'This man,' she barely looked at me, 'Oontawa will return for him. She will bring him to me.' With that she turned and walked with her handmaiden from the hall.

When the two had gone, the oldest of the ten elders invited us to talk. He was an Eskimo of very ancient lineage, a tough old ivory chief of tribes forgotten except in Arctic legend. Explaining that his English was very, very bad, he spoke through Jimmy Franklin, turning his attention immediately to Tracy.

I had noticed that the elders seated themselves carefully out of her way for an obvious reason. Now, to explain her immunity to the star-stones whose shape was the greatest symbol of benign power known to the People of the Plateau. Despite their perfectly natural dread of the real item, it was necessary that we tell our entire story right from the beginning. This we did, using Jimmy as our interpreter whenever we were in difficulties.

The elders were fascinated with our story, astounded that we had deliberately set out to track Ithaqua down, and when our tale was done they stood up to give us their applause. Then their youngest member, a man until now silent, finally said, 'Permit me to introduce myself. I am Charlie Tacomah, a Shawnee late of the Motherworld.'

'A Shawnee who speaks perfect English,' Jimmy answered him, eyeing the tall, bronzed figure whose features, though fine, were plainly American Indian. 'But Nashville and Chattanooga are a long way from the Arctic Circle, and you are a much younger man than the others here.'

'I think he's a man pretty much like yourself, Jimmy,' Whitey said. 'A man of the reservations, who figured that there might be better things in life. I guess his ambitions led him astray, though.'

The elder nodded, glancing at Whitey appreciatively. 'Yes, it was twenty-eight years ago. After the war when I got back home to Memphis, I found the same old prejudices. I wanted to do something about it, decided to write a book on all the Indian tribes, ancient and modern. I eventually travelled north, seeking out the little-known Eskimo tribes, and –'

'We can guess,' I broke in on him sympathetically. 'You fell afoul of Ithaqua. He brought you to Borea.'

Charlie Tacomah nodded. 'I lived for a few days with the Children of the Winds, then ran off and came here. The elders found out that I was something of a military strategist – I had been a major in the infantry – and I became adviser to the old warlords. Five years ago Northan took over as warlord, controlling all of the plateau's army, and I was granted a seat in the Council of Elders.

'Of all the People of the Plateau, I reckon that about sixty of them have arrived here on Borea within the last twenty or thirty years. They learn to fit in pretty quickly. Of course, the great majority of folks that Ithaqua brings stay out on the plains, too frightened to try to escape. If an escapee is recaptured,' he shrugged, 'Ithaqua has his own ways of punishing deserters.'

'And now?' Tracy prompted him after a moment's silence. 'What's to become of us?'

'Well, you heard what Armandra said. There's not a great deal we can do with you just yet. Right now, though, it is my pleasure to show you all around the plateau; a fascinating place, as you'll see. Eventually my colleagues' proposals will be put before Armandra for her approval. It is not anticipated that you will be required to contribute in any mundane fashion to the plateau's welfare. Of course, you are far different from run-of-the-mill newcomers.'

As he finished speaking Oontawa returned. Tracy cocked her head to one side and smiled wickedly at me. She whispered: 'Here comes the handmaiden, Hank. Before she takes you to Armandra, you'd better promise me you'll be a good boy. I've noticed the way you look at the Woman of the Winds.'

'Star-stones or not,' I told her, grinning, 'another crack like that, little sister, and you go over my knee – and I'll do a bit of wind-raising myself!'

And so I started out with Oontawa for Armandra's apartments, and it immediately became apparent that the Priestess of the Plateau dwelt in the topmost levels of her realm. Staircase after stone staircase we climbed, ever spiralling upward through basalt caverns and tunnels until I was sure we must soon reach the battlements of the roof; and we could not have been far short of that roof when finally we came to the first corridor I had seen with its own selected guardsmen.

During our long climb the symbols above tunnel entrances or at the feet of the staircases had been gradually narrowing down to a handful, but already I had guessed which symbol led to Armandra: that of a flash of lightning. Sure enough, above that last, guarded corridor entrance, the lightning flash was the sole remaining symbol, and I saw that beyond it even the tunnel walls themselves were draped with priceless furs.

Two huge squat Eskimo guards, each attended by a towering white bear that swayed and yawned in a rock-cut niche to his rear, stood up straight and saluted with their viciously barbed, ceremonial harpoons as we passed. Flambeaux were now absent where natural light flooded in through windows lining the vast curve of the outer wall. By 'windows' I may give the wrong impression; I paused to look out through one of them and found myself staring into a shaft, for the window was cut through a wall of rock all of fifteen feet thick!

Closer to our destination the light flooded in more brightly, and here I saw that the thickness of the outer wall was much diminished. We came to a huge, iron-barred balcony with a stone ceiling; the balcony reached out from the face of the plateau into open air. Now I saw indeed that we were at a great height above the white waste. Fighting the wind that howled in from outside, I put my head out between the bars and looked down. More than two hundred and fifty feet beneath me, the rocky base of the plateau froze into the surface of the surrounding ground. Craning my neck I looked upward and saw that the topmost ramparts were still some twenty to thirty feet higher than this level, that the solid rock above my head must form the ceiling of Armandra's rooms.

I turned to Oontawa, saying: 'A dangerous place. A careless person could be sucked out by the wind, or fall through the bars.'

She nodded. 'Yes, Armandra sometimes – walks out – from here. When she seeks solitude.'

With those innocent words, so naively spoken, the Indian girl brought back to me all that I had tried to forget of the woman who was about to give me audience. Here was I, going to Armandra's apartments almost like some fancy courtier on his way to the boudoir of a precocious princess, and yet it was not like that at all. Armandra was more goddess than woman, as much an alien creature as a human being, and I was merely a man of the Motherworld.

Oontawa chattered away as we walked the perimeter corridor, practising her English and doubtlessly trying to be very informative, but I scarcely heard a word she said; my mind was now fully on her mistress. Perhaps fifty yards beyond the great balcony we came to a curtained entrance where the lightning flash symbol was inlaid in gold: the door to Armandra's quarters. Oontawa passed through the curtains ahead of me, murmuring something as she went, but again my mind was not on what the Indian girl was saying. I followed directly behind her through the curtains.

The room beyond was gorgeously appointed, rich as an eastern sultan's wildest dreams of opulence. Delicately carved, curtained archways led off into adjoining rooms; soft furs of a texture and colouring guaranteed to delight any furrier of the Motherworld overlapped across the floor; the white walls were carved with pillars and arches and intricate arabesques; gold and silver ornaments stood in arched niches in the walls, and fretted agate and marble furniture was cushioned with white furs as soft as freshly fallen snow. But in the very centre of the room stood the greatest wonder of all – Armandra, rising naked from a crystal pool!

We saw each other and froze, and simultaneously Oontawa realized that I had followed her into the chamber of her mistress without waiting. She turned with a sharp cry of consternation, her almond eyes wide and flashing.

'Calm yourself, Oontawa,' Armandra said. 'I am sure that my guest has seen naked women before. The Motherworld is full of "fascinating" women!'

Stepping from the pool she folded herself in a white fur wrap that covered her body completely. Before her feet vanished in the robe's folds, I thought for a moment that I saw something odd about them. What it was I could not have said exactly, just that they seemed to be – scarred? It had been only a glimpse.

'Well,' she continued, shaking her red hair and sprinkling crystal droplets all about, 'you might as well sit, Hank Silberhutte, or do all men of the Motherworld stand like statues with their mouths open?'

At that I offered an awkward, embarrassed grin, in answer to which I saw mischievous lights dancing momentarily in the depths of her fjord eyes. 'Oontawa, leave us,' she told the girl. 'I will call you when I want you. Oh! –' she called out in an afterthought as, with a look of disbelief stamped upon her face, the girl turned to go. 'Though I trust you above all others, Oontawa, make sure you say nothing of this man's unfortunate eagerness to attend me; there are those it would surely enrage. You may see to it that the elders, too, remain silent about this interview. Particularly those with whom the warlord has influence.'

Oontawa bowed and went out through the curtains. I sat at a delicately carved table, hardly daring to rest the weight of my arms upon it in case it fell apart. Armandra seated herself upon the fur cushions of a settee carved of a single gigantic agate, hugging her robe about her and gazing at me curiously.

She said: 'Are your hands gentle, Hank Silberhutte?'

Again she had me tongue-tied. 'My hands?'

'Are they *gentle*,' she frowned impatiently, 'for the drying of my hair?'

'They can be gentle,' I answered, 'when they need to be.'

'Good. Come and dry my hair.'

I went to her and took the square of woven material that she handed me. She continued: 'I know that your hands can be hard, for you knocked down that strutting bear, Northan. But I expect that they are soft, too; how else would you handle all of those "fascinating" women of the Motherworld?'

I caught up her damp tresses and began to dry them, pausing to turn her head away so that I could make a decent job of it.

'Your hands *are* gentle,' she told me, laughing at me out of sea green eyes. 'Perhaps I'll find a place for you as a handmaiden, and –'

At that point I stopped her. To say what she had said to any man, which most ordinary women of Earth would know better than to do, would surely be folly. To say it to a Texan . . .

I turned her head back and kissed her fiercely, feeling her fingers fly to the back of my neck and head to tear at my hair, ignoring the shock and anger obvious in her suddenly squirming, furiously fighting body, until she no longer fought but sank her nails into my neck and drank as deeply as I.

For a moment only!

Then, as I relaxed my hold upon her, she snatched herself back from me and slapped me so hard that my ears rang.

'You beautiful *witch*!' I said through clenched teeth.

But now she tilted her head warningly and I thought her eyes were suddenly flecked with pink. Those great eyes widened and, seemingly of its own accord, the still damp hair of her head lifted eerily to float free of her shoulders. For a moment she was a goddess again, utterly inhuman. But then, amazingly, she burst into tears and buried her face in her hands!

5

Armandra Chooses a Mate

(Recorded through the Medium of Juanita Alvarez)

Her tears were the perfectly normal tears of a woman face
to face with utter mental and physical frustration. The
tears of a *woman*, not a being of supermundane powers.
Telepathically probing the edge of her emotions, gently,
so as to remain undiscovered, I found a stark island of
bitter frustration afloat in a sea of loneliness.

Whitey's words came back to me, about Ithaqua's need
for a companion: *It's a terribly lonely existence*, he had
said, *walking the spaces between the spheres*. How much
more true for a human or half-human child of the Snow
Thing with alien powers trapped in a human psyche,
framed by human emotions?

Carefully, concentrating on what I was doing, I allowed
sympathy to flow along the line of one-way communication I had established, and instantly the bleak hopelessness in Armandra's mind began to soften. She lifted
her head and leaned toward me, searching my face with
eyes as round as saucers. Her tears were already drying.

'Was it really you, Hank, that came to me when my
father held me fast?'

I nodded, answering her in a manner guaranteed to satisfy her curiosity and quell any last doubt she might have.
'Yes.' I said. '*It really was. It's a power I have.*'

And she could see that it was so, that I was speaking in
her mind. Proof of my success showed in her frown, then
in the widening of eyes already huge. 'A very dangerous
power,' she said, forming her words carefully. 'How can
any woman trust a man who listens to her thoughts?'

'She must first learn to believe that he would not listen uninvited,' I answered. Then I launched into an explanation of my telepathic power, briefly telling her what I had already made known to the Council of Elders. 'So you see,' I finished, 'that among my colleagues of the Motherworld it is considered outrageous for one telepath to "listen" to another without his permission. But in any case, my own power is rather special.'

And there I paused, for how could I say that I was limited to intercourse with alien thoughts, the hideous mental gibberings of monsters, when Armandra herself was now a vehicle for my talent? I groped for words. 'I can only detect the thoughts of – of very special Beings.'

'Other people?'

'There is one other woman I can talk to in this fashion,' I hedged, 'and she is like a sister, the same as Tracy.'

'But you have listened to my mind. Is it not so?'

'No, not really. When you spied upon your father out over the frozen wastes, it was not telepathy that trapped me there when you were trapped. It was your own power, yours and your father's, a power in no way like mine. It is far greater, different.'

She nodded, warming to the empathy growing between us. 'I believe you. I know it is true. The power I have, which came to me from my father, is not like yours. But have you not listened to my mind within the last few moments, here in this very room?'

'No,' I again denied it. 'I merely felt your hurt, your loneliness, and tried to comfort you. I have not stolen a single thought out of your lovely head, though any man might easily be tempted to try. Particularly if he thought you were thinking about him.' I stared at her pointedly.

'One day, Hank Silberhutte, I might invite you into my head,' she said, quite seriously. 'Would you come to me if I called you? If I needed you?'

'That I promise.'

'But wait,' she said. 'I have heard *your* voice talking to *my* mind, yes, but how do we know if –'

'Would you like to try an experiment?'

She nodded eagerly.

'Then think something at me, anything. See if I can read it in your mind.'

She opened her eyes wide and stared straight at me. It was very strange, that sensation, like the chiming of golden bells at the bottom of some mental well, rising slowly to the surface, forming pictures. I looked, then chuckled as the mischievous lights again lit in Armandra's eyes. 'Yes,' I nodded, 'I think perhaps Northan would be angry if he knew I was here. But it does not worry me. Do you fear him, Armandra?'

'Fear Northan? I fear only Ithaqua – but I know that many of my people, even a handful of the elders, do fear the warlord.' Her eyes narrowed thoughtfully. 'He is ambitious. And he does not like his ambitions thwarted. You must watch out for him, Hank. Be very watchful of Northan.'

'It surprises me,' I said, 'that he was not in the Hall of the Elders for your – seeing.'

'No, he would be celebrating the victory of the ships over the wolf-warriors. Sometimes the celebrations last for days. Oh, they strut and boast, as their forefathers did before them. In many ways they are like children.'

'Well,' I answered, 'the battle was well won, with your help. But without you Northan would have been hard put. And he lost a lot of face when I returned his blows. I can hardly see that he has much to celebrate!'

'Oh, he'll knock a few heads together, find excuses for your beating him on his own ship and awe his cronies with feats of strength.' Again her eyes narrowed. 'I know Northan the Warlord. It will not take him long to regain whatever face he feels he has lost. He is ambitious.' Again that word.

127

'And what is his ambition, do you think?'

'Is it not obvious?' she lifted her eyebrows. 'He desires to share these apartments with me. For while the People of the Plateau are satisfied with their princess, Northan would give them a king, a High Priest. And in a way the elders aid him, for they want me to have children.'

'But you do not want him?'

'I could do worse,' she tossed her hair, dry now, and began to comb it. 'Does the thought annoy you?'

'No,' I immediately answered, then bit my tongue and spoke in her mind. '*You damn well know it does!*'

She laughed. 'Because I am fascinating, and beautiful?'

'Those are good reasons,' I agreed.

'I am not all beautiful,' she told me, her face becoming serious in an instant. 'You saw my feet when I left the pool?'

'Your feet? Yes, they looked –'

She flicked the fur wrap so that it flew wide below her knees. 'They are ugly!' she said.

For a moment she stared down in something like horror at her feet, then said: 'My mother was stolen from your green Earth by Ithaqua. She was given into the care of the Children of the Winds until I was born. Later, in my father's absence, having learned that he had fathered a child upon a human woman, the plateau people stole me away in a raid and brought me here; my mother too, but she died from the wound of a harpoon hurled in the fighting. They say she was very beautiful.

'The elders raised me. When I was ten a physician, specially trained for ten years to perform one work, cut my feet down from the great webbed pads they were to their present shape. He was supposed to leave them looking like normal human feet, so that I would forget my origins, but the operation was not very successful. For a long time I was in constant pain.'

128

A moment longer I looked at her feet. They were the shape of human feet but with square looking, nailless toes and a covering of smooth scar tissue. Then she flicked her wrap back into place.

'When my feet had healed, about a year after the operation, I had a terrible dream of great angry winds and of the physician whose knives had scarred me. When I awakened the elders told me that there had been an accident; that same physician had fallen from a window of his room high in the outer wall of the plateau. A freak gust of wind, they said.

'When I told them that I had sent that wind to kill him – sent it in my sleep to settle a debt I hardly recognized in my waking hours – then they stood in awe of me and knew that they could never suppress that in me which was of Ithaqua. Thus I became what I am.

'But there,' she looked at me and sighed. 'Now you must go. Soon I meet with the elders again and I need a few hours sleep. The seeing drained me. Today was especially hard. I became too involved with my father's awful justice. He has never come so close to trapping me before. But, Hank Silberhutte, I am glad you are my friend. And I know that if I call you will come to me. Now go.'

'There's a lot you could tell me, many questions you –'

'Your questions will be answered, in time.' She stood up, holding her wrap about her. She held out her free hand and I took it, following her to the curtained exit. 'Only promise me,' she said, 'that however tempted you may be, you will never look into my mind uninvited. When I want you to know my thoughts, you shall know them.'

'I promise.'

'Wait!' she cried as I was about to leave. 'You gave me something I did not ask for. Now take it back.' She leaned forward, brushed my lips with hers, and quickly withdrew. Seeing the mischief rising in her eyes I reached

129

out my arms to her, and she drew the curtains in my face and was gone.

On returning to my room I felt suddenly exhausted. That experience I had shared with Armandra's psyche had severely sapped my strength, as much as the fight against her father's alien will had taxed hers. Since the others were not back yet from their sightseeing, I lay down and slept.

No sooner had I awakened than they returned. They were tired, but so full of what they had seen I decided that in the near future I must explore the plateau for myself.

'This place,' said Whitey, 'is a maze of marvels. We've seen the wells that supply half of the plateau's water, and the cavern where weeds and mushrooms grow at the edge of the geyser flats. We've seen cave pools chock-full of fish, and watched the Eskimos spearing them.'

'From the other side of the plateau,' Tracy cut in, 'we've seen the rim of Borea's sun. Like the moons, it never moves; only its upper curve shows. There's a forest of pines on that side, too, and in the distance a great stretch of woodland that reaches to the horizon. It looks like a rather flat version of Canada.'

Jimmy was less enthusiastic. 'We saw the pool of oil where they draw their fuel in wooden buckets, and we saw the dark tunnel whose entrance has a skull carved above it as a warning. We felt the horror lurking there, emanating from forbidden nether-caves. No one knows what lies at the tunnel's lower level; its mysteries have never been explored. It reeks of – fear!'

When Tracy shivered I knew it was not because of any normal chill she might feel. 'It's funny,' she said. 'Jimmy and Whitey felt this – this *thing* – and so did Charlie Tacomah. All of the People of the Plateau feel it when they are close to the tunnel. No one will enter it, not by a single step. And yet I felt nothing. Well, I felt something, but not fear. If anything, I felt safer there. But not really safe, if you know what I mean.' Suddenly she clung to my arm: 'Hank, when can we . . . I mean, do you think –'

'Tracy,' Whitey cut her off. 'Let's have it out in the open. We must all have thought of the same thing, and I've been trying my best to see what the outcome might be. You know, I've been looking for a hunch. But I haven't found one.'

'You don't come over too well, Whitey,' I told him. 'You mean we're stuck here?'

He nodded. 'I think so. It looks like we're here for good. If these people have been on Borea for thousands of years and haven't found a way back yet, what chance do we stand?'

Tracy looked miserable so I put my arm round her. 'Not much of a chance,' I agreed. Then I thought of Armandra and realized that the thought of staying on Borea hadn't really been bothering me too much.

'Still,' I added, 'never say die.'

For me the next month passed slowly. I seemed always to be waiting for a call from Armandra, but I only saw her twice, at meetings of the council to which I was invited as a courtesy. On both occasions, though, I had caught her eyes on me when she thought I was looking elsewhere. Between times my dreams were full of her.

Once I dreamed we walked together on the wind between the worlds. We moved where stars were frosted to the firmament and Borea was far away. And yet, though I saw Armandra mostly in my dreams, there was always this peculiar feeling that she was with me in the waking world also. I began to suspect that she was 'peeking' into my mind. If so then she knew well enough by now my feelings for her.

I say the time passed slowly, and yet there were diversions. The plateau's weapon-masters took me in hand and I was trained for three hours daily in a variety of weapons. I soon discovered that what skill could not achieve in a tight spot might often be realized by use of my considerable size and strength. And my strength never failed to amaze my instructors.

During one such session Northan entered the exercise cave. I was throwing a harpoon at a painted target of woven hide when the warlord came in. I saw him and his presence put me off; my throw went a few inches wide of the bull.

Northan grinned and picked up a harpoon. 'Not nearly good enough,' he said. 'If that target was a wolf, he'd be tearing you in half by now.'

He turned, casually hurled his weapon and it slammed home dead centre of the target, burying its barbs. We moved to the target together. 'Now that was a cast,' Northan chuckled.

He tugged at the shaft of his harpoon but it was stuck fast. Lifting a foot to the target, he strained. Still the harpoon would not come. He grunted, shrugged, stepped back. I caught hold of both weapons, one in each hand, placed a knee against the target and pulled the harpoons free in a snapping of leather thongs. Northan's face went grey, then darkened over. Before he could speak I said, 'That wolf you mentioned might not find me such easy meat, Northan. Perhaps, seeing you weaponless, he'd turn on you instead.'

It was just a small incident, but word of this second encounter spread as rapidly as the story of our confrontation on the snow-ship. Whitey had warned me on more than one occasion that the warlord would bring me down if he could, and having seen Northan's face as he strode angrily from the exercise cave I could only agree.

Still, I had things other than the strutting warlord to worry about.

As the weeks passed I grew almost to envy Tracy. She was with Armandra almost every day, learning the royal routine and speedily becoming the Woman of the Wind's constant companion along with Oontawa. When she was not with Armandra, Tracy spent most of her time with Jimmy. I noticed the strong bond developing between them and was pleased.

And if any member of my team was in his element, surely it was Jimmy Franklin. Apart from Tracy's attentions, he was now in a position to study the old tribes as they had really been. The Nootka and Micmac, Chimakua and Algonquin, Huron and Ojibwa, Onondaga, Chilkat, Mohawk and Tlingit; all of the northern tribes of old were represented, and Jimmy must surely have felt that he was now among the ancestors of his race.

I had asked him about the plateau's Indians, about their weapons. Why had I seen no single trace of the traditional bow and arrow? It all had to do with the nature of Borea and its people, he told me. In a world where alien, elemental powers were used as super-weapons, mere bows could easily be made useless. Temperatures could be sent down to a point where bowstrings, and even the wooden bows themselves, would break at the slightest pressure. Arrows could simply be blown aside. On the other hand, spears, harpoons and hand-axes were less susceptible to such forces.

And it was Jimmy, too, who first learned the legends of the plateau, myths that went back for something like five thousand years and maybe more. These tales had it that at a time forgotten in the dim mists of immemorial lore, Ithaqua had been prisoned in the bowels of the plateau. This had followed an act of defiance against the Elder Gods, when he had waged war on the early civilized races of Earth, striding the skies across all the dawn world and ravaging far and wide. The Wind-Walker was imprisoned thus for thousands of years before finally being released (or escaping, the legends were confused on that point) but ever since then he had been leery of the plateau, his one-time prison.

When I heard of this legend I couldn't help but tie certain facts up together. Strangely enough, Tracy featured strongly in these reckonings of mine. The fact, for instance, that my sister was the only one of all the plateau's people who possessed a positive defence against the Snow Thing; and likewise that she knew no fear when confronted with that forbidden tunnel deep in the bowels of the plateau, the tunnel whose almost physical emanations held all others back.

What lay at the other end of that dark shaft, and was it necessarily dangerous to the People of the Plateau? Tracy's star-stones, after all, were only injurious to us because we had been touched with the contamination of Ithaqua. And while we were naturally wary of the things, still they were far more dangerous – indeed lethal – to the Wind-Walker himself and his minions. Was it possible that the secret of the tunnel was that which Ithaqua also feared, the thing that held him back from destroying the plateau itself and all of its people?

Once, with Whitey, I stood at the entrance to that dark shaft, and both of us felt the thrust of forces that bade us go away or face an indefinite but very real doom. It was not only fear but a wall, a barrier real as any wall of bricks and mortar.

When I asked Whitey what he made of it, he said, 'I don't really know, Hank. I feel much the same as Tracy, I guess. On the one hand this place gives me the creeps – I don't know what's going to jump out at me, you know? – but on the other hand I feel, well, that the whole future of, oh, of *everything* is tied up at the far end of this tunnel.'

'Is that a hunch?'

'Yes, a strong one, but don't ask me to explain it. You couldn't get me down this shaft anyhow, not even for a ticket back to Earth!'

By the end of the second month I was more or less sure that Armandra had been spying on me mentally. Whether or not she was getting any clear mental pictures I did not really know; I had made no effort to project any thoughts in her telepathic direction. Nevertheless, and despite my suspicions, I stuck to my own promise not to look into her mind, though I admit that I was tempted.

Toward the end of the month, however, her prying had become so intense that I could feel her with me at almost any time in any given twenty-four hour period. At the same time I was being teased by Tracy whenever she saw me. She swore that Armandra's interest in me knew no bounds, that the Woman of the Winds had sucked her dry of all facts concerning me and my life before Borea. And I believed Tracy, for she made me promise not to repeat anything she told me; Armandra did not want me to know of her interest in me. She was no common woman to throw herself at a man.

Still, Armandra's constant presence on the borders of my mind bothered me considerably (there are things a man might want to keep secret; emotions, fears and ambitions he might not want to disclose), and so I determined to teach her a lesson if her peeking continued. It was when I had awakened from the middle of a nightmare in which I had fought to free Armandra from her father's swollen fingers, discovering her presence there at the edge of my surfacing awareness, that I found my opportunity.

'*Very well*,' I spoke to her deliberately with my mind. '*I don't know what you seek in my thoughts, Armandra, but if it is this –*' and here I projected a vivid and exceptionally erotic scene concerning the two of us, a perfectly natural fantasy which until then I had forced myself to keep out of my mind, '*– then now you know!*'

For a moment longer she was with me and I sensed sudden, explosive outrage, and something else, before she was gone. I waited a minute or two longer but the ether was completely free of telepathic influences. Later I awakened again to find strange, gentle little winds caressing my body and ruffling my hair where I lay upon my bed of furs. And I knew where they came from, for beyond my stone window the grey and white Boreal scene was calm and quiet.

And so things stood for perhaps a further week, so that it was a few days into the third month when Oontawa came to bring me Armandra's invitation to the Choosing of a Champion, when a suitable mate would be found from among all the men of the plateau. I say Oontawa came with an invitation, and yet I was ready to go before she and the others of my small party brought me the news. Armandra had already uttered these words in my mind: *'Now you can come to me, Hank Silberhutte, if you want me!'*

Simply those few words, and yet every nerve in my body was suddenly energized and fires I had only guessed to exist raced in my blood, however unnaturally cold that blood might be. She had called to me, and I would go to her, yes. But on my terms.

We made our way quickly to the Hall of the Elders, and as we went Oontawa told me things I would need to know. I knew of the ritual Choosing of a Champion, but did not know the finer details of the rite. It appeared that since women were slightly in the minority, most of them were sought after as prizes by the unmarried men. Therefore a girl would usually make known to her favourite that she intended to choose a champion, and he in turn would pick a close male friend who he could trust to accept his challenge. When the girl offered herself publicly, her lover would then have to put himself forward for acceptance or rejection, and offer a challenge to anyone else who fancied the girl. His friend would then step forward and a short fight would ensue in which the 'usurper' would be 'beaten'. That was the way the ritual usually went. Usually.

This time it would be different. For one thing it was Armandra choosing a champion. For another she had made no approaches – no physical approaches, at least – to any of the plateau's males. That would have been unbecoming for first lady of the plateau. Finally, Northan had long made known his ambition to take Armandra to wife. If any man challenged his right to the Woman of the Winds, the warlord would be merciless.

We entered the Hall of the Elders to find its amphitheatre tiers of seats already filled to capacity. Young men of all the tribes jostled each other nervously just within the door, elbow to elbow with Eskimo warriors, pure whites, and mixtures of varied background and lineage. We pushed through to a clear space where I saw that a tight circle had been chalked round the base of the dais.

At the head of the dais Armandra stood, head bowed as the ritual demanded, for she must make no sign to any man in the assembly that she favoured him. She was absolutely beautiful – white as the fine furs that concealed little of the perfection of her body, the fur boots that hid the imperfection of her feet – a gorgeously carved candle of flesh crowned with the living fire of her hair.

Across the hall, in a ring of his own admirers and cohorts, stood Northan, powerfully armoured in the manner of a warlord. Yet forbidding as his armour was, the black scowl he directed all round him would surely be even more of a deterrent to anyone foolish enough to cross him in this matter.

For the moment no one in Northan's party had seen me, and from the oily smiles on the faces of his companions I could tell that they expected no interference. Well, let them expect what they would. My chill blood had been fired; Armandra meant so much to me now that death itself would be almost preferable to the thought of her in the warlord's arms.

No sooner had the thought crossed my mind than I felt Armandra's mental fingers probing. They brushed me, lingered as if to make certain of my identity, then withdrew. She trembled where she stood, then, without looking up, she spoke.

'This woman now offers herself as wife and seeks a champion. Who will fight for me, for the glory of the plateau and its people?'

Her words were hardly out before Northan stepped forward, climbed the dais steps and took Armandra's arm. Immediately the blood raced faster in my veins. Now Northan saw me; his hot eyes lingered on me for a second, then contemptuously flicked by me to sweep the hall. There was complete silence. It seemed as if the entire assembly held its breath, waiting for the warlord to speak. And he did.

'I, Northan, her champion, claim this woman, to fight for her, for the glory of the plateau and its people. Is there a man to challenge my right?' His voice itself was a threat, a promise of violent, certain death to anyone who challenged him. I felt a movement beside me in the crush of people and held back, waiting to see what this disturbance could be.

A young brave was moving forward, hawk-featured and proud, flushed with reckless excitement. Before he could reach the forward edge of the crowd a friend caught hold of him, whispering urgently, fearfully into his ear. Their eyes went to Northan where he stood watching them, an ugly grin twisting his face. Suddenly the grin dropped away and his lips hardened. His eyes bored into those of the young brave and their message was perfectly clear. So as to make it even clearer, the warlord spoke again.

'Let any challenger come forward now, and let him know that Northan fights to the death!'

Suddenly white, the young brave stepped back and quickly disappeared in the crowd, his nerve broken.

Northan's grin returned and again his fierce eyes swept the hall. And still I waited, for I knew that the ritual demanded that a challenge be made. In threatening a fight to the death, surely the warlord had put paid to any plans he might previously have made for one of his own men to take up the challenge.

Then that which I had waited for happened; Armandra's thoughts rushed in upon me. I stared at her and slowly her head lifted. She gazed straight into my eyes.

'If you hold back much longer, Hank Silberhutte, the council might declare me Northan's woman without the ritual being fully completed. They are eager to have me wed.'

'I hold back for one reason only, Armandra, and you know that reason. I would be no mate to crawl to you when you fancied me, to father your children and then be pensioned off with a seat on the Council of Elders. If I'm to be a husband then I will be a husband, not some sort of privileged lapdog!'

Now the elders of the council had moved forward to stand at the foot of the dais. They turned outward, facing the crowd. Armandra's anger flooded into my mind for an instant before she cried out; *'Oh, you fool! Do you not know why I dared not let you look into my thoughts? I am a woman, Hank Silberhutte, but a woman can have thoughts as lustful as any man!'*

And now Northan had finally seen the two of us staring intently at each other. His lips drew back in warning and his eyes slitted with fury. I felt the hate radiating from him. The spokesman of the elders stepped up beside the warlord and Armandra. He raised his arm, opened his mouth to speak –

'I challenge you, Northan,' I shouted, moving forward. 'I challenge your right to this woman and will fight you, with any weapons you choose, for the glory of the plateau and its people!'

From behind me, completely dry and without banter, I heard Whitey whisper, 'If we ever get back to Earth, that's fifty dollars you owe me, Jimmy. Never bet against a hunchman!'

Tracy breathlessly added, 'And a hundred to me. I guess you just don't know Hank, Jimmy.' Then their whispers were drowned out in the wild and amazed clamour that roared up from the thronging audience.

PART THREE

1
Northan – Traitor!

(Recorded through the Medium of Juanita Alvarez)

At first I thought that Northan would explode. His mouth fell open and his eyes bulged in outrage and disbelief. He let go of Armandra's arm and began to descend the dais steps; then, noticing the way I was dressed – my sandals, soft leather trunks and fur-collared jacket – his eyes narrowed craftily. For a split second he paused, seeming to ponder something, and then his astonishment and rage appeared to increase twofold.

The spokesman of the elders had now left the dais but Northan's shout stopped him in his tracks as he hurried out of the chalked combat area. 'You there, elder! Do you see how this man mocks the Woman of the Winds, how he ridicules this ancient ceremony? He is recently come to us, and yet his attitude is not nearly what it should be. He even dares resent my authority as Warlord of the Plateau! Look at him. He is not dressed for combat, and if he were I could hardly lower myself to accept his challenge. He should not be in a position to lay claim to the lowliest, most miserable whore from the barracks areas, and yet here he is, offering himself as a mate for the Woman of the Winds! This is more than mere mockery,' his voice lifted to a bellow of artificial outrage. 'It is insolence – defilement!'

Now I knew what the warlord was up to, and as he finished speaking I saw a nodding of heads among his cronies. Even one or two of the elders seemed to be in agreement with him, much to the obvious disgust of others, particularly Charlie Tacomah. Well, Northan had

had his say, now it was my turn. Before the elder he had addressed could answer him, I spoke up.

'Elder,' I began, speaking to the same old man, 'in the Motherworld I was a leader of men, not given to accepting insults from puffed up dogs. I do not intend to lower my standards here on Borea. While it disgusts me to soil myself in combat with such as your present warlord, if that is the only way to elevate my position to one of acceptable status, I am prepared to do so.' I allowed a moment for that to sink in, then continued. 'Over and above the question of mere position, however, there is the fact that I believe I am in love with the Woman of the Winds. Because of this, I cannot stand and watch Northan take her unchallenged. If she is the prize of this contest, then I can imagine no more desirable prize. It is one which I will treasure always.' Again I briefly paused.

'I have been given to understand it is desirable that Armandra has children, that the Council of Elders has long been pressing her to wed. In the interest of the plateau I ask you this question: are your future princes to be strutting peacocks and boasters, or great men with powers as great as, and perhaps greater than their mother's own? That is the difference between Northan taking Armandra to wife, and –'

'I have heard of your so-called "powers", you dollop of –' Northan bellowed in genuine fury, until I stilled his tongue by turning my back on him. I addressed the thronging People of the Plateau now, letting them see that plainly the warlord was beneath my contempt.

'But if you, the people, or if Armandra herself has any objection to my challenging Northan, then I will withdraw my challenge, however reluctantly.'

Now this was what Northan himself had tried to do with his blustered insults; place Armandra in a position to refuse me as a prospective champion, on the grounds that I was unsuitable and beneath her contempt, without breaking any of the ceremonial rules of conduct. He had suspected something and wanted to see how the land lay between us, to see if she really did find my challenge objectionable.

She had not risen to Northan's bait; she had held her tongue. Well, I too had wanted the warlord to know the lay of the land, and so I had answered him myself, trying to force Armandra's hand. Now we both looked to her for an answer, and finally she said, 'You are both strong, able men. I have no preference, for I am the Woman of the Winds and above such things. There is no objection to either one of you, or to any man who would fight to be my champion.'

'*Liar!*' I told her with a sharp thought.

'*I cannot completely alienate the warlord,*' she answered.

'Alienate *him? He might kill me!*'

'*You must not let him – and you must not kill him! For all his strutting he leads the warriors well and is no coward in battle.*'

Meanwhile Northan had stepped slowly, menacingly down, approaching until we were face to face. I could almost see the dark thoughts revolving in his head. While he had insulted me, I had doubly insulted him; Armandra's little speech had told him nothing, had been completely unsatisfactory, merely explaining her acceptance of the ancient code. Things were not the way he would have them; his anger was now very real, and his face black as thunder. He clenched and unclenched his great hands.

'Will you not dress yourself for battle before I kill you, Earthman?' he ground the words out.

'I came into the Motherworld naked, Northan,' I told him evenly. 'These few rags should not hinder my exit from Borea, even if I were ready to make one. I choose to fight as I stand, unless your choice of weapon is the cutting whip, in which case I will dress as you are dressed.'

'Then let's get it over with quickly,' he snarled, hurriedly stripping himself of his armour and hurling each piece away. 'If you're afraid of the whip –'

'I don't fear the whip,' I cut him off, 'but whips are for dogs, not men.'

'Then let it be the handaxe,' he snarled. 'Either way, you die!'

Handaxes! I would rather have had unarmed combat, in which I had trained on Earth for eleven years, but if it had to be with weapons then the handaxe suited me as well as any other.

From somewhere close at hand two young Indian boys brought a golden tray bearing a pair of matched, highly decorated but nevertheless deadly, picklike handaxes. The head of each was burnished until it shone, displaying a fine cutting edge on the wide blade, and a needle tip at the end of the rearward spine. I saw that this slender, piercing spine was barbed and cut with runnels to keep blood from flowing down the shafts of the weapons to the hands of their users. I looked at the things for a long moment, and as Northan noticed the expression on my face he grinned, regaining a little of his composure.

The tray was placed on the floor between us and two more youths brought an iron chain with a manacle at each end. These clasps were secured to our left wrists. Now we were tied together, with seven or eight feet of chain between us. I waited uneasily for someone to explain the rules but apparently there were none, or I should already be in possession of them.

'Are you ready?' Armandra's voice came from the dais, trembling a little. Northan went into a crouch above the golden tray, resting the wrist of his free right hand lightly on his right knee. I followed suit. This was it then. Obviously no rules were necessary; they would be self-explanatory.

The warlord's eyes flicked sideways as he watched Armandra. I watched her too. She stood with a square of some fine weave in her hand, held high. *'When I drop the cloth, Hank Silberhutte, take up your weapon – swiftly!'*

It was an effort to stop myself nodding. I flicked my gaze from Armandra to Northan and saw the muscles standing out along his shoulders and arms; his right hand trembled over his knee in tension. Sweat suddenly burst out upon his brow. I could feel cold sweat pouring down my own face and arms.

'Now!' came Armandra's mental warning – and yet it was no real warning for she dropped the square simultaneously with her thought.

As if in slow motion I saw Northan's hand reaching down for his weapon, the glint of a razor-honed edge as the handaxe rose up and back as if with a life of its own. At the same time I took up my own weapon, feeling the shaped grip in my hand like something alive.

Then Northan jerked on the chain and I shot forward, already off balance. I saw his eyes burning fiercely as his weapon began to descend, instinctively threw myself into a dive. I passed straight between his spread legs, dragging his chained arm down and deflecting the blow he aimed at my back.

Sprawling behind him I yanked on the chain, but Northan had played this game before. He instantly tucked his head between his legs and flipped over onto his back, rolling as I directed a swift blow at the wrist of his weapon hand. My handaxe brought sparks from the floor as he jerked his wrist out of harm's way. We got to our feet together, the warlord immediately stepping forward to swing his weapon horizontally, hauling on the chain at the same time to bring me within reach.

I arched my back, felt the sharp leading edge of Northan's weapon slice a shallow groove along my belly, yanked down with my left hand to bring the warlord forward and block any backhand blow he might have planned, then leaned into a sideways swipe at his legs below the knees. He sprang high, grunting as my weapon swished through empty air.

The silence of the crowd was broken now by a succession of concerted sighings and moanings, the hissing of sharply indrawn breath. I took what little pleasure I could in the fact that what concern was being shown was mainly for me; the warlord's popularity was nothing to envy. His enemies, usually silent, were more vociferous now in the passion and excitement of the spectacle.

As we circled each other with the chain stretched between us, I noted the warlord's attitude of merciless, murderous intent. There was absolutely no doubt in Northan's mind that he would win this contest. My physical strength was greater than his, true – and he doubtless recognized that fact, however grudgingly – but his skill and experience were making me look amateurish.

So far I had been lucky: Northan had only cut me once, not seriously. Could it be that he was playing with me? Well, one way or the other, the thing must be gotten over with quickly. While the Borean warlord's skill would not diminish, my strength certainly would. In any event, brute strength can rarely compete for very long against experienced dexterity.

And as that last thought entered my head I stumbled sideways into the bottom step of the dais and went sprawling headlong. Northan had waltzed me right into it, had planned it this way, knowing I would trip myself up. All right, then let him believe that his plan had worked even better than he expected, that things were worse for me than they really were.

I forced myself to go limp on the steps. Sprawling there, I put on a look of uncomprehending, dazed bafflement. This was the work of only a second, and I never once took my eyes off the warlord.

He laughed wildly, leaping to the attack, his arms lifting to deliver the final stroke. At the last moment I threw up my own weapon to ward off the descending blow, and at the same time I threw a loop of the chain about Northan's neck. Twisting the chain, I hugged him to me.

Now I could use my strength. Gripping the chain tighter where it circled Northan's neck, I flipped him over onto his back. I locked his right arm with my own weapon and quickly trapped his right wrist in a second, smaller loop of chain. Then I applied pressure with both arms, throttling my victim while dragging him backwards up the dais steps.

Choking out curses and obscenities, the warlord flopped up the steps after me, still attempting to impale me on the spine of his weapon with repeated flicks of his trapped wrist. Near the top of the steps I put an end to that by wrapping my legs about his arm. Now his left hand stretched blindly up between my legs, reaching for me with hooked fingers. I freed my handaxe, transferred both loops of chain to my left hand and struck at Northan's left elbow with the flat of my weapon. He howled as his arm vibrated violently for a second, then flopped uselessly.

Squeezing hard and twisting the chain, I watched the warlord's face begin to go blue, purple. Slowly his right fist opened and he dropped his weapon. The handaxe went clattering down the steps. I relaxed my grip a fraction, sitting upright until I looked down into my enemy's bulging eyes. Hatred still glared out of them unconcealed.

Releasing my grip a little more, I raised my handaxe almost to arm's length and said, 'Do you admit defeat, Northan?'

For an instant indecision showed in his blood-dark features, then slyness. From his answer it was plain that he did not think I would kill him. 'It's your play, Earthman,' he gasped. 'Get it over with!'

Gritting my teeth I lifted my weapon higher yet.

The crowd gasped; Northan fainted; Armandra's voice screamed in my head: *'No!'*

I slammed the handaxe down, cutting through the knot of chain above Northan's head and sending a shower of sparks from the stone steps. Then, as a great sigh went up from the assembly, I lifted him up by his hair and put both feet to his back. Kicking him forward, I sent his unconscious body somersaulting down the steps.

'There,' I told the breathless hall as Northan landed jarringly, face down on the stone floor. 'Keep your warlord!'

I got to my feet and stepped up beside Armandra, folding my arms and taking as dramatic a stance as I knew how. 'Keep him,' I repeated. 'Perhaps now, with his strutting stilled, he'll learn to be as good a citizen as he is a soldier.'

Then, as a delighted uproar burst out all about the hall, I said to Armandra, 'And what, princess, if Northan had killed me? It seems to me a shallow sort of affection that risks a life for a barbaric code of existence!'

She leaned on me, her beautiful face pale and drawn as death. 'Have I more faith in your friend Whitey than you?' she asked.

'Whitey? You mean you –' I sought Whitey's face in the crush of people at the foot of the dais. He was grinning cheerfully, heavy eyebrows arched happily. 'But why didn't he – why didn't *you* – tell me?'

'We did not want you to relax your vigilance for a moment.'

'Good old Whitey,' I grinned.

'He has earned my eternal respect,' she agreed. 'But if you had died, I might well have had him thrown from the roof of the plateau!'

If I had thought that now the door would be open to Armandra's chambers, then I had thought wrong. I was her champion, certainly, with the right to attend her at any time during her waking hours and counsel her, and be counselled in return, but as for anything else – forget it. We could not be together; there would not be, could not be, anything other than a sort of courting between us until I had proved myself yet again, in battle against those true enemies of the plateau, the Children of the Wind. And to be absolutely sure that the opportunity would not come for us to be alone together (perhaps she did not trust herself to adhere to the plateau's ancient rules), Armandra kept either Tracy or Oontawa with her constantly.

Not only was this extremely frustrating for me but it soon began to get on Jimmy Franklin's nerves, too. Because of this, and the fact that by now Tracy was as much taken with Jimmy as he was with her, Armandra allowed the two to be together fairly regularly for short periods, but she never failed to ensure that Oontawa was there to give her moral support in Tracy's absence.

It wasn't very long before I became so unhappy with this situation that I would take myself off for long periods to the exercise cave to work off my frustrations in mock but nevertheless furious combat. Indeed, as the weeks stretched out, I began to believe – almost to fear – that all serious battling was over and done with between the People of the Plateau and the wolf-warriors of Ithaqua, that I would never again be given the chance to fight for Armandra's favours.

Certainly I did not give much thought to the possibility of any real sort of crisis developing within the plateau itself. And yet, looking back on it, I recall that there were warnings enough. Whitey was nervous and jumpy, and kept going on at me to look out for the warlord and his friends.

It was during a session in the exercise cave that Jimmy Franklin brought me word of the trouble, of Northan's treachery. Since his humiliation the warlord had slowly but surely been losing his authority with the chiefs and headmen, and now only a few of his closest friends and lieutenants remained faithful to him.

I knew of this and had already put it to Armandra that perhaps I should formally replace Northan as head of the plateau's warrior army; should become warlord in his stead. She would not hear of it. She pointed out that if Northan were deposed, stripped of rank and military power completely, this would only make him hate me more, if that were possible. Also, it would leave him free to create a variety of mischiefs on the plateau's political side. There were still those among his few cronies who, having been elevated to positions of power by the warlord, would assist him in fresh ambitions rather than risk falling into obscurity along with him. He could also compromise certain of the elders, who feared for their own positions. Even in this alien world, politics were by no means free of corruption; though from what I knew of it, Northan was at the root of everything that was bad. Well, Armandra had stressed the fact that he was ambitious . . .

I had just landed two spears in the bull from a distance of about twenty-five yards when Jimmy Franklin ran into the vast, high-ceilinged exercise cave. There was blood on the right shoulder of his fur jacket; blood dripped from a deep gash in his left thigh.

'Hank – Tracy's hurt!' he gasped it out.

'Hurt? How badly?' I grabbed him by his good shoulder, searching his face anxiously. 'What do you mean, she's hurt? Who hurt her? *How* is she hurt?'

'Northan,' Jimmy panted, 'he's defecting! He sent three of his men after Tracy. They tried to take her while she was sleeping but she woke up in time to avoid whatever they had planned. She got one of them with a star-stone. Hit him in the ear with it. Damn near burned half his head away! One of the others clubbed her unconscious. Then they split up, one heading one way to lead off any pursuit, the other making for the harbour area, where Northan's

150

ship is tied up. He tried to take Tracy with him but it didn't work out. Her star-stones are gone, though.'

'You're not making sense,' I spoke urgently, firing questions at him. 'What do you mean, he tried to take Tracy with him? Where is she now?'

'She's all right, Hank. As luck would have it I was on my way to see her. I saw this Eskimo with her across his shoulder. That was in the perimeter tunnel leading away from our rooms. When I challenged the Eskimo he had to put her down to deal with me. We had a bit of a fight and I got a few cuts,' he indicated his shoulder and leg wounds, 'but the noise attracted a couple of Indian friends of ours. One of them was Charlie Tacomah. His room is somewhere above ours. Well, the Eskimo told Charlie that he was only carrying out Armandra's orders, but I said he must be lying. He made a run for it and Charlie brought him down with a spear. Apparently Charlie and his friend were on their way here to work out with you.'

'Right. I had arranged to meet them here. But where is Tracy now? And what about the third member of the group? And where's that dog Northan?' My voice trembled with fury.

'Charlie and his friend are taking her to Armandra. They're raising the alarm along the way. Your other questions –' he spread his arms and shrugged. 'You know as much as I do now.'

Then he swayed and half fell against me. I steadied him and noticed for the first time how much blood he was losing. I caught him as he fell and carried him to a rest couch, telling the two astonished weapon masters, 'Look after him, get him attended to immediately. I'm going to Armandra.'

On my way out I turned to Jimmy. 'Thanks for everything, Jimmy,' I said. 'Are you going to be all right?'

'I think so.'

'I reckon that Tracy's just about got to accept you as her champion now, eh?'

He managed a grin. 'She was going to anyway,' he said.

Racing through the plateau's labyrinthine ways, I could see that Charlie Tacomah had been busy alerting the entire place. Indians wearing the insignia of guardsmen were hurrying to positions at the base of the outer wall; powerfully built, squat Eskimo warriors were padding along the corridors leading to the snow-ship harbours; the entire plateau was alive to emergency measures that had been in force for hundreds of years. There was no aimless milling about; these men were moving in military precision, reacting to whatever dangers the plateau now faced, hurrying to their battle stations.

'*Hank!*' Armandra's urgent thought came to me. '*Tracy is with me now and she has just regained consciousness. Charlie Tacomah has told me what he knows. Are you coming to us? Do you know what has happened?*'

'*I'm almost with you now,*' I told her, '*and I know what happened. That dog Northan; has he really defected?*'

'*Yes, with two dozen of his officers and men. His snow-ship is no longer at its mooring. They are fleeing now across the white waste, heading for Ithaqua's altar.*'

I let my disgust at the thought of the traitor flare in my mind. '*He tried to take my sister with him, as an offering to Ithaqua, no doubt. Can we get after him? I want to be aboard the first snow-ship out of the plateau.*'

'*You cannot, Hank,*' she answered as I raced by her Eskimo guardsmen and their bears. '*We are making no pursuit. My father, Ithaqua, is back on Borea. Northan was waiting for him to return. He chose the hour of his treachery well.*'

'*Then the dog gets clean away?*'

'*Not so,*' ominous undertones showed in her thought patterns. '*I am sending a wind after him even now!*'

I ducked through the curtains and entered Armandra's chambers. Oontawa was tending to Tracy who lay propped up on a couch. My sister had a bump like a hen's egg on the side of her head. Armandra, eyes closed and face grim, head tilted back, held out her arms before her while her hands described forward, stirring motions.

'Armandra,' I began, stepping forward. But at that precise moment her entire face started to glow bloodred while the hair of her head rose up to undulate above her as in an updraught of air. A wind blew out from her, thrusting me aside as it raced across the room to set the curtains flapping violently. A moment more this phenomenon continued, then Armandra's hair settled down again, the flush left her face, the wind ceased. She lowered her hands and opened her eyes.

'Come,' she said. 'We will see what games my familiars can play with Northan's snow-ship.'

'Wait,' I answered, hurrying through into a second room, Armandra's resting chamber, to fetch my binoculars. Then we went out, back along the corridor to the viewing balcony with its widely spaced bars. Tracy and Oontawa followed us. I put an arm around my sister and asked her if she was all right.

'Yes. A bit dizzy, that's all. That was quite a bump I took.'

'Not nearly as painful as the bump I'll deal the ex-warlord when next we meet!' I promised her.

'*If* you meet him again Hank,' Armandra grimly put in. We had arrived at the balcony and now she pointed out through the bars. 'See . . .'

Through the binoculars I saw the snow-ship fleeing, already two-thirds of the way to the circle of totems with its central altar. Atop that altar I could see the Snow Thing, and he too was watching the snow-ship's progress. At that distance the monster's outline was indistinct, but the flaring of his eyes was clearly discernible. I turned my binoculars back to the snow-ship, seeing that the vessel fairly leaped across the snow.

'See,' Armandra said again, 'the winds are answering my father's call and Northan's ship flies on their wings. But I, too, have sent a wind, one to vex the warlord's flight!'

Now, building up behind the snow-ship, growing out of the frozen white surface of the plain, the grey funnel of a tornado raised itself up, twisting and bending furiously as it rushed down upon the fleeing vessel. Closer to the ship the pursuing tornado roared, the howling of its passage coming back to us like the mad wail of some vengeful god.

Then Armandra cried out in anger and frustration, 'Ah! My father is curious . . . he joins the play . . . Ithaqua displays his power!'

And sure enough the figure atop the pyramid altar had held up a massive hand to the onrushing tornado, and with a sweeping contemptuous gesture he *brushed it aside!*

The tornado, towering high and threateningly over the snow-ship, suddenly swerved aside and teetered crazily, blindly in the wrong direction. The snow-ship sped on. Armandra began to close her eyes, set her jaw stubbornly and raised her arms – then shook her head and let her arms fall.

'What is the use?' she asked. 'He is not to be denied his mastery of the winds.'

Out over the white waste the tornado came to an abrupt halt. Ithaqua, from atop his pyramid altar, dismissed it with a wave of his hand. It collapsed in upon itself and spilled to the ground as a fine haze of snow and ice particles.

'But won't Ithaqua kill Northan and his crew?' I asked.

'No, Hank,' Armandra turned to me. 'Northan was the plateau's warlord; he knows all of the secret ways, the many tunnels that lead from the base of the plateau to its halls, barracks, recreation caves and dwellings. He will be a mine of information to Ithaqua's priests and soldiers. When they are ready, he will lead them against the plateau, have no doubt of it.'

'Will he try to come back for you?'

She shook her head grimly. 'No, my father would never allow it. He would destroy everyone on Borea first. Ithaqua is a lonely creature, Hank. He desires a friend to walk the winds between the worlds with him.' For a moment her face glowed with a strange passion. 'And sometimes,' her voice was suddenly far away, 'sometimes –'

Without knowing why I felt a strange chill grip me. Instinctively I focused upon the horror atop the distant altar. His eyes were burning brightly, staring directly at the plateau. I knew then that he saw us, if not physically, certainly with his mind.

'Stop that!' I cried, taking the Woman of the Winds into my arms and kissing her tenderly. 'Stop it. You're not his, Armandra, you're mine!'

She clung to me gratefully, drank of my strength, and an anger blew up in me that led almost to disaster. Without thinking I put her behind me, gripped the wide bars of the balcony with both hands and stared straight out at Ithaqua.

I screamed at him with my mind. *'You great, loathsome, alien blasphemy! When the day of reckoning comes, may the Elder Gods burn out your black heart and float your soul on a sea of fire, to fry until the end of time! Until then, know this. Your daughter is mine, mine! and neither man nor monster can ever take her from me!'*

The defiant gesture of a spoiled child! But not satisfied with that, I also conjured up a mental picture of a star-stone of ancient Mnar and, hurling that at him too, added intended injury to the insult.

Immediately, violently, the thing at the apex of the ice altar reacted. First I sensed his mental derision at the star-stone symbol, as if he already knew that we were no longer in possession of the stones; then came his anger as he lifted his arms up to the grey skies and expanded, bulging upward and outward until he towered fully a hundred feet into the air; and finally he stepped aloft to walk up the wind, reaching into the suddenly boiling sky to draw down weirdly flickering lightnings that played in his hands. For a moment longer he held that inferno of electrical energies in his hands.

'*Back!*' came Armandra's warning cry. 'Back from the bars!' She tugged at my arm until I followed her at a run, pushing Tracy and Oontawa in front of me. We had covered only a few paces when a weird, hissing blue light filled the balcony and corridor. Then the hissing became a deafening crackling as a large hand picked me up and hurled me headlong. The two girls flew with me – but not Armandra.

From where I dazedly lay I looked back at the Woman of the Winds, and at the balcony beyond her. Her hands were held up against the blue light which flickered angrily about her but did her no harm. Lightning played about the bars of the balcony, heating them a glowing white and running in rivers of sparks all about the floor, ceiling and walls. Tongues of flickering fire reached hungrily after us, but were held back by Armandra's power. For a moment longer the scene seared itself upon my mind, then the blaze of electrical fire died away.

In my mind's eyes I pictured a horrific figure striding in icy air over Borea, throwing back his head to roar with glee; then that vision too was gone and I was left knowing that Ithaqua had sent it.

Armandra came to me as I got to my feet. Chidingly she said, 'That was no way to talk to the Wind-Walker.' Then she hugged and kissed me, glad that no harm had come to me. Obviously she had heard what I said to her monstrous father, and it seemed she was no longer so vehemently opposed to someone's laying claim to her, provided I was that someone.

She kissed me again and with her kisses came a great yearning inside me. She sensed it and held me away at arm's length, turning her head confusedly to where the women had now regained their feet. She disengaged herself, asking them if they were hurt in any way. They were not.

Then, watching me out of the corner of her eye, in a very low tone she said, 'You must be very careful, Hank, how you taunt or tempt a being with the power to hurl the very lightning of the storm against you. Be it Ithaqua or Ithaqua's daughter!'

The yearning in me doubled as I saw again the mischief floating to the surface of her ocean eyes. She quickly sobered. 'Come,' she said. 'We will return to my rooms and wait for news.'

2

How Many Tomorrows?

(Recorded through the Medium of Juanita Alvarez)

News was not long in coming. An Eskimo guard soon arrived and, with much bowing and scraping, was let into Armandra's chambers. 'Good, good,' she said, drawing him upright and cutting short the formalities. 'What news?'

She listened intently to his rather slow, guttural speech – words meaningless to me, for where she had spoken in English he answered in *Eskimo* – until he was done, then dismissed him. In all of his short report I had caught only one phrase, a phrase repeated in something akin to awe and horror: 'The Madness!'

As the guardsman bowed himself out Armandra turned to me. 'They have caught the third traitor, the one who took Tracy's star-stones. He was hiding in the forbidden tunnel.'

'In the tunnel?' I repeated. 'Hiding there?' I frowned, shaking my head. 'But how could any man of the plateau ever manage to steal Tracy's star-stones in the first place? And I thought no man could ever venture into the forbidden tunnel, that its emanations were impenetrable. Now you tell me this man was hiding there!'

'Perhaps not *hiding*, then,' she looked at me pointedly. 'No, he was – trapped – there. I do not care to think about it. They had him cornered and he had only one way to go. They caught him when he came out. As for the star-stones, that was simple. He caught them up at the end of his spear, lifted them by their chains, kept them away from him so they could not harm him.'

'Even so,' I said, 'he must be a very brave man. Brave and misguided.'

'A frightened man,' she answered. 'Frightened of Northan.'

'I want to see him, question him,' I told her. 'I want to discover Northan's intentions, what he's up to.'

She shook her head. 'You'll get no sense out of him, Hank. The history of the plateau tells that once, hundreds of years ago, offenders against the common good, thieves and the like, were driven into the forbidden tunnel as punishment for their crimes. The records all show the same end result. It will be the same now; this underling of Northan's, he will not be – coherent.'

The way she said the last word found me looking at her inquiringly, but she avoided my eyes. She did not like to talk about that enigmatic tunnel in the bowels of the plateau, or of its effect upon men.

Tracy spoke up. 'And have they got the star-stones back?'

Armandra shook her head. 'No, he must have left them behind him, in that place. If so, they will remain there forever.'

At that point there came again the sound of padding feet from the corridor. Oontawa went out and returned after a few seconds. 'The man is being held in the council hall,' she told her mistress. 'The elders have tried to question him, in vain. Now they ask what you want done with him.'

Armandra began to answer, then checked herself. She turned to me. For a long moment she looked at me. Finally she said to Oontawa: 'That is not a matter for me. Better you speak to the warlord.'

For a moment Oontawa looked puzzled, but then understanding dawned in her eyes. Of course. Now there was a new warlord! Speaking to me, the girl repeated, 'The elders are holding the man; has the warlord any instructions?'

159

'I'll come to see him,' I told her, 'and I'll talk to the elders, too. Send word that I'll be there shortly.'

Oontawa left immediately and Tracy went with her. My sister knew that Jimmy Franklin had been hurt and wanted to go to him. Finally I was alone with Armandra. Now she relaxed a little, became a woman again and not a goddess.

'Big trouble is coming, Armandra,' I said. 'We don't need a hunchman to tell us that much.'

'I know,' she answered. 'And I think – I think that I am frightened, Hank. Things are all coming to a head too soon, too quickly. Troubles pile up all about us. The plateau's problems seem about to engulf us all. And now you have accepted a task that might daunt any man. You are the plateau's new warlord, and at a time such as this!'

'This was the way it had to happen,' I answered. 'In a way I'm glad. It's my chance to prove myself once and for all – to the People of the Plateau and to you. You know what that means to me.' I forced myself to grin, making light of things, kissing her forehead while she clung to me.

Her voice was molten gold when she said, 'We may not have much time, Hank. That is what frightens me most.'

'We've wasted a lot of time,' I answered, fires melting my iced blood. She pushed me away, her face suddenly flushed.

'When you have spoken to the elders, return to me,' she hurriedly said. 'Make what arrangements you must – do what must be done – then come back.' She opened her mind to me: *visions of lurking, half-formed fears and fierce, tumultuous passions!*

'I am your warrior, Armandra, your champion, but not yet truly your husband. What of the plateau's rules? The ancient codes?'

The flush left her face and disbelief replaced it. Thunderheads darkened her brows and lightning flashed in her eyes. '*Dare* you make excuses when I have offered –?'

'But the ancient codes!' I protested, unable now to contain my laughter.

'Codes! Rules!' she started to flare up, then burst out laughing with me when she realized I was playing. Suddenly we both sobered, and I saw that her eyes were now wantonly seductive, Icelandic pools beneath which volcanic fires roared. 'We will have to forget the rules, Hank.'

'Armandra —'

'*No!*' she broke away from me. 'Go to the elders now, then come back to me.'

On my way to the Hall of the Elders I found myself shadowed by two lean, powerful Indians who took up a steady, loping walk at my heels. I began to feel alarmed when it dawned on me that these could be two more of Northan's men, left behind to take care of me.

After they had followed me for at least half the distance to my destination, when it seemed that they were stealthily closing the gap between us, I turned on them. I drove my elbow deep into the stomach of the one on my right, snatching his handaxe from his belt as he doubled over, retching. Dropping to a crouch and twisting into a good position to deliver a low, killing kick at the second of the two, I was stopped dead in my tracks by the sight of the man prostrate upon the tunnel floor!

I took away his handaxe and hauled him to his feet, demanding to know what was going on. He had a fair grasp of English, speaking to me rapidly, babbling while his companion slowly managed to compose himself. They were my personal bodyguards and messengers, sent by Oontawa to attend me.

I offered my apologies and clumsily attempted to brush the winded Indian down. He assured me that he considered himself the recipient of a great honour; he could now claim to have seen and experienced the lightning ferocity of 'Sil-ber-hut-te' at first hand. His children's children would talk about me, and he, Kasna'chi, would be a part of my legend. He would doubtless have gone on had I not stopped him. It is disconcerting to say the least to find oneself growing into a living legend!

And so, with Kasna'chi and Gosan-ha close at my heels, I eventually arrived at the Hall of the Elders. The Indians waited outside while I went in to see the elders and their prisoner.

Other than the ten elders, two Eskimo guardsmen were also present in the great cave. The latter pair held between them a man who had plainly been of French–Canadian extraction. They were not so much detaining him as holding him up. I mention him in the past tense because quite simply he was no longer – anything; whatever he had been, he was no longer.

Though his body showed few of the normal signs of age, his face was deeply lined, his hair visibly greying. His eyes bulged and stared blankly and a slack grin or grimace made his lower lip seem to droop. Saliva ran down his chin. He babbled quietly, incoherently to himself. Armandra was quite right. No one would ever again get any sense out of this man.

I had him taken away. His guards were to give him into the hands of those who would do what could be done for him. Useless to punish a man who could not remember his crime, could remember nothing at all.

Then I spoke to the elders, placing emphasis on the plateau's near invulnerability, making light of Northan's defection and stating that we were all now better off without him. I told them I doubted the ex-warlord's immediate ability to attack us, that for the moment we had nothing to fear from him. While I was delivering my pep-talk, Charlie Tacomah caught my eye. When I had done he drew me to one side.

'I see what you are doing,' he told me, 'and it is good, but I hope you are not fooling yourself. Northan knows all of the plateau's intricacies, its strong defensive positions and its weak spots. Until now we have been fortunate; the great majority of the Wind-Walker's people have been weak-willed and ignorant. Northan is neither of these things. At last Ithaqua has an ally he can use.'

'And I have allies, too, Charlie,' I answered. 'You are one of them. The elders will have to do without you from now on. Tactician you once were, tactician you will be again. You are more use to me right now than to the elders.'

'What do you want me to do?'

'I want you to start by having a good look at the plateau's defences. Find me all the weak spots and devise ways to protect them. And I want to know our vantage points and cave entrances which can be made impregnable, but from which special forces might make telling forays. I need to know these things in order to prepare a plan of defence. In fact I want you to prepare such a plan, and the sooner you get started the better.'

His eyes had taken on a keen glint as I talked; a new fire now shone out of them. 'Do you think that the attack will come soon?'

'As soon as Northan can turn Ithaqua's rabble into an army, yes. They have their rough edges, the wolf-warriors, but those can soon be hammered out. I've seen them in battle and I was impressed. Led by Northan, backed up by the Wind-Walker's hellish powers – oh, yes, it's certainly coming, Charlie. I want us to be ready, that's all. If only there was a way we could get those star-stones back.'

He shook his head at that. 'If they have been left in the forbidden tunnel as we fear, then they cannot be recovered. They must – simply – remain –' He checked himself in mid-sentence, brightening. 'But wait! Haven't I heard your sister say that –'

'Forget it!' I snapped. 'She may not be afraid of the tunnel but I certainly am, for myself and for Tracy. If there's something down there that can do what we've seen done to a man – something that turns my bones to jelly just standing at the entrance to its lair – then I'm not asking my sister to face it!'

'Of course not,' he quickly replied. 'It was a stupid thing to suggest.' After a pause he added, 'I have a lot to do now, and you will be even more occupied. If you will excuse me –'

'Yes, Charlie. And let me have the answers as soon as you know them.'

After Charlie left the Hall of the Elders I had a few more words with the council before setting out to look for Whitey. It dawned on me that I had not laid eyes on him for four or five days. I wondered what he was up to, and I wanted his advice. He was my hunchman, and if anyone ever needed a few decent hunches it was me.

I found myself wondering: what kind of a hunchman was Whitey anyway? Oh, he'd warned me often enough about Northan, certainly, but there had been nothing specific, nothing definite. Whitey must be losing his touch. Soon enough I was to find out just how right I was.

Then, realizing that I need not look for Whitey myself, I sent Kasna'chi to find him, keeping Gosan-ha with me when I went to the roof of the plateau for a breath of fresh air.

All around the great flat roof, massive battlements had been cut from the solid rock. Behind them, spaced at intervals of about one hundred yards, keen-eyed watchers observed the white waste from this supreme vantage point. The scene to the front of the plateau was one which, despite its monochrome sterility, perhaps because of it, seemed starkly beautiful to me. Only one thing marred it: the obscene fingers of the distant totems pointing at a leaden sky, circling the pyramid altar like dancers frozen in some evil ritual.

And the being atop the pyramid seemed frozen too, as he motionlessly surveyed the strangely littered terrain of his territory, the white waste. A rage quickly built up in me and I had to force myself to carefully put down the binoculars, clipping them to my belt. It wouldn't do to drive the Wind-Walker into another frenzy, not while I was up here.

My mind was a muddle of conflicting thoughts, all of then having to do with the plateau's safety and future. Finally I left the roof. I walked with my thoughts, measuring the rock corridors until, almost without realizing it, I found myself on the penultimate level. There, at that entrance where Eskimo guardsmen stood in rich ceremonial robes with their bears shuffling behind them, I awoke to my surroundings. Deep in thought though I had been, busy with mad flights of heroic fancy as well as very real plans for the protection of the plateau, my feet had led me back to Armandra.

I dismissed Gosan-ha there, leaving orders with the guardsmen that I was not to be disturbed unless it was a matter of the gravest urgency, and then I went on along the richly furnished corridor.

The next morning, Oontawa awakened us. She was shocked and it showed on her face. Armandra took charge of the situation at once, saying, 'Oontawa, do you disapprove? This is my husband that fought for me in the Choosing of a Champion. Yes, and I love him.'

'Yes, Armandra,' the Indian girl began, 'but –'

'There may be very little time left for us,' Armandra interrupted. 'In the battle that must soon come we may be the losers. It is not a thought I want spread among my people but the possibility exists. You are just a maiden, a girl who has been friend and companion to me and who loves me. I love you too, for your innocence. Though not too many years separate us, our minds are centuries apart.

165

I am old in strange wisdom and you are innocent. In your innocence I have seen you smile favourably upon a certain brave. Is it not so?'

'It is so,' Oontawa bowed her head and flushed.

'And is he not the handsome brave that keeps the bears for our warlord? His name is –'

'Kota'na, my princess.'

'Just so. Then I repeat that time is very precious, Oontawa. I suggest we arrange a Choosing of Champions for you. As of this moment you are dismissed from my service, but I know you will remain my friend. Go, girl, and find your happiness, as I have found mine.'

Oontawa bowed again and when she lifted her head there were glad tears in her eyes. She turned to me. 'Lord Sil-ber-hut-te, your friend Whitey waits to see you. He is with Gosan-ha and Kasna'chi. They wait where the guardsmen stand with their bears.'

I smiled and nodded. 'I will come.'

Oontawa waited on the far side of the curtained doorway that closed off Armandra's rooms, and when I was ready we walked together to the guarded end of the corridor where Whitey and my bodyguards waited. She left me there to go in search of Kota'na, taking him the news that Armandra had ended her service so that the Keeper of the Bears could take her to wife.

I walked with Whitey, slowly pacing the fantastic labyrinths of the plateau and talking to him while my bodyguards kept a discreet distance to the rear. Whitey was up-to-date on everything, had heard of my new office, was pleased that Armandra had placed the might of the plateau in my hands. He said as much, and yet I sensed that something was bothering him.

'I feel I've kind of let you down this time, Hank,' he finally said after a long period of silence. 'Something – I don't know what – isn't right.'

'How do you mean, Whitey?'

166

'It's hard to explain, a funny thing. And yet not so funny, if you follow me. All my life, even before I was fully aware of this power of mine to, well, to gauge the mood of the future, so to speak, before I was a hunchman proper, I could kind of *sense the existence* of tomorrow. I was as much aware of the reality of the future as other people were of the past. Tomorrow was as certain to me as yesterday.' He paused for a moment, then continued, 'I suppose it must be a difficult concept for anyone who's not a hunchman. Anyway, as I've grown older the impressions of tomorrow have occasionally been clearer. Such flashes have been my hunches of course, the end results of the special talent that made me valuable to the Wilmarth Foundation. Until recently . . .'

'Oh.' I frowned. 'Well, go on, Whitey. What's the problem?'

He shrugged resignedly. 'It's a worrying thing, Hank. I feel like I just lost a leg or something. You know what I mean?'

'No more hunches, eh?'

'Right the first time. Sorry, Hank.'

'But how could it happen? Have you any ideas?'

'Yeah, I have an idea,' he grimly answered. 'My idea is, how can I see tomorrows that aren't going to be?'

'Not going to be? There'll always be tomorrows, Whitey.'

'Sure,' he said. 'But will we be here to enjoy them?'

3

The Lull Before the Storm

(Recorded through the Medium of Juanita Alvarez)

The next fortnight was one of frantic activity. Working to Charlie Tacomah's suggestions I garrisoned soldiers close to the plateau's outer walls, in temporary cavern-barracks from which they could rapidly deploy to defensive positions. The plateau's weak spots – several large and easily accessible entrances opening straight into the guts of the plateau from the plain – were specially strengthened and fortified to my orders. Quarriers worked nonstop to cut and lever massive blocks of stone into place. We did a similar job with the snow-ship keeps, those fjordlike, frozen reentries where the great skiborne battlecraft were harboured. These tasks, wherever possible, I personally supervised. If I was not available, Charlie was there in my stead. With each and every person in the plateau realizing the urgency of the situation, the work went ahead with very few complications; the plateau's peoples were all right there behind their princess – yes, and behind their new warlord, too.

Heartening as all this was, over that same period of time there were worrying things happening out on the white waste in the vicinity of the Wind-Walker's temple. The watchers on the roof of the plateau had reported the activity; I myself had seen it enlarged in my binoculars. The Children of the Winds had gathered from far and wide, were exercising in orderly military manoeuvres across the frozen terrain of their territory. Northan was flexing his new and savagely powerful muscles, making a vast and disciplined fighting body out of the entire nation

168

of Ithaqua's worshippers. And always the Snow-Thing watched over the ex-warlord's progress, and always the tension heightened.

Then, during the third week, there were two new developments. Ithaqua departed yet again, walking away across the winds and disappearing over Borea's rim, and Jimmy Franklin brought me news of that which I could only consider an act of sheerest lunacy. The latter concerned Tracy.

It was midweek and I was with Armandra, who was trying to explain to me her alien father's eternal wanderlust, his apparent inability to remain in any specific sphere for any appreciable length of time, which she explained as being simply one of the conditions of the limited freedom allowed him by the Elder Gods, when Jimmy came to us. He breathlessly told us his story.

He and my sister had been walking together through the complexes of the plateau when their wanderings had taken them to the forbidden tunnel. They had stood together at that dark entrance, and suddenly he had noticed a new light in Tracy's eyes. She was aware, of course, that her star-stones were believed to be somewhere in that sinister burrow, left there by Northan's now incurably crazed underling.

Realizing what she intended to do, Franklin had tried to stop her but discovered he was neither physically nor mentally strong enough to do so. His wounds had healed, true, but his strength was not yet back to normal. When she broke loose from him and ran off down the tunnel, bearing with her a torch snatched from the nearest flambeau, he had tried to follow her but was held back by the dreadful *power* emanating from that hideous shaft. It had been as if he threw himself against the solid wall of some castle of evil, while a brain-eating acid was dripped upon his head from the unseen battlements.

Finally, reeling and clutching at his sanity where the *power* had brought him to a halt just a few paces inside the nightmare entrance – knowing that to remain would certainly mean succumbing to madness – he realized that he could do nothing at all to help Tracy. She would not return until she either found the star-stones or satisfied herself that they were not there. Then Franklin crawled from the place on all fours, and as soon as he had recovered he hurried to me.

We returned to the forbidden tunnel immediately, Armandra and my bodyguards with us, and on our way I obtained a slender spear. Seeing that I had armed myself, Armandra clung desperately to my arm and I felt her mental fingers worriedly probing the edges of my telepathic consciousness. I closed my mind to her, though already she must have known what I intended to do – what I would at least attempt.

I expected objections but at the tunnel mouth no one tried to stop me; it would have been futile to do so. I simply ran into the tunnel, a burning brand in one hand, my spear in the other, shouting Tracy's name. And immediately the *power* was there pushing against me, trying to hold me back with fingers of fear that worked in my brain, so that with every step I felt I was leaping from a precipice, or hurling myself down the living throat of some primordial reptile. And the echoes of my cries came back to me: 'Tracy! . . . Tracy! . . . *Tracy!*'

And then I was on my knees, pushing forward, spear and torch before me, with shadows leaping on the walls and ceiling like mad demons while fear tore at my insides. And I knew I was going to go mad with fear. I knew it.

And I would have gone mad if I had forced myself on – but I didn't have to. From around a bend in the tunnel It came, waves of fear beating out from It, the horror that the plateau dreaded, hitherto unseen, unknown.

Manlike It was, an inky anthropomorphic blot that dripped namelessly; but small as I could never have expected it to be, this Thing that radiated such *fear*!

As It came closer I backed away on all fours, dropping my torch from nerveless fingers, feeling the fear eating my brain. And then I remembered Tracy.

'Monster!' I screamed. I got to my feet, drew back my arm and balanced the slender spear, which the instinct for self-preservation had made me hold on to, aiming at the thing's heart –

And the monster spoke!

'Hank? Is that you? Are you all right?'

Tracy! But if this was my sister, why should I feel the *fear* radiating from her? Why should my stomach twist and writhe with every step she took toward me?

I backed away, noting through waves of terror how the inky figure kept well away from the sputtering flame as it edged around the still burning torch where it flared upon the floor. With every step the figure advanced I had to retreat, pushed back by the *fear*.

'Tracy.' I somehow managed to force words from my parched throat. 'Is it really you? What's happened to you?'

'Of course it's me, Hank,' the figure replied, and certainly it spoke with Tracy's voice. 'Yes, it's me. I'm covered in oil, that's all.'

'But Tracy,' I pressed her, still backing away, 'why – why am I *afraid* of you?'

'What?' she stopped moving toward me and I detected the growing concern and disbelief in her voice. A moment later she laughed and I knew at last that it really was Tracy. 'Oh, it must be the star-stones!' she said in sudden relief. 'I came down here to look for two of them – and I found hundreds! Down at the other end of the tunnel there's a huge cavern, with star-shaped symbols on the walls and all over the ceiling, and the floor is literally covered with the stones. I'm carrying dozens of them with me right now, and they're heavy! It must be the stones you can sense; you're frightened of *them*, not me.'

She was right, of course she was. 'And this cavern,' I questioned, still retreating before her. 'Is it – empty?'

'Yes, apart from the star-stones and the oil. At one place the cavern wall is cracked and oil is seeping in, I guess from the place where the plateau's people draw off their fuel. I left my torch stuck in the floor while I was gathering up some of the stones. Then I slipped and fell in the oil. That's why I had to leave the torch behind and come back in the dark. Are you all right, Hank?'

Now it was my turn to laugh, weakly, almost hysterically. 'Oh, yes, I'm all right – but you'd better let me warn the others or they're likely to make a pincushion of you as you come out.'

'Yes, yes do!' she cried. 'Oh, go on, Hank, get out of here. You sound dreadful. Please hurry on ahead. And don't worry. There's absolutely nothing down here to hurt you. Oh, except the star-stones, of course.'

Of course. Nothing but the star-stones!

I turned then and ran, or rather I staggered, back along the way I had come. And all the way the *fear* snapped at my heels, right behind me. Only now I knew exactly what I was afraid of – what everyone in the plateau had feared – and though the knowledge made no difference and I was still desperately afraid, I was also jubilant!

'Let them come,' my spirit cried inside me, 'and Ithaqua with them. At least the odds are balanced a lot more in our favour now!'

And that brings us up to five days ago, Juanita. I've probably missed things, I know, but nothing that I think is of any real importance. Let's see now, how long have we been in touch? With time off for a few breaks and a couple of hours sleep, I reckon it must have been all of thirty-six hours. Is that a record for telepathic contact

172

between worlds – or – rather, between 'spheres'? I suppose it must be. You say Peaslee has given you a team of stenographers, typists, tape recorders? Methodical as ever. He doesn't miss a trick.

With you right now? Yes, I see in your mind that he is. He says to quit the casual chatter and get on with it, does he? Well, you can tell him from me that the Wilmarth Foundation doesn't carry much weight way out here on Borea. He's right, though, so I suppose we'd better get on with it. Not that there's a lot left to tell.

We're simply waiting now, there's nothing else to do. Armandra has been resting for two days, seeing no one, not even me. She says she'll need all her strength for the coming fight, and try as I might I can't convince her that she won't have any part of it. The trouble is, I know that if she wanted to join in there's not much I could do to stop her; she would only be fighting for her people after all. And for her freedom.

It can't be far off now, the fight, for Northan has quit exercising his army and holds it in readiness. And Ithaqua is back. The Wind-Walker perches atop his pyramid as always, except that he no longer stares out and away over the white wastes. Now he faces squarely in the direction of the plateau.

Tracy has been busier than anyone else since she found the star-stones in the cave at the end of the forbidden tunnel, those same star-stones that once held the Wind-Walker imprisoned deep in the guts of the plateau. That's why the horror has always held the plateau in great respect, why he himself has not yet seen fit directly to attack the place.

But to get back to Tracy: she must have walked miles, poor kid, before she let Kota'na talk her into riding one of his bears. Since then she's been getting about much faster. And her work is probably the most important of

173

all, for Tracy has been putting the finishing touches to the plateau's defences.

I suppose I could say that the idea was a group effort of Charlie Tacomah, Tracy and myself – but the truth is that Tracy's had the lion's share of the work. I had a rough idea how I wanted the star-stones used; Charlie worked out the mechanical details; Tracy is still working to finish it off, but it's just about done now.

Roughly the idea was this: that the stones be used as a secondary defence behind the new tunnel barriers, to deny entry into the plateau should the barriers be breached. Charlie designed heavy wooden frames, had them built and suspended from the ceilings of the outer tunnels. Fixed to the fronts of these frames are spears set in two rows. The bottom row consists of conventional spears fixed about two feet apart, and these are meant to impale the giant wolves. The upper rows are less conventional; in fact they're not spears at all but simply stout poles, like slender battering rams. Only nailed to the end of each pole is a star-stone – and these are not meant for wolves . . .

Tracy's hands are a mass of blisters. Because she's the only one able to handle the star-stones, by now she must have nailed up almost two hundred of the things.

Anyway, Charlie's devices work like this: swinging from the ceilings of the tunnels and operated by teams of men hauling on ropes from the rear, they should form impass-able barriers. The spears are not barbed; that is, they will impale men and wolves alike, but their victims will not pile up on the shafts. By the time a wall of bodies has built up in front of one of these fearsome devices, well, the passage will be impassable by then anyway. And when they are not in use the spear-frames can be hauled up to the tunnel ceilings to allow my warriors passage beneath them.

There have been one or two minor accidents when Tracy's assistants have come into momentary contact with

174

her stones, but once burned means twice shy. Those who suffer make sure they don't get burned a second time! I imagine that when these terrible weapons are in action, nothing Ithaqua can send against them will stand a chance.

And that is only one of the uses to which the star-stones have been put. They've also been fixed on the massive gates that guard the snow-ship keeps, and they form a five-pointed design in the battlements of the plateau's roof. All in all, I believe we've used them to their best advantage. Time alone will tell, and I think there's precious little time left.

Speaking for myself, I would prefer to hold back when the battle starts, let the Children of the Winds come to me and make them fight on my terms, but my generals tell me that to do so would be to severely demoralize the warriors of the plateau. To many of the young braves this seems their golden opportunity to distinguish themselves in bloody battle. I daren't deny them that which is their right according to the plateau's ancient codes and customs. That's why, before Ithaqua returned, I had the snow-ships out exercising and manoeuvring all about the foot of the plateau, while Armandra sent fair winds to fill their sails.

Thus, when the time comes, they will go out to attack the wolf-warriors and their battle-sledges. At the same time, foot soldiers and mounted bears will protect the tunnel entrances and keeps, while the fortified positions will be manned by strong but older men who are past their prime. Then, if things go badly, survivors of the fighting will fall back with the wounded and take over the plateau's defensive positions. They will be replaced in the field of battle by reserves, while the wounded will be passed back along the tunnels to first-aid and hospital centres. The crews of the snow-ships will simply have to fend for themselves if their vessels are wrecked, getting back to the safety of the plateau as best they can.

But I need not go on. All of this is prearranged. The plan in its entirety is complicated and would be meaningless to you, Juanita, unless you knew the plateau as I now know it; which is why I have only given you the basic outline. Now we wait.

Jimmy has just been to see me, excited about a device he's had built and positioned in the mouth of a small cave fifty feet above ground level. It's a powerful catapult on a swivelling base. He and Tracy have been practising with pebbles and they can now accurately land a stone – a *star*-stone when the time comes – almost anywhere inside a two hundred-and-fifty-yard radius. Jimmy will aim and release the 'shells', Tracy will load for him. Now she's gone off yet again to the forbidden tunnel to replenish her stock of stones.

Meanwhile, I've managed to convince Armandra that she must stay out of the fight. She promises not to join the battle unless Ithaqua himself takes a strong hand. I can't really picture him trying to do that once he sees what we have waiting for his wolf-warriors. Of course, there was a condition to Armandra's agreement to stay out of things: I have to keep out of it too, despite the fact that I've a personal score to settle with Northan. It was the only way I could make Armandra see sense.

So here I am right now where I've positioned myself in an observation cave a third of the way up the face of the plateau, surrounded by a gang of runners who will take my commands below to the fighting men once the battle begins. It's a pretty basic system of communication, but the best I can do.

And that's our present position. Jimmy and his catapult, along with a couple of runners and assistants of his own, are below me on the face of the plateau and about one hundred yards to my right, where Tracy should soon be joining them. Whitey should be up on the roof, still desperately trying to get a peek into the future and keeping a keen eye on the now very much increased activity out across the white waste. Armandra is high above in her rooms, no doubt still nervously fretting. The warriors and their bears are resting up in temporary quarters and barracks down below, and the crews of the snow-ships are ready to man their vessels at a moment's notice, though I can't see them doing a great deal if Ithaqua decides to blow in the wrong direction. That's the trouble with this situation; nothing is certain, everything is a bif *if* – everything except the one really definite fact that Ithaqua *will* send the Children of the Winds against us.

Now I'm going to stop sending, Juanita. There are a few last details I have to see to. I'll contact you again when I can, or when there's something to report.

NOTE: Following this last telepathic transmission from Hank Silberhutte, which ended at 10 A.M., June 5, nothing further was heard from him until 2 P.M. the next day. Then, from across unknown gulfs of space and time, Juanita Alvarez again began to receive his thoughts. The following, final recordings, forming as they do the last part of this document, were commenced at that time.

PART FOUR

1

The Assault Begins

(Recorded through the Medium of Juanita Alvarez)

Whitey is dead, crushed and destroyed as if he had never been, *removed* as he gave all he had, his very life, to save Armandra from her dreadful father and the alien star-voids he eternally wanders. Armandra is hurt, perhaps crippled, I don't know yet. The physicians are with her now.

Tracy and Jimmy are safe, and I'm thankful for that, but Paul White . . . poor Whitey. No wonder he could see no more tomorrows, no futures; for him there was no future.

This last day has been completely hideous! Even now that it's all over, my nerves jump and my scalp prickles at the very thought of it. I can still hear the screams of dying men and beasts, the shrill whistling of Ithaqua's man-carrying kites as they soared down upon the plateau out of raging skies, the blasts of the thunderbolts that turned the plateau's roof to an incredible inferno; and I can still smell the ozone reek of alien energies, the stench of living fear, the sordid stink of death. But let me tell you Ithaqua did not have it all his own way. And for all the plateau's losses the Wind-Walker strides by no means triumphant in Borea's skies this day. He licks an awful wound, and his warriors are scattered far and wide.

But I can't get Whitey out of my mind, poor Whitey, who will have no grave for there is nothing to bury. But, by God! – we shall raise to him a memorial where he died, a tower of stone on the very roof of the plateau, to overlook this whole demon-damned world forever.

And I'm sorry, Juanita; as yet you know nothing of all this, and here I rave like a man demented. Well, perhaps you will understand when I am finished.

It started within an hour of my last contact with you . . .

One minute the strangely 'hummocked white expanse, with all its frozen loot of the Motherworld of men, seemed empty of life, except about the totem ring and its central altar, where tents and shelters had been set up to house the army that Northan had gathered and disciplined for the Wind-Walker. The next moment the whole plain turned black! Shedding the white furs which until then had kept them hidden, the massed might of the Children of the Winds was revealed.

To think that a few moments earlier I had been wondering where all of Ithaqua's warriors had gone! Having watched them gathering for days, from far and wide, I had noticed that paradoxically there never seemed to be more than a few thousand of them visible at any one time. Now at last they showed themselves. Ten ranks deep, only a shoulder's width between them, forming a straight line that stretched for at least five miles across the wastes, I calculated that they numbered close to two hundred thousand. And these were only the foot soldiers!

Behind them, three deep and stretching in a line all of two miles long, in the next moment appeared the wolf-warriors. They too threw down their robes to reveal their great numbers, a move calculated to unnerve us. And certainly Ithaqua's army was an unnerving sight. Oh, the Wind-Walker was not playing games this time, neither him nor his new warlord, Northan.

Northan! My lips drew back from my teeth involuntarily as I thought of the treacherous hound, and almost as if I had once more thrown a challenge in his face, so the sails of the plateau's once-flagship filled out as it slipped anchor near the pyramid altar. My nails bit into the metal of my binoculars as I focused them on the ship of Northan, thought at that distance the figures crowding her decks were tinier than ants and I could never have said for certain which one was he.

The ship rode out to the forefront of the army, gathering speed as it took up a central position, and now the army itself began to move, forming an arrowhead behind the ship. I could see the wolf-warriors spurring their huge mounts to advance through the ranks of the foot soldiers. As the wolves came, so the men on foot jumped up to cling to their great sides and be carried forward.

Bringing up the rear came great battle-sledges hauled by teams of lesser wolves, and these picked up the remaining foot soldiers. I kept my binoculars upon these battle-sledges and after a few seconds managed to obtain a better view of them. They were mounted with stout, pointed battering-rams.

Finally, behind all the others, Ithaqua's priests rode in their own sledges. Forming a backdrop to that awesome army of men and beasts, the Wind-Walker himself stood atop his frozen altar with massive arms folded and terrible eyes hooded as in deep, dark thoughts.

I put down my binoculars. The V-shaped formation could mean only one thing: a direct assault upon the plateau, concentrated upon a narrow front. And the battering-rams told me that the attack must come at the gates of the snow-ship keeps, which were all positioned along an uneven half-mile of the plateau's front.

Once through those heavy gates the wolf-warriors might well manage to breach one or more of the larger tunnels that led directly into the plateau's bowels, doubly fortified as they now were. I was sure that this was what Northan intended to do, and so issued my first orders. All of the runners were fluent in English, and no sooner had the first of my messengers darted away down the steep flights of stone steps with my instructions than the next was there, eager to receive my next command. I told all of them to sit down and try to relax; orders would be issued as they were required.

That was when Charlie Tacomah entered from one of the two horizontal shafts that led back into the plateau. I appreciated his company and repeated for his benefit the orders I had given a few seconds earlier. He borrowed my binoculars, studied the advancing army and nodded.

'I think I would have done the same thing,' he said. 'It's a pity we had no time to build sufficient of our swinging weapons to completely block off the larger tunnels that enter from the keeps. They form our weakest points. Yes, I too would have sent more men there.' He paused, at length added, 'And what of our elite corps?'

'The snow-ships? I want to hold them back until Northan and his army are closer, then release them all at once. As I see it, Ithaqua is filling the sails of Northan's ship with just sufficient wind to blow him to the plateau along with the rest of the army. From here we are looking at them down a very slight slope, and in that we have an advantage. If we keep the snow-ships back until the last moment, then get Armandra to give them a push, they ought at least to be able to punch a couple of holes through that V-formation. After that –' I shook my head, frowning. 'If I had my way I wouldn't let them sail at all. Not only does it mean bringing Armandra into it, albeit indirectly, and not in any real sort of confrontation with the Wind-Walker – but I'm sure that it will be certain death for many of the lads who man the snow-ships.'

'They would not thank you for holding them back, Hank.'

'And will I thank myself for sending them out to die?'

'That has always been the lot of generals, and of war-lords.'

I nodded grimly, then took the binoculars back and put them to my eyes once more. Now Northan's army was a quarter of the way to the plateau, and already one or two stragglers could be seen stretching out to the rear. Northan's ship still rode slightly to the fore, and that must be the traitor himself in the prow, surrounded by his lieutenants. There were wolves aboard that ship too, massive white beasts that strained at their chains. An idea – a suspicion – came to me.

'Do you think it is possible,' I asked, 'that Northan intends to crash one of the gates with his ship, then release those great wolves to ravage along the tunnels? There are about three dozen of the beasts aboard, but I can see damn few handlers.'

'Wolves? Without handlers?' He took back the binoculars and a moment later said, 'You could well be right. They will be lean and hungry animals, those wolves.'

I turned to one of my runners. 'Go tell the crews of the snow-ships to be ready. The keep gates are to be opened. All are then to wait for new orders.'

As the runner hurried off I turned again to Charlie. 'It seems we'll have to deal with the ship of Northan first,' I said. 'But just in case he should manage to break into one of the keeps with those wolves of his –' I clapped the next boy in line on the shoulder. 'Go to Kota'na. I want twenty of his biggest, most powerful bears positioned in each of the keeps. The rest of them he is to use to their best advantage as soon as the fighting starts.'

Now Ithaqua's army had covered more than half the distance to the plateau and the tension was rapidly heightening. I began to pace the floor, then forced myself to sit down when I noticed the eyes of my runners upon me. Charlie opened his mouth to say something, and at that precise moment there came a swelling cry from the central snow-ship keep somewhere below and to the left of my position, a cry that was echoed almost immediately from the flanking keeps.

'Sil-ber-*hut-te!* Sil-ber-*hut-te!*'

.Obviously the runner had passed on my message to the men of the snow-ships, and now they signalled their wholehearted approval. Something swelled up inside me as once more, in unison, the men of the snow-ships roared out their new battle cry. 'Sil-ber-*hut-te!* Sil-ber-*hut-te!*'

The swelling thing inside me burst in a flood of resolution. I stood up and said to my Indian friend, 'You keep the binoculars, Charlie. You'll need them if you're to command the battle. Those men out there are calling my name. They're not going to fight without me.'

'*No!*' came Armandra's almost hysterical, mental denial in my head. '*You shall not, for if you do – then I swear I will walk out now on the winds to fight my father. Aye, even knowing that he will snatch me up and take me away with him to alien worlds. Without you, man of the Motherworld, there would be nothing for me here on Borea. Do you hear me, Hank? You shall not give your life away!*'

'But they call my name, and –'

'*They draw upon your name for its strength. They invoke your passions, your power. Why should you go out to fight, Hank, when every man of the plateau will fight with your great strength and fervour? They know you are worthy of them, now let them prove that they are worthy of you. And remember, husband, we made a bargain. If you fight, then so do I.*'

'They are closer, Hank.' Charlie's voice snatched me back to the task at hand. 'What are you going to do?'

Still torn two ways but realizing there was nothing I could do about it, I said, 'Armandra leaves me no choice. I can't let her do battle with her father, so I must stay here and command from this position of safety. You stay with me, Charlie. Two heads are better than one.'

Out on the plain, less than two miles now from the foot of the plateau, the wolf-warrior army swept toward us, its arrowhead formation slightly less pronounced. Northan had lined up his vessel on the central snow-ship keep. I slapped my next runner on his back. 'Go tell the crews of the snow-ships to move out and position their craft along the front of the plateau.' I took up my pistol. There was one bullet left in its magazine. 'When they hear a loud report from this cave, they'll go straight out and cut through the advancing wolf-warriors. The two central ships will engage Northan's vessel and try to wreck it.'

'*Armandra*,' I continued telepathically, '*we will need a wind . . .*'

'*You shall have one. With luck it will take my father by surprise.*'

'This is it, Hank,' Charlie said breathlessly. 'Only a few seconds now.'

He had the binoculars to his eyes. 'You were right about those wolves on Northan's ship. They are huge, lean, ferocious animals. They look half-wild, barely trained and certainly starved.'

I spoke to yet another runner. 'Every man of the plateau should now be in position. I want the swinging weapons set in motion and the keep gates closed as soon as the ships are out. More of our bears are to be stationed just within the gates.'

As he raced away down one of the steep shafts I stepped over to the lip of the cave and looked down to where the snow-ships would soon be lining up. After only a minute or so they began to appear from the keeps, dragged by teams of men and bears. There were eleven of them, and as they lined up the eyes of all crew members turned up to me.

Now Northan's army was little more than a half-mile away and gaining speed. The sails of the traitor's ship belled out in front, drawing the vessel straight for the gates of the central keep. The rumble of that army swept up to me as I turned to look at Charlie Tacomah. I nodded my head and he grimly nodded back. Then I pointed my weapon out over the white wastes and pulled the trigger for the last time. I said to the Woman of the Winds, '*Now we need that wind, Armandra.*'

'*You have it,*' she answered.

Flurries of ice particles swirled up all around the snow-ships and their great sails filled. They lurched forward, masts straining as the force of the wind Armandra had sent rapidly increased. And once more that massed cry came up to me as if from one vast throat: 'Sil-ber-*hut-te!* Sil-ber-*hut-te!*'

Down the shallow decline the ships sailed, their skis throwing up a silver spray, and now the wolf-warrior army also felt the wind sent by Armandra. Northan's ship visibly slowed and its sails seemed to slacken as the plateau's two central vessels bore down upon it. I had ordered that those ships engage Northan's craft; now I saw that they intended to ram him!

But if that fact was plain to me, it was equally obvious to the wolf-warriors. A battle sledge was hurriedly thrown into the path of the starboard vessel, and as its skis cut great swathes through wolves and men, so they ran into the bulky obstacle. A snapping of timbers as two of the skis were ripped away; then the screams of men and animals as the snow-ship toppled, crushing down upon the milling ranks of those around it, flinging its crew to the frozen ground where, miraculously unhurt, they quickly formed themselves and their bears into a savage fighting unit.

The other ship fared somewhat better. Its bird's-beak prow struck Northan's vessel a glancing blow that threw both ships a little starboard. As their decks passed each other, scraping together, men of the plateau leaped the gunwales to engage hand-to-hand with Northan's crew. Then I saw that indeed Charlie had been right about those wolves on Northan's ship; these were not wolves bred to be ridden as mounts, nor were they bulky for the hauling of heavy loads. They were lean and rangy killers!

And three or four of them had hurdled the rails between the passing ships and were now ravaging among the crew of the plateau's vessel, while their snarling brothers tore to pieces that brave raiding party aboard the ship of Northan. Ah, but in a few moments more the bears of the plateau's ship had turned on the attacking wolves to throw their mangled bodies from the swaying deck. The ship sailed on, leaving in its wake a crushed and bloody swath.

There were ten such swaths, red on the white plain as those heroic vessels ploughed through the wolf-warrior ranks; ten one instant, but in the next only seven as three more of the great ships were wrecked upon battle-sledge reefs. And as I watched, two more, steering wildly from their courses to pick up survivors, were flung onto their sides; in a moment only five ships remained and the plain was a tumult of fighting men and animals.

But no! Those brave men of the surviving snow-ships could not see their brothers go down alone against such odds. As their vessels slowed and stopped, brought to a halt by the sheer weight of shattered flesh and bone that clogged their massive skis, so their crews lowered the gangplanks and rushed down them onto the plain.

At last the snow-ships stood empty, while on the plain about them the Children of the Winds turned inwards on the now desperately battling, stranded crews. I turned my eyes away as that wolf-warrior tide washed over them, drowned them as a wave covers pebbles on a beach, then seethed forward again in triumph.

Gone, all those brave men gone. They had sailed out to their deaths with my name on their lips. But their lives were not wasted, for the snow was red beneath that surging tide of wolf-warriors, red with the blood of hundreds of men and wolves crushed beneath the skis, and certainly in the hand-to-hand fighting the plateau's braves had not given their lives cheaply.

Meanwhile Northan's ship, thrown off course by the glancing collision, had come about in a tight circle. Now, heedless of the scrambling men and beasts too slow to clear a path for him, the traitor returned his vessel to its previous course. Straight for the central keep gates its beaked prow was aimed, the breath of Ithaqua in its sails, and the sea of men and wolves before it parted in frantic haste as it sped to its target.

Would Northan see the star-stone where Tracy had nailed it to the centre of the great gate? Would it deter him? I had had concentric red circles painted around all such protective stars, to draw the eyes of the attacking army and fill them with dread. Surely Northan would see the star-stone. I took my binoculars back from Charlie and, with hands I could scarcely control, refocused upon Northan's ship.

There stood the ex-warlord upon the raised deck of the prow, eyes slitted and staring straight ahead, lips drawn back in a snarl. He would breach that gate if it was the last act he ever performed, and to hell with whatever awaited him on the other side!

Below me where I stood at the very lip of the cave, the forward part of the central keep and its gates were just visible. In that moment I looked down at a steep angle upon the ship of Northan. And at the same time, with something less than twice the length of his ship between him and the gates, finally Northan spotted the star-stone within its painted circles. He saw it and knew it to be genuine. I still had him in my binoculars when that happened, and the effect upon him was dramatic!

The snarl slid like butter from his face. He gabbled frenzied orders, motioned wildly with spastic arms, then hung on tight to the rail of the prow. Two of his lieutenants standing with him threw up their arms before their faces as they, too, spotted the star-stone. Then the ship slewed crazily as its crew-finally interpreted and acted upon Northan's orders. Chunks of ice flew up from the skis of his ship as they bit into the frozen surface.

Broadside, the traitor's vessel slammed splinteringly into the gate.

2
Battle for the Plateau

(Recorded through the Medium of Juanita Alvarez)

As Northan's snow-ship came to a shuddering halt at the splintered gates of the central keep, a clattering and shouting reached me from the almost vertical shafts. From closer at hand there came a savage howl as, turning, I barely found time to throw myself to one side. A hurled spear flashed past me and out through the open mouth of the cave.

Intent upon Northan's activities, I had given little thought to what was happening with the rest of the plateau. I had seen the wolf-warrior tide surging about the foot of our massive refuge; now it was made perfectly plain to me that one or more of the lesser tunnels had been breached. An Eskimo warrior, wearing on his back, shoulders and head the pelt and snarling visage of a wolf, stood astride the broken body of a youthful runner at the head of one of the steep shafts. Pulling out a long knife from his belt he stepped menacingly into the cave.

Just inside the cave, hidden from the Eskimo by a wall-like bulge of rock, Charlie Tacomah had seen the flight of the spear. He remained silent and as the Eskimo came forward swung his handaxe full in the intruder's face. The spine of that hideous weapon drove to its hilt in the fatally surprised Eskimo's forehead, splitting his skull open like a ripe melon and sending him toppling back and out of sight down the vertiginous steps. He gave a single gurgling shriek as he went.

Before I could thank Charlie, a guardsman wearing Armandra's royal insignia appeared from that same shaft.

How he had avoided being knocked from the steps by the Eskimo's falling body I was unable to think. Covered with blood – which clearly was not his own – the man bowed as he pantingly entered. Quickly he addressed me in his own tongue, which Charlie roughly translated:

'Three of the tunnels have been entered and a number of men and wolves are loose within the plateau. The rear parties and guardsmen are tracking them down. One of them has already surrendered himself and has volunteered important information. He was one of Northan's men originally and fled the plateau only under extreme pressure from the warlord. Northan's intention is to wreck the plateau and carry off both Tracy and Armandra. Even if he cannot take the plateau, he must not return without the women. Ithaqua will not allow Northan to fail him.'

A terrible foreboding suddenly gripped me. 'Charlie, take over.' I tossed him the binoculars as I ran past the bloodied guardsman and swerved into a shaft that led into the plateau's labyrinths. 'I have to get to Tracy. She's with Jimmy Franklin, and if the wolf-warriors have managed to get men this far into the plateau so quickly I'm taking no chances!'

I need not have worried. As I arrived at the head of a flight of stairs that reached down to the lower levels and the open cave where Jimmy had set up his catapult, he and my sister were just appearing from below. They were accompanied by four massive Eskimo guardsmen. Tracy was dishevelled and Jimmy had bruises and a few cuts, but aside from a superficial roughing-up neither of them seemed seriously hurt.

Relief flooded my being at the sight of Tracy's shaky but reassuring smile. 'I must be crazy,' I told Jimmy, 'to let you set up that sling of yours so close to the foot of the plateau. What happened?'

'No one's fault, Hank,' he answered. 'I guess we just underestimated the enemy's penetration power. A pair of wolf-warriors made it up to our cave.' He looked grim as he added, 'They weren't so hard, though – not after they saw Tracy's pile of star-stones. And I know just how they felt. I was pretty terrified of those stones myself.'

Excitement suddenly filled his voice. 'You should have seen it, Hank. When we started hurling the stones at Ithaqua's army – what a frenzy and a scattering! Anyway, during the scramble the catapult was wrecked, then I got one of the intruders with his own spear. But by God – spears and tomahawks are no match for star-stones! While I was occupied with my man the other one tried to get behind me. Tracy managed to hit him with a stone. It seemed to stick in him and burn there. His side seemed to roast away!'

'Oh, Jimmy, don't!' Tracy cried, the tremulous smile dropping instantly from her face. She looked suddenly very small, pale and frightened. Only her tremendous courage was keeping her going.

'A couple of seconds after that,' Jimmy finished off, 'these fellows arrived – just too late to give us a hand. They told us it wouldn't be safe for a while in the lower levels. There are about a hundred enemy warriors loose down there, not to mention some two dozen wolves.'

'That many!' I gasped. 'Look, you'd better follow me to Armandra. Two of the guardsmen will stay with you, in case you come up against trouble along the way. The other two can go and help Charlie Tacomah. He's running the show now. I have to get a move on. And look after Tracy, Jimmy. I happen to know that Northan has plans to kidnap her. He's after Armandra, too. I'll see you both later.'

No sooner had I left them, climbing in a spiral toward the uppermost levels, then I sensed Armandra's mental presence. I opened my mind and she said, *'Hank, what is happening?'*

'There are wolf-warriors in the plateau, I don't know how many. The guardsmen and rear parties are hunting them

191

down but you may be in danger, Armandra. Northan means to take you back to Ithaqua, and Tracy with you. Tracy is safe enough for now, but what about you?'

'There are eight guardsmen within hailing distance, plus Kasna'chi and Gosan-ha. All are sworn to protect me with their lives.'

'You should have ten,' I told her.

She answered, 'I sent two of them away with their bears. I ordered them to the snow-ship keeps, to the side of Kota'na, Oontawa's man.'

'Good,' I said. 'I'm sure there's a lot more of your mother's nature in you than you suspect, Armandra. Anyway, I'm on my way to you. I've left Charlie Tacomah in command; he will make a better job of it than I could. Right now I'm wondering what tricks Northan and Ithaqua have up their sleeves.'

With that thought another occurred to me: the plateau had a couple of tricks of its own. By now the wolf-warriors should be attacking in a frustrated crush all along the face of the plateau. I hoped the holes they had already found in our defences had by now been blocked. All being well, Charlie Tacomah should have ordered the pouring of the burning oil down upon the heads of the invaders. The plateau's mineral oil reserves had provided a defensive device of hideous potency.

Armandra plucked the thought out of my head.

'Yes, I have been to the balcony. The foot of the plateau is a sea of fire. The Children of the Winds are dying by the hundreds.' No trace of pleasure showed in her thoughts. Alien though her anger might be, her compassion was warm and human.

'Go back to the balcony,' I told her. 'I'll meet you there. I want to see how things are going.'

'Things seem to be going well for us indeed. But war is – terrible. The only thing in it that gives me pleasure is the thought of my father at this very moment. He must *be beside himself with rage! I will go now to the balcony. Hank?'*

   'Yes?'

   'Take care.'

Two-thirds of the way to my destination the sounds of a chase reached me. I slowed to a halt and as I stood there trying to control my breathing and listening in the light of many flickering flambeaux, it soon became apparent that the sounds of flight and pursuit were coming closer. In a few seconds more three wolf-warriors, clinging to the sides of one great wolf, burst from the mouth of a horizontal tunnel.

They saw me. As they dropped from the wolf's sides like ticks from an infested dog, one of them spoke to the beast. It sprang at me, its massive muzzle thrusting forward. I had a spear but no time to throw it. I leaned back on the shaft of the weapon until its hilt found a purchase against the uneven floor, bracing it against the wolf's spring. The great beast impaled itself on the spear, knocking me aside and wrenching the weapon from my hands.

While the wolf howled out its life in agony on the floor, the three warriors came at me in a rush. Weaponless, I threw myself up a flight of steps, turning to kick the fastest of my pursuers full in the face. He fell from the steps with a scream and crashed to the stone floor head first.

I made to climb higher and one of the remaining warriors threw himself after me. He grabbed my foot, causing me to lose my balance and fall between him and his companion. On my back, I managed to catch the wrist of one of my attackers as he aimed his tomahawk at my face, and while I briefly wrestled with him on the steps I wondered why the other man made no attempt to help his colleague.

Then as finally I overcame my attacker and throttled him with the haft of his own weapon, I saw why his friend had not helped him. The last of the three invaders was tottering down the steps, uselessly tugging at a spear that transfixed him. A second flashing spear pierced him as I watched, hurling him from the steps.

Then two of the plateau's guardsmen hurried up to me while five more positioned themselves at the mouths of the gallery's tunnels. 'Are you all right, Lord?' one of my rescuers, a strapping young Viking, asked as I climbed to my feet.

'My thanks for your timely intervention,' I answered. 'Yes, I'm unhurt. But how goes it now? How many more of Northan's warriors lurk in the plateau's caves and tunnels?'

'Perhaps a dozen of them,' he answered, 'but they, too, will soon be hunted down.'

'And their wolves?'

'Few remain, Lord.'

This man seemed well informed; he had obviously been in a position to follow the course of events closely. 'What about the plateau's losses?'

'The snow-ships and their crews are lost.'

'I know,' I answered. 'I saw it. They were brave men.'

'Within the plateau, when the first wolf-warriors found a way in, we lost some men and bears. A man for a man, a bear for two wolves, perhaps. Now that they can no longer get in –'

'I have no time now for talk,' I cut him off, 'but you have made my mind easier. Do not stop, but keep on searching the wolf-warriors out. Tell any others of the plateau's men you may meet the same thing. Now I go to Armandra.'

And as I continued on my way, as if invoked by my mentioning her name, Armandra's mental voice came to me again: *'I am at the balcony, Hank. Is anything wrong?'*

'A bit of a scuffle,' I answered. *'Don't worry, nothing came of it.'*

'The wolf-warrior hordes have pulled back from the foot of the plateau,' she informed me, *'out of the way of the*

blazing oil. But it seems to me that Ithaqua's priests are up to some trickery.'

'I'll be with you in a minute or so,' I said, entering the final gallery and crossing it to the tunnel with the lightning-flash symbol. And there I was brought up short in sheerest shock and terror. Terror not for myself, for Armandra. There, sprawled in attitudes of grisly death, lay three of my woman's guardsmen – bear, too, its spilled entrails still steaming – and the bodies of four wolf-warriors and a wolf.

Tired as I was from my race against gravity and time, my heels grew wings as I threw myself down the perimeter corridor and finally turned into the jutting balcony with its widely spaced bars. And there, his back to me, tomahawk raised to deliver a stunning blow, an Indian in the matted apparel of a wolf-warrior furtively crouched.

Beyond him, ignorant of his presence, Armandra stood at the bars, staring down at the plain where the Children of the Winds milled in confusion and frustration; but as I entered in a rush they both turned. She saw him even as he saw me, and as he leaped to meet me she cried out, *'No!'*

His reactions were quick and I was tired. His weapon caught me a glancing blow on the head that sent me dazed to my knees. Up went his tomahawk again and his wild cry was one of certain victory – cut short in strangled amazement!

He was whirled off his feet, thrust aloft and spread-eagled in midair by centrifugal force as his body spun even faster in mad currents of air. The suddenly howling wind that filled the balcony snatched at my hair, hurled me aside, slammed the shrieking wolf-warrior time and again against the uneven surface of the ceiling, finally shot him headlong, with a snapping of bones, out through the bars and away into empty abysses of icy air.

And slowly the sentient hair fell back upon her head and her blazing crimson eyes dulled as Armandra ran to me sobbing, a woman once more, where only seconds earlier an elemental of the air had commanded familiar winds!

I held her tight and for the moment there was no war in progress, no shadow over Borea. Then I became angry.

'Where are the rest of your guardsmen? I saw only three of them, all dead, back along the perimeter tunnel – what of the rest?'

'Three of my men, dead?'

'They died to stop this man and his brothers reaching you – and they almost died in vain.'

'I sent the others away,' she admitted, leading me over to the bars of the balcony. 'They wanted to join in the fighting and I felt capable of fending for my –'

'Oh, did you?' I cut her off. 'And if I had not come along when I did?'

'But you *did* come, Hank. Now come, we have no time for quarrelling. Look down there. What do you make of that?'

I took hold of the bars and looked out. The wolf-warrior army had pulled back to a distance of about one hundred and fifty yards from the foot of the plateau. There against the white of the plain they formed a deep dark band that stretched away and around the curving protective walls of rock to both sides. Between them and the fortified tunnels and keeps an ocean of fire, its warmth reaching up to me even at this height, blazed and roared. At first I could not see what was causing Armandra's concern, then I saw that the wolf-warriors were opening up to leave clear paths through their ranks from the rear to the front. They were making way for something. But what?

'My father's so-called "priests," see?' Armandra said, pointing. 'There, at the rear of the army. And now I know what they are about.'

'Yes, I've seen them cavorting like that before,' I agreed. 'Then they were calling up those tornadoes of theirs, working their devilish magic through your father.'

196

'That is exactly what they are doing now,' she said. 'See? And once they have called up their snow-devils they will throw them into the fire and smother it. And then –'

'Then?'

She turned to look at me with wide, unflinching eyes. 'Then they will hurl those whirligigs at the tunnel entrances, the keep gates. They will drive them deep into the plateau, and the wolf-warriors will follow behind!'

'Armandra, I –'

'I have promised not to fight my father, Hank, but those – *creatures* of his, his "priests" – they must be stopped!'

'If you interfere, it may draw Ithaqua into the battle.'

'And if I don't, the plateau is lost anyway.'

Down below six spinning tops had appeared, each with its own capering master behind it, urging it on. Six alien whirlwinds that grew up rapidly out of the frozen plain and moved threateningly forward, roaring along the paths cleared by the wolf-warriors, entering and obscuring in clouds of steam and smoke the field of blazing oil fires.

Armandra was right and I knew it. In another moment Ithaqua's priests would hurl those spinning pillars directly at the keeps and major tunnel entrances. They would wipe the tunnels clean of men and bears in seconds. The swinging engines that carried the star-stones might be safe enough, Ithaqua's familiar winds and powers were restricted by his own limitations. But not all of the tunnels were so well protected, and only the actual gates of the keeps carried those symbols of Eld. To simply allow these priests of the Wind-Walker to use their tools of an alien science as they desired would be suicidal.

'Armandra,' I told her, 'do whatever must be done.'

From beside me, so close that I felt her breath fanning my cheek as she spoke, and in a tone that called up visions of unknown star-voids, she said, 'It is already begun!'

197

I glanced at her and felt the hair of my neck prickle at the sight of that strange pink flush that spread outwards from the closed eyes to fill her pale face. I stepped quickly back as her hair began to rise up in undulating coils above her head and the white fur smock she wore stirred with weird life.

Gone again was the woman I loved, gone in a matter of seconds to make way for this child of Ithaqua, whose arms now reached up to beckon to the suddenly agitated sky. High above, grey clouds turned black, then blue, boiling in an instant and flashing with trapped energies. A continuous rumbling filled the pregnant air.

The fine bones of Armandra's head and neck showed redly through luminous flesh, a grinning skull of death. Her eyes opened; beams of blinding ruby radiance shot forth to the pulsating sky; she made stabbing motions with her hands, which were curved downward now like the heads of swans.

And then I was sent staggering back from the bars, away from the vicious rain of red lightning that lashed down in staccato precision from the sky to the plain below! I did not see those deadly white funnels destroyed – saw nothing of the carnage among the massed ranks of the wolf-warriors when, finished with the sundered tornadoes, Armandra simply rained her devastating energies down upon flesh and blood. I was told of it later, and then I was glad I had not seen it.

No, I saw nothing; nor, deafened from the first hellish salvo, did I hear anything, for which I am also grateful. And even when it was done, several minutes elapsed before I was able to perceive anything but the scarlet blaze burning on my retinas and the pounding of blood in my nearly ruptured eardrums.

Armandra lay huddled beside the bars, sobbing and momentarily spent. Again her terrific anger had vented itself uncontrollably, and again the human side of her nature was betrayed. I went dazedly forward to comfort her but then, as my eyes inadvertently looked down upon the plain, I froze in awed disbelief. Where an army had massed in premature triumph, a demoralized rabble now moved in blind, crippled agony.

Great black smoking craters littered the plain all along the front of the plateau, as if a squadron of bombers had unloaded their bomb bays there. Where the priests had capered to the rear, now a gutted trench lay straight as the furrow of a giant's plow in the icy ground. And in the wake of Armandra's inferno of lunatic lightnings, at last there sprang up a mournful wind that caught up the billowing smoke and steam to lay it like a veil across the whole scene, as if to hide the horror there.

Now, cradling the Woman of the Winds in my arms and rocking her, I heard drifting up to me a thousand amazed cries of utter disbelief and nameless horror from the survivors of that destroyed army. And rising above those cries came the lustful, reverberating battle cry of the plateau's fighting men:

'Sil-ber-*hut-te!* Sil-ber-*hut-te!*'

For a moment I cursed aloud, wildly and blasphemously. God, no! I would not have my name as a seal upon *that* – upon the carnage Armandra's blind fury had wrought. But then I was amazed to see that even now the remaining wolf-warriors, who still far outnumbered the men of the plateau, were rallying to the sort of battle they could understand.

And once more I felt my heart surge within me as out from the base of the plateau, from its tunnels and keeps, rushed the authors of that concerted battle cry, unleashed at last by Charlie Tacomah to earn their honour on a field of bloodied snow and ice!

3

War of the Winds

(Recorded through the Medium of Juanita Alvarez)

No sooner was the battle joined than my attention was distracted from it by footfalls sounding in the perimeter tunnel. One of the guardsmen I had left with Jimmy and Tracy hurried into view. He gave a cry of relief when he found us unharmed; he had passed the bodies of his colleagues at the entrance to the tunnel.

Now he composed himself, bowed first to Armandra and then turned to me. 'Lord, your sister, and your friend have gone to the roof of the plateau to view the fighting. They bade me come and tell you.'

I nodded. 'And your partner – did he go with them?'

'Yes, Lord.'

'Then you had better follow them. Stay with them until this is all over.'

He bowed again to me and again to Armandra, then hurried back the way he had come.

'If they wish to view the fighting,' Armandra said when he had gone, 'there are few better places from which to do so than here.'

'Perhaps they were seeking Whitey. The three of them have grown very close.'

'Whitey,' she mused, 'whose powers have deserted him. Is it a dark omen, I wonder?'

'It's a disadvantage, certainly, but I wouldn't consider it a dark omen. On the contrary, things are going very well. See, despite the odds your people are fighting an inspired battle. They are making a shambles of Ithaqua's army.'

'They are *our* people, Hank, yours and mine. And they

will be victorious because my father's wolf-warriors are demoralized. I have crippled them.' She stared for a few seconds at the milling scene below, then lifted her eyes to the distant pyramid altar of ice and heterogeneous 'trophies'. I followed her gaze as her eyes widened – and then we gasped in unison.

The Wind-Walker was raging, swelling out; his arms were lifted in a threatening attitude; his carmine eyes were blazing in his bloating face. In another moment he had stepped from his altar to stride aloft, and he was coming straight for the plateau!

'They have failed him,' Armandra gasped. 'The Children of the Winds have failed him yet again. Now he will seek vengeance upon the plateau – and upon his own men!'

'But how can he strike us?' I protested. 'The plateau is safeguarded by the star-stones.'

'Those star-stones of the Elder Gods!' she passionately cried. 'I loathe and abhor the things and the gloom they cast over the plateau and its people.'

'They are a symbol of benign power in the plateau,' I argued, 'and without them all would long ago have been lost.'

'A benign symbol, yes,' she answered, 'like the crucifix in the Motherworld. Don't you see, Hank, that all great symbols of power are horrific in their way?'

At the time I didn't give it a lot of thought, but now that I've thought about it I can see what she meant. Certainly the star-stone is benign to anyone not contaminated by Ithaqua or his hideous brothers of the Cthulhu Cycle. Of course the crucifix is a symbol of goodness, despite the fact that it is a model of a most terrible torture machine. The swastika too was an emblem of life, luck and power long before it became the outline of horror. What more innocuous than the hammer and sickle; tools of everyday life and labour?

'But look,' she said, 'perhaps you are right that my father is helpless to harm us. See, he hesitates.'

High above his totem temple the Wind-Walker hung motionless in the sky, his evil eyes glaring at the plateau. I knew that he saw – or felt – the power of the star-stones, those same stones which had held him so long impotent, and I knew that they repulsed him as surely as like magnetic poles repel each other.

'What is he doing?' I asked, as he commenced upward sweeping motions with monstrously bloated arms.

'He calls a wind,' she answered, frowning. 'But to what purpose, for surely no energies of his devising may strike us now?'

'Look!' I exclaimed. 'Those dots on the plain, black dots rising into the air, what are they?'

Rapidly the things I referred to climbed into the sky and were blown forward ahead of the Wind-Walker as he recommenced his striding toward the plateau, and a moment later I believed I knew what they were.

'Kites!' Armandra cried, confirming my own opinion. 'Kites shaped like bats that fly on my father's breath. And they carry men.'

'Man-carrying kites!' I gasped. 'But that must mean that he intends to land them –'

'On the roof,' she finished for me.

Then her eyes went very wide. 'Hank, I think it would have been better if Tracy and Jimmy had come here to us instead of going to the roof!'

'Oh my God!' I whispered, instinctively turning from her, heading for the perimeter tunnel.

She called out after me, 'Hank, wait!'

I came to a hesitant halt, half turned. 'I have to get them off the roof, out of harm's way.'

'If you go up there,' she said breathlessly, 'you will have to fight. See, already my father's man-kites approach. And if you fight. . . .' She shook her head wildly, as if shaking

202

off the dark shapes of nightmare. 'I must not lose you now, man of Earth.'

'My sister and my friends, Armandra,' I quickly answered. 'I have no choice. I could never live with myself.' Then, wasting no more time, I ran from the balcony.

In my mind, before I could shut her out, she cried after me: '*Hank! Hank! Our bargain!*'

I knew that from the gallery at the far end of the primeter corridor a long flight of steps wound their way up to the roof; it should take me no more than two or three minutes to get up there. I raced along the corridor, started up the winding steps, taking them in threes, and as I went I gave credit to the evil intelligence that was Ithaqua.

He had known the weakest spot in the plateau's defences all along; the roof, where only a handful of men, few of them warriors, kept wary watch over the white wastes. Well, I was sure of one thing at least. No matter how many of his kites Ithaqua hurled at the plateau, no matter how heavy the odds, those watchers on the roof would stand and fight to the end.

Only four passageways in all led up to the flat, ruggedly stark roof, four orifices opening into the grey light of Borea. All four were spaced out across the roof's surface, the only accesses. What if Tracy and the others had been cut off from them? These and similar thoughts ran circles in my mind as I flew up the last few steps. In fact I must have taken well under the three minutes I had allowed myself, but it seemed as though half an hour had elapsed before finally I stood panting out in the open air, where the wind rushed over the slippery stone in furious blasts.

I paused briefly to assess the situation and get my breath back. Apart from the presence of a number of kite-men, there was something very wrong with the sight that now met my eyes – something which was soon to become plain to me.

I picked out the figures of Tracy, Jimmy and Whitey

almost immediately; they were fighting with those of Ithaqua's raiders who had already effected landings. With them were about a dozen watchmen, also caught unaware by the aerial attack.

They were not together in a group. Tracy was the most distant from me; about eighty yards separated us. She held up one of her star-stones before her, a threat to any of the Wind-Walker's men who might attempt to get too close. She had found this stone still on its chain where Northan's dupe had left it. The other one was lost, gone forever in some dark crevice in the forbidden tunnel. Tracy had not yet seen me. She appeared to be trying to make her way to Jimmy. I called out to her but my shout was lost in a frenzy of winds.

Jimmy was at the forward edge of the plateau, where waist-high battlements faced out across the white waste. As I saw him he was in the act of spearing one of the raiders who was just attempting a landing. Having killed his man with a single thrust, Jimmy toppled him from the roof along with his kite.

Whitey was the closest to me. Flanked by two of the watchmen, who fought equally furiously, he was battling like a madman to hold off a handful of the invaders. There were fifteen of us in all, against about the same number of kite-men, but more of the latter were landing all the time. One thing was heartening at least: for the moment Ithaqua stood away.

Dark and bloated against the grey skies, ten times taller than a tall man, the monster trod the air half a mile from the plateau's roof almost as a swimmer treads water. With his eyes blazing avidly and his arms half reaching forward, he formed the most fantastic part of the whole scene. I knew that he noted every detail of the situation, but that as eager as he was to destroy the plateau and steal back his daughter – and take Tracy, too, for his monstrous purposes – still the star-stones held him at bay.

The star-stones! Now I knew what had bothered me about the scene on the roof. Ithaqua's raiders were not trying to break into the plateau, they were there simply to clear the way for their master. He had sent them to destroy the great protective star that my sister had traced with star-stones on the plateau's roof! With that out of the way, Ithaqua would be able to completely command the roof and land as many of his aerial warriors upon it as he could muster.

And now, out there on the wings of the wind, I could see that there were *hundreds* of the kites. The brilliance of the Wind-Walker's stratagem was obvious. Ninety-five per cent of the plateau's soldiery were engaged in the battle down below, and the rest of the able-bodied men were at their posts deep down in the rocky labyrinths. Reinforcements would doubtless come, but would they be in time?

But no, my reasoning was way off – I must be wrong! The Children of the Winds couldn't possibly have been sent to get rid of the star-stones. They were as helpless against them as Ithaqua himself!

All of these things rushed through my mind as I surveyed the roof. Then I started to run toward Tracy, slowing for a second to snatch up a tomahawk from beside a dead kite-man. As I went I called her name again, and this time she heard me. That was a wonder, for above the howling of the wind, at precisely the same time that I called her, there came a shrieking like none I had ever heard before. It was the sound of a soul in torment, a banshee howling that froze my unnaturally chilled blood even further, causing me to seek wide-eyed for its source.

And when I found that source I knew that I had been right after all, and that the fear Ithaqua inspired in his 'children' was absolute.

One of the kite-men was tearing at a star-stone where it was fastened to the battlements. The flesh was visibly blackening on his hands as he scrabbled frenziedly to tear the stone loose. His screams did not stop for a single moment but grew shriller still as his fingers began to fall off. Finally he tore the stone free and clutched it to his chest, then gave the most hideous scream of all as black smoke poured out from him. He tottered for a moment, then, as the stench of his burning reached me on the rushing wind, crumbled like rotting wood and fell from the battlements.

Suddenly the wind increased, blowing especially from that region of the roof now unprotected by the stone sigil of Eld, and at the same time I noted shrieks of mortal terror and horror springing up from four other distinct points all around the rim of the plateau. Heedless of their fatal torment – which must have been the ultimate in physical and psychic agony – Ithaqua's aerial suicide squadron was proceeding with its task of clearing the roof. And as the star-stones were removed one by one, the Wind-Walker himself came closer, suspended in the sky.

I had not quite reached Tracy when two kite-men, freshly free of the harnesses of their aircraft, sprang at her. Their weapons were still in their belts and it was plain that their task was to render her helpless and somehow bear her away. I threw my weapon just as one of them went to strike her with his clenched fist. As she ducked his blow and swung her star-stone on its chain full in his face, my tomahawk bit into his side. It is possible that he didn't even feel the bite of my weapon for the agony of Tracy's. His face caved in, black and ruined, and he went down as though a truck had hit him. The second man turned toward me but was thrown down by the force of my rush. As he started to rise I kicked him in the throat as hard as I could. Tracy freed her star-stone from the mess of the first man's face, and as I backed hastily away she began to be sick.

Looking about me I saw that almost all of the invaders had been dealt with, killed and swept from the roof as they had gone about their task of clearing its surface of star-stones. Nevertheless, they seemed to have successfully completed that task. There came a weird, shrill whistling, emanating from the hundreds of batlike shapes that still hung in the sky between the plateau's roof and the swollen figure of the Snow-Thing. The kites were soaring forward, the wind whistling its demon song in their frames of poles and stretched hides. Now Ithaqua could take possession of the roof, land the rest of his airborne forces and invade the plateau.

'Tracy!' I yelled in her ear. 'Get below. I want everyone off the roof. We'll be outnumbered in no time at all and Ithaqua himself may even make a landing here.' I pointed her in the direction of the tunnel I had used and gave her a gentle push. She started to slip and stumble away from me, barely keeping her feet as the wind's strength rapidly increased.

Having seen her on her way to safety, I signalled to Whitey, Jimmy and the remaining handful of watchmen that they, too, should get below where they could better defend the four entrances. Seeing that they understood my signals, I turned to follow Tracy and was greeted by a sight that shocked me rigid. She had fallen and was sliding in the wind across the icy surface of the roof. Ithaqua had seen her and was moving after her!

He came forward and poised himself above the rim of the plateau, his vast feet seeking purchase on the battlements. From side to side his great bloated head went, slitted star-eyes taking in every detail of what was happening. They found Tracy again and stayed upon her where she finally slid to a halt against a projection of rock. Then the Wind-Walker stepped down onto the roof and reached for her with a massive hand. Immediately she held up her star-stone against his approach . . .

Slits of burning evil opened huge and round as the horror stepped hastily back and lifted into the air. Rage filled every line of his nightmare form. He trembled with an inner fury that swelled him out more hugely yet, completely distorting his already grotesque proportions, then he abruptly thrust up a hand to the clouds that raced across the sky.

I knew instinctively what he was about. While his alien powers could not work *directly* against my sister as long as she held that star-stone, he could use them *indirectly* in a purely physical attack, and now he would simply kill her out of hand and be done with it. I tried to go after her, only to be blown off my feet and sent slithering helplessly across the roof. Fighting to find a hold on the slippery surface, I managed to keep my eyes on Ithaqua and saw him pluck a great ball of ice out of the clouds. I saw his face convulse insanely as he hurled his missile at the roof.

I thought then that Tracy was done for, but I had reckoned without Jimmy Franklin. Tracy was my sister, yes, and I loved her, but Jimmy's love was that of a man for his woman. He fought his way to where she crouched against the outcrop of rock, and dragged her behind it at the very instant that Ithaqua released his ice-bomb. Now that bomb burst like a massive grenade where she had crouched a second earlier, but in the protective lee of the great rock, she and Jimmy were unharmed.

Since she was no longer visible to Ithaqua after the flying shards of ice dispersed, perhaps the monster thought her dead. I think it must have been so, for apparently without another thought for her he turned his attention to me.

And if horror can grin, now this monster grinned; if evil can express delight, Ithaqua was delighted.

Sliding helplessly before the howling wind, flat on my back and scrabbling at the icy stone beneath me, I felt his mind probe mine. Before I could shut him out he said something to me, showed me alien pictures, made me understand. It was no sort of telepathic transmission that I could ever hope to explain, not even to another telepath, and yet I understood its meaning:

'*So. You are that man of Earth who dared set himself against me. That same one who hurls insults with his mind and threatens with powers of Eld. You are the one who would take the very seed of my being for your own, to make a mere mortal of her. You are nothing, man of Earth, and nothing you shall remain.*'

He reached one arm to the sky and pointed his other hand at me. I saw strange energies forming in the clouds, a flickering radiance that ran down his extended arm to his body and turned its barely manlike outline to an ever-changing display of crimson and golden traceries of light. In another instant that electrical nightmare would leap from his outstretched finger to me, and I would cease to be.

'*Father!*' There came a pure, bell-like resonance in my mind, a call which I heard even though it was not directed at me. '*Ithaqua – you will not take what is mine!*'

Unable to face the crackling holocaust that I knew was soon to come, I had closed my eyes. Now I opened them and lifted my head from the frozen stone surface. Of a number of things that were happening, the most important to me was that Ithaqua had partly turned away from me to face the forward rim of the plateau where now, floating slowly into view, the form of Armandra rose up. With her appearance the wind seemed abruptly to die away, to crouch down into itself and back off like a scolded dog.

'*Armandra,*' I said to her, reaching beyond the alien mask she wore to the sane and human side of her nature, '*I thank you for my life – but not at the expense of your own!*'

'*Do not distract me, Hank. All is not lost, not yet, but I need my concentration.*' To think that those mental tones of purest gold had come from the female horror that rode

209

the wind above the rim of the plateau! Her hair was floating in fiery, undulating waves over her head; her face was a death-mask. In that skull-like face, carmine pits of hell blazed in supernatural fury to match her father's own. She was tiny, compared to him, but her hatred and anger were great.

As she rose higher above the battlements, streams of guardsmen and warriors began to rush from the four exits. Pouring out onto the roof, they looked much fiercer than I ever remembered seeing them before, and I believed I knew why. One way or the other this was to be the final scene, and they knew it. They were here to lay down their lives for their princess, their world. At last they had been given an opportunity to fight, these men who had formed the rear parties, and they had arrived barely in time. Now great hordes of Ithaqua's kite-men were landing all about the roof, freeing themselves from their harnesses, moving into battle positions.

While all this was happening, I was almost unable to believe that somehow I had been spared. I came back to life, and my heart began to beat a little more freely as I saw that those energies Ithaqua had almost hurled at me were dying away, that the traceries of fire no longer permeated his dark form. He had apparently forgotten all about me; now he held out his bloated arms to Armandra in an attitude which, despite his completely alien nature, was almost humanly imploring. In answer she raised one pale arm above her head and rotated her hand, as if to spin the sky upon her fingers. And indeed the clouds immediately above her began to turn with her hand.

Undaunted, Ithaqua stepped closer, his monstrous feet treading air as he narrowed the gap separating him from his daughter. But this was no gap of merely physical dimensions. It was unbridgeable in anything other than the crudest physical sense. She floated back away from him, glowing with a scarlet flush, and faster yet her arm twirled above her head. Then, without warning, she lowered her hand to a forward, horizontal position and jabbed it viciously in her hideous father's direction.

From the whirling clouds directly above her, lightning at once struck, branching into a blinding fork that speared at Ithaqua's eyes. He never moved, but stood unblinking and still as a hawk on the wind. Only those hellish orbs of his changed; they momentarily flared brighter as twin tongues of lightning were quenched in them. He had not even bothered to ward off Armandra's initial attack; what is the blow of a child to a man full grown? Ah, but that first blow of hers had opened up floodgates of accumulated loathing.

Now she stabbed at her father again and again, her hand like the tongue of some venomous reptile, invoking powers I had once believed to belong to nature alone. Lightning flashed in an almost continuous stream from the clouds to Ithaqua's form, filling him with blue and white fire. Through all of this he stood unharmed, but if she did not hurt him, certainly she angered him.

The imploring attitude he had seemed to adopt fell away and his massive body began to tremble in rage. One of the hands he held out to Armandra clenched and rose up threateningly, swept across to strike his own shoulder in a strangely human gesture of pride. The game was over, the 'offer' was withdrawn – now the Wind-Walker *demanded* obedience! He might as well have asked it of the wide seas of Earth or the desert's sands. She simply moved farther away and continued to rain down her lightnings, whose bolts became increasingly violent.

So much I saw before being drawn into the tide of renewed battle that washed across the roof. For with Armandra holding Ithaqua's attention so completely, his aerial invaders were on their own against the men of the plateau, and where the latter were concerned, no quarter would be asked and none given. Hearing my name on the lips of every man who fought for the plateau, I joined them, hurling myself headlong into the fighting.

It was then that Whitey found his way to me through the mass of struggling bodies. 'Hank,' he gasped, dragging me behind a natural wall of rock that protected one of the openings into the plateau. 'Hank, I have an idea.'

'A hunch?'

'No, just an idea. My hunch days are over.'

'All right, what is it?'

'Tracy has a star-stone with her, right? Well, if she can somehow manage to fasten it to a spearhead – tie it firmly with a thong or something – do you suppose you could land it on Ithaqua's warty hide?'

'He makes a big enough target,' I answered. 'I suppose I should be able to do it. Come on, let's see if we can get to Tracy and Jimmy.'

Making our way across the roof was not easy. Through gaps in the tumult we got occasional glimpses of the two of them, Jimmy fighting like a madman side by side with a massive Eskimo guardsman, and Tracy behind them, her back to the same rocky projection that had kept her safe from Ithaqua's ice-bomb, protecting their flanks with her star-stone. But halfway to them we got split up. The last I saw of Whitey for a while, he was tackling a lean Viking, while I myself was faced with a pair of hatchet-faced braves.

I was lucky, managing to kill both my men without being hurt. At the same time I discovered a strange thing: though there was more than one occasion when nearby guardsmen might have stepped in and made things easier, not one of them lifted a hand to help me. I had obviously reached new heights of legend; Sil-ber-hut-te could look after himself and wouldn't thank anyone for interfering!

But if I could look after myself, the same could no longer be said of Armandra. As I cleared a path for myself through the crush of fighting men, I saw that Armandra was almost spent. The energies she drew from the whirling clouds were less powerful, her stance less steady above the plateau's rim. And her father was beginning to enjoy his invulnerability. As the lightning rained about him, so he would use his great hands to deflect the bolts into the groups of furiously fighting men on the roof. It seemed of absolutely no concern to Ithaqua where these bolts fell or what mayhem they caused; the deaths of his own followers were of no consequence to him.

In any case, within the space of a few seconds more it could be seen that with or without Ithaqua's concern, his human allies were well and truly beaten. Though they fought a desperate, ragged retreat to the battlements, where at last the monstrous shadow of their lord and master fell upon them, still the men of the plateau followed them up, determined that not one of them would escape. The end came quickly even as I watched. Taking full advantage of their opportunity the plateau's soldiers made one last effort, forming an unbreakable wall and moving inexorably forward until the remaining kite-men were simply pushed off the roof into empty space. They fell in a screaming human rain from the rim.

Then I turned my eyes again to the sky, to the bloated figure of Ithaqua and the tiny shape of his daughter as their aerial confrontation continued. But that battle, too, if such an unequal contest could rightly be termed a battle, was almost done. Exhausted, Armandra seemed to waver in the sky, her eyes dulling and brightening spasmodically, while her father waxed ever more triumphant in his mockery of her efforts.

Now there was a complete absence of movement on the roof as every eye followed Armandra's struggle. I was on the point of reaching out to her with my mind to offer whatever mental assistance I could, when above the crazed howling of the wind and following immediately in the wake of yet another deflected bolt of lightning, I heard Whitey cry, 'Hank – I've got it!'

He was making his way to me across the death-strewn roof with Jimmy and Tracy on his heels. In his hand he carried his secret weapon, its fatal head held well out in front of and away from his body. And it was at that very moment that Ithaqua suddenly reached out and snatched Armandra out of the sky. Drained of all her strength, she made no effort to escape him but seemed simply to collapse, a doll in the fist of a giant.

'*Armandra, hang on!*' I cried out with my mind. She heard me, even though she was no longer strong enough to answer me, but what I had not reckoned with was that her father would also hear me. He did, and he must also have seen in my mind's eye a picture of the weapon I intended to use against him.

The Wind-Walker immediately turned to face me. He looked down upon me, and upon Whitey as he came rushing across the plateau's roof toward me. The monster's eyes slitted as they followed Whitey, then he lifted his free hand to the sky and thrust it into the lowering grey clouds.

'Whitey – look out!' I yelled, but my friend had also seen and knew what was going to happen. He *knew*, and on this occasion needed no precognition to tell him his fate.

Ithaqua moved closer, looming large over the roof as he hurled his ice-bomb. I saw it – saw Paul White's horrible but mercifully instant death beneath ten tons of ice that smashed down upon him like a meteorite – and I also saw his last heroic action in defiance of his destroyer. Not a second too soon, he slid the spear with its star-stone tip in my direction.

Skidding across the roof that weapon came, finally to slide to a halt at my feet. I stared at it for the merest moment, almost uncomprehendingly. Then, no longer fearing the stone sigil of Eld tied to the spear's blade – I was so numb with sick horror that I no longer felt or feared anything – snatched it up. And as I felt the unevenly balanced shaft in my hand, so the sickness and the horror went out of me, *driven* out by murderous hate and a lusting for red revenge!

I drew back my arm and aimed the spear at the Wind-Walker, who seemed suddenly to lose coordination. As I hurled the spear, he began to bring his hands up to guard his face.

What happened then, is not an easy thing to tell. It seemed to me that the spear moved through the air in a sort of slow motion, and that Ithaqua's hand moved even slower, so that when the weapon shot in through the flinching slit of his left eye I could easily trace the disappearance of its length into his head. Then things began to speed up again. The dull roar that had been growing in my ears burst into a howl of approval from the warriors on the roof; the sky seemed to bend downward; the back of Ithaqua's head flew open and a stream of molten gold flooded out, through the midst of which the spear with its star-stone sigil continued its curving flight out over the plateau's rim.

It had passed through him just like the tracers we fired at him from the plane's machine gun (how many centuries ago?) during our first encounter, but with much more devastating effect! For while bullets were of no consequence to Ithaqua, the seal of the Elder Gods was very different.

The Wind-Walker reeled like a man struck in the forehead with a hammer. For a second I thought he would topple out of the sky as he fought wildly to regain his balance. Then something fell from his hand as he lurched erratically to and fro. It was Armandra, spiralling down like an autumn leaf, the dull pinkish flush emanating from her more dully yet as she slowly sank, until at a height of about twenty feet the glow blinked out and she fell like a stone.

As I ran toward her still form I saw Ithaqua throw up his hands to his swollen, pulsating head. I saw him striking his temples with the flat of his hands in a mad frenzy, while the stream of golden sparks continued to issue from his left eye and the wound at the back of his head, and then I 'heard' a cry of what could only be described as purest alien anguish. It was his mental voice crying out against unbearable psychic stress, to which I automatically closed my mind lest I too feel his agony.

By the time I reached Armandra and knelt beside her, the Wind-Walker was lurching away down aerial paths, heading for the lonely sanctuary of his pyramid altar. But in contrast to his previous lordly stridings on the wings of the wind, now he moved with the spastic jerks and twitchings of a singed moth. He might well recover, but I knew that he would *never* forget.

4

The Last Transmission

(Recorded through the Medium of Juanita Alvarez)

And for the present, Juanita, there is little more to tell.
I believe I have already told you that Armandra may be
crippled. There seems to be some injury to her spine;
Jimmy and Tracy, however – they at least are safe. Jimmy
received a few cuts from the ice-bomb that killed poor
brave Whitey, but nothing serious.

When we left the roof, Jimmy and Tracy went off
together to mourn in private while I returned to Armandra's chambers. Of course, she was not there; she
had been taken to be examined by the plateau's greatest
doctors. I stood on the high balcony looking out over the
white waste and waited for news. I stayed there, in what
must have been a state of delayed shock, for five or six
hours.

When Oontawa came to me in tears I thought at first
that she brought terrible news, but that wasn't it. She only
wanted me to go with her to where her man, Kota'na, was
lying in one of the plateau's hospitals. They had only just
found him near the gates of the central snow-ship keep.
He had been brought in with a pitiful handful of wounded
men. His injuries were severe but not fatal; he needed rest
but would not submit either to the physician's wishes or
their drugs until he had seen me. I went with her, hurrying
down into the bowels of the plateau.

Kota'na, who had a small room of his own befitting his
rank and status, was hanging onto consciousness waiting
for me. When he saw me a grim, tired smile creased
his handsome Indian features. His arms were caked

217

with blood and he bore terrible scars on various parts of his body, but he was in no way about to die. It was as Oontawa had told me; rest and recuperation were all he required to bring him back to complete recovery.

Now Oontawa translated as I bent over Kota'na's bed.

'Lord Sil-ber-hut-te, I beg your forgiveness.'

'My forgiveness? For what, Kota'na? You fought for the plateau, for its princess, and for your woman, Oontawa. You fought well and commanded the bears and the men who handle them. You have no need to beg forgiveness of me.'

Then he lifted up his hand from where it hung unseen on the far side of his raised pallet. His fingers were clenched in hair that was full of clotted blood, black hair rooted in the roughly severed head of Northan, which hung from Kota'na's fist and stared at me with wide, glassy eyes.

'Forgive me, Lord, for I knew that you would want him for yourself – and knowing it, I killed him. I tried to take him alive, but he would not let me. Take his head, it belongs to you.'

'No.' I shook my head at his offer. 'The trophy is yours, Kota'na. Let it hang in your lodge so that your children will know of my debt to you, that their father killed Sil-ber-hut-te's great enemy, the traitor Northan. For this deed, I thank you.'

Five minutes later, after accepting a drugged drink, Kota'na fell asleep and the physicians were able to begin washing him and cleaning his wounds. But it took them as long again to pry open his hand and remove Northan's head.

As for Ithaqua; he too appears to be resting. The monster crouches atop his pyramid altar and cradles his head in his hands. His left eye is half closed – yellow sparks drip from it like pus – and a dark spot is visible at the back of his head. Since his wounds were not fatal, I can only assume that he is recuperating. He has shrunk down into himself somewhat, though his size is still four or five times greater than that of a man. Even now I can see him as I gaze out across the white waste through my binoculars, and –

What was that?

Strange, I thought for a moment that –

But no, I must have been mistaken. Did you feel anything, Juanita? It seemed as though someone were listening in on our conversation. You didn't? Good. And yet I could have sworn that just for a moment I saw Ithaqua turn his head to peer evilly at the plateau out of his good eye . . .

A messenger has just arrived, sent by the physicians who attend Armandra. He seems to be quite delighted but I can't understand a word he says. It appears I am to accompany him.

I'll contact you again as soon as I have news.

NOTE:
The time was 5:50 P.M. on June 6 when Juanita Alvarez recorded that last hopeful message from Hank Silberhutte. His telepathic vibrations were then absent for some two hours, until, at 7:45 P.M., Juanita made the following, final, brief contact with him.

'Juanita, I'm back.

'*Everything is going to be all right!* I'm back on the balcony now, but I've just finished tidying up Armandra's – no, *our* – chambers, getting the place ready for her. She's conscious and they're carrying her up here right now. She's going to be fine, but she'll need a lot of rest and quiet. All she wanted when she awakened was to be with me. God, Juanita, but you must be able to *feel* how happy I am! It's as if a terrible black cloud were suddenly lif –

'*Again!* And this time there can be no doubt about it. I was watching Ithaqua through the glasses while I talked to you. It was him, listening in, and suddenly he turned and looked at me – and he smiled in a terrible way!

'Juanita, I think he saw right through me – *to you!*

'But what in the . . . this? There seems . . . sort . . . interference. It's *him*! Ithaqua is scrambling my . . . losing you! And now . . . the altar and limping off across the sky. He looks back at me and . . . hideous laughter! . . . revenge? My God, it's you, Juanita. He can no longer hurt us *so he's coming for you!*

'Tell Peaslee he has to look after you. Tell him –'

FINAL NOTE: For three long months, into the middle of September, Juanita stayed at Miskatonic and spent every minute of every day trying to reestablish contact with Hank. She never heard from him again, and having turned down my offer to take up a position with the Wilmarth Foundation, she left Arkham in the third week of the month.

When she went she took with her one of the star-stones of ancient Mnar, a genuine stone found with others by our African expeditions in 1959. We kept in contact until early the next year. When last I heard from her she was making wedding arrangements in Monterrey.

In March of the new year I learned how, along with her husband, she was killed in an automobile accident near Regina, Canada, where they were honeymooning. The car had been blown off the road and down a sheer drop in a 'freak storm'. I made inquiries and discovered that they had been returning to their hotel after a show. The gown Juanita was wearing had a plunging neckline – not the kind of gown she could wear her star-stone with.

As for Hank Silberhutte, his sister Tracy, and James Graywing Franklin: so far as I am aware they are still on

Borea, a world at the edge of strange dimensions, some-where out in remote regions of space and time.

My telepathic team at Miskatonic still occasionally try, without reward to date, to reestablish contact with Hank, and I personally will never give up hope.

– Wingate Peaslee.

IN THE MOONS
OF BOREA

For the 'Old Folks' at No. 25

1
Paths of Fate

They skirted the forest on foot, the Titan bears shambling along behind on all fours, their packs piled high so that there was no room for the men to ride. Only three of the animals went unburdened, and these were hardly bears for riding. A stranger party could scarce be imagined. Here were bronze Indians straight out of Earth's Old West, squat, powerful Eskimos from the Motherworld's perpetually frozen north, great white bears half as big again as those of the Arctic Circle, and a tall, ruggedly handsome, leather-clad white man whose open, short-sleeved jacket showed a broad, deep chest and arms that forewarned of massive strength.

To the oddly polyglot party that followed Hank Silberhutte, their Warlord seemed utterly enigmatic. He was a strange, strange man: the toast of the entire plateau and master of all its might, mate to Armandra the Priestess and father of her man-child, destroyer of Ithaqua's armies and crippler – however briefly – of Ithaqua himself. And yet he mingled with his minions like a common man and led them out upon peaceful pursuits as surely as he led them in battle. Yes, a strange man indeed, and Ithaqua must surely rue the day he brought him to Borea.

Silberhutte the Texan had been Warlord for three years now, since the time he deposed Northan in a savage fight to win Armandra. He had won her, and with her the total command of the plateau's army. That had been before the War of the Winds, when the plateau's might had prevailed over the bludgeoning assault of Ithaqua's tribes, when Ithaqua himself had been sorely wounded by this man from the Motherworld.

Mighty wrestler, fighter who could knock even a strong man senseless with a blow of his huge fist, weapons' master whose skill had quickly surpassed that of his instructors, telepath (though the plateau's simpler folk could not truly understand the concept) who could throw – had thrown – mental insults at Ithaqua, the Wind-Walker, and yet walk away unscathed: Silberhutte was all of these things. He was as gentle as his strength and size would allow; he instinctively understood the needs of his people; when lesser men approached him in awe, he greeted them as friends, equals; he respected the Elders and was guided by their counselling, and his fairness was already as much a legend as his great strength.

When he could by right have slain Northan, his hated, bullying Warlord predecessor – when nine-tenths of the plateau's peoples had *wanted* Northan dead – Hank Silberhutte had let him live, had given him his life. Later, when Northan turned traitor, siding with Ithaqua and his ice-priests to help them wage war against the plateau, Kota'na the Keeper of the Bears had taken that life, had taken Northan's head too; and even though he was wounded in the fighting, Kota'na would not give up his grisly trophy to any man but his Lord Silberhutte.

And it was Kota'na who came now at an easy lope through the long grass toward where Silberhutte stood, Kota'na, whose proud Indian head was lifted high, eyes alert as those of any creature of the wild. He had scouted out the ground ahead, as two other braves even now scouted it to the rear; for though they were well clear of the territories of the Wind-Walker's tribes, still they were wary of skulking war parties. The Children of the Winds did not usually wander far afield when Ithaqua left them to go striding among the star-voids, but one could never be sure. That was why three of the bears were not in harness; they were fighters, white monsters whose loyalty to their masters was matched only by their ferocity when confronted with their enemies. Now they were nervous, and Hank Silberhutte had noted their anxious snufflings and growlings.

He noted too Kota'na's uneasiness as the handsome brave approached him. The Indian kept glancing toward the dark green shadows of the forest, his eyes narrowing as they sought to penetrate the darker patches of shade. Borea had no 'night' as such, only a permanent half-light, whereby shaded places were invariably very gloomy.

'What's bothering you, bear-brother?' Hank asked, his keen eyes searching the other's face.

'The same thing that bothers the bears, Lord Sil-ber-hut-te,' the Indian answered. 'Perhaps it is just that Ithaqua's time draws nearer, when he returns to Borea . . .,' he shrugged. 'Or perhaps something else. There is a stillness in the air, a hush over the forest.'

'Huh!' the Texan grunted, half in agreement. 'Well, here we camp, danger or none. The forest goes on for twenty miles or more yet, Kota'na, so if we're being shadowed, we won't lose our tail until we're beyond the woods. We'll keep five men awake at all times; that should be sufficient. Six hours' sleep, a meal, and then we press on as fast as we can go. Fifty miles beyond the forest belt we'll be back in the snows, and we'll find our sleighs where we left them. The going will be faster then. Fifty miles beyond that, across the hills, we'll sight the moons of Borea where they hang over the rim. Then – '

'Then, Lord, we will be almost within sight of the plateau!'

'Where a pretty squaw called Oontawa waits for her brave, eh?' the white giant laughed.

'Aye, Lord,' Kota'na soberly answered, 'and where the Woman of the Winds will doubtless loose great lightnings to greet the father of her child. Ah, but I am ready for the soft comforts of my lodge. If we were fighting, that would be one thing – but this dreary wandering . . .' He

227

paused and frowned, then: 'Lord, there is a question I would ask.'

'Ask away, bear-brother.'

'Why do we leave the plateau to wander in the woods? Surely it is not simply to seek out strange spices, skins, and tusks? There are skins enough in the white wastes and more than enough food in and about the plateau.'

'Just give me a moment, friend, and we'll talk,' Silberhutte told him. He spoke briefly to the men about him, giving instructions, issuing orders. Then, while rough tents were quickly erected and a list for watch duties drawn up, he took Kota'na to one side.

'You're right, bear-brother, I don't come out under the skies of Borea just to hunt for pale wild honey and the ivory of mammoths. Listen and I'll tell you:

'In the Motherworld I was a free man and went wherever I wanted to go, whenever I wanted to go there. There are great roads in the Motherworld and greater cities, man-made plateaus that make Borea's plateau look like a pebble. Now listen: you've seen Armandra fly – the way she walks on the wind – a true child of her father? Well, in the Motherworld all men can fly. They soar through the skies inside huge mechanical birds, like that machine that lies broken on the white waste between the plateau and Ithaqua's totem temple. He snatched us out of the sky in that machine and brought us here . . .'

He paused, beginning to doubt Kota'na's perception. 'Do you understand what I'm trying to say?'

'I think so, Lord,' the Indian gravely answered. 'The Motherworld sounds a fine and wonderful place – but Borea is not the Motherworld.'

'No, my friend, that's true – but it could be like the Motherworld one day. I'm willing to bet that hundreds of miles to the south there are warm seas and beautiful islands, maybe even a sun that we never see up here in the north. Yes, and I can't help wondering if Ithaqua is confined to this world's northernmost regions just as he is during his brief Earthly incursions. It's an interesting thought . . .

'As to why I come out here, exploring the woods and the lands to the south: surely you must have seen me making lines on the fine skins I carry? They are maps, bear-brother, maps of all the places we visit. The lakes and forests and hills – all of them that we've seen are shown on my maps. One day I want to be able to go abroad in Borea just as I used to on Earth.'

He slammed fist into palm, lending his words emphasis, then grinned and slapped the other's shoulder. 'But come now, we've been on the move for well over ten hours. I, for one, am tired. Let's get some sleep, and then we'll be on our way again.' He glanced at the grey sky to the north and his face quickly formed a frown. 'The last thing I want is to be caught out in the open when Ithaqua comes walking down the winds to Borea again. No, for he surely has a score to settle with the People of the Plateau – especially with me!'

In no great hurry to find Elysia (Titus Crow had warned him that the going would not be easy, that no royal road existed into the place of the Elder Gods), Henri de Marigny allowed the time-clock to wander at will through the mighty spaces between the stars. In the case of the time-clock, however, 'wander' did not mean to progress slowly and aimlessly from place to place, far from it. For de Marigny's incredible machine was linked to all times and places, and its velocity – if 'velocity' could ever adequately describe the *motion* of the clock – was such that it simply defied all of the recognized laws of Earthly science as it cruised down the lightyears.

And already de Marigny had faced dangers which only the master of such a weird vessel might ever be expected to face: dangers such as the immemorially evil Hounds of Tindalos!

Twice he had piloted the time-clock through time itself; once as an experiment in the handling of the clock, the second time out of sheer curiosity. On the first occasion, as he left the solar system behind, he had paused to reverse the clock's temporal progression to a degree sufficient to freeze the planets in their eternal swing around the sun, until the worlds of Sol had stood still in the night of space and the sun's flaring, searing breath had appeared as a still photograph in his vessel's scanners. The second time had been different.

Finding a vast cinder in space orbiting a dying orange sun, de Marigny had felt the urge to trace its history, had journeyed into the burned-out planet's past to its beginnings. He had watched it blossom from a young world with a bright atmosphere and dazzling oceans into a mature planet where races not unlike Man had grown up and built magnificent if alien cities . . . and he had watched its decline, too. De Marigny had recognized the pattern well enough: the early wars, each greater (or more devastating) than the last, building to the final confrontation. And the science of these beings was much like the science of Man.

They had vehicles on the land, in the air, and on the water, and they had weapons as awesome as any ever devised on Earth.

. . . Weapons which they used!

Sickened to find that another Manlike race had discovered the means of self-destruction – and that in this instance they had used it to burn their world to a useless crisp – de Marigny would have returned at once to his own time and picked up his amazing voyage once more. But that was when he was called upon to face his first real threat since leaving Earth's dreamworld, and in so doing, he went astray from the known universe.

It was strange, really, and oddly paradoxical; for while Titus Crow had warned him about the Hounds of Tindalos, he had also stated that time's corridors were mainly free of their influence. Crow had believed that the Hounds were drawn to travellers in the fourth dimension much like moths to a flame (except that flames kill moths!) and that a man might unconsciously attract them by his presence alone. They would scent the id of a man as sharks might scent his blood, and it would send them into just such a frenzy!

Thus, as de Marigny flew his vessel forward along the timestream, he nervously recalled what Crow had told him of the Hounds – how time was their domain and that they hid in time's darkest 'angles' – and in this way he may well have attracted them. Indeed he found himself subconsciously repeating lines remembered from the old days as he had seen them scribbled in a book of Crow's jottings, an acrostic poem written by an eccentric friend of Crow's who had 'dreamed' all manner of weird things in connection with the Cthulhu Cycle Deities, or the 'CCD,' and similarly fabled beings of legendary times and places. It had gone like this:

> Time's angles, mages tell, conceal a place
> Incredible, beyond the mundane mind:
> Night shrouded and *outside* the seas of space,
> Dread Tindalos blows on the ageless wind.
> And where the black and corkscrew towers climb,
> Lost and athirst the ragged pack abides,
> Old as the aeons, trapped in tombs of time,
> Sailing the tortuous temporal tides . . .

And even as he realized his error and tore his thoughts from their morbid ramblings – as mental warning bells clamoured suddenly and jarringly in the back of his mind – de Marigny saw them in the clock's scanners . . . the Hounds of Tindalos!

He saw them, and Crow's own description of the

monstrous vampiric creatures came back to him word for word:

'They were like ragged shadows, Henri, distant tatters that flapped almost aimlessly in the void of time. But as they drew closer, their movements took on more purpose! I saw that they had shape and size and even something approaching solidarity, but that still there was nothing about them even remotely resembling what we know of life. They were Death itself – they were the Tind'losi Hounds – and once recognized, they can never be forgotten!'

He remembered, too, Crow's advice: not to attempt to run from them once they found you, neither that nor even to use the clock's weapon against them. 'Any such attempt would be a waste of time. They can dodge the beam, avoid it, even outdistance it as easily as they outdistance the clock itself. The fourth dimension is their element, and they are the ultimate masters of time travel. Forward in time, backward – no matter your vessel's marvellous manoeuvrability or its incredible acceleration – once the Hounds have you, there is only one way to escape them: by reverting instantly to the three commonplace dimensions of space and matter . . .'

De Marigny knew now how to do this and would ordinarily have managed the trick easily enough, but with the Tind'losi Hounds fluttering like torn, sentient kites about his hurtling vessel, their batlike voices chittering evilly and their nameless substance already beginning to eat through the clock's exterior shell to where his defenceless id crouched and shuddered . . .

And so he made his second mistake – an all-too-human error, a simple miscalculation – which instantly took him out of his own timestream, his own plane of existence, leaving him dizzy and breathless with the shock of it. For he had not regained the three-dimensional universe measured and governed by Earthly laws but had sidestepped into one which lay alongside, a parallel universe of marvels and mysteries. One moment (if such a cliché is acceptable in this case) the Hounds of Tindalos were clustered about the time-clock, and the next –

– They were gone, and where they had been, an undreamed-of vista opened to de Marigny's astounded eyes! This was in no way the void of interstellar space as he had come to know it, no. Instead he found himself racing through a tenuous, faintly glowing grey-green mist distantly rippled with banners of pearly and golden light that moved like Earth's aurora borealis, sprinkled here and there with the silver gleam of strange stars and the pastel glow of planets large and small.

And since his own senses were partly linked with those of his hybrid vessel, he also detected the eddies of an ether wind that caught at the clock to blow it ever faster on an oddly winding course between and around these alien spheres. A wind that keened in de Marigny's mind, conjuring visions of ice and snow and great white plains lying frozen fast beneath moons that bloated on a distant horizon. The moons of Borea . . .

2
Paths Cross

'Lord Sil-ber-hut-te! Hank! Wake up, Lord!' Kota'na's urgency, emphasized by his use of the Warlord's first name, brought Hank Silberhutte to his feet within his central tent. A moment later he stepped out into the open, shaking sleep from his mind, gazing skyward and following Kota'na's pointing finger. All eyes in the camp were turned to the sky, where something moved across the heavens with measured pace to fall down behind the horizon of forest treetops.

The Warlord had almost missed the thing, had witnessed its flight for two or three seconds only; but in that short time his heart, which he believed had almost stopped in the suspense of the moment, had started to beat again, and the short hairs at the back of his neck had lain down flat once more. Borea was no world in which to be out in the open when there were strange dark things at large in the sky!

But no, the aerial phenomenon had not been Ithaqua, not the Wind-Walker. If it were, then without a doubt Silberhutte's party had been doomed. It had certainly been a strange and alien thing, yes, and one that ought surely not to fly in any world. But it had not been the Lord of the Snows.

'A clock!' Silberhutte gasped. 'A great-grandfather clock! Now what in the – ' And his voice suddenly tapered off as memory brought back to him snatches of a conversation which had taken place (how many years ago?) in the home of a London-based colleague during the Wilmarth Foundation's war on the CCD, the 'Cthulhu Cycle Deities,' in Great Britain. At that time Silberhutte had not long been a member of the foundation, but his singular telepathic talent had long since appraised him of the presence of the CCD.

Titus Crow had been a prime British mover in that phase of the secret confrontation, and at the home of the learned leonine occultist Silberhutte had been shown just such a clock as had recently disappeared over the treetops. A weirdly hieroglyphed, oddly ticking monstrosity whose four hands had moved in sequences utterly removed from horological systems of Earthly origin. By far the most striking thing about that clock had been its shape – like a coffin a foot taller than a tall man – that and the fact that there seemed to be no access to the thing's innards, no way into its working parts. It was then that Titus Crow had told Silberhutte:

'I'm taking a chance that you'll perhaps think me a madman, my friend – certainly it will be a test of your credulity – but in any case I'll tell you what I think the clock really is. It is a gateway on all space and time, a vessel capable of journeying to the very corners of existence and beyond. That's my belief. One day I'll learn all there is to know about the thing. When I do . . .' And Crow had paused to shrug and smile, adding: 'But that is all in the future. At the moment I may rightly compare myself to an ape attempting to fathom the splitting of the atom!'

Yes, Crow had called the clock a gateway on all space and time, a bridge between worlds – between universes!

Silberhutte stared out across the forest roof where the clock had disappeared, and suddenly he was taut as a bowstring, incredible hope springing up in him, flaring bright where he had believed hope to have all but faded away. Could that thing in the sky – that coffin-shape so briefly glimpsed – could it possibly . . . ?

'What is it, Lord?' Kota'na asked, his voice low, hushed. The Keeper of the Bears was worried. He had never seen the Warlord stirred by such emotions before. Silberhutte's gaze burned – like a great hound straining at the leash, he seemed to lean toward the forest – and his fists had tightened into huge knots which he held half-raised before him.

Again Kota'na spoke: 'Was it some terrible toy of the Wind-Walker, Lord?'

'No, I don't think so.' And the great white Warlord suddenly relaxed, took a deep breath, turned to grasp Kota'na's shoulders. 'Bear-brother, I want you to come with me, you and two others and a bear. Quick as you can, choose the other men now. We get under way at once. The rest can break camp and head for home with all speed.'

'But – where are we going, Lord?'

'Into the forest,' Silberhutte answered at once. 'Where else? If that flying thing is what I think it is – by *God!* – bear-brother, if only it is!' He gave a great cry and threw his arms wide.

'Yes, Lord?' prompted Kota'na. 'What then?'

'Then?' and Silberhutte's eyes were deep as the spaces between stars. 'Then, Kota'na, the Motherworld may not be as far away as I thought.'

De Marigny set the clock down in a glade beside a pool. There was a curious absence of vegetation about that pool, and if he had been more observant, he might have noticed, as his vessel slowly descended and came to rest, a peculiar bluish *withdrawal* of something or things into the water. Before leaving the safety of the clock, he scanned the forest around him: no slightest thing moved, no birds called. That, too, might have warned him – did in fact caution him to a degree – but what could there possibly be to fear? He would only leave the clock for a few moments, and it would never be more than a pace or two away.

His reasons for coming down here, at a fair distance from the encampment of primitives he had viewed from on high, were threefold. One: he wanted the humanoid natives of this world to have time to think about what they had seen, to assimilate the fact that the clock had done them no harm, before taking a closer look at them or trying to contact them. Two: following what felt like a thousand attempts to leave this alien time dimension into which he had erroneously entered, he was feeling fatigued. All of his efforts to leave had failed miserably, highlighting his inadequate beginner's grasp of the clock's refinements; now he wanted to rest both mind and body before trying yet again. And three: the pool had looked inviting and refreshing, the glade peaceful and quiet, and the forest itself had seemed to offer green walls of protection, looking for all the world like the familiar forests of Earth.

Only now, stepping out through the clock's open frontal panel, did de Marigny become aware of the odd texture of the soil in the glade, its unnatural feel, crumbly and lifeless. A dozen or so paces took him to the water's edge where he went down on one knee, failing to note as he did so that the glade seemed to grow quieter still. Not a ripple disturbed the surface of that pool, and yet it failed to mirror the man who kneeled at its rim. He paused – his hand poised ready to dip, inches above the surface of water which carried an odd bluish tinge – and the quiet deepened tangibly. Now he felt it: the tension in the air, the sensation of a trap ready to spring shut!

He threw himself back and away from the pool, sprawling in the crumbling soil, scrambling frantically away from water which was suddenly alive with awful activity. The surface frothed and parted and lumpish blue shapes slithered over de Marigny's booted feet, fastening to his legs through the thin material of his trousers. Half-lizard, half-leech, eight inches long and shaped like flatworms or bloated tadpoles, there were thousands of the blue-veined creatures.

The water boiled with them, these *things* whose appetites had stripped the glade of life. De Marigny tore them bloodily from lacerated limbs, kicked frantically back from the pool toward the clock where it stood behind him, gasped for air as shock and horror gripped him. The farther he struggled from the pool, the less certainly they slithered after him; but their lidless red eyes regarded him evilly and their razor mouths gaped hungrily. Finally he stripped the last of them from his legs, scrabbled upright, and turned to the clock – only to stumble into the arms of an apparition out of his wildest nightmares!

Wolf-headed and terrible the figure stood, arms encircling him, staring from wild wolf eyes into his own fear-taut features. Now he saw that the figure was human and only dressed in the trappings of an animal, and that others similarly adorned surrounded the clock and gazed impassively at him. They were like Red Indians out of old Earth, and the eyes that stared from wolf heads were anything but friendly.

De Marigny mustered his strength to twist under and out of the bronze vice that held him and made a dive for the clock's open, greenly lit panel – only to be met in midair by the flat of a tomahawk that hurled him into a black pit of oblivion . . .

De Marigny's return to consciousness was slow and painful. His eyes felt full of ground glass behind closed and swollen lids. He barely stifled a cry of anguish when he tried to open them, then abandoned the attempt for the time being and concentrated instead on regaining a measure of orientation. This was far from easy for there was a roaring in his ears that came and went in regular pulses, bringing red-peaked waves of pain and surging nausea. As his mind began to clear, he tried to think, to remember where he was and what had happened, but even that small effort seemed to splash acid around inside his skull.

Very slowly the red burning died away, was replaced by an awareness of a sickly chill creeping into muscles and bones already cramped and stiff. He forced back the bile that rose suddenly in his throat and tried to lick parched lips, but his tongue met only sand, dry and tasteless. His teeth were full of the stuff; he gagged on it. Rolling his head weakly, dizzily to one side and freeing his mouth, he spat out grit and blood and what felt like a tooth, then fought to fill his lungs with air. One nostril was full of sand, the other sticky and warm with blood.

Anger surged up in de Marigny – at the stupidity of this dazed, slothful body which would not obey his commands – at his dull mind because it refused to answer his questions. Where the hell was he? What had happened to him? He seemed to be lying facedown in coarse-grained sand or loose soil – .

Then, in a series of vivid mental pictures, memory flooded back. Scenes flashed before his mind's eye: of the glade in the forest and the pool of leech-things; of the barbaric, wolf-headed warriors standing in a ring about the time-clock.

The time-clock!

If anything had happened to –

He gritted his teeth, lifted his head to shake it free of sand, then bit his lip and fought off the fresh waves of pain his actions brought. He blinked and was glad of the stinging tears that welled up to wash his eyes, even though he was blinded by the light that they admitted. It had a weak light, this strange world, true, but painful for all that and filled with a thousand bilious fireball flashes.

Nausea returned immediately, forcing him to close his eyes again. The scene he had so briefly gazed out upon – of a greenly shaded background above a sandy expanse – faded quickly from his tortured retinas, was replaced by a dull red throbbing that brought a groan of pain and despair from battered lips. Plainly he had suffered a brutal beating and kicking even after being knocked unconscious.

He wondered if there were something wrong with his limbs; while they gave him no great pain, still he could not move them. Could it be his attackers had crippled him? Again he tried to move and finally discovered the truth: his wrists were bound behind his back, and his feet were tied at the ankles. His neck, too, must be in a noose of some sort; he had felt it tighten when he shook his head. Grimly he considered his position. Having tired of their sport with his unconscious body, his tormentors had obviously staked him out – but for what purpose?

Then de Marigny thought again of the hideous pool-things and the way the slimy colouring of their internal juices had given the pool its unnatural bluish tinge, and suddenly he found himself wondering if –

He forced his eyes open again, slowly this time, to let them grow accustomed to the light, and gradually the scene before him took shape. He lay in something of a shallow depression with his chin buried in coarse sand, the soil of the silent forest glade. Beyond his immediate horizon was a more distant one of shaded greens, the forest wall at the far side of the pool. De Marigny shuddered, and not at all because of the cramped chill steadily creeping into his bones.

Turning his head carefully to the left, he saw a stretched leather thong that reached out from his neck to where it was tied to a peg driven deep into the soil. He was similarly tied down to the right. Since he could not move his legs at the knees, they too must be tethered. He struggled briefly, uselessly, then slowly and methodically began cursing himself for a fool. To have been so utterly careless, so criminally stupid as to get himself into a mess like this. It was unthinkable!

Disgusted with himself and with his predicament, he nevertheless attempted to analyse his desperate mistake. He believed he knew how it had come about.

His adventures in Earth's dreamworld – the terrible

threats and dangers he had faced and conquered there, until it had seemed he must be almost indestructible – had lulled him into a state of false security. How *could* he have come through so much only to fall prey in the end to the primitives of some nameless planet on the rim of reality?

What angered the Earthman more than anything else was the fact that he was wearing the cloak brought back by Titus Crow from Elysia, an antigravity device which allowed the wearer to soar aloft as effortlessly as any bird. He was sure that in the dreamworld his reactions would have been instinctive: to reach for and activate the buttons in his harness that would have lifted him instantly to safety. But here in this strange new world . . . things had simply seemed to move too fast for him.

If only he might free one hand and reach the controls of his cloak, he had no doubt that –

Any further thoughts of escape were aborted, driven from his mind the instant that he caught sight of a pulsating, blue-veined leech-thing that suddenly came slithering over the rim of the hollow in which he lay. It saw him at once, tiny red eyes fixing upon him hungrily, jellyish body throbbing as the creature slid and slithered down the slight declivity toward his face.

Frozen in horror, de Marigny could only think: 'My face – *my eyes*!' But even as the pulsating leech reared up in front of him, inches away, and even as a dozen or so more of the awful things appeared almost simultaneously over the lip of the hollow, still he could not avert his gaze. Hypnotized and immobilized by his unthinkable situation, by the fate about to descend upon him, de Marigny could only watch and wait for it to happen, and –

– The earth shuddered beneath him as a leather-booted foot came down on top of the menacing leech-thing in the moment that it made to strike for his face. Its juices splashed him as it was ground into the moistureless soil.

A second later and the silver blade of a wicked picklike

weapon flashed down once, twice, and the thongs that tethered de Marigny's neck were severed. He felt cold metal touch his wrists and his hands were free, his legs too. Another second and – amazing sight! – a snarling, coughing mountain of white fur, a bear almost eleven feet tall, shambled swiftly into view, stomping the now retreating leech-things and shaking the ground with its massive weight.

Then, before the astounded Earthman could even muster his thoughts to consider these miraculous developments, he was hauled gently but irresistibly to his feet. Left to stand on his own, weak and bloody as he was, de Marigny might well have fallen, but steely arms supported him and keenly intelligent eyes stared into his own first in concern, then in recognition.

He stared back – stared even harder – then gasped and shook his head in dizzy disbelief. Finally he managed to mumble: 'Hank? Hank Silberhutte? I don't – '

'Neither do I, Henri,' the Texan interrupted, 'but I'm glad to see you anyway.'

'The feeling,' de Marigny wholeheartedly, bone wearily agreed, 'is mutual, Hank, to say the very least!'

He gazed then at Silberhutte's brawny companions – two bronze-skinned Indians and an olive Eskimo – and at the monster bear which stamped and roared now at the edge of the pool. 'But where in all the corners of space and time are we?'

Knowing that the newcomer to Borea was suffering from shock, Silberhutte carefully released him, nodding in satisfaction as de Marigny staggered a little but somehow managed to stay on his feet. 'We're on Borea, Henri, one of the worlds of an alien universe. I've been here some time now, since Ithaqua brought me here. And you . . . well, I saw your arrival. So Crow was right about that old clock of his, eh?' The effect of Silberhutte's words on the other man was immediate and electric.

'The clock?' de Marigny's jaw dropped and the colour drained from his face. 'The time-clock!' He whirled about, staggering wildly, his eyes frantically searching the glade for his fantastic machine.

In the sand he saw a deep indentation where the clock had stood; leading from it, twin tracks cut deep grooves in the gritty soil, terminating where they entered the abrupt shade of the forest. Beyond, a trail of crushed leaves and grasses led away into the undergrowth. Again de Marigny whirled, once more facing Silberhutte and his polyglot companions.

'No, no!' he cried, shaking his head in denial. 'I've *got* to get the clock back. I – '

But finally he had exerted his already overtaxed body and mind beyond their limits. Bright lights flashed inside his head as, with unspoken protests still whispering on his lips, he reeled and toppled. Already unconscious, he was not to know how easily Silberhutte caught him up in massive arms to bear him out of the glade and away from the pool of the leech-things.

3
The Pursuit

De Marigny dreamed of ice stars and planets, all frozen in galactic glaciers that flowed out of deepest infinities of lost dimensions. The Hounds of Tindalos chased him along corridors of ice between razor-sharp cliffs that reached blue-rimmed needles high overhead. Without warning an avalanche of huge, jagged ice splinters crashed down upon him, cracking the time-clock open like a nutshell and spilling him out onto the ice. The Hounds were on him at once, black rags of death whose lusting, ethereal feelers found and held him fast. He fought madly to escape them, but –

– He threw his arms wide and awakened with a cry of horror, only to find himself held down by Silberhutte's huge, strangely cold hands. The Texan held him until his body relaxed, only then allowing him to fall back into a deep warm bank of furs. De Marigny felt the furs move against him and saw that his head rested against a forepaw as big as a real pillow. The warmth he felt was the body heat of Silberhutte's vast bear! He instinctively drew away from the creature where it reclined beside him on the forest's floor.

'You were cold,' Silberhutte explained from where he kneeled beside him. 'Morda was the only one who could warm you. Kota'na has rubbed you with the body grease he uses. Morda won't harm you – he thinks you're the bear keeper's little brother!' The grin quickly faded from the Texan's face as he asked: 'How do you feel now, Henri? The wolf-warriors gave you a pretty rough time.'

'Wolf-warriors? Yes, they certainly did,' the other slowly

answered, 'but I feel better now.' He licked his lips and frowned at an unfamiliar but not unpleasant taste.

'Kota'na got a little soup down you and some of his tea,' Silberhutte explained. 'The tea is good; it would straighten out a corkscrew!'

'My head still feels a bit loose,' de Marigny answered, but apart from that . . . I expect I'll live.' He stood up unaided and the great bear's paw closed possessively around him. He carefully extricated himself as Kota'na approached and ordered the bear up onto its feet.

'Morda,' Silberhutte informed, 'is not normally very gentle with anyone. He's trained for the fight. It seems you've found a firm friend there, Henri.'

Staring after the towering creature as Kota'na led it away, de Marigny answered, 'I would hate to be his enemy!'

He took hold of the Texan's arm. 'Hank, I have to get after the time-clock. It's my one way out of here. All explanations, everything I would like to know – questions you must surely be wanting to ask me – will have to wait. The time-clock is – '

' – All important, Henri?' Silberhutte finished it for him. 'Yes, I know. To me, too. I'm as much a prisoner here on Borea as you are, and I've been here that much longer.'

'Then I'll be on my way now, at once.'

'Now? On your own?' Without malice Silberhutte laughed. 'You don't seem to understand, Henri. There isn't any way you can get the clock back on your own. Even if you could, they'll be miles away by now.'

'Do you think so? Dragging the time-clock behind them? Why, the thing must weigh a ton, Hank! They'd need to be superhuman.'

'You didn't see their wolves, then?'

'I saw their wolf masks – but behind them they were only men.'

'Oh, yes, the wolf-warriors are men, Henri. Ithaqua's

245

people, the Children of the Wind. But I was talking about their wolves: creatures big as ponies – bred as mounts, as beasts of burden – and some bred to kill! We found the party's tracks, and there were wolves with them, big brutes, too. They'd easily pull that clock of yours. Yes, and there are other reasons why we can't simply go chasing after them. Ithaqua is due back on Borea at any time now, and when he returns we must all be safely back in the plateau.'

'Hank,' de Marigny answered, 'I accept all you say, though I don't understand half of it as yet, but . . .' he paused. 'Look, I've no time to explain, so I'll simply show you. You see, Titus Crow used the time-clock to journey to Elysia, and when he returned, he brought back something with him. He brought this.' He opened his cloak wide.

'Your cloak? I don't see what – '

'Do you see now?' De Marigny touched the large studs that looked merely decorative where they were set in the leather of the cloak's harness. He rose slowly at first, then shot skyward through the branches of the surrounding trees.

Now it was Hank Silberhutte's turn to stare in amazement. He knew only too well that Ithaqua could walk on the wind, as could his daughter Armandra. But this was Henri-Laurent de Marigny, a common man of Mother Earth. And yet here he soared aloft on the wind as surely as any hawk!

'All right, Henri,' he called out to the man who glided now above the treetops, performing intricate aerial manoeuvres. 'You've convinced me. Come on down.'

De Marigny alighted a moment later to find Silberhutte standing on his own. His three companions kept well back, coming forward only when they were sure that the man in the cloak intended no more immediately foreseeable flights, and they now regarded him with something akin to awe. Morda stood behind them, padding from one gigantic hind foot to the other in seeming agitation. The bear, too, had witnessed de Marigny's flight.

'I'm convinced,' Silberhutte repeated. 'Convinced that you stand a slight chance . . .' He reached out to touch the deceptively strong fabric of the cloak. 'What kind of weight can this thing carry?'

'The weight of two men,' de Marigny answered at once. 'It's speed is reduced by extra weight, of course, but even so – ' He paused, stared hard at Silberhutte, then said, 'Whatever it is you're thinking, forget it, Hank. You've done enough already.'

'I've done nothing, old friend. And listen: I've as much interest in the time-clock as you yourself. What's more, I know something of Borea, and a whole lot more about the Children of the Winds. You'll stand a far better chance of getting the clock back with me along. Yes, and while we're on the trail of the clock, I guess we've a lot to talk about. We both have tales to tell.'

For a moment, considering Silberhutte's suggestion, de Marigny made no answer. He looked into the eager, honest eyes of this white giant, a man tall as Titus Crow himself but broader yet. Without question Silberhutte must be formidably strong. And did not his companions treat him with the utmost respect, and they themselves men obviously well versed in the arts of combat?

Finally he said, 'All right, Hank, and glad to have you along. But first we'll have to make you a seat or sling of some sort that we can suspend from the cloak's harness. There's just a bit too much of you for me to carry like a babe in arms for any great length of time.'

An hour later, after a meal of smoked meat, bread, and wild honey washed down with richly spiced tea, the two were ready to take their departure. While they had eaten, Umchak the Eskimo had worked with leather barely mature, fashioning a seat which, attached to the cloak's

247

harness, would hang immediately beneath de Marigny where he himself floated in the spread of the cloak's canopy.

First they tested the cloak's strength. In ascending, it was very slow, and descent was deceptive in that the 'brakes' had to be applied that much sooner, but in level flight the loss of speed was not so great as de Marigny had feared. Manoeuvrability, however, was an almost total loss. Carrying two men, the contraption was simply too cumbersome to perform any but the most rudimentary routines of flight.

Eventually de Marigny was satisfied that he could handle the cloak adequately under the circumstances, and then they descended to say their farewells to the three who breathlessly waited below. De Marigny wrapped himself in a warm fur from Kota'na's pack while Silberhutte delivered his final instructions to his retainers. Moments later, as de Marigny hovered only a few feet above the forest's floor, Silberhutte again climbed into his own makeshift harness and they were off.

As they rose up through the forest, Kota'na called: 'And if we get back to the plateau before you, Lord, how shall I tell the Woman of the Winds what you are about?'

'Tell your mistress what you know,' Silberhutte shouted down.

'She may well be displeased, Lord, that I return without you.'

'Then tell her that you keep only the bears, Kota'na – that the Lord Silberhutte is his own man. Now begone – and all speed to you, bear-brother . . .'

And with that they were away, climbing above the treetops to circle once, twice, before setting a course that followed the way the wolf-warriors had taken.

At first they flew close to the treetops, descending occasionally to ensure that they still followed the course of the twin ruts in the forest floor that told of the clock's passing. But soon they were able to climb a little higher as the trees below thinned out and the trail became that much easier to follow. By then it was apparent that they followed a course which circled to the east, back toward the territories of Ithaqua's tribes, those lands bordering on the great white plain which lay south of the impregnable plateau.

The miles were quickly eaten up beneath them, and as they went, their elevation offered a view of great beauty and mystery. To the north the peaks of a low range showed white heads above belts of grey cloud, behind which the moons of Borea were hidden except for their uppermost rims. To the south the green forest extended unbroken until hidden by distance and a wall of mist that rose until it merged with the far grey sky. Flying over rivers and lakes, they told of the adventures each had known since last he saw the other.

De Marigny related the fantastic story of how he had gone to the assistance of Titus Crow and Tiania the girl-goddess in Earth's dreamworld; Silberhutte in turn told of all that had transpired since Ithaqua bore him away from Earth's icy northern mountains to Borea; and so they grew to know one another. They had been merely distant colleagues in the old days, meeting on no more than two or three occasions. That had been at a time when the ancient but increasingly imminent threat of the CCD had drawn so many fine men together, though there had been little enough time to spare for the founding of firm friendships.

And as time passed and they talked – or rather, as they half-shouted at each other, for they had to make themselves understood above the hum of the wind in their ears – so the terrain below changed. The trees thinned out until only the occasional pine stood up from banks of coarse grass and weeds, and finally even the last of these lone trees faded away into the distance behind them.

By then they were heading in a mainly northerly direction, still following the twin ruts where they left their mark in grasses and soil below them, and de Marigny had noticed a degree of tension creeping into Silberhutte's voice, a tautness about him where he hung in his harness directly below the cloak and its flier.

When the big Texan stopped talking altogether and began to pay even more attention to the ground only ten to twelve feet beneath him, de Marigny was prompted to ask: 'Is something wrong, Hank?'

'Yes,' the Texan answered. 'They must have joined forces with a second party along the way. There are more wolves now and about nine men. That will make things more difficult for us. Also we've been flying for at least two hours. Given that we're travelling at four or five times their speed, or very nearly so, and taking into account that the woods back there must have slowed the wolf-warriors down considerably, they can't be all that far ahead. See up front there, that narrow belt of shrubs at the foot of the hills? It's my bet that – '

He paused for a split second and froze in his harness, then cried: 'Henri, get us up – *get us out of here!*'

4

Ambush!

Too late de Marigny saw what Silberhutte had seen: a pair of wolf-warriors rising from behind covering clumps of grass. Between them, shaking off loose grasses and twigs which had been strewn over it to give it camouflage, a great wolf suddenly sprang erect. Not even in his wildest dreams had de Marigny ever imagined the existence of such a beast!

With the eyes of a wolf, yellow and gleaming, and the same lolling tongue, the thing stood as tall as a pony but yet had the low-slung frame of a wolf. Indeed it was a wolf – but its head was the size of a horse's head!

The cloak was on a course which would take the fliers immediately over the heads of the ambushers. Seeing this, de Marigny began slowly to climb, banking to one side as the cloak strained to gain height. He heard Silberhutte yell some incoherent instruction or warning, and at the same time saw the stroboscopic flash and glitter of tomahawks already twirling through the air. He saw, too, the tensing of shaggy-furred muscles as the great lean monster on the ground prepared itself to spring.

One of the razor-honed tomahawks barely grazed de Marigny's ankle as it whistled harmlessly by. The other was inches lower, slicing something that twanged, sagged momentarily, and then snapped. De Marigny had only sufficient time to realize that both weapons had been aimed at him, not Silberhutte, before all balance was gone and the cloak began to yaw wildly. At the same time a massive snarling fury launched itself with all the force of steelspring legs, clawing at Hank Silberhutte where he swung now in only half a harness, and in another moment

251

the cloak and its passengers were dragged swiftly down out of the air.

Then – a kaleidoscope of action. De Marigny was privileged to witness Silberhutte's awesome speed and ferocity. He had been right about the Texan's great strength, but he would never have guessed that so large a man might be endowed with such lightning reflexes.

For even as he struck the ground with the wolf's great paws about his shoulders, Silberhutte had sunk his wicked picklike axe into the beast's shoulder, causing it to leap back away from him with a howl of pain. One of the two Indians, rushing upon them with a spear aimed at de Marigny's middle, found the shaft of his weapon trapped in a giant's fist, wrenched from his hands, driven hiltfirst into his naked belly so that he doubled over in agony. That blow itself, crushing the bronze heathen's organs, must certainly have crippled or even killed him. But to be doubly sure, as he bent forward and his screaming face came down, Silberhutte's leather-clad knee smashed upward to cut the scream short. Face bones, neck, and spine all broke in unison and the rag-thing that had been a man flopped awkwardly over onto its back.

Desperate as he was to get into the fight and go to the Texan's assistance, de Marigny was already fighting his own battle. In fact as he struggled to make the cloak manageable, he was actually obstructing his companion's action, for one leather strap still fastened Silberhutte to the cloak's harness. At last de Marigny regained control of the cloak and commenced a laborious ascent – only to be knocked sideways by a badly aimed swipe from the partly crippled leg of the now limping wolf. Then the thing was astride him, jaws slavering, terrible fangs bared as the fetid muzzle lowered toward his face.

Silberhutte's weapon was a steely blur as he cut himself free of the restraining harness. He bounded onto the wolf's back, hooked the fingers of his free hand into its nostrils, smashed down once with the spine of his terrible weapon. The needlepoint of that picklike tool drove through skull and into brain and the wolf collapsed atop de Marigny with a final, hideous death spasm.

'Get up into the air, Henri!' Silberhutte roared, leaping from the motionless carcass. 'It's our one chance. You can try to help me later – but not if it means risking your own life. And don't worry, they won't kill me. They'll be wanting to keep me for Ithaqua. He has one hell of a score to settle with me! Now go on, man – fly!'

Fighting free of the dead wolf, de Marigny saw the Texan brandishing his bloody weapon – from which the second of the two redskins shrank back – saw him turn until he faced squarely in the direction of the scrubby bushes at the foot of the hills. Racing from that quarter and no more than two dozen or so flying paces away came a pair of wolves with riders on their backs and a third man clinging between them.

And de Marigny knew that Silberhutte was right. So far the wolf-warriors had not attempted to kill the plateau's Warlord out of hand; he would provide the Wind-Walker with a great deal of pleasure. Any ordinary death he might suffer at the hands of the Children of the Wind would only anger Ithaqua – but certainly they had tried to kill de Marigny! Well, he had no intention of dying just yet.

Now, with mere moments to spare, his fingers touched the control studs and the man in the cloak sprang aloft. Looking down, he was in time to see Silberhutte bowled over by the wolves, spread-eagled by the riders of those beasts as they fell on him in a concerted tangle of thrashing bodies and bore him to the ground . . .

For what must have been all of eighteen hours (he could only guess at the passage of time in this strange world where night appeared never to fall and the light was little better than that of an early, misty dawn), de Marigny followed the wolf-warrior party, flying above them and to their rear, well out of range of their spears and tomahawks. Unlike the Indians of the Motherworld they did not carry bows; Silberhutte had explained that slender bows broke too easily when Ithaqua was close by, that the drastic fall in temperature his presence invariably occasioned made wood brittle as chalk. Also, in a world where both Armandra and her dread sire – aye, and certain of his ice-priests, too – controlled the winds so marvellously, light and slender missiles such as arrows could all too easily be turned back upon those who dispatched them!

In its entirety the party consisted of four wolves and seven Indians. Between two of the wolves the clock was secured to a travois affair of stout poles with several layers of tough hide stretched between them; Silberhutte was strapped face-down to the shaggy back of one of the other beasts. He had been unconscious for three-quarters of the time, knocked down by the flat of a tomahawk that had all but caved in his skull when the wolf-warriors overran him, and de Marigny had at first feared him dead. When at last he had seen the Texan move, then Silberhutte's aerial colleague had been both vastly relieved and delighted, particularly when the prisoner had turned his head on one side to gaze skyward, nodding his aware-ness when he saw the cloak belling out like a great kite on high.

De Marigny marvelled at the strength of the wolf-warriors that they could go so long without resting. Four rode upon the backs of the wolves while the others half-ran, were half-dragged along beside the animals, their fists knotted in the shaggy hair of the huge beasts' flanks. Periodically they would take turns about riding, but even though they obviously relished this occasional respite, still they seemed singularly tireless. But while the stamina of the redskins was not in question, de Marigny himself was beginning to feel very tired, cold, and hungry. Time and again he thought to bless Kota'na, whose fur he wore so gladly.

Twice he had let the party move well ahead before descending to solid ground and giving himself a little exercise, rubbing the numbness from stiff limbs and shaking the weariness out of a head that still ached abominably. On both occasions he had caught up with the wolf-warrior party easily enough afterward, but now his fatigue was such that he began to despair. Surely they must rest soon, when he too might be able to snatch a little sleep?

But it was not until several more miles had been covered that the party made camp. Silberhutte was bundled down from the wolf's back and given food – the sight of which, whatever it was that the Texan was offered, made de Marigny's mouth water – following which the Warlord's hands were tied again, and he was put into the close care of three guards. The other four Indians immediately settled down on the naked ground and went to sleep, as did the wolves.

De Marigny was amazed at the apparent invulnerability of these men to the cold (even in this more or less temperate zone the temperature was well down), until he remembered what Silberhutte had told him about the Wind-Walker's effect upon those who came too close to him: the permanent alterations his presence wrought in human tissues and body temperatures. This was why the Warlord's hands always seemed so cold while he himself suffered no discomfort in the most bitter conditions. As for de Marigny: he was growing colder by the minute. His one consoling thought was that however bad his plight might seem to be, Hank Silberhutte's was so much more desperate.

As soon as he was sure that the party was settled in for a few hours at least, de Marigny flew off to one flank and sought a place to hide, shelter, and rest. He found it some miles away in a small cave whose entrance was all but covered by scrub, and there he rested down, pulling Kota'na's fur close about him . . .

When he awakened, de Marigny guessed that he had slept overlong. His limbs were stiff and he was colder than ever. Beating his arms across his chest to get the circulation going, he left his cave and came into the open. Then, with his fur wrapped about him to its best advantage, he took once more to the sky.

To the north the sky was overcast, bearing the merest threat of a storm. When de Marigny had arrived on Borea, he had flown high over the plateau, remembering it now as a grimly foreboding jut of grey rock standing massively up from a vast plain of snow. He knew that it could not be long before he flew back into that region, and that then indeed he would be hard put to survive in such low temperatures. Moreover Silberhutte had told him that was where the Children of the Wind were most densely concentrated, where they worshiped Ithaqua at his totem temple. If the Texan's captors got him that far, then there would be no further hope of rescuing him.

He returned to the now forsaken wolf-warrior campsite, passed it over without pause, and flew on, ever northward, scanning ahead and following the ruts made by the travois's runners. Flying as fast as he could, another twenty minutes saw him entering a region where the terrain began to climb. Up ahead he spied ragged-crested hills and knew that the going must now be that much rougher for the wolf-warriors.

As the hills rose up, their sides grew steeper, filled with gullies and crevasses. Great boulders stuck up here and there on the slopes, with loose shale collected about their bases. Many of the crevasses were deep with jagged sides, their floors deep-shadowed and boulder strewn. The hills were desolate and dangerous.

Then he saw the wolf-warriors. They were ahead of him and higher, their attention fixed upon the problem of getting the time-clock up onto the final ridge. All of them were there, engaged in the same task, and as yet they had not seen him. He alighted, crouched down behind a boulder, and took a longer, closer look at their problem.

Normally they would find little difficulty in scaling these heights – indeed, beyond this final rise they would begin to descend, and it would be that much easier – but they had reckoned without the weight of de Marigny's clock. The thing was incredibly heavy. Once when Titus Crow was studying the weird hieroglyphs on its four-handed dial, it had taken four strong men to move it for him.

Right now three wolves crouched at the top of the ridge. They were roped to the travois, straining to haul it up after them. Strapped to its frame in folds of hide lay the clock, refusing to budge up the rocky incline. Below, levering away at the stubborn device, five of the Indians cursed and shouted and fought to maintain their balance on the difficult surface. A sixth wolf-warrior goaded on the wolves at the top of the ridge, thumping their sides with his naked fists. The seventh and last, the leader of the party, sat on the back of the fourth wolf immediately behind Hank Silberhutte. He sat there level with the travois but on a firmer piece of ground, shouting instructions at the men who laboured to do his bidding. Silberhutte, apparently bored by the whole thing, sat silently, his hands tied behind him.

De Marigny saw his chance: a heaven-sent opportunity to fly at the back of the leader of the party and unseat him, then to pick up Silberhutte as best he could and carry him over the ridge to safety. And perhaps if Silberhutte had known that de Marigny was close and that he had a plan in mind, then all might have gone according to that plan. He did not know, however, and the Warlord had his own ideas.

Uppermost in Silberhutte's mind was a determination to make as much trouble for his captors as he possibly could, if only to slow them down until de Marigny could catch up. As a last resort he knew he could call on his woman, Armandra, the Priestress of the Plateau, but not until no other option remained. Armandra was not immortal – a tomahawk or spear could kill her just as easily as they could any other mortal – and quite apart from purely physical dangers, Ithaqua himself was due back on Borea at any time. Thus the Texan kept his mind locked tight, telepathically blank, and prayed that Kota'na and the others would not get back to the plateau before he had somehow managed to escape. If they did, and if Armandra took the notion into her head that he was in trouble, then nothing on Borea would prevent her from coming out after him.

Just as de Marigny was about to make his move, the big Texan half-turned where he sat, drove his elbow viciously into his captor's belly, and toppled him from the wolf's back. Then, somehow, he got to his feet, balanced for a moment on the beast's shoulders, launched himself headlong at the five redskins where they levered at the travois and its burden.

A second later saw complete tumult, with Indians flying everywhere, the two wolves on top of the ridge scrabbling frantically to maintain their positions as suddenly they were obliged to take the full weight of the clock, the leader of the party yelling and screaming where he had fallen to the stony slope, and Silberhutte himself, completely off-balance, hands still tied behind him, slipping and sliding diagonally down the steep incline away from the havoc he had created.

To add to the confusion, with a snapping of thongs and a rending of hide, the clock suddenly broke free. It toppled over and stood for a moment on its head, then crashed down and outward, end over end, in a series of leaps and bounds back the way it had come. Fearing that it would dislodge his sheltering boulder which would then crush him, de Marigny immediately ascended out of the clock's path. This in turn made him visible to the frantic wolf-warriors.

They saw him – and at once the air rang with their savage cries of fury and outrage. He got the impression that they half-blamed him for their present problems.

Quickly rising higher still, de Marigny took in the scene below at a glance. The clock had finally come to rest face-up where its base had jammed against a huge boulder. Already three of the Indians were scrambling down the slope after it. Two more were picking their way toward a wide crevasse. But where was Silberhutte?

De Marigny's heart almost leaped into his mouth when he saw his friend's predicament. For the Texan was stretched out full-length on the perilous slope, face-down and motionless, his head and shoulders already hanging over the lip of the crevasse – and that crevasse yawned at least a hundred feet deep! The toes of the Texan's boots were dug into loose shale which threatened at every moment to slide him headfirst into space, and there was nothing he could do – no move he could make – without precipitating his own death.

De Marigny glanced longingly once more at the time-clock, glared at the Indians picking their way down to it, then turned his attention back to Silberhutte. The shale was beginning to slip . . .

Suddenly the Texan felt the whole unstable surface moving beneath him. He held his breath, gazed straight down into the abyss, willed himself to remain perfectly still where he had fallen, and offered up a silent prayer to those lucky stars which had ever guided and protected him. The movement beneath him subsided, but not before he had moved out another inch or two over the lip of the crevasse.

He could hear the wolf-warriors cautiously approaching him from the rear but dared not turn his head to look back. If they took him a second time, then in all likelihood he'd end up in Ithaqua's clutches anyway. The pit was greatly preferable to that . . . but the fire of life burned bright in Hank Silberhutte, and it was not a spark easily extinguished.

Now he could feel fingers fumbling at his booted feet, could hear the hoarse breathing of the heathens where they crouched fearfully behind him, precariously perched on the shale. Then – impossible, miraculous sound – he heard a cry from close at hand:

'Hang on, Hank! Just another second!'

De Marigny? *De Marigny!* . . .

Yet even as hope surged up in the Texan, in the same moment he felt the shale move again, and this time there was no stopping it. He slid forward, heard the frenzied shrieks of the redmen as they also began to slide, cursed his useless hands that were bound behind him, finally plummeted into air filled with falling shale fragments.

Only at that very last second did the Warlord close his eyes – for no man likes to see death hurtling upon him – but in the next moment he opened them again as his chin sank into fur and jarred against solid flesh beneath.

Slimly muscular legs wrapped about his waist like a vice as, almost in his ear, that same triumphant voice shouted: 'Got you, Hank!'

And de Marigny did indeed have him! The Texan's descent, barely begun, was checked as the cloak took the strain and hovered back away from the sheer face. And not a moment too soon.

Whirling, screaming bronze figures shot past in a thrashing of arms and legs. Then, slow but sure, the cloak bore the two Earthmen up, up into air dark with the pent-up fury of the storm, bitterly cold air that already seemed to carry a faint tang of ozone. A single tomahawk whirled harmlessly by as they sailed up and over the top of the ridge.

Before them lay a valley and beyond that a low mountain range. Already feeling the strain on his legs where they gripped the Texan's waist, de Marigny picked an open area in the valley and headed for it. It shouldn't take too long to fashion some sort of sling or seat for the extra passenger, then they would get on their way again.

For somehow de Marigny knew that time was now of the essence, that any attempt to retrieve the clock must for the moment be aborted, that hideous danger loomed above Borea's lowering sky, and only the plateau could offer any certain refuge. With one supporting arm about Silberhutte's neck he used his free hand to manipulate the studs that controlled the cloak's flight, urging as much speed as possible from that garment of the Elder Gods as it dropped down like a great bird into the valley . . .

5

The Coming of Ithaqua

Armandra, the Priestess of the Plateau, stood high above the white waste and stared down from the plateau with troubled eyes. She saw, tiny with distance, Ithaqua's pyramid throne and the circle of totems that ringed it. Her great green eyes surveyed Borea's bleakest region, the snow plain which not so very long ago had been a battleground in the War of the Winds, but her mind was elsewhere.

In her present mood she was not fit company, and so she had sent her handmaiden, Oontawa, away. Even Tracy, the Warlord's sister, with all her assurances that her brother would come to no harm, had not been able to comfort her; neither Tracy nor her man, James Graywing Franklin, the modern Indian come from the Motherworld with Hank Silberhutte and his party. For the Woman of the Winds was filled with premonition, and the golden medallion she wore at her throat seemed to grow more chill against her milky skin with each passing moment – which was a strange sensation for a woman to whom even the most frigid temperatures made for no slightest measure of discomfort.

The trouble was that Hank Silberhutte was away from the plateau; that and the fact that Ithaqua, Armandra's alien father, was due to return shortly to this wintry world. Aye, and knowing that the Wind-Walker must soon come, still the plateau's Warlord saw fit to keep his mind closed to her. Anger flared momentarily in Armandra's breast, and the small gusts of wind that came into this lofty aerie to play with the fringes of her fur jacket stood off, grew still, as the merest tinge of carmine flecked her great eyes.

But what use to be angry about the Warlord, this man from the Motherworld who ruled her heart as surely as she ruled the plateau? What use even to love him, when all he could think of in Ithaqua's absence was to be out and exploring the woods and lands beyond the mountains? A fine father for their child, this man, whose wilful nature was already apparent in his offspring.

Then she softened. Ah, but the boy would have Hank's strength, too, and perhaps something of his mother's powers. Not too much of the last, Armandra secretly hoped, for powers such as these must eventually bring him into conflict with his monstrous grandsire, that hellish Old One who even now walked the winds between the worlds as he returned to Borea from undreamed-of wanderings.

She stood on a natural balcony of rock high on the plateau's face. Behind her a smoothly hewn corridor ran around the inside of the plateau's rocky perimeter. In the one direction it led to the mazy, multilevel tunnels, caves, dwellings, and stairways of the plateau's honeycombed interior, in the other to her own and the Warlord's private and luxurious chambers. Armandra started out between thick bars which alone separated her from a vertiginous drop to the foot of the plateau. The bars were set wide apart, allowing the winds free entry, which was as well for they loved her and were her subjects.

Yet now, with a raised finger, she instantly hushed their humming and wailing to cock her head on one side in an attitude of listening.

Nothing . . .

Still she cautioned the winds in their play, clenching her fist tight about the medallion where she wore it, searching in its sensitive alloys for those dread vibrations which were ever precursory of Ithaqua's coming. And again . . . nothing. But in her heart Armandra knew that he must return very soon, and that before then the Warlord must be back in her arms.

And where *was* the Warlord? He had not opened his mind to her since finding the newcomer from the Motherworld staked out by the leech pool in the forest. Armandra frowned when she thought of that newcomer – of him, and of the strange vehicle which had brought him to Borea. In the Warlord's mind when he spoke to her, she had detected a hidden interest in that strange device, that 'time-clock' . . .

Armandra was no fool. She knew well enough that if one man could use such a machine to enter Borea, then that another might surely use it to leave this World of the Winds if he so desired. 'A gateway between all the worlds of space and time' – that was how her man had described de Marigny's machine: 'A vehicle of the Elder Gods.'

And again she frowned . . .

She wondered who this stranger was, this Henri-Laurent de Marigny, of whom it seemed the Warlord had knowledge in the Motherworld. And did all men of Earth have such long, strange-sounding names? Suspicion and panic rose up in Armandra like a tide. What if he had come to Borea to take Hank away in his flying machine? What if they were already gone, away from Borea and out into the ether currents that wash between the worlds?

She trembled where she stood. No – she could not believe that – it wasn't so. But then where was he? Again she sent her thoughts out across the bleak white waste, threatening thoughts which she well knew she could never action:

'*You – Warlord – father of my child. Do you not know my pain? Are you so heartless that my concern for you, which wounds me, means nothing? Explain yourself, husband, or I swear I'll send a wind to blow you off Borea forever!*'

'Eh? What's this?' the answer came back immediately, like joyous laughter in Armandra's mind. '*Do you greet me with lightnings, Armandra?*'

'I greet you with – with my entire self, great fool! Oh, Hank – where have you been? What have you been doing, and why has your mind been closed to me for so long? Yes, and where are you now – and how long before you return?'

Armandra sent a host of mental questions surging out to him, demanding to know everything. And then, before he could put his own thoughts in order, she continued with yet more questions: *'And where is the newcomer's "time-clock" now? Do the wolf-warriors have it still? I hope so, for only one person has ever had the power to walk on the wind in Borea. I am that person, and I am jealous of my power.'*

'Oh?' the Warlord's thoughts finally found their way through her telepathic barrage. *'Is that so, wife? And what of your father's kite-men? – and what of Ithaqua himself?'*

'The kites are crude,' she answered, *'and could not fly without my father's breath in their sails. As for the Wind-Walker: I was talking about people, human beings. Would you call Ithaqua a human being?'*

'No,' Silberhutte agreed, *'never that – he's totally inhuman. But in any case you're mistaken, Armandra. For you see, Henri also walks on the wind, and this flying cloak which bears him up is no clumsy kite!'* And he opened up his mind to let the Priestess of the Plateau see through his eyes where he soared along, high over the white waste, seated on a huge knot of leather at the end of hastily plaited thongs that were fastened to de Marigny's harness where he flew the cloak above him.

'Do you see, Armandra? You're not the only one who can fly. De Marigny flies, too. Yes, and so do I!' Without malice, with love, Silberhutte's thoughts laughed in Armandra's mind.

For a moment she was dumbfounded by the vision his mind had opened for her. It was not the time-clock she had seen but some other device – a flying cloak. First a flying coffin, now a flying cloak! And how many more surprises did this man from the Motherworld, this de Marigny, have in store? Armandra stood high in the plateau's wall and searched the horizon minutely for the peculiar flying shape which she knew must soon come into view, for the visitor in his flying cloak, who now bore her own man safely back to her.

'*As for your other questions,*' the Warlord continued, '*I'll try to answer them now. I went off with Henri – the two of us flying the cloak – to track down the wolf-warriors and get the time-clock back. Well, things went wrong and they caught me. Henri rescued me, saved my life. As to why I closed my mind to you: as long as there was any danger or the chance of danger I wouldn't let you see what was happening. I didn't want you leaving the plateau for my sake at a time when Ithaqua's return is imminent. And –* '

'*Ithaqua!*' she cut him off, her own thoroughly alarmed thoughts turning his aside. '*Oh, no – NO!*' And high on her rock-cut balcony she clutched at the medallion cradled in the hollow of her neck where it had begun to vibrate in sympathy with the Wind-Walker's approach.

'*What is it, Armandra?*' the Warlord anxiously questioned, half-knowing the answer even before she dared express it in thought. '*Is he – ?*'

'*Yes, Hank,*' she cried, her thoughts awash with waves of fear – fear for her man out above the white waste, flying over Ithaqua's own territory at this very moment – '*he's coming back! Oh, Hank, hurry! My father comes, striding down the winds to Borea even now!*'

Now she could actually see the fliers, a double dot in the sky over Ithaqua's temple, growing larger by the second. Silberhutte had closed his mind to her yet again – perhaps to urge more speed from the man who flew the cloak, more likely to isolate himself from Armandra's mind should her dread father appear on the scene too soon, when the Warlord's thoughts would probably be the last he would ever think – and so the Priestess of the Plateau scanned the far, misted horizon for a larger, darker shape.

Then her eyes detected a movement on the plain southwest of the plateau: the shape of a snow-ship sent out earlier to patrol the far western edge of the white waste and keep a lookout for Silberhutte's party as that band returned. Since the warriors who manned the ship would not return empty-handed, Armandra knew that Kota'na and the rest of her husband's chosen men must be aboard.

She shuddered. So now there would be two targets for Ithaqua when he came: the snow-ship and the flying cloak. Wasting no more time in useless fretting, ignoring the now insistent throbbing and humming of the medallion about her neck, Armandra closed her eyes and lifted up her bare arms until they were horizontal, pointing with her index fingers out over the white waste.

Slowly, eerily, her long red hair floated up over her head, drifting lazily, weightlessly above her. Her face became suffused with a carmine tinge that brightened steadily as it burned out from beneath closed lids. The bones of her skull began to show through her flesh like an X-ray picture, and twin carmine stars blazed where her great eyes had been. Now she herself drifted up from the rocky floor, long legged, straight-backed, regal as a materpiece of some fantastic macabre sculptor, her hair and head ablaze with an inner light.

A moment later, coming suddenly upon her from the corridor at her rear, an Eskimo watchkeeper from the roof of the plateau stopped dead in his tracks at the fearful sight of his sovereign in the act of commanding the winds. Seeing that Armandra was already aware of all that transpired, without daring to disturb her in any way, he bowed himself out backward and hurried back the way he had come.

His skin crawled with the sensation of unseen energies,

powers of air and space that concentrated now about Armandra, held as yet in check by her, ready to leap in obedience of her slightest command . . .

'Henri, we're in big trouble,' Silberhutte shouted up to the man who flew above him. De Marigny barely heard the other's words before they were snatched away by squalling winds which seemed to howl now from every corner of the sky. He held the cloak on course as steadily as he could and glanced down to see the Texan twisting this way and that where he hung suspended, scanning the sky and shaking his whipping hair out of his eyes.

'Is it Ithaqua?' de Marigny shouted back.

'Yes, and any time now. Look at the sky – there, to the east!'

De Marigny looked as bidden – and saw a fantastic, freakish thing. The sky itself seemed acrawl with sentient, *deliberate* motion.

The clouds, white and grey and a mixture of both – heavy nimbostratus and wispy cumulus alike, from all strata of Borea's atmosphere – were being drawn, sucked toward some central point. It seemed to de Marigny that he gazed upon a huge whirlpool in the sky, a cauldron of boiling clouds. More strongly yet the winds howled and rushed, threatening now to drag the cloak and its passengers, too, toward that portentous and awe-inspiring aerial phenomenon.

In a matter of seconds the sky became still darker and angry, until it was as if a deep and dreadful twilight had fallen over Borea. Now the clouds jostled and careened above, blue-black and laced with brightly flickering traceries of electrical fire; while eastward, at the centre of the tumult, there seemed to be a great, continuous explosion taking place in the upper atmosphere. The clouds boiled down and outward from that point, like an inverted ocean hurled back by the emergence of a volcano of the upper air, except that where the cone should be, only an area of clear sky now showed.

The clear patch rapidly enlarged as, suddenly, the clouds took flight. They raced away from that spot, writhing and roaring their terror with thunder voices across Borea's tortured heavens, hastening one another with lashes of lightning. And finally de Marigny and his passenger saw *why* the clouds fled in such chaotic panic . . .

For now he came, striding down from vaults of space as a giant descends an invisible stairway, falling out of the sky on great webbed feet, glaring down on the white waste through huge carmine stars that burned as the fires of hell themselves in his darkly demonic head.

Ithaqua the Wind-Walker was back on Borea!

6

Traitor Winds

'Henri, can you get us out of here?' Silberhutte's shout fought the shrieking wind, reaching up to the man who piloted the cloak.

'I can get closer to the ground,' de Marigny yelled back. 'Try to stay close to whatever cover there is. But there's no way we can make more headway. Perhaps he won't see us.'

'Not much hope of that. He doesn't miss a thing. But look over there – the snow-ship. That'll be Kota'na and the rest of my men.' The Warlord paused to let the shrieking of the wind die down a little, then continued: 'That ought to give Ithaqua a tiny problem: which target to pick off first!' Unwittingly he had echoed Armandra's own thoughts.

Now the Old One's temple stood to the rear, and as the cloak dropped toward the white waste, so snow and ice crystals came up in stinging flurries to greet it. The temperature had dropped alarmingly, and de Marigny was sure that he must already be suffering from exposure. He could barely feel his fingers where they worked at the control studs, and his beard, hair, and eyebrows were rimed with frost.

With only three or four miles to go now to the plateau, still that looming refuge of rock seemed a thousand light-years away. De Marigny's exhaustion was reaching a critical stage, and he could barely keep his eyes open in the blast of ice crystals that rushed and eddied over the surface of the white waste. Occasionally, through breaks in the flurries, he would catch a glimpse of a great wedge-shaped ship that sailed on three massive skis across the icy surface half a mile to his left, but it was becoming too much of an effort to do anything other than control the cloak as it was rocked and buffeted by gust after gust of frigid air, snow, and diamond-hard particles of ice.

Then Ithaqua's shadow fell over them as they flew, and looking up, de Marigny was spurred to greater effort as he stared into the gigantic face of that living doom called the Wind-Walker. What did the old Eskimo legends of Earth say? That to gaze into Ithaqua's eyes was to be damned forever? Well then, de Marigny knew he was damned, and moreover that the threatened doom would not be too long in coming.

Hideously anthropomorphic, the Old One stood in a sky from which all clouds were totally fled now. He stood there, impossibly still, on a half-mile-high pedestal of thin air, peering down through eyes which had narrowed to the merest carmine slits.

'*My God*,' de Marigny thought to himself. '*He's seen us!*'

But no, three-quarters obscured by snow flurries as they flew low over the surface, the Wind-Walker had not seen them . . . yet. But he had seen the snow-ship and knew it to be of the plateau. The flaring, bottomless pits which were his eyes opened up wide, and his monstrous black blot of a head rocked back in an attitude of crazed laughter. His whole body shook with silent, lunatic glee – but in the next moment he was still and cold once more.

Slowly the vastly bloated figure reached a taloned hand into the sky where clouds were already forming, materializing even as he moved. His hand reached into the new formed cloud bank, withdrew holding a huge ball of ice! Lower the Wind-Walker stepped, down an invisible staircase of frozen air, and his eyes glared more hellishly yet as his arm went back, almost leisurely, in preparation for a throw.

'Get us up, Henri,' Silberhutte yelled. 'Up, man, where he can see us!'

But de Marigny had already anticipated the other's scheme, had indeed undertaken a rapid ascent on his own initiative; and up above the flurries rode the cloak, up into the view of Ithaqua where he stood poised in midair, a gigantic statue of black ice imbued with monstrous life. And the ploy – however dangerous, however reckless – worked, at least for the time being.

With the plateau no more than a mile distant, making what speed they could against the rushing wind and howling snow devils, the snow-ship and cloak with its two passengers battled their way across the white waste beneath the gaze of the Wind-Walker. And the carmine orbs of his eyes went from ship to cloak as he paused in alien approximation of consternation.

Lower still he stepped, glowing eyes huge and flecked now with sparks of gold, down toward the plain beneath. The snow-ship he finally dismissed with one last searching glance; the cloak – ah! – that was where his real interest was centered.

Ithaqua could hardly credit his good fortune. Unless he was mistaken, the flying device that fled across the snow beneath his burning gaze bore two of his worst enemies, enemies of all the Great Old Ones. Men of Earth, one brought here in great error by himself and the other . . . now *that* was most interesting. Could it be that yet a third male human being – the most hated of all human beings – could it be that he, too, was on Borea? For how else could this earthbound worm beneath, the pilot of the flying cloak, have reached Borea other than in the time-clock of Titus Crow, nemesis of the CCD?

Well then, if Titus Crow were close at hand, there was danger – even for Ithaqua of the Snows, great danger – in the shape of the weapon that Kthanid the Elder God had built into the time-clock, whose ray was as a rapier against the flesh of the CCD. Even now Crow might be rushing to the rescue of the two who rode the cloak. Ithaqua's eyes became carmine slits once more as he thought of Crow. His hand closed into a giant's fist, crushing the ice ball he carried into blue shards that flew in all directions like an aerial bomb burst.

Then his hand opened and reached down; taloned doom that closed on the fleeting pair as an eagle falls to its prey. Utterly impotent to avoid its approach, Silberhutte and de Marigny watched the descent of that vast demon claw, that hand open and reaching to snatch them out of the icy air, to crush them into raw red pulp. And knowing that this must be the end, still the Texan thought to open his mind and send one last blast of telepathic hate in Ithaqua's direction:

'*Do your worst, Hell-Thing – for it's what I would do to you given half a chance!*'

A great black shadow blotted out the sky as Ithaqua's hand came down upon them, fingers closing. Then –

From nowhere, at the last moment, a whirling snow devil enveloped the cloak, thrust it furiously toward the plateau's now looming rock face. The Wind-Walker's hand closed on thin air, and astounded and enraged, he hurled his arms wide to the skies and screamed silent threats at his minion elementals one of which, obviously in error, had whisked his enemies from his grasp. Again he reached for the pair, more in anger than eagerness this time, but once more they were rushed from his frustrated, bloating fingers by – *by traitor winds!*

The first time might have been a mistake, however stupid a mistake, but not the second. Not twice. Not after his warning. No, this was outside interference. This was . . . Armandra!

Armandra, the Woman of the Winds, Ithaqua's wayward daughter who would not accompany him on his enforced interstellar wanderings. Armandra, the Priestess of the Plateau, who had stepped out through the wide bars of her high balcony to command the winds in defiance of her alien father. And now she too spoke to him with her mind, using that telepathic power she shared with Hank Silberhutte alone, defying Ithaqua as she had ever defied him from where she stood white and wondrous on a pedestal of air in front of the plateau, her arms flung wide to the white waste:

'See, monstrous father mine, how even the small winds turn against you! And you would have me walk beside you on the great winds that roar between the worlds? No, I will stay here on Borea and command the little winds and lightnings when you are away, for while the elementals of air and space and the storm fear you, they have only love for me. Aye, and I for them; but I loathe their master as surely as they do, as surely as I am his daughter!

And now, together with the snow-ship, the men who flew the cloak were also forgotten as Ithaqua gazed upon Armandra. She was within easy reach, facing him squarely, her own eyes as carmine in their starry intensity as were his, and she stood away from the plateau's face by at least a hundred feet. One fast grab with bloated, greedy fist . . . she would be his!

Flesh of his flesh, blood of his blood. If he could only take her – carry her away from Borea and show her the wonder of distant worlds, the great ice planets on the rims of star systems whose suns were mere dying embers – then she would know the glory and the power that were his, and perhaps she would want to share them with him. Aye, and there was her child, too, a man-child. A grandson for Ithaqua, who in his turn would walk the winds between the worlds and work for the release of Great Cthulhu.

While these thoughts and others flashed through the mind of the Great Old One, both snow-ship and cloak slipped in through the gates of one of the plateau's keeps. The ship slowed to a halt as ice anchors were thrown out; men and bears hastily disembarked and were hustled by eager helpers into the plateau's familiar maze of tunnels and caves. The men in the cloak alighted, and they, too, took shelter in the mouth of a major tunnel. From there, heart in mouth, Silberhutte gazed up at the aerial confrontation taking place above.

He gazed – cried out! – as Ithaqua's hand swept forward and his fingers began to close on Armandra . . . then cried out again, this time in exultation as the Wind-Walker drew back empty-handed, throwing up taloned hands before eyes which were suddenly fearful and flinching. Like a scalded dog the Snow-Thing stood off from the plateau, and Silberhutte felt the acid blast of telepathic loathing and fear that radiated from him.

Briefly the Warlord felt these things, momentarily, and something more. Bright in his mind's eye he saw a symbol – one which was now almost as painful to him as it was to Ithaqua and all others of the CCD – the symbol of a five-pointed star ablaze with searing flames!

'Tracy!' the Texan shouted his joy as Armandra slipped back in through the bars of her aerie to safety. 'Tracy, you're a wonder!'

For he knew that somewhere on the plateau's face, even now his sister leaned out over the white waste and held up one of the star-stones of ancient Mnar to ward off the Wind-Walker, and he knew also that for the moment Ithaqua was impotent to harm any of those he held dear.

'It was Tracy, Henri,' he cried, turning to de Marigny. 'Tracy, with one of her blessed – one of her damned – star-stones. Thanks to Tracy, and to Armandra, we've all come through it!'

De Marigny managed a weak nod of understanding, but he was too far gone to find the strength to smile. His eyes were glazed slits; he was covered with rime and frostbitten from head to toe; his legs, which he could hardly feel, would not hold him up straight, and so he leaned against the tunnel's wall. Silberhutte saw his dangerous condition at a glance, picked him up, and ran with him into the tunnel toward the light of distant flambeaux. As he ran, he called for assistance, for the plateau's best physicians . . .

. . . And well away from the plateau where the power of the star-stones could not touch him, Ithaqua silently raged and blustered and bloated up more gigantic yet as he called forth the fiendish elementals of the Great Storm, the malevolence of interstellar spirits, the wrath and fury of thunder and lightning to hurl against the plateau.

But the plateau, impervious as ever, paid not the slightest heed.

Marooned

Slowly but surely de Marigny recovered from his sustained ordeal of privation. In the Motherworld he might well have died, but here on Borea, where temperatures outside the plateau could fluctuate wildly – especially under the influence of Ithaqua or certain of his ice-priests – medicine in the fields of frostbite, exposure, hypothermia, and allied ailments was far advanced. For even in an environment where the great majority of members of the various levels of 'society' were immune to all but the extreme lower levels of temperature, still the inhabitants of the plateau were human beings. Layers of human skin will crack; frigid air will shred the delicate webs of agonized human lungs, and human blood itself will freeze without a great deal of persuasion. In the plateau, as anywhere else, Necessity had been the Mother of Invention – especially of the medicines of snow and ice . . .

So the Earthman recovered, and within twenty days Earthtime he was mobile again and already exploring the plateau's mazy interior network of caverns and tunnels on all their many levels. He found his way to the gymnasiums, arenas, and great meetinghalls; to the cavern lakes of the lower regions where the Eskimo fishermen cast their nets by the light of flaring flambeaux; to the stables, storehouses, and trading centres; eventually to the roof itself, where guardsmen kept vigilant watch over the white waste and the movements of Ithaqua's acolytes and worshippers at the totem temple.

Of Ithaqua: de Marigny was told that when the wolf-warrior party with the stolen time-clock finally arrived at the Wind-Walker's temple and dragged their prize to the foot of his ice-pyramid throne, he had shown little real or immediate interest in de Marigny's space-time vehicle. He had continued to spend the greater part of his time glowering at the distant plateau from under half-lowered lids, the, carmine of his eyes as smokily pensive as lava bubbling in the throat of a massively threatening but momentarily passive volcano.

Gradually, however, as the time grew closer to his departure, when once more he must forsake Borea to go out on his endless wanderings between the dimensional spheres, Ithaqua's interest in the time-clock increased. Often he would pause in his scowling where he crouched atop his pile of heterogeneous artifacts from the Motherworld frozen into a pyramid of steel-hard ice, pause to lift up the time-clock in a massive fist and stare at it with eyes that flared murkily.

At other times he would assume the size and proportions of a man and call his ice-priests to him to converse with them (by whichever means he used), for they understood the ways of men better than he, and obviously he hatched some plot against the men of the plateau – particularly the Warlord and the newcomer from the Motherworld. Often, too, he would take a woman of one of his tribes in icy hand and stride off with her on the wings of the wind into unknown regions to the east. Those women he took did not go willingly for they were common women and not worth sparing once Ithaqua had done with them, and always he returned alone. In Armandra's own words: 'Insatiable as Space and almost old as Time, my father is as lustful – and bestial – as ever he was!'

When de Marigny was nearly mended, he was given an audience with Armandra in her own sumptuous apartments. There she questioned him minutely in all aspects of his adventures with Titus Crow, adventures of which Hank Silberhutte had already appraised her but which she seemed to find both thrilling and enthralling when retold by de Marigny. And right from the start it was perfectly obvious to the Woman of the Winds that never before had she met a man like this one. Even in the Motherworld he had been something of an anachronism – the perfect gentleman in a world where morals and all standards of common courtesy were continually falling, even in the highest strata of society – but here on Borea his like was unknown.

For while he treated her like the queen she was and behaved as the very gentlest of gentlemen in her presence, and while she quickly warmed to him who had saved the life of her beloved Warlord, still she sensed that he would be equally gallant with any lady of quality. Nor did it require much effort on the handsome Earthman's part to convince her that his presence on Borea was purely accidental, that he had not deliberately sought out Hank Silberhutte to perform some fantastic interplanetary, hyperdimensional rescue! He was on his way to Elysia, home of the Elder Gods, and only the tides of fate had washed him up on Borea's chilly strand.

As for the esteem in which he held her, which amounted to something very much akin to awe, de Marigny hardly needed to fake it. He was after all of French descent, and she was one of the most beautiful women he had ever seen. As gorgeous in her beauty as Titus Crow's own Tiania, Armandra was a young but fully mature, indeed a regal person, and it was more her great beauty that held de Marigny's appreciative attention than the fantastic powers he knew she commanded.

Shortly after his audience with the Priestess of the Plateau, because the Warlord thought it would be good therapy for his rapidly recuperating body, de Marigny found himself given over into the none-too-gentle hands of the plateau's weapon masters. And Silberhutte had been right. For as time passed, the newcomer became so engrossed in his studies that he soon mastered all

279

the elementary techniques of the plateau's weaponry and went on to develop a flair and panache quite unique in one previously unaccustomed to such arts.

Therapeutically then, his daily sessions in the gymnasiums and arenas worked wonders for the stranded Earthman, but his main reason for giving himself up so completely to his tutors was not the perfecting of physical efficiency or the mastery of murderous weapons of war. He did it to keep his mind off the fact that he was marooned here on Borea, lost on an alien world in a strange parallel dimension. For Elysia seemed farther than ever from his grasp, and the wonders Titus Crow had so graphically described were fading in his mind's eye with each passing hour.

De Marigny's living quarters on the perimeter wall of the plateau where they overlooked the white waste through a number of small windows cut deep and square through solid rock, were spacious, sumptuous, and warm. They were heated by the same oil fires that kept the plateau's precipitous face free from the layers of ice which must otherwise soon close up all entries and exits alike and deprive the great hive of its air and water supplies. The mineral oil came from a great black lake in the bowels of the place, a lake which had fed itself immemorially from some source far below ground. Along with the fresh-water lakes that teemed with blind cavernicolous fish and the well-stocked animal pens of the lower levels, the lake of oil assured the plateau its complete independence.

All in all, then, de Marigny's lot might be considered extremely comfortable, and it would not have been an at all unpleasant or even tedious existence on Borea . . . but for the fact that he could see, through binoculars loaned him by the Warlord, the time-clock where it nestled in a glittering of white rime at the foot of Ithaqua's pyramid altar.

The time-clock – his gateway to the stars, his magic carpet between worlds – so close and yet so far away.

He had his flying cloak, of course, and had demonstrated its gravity-defying skills before a thrilled audience of chieftains and Elders – its remarkable manoeuvrability in the cold air high above the plateau – but whenever he strayed out marginally over the white waste, he would feel the tentative tug of sinister winds. Then Ithaqua would stir atop his icy pyramid and stretch himself with the indolent but watchful attitude of a deceptively lazy cat.

Armandra had warned de Marigny about that, and when on the last occasion she herself had to send friendly winds to release him from the blustery clutches of one of her father's lesser elementals of the air, then she reluctantly but firmly denied him any further use of the cloak. And so he removed that garment of so many adventures, folded it, and laid it safely away in his rooms.

From that time forward, seeing the way de Marigny gradually retired within himself, the plateau's Warlord despaired for his newfound friend and cursed his own inability to assist him; and while previously he had only tentatively broached to Armandra the subject of the possibility of the eventual rescue or recovery of the time-clock, now Silberhutte gave her little respite but determinedly brought the matter up at every opportunity until she was heartily sick of it. Such was his apparent obsession that while Armandra now trusted de Marigny completely, she found herself doubting the Warlord's own motives.

Could it be that her man's ever-increasing concern for de Marigny and his Elysian quest was nothing more than a front hiding a desire to desert her and leave Borea forever? There seemed to be only one sure way to discover the truth of the matter: to assist in the clock's recovery and see what next happened. And if the Warlord did indeed desert her? Well then, if that were what he wanted, he would be free to go, but Armandra was unwilling to dwell too long upon the possibility of that ever happening.

Was he not the father of her child – and did she not know his very mind, his every thought? Ruefully she had to admit that recently she did not know his mind, for more than ever before he kept his thoughts closed to her. This could well be for her own good; he might not want her sharing his worries; but on the other hand was it not at least feasible that he secretly harboured a desire to be rid of her and Borea forever?

And always the problem returned to the same stumbling block – the question of the Warlord's loyalty, his love for her – so that in the end Armandra resigned herself to the one possible course of action. If the time should ever arrive when she could assist de Marigny in the recovery of his time-clock, then she would do so, and in so doing, she would give the man she called husband, Hank Silberhutte, every opportunity to leave her.

Having made her decision and considered its possible conclusions, she then turned her thoughts to certain inner nightmares – to dwell upon the vast spaces between the stars and the even greater voids between dimensions – and having done so, she shuddered. Long and long had her father tried to tempt her away to walk with him on the winds that continually blow between the worlds . . . and wasn't she his daughter? If Hank Silberhutte had not come to Borea when he did, then by now she might –

But thoughts of Silberhutte, her man from the Mother-world, and of their man-child, stilled her fears at once. No, it could never happen, she was sure of the Warlord's love; so sure that at the first opportunity she would put him to the ultimate test. Then she would see what she would see, for only then could her faith in him – her great love for him – earn its reward . . .

8
Rough Justice

De Marigny was asleep and dreaming wonderful dreams of Elysia, of Earth's dreamworld, and of all the strange and marvellous planets out on the very rim of existence, so that he all but cried out in anger when Hank Silberhutte shook him unceremoniously awake.

'Henri, wake up, there's something you should see. This may be our chance to get the clock back!'

Hearing the Warlord's words, the dull edge of sleep was driven instantly from de Marigny's mind. He got up and quickly followed Silberhutte to one of the square windows overlooking the white waste. Even without binoculars he could see a lot of unaccustomed activity about the Snow-Thing's distant altar. Ithaqua's peoples were there in their thousands, forming a dark oval blot on the white of the frozen earth.

Taking up his glasses and focusing them on the distant scene, de Marigny asked: 'Why has he mustered them? Is there to be an attack on the plateau?'

The Warlord shook his head. 'No, not that. He lost three-quarters of his army the last time he tried it – yes, and he learned a terrible lesson in the bargain. They've gathered to witness his departure, to be instructed in the arts of their master – and to be reminded of the penalties for any sort of treason or action in defiance of his laws. When last the Wind-Walker was away raping and murdering some poor girl of the tribes, three of his wolf-warriors – probably relatives of the girl – tried to defect to the plateau. It's not the first time; we've gained several useful citizens that way even in the time I've been here. On this occasion, however, they . . .'

He paused and shrugged. 'This time they were caught and taken back alive. Before he goes, Ithaqua will deal with them.'

'He'll kill them?' de Marigny asked.

The Warlord nodded. 'It won't be pleasant to watch, and that's not why I awakened you. My reason for doing so is simple: once Ithaqua leaves Borea, we may be able to recover the time-clock. And the sooner we get moving the better. Armandra says she'll help us – in fact she seems to have turned completely about-face on the thing. She wouldn't even talk of it at one time – now she says she'll do all she can to help you get the clock back.'

'But that's marv – ' de Marigny began, but the Warlord cut him off with:

'Look there. What's happening now?'

Again training his binoculars on the totem temple, de Marigny answered, 'The ice-priests are bringing forward three captives through the ranks outside the circle of totems. The three are struggling like madmen, but their hands are bound. The rest of the crowd seems cowed, unmoving, heads bowed. Those inside the circle are prostrated. None but the priests move, and they leap and twirl like dervishes. The first of the three captives is pushed forward right to the foot of the ice pyramid.'

'Henri, you don't have to watch,' Silberhutte warned.

'I know quite a lot about Ithaqua already, Hank. If I'm to know him fully, then I may as well see him at his worst. Whatever is to happen will happen regardless of my witnessing it.'

Watching the distant scene, de Marigny grew still as Ithaqua reached down to lift up the first of his victims. The man, an Indian by his looks and dress, had stopped struggling and now held himself stiffly erect as Ithaqua's massive fist drew him effortlessly into the air. Without preamble the Wind-Walker held the man up above his monstrous head, turning his glowing eyes upward to stare at him for a moment. Then those eyes blazed wide open and their fires flickered with an almost visible heat. The taloned hand opened suddenly and the Indian fell, a doll spinning briefly in the air before plummeting with a splash of carmine sparks *into* one of Ithaqua's eyes!

Slowly the grotesque figure atop the ice throne resumed his original position, then reached down again to take up the second wolf-warrior. Not so brave this man. He kicked with his legs and struggled violently. Ithaqua held him on high, made as if to drop him – then caught him – casually used thumb and forefinger of his free hand to pluck off one of the man's kicking, offending legs!

Sickened, de Marigny looked away, then held to his resolve and found the scene once more. Ithaqua was now in the act of tossing a limbless, headless torso into the crowd within the circle of totems. And it was now the turn of the third and final offender.

Grabbed up in massive fist, the man seemed to have fainted; his body hung slack from the Wind-Walker's fingers. Almost uninterestedly, Ithaqua threw him aloft in a high arc. De Marigny expected to see the body plummet to earth – but no, not yet. Ithaqua's fiendish elementals of the air had him, boosting him higher still, spinning him like a top until his limbs formed a cross, then buffeting him at dizzy speeds, north, south, east, and west above the white waste. Finally he zoomed skyward, a marionette jerked up on invisible wires, to be *thrown* down at high velocity into the scattering crowd.

And indeed the crowd was scattering, for who could trust in the Wind-Walker's mood at a time like this? He had been amusing himself but now . . . now the game was over.

Or was it?

He cast about, turning his huge head from side to side, and at last his eyes came to rest on the time-clock where it lay at the foot of the pyramid. De Marigny gasped as the clock was snatched up – gasped again as Ithaqua threw back his black blot of a head and rocked with the convulsions of crazed laughter. Dumb, no audible sound escaped the monster, but in the next moment he turned his face to look square upon the plateau – square, de Marigny thought, at the window where he and Silberhutte stood – and hell itself flared in the carmine fires of his eyes.

Then, time-clock firmly clenched in hand, he leaped aloft to stride up terraces of air, grew large as, still rising, he raced for the plateau, his shadow an acre of darkness on the white waste. Almost directly overhead he came to an impossible halt, stared down for a moment, and held up the clock like a toy – no, like a *trophy!* – in his great hand, his whole body shaking with massive glee. Then he was gone, out of sight over the roof of the plateau and up into higher reaches of the chill atmosphere . . .

. . . Gone from sight, yes, and gone with him the time-clock, de Marigny's one hope of ever escaping from Borea and passing on into Elysia. For the first time the man from the Motherworld was truly stranded, and there seemed to be absolutely nothing he could do about it.

Less than four hours later Hank Silberhutte found de Marigny on the plateau's roof. Approaching him, the Warlord felt satisfaction at his friend's robust if somewhat dejected appearance. Silently he appraised and approved limbs and muscles that had benefited greatly from long hours spent in the gymnasiums and arenas. Nor was de Marigny too heavily wrapped as he leaned across the battlements and stared morosely out over the white waste. He had started to grow accustomed to the bitter temperatures discovered whenever he left his apartment on the plateau's warm perimeter.

'Henri, you look miserable.'

Turning, de Marigny nodded a welcome and his agreement. 'Yes, and I feel it.' His tone was wry. 'Should I be happy?'

'I think you'll be happy enough shortly.'

There was a look about the Warlord that the other could not quite fathom, as if he harboured some pleasurable secret. Suddenly hope stirred in de Marigny and he asked: 'Hank, what is it? What's happened?'

The other shrugged. 'Oh, nothing much – except we still have a chance . . .'

'A chance – for what? How do you mean, "a chance"?'

'Ithaqua's gone, that much you know – but he didn't take the clock with him after all!'

De Marigny grasped the Warlord's arms. 'You mean it's still here, on Borea?'

Silberhutte shook his head. 'Not on Borea, no, but on one of Borea's moons. He visited both moons before he went off on his wanderings – and when he left them, the clock stayed behind. Look – '

He pointed to the distant horizon, where two vast moons showed their dimly glowing rims, permanently suspended beyond the hills as if painted there by some cosmic artist. 'That's where your time-clock is, Henri, in the moons of Borea. Which one – Numinos or Dromos – I don't know. One or the other, only time will tell.'

De Marigny shook his head, frowning, failing to understand. 'But if the clock is on one of Borea's moons, we're separated from it by at least twenty thousand miles of interplanetary space! A chance, you said, but what sort of chance is that? And how can you be sure that the clock is there in the first place?'

The Warlord held up a hand and said: 'Calm down, my friend, and I'll explain.

'First off, Armandra kept track of her father telepathically when he left. She knows that when he finished his business on the moons, he no longer had the clock with him. Indeed she believes that he deliberately let her see that he'd left the clock behind. Possibly he thinks he might trap her into leaving Borea – but I won't let that happen.'

'Do you mean to say that Armandra could walk between the worlds like Ithaqua?'

'If she wanted to, yes. That's always been her father's chief desire: to have her walking with him on the winds that blow between the worlds. If ever he managed to trap her out there' – with a toss of his head he indicated the alien star-spaces above and beyond – 'he'd never let her go again, would kill her first.'

'Then how,' de Marigny patiently pressed, 'are we ever to get the clock back? I don't see what – '

'Henri,' the other cut him off, 'what would you say if I offered you the chance to take part in the greatest adventure of a lifetime? Yes, and a chance to get your clock back in the bargain? Dangers there'll be, certainly, and your life itself may well be at risk throughout. But what an adventure – to fly out to the moons of Borea!'

'Fly to the moons of – ' de Marigny's jaw dropped. 'Hank, are you feeling well? How in the name of all that's weird could I possibly fly out to the moons of Borea? Through space? An airless void? I don't see – '

'This is Borea, Henri,' Silberhutte reminded, again cutting him off. 'It's not the Motherworld, not Earth. Things are often as different here as they are in Earth's dream-world – or so I gather from what you've told me. We're in an alien dimension, man, and things are possible which would be totally unthinkable on Earth. You want to know how you get to the moons of Borea? As I said, you fly there – in your cloak!'

'My flying cloak? But – '

'No buts, Henri. This is how it will happen:

'Armandra will call up the biggest tornado you could possibly imagine – a fantastic twister, a great funnel of whirling wind twenty thousand miles long – and we'll fly down its eye like a bullet down the barrel of a rifle!'

'A tornado?' de Marigny's imagination spun as dizzily as the wonder Silberhutte described. 'Fly down the eye of a vast tornado? And did you say "we"?'

'We – yes – of course! Did you really think I'd let you go adventuring in the moons of Borea on your own?' And the Warlord laughed and slapped his thigh. 'Now come on, we've one or two things to attend to.'

1

In the Eye of the Twister

Apart from the two heavily wrapped figures standing dead centre of the flat, frozen roof of the plateau, that elevated expanse was empty. No watchmen stood behind the low parapet walls; no sightseers gazed out over the white waste; nothing stirred but flurries of snow and rime blown about by stray gusts of wind. All well-wishers had departed minutes earlier – Tracy Silberhutte and Jimmy Franklin, Charlie Tacomah the Elder, Oontawa the handmaiden, and her man Kota'na, Keeper of the Bears, these and many others – all retired now and gone down into the safety of the plateau where the Great Wind would not touch them.

The fires that warmed the perimeter walls had been extinguished hours ago; all openings in the plateau's face were now glazed over with thick sheets of ice formed by pouring water over them, necessary in view of the tremendous suction Armandra's tornado would create; all inhabitants and denizens were safely within their caves, quarters, and stables, and the snow-ships were anchored and tied down deep in the recesses of their keeps. The two men on the roof, attached each to the other by a new double harness hurriedly manufactured by the plateau's saddlers, waited for Armandra.

She, too, had said her farewells, coming to the roof to hug de Marigny fiercely and kiss her Warlord tenderly, then departing to meditate for a few minutes alone in her apartments. Now they both waited for her and watched the rim of the plateau to the south. She would appear there, floating free on the wind as she drifted up into sight. Then she would stand off from the face of the plateau, rising high into the sky before calling up the mighty whirlwind which would thrust the two adventurers across the vast gulf of space to the moons of Borea.

And now she came – Armandra, the Woman of the Winds – dressed all in white but aglow with a carmine flush that radiated outward from her perfect form as a visible aura. Her hair swayed lazily above her head, floating to and fro in eerie undulations as she rose up in awesome grandeur. Her arms were held loosely at her sides and her loose fur robes floated about her almost as if she were suspended in some slow liquid. Then, still facing them, she receded, moved out over the white waste, lifted up her arms shoulder high, and commenced a series of summoning motions with her long white hands. At this distance her body formed a small cross of carmine fire in the suddenly darkening sky – a cross that commanded incredible powers.

Mastery of all the elementals of the air – of the winds themselves – and in her father's absence, not even the most wayward wind might defy her!

Starting far out beyond Ithaqua's totem temple and hidden from the view of the adventurers on the roof by the horizon of the plateau's rim, the surface snow and rime began to stir in agitated flurries. Rapidly, forming a circle fifteen miles across that encompassed the plateau centrally, small white spirals marched on the plateau, closing their ranks and towering higher as the circle narrowed. The line, high now as Ithaqua's ice pyramid, swept across the area of the totem temple. Several totems were uprooted like matchsticks and tossed aside, and the snow wall marched on unhindered.

Finally the sky itself began to revolve, a sea of darkly churning thunderheads all moving together, turning like a great wheel on spokes of boiling cloud. As the speed of this fantastic aerial phenomenon picked up, the two adventurers gazed dizzily skyward, reeling together while the plateau's roof seemed physically to turn beneath their furbooted feet. Now, too, they could hear the *rush* of air, the howling of the white wall as it thundered toward them; and at last its crest could be seen towering higher than the rim of the plateau.

Until now the wall had been formed of many individual snow devils, tornadoes in the making, but now these small twisters had begun to move to match the motion of the sky, had lost their individuality as they formed a single massive funnel that reached higher by the second, twisting into a whirling, swaying corkscrew shape that began to shut out the light as surely as any wall of bricks and mortar.

There came a roaring as of a tidal wave breaking on a headland . . . and instantly the massive funnel reared taller, reaching up to shut out all but a dim grey light. The tornado had climbed the walls of the plateau, was now narrowing down its diameter on the roof itself with the plateau as a base. To the many watchers who braved the winds that still roared about Ithaqua's totem temple, it seemed almost that the giant twister was an extension of the plateau, the stem of some incredible white-boled tree that swayed and writhed and went up forever; for indeed its top could no longer be seen but transcended the limits of human vision as it snaked out into the void, bending toward Borea's moons.

And within a great circle that had the plateau for its centre, covering an area of almost a thousand square miles, the winds still fought and tore, shrieking as they rushed in to support the incredible column, to push it higher still, driving its corkscrew tip across the otherwise empty void. Now the adventurers felt the first tug of trembling air in the all but still centre of the uproar – now their persons were explored by gently curious tendrils of air, caressed by scarcely definable fingers – now the flying cloak belled out about de Marigny's shoulders and he felt an upward tugging that bade fair to lift him with or without the cloak's assistance.

'Armandra's personal familiars,' Silberhutte shouted above the howl of frenzied air. 'Fair winds to protect us across the void, Henri. Now we can go. Give us maximum lift, or whatever it is you do, and let's get on our way.'

'When I tell Titus Crow about this,' de Marigny began as he urged the cloak gently skyward until the Warlord swung beneath him in the dual harness, 'if ever I get to tell him, that is, he'll never . . . *My God!*' De Marigny's exclamation burst from him when, as if suddenly released like a stone from a catapult – or, as Silberhutte had put it, 'a bullet down the barrel of a rifle' – the cloak and its passengers were shot aloft.

Up they went, ever faster, while the inner surface of the whirling white wall closed on them until it was only fifty feet or so away on all sides. And yet they felt no pressure, no friction or whipping of outraged air, for Armandra's familiar winds held them fast in a protective bubble that travelled with them. They *saw* flashing past them the dizzy wall like the flue of some cosmic chimney, and they *heard* the deafening bellow of banshee winds, but all they felt was the awesome, crushing acceleration as they plummeted ever faster up the eye of the tornado.

'He'll . . . never . . . believe me!' de Marigny finally finished with a whisper that went unheard in the mad tumult. Teeth gritted, flesh straining as the acceleration built up, the two clung desperately to their harnesses while the tube of insanely spiralling air became merely a blur, no longer white but a dark shade of grey rapidly turning black.

For Borea was far behind now and even the softly luminous auroral shades of this alien dimension's interplanetary void were shut out, excluded by the nearly solid, twisting, thrusting funnel of frozen air. Then the acceleration was over, and they fell free, weightless, while around them, silent now but working as furiously as ever, Armandra's tornado – that great-grandfather of all tornadoes – blew them toward unknown, unguessed adventures.

After a little while de Marigny's natural apprehension began to abate. The limited atmosphere was bitterly cold but bearable, by no means the icy, killing, frigid hell he would normally have expected of interplanetary space; and while doubtless the surrounding wall of the twister whirled and writhed as before, it could neither be seen nor heard from within, so that all seemed tranquil with no sensation of speed apparent. Nevertheless the travellers knew that they were speeding across space, protected only by Armandra's familiars whose substance formed about them a soft, hurtling bubble of air.

It never occurred to them that they might converse until de Marigny sneezed, but as the staccato echoes of that involuntary ejaculation died away, they recognized at once that conversation was indeed possible, moreover that it would help in further dissipating their tension and not unnatural nervousness.

'Would you like to know about Numinos, Henri?' Silberhutte's voice echoed and reverberated loudly within their protective bubble of air. 'It suddenly occurs to me that you know nothing at all about where we're going.'

'Any and everything you can tell me,' de Marigny answered. 'Forewarned, as they say back home, is fore-armed.'

'Yes,' the Warlord agreed, 'and armour is something we're pretty short of. An axe apiece, a flying cloak, and – ' He paused.

'And?'

'These winds of Armandra's. Her personal familiars that have looked after her since the day she was born a daughter of that alien, black-hearted monster and a human mother. It worries me now that she's without them. Yet if they were to leave us . . . we'd be dead sooner than it takes to tell! They're ours to command now, until we find the clock, or – '

De Marigny sensed the Warlord's shrug of resignation in the dark, picturing the other floating weightlessly close by in his harness. Then the strangeness of his situation hit him, and he wondered to himself:

'What on Earth – or off it – am I doing here? Sustained by a bubble of sentient air; speeding along on a mad voyage between alien worlds; questing after a stolen space-time machine so that I can go off adventuring again in search of Elysia? Is there any such place as Elysia, I wonder, or am I simply another patient in a madhouse somewhere? A hopeless case that the doctors despair of, keeping him quietly sedated in his own lunatic world of opium dreams . . .'

'Numinos,' Silberhutte finally continued, 'though the closest of the moons of Borea, is also a world in its own right – a world like many others, with an atmosphere, oceans, and people. On one of the largest islands dwells the principal race, sailors with a warrior instinct, worshippers of Ithaqua. From what Armandra has told me of them, it's perfectly natural that they should worship the Wind-Walker; their ancestors most certainly deified Odin and Thor in the Motherworld. Yes, they are Norsemen or as nearly Vikings as makes no difference. They control and inhabit all of the Numinosian islands except one: the Isle of Mountains.

'In the Isle of Mountains dwells a peace-loving race, not Ithaqua's people, protected in some way from the periodic attacks of the seafaring barbarians. There aren't many of these peaceful folk – a few families, a handful – but Ithaqua's interest in them has always been intense, and never more than right now. I don't know why . . .'

As the Warlord paused, de Marigny inquired: 'But how does Armandra know all of these things? Has she herself visited the moons of Borea?'

In the absolute darkness Silberhutte answered, 'No, but when she was a child – through all the years when the Elders were grooming her for her role as the plateau's first citizen – often Ithaqua would try to tempt her away from her tutors. He'd send her telepathic pictures of the secret places he knew, the distant, strange worlds where he is worshipped, feared, hated. Then, as now, he desired a companion to walk with him on the winds that blow between the worlds. Remember, Henri, that his is a loneliness lasting for aeons.

'At any rate sometimes these mental invasions of Ithaqua's upon his daughter's privacy were vivid and detailed. Particularly on those occasions when he told her of the relatively close dominions of Numinos and Dromos, worlds he was wont to visit whenever he returned to Borea from his immemorial wanderings.

'But however persuasive the monster's promises, however seductive his telepathic enticements, the Elders had brought the child up to loathe him, showing her his cruelties at every opportunity. And gradually, as she grew through her teens into womanhood, her father's tempting slackened off. After all, it must have been a great strain on him – even on the Wind-Walker – to carry on this prolonged attempt at Armandra's mental seduction, the ultimate goal of which was to be her defection from the plateau and its peoples. For you see, the plateau with its subterranean store of star-stones has always been anathema to him, and to force his mind in upon hers through barriers such as those laid down by the Elder Gods must have been psychic agony. And all to no avail, for she spurned him totally.

'His final disappointment must have been when she and I joined forces, when we took each other as man and wife; for it was then that she fought him with his own powers, inherited from him, and would have destroyed him with them if she could. Oh, yes, he must have realized then that she was a lost cause, that he could never hope to win her to him. I think that if ever he is given the chance, he will kill her. Certainly he would kill me – and, judging from what you've told me, he'd kill you, too, without hesitation.'

As Silberhutte talked, his companion noticed what appeared to be a gradual lightening effect; the utter blackness became shot with dark grey streaks, and the whole began to take on an opaquely milky appearance.

'Hank,' de Marigny called out. 'I think something is happening – or do I only imagine it?'

After a slight pause the Warlord answered: 'No, it's real enough, Henri. It could mean that we've reached the end of our – ' Abruptly, breathlessly, he again paused, then cried, '*Look!*'

At Silberhutte's excited exclamation the surrounding milkiness rapidly took on rushing motion. One second all seemed calm and silent, the next brought a resumption of the tornado's chaotic whirling; and as a dim light illuminated the two voyagers, they saw that the wall of the twister had finally extended itself to its limit, that it now whirled about them within arms' reach!

In another moment gravity returned, and with it the knowledge that they were now falling headlong *down* the narrow tube that was the whirlwind's centre. Sound, too, rushed in upon them from outside: a furious high-pitched whining that had them clapping hands to ears and gritting their teeth as the pitch rose higher with each passing second.

Then –

– The whirling wall was gone, disintegrating as at the touch of some magical wand, flying apart when Armandra, a world away on Borea, released her control over it. The mighty whirlwind was finished, done, its debris filling the higher atmosphere of Numinos as fine snow. And down through that rapidly dispersing cloud of ice particles, their ears still ringing with the sounds of the great twister's death cries, down from a height of something less than two miles plummeted the men who had ridden a tornado from one world to another.

Head over heels in a knot of leather, fur, and chill flesh they fell, the cloak wrapped about them like some tangled parachute. And yet even as their fall began, it was partially arrested; they found themselves buoyed up and stabilized by Armandra's familiar winds, those same semisentient elementals of the air whose life-support bubble had protected them across twenty thousand miles of interplanetary space.

Now, falling feet first and at a vastly reduced velocity, the two men quickly disentangled themselves, and de Marigny cautiously took control of the flying cloak. As that garment of the Elder Gods took their weight, they felt a momentary tightening of their harnesses, followed by the sensation of sustained, controlled flight.

The cloak belled out above and behind them like the membrane wings of some great bat, and down they swept toward the surface of Numinos far below . . .

2
The Vikings

The descent of the cloak and its passengers to the surface of Numinos was in itself a voyage of discovery. De Marigny soon noted that the cloak was flying with an efficiency never before experienced under the burden of a dual load. He attributed this fact to the low Numinosian gravity, which was about three-quarters that of Borea. He was also struck by the beauty of this strange moon whose far face, like that of Luna, had never been seen from the parent world and should therefore be cold, dark, and foreboding. Indeed away on the horizon great blue cliffs of ice reared like a mountain chain that stretched as far as the eye could see, and in the ocean vast icebergs drifted down from the frozen regions.

As for the Warlord: he was delighted to observe that Borea and her moons did after all have a sun of sorts, one perhaps not too greatly at odds with Earth's own. Away beyond the World of the Winds, which hung huge, grey-green, and ominously clouded in the sky, the pink and yellow orb of the luminary Silberhutte had always suspected showed more than half its disk, shooting out bursts of golden auroral streamers that flowed into the void, slowed, and were rapidly drawn back into the furnace heart.

'A sun!' Silberhutte cried once more. 'Which means that Borea's far side is probably a paradise. Armandra never knew of the sun's existence, has never physically seen it, and her father seems to have taken good care never to let her see it through his mind. I'm willing to bet that Ithaqua is confined to Borea's frozen regions just as surely as he is to the Arctic Circle and its boundaries on Earth. If I'm right . . . do you know what it means? One day the monster may return from his wanderings to find the plateau deserted and its tribes flown the coop to tropical lands beyond his reach.'

'Look down there,' de Marigny called out by way of an answer. 'Many of those islands appear to be volcanic. Is that or is it not a huge hot-water geyser?'

They were passing directly over a cluster of small islands as they headed for a greater land mass some miles distant. Close to one island a great spout of water belched up intermittently, emitting clouds of steam and boiling yellow gasses. High as they were above this phenomenon, nevertheless they smelled sulphur in the otherwise pure Numinosian air.

'Volcanic, yes,' Silberhutte agreed. 'I've seen and smelled much the same in the Motherworld – that is to say, on Earth. Look over there, on the horizon to our right. If that isn't a full-blown volcano, I've never seen one . . .'

But now something else spouted in the calm, gold-glittering sea half a mile below – many somethings – and in unison the two men cried: 'Whales!'

'Will you look at them, Hank!' de Marigny yelled. 'They're Great Blues, surely?'

'I'm no expert, Henri, but whatever species they are, I count a school of about fifty. The sea must be rich in food to support them.'

'But how did they get here, on Numinos, an alien moon in a strange parallel dimension?'

'The Wind-Walker could have brought the first pair of young ones – say, oh, maybe twenty thousand years ago.'

'But why?' de Marigny asked incredulously. 'Why should he do that, for goodness' sake?'

'Why not? If you're going to people planets, surely you have to provide food for your people, don't you? There has to be some sort of ecology. On the other hand, these whales might simply have evolved here – they might have been here since the dawn of time. Perhaps this is the source from which Earth's great schools sprang. As far as we know, the Eskimos were Ithaqua's first human worshippers – and they've been killing whales for food since time immemorial.'

'But the thought is fantastic!' de Marigny answered. 'I mean, Ithaqua is evil, as blackhearted and alien a member of the CCD as ever was. And yet here we see him almost as – '

'As a god, my friend? Well, he *is* a god, isn't he, compared with the primitives who worship him? Certainly his powers – regardless of how he chooses to use them – are godlike. And for all we know, he could well be the Earthly prototype of Odin or Thor.'

'But to bring whales – '

'Why not?' the Warlord repeated, cutting in once more. 'Don't be fooled for one minute that he couldn't do it. Down on the white waste, not far from the plateau, there's an old icebreaker – a great ship of iron – and it could only have arrived on Borea one way. For that matter, didn't Ithaqua snatch my crew and me, not to mention our airplane, right off the face of the Earth and bring us here? Don't underestimate the Wind-Walker, Henri.'

'Little chance of that, Hank. I've had enough experience of the CCD, Ithaqua included, to know well enough what they're capable of. It's just that I'm beginning to see him in a fresh light. So you reckon that he was the old Viking god of the storm, eh?'

'Not for a certainty, but he could have been.'

'And Valhalla?'

The Warlord looked up at his friend with a questioning frown as they sped in vertical tandem across the Numinosian sea toward land. Finally he answered: 'It's purely a matter for conjecture, of course, but there are certain phonetic similarities . . .'

'Yes, I can see that,' de Marigny answered. 'Using a bit of imagination, one could make "r'lyeh" sound much like Valhalla.'

'I was thinking more on the lines of Hali,' the Warlord contradicted. 'After all, Ithaqua is an elemental of air and space, not water. Perhaps the Vale of Hali? Val-Halla . . . ? Of course if I had someone even moderately versed in Old Norse matters here right now to talk to, he'd probably shoot me down in flames on the instant. But even an expert could only repeat what he has learned – what he himself believes – however erroneously. The real facts behind all myths and legends must forever lie in the unfathomable past. If your friend Titus Crow were – '

'Hank, look!' de Marigny's cry cut the Warlord off. 'How's that for a Viking settlement?'

Half a mile away and looming larger by the second, perched in the flanking crags of an ocean inlet much like a fjord, a hamlet of cabins – many of them looking curiously like the dwellings of Scottish Highland crofters – stood as testimony to the habitation of the large landmass by human beings. Smoke, drifting up from a dozen or more family fires, made the air above the settlement blue with its lazily drifting haze.

Well-worn paths ran from the comparatively rude dwellings down to the sea, while on the beach three wooden slipways showed yellow against the darker shades of coarse sand and shingle. For a background to the whole, the cliffs and hills beyond were fringed with the tall pines of Norway.

To the rear of the beach, within the confines of a tall log fence, stood a large communal or festival hall. A pair of dragonships of classical shape and size lay beached, one to each side of the log enclosure. A third longship, its dragon's head lolling above the gentle swell, stood anchored just within the fjord's mouth. Several figures, antlike at that distance, moved on the beach and along the cliff paths.

Slowing the speed of the cloak as they approached the settlement, de Marigny asked the Warlord: 'What now, Hank? Do we simply fly in and see what develops?'

'I think,' the other answered, 'that things are already developing. Listen . . .'

Drifting out to them over the sea came the deeply raucous bellow of a conch blown in warning, and immediately all of the now plainly visible human figures of the settlement turned to stare and point oceanward at the bat-shape that came down out of the sky toward the beach. Moments later, running down from their huts and houses – appearing from their places of work beneath the beached dragonships and out from behind the communal-hall's stockade, from wherever they happened to be at the time – the great majority of the settlement's people appeared, all hurrying to witness at firsthand the arrival of this strange, aerial visitor.

In between the rocky points of the fjord de Marigny flew the cloak, bringing it to a hovering halt over the sea some seventy-five yards from the beach. 'I see a large number of weapons there, Hank,' he cautioned. 'Axes and swords.'

'I see them, and a spear or two. Still, from what little I know of the Vikings, they wouldn't go to bed without taking their favourite blades along! And in any case there's no question of a fight. We're outnumbered at least twenty to one – and we're here for information, not blood. But look – what's happening now?'

On the beach the four or five dozen Vikings, including a scattered handful of women and children, were congregated about a massive slab-sided boulder that guarded the gate to the communal hall. Standing atop this great rock, a wild, long-haired, ragged female figure harangued the crowd. They cowered back, cringing in the face of her vehemence, then turned their backs on her to kneel grudgingly on the sand facing the sea and the men who rode the cloak.

'What the hell – ?' the Warlord queried. 'Vikings – on their knees before us?'

'The old woman's a "witch-wife,"' de Marigny informed. 'The Viking equivalent of both oracle and witchdoctor combined. A seer, a rune caster, supposedly endowed with all of the peculiar powers such terms dictate.'

'Very well,' said Silberhutte, 'then since she seems to be for us, I say we give it a whirl and take a run ashore.'

The beldam continued to rant at the assembled community as de Marigny flew the cloak in to the beach. There he hovered effortlessly while Silberhutte freed himself and fastened the loose ends of his harness straps at the back of his neck. Then, setting down beside the big Texan, the cloak's master allowed his marvellous garment to fall loosely about his fur-clad form. Now they stood shoulder to shoulder, the two of them, arms crossed on their chests.

Still the hag railed on, but her tone was lower now, full of awe. The eyes of the whole community fed unblinkingly, not a little suspiciously, on the men from the sky.

'That tongue she's using,' Silberhutte casually drawled. 'The more I hear, the better I understand it. There's some Norse in it, a lot of Old English, too, but mainly it's . . .' He frowned in concentration, trying to fathom the strangely familiar dialect.

'Gaelic,' de Marigny finally recognized the language. 'And those swords on the sand there. Viking craftmanship, yes, but they're designed more like claymores than anything else!'

'Yes, I'd noticed that too,' the Warlord answered. 'But right now I'm more interested in the old woman. Listen to her – she's giving them hell!'

Even as he spoke, the crone uttered one final harsh word of command that rose in pitch to a breathless shriek. Then she threw her head back and her arms wide, beginning to stumble dangerously about the uneven upper surface of the rock. At that, almost without exception, the assembled Vikings cast their eyes down and bowed their heads. The two closest to the great boulder, however, leaped to their feet and rushed to help the witch-wife.

Her eyes had turned up, and she was falling forward, a bundle of rags that would have smashed down on the shingle if the two had not caught her and placed her on her feet. Now, recovering herself, she pushed them away and staggered through the prostrated ranks of Vikings to stand before the strangers. Her aides – blood relatives, sons by their looks – followed behind her at a respectful distance. Through black, bloodshot eyes she peered first at de Marigny, then at Silberhutte, all the while nodding her head of long, matted yellow hair. When finally she spoke, not all of her words were immediately intelligible to the pair, but their overall meaning was clear.

'So you have come, as I said you would: two strangers flying in from the sea on the wings of a bat. Two whose fates are totally entwined with those of the clan of Thonjolf the Red, for good or evil I know not. Two of you, blown on the winds, emissaries of Ithaqua!'

'Aye, we have come,' the Warlord took the initiative, 'and it is good that you greet us thus.'

'You speak the tongue strangely,' the crone answered, 'but you do speak it. This, too, I foresaw.'

'And who are you, witch-wife?' de Marigny inquired.

'I am Annahilde, mother of Erik and Rory.' She placed scrawny hands on the arms of the pair now come up close behind her. 'Annahilde, widow of Hamish the Strong.'

She turned to Silberhutte. 'You are much like Hamish in his younger days. Six years gone, he too was . . . was called by Ithaqua.' For a moment her visage grew yet more bleak and her eyes filled with horror. Then she shook back her wild yellow hair and peered about her, like someone waking from a nightmare.

The prostrated Vikings were beginning to stir, their patience with Annahilde's demands almost at an end. Not all of them held their eyes averted; two or three were openly, ominously grumbling together. The newcomers had noticed this, and Silberhutte, continuing his role as spokesman, decided to relieve the situation.

'If these are Thonjolf's people,' he said, 'where is the chief, Thonjolf himself? We would speak to him. Also, get these people up on their feet. Emissaries of Ithaqua we are, but before that we were ordinary, humble men.'

'Ah, no!' she shook her head in denial and grinned, showing a mouthful of badly stained but surprisingly even teeth. 'Ordinary men you never were, nor will you ever be humble. As for these – ' She flapped a scarecrow arm to indicate the prostrated ones. 'Up, dogs of the sea – on your feet. Ithaqua's emissaries grant you this boon, that you, too, might stand in their presence.'

As the Vikings sullenly got to their feet, she continued: 'You ask for Thonjolf? Thonjolf the Red, who is also called Thonjolf the Silent? He is at Norenstadt, summoned there by Leif Dougalson, king of all the Viking clans. Word is out that a raid is in the offing. Thonjolf attends a great meeting of the chiefs but should soon return. Only his oaf of a son Harold is here, and he lies drunken in the meeting-house.' She tossed her head to indicate the enclosure to her rear.

'You talk of a raid,' de Marigny queried. 'What sort of raid?'

She nodded, grinning. 'Soon all Vikings will put on metal and sail their dragons against the people of the Isle of Mountains. Ithaqua has commanded it; he has

306

set the hand of Leif Dougalson and the Vikings against the mountain isle.'

Here she paused, then laughed loudly and grasped their elbows. 'Aye, and your arms, too, will find work on that bat-haunted isle! Have I not foreseen it? Bat wings beating in the mist – blood and terror and great winds blowing – and all in the name of . . . of Lord Ithaqua!' And it seemed to the two men that she spat the Wind-Walker's name out on the sand.

By this time the Vikings were back on their feet, and the two newcomers were able to see their Numinosian hosts more clearly; from which moment onward they began to feel a certain gratitude for the doubtful affections of the witch-wife. For the clan of Thonjolf the Red, while only four or five dozen in number, was almost without exception a clan of giants among men. Even the stripling youths of fourteen or fifteen years were well over six feet tall, while some of the full-grown men were almost seven. Silberhutte, for all his massive stature by Earth standards, was dwarfed by them!

'Another effect of the low gravity, Henri?' the Warlord asked out of the corner of his mouth.

'I would say so. By the same token their strength has probably not increased in proportion. Might even have been reduced . . . I hope!'

Now the Vikings crowded forward, eager to get a closer look at their visitors, still open-minded about Annahilde's assertions regarding these men come down from the sky. So they flew, did they? Well, so did midges! What other powers did they have? Surely the Wind-Walker's chosen ones must be of greater stature than these men? What proof was there that they were what the witch-wife said they were? They moved closer still, then –

'Ho, there! Out of my way – move, man! Where are these strangers I heard the hag ranting about, these "emissaries of Ithaqua?"' The voice was a deep, drunken bass rumble issuing from behind the massed Vikings.

As all eyes turned from the strangers and a way was cleared for the speaker, so Annahilde whispered: 'Harold, the chief's son. He's a drunkard and a bully. Beware . . . !'

3
Ithaqua's Emissaries

As large and foreboding as his voice – seven feet tall, with a middle like a barrel and a huge red face that well matched his tangled red hair and the blood in his pig eyes – Harold was a monster. He glanced once at the strangers, took a long draught from the jug he carried, then threw back his great head and burst into malicious laughter. His mirth was short-lived, however, and quickly gurgled into silence as he contemplated the two a second time. Now his peering inspection was much more thorough, more threatening; and while Harold was not as drunk as the Earthmen might have preferred, he certainly appeared to be all of the bully that Annahilde had named him.

Finally he turned scornfully on the assembled Vikings and roared: 'A trick! You've been tricked, all of you. By these two, aye, and by the hag there . . .' Harold waved a massive hand in Annahilde's direction. 'Emissaries of Ithaqua, indeed! Why, only *look* at them! They're common men, can't you see that?'

'But we all saw them fly in from the sea,' one of the younger men protested.

Harold stepped over to the youth and dealt him a backhanded blow that sent him reeling. 'Fool! Oaf! It's Annahilde's work. She's blown her powder in your faces. You'd see anything she wanted you to see. Sent by Ithaqua, my backside! These two? They look more like men from the Isle of Mountains to me . . . and we all understand the witch-wife's interest in the Isle of Mountains . . .'

Instantly Annahilde's sons, great hulking men in their late twenties, stepped forward and confronted Harold. At the same time a pair of surly looking brutes, Harold's cronies, took up positions flanking him. From one of these Harold snatched a spear whose shaft was thick as a man's wrist.

'Stand aside, bitch-sons, for I've no quarrel with you two – not yet! Aside, I say, and let's see what these strangers are made of.'

In the chief's absence Harold had a certain authority with the clan. With his cronies beside him and following his cryptic accusations – against Annahilde as well as the two strangers – it would have been purest folly for the witch-wife's sons to oppose him in earnest. Thus Erik and Rory reluctantly stood aside as de Marigny and Silberhutte separated and backed up against the hull of one of the beached longships.

Quickly then, allowing no time for thought, Harold drew back his arm and made as if to throw his spear. Instead of hurling the weapon, however, he retained it in the ready position. Silberhutte – a born fighter and greatly experienced – merely froze and narrowed his eyes, waiting for the cast, knowing he could step out of the spear's flight path. De Marigny, on the other hand, for all he had learned in the plateau's arenas, was short on practical experience. He feinted, almost tripped, and in the split second it took him to regain his balance, Harold laughed harshly and made his throw.

Without a doubt the hurled shaft should have pinned de Marigny to the planking of the dragonship, would have done so but for the intervention of Armandra's familiar winds. For when that deadly weapon was only three feet away from his middle, it met a violent, invisible force that wrenched it from its path and drove it point down into the coarse sand between the two outsiders. Silberhutte snatched the weapon up in a hail of pebbles and gravel, breaking it like a twig over his bent knee.

Harold shook his head in bewilderment, unable to accept the evidence of his own eyes. He knew his cast had been a good one. It had seemed as if some unseen hand had struck the shaft aside in midair. And now the larger of the strangers – whose strength, for all his comparatively diminutive size, must be prodigious – was striding over to him, looking up at him through eyes that were unafraid, eyes filled with anger.

De Marigny knew at once what had saved his life. Now, as Silberhutte approached the huge, red-haired Viking, he whispered his thanks into thin air, saying: 'Just keep watch over us, friends. I've a feeling there'll be more work for you shortly.'

Now the bullyboys flanking Harold puffed themselves up and gripped their weapons in massive hands. One carried an axe; the other, whose spear lay broken on the sand, had drawn a sword. Harold glanced at his brutal colleagues, turning his head from side to side and grinning. To the Warlord he said, 'You wanted to speak to me, little man?'

'The two of us,' the Texan grated out through clenched teeth. 'You and I, dog, hand to hand. After that – then we'll decide which of us is the "little" man!'

'You call me . . . *dog!*' Harold almost choked on the word, going bright as a beetroot in his rage. 'And you, a midget, challenge me in hand-to-hand combat? Breath of Itha – ' He drew back his arm to deliver a backhand blow like that dealt to the young Viking a moment or two earlier. Silberhutte ducked under the flying arc of muscle and bone, driving his rock-hard fist like a ramrod into Harold's solar plexus.

The bully immediately doubled forward, breath whistling from him. His descending chin met the clasped fists of the Warlord as they rose from knee level. It was a rapid combination of blows delivered by an expert; certainly it would have killed many a lesser man. As it was, Harold was lifted right off his feet, stretched out on the sand like a felled oak.

De Marigny had guessed the outcome of any contest between his companion and the bullying Viking, and he had foreseen the natural aftermath. Now, as Harold's henchmen made to strike – the one lifting his axe while the other drew back his sword – he cried out: 'Hold . . . or be whirled aloft by angry winds and thrown down into the sea to drown!'

And with that he made a swift motion with his hand, as if casting sand in the faces of the two who threatened the Warlord. On the instant, as their eyes swivelled toward him and their blows were momentarily checked, twin spirals of sand and pebbles grew up from the beach, leaped upon the two and enveloped them, whirling them about and casting them down. For a few seconds, where a mere moment of time ago only a breeze had whispered off the sea, the wind whined its rage and drove sand up the beach in stinging flurries. Then there was quiet again.

The two Vikings, thoroughly cowed and shaken, carefully climbed to their feet and backed off, then turned and ran, fighting their way through the crush of silent, wide-eyed observers. And not once during the confrontation had the visitors from the skies reached for their own weapons . . .

The witch-wife, herself amazed at the way things had gone, but quick to take advantage of the situation, cried: 'Now lift your blades high and give these men welcome for what they are: true emissaries of Ithaqua, Lord of the Winds!'

'Aye,' cried Erik and Rory in unison, 'here's a good strong arm for Lord Ithaqua's proven emissaries!' And the crowd on the beach joined in, lifting up their weapons and their voices in an accolade which was only cut short by Annahilde.

'And now,' she shouted above the general babble, 'to complete the day, comes Thonjolf himself.' She pointed out to sea where, from behind the tall rocks at the mouth of the fjord, the dragon prow of a magnificently painted longship had appeared. There, in the prow at the neck of the nodding dragon, stood a man taller by inches than the tallest of his clan; a man whose stature, even as seen from the beach, was obviously that of a giant among giants, his red hair blowing behind him like a mane in the breeze from the open sea.

'Thonjolf the Red,' Annahilde cried again. 'And what news we have for him, eh, lads? For he's never had visitors such as these before. Men from the skies – sent by the Wind-Walker himself – emissaries of Ithaqua!'

Later, ostensibly as guests in Annahilde's house – a thatched, single-storey affair of two small bedrooms, a kitchen half-open to the sky, and a living room of sorts where now they rested at their ease, or as best they could, on low wooden benches decked with smelly furs – Hank Silberhutte and Henri-Laurent de Marigny held a muted conversation. Outside the door to this crude but comparatively clean shelter, the two brothers Rory and Erik silently squatted like human watchdogs.

The visitors from Borea were unable to say whether they were under the quiet protection or merely the wary scrutiny of Annahilde's sons, but whichever way it was, at least they each had felt sufficiently secure to snatch a few hours sleep. While it had not been immediately apparent, their hurtling voyage through the void had been both physically and mentally strenuous; now, with a pint of sweet, sticky ale inside them along with a plate of smoky, half-cooked meat of undetermined origin, they felt up to facing their next problem as it presented itself.

Of the events immediately following on Thonjolf's return to his clan: that had been something of an anti-climax. And little wonder he was occasionally known as Thonjolf the Silent!

The chief had left his longship with his retinue of a dozen

or so men, had briefly inspected the visitors, had grunted sourly at the sight of his son snoring on the beach, and had patiently given ear to Annahilde's shrill outline of events. Indeed her ragged figure and wild-eyed look had seemed to command their fair share of respect from the chief.

Then, following an aerial demonstration by de Marigny and the flying cloak, Thonjolf had gone off with the witch-wife and several members of the clan into the meeting-house. If the chief had been impressed by de Marigny's triumph over gravity, it had not showed, except perhaps in a slight arcing of his bushy red eyebrows.

And it was the general response to their coming – or rather the lack of response – that formed the topic of conversation between de Marigny and Silberhutte in Annahilde's house.

'I don't understand it,' de Marigny said. 'I always believed the Vikings to be a fiery, volatile people. The type of folk who would make a lot of an "omen" such as we've provided. Yet here we are, a pair of near-dwarfs, flying in like something out of the *Arabian Nights*, "emissaries of Ithaqua" and all that; not to mention your knocking the chief's son out cold. I mean, by my reckoning we should either be hanging up by our thumbs somewhere by now, or else occupying Thonjolf's throne – if he has one!'

Silberhutte nodded. 'Yes, it puzzled me, too, at first. But the more I think of it – '

'Yes?'

'Well, to start with, visitors from the skies are by no means unheard of on Numinos, Henri. Ithaqua's comings and goings must be fairly frequent.'

'Not too frequent, I hope,' de Marigny answered with feeling.

'And then there's Annahilde and her hallucinatory powders,' the Warlord continued. 'You'll recall Harold mentioned them? If all of the clans come equipped with witch-wives, and if all of them know where to lay their hands on the plants or whatever they use to concoct their powders . . . little wonder it requires a lot to make your average Numinosian Viking sit up and take notice! And just suppose Ithaqua had sent us here – how would you react if you were a Viking?'

'I'd be pretty wary, I suppose.'

Silberhutte nodded. 'Sure you would – and that was more or less the reaction we got. Except from Harold, who's a pretty stupid bully. And I fancy that even he was only trying to assert himself in his father's absence. As for the chief himself: Thonjolf strikes me as a man with a lot on his limited mind, namely this big meeting he's just back from and the upcoming raid on the Isle of Mountains. What with those things, and on top of them Ithaqua sending us as emissaries to *his* clan – which must strike him as a hell of a thing despite his nearly negative reaction – and at the same time having to bear the responsibility for the actions of his oaf of a son . . .'

'I suppose you're right,' de Marigny conceded. 'But it still doesn't get us any closer to finding the time-clock.'

'No, but unless my ears deceive me, here's Annahilde now. On her own by the sound of it. This could be the ideal opportunity to fill in on background information – and at the same time try and find out about the clock. Let's see what she has to say.'

The gabble of the witch-wife's voice grew louder as she approached the house, questioning her sons about the welfare of the strangers. They answered her respectfully if non-committally, and she gave them permission to go down to the meetinghouse. Apparently the building within the stockade doubled not only as a throne room but also as a drinking place. A moment later she came through the door, closing it carefully behind her. Then she cocked her head to one side and listened, waiting for a few moments to ensure that her sons had indeed left their posts as instructed.

Satisfied, she turned at last and said: 'Now then, the pair of you, let's have it.'

'Let's have it?' de Marigny queried, doing his best to look blank.

'No games!' Annahilde cautioned. 'You are not sent by Ithaqua, I know that. I knew it from the moment I touched you.' She grasped their arms. 'See! See! You' – she stared at Silberhutte – 'ah, you have known Ithaqua's touch, his carmine gaze, his icy breath in your face, aye. But you are not his. He has chilled your blood, true, but you are your own man.'

She turned to de Marigny. 'And you – you, too, have met the Wind-Walker, but he has not touched you. Your blood is still warm. No, you are not Children of the Winds . . . so what are you? I do not even believe you to be of Numinos. But if not Numinos, where else?'

The two looked at each other, silent for a moment, then Silberhutte said: 'Annahilde, it seems we're forced to trust you. No, we are not Ithaqua's emissaries, and we are not men of Numinos. I am Hank Silberhutte, Warlord of the Plateau on Borea. My people are sworn enemies of Ithaqua. This man' – he placed a hand on de Marigny's shoulder – 'is Henri-Laurent de Marigny, and he is from the Motherworld. I, too, was born on Earth, but Borea is now my homeworld.'

If Annahilde's eyes had gone wide when Silberhutte spoke of Borea, they became huge orbs at mention of the Motherworld. 'Men of Earth, here on Numinos?' she gasped. 'And not by Ithaqua's hand! But how? Why?'

'The how of it will have to wait,' de Marigny told her. 'As for why we are here: we seek a . . . a box.'

'A box?'

'One big enough to contain a man. A box shaped like this – ' and he drew a coffin-shape with his foot on the dirt floor. 'It's mine, taken from me by Ithaqua. I want it back.'

She nodded earnestly. 'Yes, I know something of your box – but only tell me what you want with it, what you would do with it? Of what use is a box?'

'It is a device for travelling between worlds, for jumping backward and forward through time itself,' Silberhutte told her. 'My friend was questing after Elysia and had barely arrived on Borea when Ithaqua stole his travelling box away.'

'Elysia!' she seemed astounded.

'Elysia is – ' de Marigny began.

But Annahilde quickly cut him off. 'The home of the Great Elder Gods – I know, I know!' Now she grabbed their wrists tight in claws like steel traps. 'I thought when first I saw you flying in off the sea that someone had blown my own powders in my face. Now – ' She shook her head in amazement. 'Yours is the true magic!'

'Annahilde,' de Marigny urgently took her hands in his. 'Where is the time-clock – my box, I mean? I must find it.'

Her eyes narrowed and she peered at her visitors cannily before answering. 'Have no fear, you shall know the whereabouts of your box . . . in good time. Before that there is something you must do for me.'

4

The Witch-Wife's Tale

'The Vikings have been here for thousands of years,'
Annahilde began. 'I know, for I am one who can read
the old writings. It is all in the Two Books: in the Book
of Earth the Motherworld and in the Book of Numinos.
The histories were handed down from father to son until
later, when Ithaqua brought others who had writing, and
then they were written in words in the Two Books.' Here
she closed her eyes and lay back her head, so that it was
as if she quoted from a book in her mind:

'And it was Ithaqua brought the first men into Borea,
and into Numinos, and many among the latter were Norsemen. This was before the time of the iron swords, but later
they too came with men of the Motherworld brought into
Numinos by Ithaqua. And the Wind-Walker said unto the
tribes that he was their God and they would worship him,
and in Norenstadt his pyramid altar was builded where it
stands to this day.

'And the Vikings multiplied in Numinos and the tribes
were many; for the Great God Ithaqua' (she spat these
last words out, as she did whenever she spoke of the
Wind-Walker) 'had filled the ocean with fishes great
and small and had carpeted the islands with grasses
and peopled them with animals, all for the needs of the
Vikings. But Ithaqua was a hard God and cold, and at
times he would take the loveliest daughters of the tribes
for his own to fly off with them into the lands beyond the
Great Ice Wall. Aye, but he rarely brought them back, and
those he brought back were mazed and cold and rarely
lived long.

'Among those that lived, several were with child, but

318

such instances were always many years apart. Whole generations of Vikings would go by, and then, again, the Wind-Walker would get a woman with child. When born, all such spawn of Ithaqua were freaks or monsters, and all died with only one recorded exception. This child was so evil of aspect and inclination – a black vampire from birth that pulled blood and not milk from its mother's breast – that the chief of her tribe tore it from her and put it down with fire.

'And Ithaqua – when he came again to Numinos and when his priests told him what had transpired – then it was that he destroyed the entire tribe which lived in that place; and his wrath and the storms he brought, which lashed all of Numinos, were awful in their might!

'And yet the tribes knew that the Storm-God himself would have put down his child if he had seen it, for he was desirous of a beautiful child and of human form . . . why else would he choose the loveliest girls with which to mate? Then, because of Ithaqua's unending cruelties – which were such that his comings were dreaded and his goings much applauded in secret and out of earshot of his priests – it came about that the tribes turned against their God and defied him.

'Parents were wont to hide away their girl-children, especially those of lovely aspect, when they knew that Ithaqua was due to walk the winds of Numinos once more; and the God's chill-hearted priests, even those priests given over utterly to his worship, they became prone to peculiar accidents and fatal misadventures in their master's absence. But in the end the Storm-God knew how his people worked against him, and he waxed wroth indeed!

'He set the tribes one against the next until all Numinos burned from end to end, and the fires of blazing settlements were hotter than the lava that bubbles on the Islands of Fire. And at the last, when the tribes of Numinos were

319

decimated, the Wind-Walker stood in the sky and laughed. He laughed – then rained down lightnings and sent storms racing across the ravished land and caused the very seas to wash the islands.

'And so all Numinos bowed down before him, and those who lived swore fealty to him, lest he destroy the Viking tribes forever . . .' Here Annahilde paused and got her breath before going on.

'These things,' she finally continued, 'are written. It is also written that at last Ithaqua looked on Numinos and saw the tribes were penitent. Then he brought others here who were not Vikings though much like them; sturdy men and women of the Motherworld, they were, whose weapons and culture and tongue were different; and it was seen that the Wind-Walker would change the blood of the tribes, would produce women of great beauty and strength to satisfy his lusts and bear him the offspring he desired . . .'

They waited for her to go on, but she seemed to have talked herself out. Finally Silberhutte asked: 'And did he ever achieve his ambition? I think not, knowing how Armandra has never totally bowed to her father's will.'

'No, he did not,' she quickly answered, shaking her head in glad denial, 'though he surely tried. He made it law that the most handsome and strongest youths of the tribes – which were now called clans – could take only the loveliest girls for brides, so that their children in turn would be beautiful and strong and the maidens pleasing in Ithaqua's eyes. So it came to pass that after eleven generations an entire tribe or clan of chosen people had grown up and dwelled upon one especially green and beautiful island. And Ithaqua looked upon the maidens of this wondrous clan and was sorely tempted, yet he held off and bided his time while eleven more generations passed. And now at last there were two couples on the island whose perfection of form and feature was a wonder to behold even in a clan whose least handsome member was beautiful, and both women of these couples were with child. The greatest seers of the time examined them, declaring that the children would be female.

'Then Ithaqua came again to Numinos and went into the beautiful isle. There he set aside certain elders to serve the mothers of his hoped-for future brides, and having done so, he put down the rest of the clan – all of them, man, woman, and child – out of hand!

'He did this – for what good reason? – and all for naught. There had been much inbreeding in the isle's two and twenty generations, which previously had only shown itself in the infrequent birth of a beautiful idiot. Out of fear, these children the clan secretly put down. But now –

' – Not only were the children of those last two unfortunate women imbeciles, they were also hideous; aye, and both of them girls, as had been foreseen! In a single blow – a blow delivered perhaps by the clean old gods of Earth – all of Ithaqua's plans were destroyed. And he saw what was become of his dream and went away from Numinos for long and long. Then, when they thought he was gone forever and those who knew the old legends had turned again to serving the olden gods of the Motherworld, the Wind-Walker returned and brought his fearful oppressions back with him.

'He put down the worship of the Earth gods and their priests and once again was wont to fly away with and ravish the loveliest maidens, and ever and ever he sought to produce a child in his own and in Man's image. So things stood for an hundred years – until some sixty-three years gone.' Again she paused.

'Sixty-three years ago?' de Marigny prompted her. 'Something happened then?'

'Aye, for that was when he brought a ship of the Motherworld to Numinos; and in that small ship were a man and wife, two strong sons and a daughter of some twelve years. And they were the first people of Earth that Numinos had seen in over five hundred years. The wife was a lovely woman even in her middle years, the husband handsome, and the sons firm limbed and clever. And the girl-child was lovely.

'They were brought here, where Thonjolf's grandfather was the then chief, and some few years later the girl married a fine young man of the clan. Twin daughters came of that marriage, aye, and I was one of them . . .'

'You?' Silberhutte stared at her, intrigued by her story.

'Ah! – I see what you are thinking,' the witch-wife cried. 'You wonder how I could possibly come of such a mating. Let me tell you that in girlhood I was not uncomely, that even now beneath the grime and the lines of age and pain I have beauty. But I am called "hag" and that is the way the clan knows me; it is the way I live, have lived since – ' Abruptly she stopped.

'Go on, Annahilde,' de Marigny again prompted.

'I . . . I stumble blindly on, going ahead of myself,' she finally said. 'Let me continue in my own time . . .

'I grew to a woman and was taken to bride by Hamish the Strong. Two fine sons he gave me and loyal, who have cared for and protected me these six years since Hamish was taken. As for my sister, Moira: she was almost perfect in her beauty and goodness. No one was ever so kind, no soul ever so lovely, and if Ithaqua had seen her as she grew to womanhood, surely would he have taken her. But his comings were rare in those days and confined mainly to Norenstadt where he sat on his pyramid throne, and he saw Moira not.

'And so she too was wed, to a good and noble man of the clan, a learned man whose instructors were my grandparents brought to Numinos in their little ship; but she did not become pregnant by him until she was in her fortieth year. Then it was that Moreen was born, small and sweet and shiny like a little pearl – Moreen, whose tiny limbs were those of Earth and not the stretchy stilts of Numinos – Moreen of the Smile. And in her fifth year . . . then Ithaqua saw her.

'A child of five tender years, and already lovely as a flower. Fresh as the green fields and full of her mother's ways, she was the darling of her parents, the joy of the clan, the rose in the garden of Thonjolf the Elder's heart. Aye, for the present chief's father was so taken with the child that he had a house built for her family close to his own house, so that he could watch her at her play and laugh with her when she laughed, which was often.

'And when he came, Ithaqua saw her at play and lifted her up. He lifted her into the clouds in his great hand and gazed upon her curiously with his carmine eyes; and where other children would surely cry and beat their tiny fists and feet, that child of joy only laughed and pointed at the huge black blot of his head and tickled his bloated, taloned fingers! And the Wind-Walker – monstrous beast of hell that he is – seemed held in Moreen's tiny fist more tightly ever than he held her.

'Then at last he set her down close by her house and stood off in the sky above the settlement. For a long time he stood there astride the wind, gazing down upon Moreen where she played below and waved up at him, and a strange fascination glowed deep in his fiery eyes.

'Soon, unable to bear this thing any longer, her parents ran out, snatched her up, and carried her into the house; whereupon Ithaqua stirred himself up as if from a dream and walked off across the sky toward Norenstadt. And as he went, often he looked back . . .

'Some time later, two yak-riding priests came plodding from Norenstadt, and with them a retinue of Viking warriors led by Leif Dougalson himself. At first, when they went to my sister Moira's house and asked to see the girl-child, it was thought that they intended to steal little Moreen away. But no, instructed by Ithaqua, they had merely come to see the child. Then they spoke to my sister and her man; aye, and to old Thonjolf, too, come up with a body of men to protect the little one and her family if such were necessary.

'And the priests said to Thonjolf that his clan was honoured among all the Viking clans, for the Great God Ithaqua had found Thonjolf's people fair and pleasing – particularly the tiny girl-child Moreen, who one day would walk with him as his bride upon the winds that blow between the worlds!

'Then, when they heard this, though glances full of meaning passed between Moreen's elders and old Thonjolf, nothing against the plan was said; for after all nothing could be said, not at that time; and that night there was a feast and drinking and much praying for the peaceful propitiation of Ithaqua. The next day Thonjolf received Leif Dougalson's instructions to care well for little Moreen: it would go badly for all concerned were Ithaqua in any way thwarted in this matter, for it was known that the Wind-Walker would return again and again to Thonjolf's clan to watch the small one grow into womanhood.

'And the priests also spoke to my sister and her man, saying how well it were that the little one should grow up carefully protected and in innocence; and they issued a warning to all the clan that its sons be not tempted as Moreen grew to maturity. Then, before these most important visitors took themselves off to their rightful places in Norenstadt, the priests said how if they had their way, the child would go with them, but that Ithaqua himself had commanded that she be allowed to grow up within her family and clan according to her nature.

'Following their departure, how my sister cried! She wept and her man was distraught with horror, anger, and helplessness, and even the old chief shed a tear at the thought of the now inevitable fate of little Moreen. The entire clan, with the exception of a handful of callow or jealous wives, grew sad and morose, remaining thus for many a day. It was as though a great king had passed away, or as if each family had lost a favourite son or daughter all in the same disaster. And the only one to remain unchanged through all of this was the angel Moreen herself, for she was less than six years old and understood nothing at all of the matter – not yet.

'As for me: such were my own emotions over the thing that I think at times I went a little mad. And when these bouts of madness were upon me, I would see strange visions and utter weird warnings and omens. As time passed, I sensed a monstrous disaster looming – though its essence utterly eluded me – and I deliberately began to pose as a seer before the clan, so that not even my poor husband or sons saw through the trick. Yet it was not merely a mad game I played, no; for the approach of the unknown horror was very real to me, and I sought to escape it. And that escape lay in the fostering of my own image as a soothsayer and wonder-worker, a power among the people.

'Thus I set about to learn all manner of spells and conjurations, brewed vision-engendering potions, gathered the delirious pollens of rare and poisonous blooms; and because my grandparents from the Motherworld had been my tutors, passing on great wisdom and even greater curiosity to me, I also journeyed to Norenstadt and learned how to read the olden books, thus discovering for myself the legends of the Vikings and their coming into Numinos. And in this manner and by these means did Annahilde become a witch-wife.

'During these preparations of mine for that terror which I knew was coming, and which by now I knew must concern Ithaqua and his desire to pluck Moreen from the clan when she was ripe, seven years went all too quickly by. Ithaqua had been back only once in those seven years, when Moreen was not yet nine years old. And if anything the extra years had merely added to the goodness of her nature, so that she was loved by all the clan; aye, and even the wild animals of the fields and the birds of the air loved her; and never hurting anything or anyone, she herself was never hurt, nor even understood the meaning of fear . . . which was as well.

'For picture the sight of that horror winging down the whistling winds of ether to Numinos: the monster Ithaqua, his mind filled with many alien thoughts, and also one thought which is all too easily recognized by men. Aye, and if man knows the meaning of lust, how then Ithaqua? For he has known the lusts of all the ages, knows them yet, and while his burning eyes were veiled, certainly lust seethed in his black heart. But little Moreen saw it not, saw only the vast being of whom her parents and the clan spoke in shuddering whispers, the massive manlike shape in the sky whose hand came down, gentle as a falling leaf, to lift her to the high places from which, in her innocence, she could gaze down upon Numinos like some queen of the clouds – which one day, if he had his way, she would surely become. And who to say him nay?

'And on this occasion he seemed even more taken with Moreen than before and flew with her round the span of Numinos, showing her all of the places, even the icelands beyond the dark horizons. Aye, but he returned her warm and unharmed, and he smiled – if ever beast such as he could be said to smile at all! – on the clan of old Thonjolf, and the islands knew fair weather, bountiful crops, and good hunting for long and long after his going.

'But of course, three years later he came again . . .

'Now there was a lad in the clan, a mere lad, one Garven the Fair. And he admired Moreen and fancied her as is right for young men to fancy pretty girls. That was all there was to it, for Garven was good and honoured the warnings and words of his parents, and the rose Moreen herself was not yet budded. Yet they were childhood sweethearts when times allowed and would meet in the fields some miles inland at a secret place. In this one thing Garven disobeyed his elders, and Moreen hers, and in other circumstances surely the time would arrive when they would cleave each to the other as man and wife. Alas, that time could never be.

'When next Ithaqua came, Moreen was not in the village. The Wind-Walker's coming was unexpected as the rough winds he brought with him and the dark clouds of storm and thunder. He came in suspicion and found things sorely wanting. The clan's cowards rushed here and there, searching for the maid that Ithaqua might be appeased, but she was not to be found. Nor indeed was the lad Garven to be found.

'Then, as Ithaqua's rage mounted to a fury, the innocents came hand in hand, over the cliff paths from their fond wandering in the fields. And Ithaqua saw them . . .

'For all that they were children and pure as driven snow, Ithaqua's reaction was that of a cuckolded berserker! Jealousy crackled in the lightnings that played about his head, and the wonder is that his great pits of eyes did not glow brilliant green rather than their customary smouldering carmine. He snatched the two up and glared at them, and for a moment the very clouds stood still and no breath of air was felt. Then –

' – Before Moreen's very eyes, slowly and deliberately, he crushed young Garven to a tattered red pulp – squeezed the living guts from him – then tossed the red wet thing that had been a fair young lad down from on high to splatter on the beach below the settlement! While Moreen screamed and screamed, he next ripped off her clothes and examined her child's body minutely, finding no blemish, no evidence that she was ought but a child, no sign that his own evil ambitions were preempted. In the sky he nodded his great black blot of a head. So, and now he must ensure that the clan of Thonjolf understood his commands, that they obeyed them more fully in future. And who better to start with than Thonjolf himself, with whom all responsibility must ultimately lie?

'But there, what use to spell out the Wind-Walker's iniquities? The list is long as his life, which began back in the dim mists of time and seems interminable. Let it suffice to say that he murdered the elder Thonjolf's family (with the exception of the third chief of the line, the present Thonjolf the Red, who with his eldest son Harold was away hunting at the time) and also little Moreen's father, oh, and everyone and anyone he could get his great black hands on. Aye, and my man, too, Hamish, great fool that he was.

'But such a *brave* fool! Why, when he saw the carnage, Hamish ran at Ithaqua, waving his sword at him and challenging him where he stood red-handed and furious in the sky! I think my husband's mind had snapped – or perhaps he was drunk, I'm not sure. Whichever, he was very brave, and of course Ithaqua struck him down.'

Briefly Annahilde paused, before quickly continuing: 'Then, gathering great balls of snow from the dark clouds and freezing them hard in his hands, the monster rained them down upon the settlement until a third of the people were dead and their houses in ruins; and all of this the child Moreen saw. And though her screaming had stopped, her eyes, which once were so innocent, now opened wide in horror and loathing as she gazed down from her precarious perch in the crook of Ithaqua's shoulder.

'Finally he set the child down – not gently this time, tossing her naked into the shingle of the beach – before storming off into the lowering sky toward Norenstadt. Then . . . but how may I describe the agony and despair that Ithaqua left in his wicked wake? And before too long, in the midst of all that grief and mourning, back came those same priests from Norenstadt last seen seven years earlier.

'On this occasion Leif Dougalson did not accompany

them, no, for he lay grievously ill upon his sickbed. The wonder is that he survives to this day; for Ithaqua had chastised him, had pulled out his left arm by its roots in payment for his disappointment! And so the priests came quickly and in anger this time, spurring their yaks cruelly on, with no false words of praise for the clan of Thonjolf and its new chief.

'Ah, but I had not been idle in the period following Ithaqua's departure. The home of Moreen and her mother had been destroyed during the Wind-Walker's fury – along with my sister's mind – so I had taken the pair in to care for them. I had lost my own man, true, but had known for long enough that some such was in the offing and recovered quickly from the ordeal. And I had known too that the Wind-Walker's priests must soon come to remove the child into their own care. Well, that black God of Horror had already taken more than enough from the clan, and now I, Annahilde, determined he should take no more. And I had instructed the child thus and so, until she knew what she must say and how she must behave.

'So when they came and laid hands on her, she at once broke free of them, pointing at the one and crying: "When my Lord returns, I shall tell him that you tried to have me for yourself, against my will, and I shall ask him for your head to play with! And you" – she turned on the other – "I shall say to him that you plot against him, seeking a way to blind him and send him lost and stumbling between the stars!"

'"No, mistress, we beg of you!" they cried out to her, flinging themselves at her feet, her mercy. "These things are not true, as well you know."

'"Yet I will surely tell him that they are true," she answered, "if you dare to take me from the clan of Thonjolf." And she stamped her foot as I had shown her, saying: "Now – go!"

329

'Now these priests had not come out of Norenstadt at Ithaqua's command but of their own accord; for rather than face his wrath again following some further contravention of his wishes, they had decided the girl were best under lock and key and in their control. Well, that plan was now plainly out of the question, and without further ado and in great haste they left. Nor has the clan been bothered with them since . . .

'Perhaps this victory of mine over Ithaqua's so-called priests went to my head, perhaps not; but whichever, once they had gone, I set about to plan for Moreen's future, for her safety. Blood of my blood would not bear Ithaqua children to walk with him on the winds of ether, spreading his seed through all the universe – no, not if I had any say in the matter.

'And so I determined to smuggle Moreen away into the Isle of Mountains: the only place in all Numinos where her safety would be guaranteed, where Ithaqua could not touch her. That is where she is now, and that is where the pair of you enter into my plan.'

'Oh? And why should Moreen's whereabouts affect us?' Silberhutte asked.

'Your quest will never be completed without her,' she answered. 'You will find her in the Isle of Mountains, and you' – she took de Marigny's arm – 'you will surely fall in love with her; it can hardly be otherwise. I had thought that perhaps you would stay there and protect her, since Ithaqua will never give up trying to regain her for his own, but now that I know of this box of yours which flies between the worlds . . .'

'Well?' de Marigny prompted.

The witch-wife nodded, apparently reaching some unspoken decision or other. 'Yes, it shall be this way: I will give you a letter to take with you. You will not be able to read what is written – but Moreen will. The letter will tell – '

' – Where we may find the time-clock?' de Marigny finished it for her.

'Of course!' she answered. And she laughed a laugh as normal and hearty as any they ever heard, with no slightest trace of her assumed eccentricity, so that finally they saw in her much more than a mere soothsayer or seer. She was a woman of the human race, and as such was shrewd as any of her shrewdest sisters – for which they could but admire her.

5

Departure at Darkhour

'You've interested us greatly in all you've told us, Annahilde,' Silberhutte said, 'but there are a number of things we don't quite understand, things which could be important.'

'Ask away,' she replied.

'First: you mentioned Moreen's 'warmness' following Ithaqua's handling of her. What did you mean?'

'I meant what I said. The child was warm, *is* warm to this day, as if the Wind-Walker never laid hand on her. Surely you understand me? Look, you – ' She took the Warlord's hand. 'You have surely known Ithaqua's touch, for you are cold. This one, however' – and now she touched de Marigny – 'he is warm, which shows that his contact with the Wind-Walker has been only tenuous, or that he has been protected.'

'All true,' de Marigny agreed. 'It's generally accepted that physical contact with Ithaqua or lengthy close proximity will result in a permanent lowering of the body's temperature and an inexplicable immunity to subzero conditions. And yet you say that Moreen – '

' – Is warm, yes. Ithaqua did not chill her blood but left well alone. Perhaps it was all in keeping with his plan to let her grow into womanhood according to her nature, I do not know.'

'I don't understand,' de Marigny shook his head. 'Surely all of the people on Numinos have altered metabolisms, just as they do on Borea?'

'Not all of them, Henri,' the Warlord contradicted. 'Occasionally the Wind-Walker's influence breeds itself out. There are several such "warm ones" in the plateau on Borea.'

'Aye, and here on Numinos,' Annahilde agreed. 'Most of them in the Isle of Mountains.'

'That brings us to the second question,' Silberhutte told her. 'Just where is this "Isle of Mountains," and how is it that Ithaqua has no control over it?'

'Ah!' Annahilde answered, her voice dropping to the merest whisper. 'The answer lies in the shape of the island. You see, there is a symbol which is utterly abhorrent to the Wind-Walker, a symbol he has forbidden in all of Numinos. The name of this symbol has never been allowed to be spoken, and so it no longer has a name. Of course I know this symbol – aye, and its ancient forbidden name for that matter – though I've only ever spoken it to myself, but . . .'

She paused and gasped, her eyes widening, then drew quickly back as de Marigny traced out a sign with his foot in the dirt of the floor. The shape he had drawn was that of a five-pointed star!

'Are you telling us that the Isle of Mountains is in the form of a star?' he asked.

'He makes the sign,' Annahilde whispered, pointing at the star-shape, 'and speaks its name!'

Silberhutte too had drawn back from the abhorred symbol, but now, with an expression of disgust flitting briefly across his face, he quickly advanced and scuffed out the sign with the toe of a fur-booted foot. 'Is my friend right, Annahilde?'

She nodded. 'Indeed he is. Of all the hundreds of islands in the seas of Numinos, the Isle of Mountains alone is protected from Ithaqua's wrath – by its very shape! That shape is hurtful to him.'

'That is something we readily understand,' Silberhutte answered. 'But tell me, since the majority of living beings who have known the curse of Ithaqua are similarly affected by the symbol, how is it that the Isle of Mountains is not lethal to them also? How may one seek shelter in a poisoned place?'

'It is the degree of kinship that accounts for it,' the witch-wife explained. 'The Wind-Walker's priests could not even set foot upon the isle, let alone live there. But warm ones such as Henri and Moreen, and others long fled there, are unaffected.'

The Warlord frowned but remained silent.

'My friend wonders how the Isle of Mountains will affect him,' de Marigny explained. 'He has had much to do with Ithaqua, in one way or another.'

She shrugged, glancing thoughtfully at Silberhutte. 'I cannot say. I do not know. We can only wait and see . . .'

Finally the Warlord looked up, and the frown slipped from his face. He grinned, however ruefully. 'Well, I've had my share of this sort of problem before and come through it. There was a time when we turned the entire roof of the plateau on Borea into a huge star. There's nothing to be gained in worrying about it now. As Annahilde says, we can only wait and see.' He turned to her: 'But how do we go about looking for the Isle of Mountains? Will you give us directions, Annahilde?'

'No,' she shook her head. 'You will not go on your own. You will be carried there in Thonjolf's longships.'

'In the longships?' de Marigny frowned. 'Are you saying that the whole clan is defecting?'

'No, no,' she repeated. 'Oh, there was some such plan once mooted – but soon forsaken.'

'But why?'

'Because three years ago when Ithaqua came to Numinos and discovered Moreen fled, he told his priests in Norenstadt that it was his intention in the near future to send all the Vikings against the Isle of Mountains – to kill all therein except the girl – which means that to flee there now is to commit suicide. And the meeting of chiefs from which Thonjolf has just returned confirms the Wind-Walker's intentions. However . . .,' she paused.

'Go on, Annahilde,' Silberhutte urged.

'You two will be there *before* the Viking hordes. I have convinced Thonjolf that you are come here to lead his clan in the first assault upon the island – that you wish neither to wait for nor to join the main attack under Leif Dougalson – and that in this way, and by fetching Moreen out of the Isle of Mountains, the clan may regain Ithaqua's favour. I said these things to explain why you are here; also to ensure you reach the island before the bulk of the Vikings.'

Now it was once more the big Texan's turn to frown. 'Surely we could get there much faster on our own?' he said.

'Perhaps you could – if you knew the way,' she answered. 'But that is the one thing I cannot tell you. Only the sea captains know the location of the Isle of Mountains, and of course they have always shunned it – except for a trickle of refugees from Ithaqua's tyranny.'

'And when do the longships leave?' de Marigny asked.

'The men prepare them even now,' she replied, 'and they set sail at the next Darkhour.'

'Darkhour?' Silberhutte queried.

'That is the time when the sun is more than half-eclipsed by Borea. Always the sun hangs close behind Borea, but when the two seem to merge in the sky until the sun is two-thirds obscured, that is Darkhour. On the other hand, 'Lighthour' is when the rims of the sun and Borea separate, however fractionally. From one Lighthour to the next is a 'day' on Numinos. According to the old books about one hundred such days are equal to one "year" in the Motherworld.'

Here de Marigny spoke up. 'I know a little astronomy – a little science, physics,' he said, 'and by all Earthly laws this planetary system can't work.' Then, seeing that Silberhutte was about to voice his usual protest, he added: 'Oh, I know, I know: this isn't Earth, not even the same universe we were born in – but it's baffling nevertheless.'

335

'That's as it may be,' Silberhutte mused, 'but what Annahilde says explains a thing or two. Borea and its moons – if they really are moons and not a couple of minor planets – occupy fixed positions on a slightly crooked line, at the inner end of which stands the sun. That's why, seen from Borea, the moons are always partially eclipsed. The plateau must stand just sufficiently far around the curve of Borea to permanently hide the sun from view, which is why the plateau exists in a permanent half-light. When the moons are in Borea's shadow, there's always a false-dawn effect caused by the sun getting as close as it ever comes to rising. And when the sun shines full on the moons, they reflect its light upon Borea, maintaining a sort of balance. If my own knowledge of astronomy had been a little better, I might long ago have realized that there must be a sun. The regular shadow that half-obscures the moons should have told me as much on its own!'

'But you've always more than half-suspected it,' said de Marigny.

'Yes, I have. And just think: if on my expeditions I had ever managed to push on a few more miles away from Borea's twilight zone – why – I might well have seen my first Borean sunrise!' He paused for a moment and his expression grew more serious. 'Right now, however, we're more interested in the next Darkhour than in any future sunrise.'

'That's right,' de Marigny agreed, turning back to Annahilde. 'So we set sail for the Isle of Mountains at Darkhour. And when we get there and find Moreen? And after she translates your letter and tells us where we may find the time-clock? What then?'

She shrugged. 'That is out of my hands. But Moreen must not be harmed, and she must not be brought back here where Ithaqua can find her. She is a woman now. He would not hesitate . . .'

336

'About Moreen,' de Marigny said. 'There's one more thing I don't understand. One thing about her, and one about Ithaqua.'

'Say on,' she nodded, 'but be quick. I must report to Thonjolf. Later there will be feasting and drinking, then all will sleep – including you two, for you'll need your strength – and when you next awaken, it will be Darkhour.'

'Two questions, that's all. How is it that the clan, which you say loved Moreen, now turns so readily against her? And why did Ithaqua not take some terrible revenge on discovering that the girl had fled from him? I would have thought he would utterly destroy the clan of Thonjolf.'

'Ah, but that was some three or four years ago,' she answered, 'and when Ithaqua visited Numinos at that time he had other things to worry about. I was studying the books in Norenstadt when he came, and I saw him. I believe he was wounded!'

'Wounded?'

'Aye, for he sat on his pyramid throne and rocked to and fro and he held up a great hand to his eye, from which trickles of carmine fire dripped like vile blood!'

The Warlord nodded. 'That was my doing,' he said, showing neither pride nor modesty. 'When Ithaqua attacked the roof of the plateau with his kite-warriors, I struck him through the eye with a star-stone-tipped spear.'

'Your doing?' Annahilde was astounded. 'You struck him? A mere man against the Wind-Walker?' For a moment she was dumbstruck, then she laughed delightedly. 'And did I not say you reminded me of Hamish?'

Again the Texan nodded. 'You did, but my weapon was far more potent than any sword, Annahilde. Your Hamish was a hero, while I was merely desperate! But in any case you were going to tell us about the clan's change of heart toward Moreen. How did it come about?'

She shrugged fatalistically. 'There were always the

jealous ones. Then, after the near-slaughter of the clan and the destruction of the settlement when Ithaqua found Moreen and Garven together – aye, and once she was fled, the sure knowledge that Ithaqua must sooner or later exact an even more terrible vengeance – ' Again she shrugged.

'Moreen was a loved one, yes, but the families of the clan have their own loved ones to worry over. It has been four years since I sent the lass away; sufficient time for the clan to transfer all the blame upon her innocent head. They forget that the only one to blame is the one who walks on the wind. But who am I to judge them? Now, with your coming, they grasp at their one chance to redeem themselves in Ithaqua's eyes. No, I do not blame them – I pity them.'

After pausing reflectively, the witch-wife continued in a lighter tone. 'Now then, before I report to Thonjolf – and just in case no further chance presents itself between now and Darkhour – I have something to give you.'

From pockets hidden in her ragged clothing she drew out two small skin pouches. 'This one,' she said, passing it to de Marigny, 'is for you. It contains herbs and salts crushed to a powder. Individually the ingredients are of no consequence; as I have prepared them, they form a powerful potion. The powder is to be taken carefully and sparingly.'

'But what does it do?' de Marigny asked, weighing the pouch in his hand. 'And why do you give it to me and not the Warlord?'

'He has no need of it,' she answered, 'for he feels only the utmost extremes of cold. You, on the other hand, are a warm one. The powder will keep you warm when the cold would otherwise kill you!'

Silberhutte eyed the other pouch. 'And that one?' he asked.

She smiled cannily. 'Ah, this one is a small magic in

support of those you already possess. No mage in all Numinos prepares a more effective dreaming powder than Annahilde the witch-wife. Nor is it necessary for a man to sleep in order to dream. Simply blow the powder in the faces of any you would confuse or dismay. Look – '

She opened the neck of the pouch and took the merest pinch of a blue powder from it, blowing it from her palm into their faces before they could turn away. The powder settled on their lips, in their eyes. It entered their nostrils.

Then –

Silberhutte reeled as if struck with a sledgehammer. He threw himself against a wall, weaving, dodging, feinting, his arms and hands a blur as he batted away the myriad axes that flew at him from all directions, hurled by invisible hands. At the same time de Marigny leaped back from a black chasm that gaped open at his feet, where far below he glimpsed needle peaks that seemed to pull at him with a weird magnetism, demanding that he hurl himself to his death! Instead of 'escaping' from the chasm's edge . . . he fell backward over a bench to sit jarringly on the dirt floor.

For both men the uncanny experience of being removed instantly from Annahilde's house into unknown realms of terror was totally real; so that when, scant seconds later, the powder-inspired visions faded and were replaced by the room they recognized and their laughing hostess, then their astonishment was complete.

She gave them no opportunity for comments or further questions, however, but clasped their strong arms to assure them that reality had indeed returned, then briefly studied their startled faces with bright eyes. Satisfied with what she saw, she nodded. 'Most effective, yes?'

Without waiting for an answer, she continued: 'The

freedom of the settlement is yours. Only ask no more questions – certainly not of the common folk – for of course you are near-omniscient and therefore need no questions answered.' With that she opened the door and slipped out of the house.

'A pity,' de Marigny at last managed to say as the door closed behind her.

'What is?' the Warlord turned to him, fully recovered now from his brief ordeal.

'I meant to ask her about the bats. Don't you remember? She mentioned them in connection with the Isle of Mountains when first she met us on the beach. "That bathaunted isle," she called it. "Bat wings beating in the mist – blood and terror and great winds blowing!"'

'Yes, I remember,' the Warlord nodded thoughtfully. 'Perhaps we'll get a chance to talk with her later. Then we can thank her for these "small magics" she's given us . . .'

Darkhour . . .

Darkhour, and chill grey mists had come up off the sea, changing the shapes of the grim-faced men who boarded the longships into those of weirdly horned monsters. Leather and metal helmets glistened with moisture, and furs clung damply to brawny backs and arms. The mist seemed to form a film of slime over everything; the timbers of the ships were slick with it.

The temperature had fallen until it stood not far above freezing; even the ocean, normally slightly warm from the high incidence of submarine volcanic activity, was more chill than its medium. Outlines were soft and blurred, and sounds were muffled.

The Warlord, where he sat beside de Marigny toward the stern of Harold's ship, had been quiet for some time, had uttered no word since boarding. Now he shuddered involuntarily. He felt no natural chill but an ominous foreboding, engendered perhaps of the quiet, sullenly lapping waters and the leaden mist.

De Marigny was more cheerful. He was filled with warmth and feelings of well-being, the result of putting his tongue gingerly to the merest pinch of Annahilde's warming powder. The blood flowed in his veins like red wine and his features, pale and waxy since first he set foot on Borea, were now ruddy and seemed almost to glow. He turned to his silent companion.

'Hank, Annahilde's warming powder is certainly the Great Equalizer where I'm concerned. I never felt so warm and well. I feel almost reborn, well up to anything Borea and its moons may throw my way. Even in the plateau the cold was a damnable handicap – but no longer.'

As if waking from a daydream, the big Texan had started nervously when de Marigny began to speak. Now he shook himself and nodded his approval. 'Good,' he grunted. 'I only wish I felt as comfortable and as confident.'

De Marigny searched the other's mist-damp face. 'Is something wrong?'

'Several things. For one, I don't like being on Harold's longship. He hates us and it shows. You saw the way he watched us all through that shindig they threw for us? If he can, he'll do away with us at his first opportunity. No, I don't like him; and I don't care much for this mist, either. It hides too much. Also I've a strong premonition of trouble looming. And finally – '

'Yes?'

'Armandra has me worried.'

'She's been in contact with you?'

The Warlord nodded. 'We agreed only to "talk" to each other if there was real danger or something important to say. Well, she too has been bothered by dark premonitions. She thinks Ithaqua is close at hand, standing off in the void and riding the ether wind like a great hawk.

She thinks he's watching us, that we are his quarry, his prey.'

'Are we that vulnerable?'

'We're completely vulnerable. Oh, with luck Armandra might be able to snatch us back to Borea faster than her father could come for us. But on the other hand . . .' He shrugged.

'You mean we might be out of luck?'

Again Silberhutte nodded. 'Could be. And you'll note that Annahilde's boys aren't coming on the raid? She made damn sure they were to remain with the rear party, didn't she? What does she know that we don't, eh?'

De Marigny refused to be subdued. 'I'm sure I don't know,' he said. 'But about Ithaqua: personally, I think he's gone off on his wanderings again. I mean, if he were really interested in taking us and knew of our whereabouts, surely he'd have done it by now. What do you think?'

The Warlord shrugged. 'I wish I dared seek him out with my mind, telepathically,' he said. 'But if he's close, he might recognize me and track us down by my thoughts. As a matter of fact I think Armandra's right and he is somewhere out there, not too far away. I also think he knows much of what's going on. He won't make his move yet, though, for he holds all the trump cards and he's very greedy.'

'Greedy?'

'Sure. Why should he step in now and spoil it all? Why take us now when he might yet get his hands on Moreen – and the two of us in the bargain? And what a coup it would be if he could lure Armandra herself away from the plateau and Borea.'

'You think that's his plan?'

'It makes sense.'

Suddenly deflated, de Marigny said: 'If it wasn't for my stupidity you wouldn't be in this spot.'

The Warlord looked at him and grinned wryly. 'Don't flatter yourself, Henri. I'll go out of my way to help a friend, yes, but don't forget that you're the one man who can help me . . . you and your time-clock. That machine of yours isn't just a gateway out of Borea and this alien dimension we're trapped in – where at the moment I'm as surely a castaway as you are – it's also a powerful weapon. The ultimate weapon against the Wind-Walker.'

'True enough,' de Marigny answered. 'If any weapon can destroy Ithaqua, the time-clock can. Is that what you want, to kill him? Or is it that you want to escape from Borea and get back to old Earth?'

The other shrugged again. 'I'll tell you better when we've recovered the time-clock – if we ever do recover it. As for now, it looks like we're on our way.'

With a shout that roared out from sixteen throats as if from one – a shout whose echoes vibrated eerily through the mist – the oarsmen lifted up their oars vertically, poising them momentarily like twin rows of masts above the deck. Then the oars were lowered into oarlocks and dipped deep into darkly swirling ocean; and flanked by its dragon sisters, as a pacemaker in the mist-wreathed prow took up the beat with his hardwood pounding blocks, the longship pulled sluggishly away from the beach.

In the wake of the ships the settlement with its back-drop of cliffs quickly merged with the mist, and soon the three vessels passed out through the mouth of the fjord into the open sea. There, for all that the mist lay thick and menacing, the sails were unfurled and soon filled out as the dank, moisture-laden air swirled into them.

Finally, as they emerged seaward of the grey bank of fog, Harold roared a command from where he stood swaying in the prow. Echoing cries came back from the other ships; the pacemaker stopped his pounding; the sail belled out with the freshening breeze; and as the longships surged

343

forward into the gloom of Darkhour, so the oars were lifted up once more and stowed away.

The longships were now fully under sail, creaking through slapping wavelets toward unseen horizons. Overhead, a dull-glowing crescent of sun showed golden-red from behind Borea's shadowy bulk.

6
Wings in the Mist

They sailed out of one Darkhour toward the next, always holding the same course, three ships abreast under strange auroral skies. To the port side sailed the chief's ship with Thonjolf himself in command; to starboard his cousin Hanarl's dragon clove the wave crests. Pride of place, though, went to Harold's ship, for it was the craft that carried Ithaqua's emissaries and rode to sea flanked by the other two.

Only once, when the wind failed, did the Vikings unship their oars, and then briefly. For growing impatient, the Borean Warlord (a genuine high priest of the Wind-Walker in the eyes of most of the Vikings, though Harold and his closer colleagues obviously maintained certain reservations) saw fit to call up Armandra's familiar winds to fill the slack sails and drive the ships on. To witness again at firsthand the strange powers of these men from the skies, and this time to be completely sober, was galling for Harold and his cronies and astonishing to the crewmen; nevertheless, as time passed, proximity bred something of contempt among the crew of the longship.

True, the small-statured strangers seemed to command the very spirits of the air, and it certainly appeared that they carried the word of the Storm-God, but in the end they were only men. And so the bearded giants of the ship soon grew tired of peering wonderingly at the pair where they sat in the stern, and on occasion one or other of the Vikings would even venture so far as to ask of them a gruff question. For their part they always answered carefully and with a paucity of words so as not to demean their assumed standing.

Harold himself, exercising his trunklike legs by walking the wide central way that separated the oar banks, often strode close to the strangers. Whenever this happened, he would pause, legs braced and arms akimbo, scowling down at them. Invariably, though they returned his gaze blandly enough, de Marigny could sense the Warlord's desire to hurl himself at Harold's throat. Silberhutte's experiences on Borea had taught him well enough the best way to deal with treacherous enemies. To challenge Harold here, however, would be to challenge the entire crew – not to mention the crews of the other ships – and it would not bring their quest any closer to its conclusion. Thus Silberhutte bided his time, though now and then his companion could almost swear he heard the grinding of the Warlord's teeth.

For all their intense distrust and dislike of Harold, in one respect the pair followed his example: they, too, in a limited way, managed to spend some little time in exercising. De Marigny's method was to stroll out onto the walkway and limber up in the manner taught him in the plateau's gymnasiums: 'physical jerks' which were initially greeted with loud hoots of derision. The Vikings soon grew bored with such 'caperings,' however, and left him to get on with it.

Silberhutte's exercises were rather more spectacular. Using his fantastic skill, he juggled with his own and de Marigny's murderous picklike weapons; or at other times he would hurl himself furiously from one end of the walkway to the other in whirlwind feats of gymnastic agility. For all that displays such as these were performed solely as a means of loosening up otherwise inactive muscles, still the warrior crew would look on in open awe and admiration, much to their captain's envious chagrin.

During those infrequent periods when the Warlord sat nodding with his broad back to the curving side of the ship, then his companion would ensure that he stayed awake and mentally alert, and vice versa. Both men were certain that their position was very tenuous – the look in Harold's pig eyes said as much – which was sufficient in itself to keep them on their toes.

So Lighthour came and went, and gradually the sun crept once more into Borea's shade, and slow but sure the mists rolled up off the sea to deaden the slap of wavelets and shroud the ships in undulating milky billows. Darkhour was coming on again, and according to things the Earthmen had overheard, that was the time estimated for their arrival in the forbidden region, that area of ocean where loomed the rocky star-shaped bastions of the Isle of Mountains. They had heard other whispers, too, concerning devilish creatures that came down out of the sky to murder unfortunate sailors and drive venturesome ships away, but of these they could discover no further details . . .

Almost completely immunized against the cold by Annahilde's powder, de Marigny enjoyed as best he could his newfound comfort; nevertheless, and not wanting to become too dependent upon the drug, he used it sparingly as directed. In that period before and after Lighthour corresponding roughly to one Earth day, he had not taken a single sniff of the stuff, but as Darkhour drew closer, so he resumed his wary consumption of the warming powder, keeping at bay the freezing chill that came with the billowing mists.

Once, before the mist came down in earnest, they had thought to see in the distance a jagged wedge of land against the horizon, and at sight of those distant spires rising, the Vikings had grown silent. Too, there had been a cloud of tiny dots in the lowering sky above the far-off landmass, dots that seemed to circle sentiently but with motions unlike those of birds. Then the damp miasma of ocean had washed over the ships, covering them with a grely swirling blanket.

And it was then also, with the Isle of Mountains comparatively close at hand and visibility down to only a few feet, that Harold decided to have done with these so-called emissaries of Ithaqua. It would have to be now, under cover of the mist, so that Thonjolf would never know the truth of it; he was a strange old dog with an odd sense of honour. Harold could always fabricate some tale or other with which to satisfy the old chief, and he knew well enough how to cow his men into complete silence. He had long ago decided that if anyone were to receive Ithaqua's blessings for fetching the girl Moreen out of the Isle of Mountains, that one would be Harold. The reward must certainly not go to a pair of strangers of doubtful origins . . .

De Marigny was on watch while Silberhutte lay wrapped in sleep in the very stern of the ship. For some little time the Warlord's sleep had been restless, and he had tossed and moaned, so that de Marigny had thought to waken him. He had resisted the impulse, reckoning it was best for Silberhutte that he slept his fill in spite of whatever bad dreams disturbed him.

Moments after making this decision, however, he reconsidered. Suddenly there was a tension in the air not at all to his liking, an ominous, almost physical weight that seemed to press down upon him. The figures of the Vikings closest to him, where they sat in their places behind the round shields that lined the sides of the ship, were almost obscured by writhing tendrils of mist; they seemed like grim-horned phantoms sitting there, and their sullen silence only served to accentuate de Marigny's growing premonition of creeping doom.

Then, before he could stretch out a hand to shake Silberhutte's shoulder, there came to his ears a clear and distinct sound. An unmistakable sound which issued neither from the too-calm sea nor the ships that lolled upon it but from above, from the banks of mist that rolled over them. The sound of great wings in the mist, beating steadily, eerily over the longships.

De Marigny started, his heart leaping, as Silberhutte's hand grasped his wrist. 'Henri! I . . . I was dreaming. Or was I?'

'More like a nightmare,' the other retorted in a strained whisper. 'But this – whatever it is – seems real enough. Listen!'

The Warlord needed no urging; his face was already tilted upward. 'Bat wings beating, the old girl said,' he recollected. 'But I don't believe she told the half of it, and we forgot to ask!'

Harold, too, heard the wings in the mist. Halfway down the walkway toward the strangers, sword to hand and flanked by two of his flunkies while a third followed up behind, he paused; his darkly suffused face blanched and his pig eyes grew wide.

'They've come,' he whispered, his voice a half-croak. 'Well then, so be it. But before the winged ones tackle us, we take the imposters . . . *Now!*' And with that cry on his lips, crouching as he rushed forward through the shrouding curtain of mist, Harold led his men in a treacherous attack.

Surging out from the swirling grey wall that obscured the deck, startling the crew almost as much as the outsiders they attacked, Harold and his homicidal colleagues were a fearsome sight. He himself wore no helmet and his long damp hair was plastered back on his head. His mouth was open in a twisted, hideous snarl, and his tremendous stature and sheer bulk – plus the fact that the great, dully glinting sword he held on high was all of five feet long – put the finishing touches to the paralysing shock of his appearance.

All in all the element of surprise itself ought to have been sufficient to see Harold's murderous intentions carried through, would have been sufficient but for unforeseen circumstances. One: the bully had made a mistake in allowing his cronies to flank him so closely. The walkway was not wide enough to accommodate three men abreast, certainly not men as huge as the Vikings. Even as they rushed into view of their intended prey, the man on Harold's right slipped on the damp planking, lost his balance, and fell, bringing down the one to the rear. By then de Marigny and Silberhutte were on their feet, reaching for their hand axes, automatically taking up defensive stances.

Then came the second unforeseen circumstance – the sudden intervention of an outside agency. For down out of the mist came Nightmare borne on leathery wings, Nightmare with the pointed ears and dripping fangs of the devil himself. The creature was a bat – fur bellied, yellow-eyed, with a wrinkled black-leather face – but it was almost as big as a man!

Flying between attackers and attacked, the giant bat used the talons of one of its hind limbs to rake Harold's face, opening his cheek in a red slash. He cursed and hacked at the thing with his great sword, but the creature was agile as its smaller cousins of the Motherworld and avoided the Viking's blade without difficulty.

Again and again Harold struck upward at the huge bat until suddenly, following fast upon his last thrust, its talons reached down and caught at the blade near his wrist, snatching it from him. He cursed as, with a shrill whistle of triumph, the creature tossed the weapon aside so that it fell into the sea.

By then the man on Harold's left, who had momentarily stepped back to give the chief's son elbow room, was once more coming in to the attack. He leaped high in the air, striking at the bat and missing, then followed up his action by turning his attention once more to the strangers. Landing in a crouch, he straightened up and whirled his sword at de Marigny. Instinctively, with skill born of his many lessons in the plateau's arenas, the Earthman ducked under the deadly arc to swing the needlepoint of his weapon into the giant's neck. In the next moment blood gushed in a crimson fountain, and the stricken man gave a single, gurgling scream before toppling overboard.

But now more bats had descended from the mist and were flitting hugely over the heads of the Vikings, striking at them with wickedly sharp talons as they rose up from their seats to fight back with savage blows. All was confusion; the mist swirled everywhere; the air was filled with shrill whistlings, screams, and bull roars of rage and pain as the bats took advantage of the momentary havoc to tear and rip.

Harold, defenceless now, still faced the first of these horrors from the sky, and as the great bat struck at him yet again, de Marigny stepped forward and made to intervene. The Earthman was in no way interested in saving Harold's skin, but it fully appeared to him that unless the bats were driven off, all aboard the dragonship were surely doomed.

Before he could strike, however, the Warlord – until now curiously inactive – caught at his arm and stayed the blow. 'No, Henri,' he shouted, 'leave it. If we don't bother them, they won't bother us. It's the Vikings they're after!'

But freely given or not at all, Harold needed no assistance. He was far from crippled by the loss of his sword, and as the bat tore at his chest with its talons, he struck it a massive double-fisted blow in the face. Half-stunned, the creature thudded to the deck, and taking advantage of this brief respite, the chief's son roared: 'Do you see what these so called "emissaries of Ithaqua" are up to, lads? Why, it's *them* called these monsters down on us! See here, they've sided with the bats! Now fight, you dogs, and when we've driven off the fliers, then we'll deal with the traitors . . .'

As he finished yelling, the dazed bat on the deck seemed to recover its senses. Wings outstretched, it flopped toward him and attempted to knock him from his feet. With a blustering battle roar, seeing that the thing was half done for, Harold stepped inside the span of its wings and caught at its soft throat. Forcing its dripping fangs to one side and well away from his face, he locked his mighty arms about its neck.

His remaining pair of cronies, having been amply engaged in their own right prior to this moment, now rushed to assist him. They stabbed at the bat together, their swords passing through its membranous wings and into its soft body. Blood gushed from its wounds and from its gaping mouth, drenching Harold from head to foot; but a moment later he heaved its corpse over the side of the ship to stand there red with gore and furious in the berserk rage that now gripped him.

The mist was lifting a little, and the bats were retreating with it, but in their wake they left a dozen dead or dying Vikings. Nor had the crew of the longship failed to take its toll. The deck was littered with the broken bodies of great bats, and those that yet lived were even now being put to the sword.

'Time we abandoned ship, Henri,' Silberhutte said as Harold's pig eyes lighted upon them where they stood in the stern. 'The big fellow's tasted meat, and we're next on the menu. Can you fly us out of this? The bats are waiting for us.'

'Waiting for us?' the other repeated. 'Then maybe we'd do as well to take our chances here.'

'No, you don't understand. They're waiting to lead us to the Isle of Mountains – to the great cave where the people of the island live – to Moreen . . .'

'But how do you – ?'

'No time now, Henri. Later. And here comes Harold – *look out!*'

Harold had taken two paces toward them, his massive hands reaching. Then, finding himself weaponless, he smatched a sword from one of his men. As he did so, de Marigny shrugged out of his fur jacket and let down his cloak from where he had gathered it at his waist.

As the Earthman's fingers brushed the studs that controlled the cloak in flight, so the Warlord yelled: 'Get aloft, Henri. Quick – I'll grab your legs!'

'They're trying to get away!' Harold roared, and he rushed forward, swinging his sword around his head. De Marigny was already airborne over the deck and bringing the cloak under his expert control when Silberhutte and the chief's son came together in a clash of steel and flying sparks. He looked down and was barely in time to see the fight finish as quickly as it began. For such had been the violence of the shock when the two crashed together that their weapons had shivered into fragments; the metal of their blades – axe and sword alike – had actually shattered!

Harold had then stepped back to hurl the heavy, jagged hilt of his sword at Silberhutte's face. But the Warlord, avoiding the deadly missile, had stepped in close to use the splintered haft of his axe as a club. Swinging it against Harold's neck, he had battered the giant to his knees. Then, as the Texan leaped to grab at de Marigny's legs, so he simultaneously contrived to smash his knee into the Viking's forehead. Once again this combination of blows must surely have killed any normal man, but even as Silberhutte secured his hold on de Marigny's calves and the two drifted aloft, so they could make out the shape of the fallen man moving on the deck below, trying to climb to his feet.

'He must be made of iron!' Silberhutte muttered, shaking his head in disbelief as the cloak now bore them more surely upward into the dispersing mist.

And now, too, the remainder of the crew awoke from

the stupefaction of seeing Harold so swiftly dealt with for the second time by the 'little' stranger. But their awakening was too late, and their cries of rage were of no avail as the cloak-fliers quickly soared out of range. Only one of the many spears thrown after them passed close; the remainder fell well behind, splashing into the sea. Then the ship was momentarily lost to their view as they rose swiftly upward into the chill but rapidly thinning mist.

Seconds later they climbed into open air. Circling high overhead, the bats were beginning to disperse, heading for that island briefly glimpsed before the mist had come down. At this distance and from this elevation, the island's shape could not be discerned, but the cloak-fliers had little doubt that it was the Isle of Mountains.

'Will you be all right, Hank, hanging onto me like that?' de Marigny called down to his passenger.

'I'll be okay,' the Warlord answered. 'Don't worry about me. Just follow the bats.'

'Just as you say – but what makes you so sure they won't turn on us?'

'Because they told me so,' the Warlord returned, laughter in his voice.

'They *what?*' de Marigny shouted. 'How in the name of – '

'They're telepathic, Henri. Most animals are, to one degree or another. Dogs and dolphins are, for sure. You must have noticed how a dog reacts when it senses you're afraid of it? Well, the bats are telepathic, too, only more so. They're highly intelligent, cleverer than dolphins, I'd say. They're probing my mind right now, as they were when I was sleeping. That's why you thought I was having a nightmare. And watch what you're thinking, for they're probably probing you, too!'

'And do they know why we're here, that we're looking for Moreen?'

'Yes, and they know we mean her no harm. If we did . . . well, that would be just too bad.'

For a moment they were quiet and only the whine of the wind in the cloak disturbed the silence. Then, noting that the mist had finally dispersed, leaving the surface of the sea a dull and wave-flecked bronze colour, de Marigny called: 'Hey! Look down there. The bats didn't just pick on Harold's ship.'

Far below the three longships showed against the sea, though height and distance now made it impossible to pick out individuals among the antlike figures that scurried about the decks. One of the ships – drifting quite aimlessly, crippled, with its sail torn and askew – seemed to be completely void of human activity. The other vessels moved in, throwing lines aboard and closing with her.

'Hanarl's ship,' the Warlord grunted. 'She must have been taken completely by surprise. Well, there's nothing we can do – and you must know how we'll be dealt with if ever the Vikings get their hands on us after this. Let's hope they don't catch up with us.'

'You think they'll try?' de Marigny asked, urging more speed from the cloak as the great bats began to draw away.

'Sure of it,' Silberhutte declared. 'It's Thonjolf's one remaining chance to save face – Harold's, too. And don't forget, Henri, somewhere out there, possibly at this very moment, a thousand longships are making sail in this direction. Oh, yes – we'll do well to find Moreen and be far gone from here when those ships arrive . . .'

7

The People of the Cave

When they were well underway and de Marigny could give his attention to things other than the firm control of his flying cloak, he managed to reach down and receive from Silberhutte the fastenings of the other's harness. Not without some difficulty he then clipped his passenger's straps safely into position. Now at last, while the big Texan hung in comparative comfort below, de Marigny was able to work his own dangling legs and stretch them, bringing life back to them after their crushing by Silberhutte's mighty arms.

The three dragonships were mere matchsticks floating far below and behind them by then, while ahead the rocky, natural bastions of the island loomed ever closer. Gradually climbing higher into the sky of Numinos, they had at last seen that indeed the island was in the shape of a regular, five-pointed star. It appeared that in some bygone age there had been five mountains, all of a height and probably volcanic. As time passed, the elements had whittled the formation into a single star-shape on the outside while forming an irregular lake within. Steam and a little smoke, puffing up still from the centre of the vast, still lake, showed that volcanic activity was not yet extinct in the area; but soon, as the bats began a breathtaking descent and de Marigny followed suit, the central lake was lost to sight behind the topmost spires of the exterior mountains.

Down the great bats fell in a spiralling stream, and rushing up to greet them came the jagged fangs of secondary peaks, crested now with tufts of white cloud that formed ever faster as Borea slipped in front of the sun to shut out its light and warming rays. Darkhour was almost here, and so chill the wind howling over the mountains that de Marigny felt obliged to take yet another pinch of Annahilde's warming powder.

Then the winds were suddenly shut off, and the view beyond the mountains disappeared in an instant as the fliers fell below the level of the range to continue their descent oceanward. They were coming down in a bay formed of two of the island's starfish arms, and they could now see and hear the wash of ocean on the rocks far below and marvel at the gaunt appearance of the inhospitable coastline. Here the ocean-facing cliffs rose black and threatening, almost perpendicular from the sea, so that it seemed almost impossible for anyone approaching by ship to gain any sort of foothold upon them.

Stark and bare, the place looked uninhabitable, and yet the fliers were certain that there were people here: the people of the cavern that Silberhutte had seen in telepathic pictures snatched from the minds of the great bats; those same creatures that now skimmed unhesitatingly toward a shadowed entrance whose mouth loomed darkly ominous in the rocky wall some forty feet above the level of the choppy sea.

A few seconds later, hot on the trail of the hindmost bat, the fliers entered a deep high-ceilinged cave. From the entrance to a depth of some fifty feet, the ceiling had been propped up with stout beams fashioned from whole pines – wood which was now black with age, decayed, and sagging – and brackish water dripped from above, splashing on the slimed stone floor. Overhead, showing through a crisscross of heavy beams, the pair saw how badly rotted was the rock of the ceiling, how saturated with the salts of ocean and the nitrous drip of acidic moistures.

Beyond this point de Marigny was forced to cut back their velocity to little more than walking speed. The bat they followed made no attempt to wait for them but disappeared with an amplified burst of fluttering into the darkness of the cave's winding tunnel. In its wake a single high-pitched whistle echoed eerily back to them. Finally, finding themselves flying blind as the light quickly diminished, they were obliged to settle to the moist shingle floor where they waited until their eyes grew more accustomed to the gloom.

'People live in here?' de Marigny inquired as his eyes began to pick out details of the fissurelike tunnel. 'They actually *live* here?'

'No, this is only the entrance,' the Warlord stated matter-of-factly. 'We've some way to go yet before we reach the cavern where the people live. The tunnel goes right back to their cave and even continues beyond it, in the form of old volcanic vents which come out on the inner slopes above the central lake. That lake feeds a lesser pool in the great cave, where the cavern people do their fishing.'

De Marigny looked at his friend in astonishment. 'You got all that telepathically, from the bats?'

The other nodded. 'Yes, and I'm getting other stuff right now.' He peered into the gloomy reaches of the tunnel. 'Actually I should feel quite at home here; there's much about this place that has the atmosphere of the plateau on Borea. And yet . . .'

'Yes?'

'Well, Annahilde was right. It's an effort to stop myself running right out of here. The island's star-shape, you know . . .'

De Marigny nodded. 'I forgot about that. Of course I personally feel nothing.'

'No, you shouldn't. It's just something I'll have to live with for now; but after all, I've had it worse than this before. I was once inside the plateau's forbidden tunnel, which leads down to a cave full of star-stones – the genuine articles – beneath the very heart of the place. By comparison this is only a very small fear.'

De Marigny looked at his companion's dusky outline and found it hard to imagine that the Warlord could fear anything. Presently he said, 'I believe I can see a little better now. Should we press on?'

'Do us good to stretch our legs,' the big Texan nodded. Then: 'Henri, do you mind if I take your axe? You've learned to handle it pretty well, but I've had a lot more firsthand experience. We don't really know for sure what's up ahead, and – '

'Take it by all means,' de Marigny cut in, handing his weapon over. 'In my hands it's only a pick – or an axe, or whatever you want to call it – but with you behind it, the thing's almost an arsenal!'

Moments later, having wrapped the cloak about his waist, de Marigny was ready. Silberhutte, clipping the straps of his harness securely behind his neck, hefted the axe once in his hand and said, 'Well, ready or not, here we come. While we walk, I'll probe ahead and see if I can pick up the bats.'

The Warlord managed a grin that de Marigny sensed rather than saw. 'It was quite a shock for them when they found I could read their minds almost as well as they read mine. They never met a human telepath before. Come to think of it, apart from Armandra's and the mind of one other girl I knew – and not forgetting the alien cesspits of the CCD minds – these are the first genuine telepaths I've been able to contact. One thing I'm sure of is that they're good guys. They don't dislike people.'

'Oh? What of their attack on the longships?' de Marigny asked.

'Their allegiance lies with the people of the cavern,' the Warlord answered, 'especially with Moreen. They knew why the Vikings were coming, and their attack was to show how strongly they disapproved. I don't know what that girl has, but I reckon the bats love her dearly.' After a moment he added: 'Hey, Henri, you'd better worry about that, eh?'

'About what? How do you mean, Hank?'

'Well, didn't old Annahilde say you'd fall for Moreen? It certainly seems like the girl's got something worth falling for!'

'Is that so?' de Marigny soberly answered. 'Well, whatever she's got, surely the last thing we want is any sort of complication. Just look at the circumstances. Can you really see an affair brewing between me and some unknown girl – here on Numinos, in an environment alien as this – as if the trouble we have already isn't enough?'

'Just kidding, Henri,' the Warlord nodded, stepping out a little faster along the tunnel. 'But you have to admit Annahilde's prophesies have been right on target so far, eh?'

When no answer came, he added: 'Forget it.' But de Marigny was pleased to hear the Texan's low chuckle sounding in the darkness. Already his massive companion was forgetting his deep, subconsciously rooted fear of the place, and that could only be a point to the good.

So they set out to walk down the dusty, guano-smelling passage through the mountains, moving in comparative silence, with only the dull echoes of their footsteps to accompany them.

After traversing the first two bends, all remaining exterior light was shut out, but they were thankful to note that the gloom was relieved, however faintly, by a fungus phosphorescence that glowed from the flaky walls. If anything, they were able to go ahead a little faster, though there were stretches here and there where the absence of the patchy fungus threw them into pitch-darkness. Gradually they became used to feeling ahead with their feet and hands; and so they progressed.

Midway through one of these regions of Stygian darkness, where they were to each other's eyes vague outlines seen against a very faintly glowing background, Silberhutte fetched an abrupt halt and grasped his companion's arm. 'Henri, I just got something from the bats. There's danger up ahead . . . Wait a minute . . .'

'Yes?'

The Warlord grunted. 'Some sort of trap. No, it's not meant for us after all. We just have to step warily, that's all.'

Moving even slower now, after some time they reached a spot where a steady breeze blew in their faces. Soon after, from high above, the dim light of Darkhour filtered down through a fissure that reached clear up to the open air. By that feeble light they saw that the tunnel had widened out considerably, that to their right a subterranean ravine now opened, at the foot of which unseen waters gurgled and rushed, hurrying blindly to some unfathomed destination.

Once the fissure was behind them, the breeze all but disappeared, and with its passing, the gloom descended once more; the wide ledge they trod seemed to vanish in the darkness ahead, as did the chasm to their right; the silence was relieved only by the sound of their hushed breathing and the far-off *drip, drip, drip* of falling water. Then, in the distance – a mere flicker at first but quickly brightening – they spied an orange-burning flame whose light beckoned them more rapidly on.

The flambeau – of seaweed drenched in some slow-burning, glutinous resin – was set in a blackened hard-wood bracket fastened to the wall of the tunnel. Its sputtering flame illuminated the ledge, the rough lip of the ravine . . . and something else. A trip wire had been stretched inches above the floor across the entire width of the ledge. Climbing the craggy wall to their left to a height of some thirty feet, the trip was fastened to a wooden beam that protruded from a V-shaped crevice.

Piled above this beam, precariously balanced, great boulders filled the crevice in such a way that even a gentle tug on the trip wire would bring them tumbling down in an avalanche that would sweep anyone on the ledge over the lip of the ravine into oblivion.

'Hardly what you might call a friendly welcome,' the Warlord dryly commented, 'but at least we were warned about it.'

De Marigny nodded. 'It would have been a sight less friendly if they'd left the torch unlit for us! Careful how you go, Hank.'

Gingerly they stepped over the trip wire, uncomfortably aware of the great weight of boulders above, and quickly continued on down the tunnel for a further hundred yards or so. There, rounding a gentle bend and plunging once more into darkness, they spotted in the near-distance the flickering glow of a second torch. Now their progress became much more rapid as they moved between a succession of sputtering torches, evading the booby traps their light invariably disclosed, until at last the tunnel narrowed down to a mere shaft, and the ravine disappeared altogether. Then it was that they emerged into a cave of truly fantastic proportions, where a party of the cavern dwellers awaited them.

At first they did not see the men who waited, so stunned were they at the sight that greeted them as they came out of the tunnel into the vast cavern. Flambeaux seemed to burn everywhere – forming a rough circle around the floor of the cave some fifteen feet or so below them, a circle at least fifty yards across which marked the perimeter of the cave's walls; blazing brightly higher up in the walls of the place, from where the mouths of lesser caves looked down; burning in braziers borne on the decks of rafts that floated on the rippled surface of a pool which occupied at least one-third of the cavern's floor space; and, across the cave proper, illuminating the mouths of a hundred smaller caves which were plainly the dwelling places of family units – so that the whole scene was as of some Troglodyte grotto, or perhaps a diamond mine of the fabled King Solomon. The smoke from all of these sources seemed drawn on a draught of air to a central vent high in the ceiling, so that the atmosphere was surprisingly clean and free of debris.

But even as they gazed at the scene in silence – watching fire-bright fishermen casting their nets from the decks of the rafts and listening to the low chanting of figures where they squatted in some sort of ceremony around a blazing fire – so they became aware of their reception committee. Out from the shadows they stepped, forming a ring about the pair, and a moment later sparks were struck from flints to ignite yet more torches.

Not quite so tall as the average Viking and carrying far less weight, the men of the cave were pallid, their eyes showing a distinct lack of colour. They were clothed in garments made from animal skins or furs, many of which appeared to have been woven from the soft fur of the great bats. None of them were youngsters, the majority appearing to be in their thirties or older; and all of them seemed to have stooped shoulders, a stigma which was very prominent among the more obviously aged.

'We come in peace,' de Marigny offered when a few moments had passed in uneasy silence.

'Aye, we know that,' said one greybeard stepping forward and holding his torch high. 'If you did not, then the bats would have struck you down.'

The same man turned to Silberhutte, eyeing first the hand axe and then the face of the man who held it. 'Since you come in peace, you will surely not need that.'

'Ah?' the Warlord started, then saw the old man's meaning. He quickly put the weapon away in his belt. 'Your pardon,' he said. 'We did not know what to expect.'

Now a somewhat younger man stepped forward, his face firm but friendly in the light of the torches. 'Before we welcome you more properly,' he said, 'there are certain formalities of ritual. We will tell you what we have to offer you, and you will say how you will make payment for our hospitality.'

As the other two stepped back, so a third man came to the fore. He said: 'We offer you the shelter of the cave and its warmth, the fellowship of the bats, the flesh of the beasts of the inner slopes and their furs, the mushrooms of the caves, the water of the pool that you may drink and its fishes that you may eat. All of these things we offer. How are you to make payment?'

The two looked at each other. Finally de Marigny spoke. 'How shall I answer?' he asked.

The greybeard who had first spoken came forward again and grasped his arm. 'Answer in your own way,' he advised.

'Very well . . .' De Marigny considered for a moment, then said: 'We thank you for all you offer. For however short a span we remain with you, we gratefully accept these things. We will pay for them with our friendship, with our respect for your laws, and with – with – '

'With information,' the Warlord cut in, seeing de Marigny's difficulty. 'Information which could well mean life or death for all of you!'

'Information? Life or death? Speak on,' commanded the elder.

'The Vikings are coming – all of them,' Silberhutte continued. 'A thousand longships sent by order of Ithaqua against the Isle of Mountains. They'll find your cave – from the sea or by climbing the mountains to the inner slopes, it makes little difference – and they are sworn to kill all they find. All except the woman Moreen, which Ithaqua the Wind-Walker claims as his own. That is the information we bring.'

The elder slowly nodded. 'Aye, we thought that might happen sooner or later.' Then, more urgently he asked, 'How much time do we have?'

Silberhutte shrugged. 'Not long. We believe that the Vikings may be converging on your island even now. Certainly three ships from the clan of Thonjolf are already in these waters.'

'Then there remains only one more question, or perhaps two,' the elder muttered. Suddenly he seemed lost for words, strangely embarrassed, but at last he found his tongue:

'We keep watches on the sea approaches; the higher peaks are constantly manned, as is the passageway from the sea. Just before you came, we were forewarned by the young man on watch at the mouth of the tunnel. He is a very young man and easily excited, but he says that when you came, you followed the bats, and that like the bats you – '

'Like them we flew, yes,' de Marigny spoke up, anticipating the question. 'This cloak I wear has the power of flight. It carries us through the air at great speed. I brought it with me from the Motherworld. The Warlord, too, is a stranger in your world, for he hails from Borea, the World of the Winds. Our purpose in coming here is to find the woman Moreen, for we think she may be able to help us in our quest . . .' Here de Marigny broke off, for as he had spoken, his voice had been progressively drowned out by a rapidly rising babble from the surrounding circle of cave dwellers.

His and Silberhutte's revelations, coming thick and fast, had finally broken through the reserve – real or assumed – that the men of the caves had initially displayed. Now the air was full of such muttered words and phrases as: 'The Motherworld! Borea! A *thousand* longships! The woman Moreen! A flying cloak!'

At last the hunched-up old greybeard – who appeared to

be the main spokesman for the group, possibly the leader of the entire subterranean clan – held up his hands and cried: 'Hold! There is much to be said and little enough time for saying it. There must be an orderly council meeting as soon as one can be arranged, but before that – ' He turned back to the strangers.

'You,' he spoke to Silberhutte. 'You have the appearance and the build of a great warrior, even though you are not a very tall man, and your friend calls you "Warlord." And you,' he looked at de Marigny. 'You wear a flying cloak that carries you through the skies like a bird. That is a wonder I must see. And in addition, though you would not seem to be wizards, you say you come from distant worlds! Very well,' he nodded, 'we accept that you control great powers; it remains to be seen how well you use them. And so, before I call a grand meeting of the council, there is one more thing I must know. When the Vikings come, will you – '

'Yes, we will,' Silberhutte interrupted. 'If we are still here when the Vikings come, we'll help you defend yourselves as best we can.' He turned to his companion. 'Right, Henri?'

'Right!' said the other. And from somewhere high in one of the many deep dark recesses of the ceiling, a series of shrill, eerie whistlings greeted their decision with approval . . .

8
Moreen

From that time onward – following the meeting of the council and during the feast prepared in their honour that followed it; and then through the drinking, talking, and great round of introductions – time and again the newcomers would ask to see Moreen, only to be told that for the moment this was out of the question. Darkhour was not long passed, and no one would venture to guide them to Moreen until the way was fully lighted by the strange auroral rays of the sun.

For she did not dwell in the cavern itself – was unable to bear the weight of the mountain above – but preferred the air of the inner slopes, of the forest and the five mountains, particularly that peak whose inner face housed her in a cave of her own. There she dwelled, far across and high above the deep central lake, and there they would doubtless find her with her retinue of great bats – but not until after Darkhour. Now they must rest themselves and benefit from the good food and drink they had consumed. They could sleep easy in the knowledge that they were with friends, and when they awakened, that would be time enough for them to go out and seek Moreen.

For all that, the proposed itinerary of the cavern folk seemed to make good sense. The thought of finding the mysterious Moreen remained uppermost in de Marigny's mind; of finding her, yes, and of having her decipher those cryptic symbols scrawled upon a scrap of soft hide by Annahilde. Surely, he told himself, he must be closer now to recovering the time-clock than at any time since leaving Borea; and such was the mental fever this thought wrought in his mind that sleep seemed almost impossible.

Nevertheless he did sleep, finally succumbing to the combination of weariness and strain that hung over from the nerve-racking journey through the midnight tunnel; and to the soporific effect of an amount of ale consumed during the feast; but it was in no way a peaceful sleep.

Twice he started awake from unremembered nightmares upon his bed of furs, bathed in the glow of the fire that burned brightly before the hollow in the cave's wall that housed his own and Silberhutte's recumbent forms. On both occasions he cast about nervously with his eyes in the gloom beyond the flickering flames, observing on ledges across the great cave the moving fires that told of patrolling watches. But it was not until he awoke for the third time that he noticed the huge bat where it hung upside down, clinging to an overhang of rock like some weird watchdog not far above where he lay.

The eyes of the creature, inverted, burned upon his briefly, then turned to Silberhutte's still form. The Warlord stirred for a moment and his body tensed . . . but then he settled back on his furs, sighed deeply, and relaxed. After awhile the great creature turned its eyes once more upon de Marigny, and he fancied it sensed his restlessness.

At once, as if from nowhere, driving out all agitation and frustration, comforting sensations began to fill his mind. Without feeling any resentment, he knew that indeed this monstrous creature, whose smaller cousins of Earth were synonymous with Night and all the terrors of midnight abysses – was lulling him to sleep, soothing his fears, and calming his troubled mind; and so persuasive was its hypnotic power that he gave himself up entirely into its care and quickly fell into a deep, satisfying, and dreamless sleep.

. . . And it was the leathery beating of that same creature's wings that awakened him hours later; that and Silberhutte's terse command, breaking into his subconscious, that he should get up. Raising himself onto one elbow, de Marigny saw the Warlord crouching upon his own bed and staring into the eyes of the huge bat where it hovered, buffeting the air with mighty sweeps of its wings. The creature's movements were full of a visible urgency, de Marigny could see that, but the nature of what it imparted to the Texan was far beyond his grasp. Though Titus Crow had once hinted that he was slightly telepathic, de Marigny had little practical knowledge of the art.

He could guess, however, and guessing, his heart sank. For the Warlord had made a promise, and de Marigny knew that it could not be broken. 'The Vikings?' he queried.

Silberhutte, without taking his eyes from those of the furred monster whose motions scattered the ashes of the fire and caused its embers to glow bright red, merely nodded for an answer.

'They're here?' de Marigny pressed. 'Already?'

'Only hours away, Henri, and there's much to do.'

'I know,' a trace of bitterness crept into de Marigny's voice. 'We promised we'd help . . .'

'No,' the Warlord quickly answered, turning toward him, 'I promised.'

The great bat, satisfied at last that its message was understood, flew off into the cavern's gloom as Silberhutte grasped de Marigny's shoulder. 'I promised, Henri,' he repeated, 'and it's up to me to make that promise good.'

'But I – '

'No buts, friend. I fixed it with old Skaldsson the chief, right after the feast. You are to go hunt out Moreen, while I take a closer look at the tunnel's defences. The peaks should be easily enough defended – a dozen men could start avalanches down the outer slopes that would keep out the entire army of Vikings for a long time – but the tunnel is different again. Those booby traps they've rigged up will create all hell when they hit, but only for a moment. When the boulders stop rolling the Vikings will come on again, more angry than before, and they'll take it out on the cavern folk.'

'You think they'll get this far?' the other asked.

Silberhutte nodded. 'I don't doubt it. There are too many of them: thousands of them in a great fleet of long-ships with Harold bringing them in. I was shown them through the mind of the great bat. Some of its brothers are keeping an eye on the fleet even now, picking off Vikings whenever they get the chance – and paying dearly for their audacity!'

'But I can't just go off chasing this girl while you – '

Again the Warlord cut him off: 'You have to, Henri. We have to get that cryptogram deciphered before we can find the time-clock. For all we know the clock is within easy reach, and with it – '

'We could turn back the entire Viking force!'

'Right!' The Warlord clapped him on the shoulder. 'While you're away, I'll get in touch with Armandra. With or without the clock we may have to be out of here quickly. Also I have my work cut out in the tunnel. There must be dozens of places where additional booby traps can be rigged up. If I take a gang of the cavern folk and start near the entrance, we can play a delaying game all along the tunnel's length. By then, using the flying cloak, you should be safely back from your meeting with Moreen.'

'But surely I should be back long before then,' de Marigny protested, frowning. 'I mean, the Vikings are still hours away.'

'That's right, and you still have to get out of here. The exits from here to the inner valley are long, dark, winding, and treacherous. But . . .' The Warlord paused. 'Wait, I have an idea.'

'An idea? About what?'

'We've been thinking in terms of a human guide to get you to Moreen. However . . .' Again he paused, then frowned and half-closed his eyes. He held up his hand to silence de Marigny as the other started to question his meaning.

Moments later there came the throb of leathery wings and one of the great bats hovered close by. The Warlord opened his eyes wide and stared at the bat, and once more de Marigny watched their silent 'conversation.' Finally the bat flew off and Silberhutte turned to his friend with a grin.

Before the Warlord could speak, de Marigny guessed: 'A bat? My guide is to be a bat?'

'Right. There's one on its way from Moreen right now. Flying your cloak, you'll follow it out along one of the exit tunnels to the inner slopes. Once out in the open, it will take you straight across the lake to Moreen.'

'I'm to fly blind through the tunnel?'

'Carry a torch,' the other answered. 'Is that feasible?'

'I wouldn't really care to try it,' de Marigny replied. 'What if the cloak catches fire? I don't know how – '

'Then try to attach yourself to your guide in some way or other,' Silberhutte cut in. 'Give it some thought. Getting to Moreen has to be your problem, Henri. As for me: I'm off to get things moving. The cavern folk are not telepathic; so far they don't know that the Vikings are almost here. Well, they should have recovered from their feast by now. I certainly hope so. They're going to need all of their strength and wits before very much longer!'

Flying in darkness behind the great creature to which he was loosely tethered – not having to worry about obstacles but merely ensuring that his forward speed and direction were compatible with those of the bat; being towed, if anything, like some blind, sentient balloon behind his constantly, weirdly whistling 'guide' – de Marigny thought back on that period of activity immediately preceding his departure from the great cavern. He had gone with

Silberhutte to warn the cavern folk of their imminent danger, and while the Warlord had assumed command of the fighting forces, he had spoken long and earnestly with the chief, old Arnrik Skaldsson. Their topic had been Moreen.

The chief had been able to tell him much. Since her coming to the Isle of Mountains, Moreen might easily have had her pick of the younger unattached men of the cavern, of which there were several, but had preferred a lone existence accompanied only by her bats on the slopes of the inner valley. It seemed that before she came here, a witch-wife had promised her that the time would come when a man would find her – a man as good and free in spirit as she herself was good and free – one she could love. And of course she had shunned the great cavern from the first, had hated the idea of being shut in; for she was a 'warm one' and her love of open skies and freshening breezes could not be fulfilled below ground.

The cavern folk, on the other hand, for the most part could not bear to be too long out in the open. They feared Ithaqua mightily, most of them having fled his wrath to come to the island in the first place, and they associated the Wind-Walker with vast, wide-open skies. Their agoraphobia could not, however, preclude their essential watch duties on the peaks, nor did it stop certain persistent types from visiting Moreen when circumstances permitted and attempting to woo her over.

She would have none of it; for to give herself to a man of the cavern would mean following him into the constant gloom of the cavern world, and hers was an exceptionally free spirit. Why should she take a husband when already her bats provided so adequately for her? Five in number, those creatures which had bound themselves to her brought her wildfowl from the wooded inner slopes, fishes from the deep lake; even her clothing was woven of their soft fur. They were her constant companions.

Aye, and they were her protection, too, or so old Skaldsson had told de Marigny. Twice when men had thought to bring her forcibly to the cavern (they were, after all, Vikings or the sons of Vikings, and as such wilful and less than diplomatic in dealing with women), they had returned scratched, bruised, and bloodied from their encounters with Moreen's providers and protectors.

She could have had those men killed, little doubt of that, but such was not her nature. She was kind and gentle and free, and she intended to stay that way. She desired neither the cavern's safety nor its restrictions, nor indeed the caresses of any dweller therein. But if de Marigny had questions to ask of her, surely she would answer all of them willingly and truthfully if she could, and certainly she would enjoy his company for a little while, she who lived apart from the cavern clan and dwelled halfway up a mountain.

These things that the chief had told him, together with many other scraps of knowledge, passed in kaleidoscope review through de Marigny's mind as he automatically answered the gentle tug of his guideline in the dark. Quite apart from Moreen he thought of Silberhutte and his plan to fight a delaying action along the length of the tunnel from the sea. He could not help feeling a little guilty that he was to have no part in that fight. Perhaps if he could get this meeting with Moreen quickly and satisfactorily over and done with . . .

The Warlord had said he would contact Armandra, ask her to conjure up another tornado – one with its roots right here on Numinos – to carry them to their final destination, wherever that might be. Just how the Woman of the Winds would contrive to do that, de Marigny could hardly guess, but Silberhutte seemed sure enough of the thing's mechanics. According to him the idea's feasibility was not the crucial factor; the crux of the matter lay in their ability to rendezvous with the tornado when it came.

All of these things had passed through de Marigny's thoughts several times before he spied ahead, partly obscured by the nightmare shape of his guide as it manoeuvred the jaggedly tortuous sinuses of this long-dead volcanic vent, a distant fragment of dull daylight that hung in darkness like a damply luminous rag. Soon, as the light improved, he was able to pick out the features of the treacherous walls as they moved slowly by, following which the passage rapidly widened and the bat picked up speed.

De Marigny could almost sense the relief of his huge 'blind dog' as it now sped ahead, no longer constrained by concern for its merely human charge. The muscles powering its wings must have been close to exhaustion. No bird, except perhaps the hawk with its ability to hover, could have managed the job; even a hawk must surely have crashed and come to grief in the absolute darkness.

Now there was no holding the bat, and such was the turmoil of air left in its wake that de Marigny's control of the cloak was in constant jeopardy. He quickly cut himself loose from his guide, then accelerated to maximum velocity as the bat, free at last of its aerial anchor, shot ahead on throbbing wings.

Out they sped across the inner lake, the five peaks towering overhead. Straight as the path of an arrow flew the great bat with de Marigny not too far behind. Somewhere over there, at the other side of the lake, the woman Moreen had her cave. It would not be long now before de Marigny knew the answer to his one, all-important question.

Moreen . . . The 'woman' Moreen, in actuality little more than a girl. Almost twenty years of age and all of them spent on Numinos, an alien moon in an alien universe.

Moreen of the golden hair, shoulder length and shining with its own lustrous light; Moreen of the wide, bright blue eyes. Her natural, intrinsic warmth covered her like a blanket only ever torn aside by Ithaqua, black walker on the winds that blow forever between the worlds.

Tiny Moreen, at least by Numinosian standards. Sixty-four inches of unaffected grace, loveliness, youthful lithe-ness, and not-quite innocence; for she had seen the Wind-Walker at his worst, and no one could remain wholly innocent after that. To be audience to it, even captive audience, was to be defiled.

Moreen: mortal and fragile as are all human beings, nevertheless carrying a strength within her which, merci-fully, made it possible for her to put aside the past – blot it from her mind to a wide extent – until those long-lost loved ones, her father and poor, maddened mother, aye, and Garven too, all of them were only bright memories that terminated where the Wind-Walker had intruded to score them from her mind.

Moreen of the mountain – laughing Moreen – who had a love of all living things with but one exception: the monster Ithaqua, for whom her heart held only hatred.

Moreen . . .

At Darkhour, as was her wont, she had lain in the mouth of her cave on a comfortable bed of bracken covered with soft skins, her body bathed in the glow of a fire that burned ruddily in a hearth of piled stones. She had absently listened to the rustle of great wings from the rear of her cave where her bats hung together from the stalactite ceiling like a cluster of strange fruit; and she had watched the reflective surface of the still lake far below for the ripple and wash of auroral heavens and the images of pale stars which only ever showed at Darkhour.

She had observed, too, the campfires of the watchers on the peaks across the lake. Such fires told of the presence of men from the great cavern; and she had shuddered at the

375

thought of that vast and (to her) tomblike subterranean grotto.

Oh, periodically they would come to her, those younger men of the cavern, boasting and strutting and attempting her seduction, to no avail. Though loneliness hurt her more and more, she would not go with them; not to their cavern world, to the smoky, airless pits of darkness where they hid like pallid cockroaches from a giant's tread – from the wrath of Ithaqua.

Yet their campfires at Darkhour comforted her, making her feel less lonely. And on those rare occasions when she recalled how some of her suitors had been fairly handsome men, for all their pallor, then she would remember Annahilde's promise: that one day a real man would come to her – a *man*, not some stooped, burrowing mole in man's guise.

Well, her witch-wife aunt's prophesy had best reveal itself soon, for the warming powders were four-fifths used up. Without the powder, given her by Annahilde, Moreen were long since dead; or at least gone from here to seek warmth at the fires of the cavern, which to her seemed worse than death. She knew this all too well and constantly wore the precious packet about her neck, fingering it now and then for reassurance. She wore very little else, for their seemed nothing of value in false modesty (who was there to see her near-nakedness here?), and the warming powder turned even the chillest wind to a balmy breeze. But when the last of the powder was gone, which it would be before she was very much older, what then?

Perhaps her man would find her before then. Annahilde had said it would be so.

With these thoughts in her mind and lulled by the soft glow of the distant fires and the whirl of pastel reflections in the lake, Moreen had slept, only waking when it was lighter and the weirdly streaming orb of the sun was visible as a glowing bulge on Borea's grey flank.

She had noticed at once that the bats were active again with an unaccustomed agitation and wondered why. They had been acting this way on and off for some time now, and their excitement puzzled her. If only she could read their minds, as she knew they read hers. Then, for no apparent reason, one of the bats had left in great haste, flitting hugely across the lake toward the opposite shore. Something was in the wind, that was plain, and Moreen guessed that it must somehow concern her.

Normally she might have gone down to the lake to bathe, picking her way down the steep path she knew so well, but on this occasion she had not done so, being satisfied merely to splash her face and breasts with the chill waters of a streamlet cascading from on high. Up here she could keep watch over the entire lake and its surrounding inner slopes, though she knew not what she expected to see.

Then, after a long time, she had grown bored and thought to make her way down to the trees that grew tall and dense where the slope was less steep not too far below and to one side of her lofty aerie. There she could play with the smaller animals that lived in the trees, and with the tiny coloured birds, all of which came to her as household dogs answered the calls of their masters in the Viking village she had known as a girl.

It was as she was putting on knee-length trousers made from the pelt of a white fox, with a halter to match, that she noted increasing activity in the four bats within the cave. Suddenly they fell in rapid succession from the shadowy ceiling and glided out of the cave on still wings, barely disturbing the air. Outside in the wan Numinosian light, they circled overhead before heading out over the lake. Gazing after them, Moreen frowned – until she picked out the oncoming form of the fifth creature.

So, they had gone to welcome their brother on his return: four forms converging on a fifth high over the grey lake. Five of them now, her five familiars, who had followed after her like faithful watchdogs when she left the great cavern to come and live here. Five monstrous bats that loved her as –

Five?

No, six!

Six of them? Moreen's eyes narrowed and her frown deepened. The single bone button of her halter slipped unfastened, forgotten, from her fingers as the flying figures drew closer. They wheeled high overhead, almost level with the rocky saddle between the two nearest peaks, then began to descend.

At last Moreen could see all six figures quite clearly. Now her mouth fell open and she froze where she stood, trembling in every limb, close to the mouth of her cave. The blood had seemed to drain from her in a moment.

The sixth flier was . . . a man?

Moreen's hand flew to her mouth. A man – or a monster! Her experience of man-shapes that walked on the wind in no way concerned human beings. Only Ithaqua to her knowledge could do that. But this could hardly be the Wind-Walker, neither him nor any manifestation of him. No, for a bat – one of *her* bats – had brought him here; and while all of the huge creatures were excited, none of them seemed afraid or concerned for her safety.

It must then be a man, a man in a cloak with wings almost as big as those of the bats themselves. A handsome man, more young than old, who smiled at her now as he made an expert landing a half-dozen paces away.

The bats, hovering nervously, thrust the air this way and that with their throbbing wings. Facing the stranger, still frozen in amazement, Moreen saw his lips form her name, heard him say it as a question:

'Moreen?'

She shook off her paralysis. 'Yes, I am Moreen.'

A gust of disturbed air tugged aside her halter, which she automatically trapped with her elbow before it could blow away altogether. For a moment, caught unawares, de Marigny stared at her. Then, colouring, he averted his gaze.

Moreen, seeing his confusion and knowing its cause, laughed and finally managed to button her halter. She said: 'You know me – and yet you are a stranger.'

'Yes,' he nodded, stepping closer. 'I'm a stranger – but I'm a friend, too.'

'You're no Viking,' she stated with certainty. 'Nor are you of the cavern folk. Your back is too straight, and your skin's not pale like theirs. Do you have a name? Who are you?'

'I'm called Henri,' he answered. 'And no, I'm not a man of Numinos. It's a long story, one we've really no time for now, but I hail from the Motherworld. Annahilde sent me to – '

'Annahilde?' In a moment the look on her face went from puzzlement through astonishment to sheer joy. 'Annahilde sent you?' She breathed the words.

A moment more and she had flown into his arms, almost throwing him from his feet. 'Then you must be the one!'

'I must?' de Marigny repeated, not quite knowing what to do with his hands. Then, from nowhere, certain words of the witch-wife, forgotten until now, came back to him:

'*You will surely fall in love with her; it can hardly be otherwise!*'

'You are the one, aren't you?' the girl asked, her wide eyes anxiously searching his face.

'Why, I – ' He paused, lost for words, brain whirling, before finally wrapping his arms firmly about her suddenly snuggling form.

'Yes?' she pressed him, sweet breath fanning his neck, the smell of everything good filling his nostrils, his heart.

And de Marigny knew then what Annahilde had meant, and that seer or none she had been absolutely right.

'Oh, I'm the one, all right,' he answered at last. 'It could hardly be otherwise . . .'

379

9

Under Attack!

Long before Hank Silberhutte and his ten men of the cavern had reached the seaward entrance to the fissure, the Warlord knew the worst: that the Vikings were closer than he had believed and that there would be no time to build further defences against them.

This bad news came to him first from the lips of the lone watchkeeper from the mouth of the tunnel, racing back to the cavern with the grim news; secondly, it was relayed to him via the minds of a pair of wounded bats limping home from a fight aboard one of the longships. The bats were the sole survivors of a party of six of the great, intelligent creatures, and they were able to tell Silberhutte much.

The enemy fleet was closing rapidly with the island (the bats informed), ringing it about and sailing in from all sides. Furthermore, while there were those aboard the ships who knew of the tunnel entrance to the cavern and while doubtless many of the Vikings would land there, the tunnel could only accommodate so many. The invaders appreciated this fact too; thousands of them, believing that the ridges between the peaks would be mainly unguarded, intended to scale them and thus make their way to the inner slopes. By now there would be many defenders in the mountainous heights, and many more climbing the inner slopes from the volcanic vents, but there could never be enough.

Quite simply, the men of the cavern were outnumbered by at least thirty to one! Therefore, while the main shaft from the sea could probably be held for a very long time, plainly the crucial battles must in the end be fought on the heights and in the volcanic vents. To place too much emphasis in the main tunnel would therefore be a waste of time and manpower. Instead it would be better if that tunnel were blocked completely, and the way to do this was readily at hand.

Years ago the cavern folk had prepared for just such an emergency, propping up the unstable and rotting ceiling of the fissure at its entrance. The Warlord recalled having seen the evidence of this operation when first arriving on the island with de Marigny – the massive beams and props that held up the slimy, nitrous ceiling. Now those supports must be removed, allowing gravity, nature, and thousands of tons of rock and ocean-rotted debris to seal the fissure forever. Once that was done, then the party could return to the cavern, and pass through the volcanic vents climbing the inner slopes to reinforce the defenders of the saddles between the five peaks.

Less than one hundred yards from the tunnel's mouth, however, with the sound of the ocean loud in their ears, they knew that before they could destroy the entrance, they must first clear it of invaders. For a handful of Vikings were already in the tunnel and more were climbing the sea cliff from their longships. Waiting in the gloom, invisible to the silhouetted, helmeted Vikings, the Warlord and his party listened for a moment to the loud, boastful conversation of the invaders – and to the frightened voices of more than a few whose dread of the Isle of Mountains was obviously a terror within them – before making a hurried, whispered plan of campaign.

Silberhutte measured and cut a length of heavy rope, knotted one end, and stood with it close to a wall of the tunnel. The heaviest of his colleagues did the same with the other end of the rope, taking up a like position by the opposite wall. Then, with the rope held taut between them and the remainder of the party following up behind, uttering bloodthirsty shrieks and war cries which the tunnel magnified tenfold, they rushed forward upon the startled, unsuspecting Vikings.

Half a dozen of the invaders were speared where they stood; the rest became caught up in the rope and were hurled by it and the crush of men behind it from the mouth of the tunnel to fall into the sea. At once axes and spears were flying between the tunnel's mouth and the decks of the dragonships bobbing below, and the air became thick with curses, screams and shouts.

Moments later, avoiding the flying weapons that clattered all around them, the Warlord's party tossed the corpses of the slain Vikings down into the sea. Then Silberhutte was able to take stock. Two of his men had lost their lives, and one other had a bad wound. The Warlord quickly ordered that the injured man be helped back to the cavern, which left only himself and five others to attend to the sealing of the entrance.

While Silberhutte and two others collected shields and spears of fallen Vikings with which to guard the narrow ledge in front of the entrance, the remaining men formed a demolition team and began tying ropes to the bases of the lesser beams that supported the rotting ceiling. Throughout, heavy grappling irons continued to land on the ledge and in the entrance, several of which found purchase. The Warlord and his colleagues were responsible for disengaging these grapples, thus ensuring that no more of the raiders gained a foothold. This was in no way a simple task; every grapple that flashed into the wide entrance was accompanied by half a dozen spears and the occasional axe.

Just as the demolition party was completing its preparations, a hurled grapple struck the man on Silberhutte's left, one of its barbed tines hooking into his thigh. Before anything could be done, he had been yanked screaming into empty air, his shield and spear flying free. He landed half-in, half-out of a longship forty feet below, breaking his back and dying instantly.

Now the Vikings redoubled their efforts, and two of them actually struggled their way to the rim of the ledge before Silberhutte cut them down. The Warlord was completely dispassionate and efficient in his killing, ruthless as his early days on Borea had taught him to be; but he was just as ready to disengage when the toiling team behind him called for his assistance.

Drawing back into the entrance, he cursed as a spear flashed into view and skewered his right-hand man through the breast, killing him outright. Then, wasting no more time, he joined the remaining trio of cave dwellers where they strained at the heavy ropes. By the time Silberhutte was able to wrap a rope round his waist and add his weight to the effort, more of the invaders were clambering up onto the ledge. Their energies had been spent in vain, however, for no sooner were five or six established and moving cautiously, blindly into the dark interior of the tunnel than – with a snapping of timbers and a rumbling of fractured rock – the first section of the ceiling crashed down upon them, burying them beneath untold tons of boulders and rubble.

Deep within the tunnel, momentarily suffocated by complete darkness and billowing clouds of dust, the jubilant four moved quickly back as debris continued to rain down from the sagging ceiling. Finally a torch was struck and, as a second section of the tunnel collapsed behind them, Silberhutte and his small force hurried back the way they had come.

It was time now for the Warlord to seek out de Marigny. Pressure was building up far too rapidly in the cauldron that was Numinos, particularly on the Isle of the Five Mountains. The sooner the secret of Annahilde's runes was revealed – and the time-clock discovered and reclaimed – the better . . .

* * *

Silberhutte got back to the cavern minutes after de Marigny's own arrival. The latter, having flown up above the peaks on leaving Moreen (who still would not go down into the island's interior), had seen the longships in their hundreds where they were anchored about the island, their crews grimly preparing for their assault upon the arduous slopes. He had warned the cavern folk of the enormity of the peril and had then sent out the cavern's rear guard, a pitiful band of one hundred and fifty men, to strengthen the thin ranks of the three hundred already gone to defend the ring of mountain peaks.

While Moreen's own mountain – farthest from the cavern and unguarded when last de Marigny had seen it, though a stream of men from the cavern had been heading toward it along the high saddles – was also the tallest of the five peaks and the most sheer oceanward, nevertheless the Earthman was frantic with worry over the girl. He had promised to return for her, would not have left her in the first place but for the need to carry her translation of Annahilde's message to Silberhutte.

She had however assured him that she would be safe – that if the Vikings came in his absence, her bats would protect her – before wishing him well as he went reluctantly off again, once more in tandem behind the strongest of her retainers. The trip back through the volcanic blow-hole had been quicker this time, the way lighted by flaring flambeaux by whose light parties of the cavern's women worked to fortify the vents against attack; and de Marigny had reckoned not unreasonably that indeed this was where the final battles would be fought.

All of these things de Marigny told to Silberhutte in return for the Warlord's own news, but when he paused, there were several very important things left unsaid. Now Silberhutte pressed the other for additional information:

'And the time-clock? Did you find out where it is?'

'Dromos,' answered the other, seemingly surprised.

'Didn't I mention it?' He was visibly on edge and kept eyeing the shadowed mouths of the vents close to where they stood. 'The Ice-Priests of Dromos have it. But – '

'But what, my friend? I half-suspected that Ithaqua hadn't left the clock here on Numinos. What I didn't suspect was that Annahilde's prophesy would work out so well – that she'd get all her own way.'

'Her own way?' de Marigny repeated as the Warlord donned his part of the cloak's harness.

'She was hoping and praying that you'd fall for the girl,' Silberhutte explained his meaning. 'Well, it seems to me that you have. And you're the one who wanted "no complications!"'

'Listen,' de Marigny ignored his friend's knowing grin. 'I have it all worked out. We two weigh something less than normal here on Numinos, right?'

'Three-quarters normal, yes.'

'Well then, that means – '

' – That the cloak can probably manage all three of us? Yes, it probably can, at least here on Numinos. I'm way ahead of you, Henri, and it looks like I'll have to go along with you. I only hope that this girl of yours doesn't slow us down, that's all. Dromos is different again from Numinos – but I'll tell you what I know about that when we're on our way. Right now we have to get out into the open air before I can start things moving.'

'How do you mean?' asked de Marigny, lifting the cloak up above the floor of the cavern and taking the other's weight, then flying slowly into the main vent. 'What's your plan?'

'My plan? Any plan I might have had would be changed beyond recognition by now. The idea was that if we found the clock here on Numinos, we'd pick it up and that would be that. But, having an idea that Ithaqua might have taken it to Dromos, I put it to Armandra, and she told me how we could go about getting there if we had to. Well, now we have to – but it's going to be a hell of a job, that's a promise. And it won't be any easier now we've the girl to allow for.'

'About Moreen – ' de Marigny began.

'Don't tell me,' the Warlord cut him off. 'It's written all over your face. Anyway, if she's half what Annahilde described, a man would be a fool to leave her behind.'

'When you see her, you can judge for yourself,' de Marigny answered. 'As for now, I'll have to concentrate on what I'm doing, get us through this damned snake of a hole as fast as I can.'

'Yes. Well, I won't bother you,' the other grunted. 'I'll spend the time "chatting" with my better half, let her know what's going on.'

Now in silence the cloak flew rapidly between a string of flaring, shadow-casting torches, passing the occasional group of frantically toiling women along the way. Without exception the women wished them all speed, urging them onward with approving cries and gestures; and so they swept eerily on through the winding volcanic flue.

De Marigny's urgency was clearly visible in the way he took chances in the darker stretches of the vent, but his handling of the cloak was now inspired. Despite the fact that his hideous guide had long since deserted him to return to Moreen, he flew faster than he had on either of his previous trips. Even so, it seemed to take hours before they finally flew out into daylight.

And it was at once apparent that fighting was already in progress. Even in the dim light of Numinos the glint of metal could be seen in the saddles between the three lesser peaks, and the faint shouts and screams of furious contests echoed down to the fliers through the ominously still air.

Gaining height the better to see the action in the saddles, the pair were relieved to note that the cavern folk were getting the better of their adversaries. At present only small groups of Vikings were reaching the ridges, and that only after fighting their way through continual avalanches of boulders released by the defenders. Tired from the climb and bruised by flying rocks, they were easily picked off as soon as they attained the saddles; but greater numbers were not too far behind. It would not be long before they were too many for the defenders to handle.

Racing high over the lake, the adventurers felt a warm updraught from its still volcanic centre; then, ahead, Moreen's peak rose up before them; and –

– And on its uppermost slope there was a clouding of dust, the glitter of whirling weapons, and a vast and frenzied throbbing of bat wings!

Ten, a dozen Vikings engaged Moreen's monstrous protectors at not too great a height above her refuge; and two more, armed to the teeth, slid recklessly down a shale slope immediately above the low overhang that sheltered her cave. Then de Marigny saw the girl herself, hair streaming behind her as she plunged in a near-panic flight down the steep slope toward a green stand of tall, thickly grown pines.

They were after her, those two heathens, and their prime reason for being here seemed completely forgotten in the excitement of the chase. There was no saying what they would do to the girl when they caught her . . .

10

Warlords of the Winds

Unseen, swooping down upon Moreen's pursuers from above and behind, the fliers made to deliver a surprise attack. De Marigny felt the cloak yaw slightly and saw that the Warlord had freed himself from the harness, that he hung now by his arms alone. Then, close in behind the excited, scrabbling raiders, the cloak yawed again, more wildly this time, before shooting skyward as Silberhutte cast himself free.

Hurtling between the unsuspecting Vikings, whose eyes saw only the fleeing Moreen, Silberhutte caught them up in his powerful arms. This had the effect of braking his own speed while rapidly accelerating theirs, so that they shot headfirst out over the overhang to crash down in front of the girl's now empty cave. The Warlord landed light as a cat between them, noting that one lay still, his head at an odd angle. Better for the other if he, too, had shown no sign of life; instead he made to climb shakily to his feet, his helmeted skull offering itself as a target for the exiled Earthman's weapon.

Up above, once more in control of the cloak, de Marigny saw metal shatter, blood and brains flying, heard a single gurgling shriek, then glided on after the stumbling, fearful girl.

'Moreen, it's me – don't run!'

At the sound of his voice she fell back onto her fur-clad rump, skidded a few feet while clutching at tufts of tough herbage, then slowed to a halt, and looked back. De Marigny swept down upon her, landed close by in time to catch her up as she threw herself into his arms.

'Hang on,' he told her. 'Tight now!' And again he

was airborne and winging back up the slope to where Silberhutte waited.

'She stays here for now,' the Warlord yelled before de Marigny could once more set down. 'Henri, we have to take that peak up there. It has to be our launch site. The bats are doing a good job – but not quite good enough. We'll need to give them a hand.'

To Moreen de Marigny said: 'Climb up after us – but be careful.' And when she would have questioned him, he earnestly added: 'Trust us, Moreen.'

She stood then for a moment, looking lost and lonely as the pair flew off toward the peak . . .

Bloody battle still raged at the mountain's crest, but the bats had done well. Only three of the dozen Vikings remained on their feet, and of those that had fallen, all but one were dead. The bats had paid dearly for their selfless service to the girl, however, for only two of them remained aloft. Pounding the air, they wheeled and hovered, buffeting and tearing at the bloodied Vikings who desperately hacked at them with whistling blades.

Alighting, the Warlord rushed in to support these weird defenders of the peak. De Marigny quickly shucked off his marvellous aerial garment, and snatching up a fallen foeman's sword, he, too, joined the fray.

First blood went to Silberhutte as he ran past a crippled but still active invader where he lay with the tendons of his legs slashed through. With a savage cry and a wild sweep of his sword, the man made to sever the Warlord's own legs. But leaping above the deadly arc of metal, the Earthman came down with both feet on the other's outstretched arm, breaking it close to the elbow. In the next moment the Viking's scream of agony bubbled into silence as Silberhutte sliced open his jugular.

Simultaneous with that bubbling shriek came another – but not from an enemy. This dying scream came from one of the two remaining bats, skewered through the eye by a Viking sword. Down the great creature fell with the sword stuck fast in its head, so that the owner of that weapon had to leap astride the body of the bat to drag his blade free. As finally the sword came loose and its wielder turned toward the onrushing de Marigny, so the last bat settled with a piercing whistle of rage on the Viking's shoulders, literally decapitating him as it hurled his body to the ground.

Both of the remaining Vikings fell on the creature from behind, dispatching it in a moment, then backed away from the oncoming Earthmen. Silberhutte and de Marigny, however, giving the invaders no time to recover from their terrific exertions, leaped in upon them with war cries and whirling weapons.

The Warlord battered aside his man's buckler and blade, splitting his skull in the time it takes to tell, and de Marigny took only slightly longer. At the end, gore spattered and wild, the victors stood breathlessly back to back and surveyed the now silent field of battle. Broken bodies and bloodied weapons lay scattered about; great bats lay like crumpled heaps of dark fur together in a tangle with white-limbed Vikings; but finally the peak, that topmost summit of Moreen's mountain, was free of all living invaders.

As for the girl herself: she came quickly, nimbly up the steep slope toward the gore-streaked pair, a little out of breath and dishevelled but otherwise unharmed. Before she could reach them, Silberhutte moved apart from de Marigny to stand alone, his eyes closed and his mind far, far away on another world, in mental conversation with the mind of his woman.

For a moment he stood thus, then opened his eyes, turned to de Marigny and said: 'Well, this is it, Henri. Let's hope there's time enough.' He nodded, directing his gaze down the outer slope. There, rapidly toiling upward, came a large body of Vikings. Among them, one stood out like a tree among saplings.

'Harold,' de Marigny grimly noted. 'I was expecting him. Those two' – he indicated a pair of corpses with the fatal marks of the great bats fresh upon them – 'were from his ship. Did you recognize them?'

The Warlord nodded an affirmative. 'If Harold gets up here before we can lift off – well, it will be up to you. I'll be busy and of no use to you. You'd better get your cloak on and clip me in while I work.' He paused, added: 'And Henri – no distractions. This has to be all systems go first time . . . or not at all!'

There were questions de Marigny would dearly love to ask, but he put his faith in the Warlord and remained silent. As Moreen came closer, climbing the slope to a destiny she would never have believed, he ran to where he had thrown his cloak and donned it. Then he flew to the girl and returned with her to Silberhutte.

And approaching, seeing his friend standing there alone atop the peak, finally de Marigny understood. He had not wondered how Armandra might go about sending them a tornado, for he knew well enough that she was capable of that. What had puzzled and worried him was how such a whirlwind could possibly pick them up and then power them on their way to Dromos; and, with fighting still in progress and increasing in ferocity along the ridges, how such a rescue could be achieved in time. Now he saw that no such intervention from Borea was planned, that their passage to Dromos would have its origin right here on Numinos!

For Armandra controlled the winds with her mind, and now the giant Texan had given himself completely over to her – *so that his mind was merely an extension of hers!*

The Warlord stood – legs apart and arms reaching out to the sea and sky, eyes closed and face a death mask – flesh white as a candle's wax and chill as an icicle. He stood there under a sky that darkened visibly, rapidly, as Armandra worked her will on the elements through his mind.

Far out at sea, from a leaden sky shot with the golden traceries of electrical energy, searing lightning suddenly lashed down to lighten the surface of the darkly roiling sea. Then another bolt, and another, and in rapid succession a fourth, fifth, and sixth – becoming a torrent of bolts that turned Numinos bright with their fire as they strode about the Isle of Mountains on forked and fiery legs – until, in a final concerted blast that left the atmosphere reeking of ozone, the fires from the sky were done.

Armandra was satisfied for the moment. She had successfully tested her powers . . .

Moreen pressed close to de Marigny and gazed awestruck at the Warlord. Unseen forces lifted his long hair and floated it up about his head as if it drifted in deep and languid waters. Then de Marigny felt the tug of familiar, invisible fingers at the fabric of his fabulous cloak: Armandra's little winds, eager now to add their own effort to the greater tumult to come.

'Go on then,' de Marigny whispered to them, unheard by Moreen. 'Do what you can.' And a flurry of dust spiralled up at his feet to race away and dwindle into the gloom that now hung everywhere like a harbinger of Doomsday.

All lightnings had ceased now, as had the golden flickerings in the clouds that heralded them. Strangely, while the sky boiled darkly, about the peak the air was still. Steadily the mass of invaders, who as a man had paused to witness the aerial phenomenon, continued their climb toward the peaks and saddles, drawing closer with each passing moment. But now –

– Now it was time to go, and now too an utterly weird thing began to happen far out at sea. At first it appeared that a wall of mist had sprung up in a vast circle about the mountainous island, a wall that deepened and whirled and came closer by the second. But soon it could be seen that the entire ocean was in motion, turning like a tremendous disc about the hub of the island, and that rushing wall of mist formed the disc's outer perimeter.

In fact the mist was moisture ripped from the ocean's surface by the winds of Numinos under Armandra-Silberhutte's control, the same force that drove the sea in its rapidly accelerating whorl about the island. And that motion had reached the ocean cliffs of the island now, was already lifting the sea in a huge swell, tossing the Viking longships at anchor and threatening to smash them against the cliffs. A few moments more and they were being reduced to kindling as the waves reached higher yet up the rocks. Some of the ships parted with their anchors, went careening and dipping on the wild ocean until they, too, were battered against the cliffs and flew asunder.

For a moment the Vikings on the slopes were awestruck, paralysed by the destruction of their ships; and in the saddles the island's defenders took advantage of the diversion to wipe out those invaders who had recently reached their positions. Then, realizing that some nameless doom was about to befall them, the men of the caves turned and fled back down the inner paths toward the vents. They would gather ranks there, make a stand against the Vikings at the mouths of the vents, then fall back and fight delaying actions along the lengths of the subterranean channels to the great cavern itself. That was probably how they planned it – but they were not to know that they would be spared any further fighting.

The rising, towering, whirling wall of vapour was half as high as the mountains now, closing with the island, sucking more water up from the frenzied ocean. It was a fearsome sight, completely unnerving, and the effect it had on the Vikings was electric. They were afraid, yes, even unto flight – but where should they flee? With the alien wall of vapour rising at their heels, threatening to suck them up and blow them away, and their ships gone in a maelstrom of wind and water, they could only come forward, up the last few feet of shale-covered slope to the saddles and peaks.

And come they did, howling their berserker rage to the more loudly howling sky, foaming through their beards in fear and bloodlust. And the mountain peaks deserted and empty now of life – all save one.

Carefully de Marigny fastened Silberhutte's harness about him, stood close to the Warlord, gathered Moreen to him and hugged her, telling her to cling to him tightly, more tightly than she ever clung to anything before.

And still the Warlord stood as petrified, and faster whirled the great spout and higher still. Now the wall had breasted the far range of peaks and saddles, dipping down into the valley and moving rapidly across the central lake, whipping that, too, to a white-foaming fury.

It was abundantly clear that the peak whereon the three stood was the centre of the tremendous spout, but as such it was utterly, incredibly calm. Calm, despite the fact that the sky was quickly being shut out – calm, while rushing ever closer the inner wall of the funnel wore a glassy mirror sheen – calm, when above and all about the sky, ocean, and central lake were a howling, banshee tumult.

Then, as de Marigny felt invisible but familiar fingers returned to tug at the trappings of his cloak and freed one hand to find the controls of that fabulous garment, Moreen gasped in his ear and pointed to where a burly, red-haired Viking warrior now toiled toward them up the crest of the ridge less than one hundred yards away. Harold, alone of all his comrades, driven on by a berserker rage – an all-consuming hatred for the strangers who had upended his plans and his world – had finally arrived on the scene in time to be part of its conclusion.

He seemed oblivious to the rushing wall of water that climbed the slope behind him, tearing up trees and boulders alike and rushing them aloft; he saw only the Earthmen and the girl, and, possibly, in his mind's eye, the destruction of the longships and the fantastic doom which had already overtaken his comrades in their thousands.

'Emissaries of Ithaqua!' he roared, his voice somehow coming to them over the howling of tortured elements. 'Aye, perhaps you are after all, for surely have the winds protected you. Well, if the Wind-Walker is in truth your Lord, then he is no longer mine! Damn Ithaqua, and damn his carmine eyes! His winds shall not protect you this time – *not this time!*' And he lumbered forward, red-eyed and foaming at the mouth.

When Harold was no more than fifty paces from the little knot of people on the peak, the whirling wall caught up with him. Perhaps at the last he sensed his doom, for in the moment before that almost solid sheet of revolving air and water struck him, he turned to face it, throwing wide his arms as if to enclose it and uttering a wild shriek. A shriek of horror, perhaps, or maybe rage – rage that indeed the elements had won the day and robbed him of his prey.

And a second later he was gone. Only a brawny arm showed itself to the horrified watchers, an arm that stuck out from the glassy surface briefly and was then sucked under. An arm, and the dull glint of Harold's great axe caught up in the rush and swirl. These things they saw, and heard the drowning echo of Harold's final shriek, soon lost in the cacophony of insane elements.

Then, with a rush and a pounding of pressure that threatened to burst eardrums and pop eyes from their sockets, the cloak belled out and rocketed aloft, and Moreen's legs wound about her Earthman's waist in a scissor grip as the trio fled down the eye of the waterspout and out beyond the rim of Numinos.

To an observer, had there been one far out in the Numinosian sea, it would have seemed that the great spout stretched itself impossibly thin as it speared the heavens – that high above the outermost layers of atmosphere it twisted tortuously and bent its neck like a great serpent – before striking across space at a huge and dully glowing orb hanging low on the horizon.

Dromos . . .

1
Ice-Planet

Wrapped safely in a bubble of air formed of the substance of Armandra's familiar winds, the trio sped down the eye of the fantastic waterspout-cum-tornado. The journey would be shorter this time, for the distance between Numinos and Dromos was not so great. In the almost complete darkness the inner wall of the twister was a bluish sheen of incredible motion viewed beyond their protective bubble; and now, recovering from the heart-stopping, strangling effects of nightmarish acceleration, de Marigny comforted the girl in his arms and tried to explain, as best he could, what they were about.

They each took a pinch of Annahilde's warming powder, and as it gradually took effect and apprehension of the unknown waned a little in Moreen's heart, so she began to question de Marigny, to absorb and believe the many wonderful things he told her. Then, surprised at her rapid recovery and acceptance of her present position, he asked her if she were not afraid.

'Afraid?' her voice was tiny in the darkness. 'There are so many things I don't understand, and Annahilde used to say that ignorance is fear. In that way I suppose I'm afraid. But afraid of flying to Dromos and of what we might find there? No, I think not. Should I be afraid when you are here with me, who came from the Motherworld to fetch me out of the Isle of Mountains?'

'Moreen,' he began, 'you should know that there may well be dangers ahead, and that – '

'Dangers we will face together,' she put her fingers to his lips. 'You and I and the Warlord, until we find this box you seek so urgently. And of what dangers do you speak? No creature of flesh and blood will harm me, nor you when you are with me – except perhaps evil men or Lord Ithaqua . . .' She paused and de Marigny felt her shudder where she lay weightless in his arms.

'I have flown with him, too,' she finally continued, 'in the skies over Numinos. But he is not like you. No one – no *thing* – is like unto Ithaqua.' She found de Marigny's mouth and kissed it.

Then for a while they were silent, Annahilde's powder producing warm sensations of well-being within them, and soon de Marigny became very conscious of the girl's lovely body pressed tight to his, of her form that clung to him and set his flesh tingling despite the thick fur garment he wore.

Moreen, too, for all her innocence, felt the fire that burned in her Earthman's blood. Now she knew him for a real man, and her pulse quickened to match his. Then –

Breaking the spell, coming to them from the darkness close at hand, faint stirrings and a sighing groan!

'Hank!' de Marigny whispered, horrified at the thought of what would happen if the Warlord should inadvertently waken from his telepathic trance and lose control over the vast funnel that bore them through the void. '*For God's sake!*'

'No panic, Henri,' came the Warlord's waking rumble. 'Armandra has it in hand. She only needed me to help out with the takeoff – to supply a one-hundred-percent location statement and to get things started. Now she's completely taken over. She'll get us to Dromos, all right, and help set us down safely, too – but from then on we're on our own. Dromos is too far out, at the very extremes of her reach. You may as well know it right now: if we fail to find the clock, we're stuck.'

Sighing his relief that all was well, at least for the moment, de Marigny answered: 'And meanwhile Ithaqua just sits somewhere out there and watches us wriggle, right?'

'That's the way I read it, yes. Right now, if he wanted to, he could take me, you, Moreen – all of us and the time-clock too.'

'Then why doesn't he do just that?'

'There's something else he wants.'

'Armandra?'

'Right – but that's not going to happen.'

'Armandra?' came Moreen's voice in the darkness. 'She is your woman, Warlord?'

'Call me Hank,' he answered. 'She's my woman, yes, and a daughter of Ithaqua, too. He wants her more desperately than all three of us together. But he'll never have her, not while I live.'

Silberhutte paused, and when next he spoke his tone had lightened somewhat: 'About our destination, Henri. Now is as good a time as any to tell you what I know of Dromos – possibly the only chance I'll get. Moreen, you'd best listen in, too, and learn what you can . . .

'Armandra tells me that Dromos is an ice planet, and that the habitation of its dwellers lies far below the surface in huge caves of ice in the bowels of a vast, near-extinct volcano. That's one of the reasons she won't be able to help us leave when the time comes, for we'll probably be deep underground – or at least, under ice.

'As for the inhabitants of Dromos – they were men, once.'

'Were men?' de Marigny questioned. 'What are they now?'

'Surely men are men,' Moreen added. 'What else could they be?'

'I honestly don't know,' the Warlord replied. 'I know only as much as Armandra has told me. I'll try to explain.

'The ice-priests of Dromos were first taken there millions

of years ago by Ithaqua in his youth. Like all men, they had their origin on Earth the Motherworld, but at a time predating the dinosaurs. If Atlantis was yesterday, their world was years ago! They were of a primal continent at the dawn of Earth's prehistory, lost in such unthinkable abysses of the past that you could never convince any modern scientists back home that they ever existed at all.

'All of these things Armandra plucked from her father's mind when she was a child and he used to tempt her with telepathic tales of his deeds and his wanderings between alien spheres. She even learned the name of that primal continent, and that of the city which the ice-priests ruled with cruelty, terror, and through their skill at casting monstrous visions, mass hallucinations with which to confuse the minds of the common people.

'The land was called Theem'hdra, and the city of the ice-priests was Khrissa, a place of massive basalt slabs in Theem'hdra's frozen northern regions. There the ice-priests conjured their evil illusions and worshipped dark gods, among which was this same Ithaqua we know now. And indeed all of this was so long ago that the Wind-Walker himself has all but forgotten the details. For while he is very nearly immortal, ageless, yet all of this was in his youth.

'Of the ice-priests themselves: they were a tall, thin, hairless race, white as death and cold and cruel as ice itself. They set themselves up as the saviours of Theem'hdra, saying that only their black prayers could keep the ice at bay, that great wall of ice that crept down from the north each winter and grudgingly retreated as the seasons waxed warmer. But those must have been monstrous prayers indeed, for in company with them the priests would kill off hundreds of women, human sacrifices to propitiate their hideous gods.

'And you ask, Moreen, how men can be other than men? I don't call such as these things I've described men.'

Here de Marigny asked, 'And Ithaqua brought these ice-priests to Dromos, you say? How many of them and why?'

They could almost sense the Warlord's shrug in the darkness. 'I'm not sure, but you may be certain he had his reasons. Armandra tells of a great war that raged between certain of Theem'hdra's barbarian nations and the people of Khrissa, when the city lay under seige for many years while the barbarians bided their time outside the massive basalt walls. Perhaps that had something to do with it – perhaps Ithaqua took his priests out of the doomed city as repayment for their tainted worship. Who can say?

'At any rate, there's little more to tell. As I've said, Dromos is an ice planet, perpetually frozen, but it wasn't always so. Armandra tells that simultaneous with the coming of the ice-priests into Dromos, Ithaqua wrought a fantastic climatic change in the moon. Prior to that time there had been a great volcanic belt about Dromos, which was not to the Wind-Walker's liking; he finds all sources of warmth abhorrent.

'As time passed, however, the volcanoes became extinct until only one remained: the hugest cone of all, still rumbling threateningly, with a throat that went down almost to the moon's core. When he brought the ice-priests from doomed Khrissa, Ithaqua made it a condition of his mercy that they become instrumental in damming up that last great vent, thus turning Dromos into the frozen world which it is now. How he or they achieved this, I'm at a loss to say; but as we all know well enough, Ithaqua defies all Earthly laws and sciences . . .'

Following Silberhutte's narrative, for a few moments there was silence, then de Marigny said: 'Well, if that's Dromos as you've described it, it sounds like a pretty inhospitable place to me. And I can't say I much fancy the idea of these ice-priests, either!'

'Neither them nor their priestesses,' added Moreen.

'Priestesses!' de Marigny repeated her, surprise showing in his voice.

'The facts of life, Henri,' came the Warlord's humourless chuckle. 'Your girl has a head on her shoulders. Perhaps the ice-priests are less inhuman than we picture them.'

'Yes,' the other replied, equally dryly, 'but then again, perhaps they're not . . .'

Not long after, their journey came to an abrupt end. On this occasion, however, de Marigny was ready for it, was prepared at any moment to use his cloak in the manner accustomed, so that it came as no surprise when the vast and whirling tube fell apart around them.

Down they swept through the debris of the collapsed funnel – which drifted as shimmering ice-crystal curtains and flurries of fine snow – toward glacial Dromos. The air was thin and icy, though mercifully no winds blew, and so the surface of the world a mile below was crystal clear to their eyes in every minute detail. Had the scene been other than utterly barren and white, then it might have been beautiful. It *would* be beautiful, but not to any lover of life. For Dromos, at least on the surface, was quite dead.

What little light filtered its way out here from the sun, or down from the weirdly lucent heavens, was reflected in millions of tiny points of light from the frozen surface. Great drifts of snow – forming white and blue dunes whose slopes scintillated dazzlingly, with crests miles apart – marched to the distant horizons and formed the only topographic features to be seen . . . almost.

For as they dropped down closer to the surface, they now saw against the horizon a series of distant mounds silhouetted against the subtly auroral backdrop of the sky. Since these huge domed hills were obviously not merely gigantic snowdrifts (which everywhere else seemed perfectly uniform in height and formation), they must be rounded mountains, perhaps the range of dead volcanoes for which the trio searched.

And so for more than an hour they followed in silence the cloak's strange shadow across the deep snows, buoyed up and assisted on their way by Armandra's small friendly winds; until at last they were in the frozen white foothills that led upward to vast, extinct volcanic cones. They flew high above a range of six such bowls, each one filled to its craterlike brim with drifted snow, before spying some miles ahead a dome almost twice the size of any of the others. This could only be – must surely be – that final prehistoric vent into whose throat, in countless ages past, Ithaqua had transported the Khrissan ice-priests. And according to Armandra this was where the ice-priests dwelled to this day.

And now, as they gained elevation to fly across that looming crater wall at a height of many thousands of feet, they saw . . . an impossible sight!

For here was no great bowl of drifted snow but a spiralling ice-cut stairway that coiled down and down into that terrific throat and finally disappeared far below in a dark blue gloom. Hardly daring to believe their eyes, the cloak-fliers descended into that mighty blowhole, and as they drifted slowly down past the first of those Titan-carved steps – each one of which had a rise as tall as a tall man – so their senses once more were astounded.

Not by sight this time but sound!

Or was it purely *physical* sound? No, not sound as ordinary men know it; though certainly Silberhutte recognized the phenomenon at once, and his companions took only a little longer. For it was a voice they heard – a deeply booming, clinically cold and correct voice – and while it seemed to have its source deep down in the volcano's throat, the trio knew now that they heard it only inside their heads!

A voice, yes – a telepathic voice that said: '*Welcome, strangers – welcome to Dromos. The ice-priests await you, as they have waited since the dawn of time!*'

2

Beneath the Volcano

Beckoned on by the voice that called in their heads from unknown depths below, the trio drifted down past tiers of descending, colossal steps that swept around the perimeter of a vent all of a mile across. After 'hearing' the voice that first time, they had heard no more, but still eerie mental echoes reverberated in their minds.

To say that the three were wary would be to severely understate the apprehension they felt, particularly Silberhutte. For the Warlord was experienced in telepathic communication, and he had detected behind the voice's welcome certain sinister undertones. 'The ice-priests await you,' the voice had said, which was to admit knowledge of their coming. Who, then, had foreseen and foretold their eventual arrival on Dromos, when they themselves had not known of it for a fact until so recently?

Who else but Ithaqua himself, when he deposited the lure here, the time-clock, knowing that they must follow on behind sooner or later! Little wonder that the Wind-Walker had been so crazed with lunatic glee when last they had seen him high over the plateau, his mighty fist clenched about the time-clock.

'The ice-priests await you, as they have waited since the dawn of time.' Since the dawn of time? Merely for the arrival of three mortals come to Dromos on an impossible quest? But then again, perhaps that was it exactly; perhaps any mortals would suffice, would satisfy the needs of the ice-priests – whatever those needs were. Such were the thoughts that passed through the Warlord's head; and because of them he grasped his massive axe, rescued from the debris of battle atop Moreen's peak, more tightly as he hung in his harness below de Marigny and Moreen.

As for de Marigny: he now wore in his belt his original picklike weapon, reclaimed when the Warlord discarded it, and its presence there comforted him inordinately. While he had taken the voice's welcome at its face value, (for the moment at least,) and while he did not have Silberhutte's acumen in matters of mental communication, still he remembered well his friend's tale of the cruelty of the ice-priests. And his arm tightened protectively about the girl whose slender legs encircled his waist and whose arm hugged his neck.

Moreen, too, was full of doubt, but she must now go where the men from the Motherworld went, placing herself entirely in their care. If that meant exploring the bowels of a huge volcanic vent, wherein as yet unknown intelligences – 'men,' perhaps – had their lair, then that must be the way of it. Still, she comforted herself, while Dromos was a strange, cold world and most mysterious, Numinos had never been a paradise. She had known hardships before and would probably know them again before finding that Elysia of which her Earthman had spoken and which he sought so avidly. And, she reminded herself, it was by no means certain that they ever would find Elysia; for de Marigny had told her that there would be dangers, and he had tried to hint that they could well be insurmountable. Well, she had been brave enough when she shrugged his warning off – but now?

Now Silberhutte interrupted the thoughts of his companions to say: 'Henri, if we can be contacted that way by the ice-priests, then it should be just as easy for us – for me at least – to contact them. While it's obvious we can't stay up there on the surface, that we must get on as quickly as possible and find the clock, still I would like to know more about where we're going and what we're letting ourselves in for. So steady as you go and give me time to get a few answers, or at least time to pose a few questions.' And with that he fell silent.

Knowing his friend to be probing telepathically ahead, searching for the minds of the as yet unknown ice-priests, de Marigny slowed the rate of the cloak's descent to little more than a gentle drift and waited breathlessly for the Warlord's report. And almost immediately Silberhutte's sixth sense detected something in the dark blue gloom below. A mental *motion*, a purely psychic seething – a lurking presence . . . no, many presences – a conclave of shadowy minds, a cesspit of evil influence!

For a split second he had caught the ice-priests, who or whatever they were, unawares; but that was all the time it took for him to determine their purpose – which was, as the Warlord had feared, nothing less than to snare the three who now descended toward their subterranean lair! A split second only to divine not only this but also something of how it would be done.

These things Silberhutte learned from that single moment of telepathic contact, these and one other: that while the ice-priests may well have been men once long ago in fabulous Theem'hdra, they most certainly were not men now! No race of men could possibly have minds like these, which reeked of an evil as ancient as the CCD themselves.

This was as much as he was allowed to know, for no sooner was his presence felt by the ice-priests than they shut his mind out, blocking his telepathic power as surely as if it had never existed. Silently the Warlord cursed himself for letting the ice-priests discover him, then gripped his harness tightly and turned his face up to look at de Marigny and Moreen where they swung together beneath the canopy of the cloak above him.

'*Get out of here, Henri!*' the Warlord shouted. 'Take us up, man – before it's too late!'

But a moment later, as de Marigny desperately tried

to manipulate the studs that controlled his wonderful garment, he knew the worst: that they were already too late. For now, as if somewhere below the blades of a great fan had begun to turn, air was being sucked down the narrowing bore of the volcano in huge gulps, creating too much of a drag for the already overloaded cloak to defy.

For a few moments de Marigny fought the rapidly increasing suction but then, as the turbulence became such that he was obliged to seek the centre of the bore where there was less danger of being tossed against the steep steps of ice, he gave up the unequal struggle and fought instead to keep the cloak stable as it was drawn down toward whatever fate awaited it.

Down they spiralled, helplessly, like ants trapped on a leaf and whirled in a gale, and even Armandra's little familiar winds could do nothing to help them . . .

Minutes passed and still the power of the vortex increased, so that twice de Marigny felt Moreen's legs slip where they gripped him. On both occasions he released all control over the cloak to grab the girl to him, gritting his teeth in the face of the now howling current of air that rushed them ever faster into nightmare bowels of ice and stone.

In the same interval of time Silberhutte, too, was active, partly freeing himself from his harness and then fighting the suction that threatened to tear him bodily loose from his straps. He would part with the cloak soon enough – but when he chose to do so and not before. When he went to the ice-priests, he would go as his own man, not hooked and wriggling like some fish on a line.

But now, as the bore narrowed until its huge, blue-glowing ice steps were less than fifty feet away on all sides, the cloak and its passengers were caught up in a chaos of crazed air that immediately checked their sickening plunge, whirling them in a circle that took the trio ever closer to the smooth ice walls. Finally, when it seemed they must surely be dashed to pieces against the lowest tiers of steps at the very bottom of the pit, then the mad winds hurled them irresistibly along one of several horizontal shafts that lay at right angles to the main bore.

They were rushed into a region of eerie, blue-lit caves hung with ice stalactites that glowed phosphorescently, and as the frenzied current of seemingly sentient air slackened off a little to thread them safely through this maze of descending daggers, so Silberhutte decided that the time had come to part company with his friends – at least for the time being.

He finished unfastening himself and, ignoring his great speed, cast himself free. His arms, thrown wide, momentarily embraced a pair of icicles almost as thick as his thighs, which might have withstood his body's weight but never its hurtling velocity. They snapped from the ceiling and crashed down with him to the floor of the tunnel in a massive shivering of ice. In the next moment there came a veritable deluge of crystals shaken loose by the reverberating echoes of Silberhutte's collision and fall; following which, as the howling subterranean winds bore the cloak swiftly away into the distance, the tunnel became still once more and coldly silent.

As for the two who still clung together beneath the cloak's straining canopy, they did not even know that the Warlord had left them. They knew only the nausea of their buffeting rush through bowels of earth and ice – a kaleidoscope vista of weirdly carved ice caves, lit now by blue luminosity, now dark as Stygian tombs – the irresistible wind and, in deep mental recesses, the obscene tittering of telepathic voices which could only belong to the ice-priests of olden Khrissa.

When the Warlord's senses returned, (he knew not how long after his fall,) he found himself lying in a pile of ice fragments, large and small; but while his body was a mass of bruises and abrasions, nothing seemed to be broken, though a painful and lumpy forehead explained his splitting headache. He climbed carefully to his feet and examined his body minutely, easing the aches and pains out of stiffened joints and battered limbs.

Then, as he made to follow a trail of ice debris brought down from the ceiling of the tunnel by the demon wind and the cloak's passing, he cast his mind back over the most immediate past. Uppermost in his memory was the wind that had dragged the cloak down the bore of the dead volcano and into this icy underworld, a wind which had doubtless been called up by the ice-priests. Ithaqua had obviously conferred certain of his powers on the ice-priests, much as he had on Borea.

Ah, but these priests of Dromos were different again from those the Wind-Walker occasionally elevated from the ranks of his common worshippers on Borea; they had been real priests in their time and were still, however dark the powers they served. Moreover they were telepathic. For this latter reason Silberhutte kept his thoughts carefully guarded as he traversed the tunnel, which in reality was not so much a tunnel as a series of domed caverns or galleries, natural in appearance and of unknown extent.

So the ice-priests were telepathic; they served Ithaqua and commanded, to one degree or another, a certain control over the elements; and they were basically evil in nature, as Armandra had forewarned. In short, and in the light of what the Warlord had glimpsed in their minds, they were certainly inimical to de Marigny's quest and both he and the girl Moreen could well be in the most dire trouble at this very moment.

With the latter thought strong in his mind, Silberhutte found himself increasing his pace as he passed through successive caverns of blue-glowing ice, always following the trail of crystalline debris. The air was absolutely calm now and completely icy, with a temperature well below zero, so that for all the masses of ice that hung from the ceiling and festooned the walls and floors in fantastic formations, no water moved or dripped anywhere. Silberhutte, however, felt no discomfort; his metabolism had been permanently altered long ago, so that he was perfectly at home in this frigid place, but he worried about de Marigny and Moreen. He knew that they had Annahilde's warming powder but wondered if they had retained their freedom to use it. By now they might well be in the clutches of the ice-priests.

Feeling almost fully recovered and having worked all of his aches and pains out of his system, the Warlord now forged ahead at a rapid pace, surefooted despite the treacherous surface on which he trod. Once or twice as he went, he felt tentative, searching mental fingers groping at the edges of his mind, but he kept his thoughts completely shielded from whichever minds sought his in this alien underworld. The very fact that they sought him, however, told him that his fears for the safety of his companions were realized; that they must have fallen into the hands of the ice-priests and that his own absence had been noted. That simply meant that he must proceed with great caution. And yet how could he do that and maintain his speed? No, speed was of the essence and caution must for the moment take second place in matters of precedence.

At least he could not complain of misplacement; on the contrary, for he was used to a subterranean or semisubterranean existence. These were different caves from those he had known in the plateau on Borea, certainly, and different again from the volcanic system of caverns and vents in the Isle of Mountains on Numinos, but they were caves nonetheless. Thus he was not at all dismayed when he was obliged to traverse several darker caves where the illumination was little more than a dull blue glow around the perimeter of the walls (he had known darker places in the plateau), though of necessity he had to slow his pace in passing through such areas.

411

Before long, however, he came to a large gallery where he was brought up short in unaccustomed indecision. Here the ceiling receded into frosty heights from which massive ice pillars, many of a thickness three or four times as great as his waist, joined with columns that grew up from an oddly corrugated floor; but the size and configurations of the place were not that which stopped him. What caused his consternation was something entirely different.

For some time the ice-crystal spoor of the cloak's passing had been diminishing, but here in this huge cave it petered out altogether. That might well mean that Silberhutte's search was almost at an end, but at the same time it confused matters greatly. For the place was like some sort of underground junction from which several shafts led off in different directions. One of these tunnels had been the cloak's exit route from the gallery, and its discovery would certainly lead the Warlord to his vanished friends.

But which one?

Lair of the Ice-Priests

Following the perimeter of the vast ice hall, Silberhutte peered into each of the tunnel entrances in turn, examining their floors for sign of the cloak's passing. He discovered nothing to suggest the way his friends had gone, but he did detect at the last entrance a certain odour. For a single second in the frozen, sterile atmosphere of the place, the strange smell – of incense, perhaps, and yet sulphurous, too – assailed his nostrils, then was gone.

Wasting no time, he moved forward into the tunnel, going as silently as possible between bluely luminous walls of ice, and as he went so the peculiar smell came stronger to him from some as yet unknown source. A minute more, and as the Warlord carefully came around a bend, he froze, baring his teeth in a half-snarl, half-gasp of surprise.

Slowly, great axe upraised, he emerged into view of a fantastic scene. Then he allowed himself to relax, his body coming erect from its half-crouch as he again moved forward, disbelief growing on his face. For this was the tunnel's end, the very lair of the ice-priests. And indeed there were ice-priests here – but they were the last thing Silberhutte had expected.

Armandra had said they were tall, hairless, thin, and cold. Yes, and so they were, but her description simply did not do them justice! They stood all of eight feet tall, were thin to the point of emaciation – mere bones with an outer layer of naked, heavily wrinkled skin – and their colour . . .

They were white, but not the white of clean snow or of good milk or of any normal thing. They were *corpse*-white, the sickly white of the destroying angel, Amanita

413

Phalloides, the mushroom of death! And not only in their unwholesome colour did they match that terrible fungus, for their heads, too, were of a loathsome mushroom shape; with foreheads that overhung their faces, and skulls that were much too squat and flat.

Like grotesque, alien mummies they were, and preserved just as surely – though not wound in bindings or lain in carven sarcophagi. No, they were preserved in pillars of ice! And like mummies they too were ancient; but somehow Silberhutte knew that they predated any Earthly mummy, that indeed they were the original ice-priests of Theem'hdra, and that time itself had wrought in them their hideous desiccation.

Nine in number – standing upright, monstrous heads drooping upon bony, shrivelled chests, spindly legs together and stick-arms hanging by their sides . . . and all encased in ice, except for the domes of their projecting heads and their turned-down faces. At first the Warlord thought that they were dead. Stepping closer, however, he saw that they were merely in a state of suspension, a cryogenic limbo; for even as he stared at the awful skull of one of them, he saw the distended blood vessels darkening as the ice-priest's circulatory system worked. They were alive, yes, but their metabolisms had been so slowed as to be almost at a standstill.

They stood (were encased) each to his own icicle in a ring about a central pit, facing outward. The pit was the source of that peculiar odour – much stronger here – that had attracted the Warlord's attention to the lair in the first instance. He now found himself thinking of the place more positively as a 'lair,' as if the ice-priests were more animal than human; nor did studying them briefly at close quarters change his opinion of them in this respect.

Basically human they might well be, but their branch had grown apart from the great tree of humanity in an age predating the coelacanth, and from that day to this they had remained unaltered and irretrievably, yes, alien! They *were* human – as was Neanderthal, as is the pygmy and the aborigine – but their evolution had taken them much farther from the main stem than any of these.

Carefully, still more than a little wary, the Warlord stepped between two of the refrigerated figures to stare down into the central pit. Here the fumes from below were understandably stronger, cloying almost, so that he held his breath as he looked down upon the slow, glutinous bubbling of some thickly viscous lavalike substance fifty feet below. Then, seeing that the walls of the pit at its bottom were glowing a dull red, he decided that it must indeed be an as yet active volcanic source, the valve of some larger vent, and further that the fumes it gave off must somehow be essential to the process of suspended animation.

Finally he straightened up to walk silently around the circle, only halting when he came to a wide gap in the ring of ice-blurred figures. Here, where instinct told the Warlord that there should be more pillars of ice reaching from floor to ceiling, he saw only the stumps of three great icicles which formed uneven mounds upon the floor. And deeply indented in them were the marks of wide, wedgeshaped feet . . . such marks as the feet of the ice-priests would make. Now the Warlord knew that there must be twelve ice-priests in all – an even dozen – of which three were even now awake and abroad in the ice-cave complex!

So absorbed was Silberhutte with these observations that for a moment he inadvertently left his mind unguarded, only realizing his danger when alien thoughts rushed in to detect his presence. Before he once more closed the shutters on his mind, he read disbelief, rage, and something akin to panic in the thoughts that crowded in upon his own; panic that he had managed to reach the lair itself. These disordered, frightened thoughts were strangely sluggish and came from close at hand – from the minds of these very figures ringed about the volcanic blowhole – but the others, whose sources he noted with alarm were also fairly close, though he could not place them exactly, were much more active and immediately purposeful.

Silberhutte again cast his glance across the space where those oddly indented stumps of ice stood up from the cave's floor, and as he did so, he spied a small motion among the ranks of silent, petrified ice-priests. Again the Warlord froze . . . then watched in morbid fascination as jerkily, one by one, the domed heads of the encased ice-priests came up and their slowly opening eyes, which seemed to have no pupils and were uniformly crimson, swivelled to stare in his direction!

And immediately it was as if chains had been thrown about the Warlord's massive shoulders, as if his feet were suddenly shackled to the ice-layered floor. He had never before met with hypnotism in any form but knew its principles, knew that what he now felt was not a physical power but the purely mental one of mind over matter – the minds of the ice-priests over the material of his being! It was not even telepathy, which he could understand and handle more than adequately, though certainly there were parallels. For while his mind now worked swiftly and lucidly to free his body from the ice-priests' hypnotic shackles, still those shackles tightened about him, denying him the use of powerful sinew, muscle, and bone. It was as much as he could do to back away from the pit, stumbling and barely managing to remain upright, holding on grimly to his great axe as those crimson eyes bored awfully into his own.

Finally, concentrating all of his mind on the breaking of his invisible bonds, the Warlord could no longer hold in place those shutters that protected his thoughts from external influences. Down crashed his mental barriers – and in rushed the concerted sendings of a dozen evil, powerful minds, the chaotic and monstrous imaginings of this nightmare Brotherhood of Ice.

But the ice-priests, too, had their limits. Now, as they concentrated on the Warlord's mind, they were obliged to relax their hypnotic hold on his body. He found himself free to move, to flee, and turned to do just that –

– Only to find himself face to face with that trio of monsters whose footprints were melted into the three ice mounds at the rim of the pit. There they stood, and while Silberhutte believed that he might handle them easily enough (for what were they but skin and bone?), he was not so sure about the *things* they had with them!

About the feet of the ice-priests, crouching like great hounds at the ends of their leads, were three fantastic creatures unlike anything the Warlord had ever thought to see. Six-legged, like huge insects – protected by black, chitinous plates which sprouted short, coarse red hairs, and with lashing forked tails whose barbs dripped a clear fluid that set the icy floor steaming poisonously – the things were the stuff of a madman's dreams!

The advancing ice-priests smiled (if such a word may rightly describe what they did with their alien faces) in hideous anticipation as they drew closer, drawn on by the straining of their awful servitors. Silberhutte, turning to left and right, could see no escape; the cave was a dead end, containing only the broken circle of ice-priests frozen about the central pit. And now, as the leashed hounds and their masters blocked his single route of egress, so the Warlord found himself backing toward that pit.

Then, quick as thought, one of the terrible creatures slipped its leash and hurled itself straight at the Warlord's throat. He cried out once – no cry of horror, though he felt great horror; not even a cry of rage, though certainly he was enraged to be trapped here like a rat at the mercy of beings whose instincts he knew to be more savage, merciless, and cruel than the instinct of any rat – no, none

417

of these, but a battle cry. And with the echoes of that cry reverberating and setting the lair of the ice-priests to a tinkling of startled ice, he lifted his great axe, smashed the slavering cockroach thing to one side in midair, and threw himself headlong into battle . . .

De Marigny and Moreen regained consciousness together. They had been literally whirled unconscious at the end of their subterranean flight, driven round and round in a tight circle until they had blacked out. The wonder was that the girl had not been torn from the Earthman's arms by centrifugal force, to be dashed against the blue-glistening walls of their ice prison, but she had not. Now, recovering but still filled with a whirling nausea, they clung together as before; and for some little time that was as much as they could do.

It was as de Marigny became cognizant of their immediate surroundings that the full extent of their plight was brought home to him. To begin with, the Warlord was no longer with them; whether of his own volition or at the will of some other, Silberhutte had parted company with them. Equally disconcerting to de Marigny was the fact that he no longer wore his flying cloak – but there was worse yet to come.

The girl had her face buried in the furs that covered his chest, and so she knew nothing of their whereabouts, was not aware that they lay upon a hard, cold floor of ice in a small cave. De Marigny knew, however; knew moreover that there was only one exit, and that it was guarded . . .

But what guards!

There were two of them, two huge insect-things that crouched down for all the world like guard dogs – except that they bared no teeth but hissed warningly through jaws like those of great reptiles. De Marigny saw them and was relieved to see also the stretched chains attached to their collars and fastened to iron staples hammered into the ice of the walls. The – hounds? – were at the fullest extent of those chains, uncomfortably close to his feet.

Drawing breath in a huge gasp, he snatched back his feet and hugged the girl to him all in one movement. Shaken from her exhausted half-sleep, Moreen opened her eyes to peer into those of the two monsters that now snapped and slavered only feet away. Galvanized into action by de Marigny's movements, they hissed loudly and hauled dangerously on their chains, scrabbling at the ice floor with legs like hairy, jointed bones.

Then an astounding thing – for before de Marigny could stop her, Moreen had slipped from his arms to hold her hand out to the chained creatures, as if she were about to pet a pair of domesticated animals in a Viking settlement on Numinos!

'Moreen, no!' he cried, stark horror in his voice.

She pulled her hand back from the snapping snake jaws of the things and turned to him in seeming surprise. 'But why? They will not harm me.'

'Not harm you?' he cried, dragging her back bodily from the chained monsters. 'Girl, they'd kill you! That's why they've been put on duty here, to keep us in. They're killers.'

'You don't understand,' she told him patiently. 'No lesser beast would ever harm me. They sense something in me – something which I myself do not understand – and even the wildest of them are calmed when I speak to them. The great eagles of Numinos have perched on my shoulders, and the wild dogs of the hills have accepted meat from my fingers.' She turned back to the hissing cave-things and shrugged. 'These creatures are – different – yes, but for all that they are living creatures. Therefore I am safe with them.'

Her logic baffled de Marigny. 'But *look* at them!' he cried. 'Do they look harmless?'

'Henri,' she answered, kissing his brow, 'I have trusted

419

you – with my life. Now you must trust me. Indeed there is something very strange about these creatures – for see, they continue to snap and hiss even now that they know me. Still I say to you that they will not harm me.'

Frowning, she turned from him, approaching the insect-things on all fours. They reared on their chains, jaws slavering and barbed tails lashing as, unhesitatingly, she again stretched out her hand to them.

'*For God's sake!*' de Marigny whispered, fighting the urge to grab her and drag her back. Ignoring him, she drew closer to the hideous creatures; and as she did so, they arched their necks and drew back their flat reptilian heads – for all the world like angry snakes about to strike.

And strike they did, so swiftly that the eye could scarcely follow their movement. Moreen had no time to snatch her hand back out of harm's way. Razor fangs opened her flesh, injecting yellow poison. Wide-eyed in disbelief, her mouth forming an 'O' of surprise to match de Marigny's expression of horror, she fell back into his arms. No living creature would ever have done this to her, she knew that, and so –

'Not real!' she gasped as de Marigny feverishly took her hand and gazed at it in amazement, his jaw dropping. Then they both stared at the clean, unbroken flesh of her hand and wrist. 'They are not real!'

As one they turned their heads to look again at the monstrous hounds – seeing immediately that she was right. The creatures had disappeared, vanished into thin air, and with them the chains that had seemed to tether them to the frozen walls. They had not been real, had existed only in their minds, illusions placed there by the evil genius of the ice-priests.

Suddenly de Marigny recalled what Silberhutte had said about Theem'hdra's ice-priests being greatly skilled in the arts of illusion and mass hypnotism, and at last he understood. Well, it was a lesson learned, knowledge which would doubtless prove very useful in the near future.

As for the immediate future: there were things to be done, and at once!

'Come on, Moreen,' he helped the girl to her feet. 'We have to find Silberhutte – and then the time-clock.' And as they hurried together down the unknown ice tunnel toward whatever terrors or triumphs lay ahead, he pictured in his mind's eye an upturned hourglass in which the sands of time flowed swiftly indeed – sands which were rapidly running out . . .

Within a very short time the pair emerged from the prison tunnel into that same great ice gallery whose many exits had so recently baffled the Warlord. For them, however, there was to be no indecision; coming to them clearly from close at hand, sounds of battle pointed the way as surely as any signpost. There was the clash of iron and the splintering of ice – but above all else, clear and resounding, came the enraged if somewhat frustrated roar of Silberhutte's bull voice! As they skirted the great hall, it was easy to discover the mouth of the tunnel which issued these furious reverberations.

All caution to the wind – ignoring the fact that his weapon had been taken from him along with the flying cloak – de Marigny rushed down the vast natural tunnel of blue, softly glowing ice toward the lair of the ice-priests; and as he came round the final bend, with Moreen hot on his heels, there opened to his eyes a scene strange and macabre. He took in the circle of frozen ice-priests at a glance, then concentrated his amazed attention on the actors and the action. As Moreen pantingly caught up with him, her gasp told him that she, too, was struck by the weirdness of the scene.

One ice-priest – tall, naked, spindly as a stick-insect – stood with his wax-white back to the pair. His arms were raised shoulder high, his hands alive with mesmeric motion, outstretched toward the Borean Warlord. But the mushroom-headed ice-priest was not the sole source of de Marigny's and Moreen's astonishment; no, that doubtful honour went to the insane activity of Silber-hutte. For the Warlord had obviously gone stark, staring mad!

He crouched between the lone ice-priest and the central pit with its perimeter of frozen figures, his eyes wide and full of darting motion, his great axe held out before him. Every few seconds he would turn, leap toward a wall, and strike at it shatteringly, all the while yelling his rage. But it seemed to the astounded watchers that there was as much terror as rage in the Warlord's savage battle cries . . .

'Where is the Time-Clock?'

Now Silberhutte embarked upon a series of dodges, feints, wild turns, and tumbles, his axe flashing in a blur to left and right, as if he fought half a dozen fleet-footed foes which only he could see; and through all of this the solitary ice-priest pivoted to follow his every movement, long-fingered hands tracing mystic passes in the air. This could only possibly be one thing – and de Marigny already had ample evidence of the mastery of the ice-priests over magic and illusion. The Warlord had become the latest victim of that power, as had been his friends so very recently. He had not seen them enter the terminal cave, saw nothing now but the illusions engendered of the lone ice-priest's mesmerism enhanced by the telepathic embellishments of that being's now wakeful, ice-encased brothers. And his plight was indeed a sore one.

Following the attack of the first creature, the other priests had deliberately released their 'hounds' upon him, and since then they had called for the reinforcements with which Silberhutte now battled. And no matter how many of the insect-dogs he cut down or smashed aside, others were there to take their places, supplied from some seemingly inexhaustible source to the rear of the 'three' priests who continued to bar his exit.

One thing was certain: he was losing the battle and knew he must soon fall before the concerted savagery of the pack. Constantly he tripped over their fallen, broken bodies, and only a series of miracles had sufficed so far to protect him from their slavering jaws. On more than a dozen occasions their barbed, venomous tails had come close to splashing him with their acid, and already he was beginning to feel a mental and physical weariness as his great strength was put to this most gruelling test.

Finally that which he most feared occurred: stepping back from a frontal attack by one of the hounds, he tripped over a broken carcass and sprawled on his back between two of the frozen priests, his head and shoulders over the lip of the pit that went down to the glowing, sluggishly surging lava. Instantly the hounds were on him, closing from all sides. Then –

'They're not real, Hank!' came de Marigny's warning cry in the Warlord's ears, strangely hollow and echoing. 'Whatever you see, none of it's real . . . not real . . . not *real!* It's an illusion . . . illusion . . . *illusion!* It can't harm you . . . can't harm you . . . *can't harm you!'*

And at once the hissing, slavering snake faces surrounding the Warlord began to fade, to dissolve away into mist, so that he instantly knew and understood de Marigny's message.

Illusions, his friend had called out to him. The mental mischief of the ice-priests. Visions called up to sap his strength and render him helpless – to kill him! Well, the warning had come in the nick of time, for struggling against the hounds, the Warlord had been at the point of falling backward into the lava pit. Now he sprang to his feet, mentally brushed aside the rapidly dispersing mist of nightmarish chitinous bodies and slavering, ethereal jaws, gazed up into the monstrous crimson eyes of the lone ice-priest whose evil skills had conjured the visions.

For a moment Silberhutte paused . . . Then, with a grunt of exertion – even as the naked ice-priest frantically recommenced his esoteric passes – he narrowed his eyes, lifted his great axe, and drove its keen edge into the willowy giant's fragile chest. With a single, high-pitched, whistling shriek of agony and disbelief the ice-priest died, felled as a grass-blade before the scythe; and a moment later the Warlord stepped over his crumpled body, freeing his axe and almost absently cleaning its edge on the sleeve of his jacket.

Finally the red haze of battle and illusion-engendered weariness cleared from Silberhutte's eyes, and for the first time since releasing himself from the cloak in mid-flight, he saw his friends. They hurried toward him, their faces drawn and anxious, and he caught them to him crushingly. Then he drew a deep draught of the cold cavern air, released them, and said:

'Thank you, Henri, Moreen. When I cut loose from the cloak, my idea was to track you down and come on like the cavalry. But you outflanked me – thank goodness!' He turned back and gazed grimly on the broken circle of ice-priests. 'Now there are one or two things these fellows are going to tell us. We already know they're telepathic, so – '

'*We underestimated you, Warlord, that much we grant you,*' came a cold, booming voice in their heads, cutting short Silberhutte's words. '*There were none such as you three in Theem'-hdra. Strength such as yours – aye, and powers such as you possess – made men mighty in the Old World. Such men were wizards whose words were law, whose law was – *'

'Cruel and corrupt!' Silberhutte spoke out lord. 'Now listen, you ice-priests. We've no time to waste, so I'll make it short. We came to Dromos to find a box, a machine stolen from us by Ithaqua. One of you is already dead. I killed him and I'm glad of it. I don't care how many more I have to kill to get the machine. We three,' he indicated Moreen and de Marigny, 'we're all of a like mind.' Flanked by his friends, he hefted his axe in his huge fist and strode closer to the circle.

The three could not see the awful corpse faces of the four beings whose backs were to them, but the remaining five gazed at them with eyes red as the fires of hell. The veins that stood out in the domes of their mushroom heads were visibly pulsing now, and suddenly there was a tangible electric tension in the air which had not been present a moment earlier.

Moreen gasped and moved behind the Warlord, catching de Marigny's hand. He wrapped an arm about her, said: 'Something's coming, Hank – I feel it!'

'No tricks,' Silberhutte warned the ice-priests sharply, carrying his axe as if it were weightless and stepping closer still to the frozen figures.

'*Tricks? You dare relegate the magic of the ice-priests of olden Khrissa to mere trickery? Fools – you know nothing of us – nothing!*' Now the eyes of the five were boring into theirs with increasing intensity, crimson orbs that seemed to protrude obscenely as their owners concentrated . . . concentrated.

'Mind over . . . matter!' gasped the Warlord, experiencing again that iron constriction he had known earlier. 'Telekinesis – or something much . . . like it.' He tried to lift his axe but froze with the great blade only half-upraised. Though the muscles of his mighty frame bulged and strained, his earlier exertions had all but sapped him, making him easy prey to the mental 'magic' of these masters of weird phenomena.

Moreen, too, was held immediately helpless. Though she was young and strong, she had only a woman's physical strength; nor was her mind sufficiently sophisticated to grasp readily the nature of the forces involved. Only de Marigny, as yet untried by any real physical exertion in this frigid subterranean complex, found himself capable of the slightest movement.

Illusion, 'magic,' mind over matter, hypnosis – whatever powers these ice-priests possessed and however they chose to use them – there must surely be rules to the game. All actions have *counteractions*, produce *reactions*. De Marigny, unable to defend himself, knew that he must attack; but how? Then, like a glimmer of light in

426

a maelstrom of darkness, he remembered Annahilde's dreaming powders. And that single spark rapidly fanned itself to a flame, for he knew that the dreaming powders – together with the warming powders – were still tucked away in his clothes where the ice-priests had failed to search.

'*Fight fire*,' he told himself, '*with fire!*'

Slowly, agonizingly slowly, he forced his hand to the pocket that contained the dreaming powders, brought forth the pouch, lifted it toward his face. And all the while his eyes were held by the crimson gaze of the ice-priests, and each slightest movement of his body was slower than the one preceding it. Then, before he could even give thought to the task of disseminating the powders, the pouch was snatched from his hand and thrown down on the ice of the floor, taken from him by no visible power. Telekinesis – 'magic' – the mind power of the ice-priests!

Despair filled de Marigny – despair and the mad, triumphant laughter of the ice-priests, booming and mocking in his mind – until suddenly he became conscious of a frenzied tugging at the hair of his head and the fur fringe of his jacket. Armandra's familiar winds!

In a flash he saw his salvation – his, the Warlord's, and Moreen's. 'The . . . pouch,' he managed to whisper. 'The . . . powder!' And instantly the cave was filled with a tinkling of disturbed ice as frantic winds lifted the pouch from the floor, hovered it before the stricken Earthman's eyes, plucked at it until its contents spilled in air and formed a cloud.

'In their . . . faces,' he commanded. 'Blow it . . . in . . . their faces!' And the whirling cloud of powder was immediately rushed away, driven into the faces of the ice-priests by sentient winds. They breathed air, those chill, soulless beings – and now they breathed Annahilde's dreaming powders . . .

The effect was instantaneous.

For a brief moment the three beleaguered adventurers were granted a fleeting glimpse of the terrors that threatened the ice-priests – a single glimpse that leaped to their minds telepathically and involuntarily from the minds of the ice-encased ancients – but that one glance was sufficient in itself to testify to the efficacy of Annahilde's powders. Silberhutte, had he so desired, might easily have remained in telepathic contact with the stricken ice-priests, might have probed their stunned and hag-ridden minds to witness at firsthand the monstrous illusions that now enmeshed them; but that would have meant sharing their terror of the incredible nightmare hordes which now pressed in on them from all sides. Rather than suffer that, he withdrew, shuddering at what he had so briefly glimpsed.

Masters of illusion the ice-priests were, but theirs were illusions of the mind, born of advanced development of the ESP areas of the brain. Annahilde's powders, on the other hand, produced hallucinations which were external, 'artificial,' as it were; and the difference was that between a disturbing dream and a drug-induced hallucination.

For the powders worked on those areas of the mind that govern an individual's capacity for fear – his capacity to suffer it as determined by his capacity to inflict it. In the olden times the ice-priests had been masters of terror, and now they paid the price. What kind of horrors would terrify a ghoul, a mass murderer, a torturer, a homicidal maniac, a soulless monster? Whatever the kind, those were the horrors – indescribable in mundane terms – which now threatened the ice-priests of primal Theem'hdra.

The reactions of the three to their sudden release from the mind chains of the ice-priests were varied. De Marigny, to say the least, was relieved and delighted that his ruse had worked so well; Moreen was mystified and frightened, stumbling and clinging to her man's arm as the numbness abruptly left her limbs; and Silberhutte: he knew only that his anger, the rage and frustration he felt at the mere thought of these vilest minions of Ithaqua, had trebled. Given another chance he doubted that they would hesitate to kill himself and his friends out of hand; or worse by far, they would hold all three and wait on the return of the Wind-Walker. Plainly they must not be given that chance.

Showing that ruthless efficiency of which he was more than capable when circumstances demanded, commencing before the effect of Annahilde's dreaming powders could wear off, the Warlord waved de Marigny and Moreen back from the broken circle of tormented figures and swung his great axe high against the upper part of the nearest column. The massive icicle shattered where the axe bit. Pausing only to gauge his aim, Silberhutte next swung at the base of the pillar, then threw his weight against the collapsing slab of ice and toppled it bodily into the pit. A moment later and, with a belching roar, a great gush of steam came up mephitically, flowing outward along the tunnel's ceiling and settling as fine snow in a matter of seconds. The desiccated prisoner of the pillar, already immersed in hideous hallucinations, had known nothing at all of his final, fatal immersion. That at least had been a mercy.

But now the remaining eight were rapidly recovering, blinking their crimson eyes, and moving their heads from side to side, groping dimly with their minds ... and finding the mind of the Warlord open and waiting for them. He spoke to them with his mind, at the same time speaking out loud so that his friends would also hear him:

'Mercy is something of which you've no knowledge, ice-priests. You could no more understand mercy than you could show it. So be it. Your destruction here and now should come as no surprise to you; it's what you would do to us if the roles were reversed. Even so, you'll decide how many are to die; the matter is in your own hands. There are questions I will ask – to live you must supply the answers. But before we begin, just to be sure we understand each other – '

He again lifted his axe and struck mightily at the second pillar. The blow failed to completely shatter the icicle but severed the neck of the shrivelled being encased within it. That dweller in the ice was not so lucky as the first, was briefly aware of the doom rushing upon him, and his mental shriek was awful to hear in the moment before the keen edge of Silberhutte's axe cut it off. One more shattering blow followed – and a further creaking of ice, a toppling of frozen flesh, a second vast puff of poisonous vapour and settling cloud of fine, blasphemous snowflakes – before the thing was done.

Now only two figures remained on the nearer rim of the pit, but the crimson eyes of the five who now twisted their necks to gaze across from the other side of that volcanic blowhole – which, through nameless centuries had sustained the evil lives of the ice-priests and now, with utter equanimity, was taking them – surely mirrored their disbelief, their fury and hatred, their fear of these strangers come across the lightyears to exact a vengeance for deeds ancient, monstrous, and without number.

'*In what you have done,*' came the booming voice in their heads, weaker now but still full of acid hatred, '*you have signalled your own unenviable end!*'

'You take,' grunted Silberhutte, again lifting his avenging axe, 'a lot of convincing. Don't you understand? You're in no position to threaten. You're beaten!' And moments later yet another ice-priest screamed his last and toppled to boiling oblivion.

Now the eyes of the remaining six were bulging as before, the veins of their awful heads pulsing malignantly, and again there came that tension in the air that forewarned of a further manifestation of their power.

De Marigny, snatching up the pouch from where it had fallen, shook the dregs of Annahilde's dreaming powders into his palm and held up his hand where the ice-priests could see its contents. Then, clenching his fingers over the small heap of precious grains, he cried: 'No more of your tricks – or I'll send you straight back to hell! You're not the only ones who deal in nightmares, but I fancy mine are worse than any you might dream up . . .'

For an instant the tangible *electric* feeling went out of the air, and de Marigny believed he had convinced the ice-priests against any further use of their powers. Then –

With a roar and a crash fire licked up from the central pit, a mad gout of leaping flame that indiscriminately enveloped both ice-priests and adventurers in a moment, overwhelming all and spilling them in a blazing torrent down the length of the tunnel! Burning, feeling his skin cracking and peeling from him even as he heard Moreen's scream and saw her hair blossom into licking flames, still de Marigny thought to open his hand, thought to hoarsely utter one last command to Armandra's familiar winds – if indeed the winds themselves were not already consumed in the devouring fire.

'Go,' he told them, his voice a cracked whisper in the inferno. 'Again – the powder – in their faces!'

And perhaps because he felt those precious powders snatched from his palm by eager, frantic gusts of air, and so knew there was at least a chance that this was some ploy of the ice-priests and not a genuine eruption brought on by Silberhutte's feeding of the lava pit, de

Marigny was the first to recover from the effects of the illusion. Even so he was awed by the power these beings commanded, that depleted as they were, still they could so readily employ man's elemental and immemorial fear of fire.

For he had actually *felt* the terrific heat of the thing, had *felt* his eyes melting and his skin being crisped and stripped from his body. He had *seen* the ice-priests themselves engulfed and had *heard* in his head their telepathic shrieks of agony. And all a great illusion, a living nightmare conjured by these sole survivors of ancient Theem'hdra.

And so de Marigny recovered first . . . to see Moreen, unburned, curled on the cold floor where she had fallen, mercifully fainted away from all shock and terror; to see the Warlord frenziedly beating at himself, at his clothes, in a final attempt to quell the 'fires' that smothered him and consumed his flesh; to see the mouths of the ice-priests snap open in a concerted rictus of horror as once again the even greater horrors born of Annahilde's powders gripped them; and also to see the cave of ice, unaltered, blue and luminous and bitterly cold as ever!

And it was de Marigny, too, who, as the Warlord was released from his private hell of flames to fall trembling and white as snow to the icy floor, grabbed up his friend's great axe and cut down one, two, three of the stricken ice-priests, toppling their encased figures into the pit in a passion of loathing more desperately ruthless even than that displayed so recently by Silberhutte himself. Only the choking *vapours* that rushed up from the seething pit forced him back from his task – the vapours and the hideous 'snow' which they immediately formed – but then he stepped forward again to cut down a fourth and fifth ice-priest, and would have continued with the sixth and last had not Silberhutte, recovered but staggering still, stayed his hand and wrested the axe from him.

Only then did de Marigny fall back to lean panting against the glistening wall, nausea growing in him as he realized that he of all people – a truly 'civilized' man – had been gripped in what could only be described as a berserker rage. He who had so recently wondered at the Warlord's – inhumanity? – now knew that he would nevermore criticize his friend's instincts, for indeed the ice-priests more than deserved each and every stroke made against them.

'Not this last one, Henri,' Silberhutte was panting, shaken but sound, still astounded to find himself unblackened by fire. 'Not him, my friend, for he's all we have left, and he has the answers we need. He'll supply them, too – by God he *will!* You tend to the girl – I'll see to him.'

With that the Warlord lifted up his great axe before him and poised it inches in front of and level with the pulsing, bluely veined dome of the ice-priest's head. Then he lowered it until its keen, slime-spattered blade was almost resting on the forepart of that being's loathsome skull. The eyes of the ice-priest opened wide in terror, and he audibly sucked in air as Silberhutte began to speak:

'The weight of this weapon is not inconsiderable, ice-priest. If I let it fall, it would probably crack your head wide open. And if I added my own weight to it – then it would split you to your rib cage! At this very moment I am tempted to do just that, and at the first hint of any further trickery I will. If you doubt me, try me. It will be the last thing you ever do. Do we understand each other?'

Slowly the obscene head nodded, crimson eyes focusing briefly, shrinkingly on the blade of the axe where it glittered dully through thin, pinkish blood and drying brain matter.

'Good,' said the Warlord, his face cold as the ice that formed the walls of this inner adytum of evil. 'Now then, before my arms tire as the weight of the axe numbs them – where is the time-clock? Where is it, ice-priest? And if you would live, you'd best tell me no lie!'

5

A Mind Unlocked

'Hold your axe steady, Warlord, and believe me when I say there is much I can tell you,' the ice-priest answered. He looked down from his great height, ignoring as best he could the thin edge of sudden death poised before his face; but the booming power was gone from his telepathic voice and it was more like a whisper now, running frightened through the minds of the adventurers. *'If the time-clock is your primary concern, then its secret is easily told. It is close by, not far from here – you can reach it in a very little time.'*

'Where is it, exactly?' Silberhutte demanded, placing menacing emphasis on the last word.

'Do not rush me, Warlord, for I will not lie. And once more I beg you, hold well your axe. If it falls, your questions go unanswered and I simply . . . go!' Now the ice-priest seemed more in control of himself, had gauged the urgency of his enemy's need and was using it to prolong the questioning.

'He's stalling!' said de Marigny. 'He's avoiding giving direct answers.'

'Could it be,' the Warlord spoke to the ice-priest low and dangerously, 'that you believe your two brothers will return to rescue you? If they do come back before we know what we need to know, then you will surely die.'

'And should I fear this?' the crimson eyes of the ice-priest went from Silberhutte's face to the blade of the great axe. *'Warlord, I am already dead! If you do not kill me, Ithaqua will when he returns.'*

'Why should he do that?'

'He will surely kill any that you leave alive, for we will

435

have failed him. He has no patience with failure. However, if you and your friends are still here when he comes – then he may let us live.'

'It was your task to trap us for him?'

'What profit to deny it?'

'When will he return?'

The ice-encased figure offered a mental shrug. *'You might as well ask when will the wind blow. He commands his own comings and goings.'*

Listening to this conversation, de Marigny found his natural curiosity becoming piqued. Also, now that there seemed to be no further immediate danger, he felt the cold beginning to grip him, biting to his very bones. Quickly he took a pinch of Annahilde's warming powder, offering another to Moreen as, rapidly recovering from her faint, she got to her feet and began uncontrollably to shiver.

Silberhutte, too, had sensed the relaxation of danger; now he lowered his axe to the frozen floor. After all, what possible harm could this one ice-priest do them, when they had already disposed of nine such monsters?

By now de Marigny's curiosity had the better of him and he took up the questioning. 'Why are you here on Dromos in the first place?' he asked.

'We were "rescued" from olden Khrissa by Ithaqua – who may say how long ago? – when the common people turned against us. They would have overwhelmed us by sheer weight of numbers, and so we fled to Ithaqua whom we worshipped. He brought us here. I tell you this happened, indeed I know that it was so, but I personally remember little of it. My memory does not extend beyond the ice of the caves, the great snows of the upper world, the lava pit and its sulphur fumes.'

'Then how do you know it was so?' asked de Marigny.

'Ithaqua has on occasion reminded us of our debt.'

'Debt? He has kept you here on this great snowball of

a world – encased in ice for millions of years – and you consider yourself to be in his debt?'

'*Without him, we would have been dust aeons gone,*' the ice-priest reminded, and after a pause continued: '*Occasionally he provides diversions . . .*'

'Diversions?' de Marigny repeated. 'Here on Dromos?'

'*Of course. He brings us women from time to time, from Borea and Numinos, but they are nothing more than brief amusements. On the other hand he promises that once he has you three in his power – then that he will give us a green world of our own to rule. Perhaps Numinos, or Borea – even the Motherworld.*'

'Well,' said the Warlord, 'that's one mad dream we've put paid to.'

'*Three of us yet remain,*' the ice-priest retorted. '*With our powers, three should be sufficient – at least for any minor world.*'

'Three,' the Warlord mulled over the number, frowning as it set him to wondering. 'Why were only three of your brothers free and wandering abroad in Dromos when the remaining nine were encased in ice?'

For answer there came another mental shrug and the ghost of a laugh. '*Ithaqua made the rules, Warlord. Perhaps he feared to have more than three of us free at any one time. Fit and well and working as one – strong and mentally alert and not drowsing in the ice – who can say what our limits would be? Such illusions as we could create might fool even the Wind-Walker himself.*'

By now Moreen was almost fully recovered from her faint and already the warming powders were working in her blood. She had only half-heard the conversation between the two men and the ice-priest; her naïve mind was still staggering from the dizzy turns events had taken. But as she became more conscious of her surroundings and what was taking place, she realized that something was very wrong.

The Warlord – that massive and sometimes brutal man – as if engaged in casual conversation with an old friend, leaned on his axe and gazed up at the ice-priest with an almost bemused expression on his face. De Marigny, one arm loosely about her waist, seemed equally unconcerned. The entire atmosphere was completely unnatural – the more so because the crimson eyes of the lone ice-priest blazed hypnotically and bulged in their sockets as if at any moment to leap from their owner's monstrous head!

Moreen felt the hypnotic spell of those eyes and instantly averted her gaze. What was it the ice-priest had said? That his illusions might fool even Ithaqua himself?

'*He's fooling you!*' she screamed, tugging at de Marigny's arm and lashing out with her foot at the Warlord's shins. 'Don't look at his eyes!'

For a moment, caught off-balance, the two men looked startled; then their eyes met and their jaws dropped in spontaneous astonishment. It had been so close, and they had been so completely hoodwinked. But now their faces hardened as they too averted their eyes from the hypnotic gaze of the ice-priest.

The awful head of that ice-encased figure had commenced to shake violently from side to side – one of the very few movements its owner could readily perform – in frustration and rage. Triumph had indeed been close, only to be snatched away by a slip of a girl. Carefully, insidiously the ice-priest had worked his hypnotic spell, drawing the Earthmen into a web of false security – but now that web was torn aside, and the evil spinner himself stood exposed to the gaze of the adventurers.

Silberhutte quickly stepped around behind the last ice pillar, out of range of the evil, powerful eyes of its prisoner. He reached around to the front of the icicle with one hand and cupped the ice-priest's small chin, trapping his head and holding it still. With his other hand the Warlord gripped his axe close to its heavy head, reached around and pressed the naked blade of his weapon to the spindly giant's trembling throat.

'Look away, Henri, Moreen,' the Warlord commanded. 'It's between the two of us now. *You!*' He spoke to the ice-priest in a withering telepathic blast of anger and loathing. 'I want all of it, everything, and no holding back. Open up, ice-priest, and let me see what's hidden in there, in that black pit of nightmares you call a mind. Do it now, creature, while I'm still fool enough to let you live!'

And so powerful was the Warlord's command that it could no longer be denied. For a single moment only he probed at the innermost recesses of the ice-priest's thoughts, at the tightly guarded core of that being's mind – then broke through triumphant to the secrets hidden within. He looked – and he saw!

He saw all the pent-up evil of nameless aeons, the festering frustration of centuries unnumbered, the lightless horror of a million lifetimes spent in the abstract – but not *always* abstract – contemplation of hideous tortures and the endless plotting of mad dreams of conquest. He saw what the final destiny of olden Theem'hdra was to have been beneath the crushing heel of the ice-priests had they gained full control in that primal continent; and not only that but the fate of the universe itself if ever beings such as these were allowed to expand and overflow like pus into the clean and healthy worlds of space and time. These things and many others he saw and knew now why Ithaqua himself had seen fit to restrict the activity of these ice-priests whose depravity, whose lusting after all things loathsome, whose delight in the diabolical and sheer *potential* for total horror were so immeasurable.

He saw the many possible fates considered by the ice-priests for himself and his companions, the insufferable tortures and degradations plotted for them; and if he shuddered at what had been planned for himself and de Marigny, he positively shrank from the diseased diablerie

439

of Moreen's unspeakable fate. For the ice-priests had been promised the girl when Ithaqua was done with her, and their intentions toward her were far more complex, detailed, and depraved than his. It was surely a terrible thing in itself to envisage the girl ravaged and brutalized by the Wind-Walker, yes, but then to be thrown to the ice-priests with their less mentionable anomalies and deviations – including at the end, group anthropophagy *while yet the girl lived!* – that was to glimpse the essence of hell itself, pulsating like sentient slime in the cesspit minds of these most foul and detestable creatures.

Yet even now the ice-priest held back, refusing Silberhutte access to one final pocket of closely guarded knowledge, an almost complete set of answers to the Warlord's all-important questions. Closing his eyes and baring his teeth in a grimace of concentration against the frozen surface of the ice pillar, the massive Texan wrapped a knotted mental fist about the ice-priest's mind and squeezed . . . squeezed . . . and once more crashed through to a treasure trove of secrets.

Primarily he was seeking the time-clock; yes, and at last, finally he knew its location. For all at once he became aware of the most intimate details of this entire subterranean labyrinth of ice caves and tunnels, became heir to a plan of the frozen underworld which was immediately and as plainly recognizable to him as the lines in his own palm; so that now, in his mind's eye, he could see the time-clock where it stood, not too far distant, with de Marigny's flying cloak thrown carelessly about its base.

But if sight of the time-clock was a glad thing, not so the other secrets prised from the ice-priest's ravaged brain; secrets which, when the Warlord knew them, drove all else from his mind in a passion of horror and fear –

Fear not for himself but for Armandra, the Woman of the Winds, wayward daughter of Ithaqua the Wind-Walker. Armandra, on her way to Dromos right now, at this very moment, *and closely pursued by her monstrous father!*

For this was what the Warlord had most feared – that Ithaqua had deliberately brought the time-clock to Dromos solely in order to trap Armandra – and now his fears seemed fully realized. He saw how the ice-priests had blocked Armandra's every telepathic attempt to contact her man, how they had insinuated their own doom-laden suggestions into her mind until she suffered continually from hideous doubts as to Silberhutte's well-being. Finally, when her spirit had been at its lowest ebb, then they had sent out a desperate cry for help, a cry cut short before Armandra could discover their deception, that this was not the Warlord who cried out in distress.

And of course the Woman of the Winds had not hesitated for a single moment but had set out at once to walk those eerie winds that constantly blow between the words. That act which Ithaqua had never once managed to persuade her to perform – despite his countless enticements, his myriad threats – she now undertook without a second thought. For she went, or so she thought, to the aid of her beloved Earthman, caught up in some nameless evil.

Silberhutte saw how well the plot had been laid and executed, and he heard the cynical, sniggeringly gleeful laughter of the ice-priest whose mind he had forced to reveal these things. He heard that laughter – heard it turn to a mental shriek, a cry of horror that went on and on, threatening to tear his living soul from him and drag it down to hell –

– And then de Marigny was pulling him away from the pit, away from the headless ice-encased *thing* whose thin blood drenched his hands and arms and pinkly patterned the broad blade of his axe.

'Hank!' de Marigny cried, 'what in all – ?'

'No time, Henri,' the Warlord answered, his voice a cracked whisper, his eyes suddenly deep sunken in a chalk-white face. 'No time for explanations. Armandra is coming here – Ithaqua, too – and before they get here, we have to find the clock. I know where it is, and it's close. But remember: there are two more of these creatures on the loose down here. If we meet up with them . . . then we must kill them by whatever means are available to us. And be sure about one thing, Henri,' he gripped the other's arm fiercely. 'They *must* be killed; we daren't leave one of them alive! The universe will never be safe or sane as long as things like the ice-priests live . . .'

6

The Last Ice-Priest

At very best any sound, a glow that echoed the ice walls, that crossed their blue sheen in bursts... ... a world, a maze... ... the victory along that setting to drip as they slowly melted and finally the head was behind them while ahead they saw – the trio clearly.

The trio of adventurers hurried from the shattered lair of the ice-priests, along the blue-glowing tunnel and out into the great gallery. As they went, the Warlord related all he had seen in the secret inner mind of the ice-priest. De Marigny immediately grasped most of what his friend had to say, but Moreen found Silberhutte's revelations much harder going.

The girl had no experience of Armandra, the Warlord's mate, and so found the idea of a mere woman walking on the winds that blow between the worlds hard to accept. And yet perhaps it really was so; indeed Moreen was not yet over the amazing way in which she herself had been transported between worlds; and had not that, too, been the work of this daughter of Ithaqua, this Armandra? But there would be time later, she told herself, for the pondering of such problems; for the moment it was an effort merely to keep pace with the two men, who seemingly raced against time itself.

Hurrying one-third of the way around the gallery's perimeter and ignoring several lesser burrows that branched off from it – including the one where the illusory insect-hounds had held Moreen and de Marigny prisoners – the Warlord unhesitatingly plunged headlong into a tunnel whose arched, icicle-festooned entrance was somewhat taller and wider than the rest. Racing along behind him, de Marigny and the girl followed the winding corridor of ice until, suddenly, they found themselves on a declining gradient down which it was as easy to slide as run. In a little while the sloping floor levelled out and then, coming around the final, gradual bend –

At first there was a reddish glow that lighted the ice walls and drowned their blue sheen in bronze tints, then a wash of heat that set the air to shimmering and caused the icicles of the high ceiling to drip as they slowly melted, and finally the bend was behind them while ahead they saw – the time-clock!

They saw it . . . *across a river of sluggishly moving lava!*

De Marigny was stunned, brought up short beside the Warlord where he had skidded to a halt on the wet ice not ten paces from the oozing flow of molten rock. The channel the lava followed entered the tunnel from a low, wide archway to the right, cut straight across the floor at right angles, and disappeared under a similar arch on the left. It was all of forty feet across, with a surface of powdery pumice that continually quivered and formed cracks, from which hissing clouds of steam emerged and an occasional tongue of red fire greedily licked.

Beyond the lava stream, leaning against a low mound of rocks and pebbles, with de Marigny's flying cloak in a heap at its base, the clock stood and seemed to waver in the heat haze rising from the lava barrier. De Marigny gazed longingly at the clock and knew it to be completely beyond his reach. He took a pace forward as if to defy the heat that already was searing his legs.

'How solid is that stuff?' he spoke over his shoulder to the Warlord. 'I mean, would it take my weight if I – '

'No way,' Silberhutte answered, placing a hand on the other's shoulder. 'Look.' He quickly shrugged out of his fur jacket and twirled it round his head, then let the heavy garment fly out over the lava to fall in the middle of the stream. It alighted, glowed instantly red at its fringed edges, burst into flame even as the scum of surface pumice quivered and parted beneath its weight.

The sight of Silberhutte's jacket sailing out across the molten rock had given de Marigny an idea, however, and now he moistened his dry lips as he turned to the Warlord. 'Armandra's little winds!' he exclaimed. 'If they could lift my cloak, float it across here – '

Now the Warlord was interested; a gleam of hope came into his eyes as he gripped de Marigny's shoulder. 'Right!' he cried, turning to left and right, lifting his face and casting about in the sulphurous air for Armandra's familiar winds, finding – nothing.

'Not here?' de Marigny's voice echoed his disbelief, his disappointment. 'Then where are they?'

Hearing his words, the Warlord started as from some sudden shock. The haggard look came back into his eyes as he turned to his friends. 'I haven't contacted Armandra since we arrived on Dromos,' he said. 'At first I didn't want to, for if there was going to be trouble, I didn't want her following us here – better if she knew nothing of how things were. Now – well, she's coming anyway, called by those damned deceiving ice-priests. Yes, and she must be pretty close at that. Why else would her familiars leave us?'

'You think they've gone off to meet Armandra?' said de Marigny.

The Warlord nodded. 'They must have. Wait – ' He closed his eyes and a frown of mental effort gradually grew on his face.

De Marigny, not wanting to disturb the Warlord's concentration – knowing that he was attempting to contact Armandra telepathically, that the outcome would probably be vitally important – signalled Moreen's silence and himself kept perfectly still.

With the passing of a few more seconds the lines of effort on Silberhutte's face changed to lines of puzzlement, then of anger. Under his breath he said: 'There's interference . . . those damned ice-priests . . . but I'm reaching her . . .'

In the next moment the words, 'Ithaqua – *damn his*

445

black heart!' burst from Silberhutte's lips as, galvanized into
frantic activity by what he had seen through Armandra's
mind, he sped away back down the ice tunnel.

So as not to leave his friends completely in the dark as to
his intentions, before passing out of sight around the curve
of the frozen walls, he hoarsely called back: 'Stay here,
Henri. Do what you can. Armandra is almost here – but
Ithaqua is closing in on her fast! I must see what I can do.'
Then he was gone, but echoing back to the two at the edge
of the lava river came his final words: 'Good luck . . . !'

'Luck, Hank!' de Marigny yelled back, frustration and a
clutching sickness welling up in him that there was nothing
he could do to help the situation. In desperation he turned
his attention once again to the lava barrier that alone kept
him from the time-clock.

For locked in that machine, built into it by Kthanid the
Elder God, was a weapon whose power could stop even
the awesomely powerful Great Old Ones – the Cthulhu
Cycle Deities themselves, of which Ithaqua was one. If
only there were some way to cross this slow-moving flood
of molten rock, then the rest would be a matter of the
utmost simplicity. But there was no such way across . . .
was there?

Yes, there was, but it made de Marigny's mind, his soul
and entire body cringe merely thinking of it. He knew if he
dwelled upon it too long that he could never bring himself
to face it. But face it he must, for there was too much at
stake here.

He turned from the river of lava and took twenty
deliberate paces up the ice corridor before halting and
turning back. Moreen saw his intention and ran toward
him. 'You can't,' she cried, 'you can't! No man could leap
that distance – it's too far.'

'A hop, a skip, and a jump,' he answered, gritting his
teeth. 'I could have done it once; perhaps I still can.'

Trembling with horror, she stood back from him. 'You'll

446

broil your legs – the lava will strip them to the bone! – and what if you slip and fall?'

'Don't, Moreen!' he almost snarled. 'I have to try.' He faced the lava river, went into a half-crouch, and –

'*No!*' came a sharp mental command, booming and echoing in de Marigny's mind. '*No, Earthman, you are not to die here, not now. Ithaqua would not wish it so. He has his own plans for you – and for the girl.*'

Maintaining his crouch and whirling into a defensive position, de Marigny's wide eyes found the crimson orbs of the ice-priest where the spindly giant had stepped from jagged shadows cast by a row of icy stalagmites. He prepared to launch himself at the gaunt creature, whose hands already were weaving strange patterns in the air; but a freezing coldness, a numbing paralysis was rapidly spreading through his limbs. In a moment the metamorphosis was complete; and with his muscles frozen into immobility, he toppled forward and crashed to the floor like a stone statue.

Now the ice-priest turned to Moreen, trapping her between himself and the molten rock river. Before he could fix her with his crimson eyes, however, or fascinate her with the mesmeric motions of his hands, she spun away from him and sped toward the lava. He swiftly followed, his eyes bright with a timeless lust, only pausing in his bony striding when the girl skidded to a halt close to the Warlord's discarded axe. She cast one terrified glance at her pursuer, then bent to grasp the great axe with both hands.

Laughing hideously in her mind, the ice-priest came on. She was a mere girl and could hardly lift the axe, much less put it to any use. Thus the incredibly ancient being believed, and possibly that was the way girls had been in olden Theem'hdra. This was why he now resorted to purely physical methods to take her, when he might easily have caught her by spinning a telepathic mind web.

But he had not reckoned with Moreen's desperation, her determination.

As he came up to her, the girl straightened, turning to face him and dragging the axe with her. Such was the weapon's weight that she had to lean backward to control it as, rising up with her turning, the axe pulled her arms out straight. The great blade passed in front of the ice priest's middle and pulled the girl around with it. He moved closer, intending to throw his arms about her and put an end to this farce – until at last he saw his danger.

She had increased her rate of spin and already the blade was flashing around again, faster, inexorably, to the point where it would make a deadly connection. The ice-priest saw this and could not believe his eyes – saw, and the evil smile of triumph died on his monstrous face – died even as he was to die. The blade of the axe, still sharp for all its grisly work, came leaping around and sliced into his side, crippling him and knocking him from his feet. Before he could do more than writhe in agony on the floor, Moreen hauled the axe free and used her last ounce of strength to swing it at his mushroom-domed head, splitting it like an overripe melon . . .

Moreen was still being sick when de Marigny limped up to her, his face a mass of bruises and small cuts. He paused to touch her shoulder – then looked beyond her with eyes which could no longer credit the truth of anything they saw. For when the ice-priest had died, so too had died the illusory river of lava!

A few paces away, Silberhutte's jacket lay on the frozen floor of the tunnel untouched by fire. The clock, its four hands moving on their great dial in completely incomprehensible patterns, seemed almost to wait in silent sentience beyond. But at last its waiting was at an end.

Silberhutte had entered the great ice gallery and was on the point of plunging into that tunnel which led back to the volcano entrance to the frozen underworld. Such were his exertions that his breath came in great gasps and his legs and arms moved like massive pistons. All the time he sought mental contact with Armandra, but telepathic intrusions from some undetermined source close at hand kept interfering. Then, suddenly, his and his woman's minds locked onto each other, became as one, and he skidded and slid to a halt just within the mouth of the tunnel as Armandra herself came around a curving wall of ice toward him.

Armandra, the Woman of the Winds! And borne up by the very air, she floated into view, inches above the floor of the tunnel, her hair a golden halo that drifted above her, her face a carmine skull that glowed through her flesh, her white fur jacket and skirt alive with eerie motion. She came, and recognizing her man's presence, a shudder passed through her as she settled to the floor and the carmine light died in her eyes.

Then they were locked in each other's arms, locked physically and mentally, and their telepathic exchange was a barrage of passion and fear, of love and loathing as they told their tales in lightning-fast disorder; until at last the present loomed in on them and only one all-important fact remained uppermost in their minds. The fact that Armandra's awful father was close behind.

'How close?' Silberhutte asked out loud, taking her hand and hurrying her back along the way he had come, across the ice gallery toward the tunnel that led back to his friends, where – to his knowledge – they waited at the edge of a river of lava.

'He keeps his mind closed to me,' she gasped, exhausted by her journey through the interplanetary void. 'I don't know how close he is – but he's close, Hank, so close! I had the feeling he could have taken me at any moment, but that he deliberately held back. Now – '

She paused, her now green eyes opening wide as an

449

almost electric shock of horror passed through her. They froze at the entrance to that tunnel whose sinuous folds contained the time-clock and fearfully looked back. A blast of cold air – so cold that even they could feel it – blew snow and ice particles into the gallery, setting the myriad hanging icicles to an eerie creaking, a tinkling and chiming. The temperature dropped further still, plummeted, and the white rime upon every surface visibly deepened, turning the blue glow from the ice walls to a scintillant glare of madly winking diamonds.

'*He's here!*' she cried, even as an awful shadow fell across the gallery, flowing like ink from the tunnel mouth where so recently they were reunited.

'Close your mind to him!' the Warlord warned. Then, the paralysis broken, he caught Armandra up and ran into the tunnel, ran to where a huge hump of ice loomed up from the floor, and carried Armandra into the temporary protection of its shadow. From that position he watched the gallery, saw the monster Ithaqua – shrunken now but still three times greater in size than any man – stride into view.

Ithaqua! Anthropomorphic, black figure of hell, cold and dark as the spaces between the stars which spawned him, inky blot of a head turning this way and that, carmine eyes gazing – but only for a moment – into the very tunnel where Silberhutte and Armandra hid from him. Then, when the monster would have passed them by –

'*They're here, master, here!*' came that treacherous telepathic voice in their minds, in Ithaqua's mind, too, from a source which only now made itself apparent.

It was as if the ice-priest had stepped out of thin air, or out of the walls of ice themselves; but now this sole survivor of his kind cast aside all magic and illusion to show himself, tall and gaunt – and cringing like a whipped dog before his monstrous master! One hand he used to fawningly beckon Ithaqua into the tunnel, urging him to hurry, while with the other he pointed out the hiding place of the Warlord and his woman.

And now Ithaqua came, webbed feet finding purchase on the icy floor, carmine eyes glaring suspiciously and massive fists clenched threateningly where they hung at his sides. He came, and the chill of empty space came with him, riming the walls and floor of the tunnel inches deep with frost in the space of only a few seconds. The ice-priest ran to greet him, held out spindly trembling arms to him in supplication – was paid for his services with one lightning sweep of the monster's arm that flattened him to the iron-hard ice of the wall like a swatted fly.

Thus the last of the ice-priests died.

7

Eruption!

And as if that sole survivor of the immemorially ancient ice-priests had never existed – as if he had not been born evilly, lived evilly, and grown into the evil priesthood, finally to be snatched from the wrath of honest people and carried here by Ithaqua himself, only now to die so abruptly at the hands of that self-same storm-spawn – so the Wind-Walker ignored his shattered corpse and advanced into the tunnel.

His carmine gaze seemed to penetrate the ice-layered walls of volcanic rock, causing the tunnel to glow a dull pink, like a gateway to hell. And high though the ceiling was, still Ithaqua had to stoop to fit his monstrous manlike form into the icicle-festooned tunnel; and his vast blot of a head rocked from side to side as he advanced, step by step, toward that massive stump of ice that hid his quarry from his gaze.

Except that it seemed no longer to hide them . . .

Perhaps it was that he detected certain telepathic traces that they were unable to conceal – or that he sensed their fear – or simply that he knew instinctively where they were. Whichever, he ignored a dozen other great fangs of ice where they stuck up from the floor and made straight for their particular refuge. And as he came, so his head ceased its inquisitive side-to-side movement and he began to stretch out his fearful arms before him.

'*Run!*' Silberhutte commanded, his voice ringing in the shocked air like a pistol shot.

Taking Armandra's hand, he raced away with her down the frozen burrow toward the lava river, hidden from view by half a mile of winding, curving walls of ice. Ithaqua saw them at once and sent a blast of telepathic derision coursing after them – then came on himself, his vast strides effortlessly closing the distance between them as the two he pursued slipped and slithered in their haste, scurrying like mice before the sure tread of some demonic cat.

Looking back as Ithaqua's shadow began to overtake them, Silberhutte saw the monster pause, reach up, and snatch down from the ceiling an icicle with the girth of a barrel. In the next moment, guessing correctly the Wind-Walker's purpose, he gathered up Armandra on the run and leaped high as a ton of ice came crashing and careening down the corridor after them, bouncing and slithering like a juggernaut over the rippled floor. Another moment and the pair fell, Silberhutte cushioning Armandra's soft body with his own, amidst a chaos of shattering ice.

Half-stunned from the roaring of tortured ice – loud as an avalanche in the sounding walls of the tunnel – still the Warlord protected his woman as their bodies slowed to a halt, a tangle of arms and legs in a shivering of frozen fragments. Half-stunned he lay there as Ithaqua drew near and finally towered over them, his carmine gaze searing their very souls. Then, acting instinctively and with incredible bravado – despite the hellish ringing of mad, alien laughter in his head and the sure knowledge that this *must* be the last thing he would ever do – Silberhutte shook a mental fist in the face of the monster and charged his mind to fire one final telepathic salvo:

'*Hell-Thing!*' he cried. '*Star-born spawn of an unholy mating between –* '

But the Wind-Walker would hear no more. His eyes were sputtering pools of fiery rage as he reached down to sweep Armandra aside, sending her spinning half-conscious across the debris-littered floor. Then, deliberately, he lifted up one great webbed foot and poised it

453

over the head of his mightiest mortal enemy – but before that awesome club could fall . . .

. . . A beam of purest white light lighted the tunnel, its needle tip searing the Snow-Thing's shoulder and sending him stumbling back, staggering away from his intended prey. Only for a single instant did that beam lick out, but in that solitary moment of time the changes wrought in Ithaqua were astounding. From a dumbly snarling, murderous beast-god he became a cringing, vaguely anthropomorphic shape that wavered like smoke, mewling telepathically as he backed away, holding his hands up before a bloated black face in which flinching carmine eyes were slitted now and full of – fear?

Fear, yes – even Ithaqua – for this was that power against which he could not stand, the power of the beneficent Gods of Eld – the cleansing beam of the time-clock's weapon!

Then Ithaqua turned and fled, bounding away down the ice tunnel, rapidly shrinking as he made of himself a smaller target, careening heedlessly from wall to wall as he sought to avoid that purifying needle of light which licked out after him again and again until he disappeared around the curve of the wall and was gone. And as de Marigny set the time-clock down on the ice-littered floor the Warlord was already helping Armandra to her feet, hugging her to him and offering her comfort as any man might comfort his woman.

Leaving the time-clock, it took de Marigny only a few seconds to convince Silberhutte and Armandra that they would suffer no harm from his fantastic machine. For all that it was a creation of the Elder Gods, it was not an extension of their power (except in the form of its single weapon) and could not cause them physical pain such as would be caused by one of the star-stones of ancient Mnar. Then it was simply a matter of bundling them in through the opening of the clock's panel, into that place where Moreen waited for them, an utterly fantastic place whose dimensions were greater – infinitely – than external appearances might ever account for.

Quickly de Marigny demonstrated the use of mental *rapport* in binding his passengers to the clock's sensory systems, and once they had the hang of it and were over their initial astonishment, then he flew that incredible vehicle of the Elder Gods out of the frozen underworld, up the massive throat of the volcano, and into the outer world of Dromos. There, stationary in the air above that mighty vent, he briefly explained his purpose in directing the clock's beam back down into it:

First, that if Ithaqua yet hid in the underworld, he might permanently be sealed in down there; and secondly, that the underworld itself was and had been a place of evil for so long that its door should not be left open on any sane or ordered universe. Then he said no more but triggered the clock's weapon to pour its ray with an ever-brightening glare into the volcano's vent.

For minutes he played the beam into the root of the volcano, continuously increasing its power until his passengers were obliged to quit the time-clock's scanners; for even though they viewed the scene outside with their minds, the sight threatened the mind's eye itself! And although he had used that awesome weapon before, even the clock's master did not know the full extent of its power, so that the great gout of flame that suddenly licked forth from the volcano's rim came as a complete surprise to him.

He lifted the clock high into the skies of Dromos then and watched that ancient cone fill with fiery life, spewing its molten heart miles into the air. A river of lava coursed down the side of the volcanic mountain, hissing and obscuring the view in clouds of steam from melting drifts of snow. In another moment a fantastic pyrotechnic display commenced – with lava bombs and flaring streamers of fire hurled in all directions – out of which, rising like a dread phoenix from the flames, came the black and once more gigantically bloated figure of the Wind-Walker, fleeing the fire and racing madly for those high-blowing currents of etherwind which only his feet knew, whose ways only he had ever wandered.

And as he cleared the rim of Dromos, so he saw the time-clock where it seemed to wait for him on the reaches of the void; and he threw up his great hands before his flinching eyes, knowing full well his vulnerability and that at any moment he must surely feel the fatal sting of de Marigny's ray. But no, the beam did not come, and slowly the Wind-Walker lowered his hands to stare in alien amazement at the time-clock where it faced him squarely across a distance of less than two hundred yards.

Now, in his expanded size, he dwarfed the clock completely, made of it the merest toy, which in his hands it had once been. But in de Marigny's hands, for all that it seemed so tiny, the clock was the most awful weapon. And still the beam did not come.

For long moments they stood thus high in the sky over Dromos – darkly looming Wind-God and coffin-shaped vehicle of unbelievable journeys and near-infinite power. Then, as at a mutual signal though none was given, they broke apart and went their separate ways; Ithaqua striding off, bemused beyond a doubt, into unknown star-spaces, and the time-clock winging ever faster inward, away from Dromos, past Numinos, down toward Borea itself . . .

Much later Silberhutte was to ask de Marigny: 'When you could have finished the monster for good, you didn't. Why?'

De Marigny was to shake his head in answer, replying: 'No, something told me that that wasn't the way into Elysia. I remember that Titus Crow once told me much the same thing. And of course we don't know for sure that

I could have killed him. Better to retain the threat of his extinction, I think, than to try to destroy him and fail.'

But the Warlord's patience had left him. 'I don't understand,' he grated. 'After all we've been through, couldn't you – '

'I am glad,' Armandra had broken into the conversation, 'that you let him go, Henri. My father always was, he is now, and he must always be. He is one of those elementary evils which *must* exist, so that we lesser sinners may be reminded where our ways may ultimately lead us.'

'And I, too, am glad he lives,' Moreen had added in her turn. 'Once he flew with me all around Dromos, and he was gentle. Perhaps if we knew how to make him so, he would be gentle again . . .'

'Perhaps,' the Warlord had then grunted, subdued but unable to keep the cynicism out of his voice. 'And perhaps not.'

Epilogue

It was all of three weeks later (Earthtime, for de Marigny still used the chronology of the Motherworld) when at last the time came around for him to take his departure from Borea. Three weeks, but it might easily have been a much shorter period had he felt able to tear himself away from the plateau and its polyglot tribes and peoples.

Now the adventurers stood together on the roof of the plateau surrounded by the many thousands of its inhabitants come to see the departure of the time-clock and its crew. The talking was all done, the farewells all said; and only the wind any longer had voice, blowing a thin rime of fine snow crystals across the flat roof and between the massed ranks of spectators, piping an eerie, far-distant tune.

Much had happened in the days since the return of the four to Borea. There had been a second visit, however brief, to Numinos to see Annahilde and carry her and her sons into the safety of the Isle of Mountains; several trips to the sunward side of Borea, where Silberhutte had discovered those tropic islands and lands so often dreamed of; one short mission of vengeance in the time-clock, undertaken solely on the insistence of the Warlord, to destroy utterly Ithaqua's totem temple out on the white waste and recruit the Children of the Winds in their thousands into the brotherhood of the plateau; yes, and banquets and tournaments and pleasurable things galore –

– Until finally de Marigny had said: 'It's time,' and had gone off with Moreen to their rooms high on the plateau's rim.

And later Silberhutte had followed and the two men had

talked, when for once Armandra kept out of her man's mind to let him make his own decisions. For this was the way she had known it must be sooner or later.

'Hank,' de Marigny had said, when finally the conversation had led them to it, 'I think your decision is the right one. If I were you, I would do the same thing.'

'You don't know what I've decided,' the other pointed out.

'Oh, I do,' de Marigny answered. 'And if ever I return to the Motherworld, I'll tell them that you're a king in Borea – that you rule all the tribes of the south, where an auroral sun always shines, however strangely – and that your queen is strange and beautiful beyond belief. I'll tell them that you walk on the wings of the wind there together, and that no man was ever so loved . . . or so lucky.'

'That we walk the winds together, Henri?' the Warlord had raised his eyebrows in question. 'Armandra is Ithaqua's daughter, yes – and she walks the wind when the fancy takes her, granted – but I remain earthbound, my friend.'

'No more, Warlord!' the other had laughed, handing over a silken bundle which Silberhutte at once recognized as being the flying cloak.

'Henri, I couldn't accept your – '.

'Why not? I've no further use for it now that the time-clock is mine again.' And before the other could further protest, de Marigny had asked: 'Will you tell them that Moreen and I are leaving, and that we'd like everyone to see us off from the roof?'

And now they stood together on the roof: Armandra and the Warlord, Tracy Silberhutte and Jimmy Franklin, Oontawa and Kota'na, with all of the plateau's Elders ringing them about and the tribes thronging behind. Only the sad winds spoke, until Armandra, unable to bear the silence any longer, her golden voice full of anguish, begged:

'Must you go?'

As if in answer, of its own accord, the panel in the front of the time-clock swung open, and the four hands on its weirdly hieroglyphed dial commenced moving in a different pattern, a new and unfathomable sequence.

Then, without another word, de Marigny and Moreen passed into the clock and became part of the purple light that softly pulsed within.

Behind them, the panel clicked shut . . .

ELYSIA
THE COMING OF
CTHULHU!

For W. Paul Granley, who was
there at the christening . . .

1
Borea

Kota'na, Red Indian straight out of America's Old West –
Kota'na, Keeper of the Bears – watched Moreen at play
with a pair of cubs each bigger than herself and shook his
head in admiration and amazement. The mother of the
bears, huge Tookis, almost ten feet in height when she was
upright, grunted and pawed the floor of the exercise cavern
where she stood beside her master. Her mate was Morda,
Kota'na's favourite among all the fighting bears, but Morda
was not here. No, for he was out hunting with a pack of
his brothers and their keepers, butchering food-beasts
around the foot of the plateau for the larders of its tribes.

But the way this girl played with these cubs – without
fear, laughing and biting their ears, and slapping their noses
where they tumbled her – and them retaliating with howls
and clumsy bounds, like puppies, but *never* going to strike
her! Striking each other, certainly, with mighty, resounding,
bone-breaking clouts; but not the girl, never the girl. And
mighty Tookis, the mother of the cubs – the way she
seemed to enjoy all of this, snorting her encouragement
and thumping the floor – but if anyone else had dared to
try it, maybe even Kota'na himself . . . well, good luck to
him!

And at last Moreen had had enough. Laughing and
panting she struggled free of the boisterous mounds of
snowy fur which were Tookis' cubs, then leaned against
the wall of the cavern to catch her breath. 'They're too
much for me!' she panted and laughed, shaking back her
shoulder-length, golden hair. 'Why, I'd bet they're even
too much for their own mother! Eh, Tookis?' And she flung
an arm round the great bear's neck.

Tookis thought otherwise. With a low growl she shook Moreen off, shambled forward into the fray, raised a cloud of dust where she merged with the cubs; until their massed, tussling, rumbling bulk resembled nothing so much as a small white unevenly mobile mountain. Kota'na grinned and let the play of these giant descendants of Polar bears continue for a moment or two, then stopped it with a single word. Until now the animals had been completely free, harmless in the presence of their master, but Kota'na dared not leave them alone like that. The cubs were at that curious age and would explore if they could; it would never do to have them wandering free through the many levels and labyrinths of the plateau, with mighty Tookis shambling along behind them! And so now he chained all three by their collars to the wall, on tethers long enough they might continue their game, then stepped back and let them get on with it.

'There,' he said, as the snarling, slavering and tumbling recommenced, in a very convincing imitation of the real thing, 'let them weary themselves with play. It's the best exercise I know. And while they play, will you not sit with me on the high balcony there, and look out over Borea while we talk?'

Moreen had her breath back; she stood up straight, all sixty-four inches of her, and dusted herself down. Then she gazed up in open admiration at the tall, bronzed Indian brave. He wore his shiny black hair in pigtails that fell forward to the ridges of his collarbones, and his naked arms and deep chest were marked with the unfaded scars of many a battle. For Kota'na was a great hero of the plateau's wars with Ithaqua's wolf-warriors and his Children of the Winds, and his deeds were already legended as the deeds of any mere man may be. Now he kept the bears for Hank Silberhutte, the plateau's Warlord; but more than that he was Silberhutte's friend, the highest honour to which any man of the plateau might ever aspire.

And as Moreen regarded him, so Kota'na's keen brown eyes stared back in mutual appreciation. De Marigny, man (or possibly magician) of the Motherworld, had got himself a fine woman here. She should bear him many strong sons.

The girl was lithe and supple as a withe, with wide, bright blue eyes and skin like the pale honey of wild bees. She had about her an aura, a warmth she wore like some fine fur; which had only ever been torn aside by Ithaqua, black stalker between the stars. Now, in her brown jacket and trousers of soft leather, she seemed almost boyish, and yet fragile for all that. But her unaffected grace and loveliness, and her youthful litheness, were perhaps set off by a not-quite innocence; for Moreen had seen the Wind-Walker at his worst, and no one could remain wholly innocent after that.

To have seen Ithaqua raging – to be witness to his mindless slaughters – was to have the innocence mercilessly ripped from you. And yet she had come through all of that, had succeeded against all odds to be one with The Searcher, Henri-Laurent de Marigny. Aye, mortal and fragile as all human beings are, nevertheless Moreen bore a strength in her and a power; she was a free creature of Nature, and could commune with all creatures of Nature wherever she found them. This was her power, and thus her seeming familiarity with Tookis and her cubs.

As to Kota'na's invitation: 'Very well,' she said. 'But what shall we talk about? – and please don't ask me to tell you *again* about Numinos, or of our adventures in the ice-caves on Dromos. That was a very frightening time and I would like to forget it ...' And for a moment, anyway, the laughter went out of her wide eyes.

It was mid-morning on Borea, and the day was still and uncommonly bright. But 'bright' is hardly the right word, for Borea has no real daylight as such; it is a world which dwells in a permanent half-light, certainly in its northern regions. And that was where the plateau's vast hive

465

of alveolate rock stood: in Borea's northland. There it towered, mighty outcrop thrust up in ages past, flat-roofed and sheer-sided, the last redoubt of Borea's free peoples against Ithaqua and his Children of the Winds.

The balcony Kota'na had mentioned lay through an archway in the wall of the great bears' exercise cavern, cut through where the cavern's wall came closest to the plateau's face. One of many such observation points, it was a wide ledge where benches had been carved from the solid rock; and beyond – only a chest-high wall separated Moreen and Kota'na from empty air and a sheer face that fell for well over a hundred feet to the icy, scree-littered foot of the plateau.

It was cold there, where the occasional draught of frigid air would come gusting in from the northern plains; and so Moreen kept on the move while they talked, hurrying to and fro on the precipitous balcony and only pausing now and then to peer out and down at some freshly discovered feature spied on the gentling snow-slopes far below. Kota'na, on the other hand, impervious to the cold, as were most of the people of the plateau, simply stood stern-faced, his arms folded on his breast.

'No,' he said after a moment, 'I will not ask about the moons of Borea: Numinos, where you were born, or Dromos, where the Lord Sil-ber-hut-te and you others destroyed the ice-priests. I have remembered it well from your other tellings, and from what the Warlord himself has told me. It is a tale I shall pass down to my children, when they are old enough to understand it; and when Oontawa their mother is old, and when I am a wrinkled, leathery Elder, then *our* children will tell it to theirs. That is the way of legends; it is how they live. No, this time I would know of the places you have seen since last you were here, and what brings you back here? And if it is not impertinent of me – for I know your man is a wizard, whose ways are hard to understand – I wish you would also say what ails him? Doubtless it is a pain I cannot ease, but if I could –'

Impulsively, Moreen stood on tiptoe and hugged the tall Indian's neck. 'No wonder Hank Silberhutte loves you!' she burst out. 'And Oontawa and the great bears and your people, too. That stern look you wear can't fool me, Kota'na; it is a mask. You and your legends and tales·of derring-do. You're a romantic, that's all! You'd take the entire weight of the plateau itself on your own shoulders, if you could. The way you talk about Hank, as if he were a god! He's a man of the Motherworld. But how can I blame you when he is exactly the same? You should hear *him*, sometimes, when he talks about how you killed the traitor Northan – and then would not give up his head until Hank had seen it and forgiven you for stealing his glory?'

Kota'na held her at arm's length and raised an eyebrow at her impetuosity; but she could tell that he was pleased. He very nearly smiled. 'The Lord Sil-ber-hut-te ... says these things?'

'What? Of course he does! He can't talk about his "bear-brother" without puffing himself up first. You men!' Then she stepped back a little, hugged herself and shivered. And: 'Come on, let's walk in the plateau,' she said; and in a moment her voice was serious again.

Back under the arch and into the exercise cavern they went, where Tookis and her cubs were sprawled, panting, for the moment spent. Kota'na stopped and spoke briefly to a young Eskimo keeper, told him to tend the bears, and then he and Moreen passed on into the plateau's labyrinth. As they went, she said:

'You ask what ails Henri. Well, I'll tell you. Except, believe me, he is not a wizard. His time-clock is a wizard's device, or would seem to be, I'll grant you; and its previous owner, now perhaps he really *was* a wizard! – or so I'd judge from what Henri says of him. But not de Marigny. He's just a man, albeit a very wonderful man, and I love him. And you're right, he *is* unhappy. Which is a hard thing to understand, I know. Through the time-clock he has all space and time at his command; they are his to explore endlessly. And yet – '

'Yes?'

She shrugged, and now Kota'na could see that Moreen, too, was unhappy. Because of her man's unhappiness. 'The one thing he most desires,' she finally continued, 'it is forbidden to him. The one place he would find, that remains hidden. The one voice he would hear, even across kalpas of space and time, stands silent. Indeed, the entire universe seems indifferent to his endless searching, even heedless of it. Do you know, but Henri is known as The Searcher now, on a hundred strange worlds? What ails him? It is this: someone once showed him a bright jewel place, where miracles are frequent and the impossible is commonplace – a place beyond imagining, called Elysia and said to be the home of the gods – and all Henri finds are balls of mud and rock twirling endlessly about their heart-suns. Worlds countless as grains of sand – and to him just as tasteless. Ah! – I will tell you, Kota'na – but we have seen *wonderful* worlds in the three years you say have elapsed since first we left here in the time-clock. Huge worlds of ocean, teeming with islands of turquoise and rose and agate; mountain worlds where cities stand in the clouds atop the highest peaks; forest worlds, where the air is laden with scents of a million orchids, and the nights lit with organic lanterns glowing in the beacon-trees. We found friends on these worlds you would not believe, because of their strangeness; and so many of them took us to their hearts. But no, the one friend Henri seeks has a machine for a heart!'

'*Huh!*' grunted Kota'na. 'He would seem perverse, this man you love. And yet he cannot be, because you love him. Perhaps he is under the spell of a mightier wizard yet?'

And at that Moreen had to laugh. 'Oh, he is, he is!' she

said. 'Or so Henri would have me believe, anyway. But remember, Kota'na: my fostermother, Annahilde, was a "true" witch-wife – and yet even her magic was only trickery. So you see, I don't really believe in magic, and neither must you. There are only strange people – people with weird and fantastic powers – but there is no magic. And that is a fact for Henri told me himself. No magic at all, but forces and powers and something called "science".' But as she finished speaking, and even though she continued to smile, still it seemed to Kota'na that the girl's eyes had clouded over a little.

And in her heart:

Magic? she thought. *Perhaps there is after all. For certainly Henri is ensorcelled. By a place called Elysia, and by the visions of a man called Titus Crow . . .*

At that very moment, Hank Silberhutte and Armandra, the Woman of the Winds, were having much the same conversation. They were in their cavern apartments near the very roof of the plateau, and there was a rare tension between them which had its source in Armandra's natural suspicions and preternatural senses, and in the Warlord's most *un*natural predilection for adventure.

They were telepathetically attunded, these two, but had an agreement: their mental privacy was paramount. Only in their most intimate moments together, or in time of danger or matters of pressing urgency, did they mingle their minds. For they had long since discovered that it is not well for man and wife to live in each other's pockets – nor constantly *in* each other's thoughts, literally! But now Armandra was tempted to look into her man's mind, and perhaps not surprisingly.

The time-clock was back on Borea after an absence of three years, and with it an air of adventure. And that, thought Ithaqua's daughter, was Hank Silberhutte's trouble. It was what gave him restless nights, filled his head with thoughts of a Motherworld; Earth, else long forgotten, brought him dreams of quests and adventures out beyond the farthest stars.

'Armandra,' the Warlord sighed now, pausing in his troubled striding to reach out and gently grasp her shoulders in his massive paws – the delicate-seeming shoulders of this incredible woman, human spawn of the vastly inhuman Wind-Walker – 'we've had all this before. Don't you remember the last time? And didn't you entertain just such doubts then? And what came of all your fears, eh?'

As she gazed back steadily into his eyes, so his words brought memories:

When last de Marigny was here and before they had all four – Henri and Moreen, Hank and Armandra – gone out on their impossible, peril-fraught mission to the moons of Borea, she had had plenty of time to talk to de Marigny and get to know him. She had questioned him minutely in all aspects of his past and his wanderings in the time-clock, adventures of which the Warlord had already apprised her, but which she found more immediately thrilling when retold by de Marigny. And it had been perfectly obvious to the Woman of the Winds that never before had she met a man like this one. Even in the Motherworld he had been something of an anachronism, the perfect gentleman in a world where morals and all standards of common courtesy were continually falling, but here on Borea his like had been unknown.

It had not required much effort on the handsome Earthman's part to convince her that his presence on Borea was purely accidental, that he had not deliberately sought out Hank Silberhutte in order to perform some fantastic interplanetary, hyperdimensional rescue! No, for he was on his way to Elysia, home of the Elder Gods, and only the tides of Fate had washed him ashore on Borea's chilly strand ...

Armandra came back to the present. 'Oh, yes, I

remember,' she said, unsmiling. And she tossed her long red tresses and flashed her oval green eyes. 'And I remember what followed. It finished on Dromos in the caves of the ice-priests, where you and Henri very nearly died and I almost became handmaiden to my monstrous father! As for poor Moreen, if that *beast* had had his way . . .' She shuddered and left it unfinished.

'But none of that happened,' the Warlord patiently reminded. 'Instead we taught Ithaqua a lesson. That was the second time he'd tried it on, and the second time we'd bruised his ego. And now he stands off, regards the plateau and its peoples with a little more respect, spends his time and energies in more profitable pursuits. In other words, the last time de Marigny visited here it worked to the good of the plateau. Remember, too, he saved my life, snatched me from Ithaqua's wolf-warriors – who without a doubt would have given me into the hands of their terrible master.'

'He saved *your* life?' she flared up, and for the briefest moment a tinge of carmine flashed in her green eyes. 'And how often did you save his, at great risk? Oh, no, Lord Silberhutte,' (she only ever called him that when he was in the wrong), 'there's no debt between you there!'

'He hasn't come back to collect on any debts, Armandra,' the Texan released her, turned away, clenched his great hands behind his back. 'He wants nothing of us except our hospitality. He's come back as he went: a friend – come back to be with people, for however short a time – before he goes off again on this crazy quest of his. Next to Earth, which he put behind him the day he left it, we're the closest he's got to family. That's why he's come back: because this is as near as he'll get to home. At least until he finds Titus Crow in Elysia. *If* he finds him!'

Armandra stepped round in front of him. Draped in a deep-pile, white fur smock, still her figure was the answer to any man's dream, the body of an exceedingly beautiful

471

woman. Almost unchanged from the first time Silberhutte had seen her nearly six years ago, Armandra was Complete Woman. Her long, full body was a wonder of half-seen, half-imagined curves growing out of the perfect pillars of her thighs; her neck, framed in the red, flowing silk of her hair, was long and slender, adorned with a large medallion of gold; her face was oval as her eyes and classically boned. With her straight nose, delicately rounded at its tip, and her Cupid's bow of a mouth, perfect in shape if perhaps a shade too ample, the Woman of the Winds was a beautiful picture of femininity. But where her flesh was pale as snow, those great eyes of hers were green as the boundless northern oceans of Earth. Yes, and they were just as deep.

That was Armandra. When she smiled it brought the sunlight into the Warlord's darkest hours, and when she frowned ... then the fiery hair of her head was wont to have an eerie life of its own, and her eyes might narrow and take on a warning tint other than ocean green: the carmine passed down to her from her inhuman father.

She was frowning now, but not in anger. In fear, perhaps? Fear of losing this man of the Motherworld, this Warlord, this Texan whom she loved so desperately.

'And what of you, Hank?' she asked at last. 'What of *your* home?' Her frown did not lighten, and Silberhutte knew what was coming next: 'Do you, too, feel trapped here, marooned? You guard your thoughts well, my husband, but I would know the truth. The plateau must seem a very small place compared to what you've told me of those mighty city-hives of the Motherworld. And now, with de Marigny returned – him and his time-clock – '

He took her in his arms, lifted her up as surely and as easily as her familiar winds when she walked in the sky, then lowered her down until his mouth closed on hers with a kiss. And after long moments he slid her down his hard-muscled body until her sandalled feet touched the furs of the floor; and before she could speak again, he said:

'This – is my home. You – *are* my life. Borea's my world now, Armandra. My woman, my son, my people are here. If I could go down to the pens and take Morda and ride him out a single mile across the plain and into the Motherworld – if it was as easy as that – I wouldn't do it. I might ... but only if I could take you with me. And for all its many wonders, the Motherworld is a common place. It has nothing like you. What would its thronging people make of a woman of unearthly beauty who walks on the wind and commands the very lightnings?' And he paused.

He might have said more: how Armandra would be lost on Earth, bewildered, a complete outsider. An alien. A curiosity. A seven-day wonder. And finally a freak. But saying it, even thinking it, hurt him worse than it would hurt her. Which was too much. And so instead he finished with:

'I love and *will* love only you. Where you are I must be. Be it Borea, heaven or hell, if you are there it's the place for me. But surely you can see that while I have found my home – the only home I need – our friend Henri-Laurent de Marigny has not yet found his. What you call my "trouble" is in fact his trouble. If you see pain in me, it's only pain for him. Moreen says he's known as The Searcher in a hundred inhabited worlds. Beings who are not men, who don't even *think* like men, understand his quest and have named him for it. They feel for him. And should I hide my feelings? No, Armandra, I'm not a child to be homesick. Nor is de Marigny, not for a home he's never seen. But it's his destiny – yes, and it's driving him to distraction. My pain is this: that I don't know how to help him.'

Now Armandra felt wretched. She knew that she did not have to look into her man's mind, that everything he had said was right in there. Yes, this strange world with its weird auroras and inhabited moons *was* his world now; but he was still a man of the Motherworld, and so felt for his fellow man, de Marigny The Searcher.

'Hank, I – ' she began, her voice full of shame. But before she could continue, and because he would not let her humble herself:

'I know, I know.' And he patted her head.

'But how can we help him?' She desired only to put things right now. 'Should I commune with my familiar winds? For they have talked to winds from across the farthest reaches of eternity. Perhaps they have heard of this Elysia.'

Silberhutte nodded. 'It's worth a try.' Then he stood up straighter and squared his shoulders, finally gave a snort and chuckled to himself. Armandra looked at him quizzically, but he only smiled and shook his head.

'What is it?' she asked, raising the corner of a golden eyebrow.

He chuckled again, then shrugged. 'Once – oh, six years ago – I set out on a vengeance quest to track down and destroy your father. I knew Ithaqua was real: not supernatural but a Being of alien spaces and dimensions. That was my *total* belief in matters concerning things not of Earth: that Ithaqua was real, and with him others of an incredibly ancient order or pantheon of Beings, the Cthulhu Cycle Deities. Also, I was a telepath. But the rest of me was Texan, and *all* of me was Earthman, in many ways mundane as any other. And instead of tracking Ithaqua he tracked me and carried me and my crew here to Borea. Since when – '

'Yes?'

'Why, see how my spheres have widened! And what's become of this vengeful, telepathic but otherwise "mundane" Texan now, eh? Warlord of polyglot peoples on an alien world; adventurer in strange moons; mate to the daughter of the one he vowed to destroy, a woman who walks on the wind and "communes" with puffs of ether

474

from the stars? And when you say: "I'll have a word with some winds I know from the other side of eternity," this man nods and answers, "sure, it's worth a try!" ' And now he burst out laughing.

Barely understanding this sudden bout of self-directed humour, but carried along by it anyway, Armandra joined the laughter; and she hugged him and clung to him for a moment. Then, arm in arm, they set out together to find de Marigny and tell him how she would try to help him ...

Henri-Laurent de Marigny was aware of some of the concern he caused in the plateau and among its inhabitants, but aware of it only on the periphery of his consciousness. His ever-advancing obsession would not allow for more than that. No, for now the quest was all that mattered. He knew it, and could do nothing about it. He suspected, too, that but for Moreen he might well have cracked long before now, that she alone was his sanity. Together they had visited many worlds with near-human, half-human, and totally inhuman inhabitants, might easily have settled on several. Oh, yes, for there were wonderful, beautiful islands galore out there in the infinite seas of space. But while they'd rested in these planets and found peace in them, it had never lasted. Always de Marigny would wake with a cry one morning, sit up and cast about, discover that yesterday's wonders and last night's marvels had turned drab on him and lost their flavour, and his eyes would grow dull while the bright dream he had dreamed receded. And then they would go to the time-clock, and at his command its panel would open and spill out that familiar, pulsing purplish glow, and it would be time to move on.

And of course he knew that it would be exactly the same here on Borea. But at least there were friends here, completely *human* friends; which was why, after these last three years of futile search, he had returned. Earth ... ? That thought had never seriously occurred to him. The

Earth was beautiful but diseased, polluted by men, the one planet of all the worlds de Marigny knew whose inhabitants were systematically raping and ruining her. Indeed, even Earth's dreamlands were beginning to suffer!

And that *was* a thought, an idea, which had occurred more than once: why not give up all Elysian aspirations and dwell instead in the lands of Earth's dreams? Fine, but there are perils even in the dreamlands. And the very least of them lay in waking up! For de Marigny knew that there are certain dreams from which men never wake ...

The dreamlands, strange dimension formed by the sub-conscious longings of men. A *real* place or world, as de Marigny now knew.

Gazing down from a rock-hewn bartizan at the rim of the plateau, now he smiled – however wryly – as his mind went back again to the adventures he had known in Earth's dreamlands with Titus Crow and Tiania of Elysia. For peering from on high like this was not unlike (and yet, in another sense, totally unlike) the vertiginous view from cloud-floating Serannian's wharves of pink-veined marble, where that fabulous city was built in the sky and looked out over an ethereal sea of glowing cirrus and cirrocumulus.

And remembering that wonderful aerial city, de Marigny's mind could not help but conjure, too, Kuranes: 'Lord of Ooth-Nargei, Celephais, and the Sky around Serannian.' Kuranes, yes! – and Randolph Carter, perhaps Earth's greatest dreamer, a king himself now in Ilek-Vad – and who better for the job, since he himself had probably dreamed Ilek-Vad in the first place?

Other lands and cities sprang to mind: Ulthar, where no man may kill a cat, and the Isle of Oriab across the Southern Sea, with its principal port Baharna. Aye, incredible places all, and their peoples fabulous as the dreams that made them; but not all dreams are pleasant, and the dreamlands had their share of nightmares, too.

Now de Marigny thought of Dylath-Leen in the Bad

Days and shuddered, and he tasted something bitter in his mouth as he recalled names and places such as Zura of the Charnel Gardens, the Vale of Pnoth, Kadath in the Cold Waste and Leng's forbidden plateau and hideous hinterland. Especially Leng, where squat, horned beast-men cavorted about balefires to the whine of demon flutes and the bone-dry rattle of crazed crotala . . .

No, the dreamlands were no fit habitation for such as Moreen and de Marigny – who in any case had never considered himself an expert dreamer – not yet for a while, anyway. Perhaps one day on his deathbed he'd dream himself a white-walled villa there in timeless Celephais, but until then . . .

. . . The dimension of dream, glimpsed briefly in the eye of memory, slipped away and de Marigny was back on Borea, on the roof of the plateau. Chill Borea, where for ten days now he and Moreen had been feted like prodigals until, as always, the pleasures had begun to pall; even the great pleasure of human companionship, the company of men such as Silberhutte, Kota'na, Jimmy Franklin and Charlie Tacomah.

And suddenly de Marigny knew that he was tired of his quest, and he wondered how much longer it could last before he gave in, surrendered to the hopelessness of the thing. Indeed, sometimes he wondered what had kept him going so long . . . but no, that was a lie, for he already knew the answer well enough. It lay not alone in what Titus Crow had told him of Elysia, but also in what he'd said of de Marigny himself:

'You are a lover of mysteries, my friend,' (Crow had said), 'as your father before you, and there's something you should know. You really ought to have guessed it before now, Henri, but there's something in you that hearkens back into dim abysses of time, a spark whose fire burns still in Elysia . . .'

It had been like a promise, as if in those words Crow

477

had willed to him a marvellous inheritance; but what of that promise now? Or could it be that Crow had simply been mistaken, that de Marigny ought never have set his sights on Elysia in the first place? What else had Titus Crow said?

'You will be welcome in Elysia, Henri, but of course you must make your own way there ... It may well be a difficult voyage, and certainly it will be dangerous, for there's no royal road to Elysia ... The pitfalls of space and time are many, but the rewards are great ... When there are obstacles, we'll be watching in Elysia. And if you are where I can't reach you without aid, then I'll ride a Great Thought to you ...'

De Marigny could not restrain a snort of derision, however inwardly-directed. Obstacles? Oh, there'd been 'obstacles,' all right! Time-travel in the clock was invariably complicated by running battles with the Tind'losi Hounds; certain worlds of space seemed friendly but were in fact inimical to human life; the space-time fabric itself had focal points mysterious and dangerous beyond reckoning; and, neither last nor least, there was no dearth of places in the continuum wherein were contained the 'houses' or 'tombs' of the Great Old Ones (more properly their prisons), where they had been locked in untold aeons past by the beneficent Gods of Eld. This had been their punishment for an act, or the massed threat of such an act, monstrous beyond imagining. The Elder Gods had pursued Cthulhu, his ilk and their spawn, through space and time and dimensions *between* the spaces we know, prisoning them wherever they were found. And so they remained to this day, in greater part: imprisoned but immortal, only waiting out the time of their release, when the stars would wheel in their great celestial orbits and finally stand *right* in pre-ordained positions in the firmament. And then, when the stars were right –

– A great hand fell on de Marigny's shoulder and he

gave a massive start, clutching at the rim of the open viewport where he gazed out from the bartizan. All doomful thoughts were snatched from his mind at once, and he himself snatched back to the immediate, the now.

'Henri,' Hank Silberhutte's voice was deep where he stood with an arm around Armandra, 'we thought we'd find you here. Did I startle you? It seemed you were miles away just then, right?'

'Light-years!' de Marigny agreed, turning. He managed a smile, nodded a greeting to Hank, bowed formally to Armandra – and at once felt something of their concern for him, the pain and worry he was causing them. Words of apology would have tumbled out of him then, but the Woman of the Winds had quickly taken his hand in both of hers, to tell him:

'Henri, if you wish it, I think I may be able to help you find Elysia. At least, there is a chance.'

'And what do you say to that?' the Warlord grinned at him.

For a moment, maybe two, de Marigny simply gaped at them. He knew that Armandra had senses beyond the mundane five, was aware that if anyone on Borea could help him, she was that one. And yet he had not even considered asking for her help because ... because he was de Marigny and she was his friend, and he knew that you can only beg help from real friends just so often before losing them.

'Well?' the Warlord waited for his answer. And now de Marigny gave it.

Stepping forward, he briefly, fiercely hugged the Woman of the Winds, then lifted her bodily up above him. And still words would not come. 'Armandra, I ... I ...' Then, ashamed of his own emotions, he set her down again, dumbly shook his head and backed off. And under Armandra's stern, steady gaze, finally he lowered his head.

At last she said: 'You men of the Motherworld would

all seem much of a kind: you have the same strengths and the same weaknesses. Fortunately the former outweigh the latter, which in any case are often ... endearing?' Looking up, de Marigny saw that her great green eyes were sparkling.

At which her husband put arms round the shoulders of both of them and began laughing uproariously ...

2

Elysia

There were strange stirrings in the Elysian ether, ominous undercurrents more psychic than physical, which weighed on the souls of certain dwellers in that weird and wonderful land. The source of this dawning – dread? – was intangible as yet, but to those few who sensed it, its approach was anticipated as surely as the bite of a mosquito in the darkness of a room, in those taut moments after its hum fades to silence. Titus Crow had come awake to that silence, and had known instinctively that the bite was still to come. Not immediately but soon, and not merely the sting of a mosquito ...

Outwardly ... all seemed ordered – as it had been immemorially in Elysia – but inside:

'There's a knot in my stomach,' said Crow, hurriedly dressing in forest-green jacket and bark-brown, wide-bottomed trousers, tightening his belt and peering out at the sky through the stone windows of the aerial castle which he and Tiania called home. And scanning that sky he frowned, for even the synthetic sunrise seemed wrong this morning, and on the far, flat horizon, the wispy clouds were tinged a leaden grey.

Tiania was only half awake. 'Ummm!' she said, not wanting to argue, her head deep in pillows.

'Something's up,' she heard her man declare. He sniffed at the air and nodded to himself. 'Why, even the clouds are grey!'

Now she was coming awake. 'Did you never see grey clouds before?' she mumbled. 'Perhaps it will rain! It's good for the gardens.'

'No,' he shook his leonine head, 'it's not that *kind* of

481

grey. It's more a feeling than a colour.' He went to her, gently lifted her head from the pillows, kissed her soft, unwrinkled brow. 'Come on, Tiania. You're a child of Elysia, and a favourite child at that. Can't you feel it? It's in the air, I tell you, and it's been there for some time. Something *is* wrong!'

At that she sat up, and Titus Crow was frozen by sudden awareness of her nearness, her beauty. It was the same each morning, the same every night: he looked at her and knew she was his, and every fibre of his body thrilled to the knowledge. Tiania had the perfect shape of a beautiful girl, but that was where any further comparison with a female of planet Earth must surely end. Most definitely!

To describe her in detail would take many thousands of words, most of them superlatives. The mind tires of searching for them, and the reader's mind would weary of absorbing them. And so, to simplify matters:

Tiania's hair was a green so dark as to be almost black, with highlights of aquamarine and flashing emerald tints. All coils and ringlets, it reached to her waist, which seemed delicate as the stem of a wineglass. Her flesh was *milk*-of-pearl, not the nacreous gleam of shell-heart but the soft glow of a pearl's outer skin. Her eyes were huge, the colour of beryl and infinitely deep, under arching emerald eyebrows in a slender, pixie face. Pixie, too, her ears and delicate nub of a nose, so that when she smiled she might well be some tomboy elf – except that she literally radiated Essence of Woman. She *was* plainly human, and yet quite alien; a girl, yes, but one whose genes had known the mysteries of Eld.

Crow shook his head in silent wonder, a ritual of his that she'd grown used to even if she didn't fully understand it. And: 'Nothing so beautiful lived before you,' he said quite simply.

'Ridiculous!' she answered, rising up and shaking back

her hair – but at the same time blushing rose. 'Why! There are flowers in the Gardens of Nymarrah – '

'Nothing human,' he cut her off.

She kissed him, began to dress. 'Then we're a match, for you're a fine, big man.'

'Ah, but just a man for all that,' he answered, as he invariably did. Which was far from true, for Crow was wont to forget now and then that since his transition he was rather more than a man. But whichever, she returned his appreciative gaze with equal raptness, for Tiania never tired of Titus Crow. What she saw was this:

A man, yes, but a man glowing with health, ageless as a rock. He looked a young forty, but that would be to grant him more than a quarter of a century! And even *that* would be a false reading, based solely on Earth-time. For rebuilt from his own pulp by a robot physician on a robot world, he had spent more than sixty years in T3RE's vats alone! And that was where he had undergone his transition proper: in the laboratory of T3RE, whose robot hands and tools and lasers had built him the way he was now. And almost literally ageless, too, for in Crow the ageing process was slowed down in a ratio of one to ten. Twenty years from now he would look more or less the same, but Tiania would have started to catch up with him. That was a problem they would face as it arose . . .

While she finished dressing he pulled on boots and tucked his trousers into their tops, forming piratical bells. It gave him a swashbuckling air which he admitted to liking. But appearances were secondary in his mind now, where his thoughts were too sombre for theatrical posing. By then, too, Tiania was ready. And:

'Where are we going?' she asked innocently.

'We? *We?*' he teased her, playing down his as yet unfounded fears. 'Who said anything about "we"? But as for me, I'm off to see if I can arrange an audience with Kthanid in his glacier palace.'

'Oh?' she raised an eyebrow. 'And I should stay home and prepare a meal for you, right?' And she put her hands on her hips, pretending to scowl.

Inside Crow his mechanical heart picked up speed; something gnawed at him, worried at his guts; time was wasting and a monstrous cloud loomed ever closer. But still he played this lover's game with Tiania. 'Of course, woman, what else?' he barked. 'And doesn't a man deserve a good meal when he's been out working all day and returns home to . . . to . . .'

The smile had fallen from her face. For all their banter, now Tiania had sensed something of her man's apprehension and knew it was real. And perhaps for the first time, she too felt that leaden, stifling oppressiveness, an as yet vague but steadily increasing sensation of DOOM in the atmosphere of Elysia. Suddenly frightened, she threw herself into his arms. 'Oh, Titus! Titus! I feel it now! But what is it?'

He hugged her, comforted her, growled: 'Damned if I know. But I intend to find out. Come on!'

They hurried out from their bedroom in the base of a turret onto ornamental 'battlements' that offered a fantastic view of Elysia – or part of Elysia, anyway. To the east a synthetic golden sun burned behind a lowering bank of cloud, and an unaccustomed chill wind rippled the fields far below. There was more than the usual movement in the sky, too, where from all quarters flights of lithards could be seen wearing the bright colours of dignitaries and bearing their favoured riders north.

North? Across the Frozen Sea to the Icelands?

Crow and Tiania glanced apprehensively, speculatively at each other. This would seem to confirm their private thoughts and suspicions. He nodded his leonine head. 'And didn't I say I wanted an audience with Kthanid, in the Hall of Crystal and Pearl?'

Before she could answer there came a throb of wings

and rush of air, and up from below there soared a monstrous, magnificent shape well known to both of them. A great lithard, the veriest dragon, flew in the skies of Elysia! Oth-Neth, first representative of his race – intelligent dinosaur of doomed Thak'r-Yon, a world long since burned up in the heart of its exploding sun – alighted in a flash of bright scales, a sighing furling of membrane wings, on the battlements close by.

'Oth-Neth!' cried Tiania, and she ran to the great beast and threw her arms about his neck.

'Tiania,' the creature returned, soft-voiced, lowering its great head to facilitate her fondling.

Crow might witness this same scene a thousand times and still be awed. Here was a monster out of Earth's oldest mythologies – a *draco* out of Asian hinterlands, and all of a natural green and gold iridescence – and Tiania caressing the beast as if it were a favourite horse. No, he automatically corrected himself, greeting it – greeting *him* – like an old friend, which he was. Oth-neth, green and golden dragon from the Tung-gat tapestries, a creature such as might sport in the Gardens of Rak. And here on a mission.

Oth-Neth wore green, the emerald saddle and reins of Tiania's household. He had been sent to collect her.

'What about me?' Crow strode forward, rested a hand on the creature's flank.

'You?' Oth-Neth bent his head to look at him. 'You, too, Tituth.' (The lithard's command of human languages was imperfect: he lisped, as did all his race.) 'But you go quick, direct to Kthanid! Flying cloak ith better for you.'

Crow looked him straight in his saucer eyes. 'Do you know what's happening?'

'No,' an almost imperceptible shake of the great head. 'But ... I think trouble. Big trouble! Look!' He turned his head to the skies. High above Elysia, beyond the flying-zones of lithards and cloaks and winged creatures alike, time-clocks in all their varieties were blinking into existence in unprecedented numbers. And all of them wending east toward the slowly rising, strangely dulled sun, to the Blue Mountains and the subterranean, miles-long corridor of clocks. Elysia's children were returning from a thousand voyagings and quests, answering the summons of the masters of this weird, wonderful place.

Crow stared for a moment longer, his high brow furrowed, then hurried back into the castle. He returned with a scarlet flying cloak and quickly slipped into its harness. Tiania had already climbed into the ornate emerald saddle at the base of the lithard's neck, but she paused to lean down and kiss Crow where he now stood poised on the battlements.

'Titus,' she began, 'I – ' but words wouldn't come.

He looked at her beautiful face and form, only half-concealed by an open jacket and knee-length trousers of soft grey, and felt her fear like a physical thing; not fear for herself or Elysia, nor even Titus Crow himself – who in any case had often shown himself to be near-indestructible – but for *them*, for they had become as one person and could not be apart. And: 'I know,' he said quietly. And then, brightening: 'But we don't know what it is yet. It may be ... very little.'

They both knew he deliberately made light of it, but she nodded anyway. Then Oth-Neth launched himself from the castle's wall and soared north; and Crow's fingers found the control studs of his cloak, which at once belled out and bore him aloft; and in the next moment girl, dragon and man were flying north to join the streams of other fliers where they made for Kthanid's glacial palace ...

Crow sped on ahead. He guessed that Oth-Neth deliberately held back, letting him gain a lead and a little extra time. For what? So that he could talk to Kthanid in private? That seemed unlikely, with all these others heading for that same rendezvous. But Crow accelerated and shot ahead anyway.

And as he flew his cloak, so it was suddenly important to Crow that he look at Elysia again, let the place impress itself upon his mind. It had dawned on him that if ever he had known a real home – a place to be, where he *wanted* to be – that home was here. Now, for the first time, he consciously desired to remember it. Knowing his instincts, how true they ran, that was a very bad omen indeed. And so, until journey's end, he deliberately absorbed all he could of Elysia, letting it soak into him like water into a sponge.

Elysia was not a planet; if it had been, then it would be the most tremendous colossus among worlds. But there was no real horizon that Crow had ever seen, no visible curvature of rim, only a gradual fading into distance. Oh, there were mountains with towering peaks, and many of them snow-clad; but even from the tops of these Elysia could be seen to go on endlessly into distant mists, a land vast as it was improbable and beautiful.

Beautiful, too, its structures, its cities. But *such* cities! Fretted silver spires and clusters of columns rose everywhere, fantastic habitations of Elysia's peoples; but never vying with each other and always with fields and rivers and plains between. Even in the most abstract of cities there were parks and woodlands and rivers and lakes like bright ribbons and mirrors dropped carelessly on the landscape, yet always complementing it perfectly. And away beyond lines of low, domed hills misty with distance, yet more cities; their rising terraces of globes and minarets sparkling afar, where dizzy aerial roadways spread unsupported spans city to city like the gossamer threads of strange communal cobwebs.

Sky-islands, too (like Serannian in the land of Earth's dreams, or Tiania's castle and the gardens around it), apparently floating free but in fact anchored by the same gravitic devices which powered Elysia and kept her positioned here in this otherwise empty parallel dimension; and all of these aerial residences dotted here and there, near and far, seemingly at random and at various heights; but perfectly situated and structured to suit their dwellers, who might in form be diverse as their many forms of gravity-defying architecture. And yet the sky so vast that it was not, could not be, cluttered.

Flying machines soared or hovered in these skies whereever the eye might look (or would in normal times), and through tufted drifting clouds green and golden dragons, the lithards, pulsed majestically on wings of ivory and leather. Nor were the lithards and flying craft sole users of their aerial element: a few of Elysia's races were naturally gifted with flight, and there were even some who might simply will it! Then there were the users of flying cloaks, like Crow's; and finally, today especially, there were the time-clocks ...

But Elysia was not all city and sky and mountain; she had mighty forests, too, endless valley plains, fields of gorgeous green and yellow, and oceans more beautiful even than the jewel oceans of Earth. The Frozen Sea was one such: patterned like a snowflake one hundred miles across, its outer rim was cracked into glittering spokes of ice, while at the core a nucleus of icebergs had crashed together in ages past to form a mighty frozen monolith. Titus Crow flew across the Frozen Sea even now, and beyond it –

– There in the Icelands, whose temperature ideally suited certain of Elysia's inhabitants – there dwelled Kthanid in his palace at the heart of a glacier. Kthanid, spokesman of the Elder Gods themselves.

'Elder Gods.' They were not gods, and Kthanid himself would be the first to admit it, but so many races down all the ages of time and on a thousand different worlds had seen them as gods that the name had stuck. No, not gods but scientists, whose science had made them godlike. Beneficent Beings of Eld, they were, but not *all* of them had been benign.

Crow was across the Frozen Sea now and began to feel the chill of the Icelands. Oth-Neth's body-heat would warm Tiania, he knew, until they were down in the heart of the great glacier; and as for his own welfare: this body T3RE had built for him would come to no great harm. And in any case, it was more a chill of the spirit he felt than the frosty burn of bitter winds. For still that leaden feeling was on him.

Away in the west, beyond the ice-shard glittering rim of the Frozen Sea, he glimpsed the blue waters of a somewhat more temperate ocean, where majestic icebergs sailed and slowly melted, but then in another moment the view was shut off as he soared down over frozen foothills and set his course parallel to a procession of lithards who bore their riders doubtless to the same destination: Kthanid's council-chamber in the great Hall of Crystal and Pearl.

Kthanid: super-sentient Kraken, Eminence, Sage and Father of Elysia. And benign ...

But there was that One born of Kthanid's race and spawned in his image who was *not* benign, that bestial, slobbering bereft Great Old One whose cause and cult Crow had fought against all his days, that one true prime evil whose seat for three and a half billions of years had been drowned R'lyeh in Earth's vast Pacific Ocean – Cthulhu! And now Crow wondered: why did *that* thought spring to mind? From where?

And he once more quickened the pace of the cloak as finally he spied ahead a frozen river of immemorial ice and the jagged crevasse that guarded the entrance to Kthanid's sub-glacial palace.

Normally Crow would show his respect, enter cautiously and continue on foot to the council-chamber, but these were not normal times. He flew the cloak dexterously into the mouth of a fantastically carved cavern, then down sweeping flights of ice-hewn steps into the heart of the glacier, until at last he swooped along a horizontal tunnel carved of ice whose floor was granite worn smooth by centuries of glaciation. And now he smelled those strange and exotic scents only ever before smelled here, borne to him on a warm breeze from inner regions ahead.

It grew warmer still as the core of the glacier drew closer, until suddenly the dim blue light of the place came brighter, as if here some secret source of illumination was hidden behind the soft sheen of ice walls. Then those walls themselves, like the floor, became granite, and finally Crow arrived at a huge curtain of purest crystals and pearls strung on threads of gold. And he knew that beyond the curtain – whose priceless drapes went up to a dim ceiling, and whose width must be all of a hundred feet – lay the vast and awe-inspiring Hall of Crystal and Pearl, throne-room and council-chamber of Kthanid the Eminence.

Crow had been here before, on several occasions, but they had never been ordinary times; and now once more he felt himself on the verge of momentous things, whose nature was soon to be revealed. But . . . here was no longer a place for flying. He alighted, slipped out of the cloak's harness and folded that device over his arm, finally parted the jewel curtains and stepped through.

And now indeed he knew that Oth-Neth had been correct, that trouble, 'big trouble,' was brewing in Elysia.

Again, as always, Crow felt amazement at the sheer size of the hall, that inner sanctum wherein Kthanid thought his Great Thoughts. He stood upon the titan-paved floor of massive hexagonal flags of quartz and eyed the weird angles and proportions of the place, with its high-arched ceiling soaring overhead. Enormously ornate columns rose up on all sides, supporting high balconies made vague by the rising haze of light; and everywhere the well remembered white, pink and blood hues of multi-coloured crystal, and the shimmer of mother-of-pearl where the polished linings of prehistoric conches decorated the marching walls.

The only thing that seemed different was the absence of the customary centrepiece – a vast scarlet cushion bearing the sphere of a huge, milky crystal. Kthanid's 'shewstone' – but all else was just as Crow remembered it. Or would be, except that on those previous occasions Kthanid had seemed alone in his palace; whereas now –

– Now, where mighty Kthanid sat in his private alcove, its pearl-beaded curtains thrown back – now he gazed out upon a multitude!

At first glance it appeared to Crow that half of Elysia must be here – including several who ranked almost as high at Kthanid himself, and whose appearances were similarly or even more *outré* – for the great hall was packed. No simple council-meeting this, for not only were these High Eminences here but also representatives of a dozen different races, and lords and leaders from all of Elysia's many cities and lands and parts.

Among those assembled were several high-placed lithards, wearing their black leather neck-bands of office; and Crow at once recognized Esch, Master Linguist of the bird-like Dchi-chis, a man-sized archeopteran who bent his plumed head in a silent nod of greeting; and then there were several 'Chosen' ones: usually but not always members of manlike bipedal races whose natural beauty was favoured by the Elder Gods, including several fragile-seeming varieties Crow could only ever think of as pixies, elves or fairies. There were insect-beings, too, and squat, amphibian fin-creatures; even a solitary member of the D'horna-ahn, an energy spiral who gyrated close to Esch where they hummed electrically at each other in muted, cryptical conversation.

Of the handful of Elder Gods who were there: Crow

491

spied a great, gently mobile congeries of golden spheres that half-hid a writhing shape of sheerest nightmare, and he knew that this was Yad-Thaddag, a 'cousin' of Yog-Sothoth, but infinitely good where the latter was black and putrid evil. Also, in an area apart from the rest, a lambent flame twice the height of a man, tapered at top and bottom, twirled clockwise where it stood 'still' upon its own axis and threw out filaments of flickering yellow energy; and this too was a member of the elite Elder Gods, a Thermal Being born in eons past in the heart of a star, whose half-life was five billion years! And all of them here to talk, exchange thoughts or otherwise commune with Kthanid.

And Titus Crow, a mere man, summoned to a meeting such as this . . .

'*Mere man?*' came Kthanid's thoughts from where he sat upon a throne in his arched alcove. '*That you are not, Titus Crow, and well you know it. Men are not "mere" creatures; you, of all men, are not "mere." Indeed, this entire assembly has waited on your arrival more than that of any other.*' Crow's entrance had been noted, and in more ways than one. Now he felt the golden orbs of Kthanid's eyes full upon him, and the mainly silent throng parted to let him come forward. This he did, losing count of the strides which took him across those great hexagonal flags to the alcove where Kthanis sat at an onyx table. And there before the Elder God, a scarlet cushion; and upon the cushion, the milky shewstone . . .

3
Kthanid

Crow arrived at the foot of the huge steps up to the dais, paused there and stood straight as a ramrod, his hands at his sides, his head bowed. It was a measure of his respect; his stance told eloquently of his recognition of Kthanid, that he stood in the presence of a superior Being. Then:

'*Yes*,' said Kthanid, but directing his thoughts at Crow alone this time. '*Well, we're one and all superior in our way, else we'd not be here in Elysia in the first place. Titus, come up here to me. We need a little privacy.*' Crow lifted his head, climbed the steps. Behind him the curtains swept shut and closed the alcove in; but not before Kthanid sent out a final thought in the direction of all those gathered there: '*Please wait. Accept our apology that we exclude you from this, but its nature is such that it involves only the Earthman and myself. Only be sure it is a matter of great moment . . .*'

Now he spoke openly (albeit telepathically) to Crow, saying, '*Titus, we now stand in a completely private place. Here we two may converse, and none hear us. Wherefore you may answer as you please, without consideration to my position here.*'

'You know there's no one I hold in higher esteem,' Crow answered without hesitation. 'What could you ask me that I could refuse, or to which I might answer no?'

'*Perceptive, aye!*' Kthanid nodded. '*Indeed the seed of Eld runs strong in you. As to what it is I must ask of you –*' and he paused.

During that pause, however brief a moment, Crow took the opportunity to look fully upon this great alien scientist, truly a Great Old One, and marvelled at what he saw. There had been a time when such a sight had almost unmanned

493

him, but now he could look at Kthanid and ignore his monstrousness. For indeed beauty lies in the eyes of the beholder, and knowing what Crow knew, Kthanid *was* beautiful.

That itself was an incredible thought, for this might well be Cthulhu himself, this mountain of semi-plastic flesh, this pulsing Kraken. But where Cthulhu's eyes were leaden and lustful, Kthanid's were golden and wise beyond wisdom; and where Cthulhu's thoughts were creeping hypnotic poison, Kthanid's were the very breath of life, Beneficence in the fullest meaning of the word. Oh, kin to the Lord of R'lyeh, that blight on universal life and sanity, this Being most certainly was; close kin at that. The folded-back wings, the great head with its proliferation of face-tentacles, the clawed feet: all told of their kinship. But where Cthulhu was mad and corrupt, Kthanid was the very soul of goodness and mercy, and his compassion enveloped all.

His compassion, yes, which even now worked against him like an acid, betraying him in what he must do, filling him with – guilt! Crow felt it flowing out from him, and was astonished. 'Kthanid, what is it? Why have you brought me here? What is it you want me to do, which at the last you can't tell me face to face?'

'*What I want you to do? Nothing. It is what I must do, for which I need your permission!*'

Impossible! Crow's mind itself must be deceiving him. Kthanid needed *his* permission before he could perform some act?

'*Titus, in your homeworld you had a friend, the man de Marigny. A good man; I myself sent him questing after you and Tiania when you were trapped in the lands of Earth's dreams. Aye, and I promised him a welcome in Elysia, even as a son, if only he return you both alive and sane to me from your travails.*'

Crow nodded. 'He did those things. More, we purged

494

the dreamlands of certain evils – though in the end that was as much your victory as ours.'

Kthanid gave a mental groan and turned his great head away. *'You cannot know the pain your words bring me . . .'*

'What?' Crow was at first bemused – then mortally afraid. The blood drained from him in a moment. 'Henri?' he whispered, 'Something has happened to Henri?'

'No, no,' the great Being was quick to answer. *'Be at ease over his well-being. He is well, I promise you. Indeed, soon I shall ask you to ride a Great Thought to him, in Borea on the rim of the bitter ether winds.'*

Crow relaxed a little, allowed himself a sigh of relief. 'Then you intend to keep your promise, bring him here? Whatever it is that threatens Elysia, I can assure you that de Marigny will be a useful force against it!'

'Useful, yes,' again Kthanid nodded. And: *'Bring him here? Use him? Ah! – and indeed I intend to use him – but in such a way! And that is why I need your permission.'*

Crow frowned, shook his head. 'Kthanid, I don't think I fully – '

'Let me remind you,' Kthanid broke in, *'of things you know well enow but perhaps have forgotten – or at least put to the back of your mind – during your time in Elysia.'*

And then the great Being used a skill of his to throw into Crow's mind a mass of detail, a host of memories revived, and all so thick and fast that even the mind of Titus Crow reeled at this assault on his senses; at the assault itself, and in the face of the evils it conjured.

He was reminded of the ongoing struggle between the intelligent races of the multiverse and the prime Forces of Evil, those prisoned beings of the Cthulhu cycle:

Yog-Sothoth, 'the all-in-one and one-in-all' – a slime-thing frothing forever behind his shielding congeries of iridescent power-globes, co-existent with all time and con-terminous in all space – stood high in their ranks; likewise

495

Ithaqua the Wind-Walker, stalker between the stars; and Hastur the Unspeakable, half-brother and bitter rival to Cthulhu, dweller in the ill-omened Lake of Hali in the Hyades. Crow knew and had had dealings with all of them, so that Kthanid's sendings merely reinforced his knowledge of them.

He knew the others of this vile pantheon, too, some of them standing on a par with the prime powers, others lower in the scheme of things or subservient to the principal beings and forces. There was Yibb-Tstll: gigantic, grotesquely manlike lord of an alien dimension beyond the borders of sanity; and Shudde-M'ell, nest-master of the subterranean Cthonians of primal Earth; and Cthugha, whose thermal flux had reversed itself and so deranged the once ordered working of his radioactive mind. There was Dagon, fish-god of the Philistines and the Phoenicians and ruler over the Deep Ones, degenerate subaqueous (and sub-human, or *once*-human) servants of Cthulhu and his ilk. Nyogtha, too, and Zhar, Lloigor, Tsathoggua and Bugg-Shash ...

The list went on, menacing and monstrous, but central and towering over all, always there was Cthulhu, 'an utter contradiction of all matter, force, and cosmic order,' whose lunatic telepathic sendings from R'lyeh in the deep Pacific were of such morbid potency that they were responsible for much of Earth's madness, and almost all of men's nightmares in the land of Earth's dreams.

Basically the legend or history of this ancient order of near-immortal beings was this: that at a time so remote in the past as to defy comparison or definition, they had risen up in a body and rebelled against Order, invoking Chaos as the natural condition. After committing an act so heinous that even they themselves were shocked, they fled and hid in various places and on many parallel planes of existence. Outraged, the Elder Gods regrouped, followed on and tracked them down each and every one, 'chaining' them wherever they were found and placing 'spells' to hold them in their prisons or in selected regions of space-time: Hastur in the Lake of Hali in Carcosa, Cthulhu in sunken R'lyeh, Ithaqua to dwell in frozen interstellar winds and above the ice-wastes of Earth's Arctic, Yog-Sothoth and Yibb-Tstll to chaotic continua outside any known design of science or nature, Tsathoggua to black Hyperborean burrows, and likewise Shudde-M'ell and many of his Cthonians to other buried labyrinths in primal Africa.

All commerce was lost between them except for the contact of disembodied thought. In their infinite wisdom and mercy, the Elder Gods had not taken away the mind-powers of the Great Old Ones, but had merely set up barriers to keep the evil potency of such telepathic wave-bands down to a bearable level. Thus, in the loneliness of their punishment, the Great Old Ones could still 'talk' to one another, even if the power of such communications was much reduced . . .

The flow from Kthanid's mind lessened, finally ceased. And still Crow was puzzled. Why had the great Being shown him these things he already knew so well? Why refresh his memory in these morbid areas? Unless –

'Is de Marigny threatened by the CCD?' he asked. 'Is that what this is all about? Frankly, I don't see how it can be. We've *always* been under threat, de Marigny and I. No, it must be worse, far worse than that. And how is Henri involved?'

'*We are all threatened, Titus,*' Kthanid's thoughts were utterly grave now. '*Your Earth, all other worlds of the three-dimensional universe's intelligent races, the parallel places and subconscious planes – even Elysia!*'

Crow's eyes widened. 'They've risen again,' he whispered. 'Is that what you're trying to tell me? They're free again, and more powerful than ever. The Great Old Ones are back!'

'*Very nearly correct,*' Kthanid answered at once. '*But no,*

497

they are not yet "free", as you have it – not yet. But their time is close now; soon they will have the power to be free; even now the constellations move into certain patterns which never should have been. Azathoth, which you knew in your world as the power of nuclear fission, is the betrayer. The mindless nuclear chaos and confusion which spawned us all is a force of Nature and may not be denied. Out there in the vasty voids, gas clouds gather and Azathoth lights them to suns; stars are born which complete a pattern whose configuration is the one thing come down to us from a time beyond all other times; and yes, it would seem that for Cthulhu and those you choose to call the Great Old Ones – after all these eons of time – at last the stars are coming right! Look!'

Face-tentacles reaching out toward the huge ball of crystal on the onyx table between them – that milky shew-stone whose entire opaque surface seemed slowly mobile, like a reflection of dense clouds mirrored in a still lake – Kthanid showed Crow a distant scene. For as the Earthman stared at the crystal, slowly the milky clouds parted to reveal a picture of an almost sacred place:

Elysia's Vale of Dreams, at the foot of the Purple Mountains far to the south. Tiania had taken Crow there once, to that mysterious place. Mysterious, aye; for there, cut into the royal basalt, were the Thousand Sealed Doors of the N'hlathi, hibernating centipede creatures whose slumbers had already lasted for five thousand years and were not due to be broken for as long again. And the pattern of the doors – each one of which was thirty feet in diameter, sealed with bands of a white metal that no acid might ever corrode – was as the shape of a huge whorl against the face of the mountain, like the spiral of Andromeda.

'*It is the spiral nebula in Andromeda!*' came Kthanid's thoughts in answer to Crow's own, however unspoken. '*Each portal indicates an especially bright star in that mighty whorl. Now let me show you something else –* ' and again he reached out with his face-tentacles.

Now, superimposed over these thousand portals to the burrows of the immemorially dreaming N'hlathi, Crow saw Andromeda, how perfectly its principal stars matched the pattern of the doors. '*But see,*' Kthanid indicated where Crow should look, '*there are three doors where no stars exist; but at this very moment spatial debris gathers in one of these places, and in the others ancient suns bid for rebirth. Gravity forms mass . . . and soon the raw and elemental power of nuclear genesis will do the rest. Ah! See!*'

For even as Kthanid had spoken, so another star had blazed up, newborn and bright, central in the circular panel of one of the great basalt doors. And now only two spaces remained to be filled . . .

Kthanid turned his great head from the crystal, and at once milky clouds rolled as before across its surface. And: '*So you have seen for yourself,*' said the Elder God, '*how time narrows down for us.*'

Crow kept his patience, knew that Kthanid constructed his case this way the better for him to grasp the whole picture. And sure enough:

'*Another portent,*' said the golden Kraken in a little while. '*The giant poppies put up their shoots in the Vale of Dreams. Aye, and the N'hlathi stir in their burrows. It would seem that their ten-thousand-year cycle is broken. Soon the N'hlathi will waken and graze on the seed of the poppy, but utterly out of their season. And it is a matter of legend that this has only ever once happened before – when Cthulhu and his cohorts rose them up against universal sanity! And so you can see, this too is a bad omen . . .*'

Now Crow must speak; he controlled his mental agitation, tried to ask only ordered, logical questions: 'Then the N'hlathi are harbingers of doom? I've heard it said that the history of the giant centipedes has never been written, their tongue never understood, the inscriptions on their

499

doors never deciphered, not even by the Dchi-chis. But since they would seem to have had knowledge of this now imminent coming of the Great Old Ones, to such an extent that they deliberately, correctly forecast the pattern of this fantastic omen, as a warning, surely – '

' – Surely we should have made every effort to decipher the legends of their doors long before now? Titus, our greatest scholars, linguists, calligraphers and cryptographers have worked on those inscriptions for a thousand years! It is only through the work of such masters as Esch that we recognized the pattern in the first place. Aye, and his work progresses well – work which I have only disturbed in order to bring him here, so that the Dchi-chis, too, may know of the doom hanging over us all. And so I hope to hasten him and others of his race in their work . . .'

'Why not simply wait for them to wake up?' Crow asked.

'Who can say how long their waking will take – or if it will be soon enough? Indeed, we might contact them in their dreams, but their minds are different; to disturb their hibernation might be to destroy them. We cannot risk that.'

Crow nodded, frowned, said: 'But still you haven't told me what Henri has to do with all of this. How exactly do you intend to use my friend, Kthanid? What is it you need my permission to do? And remember: it was you promised him a welcome here.'

Yet again Kthanid's mental groan. 'I remember it well enow, Titus Crow. But as you well know, there's no royal road into Elysia. Still and all, yes, I greatly desire for him to come here now – but by a route extraordinary!'

Dark suspicions growing, Crow waited, and:

'First let me say this,' Kthanid continued. 'The last time Cthulhu rose him up, we put him down. If it goes our way, this time will be the same. If not – ' Crow sensed a mental shrug.

But something which had been bothering the Earthman at the back of his mind now surfaced. 'That's it!' he cried.

'That's what puzzles me. If you had the measure of the Great Old Ones way back there at the dawn of time, and if you beat them then, why not use the same process over again? After all, they've been prisoned for billions of years while your science has gone on, improving almost to infinity. So how can they possibly form any real threat now?'

'*Their threat comes in two forms,*' said Kthanid, patient as ever '*Against Elysia and us Elder Beings, whom they detest and are sworn to destroy, and against your Earth and the lesser worlds and planes of existence. We in Elysia are far from helpless against them, but what of the rest of the sane, ordered universe? Aye, and against us they have a great advantage: for while they may kill or try to kill us, our laws utterly forbid us to kill them!*'

'I begin to understand,' said Crow. 'You may defend yourselves – defend Elysia, Earth, the other places – but you may not attack, not kill. You can only trap them, prison them as before. And you don't know where they'll strike first, right?'

'*That is correct, and so we would like to be able to direct their first strike! More of that in a moment, for that's where your friend de Marigny comes in – with your permission. Without it – then we must seek another way. But first let me explain something else:*

'*You have asked why we do not use the same forces – the same methods – against the evil Great Old Ones that were used before. The answer is this: that we are no longer certain exactly how we defeated them!*'

Crow was utterly dumbfounded. 'But you were part of it – you engineered it – you *are* the self-same Elder Gods, the same great scientists who brought them down! Are you saying you've forgotten how you achieved your victory?'

'*That is precisely what I am saying! Oh, we remember the last million years with considerable clarity, but what of the three and a half thousand million years before that?*'

While Crow absorbed that fantastic thought, that vision of eons, so he felt the Elder God searching delicately in his mind for parallels: looking for ways to make his meaning clear. And finally:

'No single atom of my body is the same – every single one of them has regenerated many times – in three and a half billion years! Memory? Do you remember your first week of life on the planet Earth? Listen, in a time of your planet's history which I consider yesterday, many peoples spoke Latin – and who remembers how it was spoken now? Certain scholars guess. Some of them fairly closely. Your "ancient" Egyptians built great pyramid tombs, and who is there "today" to say how they built them? Your scholars guess. Indeed, you have only recently rediscovered their writing! And what man of you remembers the time when the Elder Gods shaped themselves like men and came down to mate with your daughters, which made you great? Not a one; it is the merest echo of a legend. But indeed there were giants in the land in those days. Yes, I have forgotten!'

Still Crow's mind, keen as any, could not accept it. 'There are no records?'

'Records? Do not think thoughts at me of primitive books and tapes and plastic disks, Titus Crow! The finest memory crystals turn to dust in a billion years. Metals transmute. Sand becomes stone and is worn down to sand again. Indeed, entire worlds may be born and die in that span! The records are gone, forgotten, erased, eroded, extinct. Now, like man, we live with myths and legends . . .'

'Except the N'hlathi.'

'Exactly, for they have "lived" only a few hours out of each ten thousand years. Their minds are the original minds and uncluttered, eneroded. They remember everything. And the legends are writ on their sealed chamber doors.'

Suddenly Crow felt infinitely tiny before this mighty Being and the concepts he conjured. 'You've literally forgotten more than my entire race shall ever learn,' he mumbled then. 'And yet you call me here to ask my permission ... for what?'

And at that point Kthanid told him how he would 'use' de Marigny. Crow might have argued, might even have denied him. The dangers to his friend would be ... enormous! But at least Henri would have a chance, however slim. He'd taken slim chances before, run the gantlet and lived to tell the tale; and as Kthanid had pointed out, there was no royal road into Elysia.

Finally, after long moments of thought, Crow nodded, said: 'I'll ride your Great Thought to de Marigny, Kthanid. Yes, and I'll tell him what I must tell him.'

The Eminence seemed to sigh, nodded gravely. *'I thank you, Titus Crow. Indeed, all Elysia thanks you. But before that there are things that must be done, messages to be run. Now stay here beside me and hear what I shall tell my messengers, and then we shall think a Great Thought to carry you to Borea.'*

He motioned and the curtains hissed open, and the sounds of the assembled peoples of Elysia flooded in. Then Kthanid called certain of them to attend him ...

... Some little time later four 'messengers' went out from the Hall of Crystal and Pearl and made their ways at once and swiftly to various parts of Elysia. One of these was the Thermal Being previously noted by Titus Crow among the throng, another a gossamer-winged, insect-like and ephemeral creature who carried a memory-crystal hurriedly prepared by Kthanid; both of these flew under their own power to the Corridor of Clocks beneath the soaring Blue Mountains.

Of the two remaining messengers: one was Tiania herself, who flew Oth-Neth to The Tree in the Gardens of Nymarrah; the other was a Dchi-chi pupil of Esch, specializing in the cryptic codes, enigmatic and riddlish conversation of wizards, who flew a gravity-defying airform to the spherical aerie of Ardatha Ell at the uppermost limits of Elysia's atmosphere.

In the Corridor of Clocks, the Thermal Being paused before a huge time-clock of near-indestructible glass. The four curious hands on its great dial were tipped with gold to make them more conspicuous, but their *motion* about the hieroglyphed dial was utterly eccentric for all that, which is the way of such devices. The Thermal Being considered his instructions one last time; he would carry them out to the letter, not returning to Elysia until ... until this thing with the Great Old Ones was finished. Which meant that he might never return. So be it.

All done, he opened and entered the time-clock, flew it out of the subterranean corridor, up over the Blue Mountains, to a point in the upper atmosphere where clock and passenger both blinked out of existence in this plane and so left Elysia. And his destination was far, far away in the deepest voids of space ...

The clock chosen by the fragile fairy-insect creature was a small grey metal cube of nine-inch sides – more conveyance than vehicle proper, and featureless except for the inevitable dial with its four bizarrely wandering pointers – into which he placed Kthanid's memory-crystal before whistling a sequence of instructions which the clock, in some mysterious way, accepted. For all its unspectacular appearance, this leaden cube was a very special clock indeed: it was not constructed to operate in the physical space-time continuum at all but in those subconscious dimensions formed by the minds of all creatures who dream. It was, quite literally, a clock of dreams, a mechanical monitor of many of the dreamlands of the psychosphere. And it, too, had a special quest: to seek out and deliver its cargo to a very special mechanical being. No sooner were the whistled instructions concluded than the grey cube grew less solid, became transparent, finally disappeared in a rush of displaced air. Satisfied, the insect creature took wing and departed . . .

And in the same moment that the dream-clock passed from Elysia's conscious world, high above her cities and oceans and fields, Esch's favourite student approached the silver sphere which was Ardatha Ell's retreat. The comb-headed creature flew his airform close to the wind-riding, highly reflective surface of the sphere, adjusted his vehicle's controls to 'hover,' rapped upon a curved silver panel with the bony knuckles at the end of a vestigial wing.

'Who knocks?' the sphere dolefully inquired after a moment, asking its question in three mechanically-created languages, all of which the Dchi-chi understood.

'No one,' he at once answered, likewise in triplicate, knowing how much Ardatha Ell would appreciate so cryptic a statement.

'No one knocks, and speaks to me in three tongues? Well, then, the equilibrium is maintained, for I am not at home.'

The Dchi-chi did not even pause to consider this (Kthanid had already apprised him of the wizard's absence, at least of his part-absence) but said: 'I meant that I am no one in the great scheme of things, as I'm sure you well know, wizard. But my message is from a definite someone.' This time he had used only one language, the English of Earth, widely known in Elysia.

'And am I acquainted with this someone?'

'Should I name him, or would you prefer to fathom his identity?'

'You may couch his name in terms, if it please you.'

Knowing that it would please Ardatha Ell even more, the Dchi-chi said: 'Very well, let me say that if your cap was a conical titfer of white wizardry, his would be a crown of mighty beneficence.'

'I do not wear a head garment,' said the sphere, speaking for Ardatha Ell.

'Nor does he.'

'*Hmm!*' said the sphere, thoughtfully. 'He is mighty, he sends out messengers to do his bidding, he is good, and if he wore a crown it would be a kindly one. Hah! Clues galore – and an anagram, too! "Kind hat," indeed! Kthanid!'

'Excellent!' declared the Dchi-chi.

'What's more,' said the sphere, 'you are a Dchi-chi and likely one of Master Esch's best pupils. This is a simple deduction: who else but a Dchi-chi would be adept in so many tongues, and practised in the curious ways of wizards to boot? Oh, you are Dchi-chi, certainly, but not the very master. No, for while your riddle was merely middling, *his* are ever desperately difficult.'

'Still, I do my best,' answered his visitor with a shrug.

'Indeed, and who could ask more of you than that?' agreed the sphere on behalf of Ardatha Ell. 'And now you may enter.'

The curved panel opened outwards and formed a ramp with steps, which the Dchi-chi climbed without hesitation. And: 'Use my house as you will,' the machine voice continued, as the bird-man made his way down a shiny metal corridor toward the centre, 'even though, as you were warned aforetime, I myself am not at home and so may not welcome you.'

'Nor likely to be at home,' answered the other, arriving at Ardatha Ell's innermost apartments. 'Not yet for a while, anyway. But tell me pray: since you are not here, where then are you?'

'In the manse of Exior K'mool, a sorcerer late of Theem'hdra in the primal planet Earth, now Lord of Lith in Andromeda. We amuse ourselves with cryptical conjecturings ...'

'Pray offer your friend my compliments,' said the Dchi-chi, staring about in amazement, 'and tell him that if ever he has need of a half-decent linguist – '

'What?' Ardatha Ell chuckled. 'Why, Exior K'mool was unriddling the stars when your remote ancestors were eggs in the nest of Archaeopteryx! But say, what bothers you now?'

'Only this,' answered the Dchi-chi with something of a gulp, 'that apparently the greater part of you is here after all!'

For there, suspended on a gravitic bed of air in the centre of this central room, surrounded in the soft green haze of glowing emerald globes that floated around him, lay the body of the wizard, horizontal where his clothes drifted lazily, weightlessly outward from him. All of eight feet tall, Ardatha Ell, but slender as a wand in his robes of floating, fiery bronze mesh. Young-seeming, and yet white-haired and with skin pale as death; his eyes were closed and sunken under purple lids, like those of a corpse. Six-fingered, his hands, with thumbs on both inside and out; and the nails of his long fingers white as wax, and lacquered black at their pointed tips. Sharp-pointed his chin, his nose too, and the bronze mesh slippers on his feet curled at their toes.

No beat showed in his breast, or if there was one it was imperceptibly slow; no breath seemed drawn or to issue from his lips; no proper signs of life were in him at all. And yet:

'I beg to differ,' came that voice from some unseen mechanical source, causing the Dchi-chi to start. 'The lesser part, surely? For this recumbent shell here is only the flesh of Ardatha Ell. The mind – which is greater by far, which is more truly *me* – that is in Exior K'mool's manse in Andromeda.'

The Dchi-chi gulped again, his gizzard contracting, and gazed all about at the room's crammed shelves and sorcerous appurtenances: the ancient books and bottles, charts and charms, even a shewstone like that of Kthanid in the Hall of Crystal and Pearl. And: 'Of course!' he concurred

507

with a nervous *chirrup*. 'Why, this must be the very least part of you, I see that now. But, good sir, time waits for no creature and I carry Kthanid's message, and – '

' – And you must fly, little bird? And the secret of your cryptic statement – that for the time being I shall not re-enter Elysia – lies hid in Kthanid's message, eh?' The voice seemed far less mechanical now, much more vibrant and forceful. Even ominous, in a way. 'Very well, let's have that message now. Merely place your hand – or whatever you have which passes for one – on the pale brow of that sleeper there. Then think your message, or chirp it if you will, or even couch it in rhyme or riddle, and I shall receive and understand.'

Gingerly the Dchi-chi did as instructed, placed his bony bird-hand upon the brow of the suspended wizard, and ... instantly it was as if his claw was glued there, taken root in Ardatha Ell's skull and held fast by some irresistible force! He felt his message, which he would have passed anyway, *sucked* out of him in a moment – following which he was at once released. Staggering backwards he heard the wizard's dry, mechanical chuckle. And:

'There, all done,' said Ardatha Ell. But in the next moment, in a voice more grave: 'Aye, and this is an important task Kthanid has set me. You should have said so before now, little bird, instead of posing and parroting.'

But the Dchi-chi was already fluttering his way back down the shining corridor to the outer portal. Out into the gusting higher atmosphere of Elysia he went and down the metal steps to his airform, and only then did he pause to say: 'I thank you for your hospitality, wizard. Alas, my wit is small and likewise my talent, when compared with such as yours.'

'Not at all,' said the sphere through the bluster of air, once more completely cold and mechanical. 'We all have to begin somewhere. But when next you call, first make sure I'll be at home in person to greet you, eh? Or perhaps I'll speak to your master, Esch, and tell him to let you come more often; and we can test each other's mettle with riddles, or I'll teach you some tongues you haven't even heard of yet. What say you, Dchi-chi, who fancied himself proficient in the many ways of wizards?'

Casting off, the Dchi-chi answered: 'I thank you, sir, and hardly like to appear ungrateful – but Esch keeps me very busy, and I haven't much of a head for heights – and truth to tell, I'm afraid I'd bore you very quickly!' He dipped his airform toward the fields far below.

'Ah, well! So be it,' the sphere called after him. 'Farewell, then, little bird.' And the steps flattened themselves and folded back, becoming a panel in the sphere's silver flank as before.

. . . And in the fire-floating manse of Exior K'mool where it drifted over the bubbling lava lakes of Lith, two great wizards nodded and chortled, amused for a moment by this diversion whose source lay in Elysia on the far side of eternity. And then they returned to their game of chess . . .

Tiania, the fourth messenger, sat high in the branches of the Tree in the Gardens of Nymarrah. The fork where she perched was broad as a branching path, but even if she slipped she would not fall very far. The Tree's sensitive tendrils were never far away; indeed the one that carried his powerful thoughts and emotions lay on Tiania's pulsing wrist. His leaves were huge as blankets and just as soft; his smaller branches were bigger than the oaks of Earth; all of his care and attention were centred now on this favourite child of Elysia.

Six hundred feet below, there the Tree's vast roots spread out in Nymarrah's rich soil, while as high again overhead his topmost leaves, small and lush green, trembled in Elysia's synthetic sunlight; but here in his heart sat Tiania, talking with him as they had talked a hundred times before, though rarely so seriously:

'And you *will* speak to that Tree in the land of Earth's dreams, and pass on Kthanid's message as I've told it to you, word for word?' she begged for at least the tenth time, while the Tree caressed her with the soft-furred edge of a leaf.

'I sleep and dream, too, child,' he answered in her mind. 'If that dream-Tree may be found – even on a world as far away as Earth – then I shall find him. Aye, and I'll pass on Kthanid's message. Now be sure of that: if I must dream all night, I'll find him.' He was silent for a moment, then said: 'He must be very dear to you, this Searcher?'

'He's a friend like no other,' she answered, sighing. 'But for Henri I'd not be here. He's a brother to me, a lifelong friend and companion to my man, a champion to all lesser creatures. And we treat him like this!'

'Well, then,' said the Tree's gentle 'voice' in her head, 'if he's all of these things my task is made doubly important. And lifelong friend of Titus Crow, you say? That alone were more than enough! No, I shall not fail you. But why are you alone today? Where is your Titus?'

'With Kthanid,' she answered in a whisper, 'in the Hall of Crystal and Pearl. He's there, and by now he's very likely somewhere else.'

And with that she fell silent and was satisfied to let the Tree comfort her . . .

510

4

Familiar Winds

Ithaqua The Wind-Walker was back on Borea.

Once, three years ago, this Great Old One would have sat atop his totem temple throne four or five miles from the foot of the plateau out in the white waste; he would have sat there and scowled at the plateau – threatening occasionally with raised, massive club-like fist, or lightnings called from living, lowering skies – while his wolf-warriors and the wild Children of the Winds howled and cavorted at his great splayed feet and made sacrifice to him. And when the mood took him he would have raised up tornadoes of snow and ice, gigantic wind-devils tall as the plateau itself, to hurl shatteringly against the hollow mountain's impervious flanks.

Three years ago, aye . . .

But Ithaqua's totem temple was no more; at Hank Silberhutte's bidding, Henri-Laurent de Marigny had used the time-clock to destroy it utterly, a crippling blow to Ithaqua's monstrous pride. More than that, Ithaqua himself had felt the sting of de Marigny's weird hyperdimensional vehicle, had come to understand that the plateau's Warlord and his friend from the Motherworld had his measure. And so now he stood off and kept his distance, especially since he sensed that de Marigny had returned, and that once again the time-clock and its near invincible weapon of the Elder Gods were resident in the plateau.

Like some toxic breath of ill-omen, the Wind-Walker had come back to Borea in that same hour that Armandra called her council of tribal chiefs to attend her in the Hall of the Elders, to witness her intended communication with ether winds from all corners of space and time. And while they had gathered there at the counselling place, so he had come striding down the star-winds to Borea, evil burning in his black heart and the unquenchable lust for revenge fevering his alien blood.

And because his totem temple was no more, and also because he hated and feared the time-clock, now he perched a good six miles from the plateau on the rusting steel hulk of a British ice-breaker of the late '20s; a once-proud vessel, fashioned perhaps in the shipyards of the Weir or the Tyne and long since paid for by Lloyds of London: 'lost with all hands, somewhere inside the Arctic Circle', stranded now in the ice and snows of the white waste. There the ship lay – half-shrouded in ice, her once powerful propellers jutting up at an odd angle, monument to Ithaqua's enormous cruelty – snatched up by *him* in deranged glee and borne here through alien voids, finally to be tossed down in the snows of a strange world like some discarded toy.

And the beast himself, crouched upon the ship's flank, the carmine stars of his eyes thoughtful in his dark blot of a head where they burned on the distantly jutting rock of the plateau. For aye, he knew that Armandra talked with the winds, those traitor winds (to him) of time and space. But what his half-human daughter could do gently and without coercion, he would do brutally with blows and curses. And what secrets she could learn by simply asking, he could likewise learn with demands and threats of doom . . .

In the Hall of the Elders, Armandra was in trance.

To call that place a 'hall' were no misnomer: it was a huge cavern of a chamber, lit by many flaring flambeaux; and at its centre a fur-decked dais supporting a carved, massively ornate throne. There sat Armandra, her white hands curved over the throne's stone arms, eyes closed and regal head upright, breast slowly rising and falling under a white fur jacket.

Before her face, hanging down from the forward-curving back of the throne and suspended on a chain of gold, was the large medallion she normally wore at her neck, sigil of her supremacy over the winds. Slowly the medallion turned, its gold burnished to a blaze in the bright glare of the hall's flambeaux.

Descending tiers of stone benches encircled the Hall of the Elders, giving it the rich acoustics of an auditorium; so that now, in the near-absolute silence, even the steady sussuration of Armandra's breathing could be heard in all quarters. And certainly there were sufficient elders there to hear it! Chiefs of all the plateau's peoples they were: Tlingit, Blackfoot, Esquimaux, Chinook and Nootka, and all the old Northwest Tribes of old Earth, their ancestors brought to populate Borea in primal times by Ithaqua the Wind-Walker. There they sat in full ceremonial regalia, just as they might have sat at some meeting of the great chiefs in a northern forest of the Motherworld, watching Armandra with their eagle eyes and breathlessly awaiting her words and works.

To the left of Armandra's throne kneeled Oontawa, lovely Indian handmaiden and squaw of Kota'na; she was there in case the plateau's priestess should require assistance in this task she'd set herself: to call down before her those strange winds which forever wander between the worlds. And at the foot of the dais, at its front, there stood the warlord's small party: Silberhutte himself, his bear-brother Kota'na, Tracy (Hank's sister) and Jimmy Franklin, and The Searcher, Henri-Laurent de Marigny, and his woman Moreen. With them stood Charlie Tacomah, a modern Shawnee late of the Motherworld who had befriended Silberhutte and co. when first Ithaqua had brought them across the star-spaces to Borea – a mistake the Wind-Walker must surely rue to this very day. After the war in Korea, Charlie had travelled north in the Motherworld to write a book on the old Indian and Eskimo tribes, and there on the fringe of the Arctic he'd run foul of Ithaqua. Korea to Borea, as simple as that! He'd spent some time in the camps of the savage Children of the Winds, had finally run off to the plateau. His military experience had been useful, for he'd been a strategist; now he had a seat on the Council of Elders. But his high-ranking friends preferred that he stand here with them.

And so they all waited, and in a little while ... so it began!

For now de Marigny and the others began to hear, as if from far, far away, a keening as of winds blowing between the worlds, and the sounds issued from that now vibrating medallion where it turned on its golden chain before Armandra's drawn white face. What few hushed whispers had sounded before from the audience of elders now ceased; and as if to compensate, the humming and roaring of the throbbing medallion increased. Then –

– It seemed to de Marigny that a host, a torrent of sighing ghost-winds rushed through the chamber. They plucked at his and Moreen's clothes, played in their hair, rushed on in a curious swirl. And yet surely it was all delusion, for the flambeaux flickered not a jot but burned steadily as before! An illusion, yes, like the crashing of distant breakers heard in a shell, this moaning of winds plucked down from between the stars – or was it?

'This never fails to get to me,' came Hank Silberhutte's hoarse whisper in de Marigny's ear, causing him to start. 'She's all woman, Armandra, but there's plenty of the stuff of her father in her, too. Still, I don't have to tell *you* that!'

Indeed he didn't, for de Marigny had previous experience of Armandra's works a-plenty – but this at least was new to him. New, too, the sudden shock of her voice, where before she had been silent – that golden, bell-like voice, breaking over the ghost-ridden rush of weird winds.

The short hairs of de Marigny's neck prickled as she spoke, and he felt an electric tension in the air:

'Ithaqua has returned to Borea,' she intoned, her eyes still closed, her face white as driven snow. 'Drawn back before his time, he watches even now from the white waste. I feel his mind probing at my own, which now I fortify against him!'

Whispers of inquiry and alarm passed between the elders. Ithaqua had not been due back for a three-month yet! What, Ithaqua, back so soon? And no use to ask for what good reason, for there was never any *good* reason where the Wind-Walker was concerned. This was ill-omen indeed!

Armandra gave them no more time for speculation, however, for: '*There!*' she continued, giving a curt nod of satisfaction. 'Now I have shut him out, whose greatest desire is to know our every secret. And now I may converse with the small, friendly winds that wander all the starlanes. Not the mighty whirlwinds of time and space, spawned in the great holes and angles of existence, but their little cousins who play in the vasty voids, whose wanderings have taken them every where and when . . .'

For a moment she was silent, breathing deeply, her brow furrowed in concentration; but then her face lightened, she smiled strangely, her right hand lifted and beckoned. 'Come then, little wind. Come talk to Armandra, and tell her of your travels. And speak, if you will, of the ways of Elysia and the roads that lead there.'

Her eyes remained closed but her burning hair stirred eerily, apparently of its own accord, and began to drift up weightless from her alabaster neck and shoulders. The fur of her jacket grew ruffled, as by a breeze, and her smile became broader at some small secret she alone heard whispered. And:

'This one has returned from Arcturus,' she said, 'where ten thousand ice-planets whirled about a frozen hollow sun.

515

And so fragile that great frozen star, that when he ventured inside and blew about its icicles and brittle stalactites, all crumbled and fell in and shattered into shards and motes of ice. And when the frozen sun collapsed, so its many worlds, released like shots from a sling, went bounding off into space to seek new suns; and so this small wind is very likely a father of future worlds! So he says, but I think it a clever fantasy, with which he hopes to please me. As for Elysia: *there* lies the fable, he says, for never did he talk to a wind who ever ventured there.'

Her smile faded a little as she slowly cocked her head to allow a very small breeze to rest a moment like a kitten in the crook of her neck. Invisible, that ether-gust, but it smoothed out the ruffled fur of her collar and caused her copper hair to billow there. 'And this one is sad,' she said, 'for he lost his brothers in the maw of a black hole, where they strayed too close to its rim. Now they are sucked through the hole to some other place far removed, and he fears he'll never more gust with them out in the stars we know. He supposes they might just possibly have found their way into Elysia – whereof he's heard it said that all the winds are fair – but alas, of the location of that place he can tell me nothing.'

And so it went: the ether winds came and departed at her bidding, breezes and breaths, puffs and pants, gusts and gasps of wind come to talk to Armandra. She spoke with bitter winds from the deepest regions of space, and others warmed by the exhalations of suns where they'd played. There were winds born in the mountains of green worlds on balmy summer evenings, and others whose worlds were dead now and mourned their passing as winds do. Infant breezes there were, and soughing winds almost as old as time, and all of them with their own tales to tell.

Until at the last, and just as de Marigny began to despair of ever hearing anything useful –

'– *Ah!*' sighed Armandra, clasping the arms of her

throne and sitting up yet more regally erect. 'Now here's a rare wind indeed, and a *frightened* one at that!'

Hank Silberhutte grasped de Marigny's elbow, reminder that he was not merely lost in some impossible dream or hallucination. 'This might be just what you're looking for!' the ex-Texan whispered. 'I thought she was beginning to flag, but now she's fully alive again – *see* . . . !'

De Marigny saw. A faint bloom was suddenly visible on Armandra's pale cheeks, like the flush of some strange excitement. Some unseen thing – a panicked gasp of air, perhaps – hid for a moment in a sleeve of her jacket, causing it to bell out, then burst free to rush round her head in a veritable frenzy of fear. Until: 'Be still! Be calm!' she cried. 'You're safe here, little one, from whatever it is that pursues.'

De Marigny was drawn to lean closer, caught up in what was happening.

'And this one,' said Armandra, with something of triumph in her voice at last, ' – this last small wind – he has had all the bluster knocked out of him! He's fled far and fast from a very terrible thing, almost exhausting himself entirely in the process. He is not pursued, no, but he has heard the shrieking of a gaseous intelligence out beyond the Red Medusa who *was* pursued – by the Hounds of Tindalos!'

De Marigny caught his breath as his flesh began to crawl, but he must hear this out.

'A cloud of gas, yes,' Armandra continued, 'a vapour in the voids travelling half as fast as light, and pursued by the hounds. He had a name, this intelligence, which was simply a hiss – Sssss! Or if not a name, at least that is how he thought of himself. And as he fled, so this small wind thought to hear him praying to the Great Gods of Eld in Elysia, begging of them their assistance! Then he saw the hounds where they pursued, saw them devouring the trailing wisps of the gaseous being, and when he saw how

517

hideous they were he too fled. And so he is come here to rest and recover his strength . . .'

Armandra sighed, lay back her head a little, opened her great green eyes. Her lustrous copper hair settled down upon her head and round her shoulders, and suddenly the chamber was still and the winds were gone from it.

Then someone coughed and the silence was broken. The spell, too. De Marigny shook himself, considered all he'd heard – especially the tale of the final visitation.

It wasn't much to go on, he thought, but it had to be better than nothing. Or was it? What was he to make of it after all? A cloud of intelligent gas out beyond the Red Medusa Nebula? A vapour-being who prayed to the Gods of Eld? And yet if that incredible gas intelligence knew enough of the Elder Gods to call out to them for their aid, perhaps he (it?) might also know where they were. It was a possibility, however remote, that de Marigny couldn't ignore – made all the more urgent by the presence of the Hounds of Tindalos. Maybe out there in the star-voids a door was closing even now, a gateway to Elysia, slammed shut forever by the Hounds of Tindalos!

Oontawa was helping Armandra down the dais steps. The Woman of the Winds was not so much tired as dizzy from her efforts. Tracy, too, had gone to help support her; both girls were anxious for her, until the Warlord reached up and lifted her easily down the last two steps into his arms. She hugged him, then turned to de Marigny.

'I'm sorry, Henri, but that's as much as I can do. It seems that this Elysia is a very special, very secret place.'

He took her hand, kissed it, said: 'Armandra, you've probably done more for me in half an hour than I've been able to do for myself in three long years! At least I've something to go on now. But the effort has wearied you, and I had no right to ask you to do it anyway. So how can I ever find words to thank you for – '

He paused as there came a sudden buzz of excitement

518

from the elders close to the chamber's entrance. An Eskimo runner stood there, gasping his message. Kota'na recognized him not so much as a messenger but one of the keepers he'd left in charge of the bears that guarded the time-clock in de Marigny's chambers, and went to him at once. He returned in a moment.

'Henri,' he said, his Indian's eyes wide and very bright. 'It is the time-clock!'

'What?' de Marigny's jaw dropped as he grasped Kota'na's brawny arms. 'The clock? What of it?' His anxiety was very real, for he remembered that time from three years earlier, when Ithaqua's wolf-warriors had stolen his vehicle. 'Don't tell me something's happened to – ?'

'Happened to it?' Kota'na cut him off, shaking his head in denial. 'Oh, no, my friend – and yet, yes. The clock is where you left it under guard – but its door has opened, and a purplish light spills out!'

5

Great Thought Rider

Time-clock: a totally inadequate misnomer, thought de
Marigny, as he hurried with Hank and Moreen through the
plateau's labyrinth to the dwelling-caves near the perimeter
where the clock was temporarily housed. It did look like a
clock at first glance, like a fine old grandfather in the
somewhat macabre shape of a coffin, and it did have a dial
and hands; but there any resemblance to a clock in the
mundane sense of the word ended.

Its weird ticking was quite irregular; its four hands moved
about the hieroglyphed dial in spastic patterns patently
divorced from any chronological system known or even
guessed at by man; it was certainly *not* an instrument for
measuring the orderly passage of time at all but rather
ignored and even transgressed temporal laws. And because
time is part and parcel with space – the other side of the
same coin, as it were – so the time-clock transgressed
against spatial laws, too.

In short, it was a vehicle for space-time travel, a gateway
on all possible worlds and levels of existence, a not entirely
mechanical magical carpet. Einstein would not have believed in the time-clock, and what he would have made of
a gaseous intelligence riding the solar winds through space
at half the speed of light . . . who can say? But then again,
a sea-urchin would probably experience the greatest difficulty believing in Einstein.

De Marigny, on the other hand, did believe in the clock;
each time he used it his life, Moreen's too, hung by the
thread of that belief. He believed in it, and he trusted it,
even though many of its complexities remained way beyond
his grasp. This was hardly surprising; it had been that way

for Titus Crow too, in his time. But the more de Marigny used the clock, the more he learned; a slow process, true, but a sure one. It was like being a learner-driver in the latest model of some high-technology motor-car; there was always a new button or switch one had never tried before, which might well be a device for steaming rain off the windows ... but might just as easily jettison the driver through the roof!

... Finally the three arrived at de Marigny's and Moreen's quarters, passed the Eskimo guard and keeper where he stood with a pair of massive, rumbling bears, and so into the chamber where the time-clock waited. Here small circular 'windows' looked out over the white waste, and on a bleak horizon Ithaqua crouched atop the derelict ice-breaker, watching the plateau just as Armandra had seen him in her trance. Time for only a cursory glance at the Wind-Walker, however, for here was an even greater wonder; and perhaps one just as fearful, in its way.

For indeed the time-clock's panel stood open, its eerie purple light pouring out in rhythmic pulses from within. Just what this might signify was hard to say, but de Marigny could soon find out. 'Wait,' he said to Moreen and Hank as he stepped forward and made to enter the clock. Except –

– Even as his hand gripped the frame of that narrow portal, *so a figure materialized there and stepped out!*

Taken by surprise, de Marigny gasped, jumped back and almost collided with Hank and Moreen. Then he grasped and restrained the Warlord's hand where already his knuckles were white, clenched on the haft of a bright pick-like weapon snatched from his broad belt.

'No, Hank!' The Searcher cried then. 'There's no danger here. Can't you see who it is? Don't you recognize him? It's Titus Crow!'

On legs suddenly weak as jelly de Marigny went to embrace the newcomer – fell against nothing and staggered right through him. Crow was insubstantial as smoke, a mirage – a hologram!

'A ghost!' Moreen gasped. 'Is this your Titus Crow, Henri? A phantom whose grave is the time-clock? Is that why it's shaped like a coffin?' And for all that she was only half-serious, still de Marigny sensed something of fear in her voice.

Silberhutte, on the other hand, was quicker to grasp the true picture. '*Shh*, Moreen!' he whispered, putting a protective arm round her shoulder. 'This is no ghost. It's not magic but science. And Henri's perfectly correct: wherever this 3-D picture is coming from, it's certainly a picture of Titus Crow.'

De Marigny had meanwhile recovered himself and stepped back from the apparition; and as for Crow, he seemed just as bemused as the three whose eyes followed his every movement. For a moment utter confusion was written on his face; then, like a man suddenly blind, he groped his way backward until once more he stood inside the clock and was bathed in its ethereal glow. Then came his voice, that deep, rich and oh so well remembered voice from the memories of de Marigny and Silberhutte both:

'Henri? I saw you then, but just for a moment. If that was really you out there, please come inside the clock where we can talk. I'm riding a Great Thought sent by Kthanid. Outside the clock I'm largely immaterial, but in here I'm much less a spectre. Only be quick, Henri, for Kthanid can't keep this up for very long.'

De Marigny needed no further urging. With a second 'Wait!' to his friends, he stepped inside the clock and was engulfed in its pulsing light. Then for a moment two old, true friends peered anxiously at one another – and at last smiles broke out, and laughter – and finally they pounded each other's backs.

'It's you,' said de Marigny, 'in the flesh – of a sort, anyway! But how?'

'You haven't changed, Henri,' said Crow then, holding him at arms' length. 'Not a jot. Still full of questions I never have the time to answer.'

'And you,' the other returned. 'Why, if anything you seem even younger!' And then, with less levity: 'But you're wrong, Titus, for I have changed. I've been changed. It's not simply my own skin I've to care for now. But . . . I want to show you something. How long do we have?'

Crow's smile also fell. 'Minutes,' he answered. 'I'll get the very briefest warning, and then I'll be on my way back to Elysia.'

'Time enough,' said de Marigny; and over his shoulder he called, 'Moreen, will you come in here, please?'

She came at once, innocent and charming as always. Face to face with the girl, Crow's eyes opened wide in wonder and appreciation. And: 'This is Moreen,' said de Marigny. 'Born in Borea's moons of Earth stock taken there by Ithaqua. Funnily enough, she was mine even before I found her, much like your Tiania. Now we travel together.'

Crow gave the girl a hug, said to his friend: 'You'd have been pushed to find her like on Earth, Henri – or even in Elysia, for that matter.'

'Room for another in there?' came the friendly, growled query of the plateau's Warlord. And a moment later Hank Silberhutte, too, stood bathed in the clock's weird illumination. For that was another anomaly of the time-clock: that the space within it was very nearly as great as that outside!

And now for the first time it was Crow's turn to display amazement. 'What?' he said, his eyes incredulous where they looked Silberhutte up and down. 'Hank? Is it really you? My God! And how long ago since we all went at the Burrowers together, eh? And how much passed between?'

'That was . . . another world,' said the other. 'Hell, it really was! But from what I've heard, it hardly seems we'll have the time now to fill in the gaps. So Moreen and me, we'll simply stand here and listen, and try to keep patient until you and Henri get done. You're not here for the fun of it, eh, Titus?' .

Crow's face quickly became grave. 'Not for the fun of it, no. My reason for being here is probably the best any sane human being could have.' He turned more fully to de Marigny. 'I might have come sooner, mind to mind, but you weren't receptive. You were preoccupied, Henri, your mind full of other things. But I know that wherever the old time-clock was, then that you'd be there too. Also, I might have simply come here – more fully "in the flesh" – in another time-clock or via this one. But with very few exceptions all the clocks are back in Elysia now, where for a little while at least they're destined to stay. This clock of yours is one of those few exceptions. Also, to use this clock as a gateway and come here physically, that would mean returning the same way: transmitting myself *physically* into Elysia. And right now nothing physical is allowed into Elysia. Which is why I rode a Great Thought, between Kthanid and the clock. It was the only way.'

'You seem physical enough to me,' said de Marigny, and the Warlord nodded his agreement.

'I felt your arms around me,' said Moreen.

'That's the clock, reinforcing my presence here. But you saw what happened to me outside – I was thin as a spook!'

'Wait a minute,' said de Marigny, frowning. 'Are you saying that something's happened in Elysia? Nothing physical is to be allowed in? And does that include me?'

'Elysia is under siege, Henri,' said Crow, 'or as good as. It's just a matter of time, that's all.'

'Under siege?' This was plainly beyond The Searcher. 'But how could a place like Elysia possibly be under siege? From whom? I mean, I – ' He stopped dead and his eyes suddenly opened wide. Then: 'This has to be some sort of perverse joke, Titus, surely?'

Crow shook his head. 'No, my friend, no joke. They're rising – and soon!'

'Who?' the Warlord could keep silent no longer. 'What is this threat? Who or what is rising?'

'*They* are rising,' Crow repeated. 'The primal threat, the Great Old Ones themselves! The stars are very nearly right, and the Cthulhu Cycle Deities are on the move again. But that doesn't mean you're excluded, Henri, on the contrary. Indeed, both you and Moreen will be welcome in Elysia. It was Kthanid himself promised you that, remember?'

'Oh, I remember all right,' the other answered, a little sourly. 'But how does one *attain* Elysia? Titus, I've searched so hard. Believe me, I've tried. Man, I've found out what you meant when you warned me that there was no royal road into Elysia. In fact, I had almost given up hope.'

Crow bit his lip, and for the first time de Marigny knew that something gnawed at him, something other than the trouble brewing in Elysia. Crow covered it quickly, said: 'You can't give up hope now, Henri, not now. No, for now you're really needed in Elysia' (and again that tortured look). Then: 'Listen, you're right about there being no royal road. I can't take you by the hand and lead you there, especially not now. But there is still a way. It's a pointer, that's all, a couple of clues, and they're the best I can do for you.'

'I'm listening,' said de Marigny eagerly. 'Whatever it is, it has to be better than groping in the dark. Just keep talking, and believe me I won't miss a word.'

'Very well,' said Crow. 'First, there are places you can try looking in Earth's dreamlands. Now we both know a little about the dreamlands but we're not expert dreamers, so don't go jumping to any wrong conclusions. It's just a place to start. Then there's – '. He paused, looked startled, grasped de Marigny's hand and held it tightly. For a moment his outline wavered, and at the same time his grip on de Marigny's hand seemed gentle as a girl's, but then he firmed up strong again.

'Titus, I – ' de Marigny was alarmed.

'The warning I told you about,' Crow cut him off. 'We only have a minute now. So listen: back in Theem'hdra at the dawn of all Earthly civilization, there was a wizard called Exior K'mool. He, too, might know something – if you can find him. And finally – '

The light in the clock was pulsing faster now, and its colour was changing through all the shades of purple to a strange foxfire blue. Crow wavered again, grew wispy as smoke, tried to grab de Marigny and hang onto him. His hands went right through; de Marigny's and Silberhutte's, too, where they tried to hold fast to their old friend. And now, at the last, Crow's voice was thin as a reed:

' – Finally there's a cloud of luminous gas out beyond the Red Medusa Nebula,' he said, as from a million miles away; but on the last word his voice grew fainter still and petered out altogether.

'I know it!' de Marigny cried. 'It has intelligence. It's fleeing from the Hounds of Tindalos . . .'

Crow was still mouthing something but the words were lost. Suddenly he seemed snatched up, whirled away. Pin-wheeling down a whirlpool of throbbing blue light, he grew small in a moment. But before he vanished completely, his voice came back one last time:

'But if you know that much, maybe you'd have discovered the rest, too. That's good! I don't feel so bad . . . about . . . it . . . now . . .'

'About what?' de Marigny frantically called after him, but only echoes came back. Titus Crow had gone, drawn back on Kthanid's Great Thought to Elysia.

Gone too the whirlpool of blue foxfire, and the interior of the time-clock pulsed purple as before . . .

6

Sssss!

When a hedgehog is trying to cross a motorway, there has seemed very little purpose. Even into the Primal Land is the domain of Earth. Its name and the land of Earth however, that the faintest gas cloud was threatened by the Turquoise Firmament, or (if) backwashed on the Eden I see me then and, perhaps – and for all de Marigny knew –

Named after a creature of incalculable evil, nevertheless the Red Medusa Nebula was a thing of incredible beauty.

Way beyond the range of Earthly telescopes, in whose eyes it was the merest smudge of ochre light or series of faint radio blips, the Medusa was aptly named: not only did it have the outlines of that Gorgon's head, but also a mass of snaky filaments which could be her hair. More, it had a certain trick of hers, too: in a manner of speaking, it could turn things to stone.

The Medusa was a cancer which was eating itself; its filaments had not been flung outwards but were being *drawn* out, by a ring of great black holes where they circled the nebula and sucked off its countless billions of tons of matter into nothingness. Theory has it that matter falling into a black hole, as it approaches the speed of light, becomes motionless as time itself is frozen. And so it can be seen how this great cosmic Medusa 'petrified' her victims. But of course that was only theory, and since coming to know the time-clock de Marigny was given to mistrust much of what theory says.

Nevertheless the Medusa was a place to avoid, and so now the time-clock winged around it, hurtling at many times the speed of light (and in so doing, ruining another theory) and heading for the far side. 'Beyond the Red Medusa Nebula' had seemed to The Searcher's way of thinking to cover a very large and largely unknown region; but at the same time he (the clock) was equipped with the most sensitive scanners, and so it should not prove too difficult to locate the luminous and comparatively slow-moving Sssss . . .

When it had come to choosing a place to start there had seemed very little of choice. Theem'hdra, the Primal Land in the dawn of all Earthly civilizations? The land of Earth's dreams? But the sentient gas cloud was threatened by the Tind'losi Hounds; he (it) had called on the Elder Gods for their aid; perhaps – and for all de Marigny knew – this mission of his was simply Kthanid's way of answering that call. Another good reason was that Moreen had wanted it; indeed her love of all (or most) creatures, no matter how strange, had driven her to insist upon it. The Hounds of Tindalos were devouring the gas-being, and that was good enough for her. In the three years she had loved and travelled with The Searcher, Moreen had come to know the hounds very well; to know them, and to be repulsed by them – even Moreen.

In those same three years she'd learned something of the clock's handling, too, so that along with de Marigny she now exhilarated in its flight as they sped in that near-fabulous craft across the vast curve of space. And so at last, when the Red Medusa sprawled far in their wake: 'There!' she cried, first to detect the drama that lay ahead.

De Marigny saw it a moment later, drew it close in the clock's scanners: a glowing green cloud like some mighty comet, with a hard bright nucleus and a long gossamer tail flaring far behind. Fifty thousand miles long, Sssss, and seeming to expand enormously by the moment as de Marigny slowed the time-clock and brought it about in a great semi-circle to parallel the path of the nucleus. And back there in the tail –

The time-clock's rearward scanners left little doubt as to what was happening back there.

It was without question the hounds, but in such numbers – so vast a pack – as de Marigny had never imagined in all his wildest hound-ridden nightmares! 'By all the gods in Elysia,' he whispered to Moreen then, 'just *look* at them!'

'I have looked,' she answered with a sob, 'and I've seen.

They are like no other creatures, these hounds. They know only two things: destroy and devour.'

De Marigny nodded. 'They're the stuff of the Mythos, all right,' he agreed. 'The CCD's trackers across time's wastelands!'

To see the Hounds of Tindalos was to know them at once, but a man might see them a hundred times and still find difficulty in describing them. They were that alien! Like some monstrous four-dimensional plague, they were vampires of time that haunted its darkest angles, foraging abroad from the temporal towers of wraithlike Tindalos to hunt down unwary travellers. An uncleanliness lacking any real, living form, yet they were embodied in vague batlike shapes. They were flapping rags of evil, thirsting drinkers of life itself. And insatiable.

But since their true habitation was time itself, de Marigny found a strange anomaly here. 'A weird pack, this,' he said to Moreen. 'They run in space! I knew that in certain circumstances they can cross the time-barrier into three-dimensioned space, but this is the first time I've actually seen it. Maybe those black holes back there on the rim of the Red Medusa have something to do with it. Perhaps they've welded space and time into one here.'

But Moreen was hardly listening. Rapt to her scanners, she murmured: 'He is alive! He is . . . *aware*! And Henri, he is in pain! Not pain as we know it, but hurtful nonetheless. The hounds are a slow acid that sloughs away his being, reduces his life force, slows him down and ever more speedily devours him. They are a disease eating into him, corrupting him, killing him. It may take a thousand years, but what is that to them? Time is on their side. And all the time his agony increasing, until the hounds reach his nucleus. Then the final rending as they bring him down, the last spurting of the forces which power him, and the black debris of his passing seething forever in an endless orbit round the Red Medusa.'

De Marigny found and squeezed her hand. 'Not if I have anything to do with it,' he told her. 'We'll see about that in a little while. But first ... Moreen, can you actually talk to it – to him?'

'Did you ever see a creature I couldn't talk to?' she asked.

'Only the hounds themselves,' he answered.

'Because they are *not* life,' she explained. 'Because they are anti-life. But Sssss is alive and beautiful. His colour, even his size is ... beautiful! Of course I can talk to him. Only adjust your receptors, Henri, and hear him for yourself.'

Receptors: another misnomer. Like the scanners, these were not wholly mechanical; both words were simply terms for devices almost beyond mundane comprehension. To meld one's mind with the clock was to enhance one's perceptions ten-fold, while to use its sensors was to achieve the square of that effect. Through the clock's scanners human eyes might well be telescopes, or on a different scale microscopes. Hearing was so sensitized that the human ear might detect the abrasive rasp of one snowflake against the next. Tuned to the time-clock's senses, a man might 'smell' the scents of distant moons, or the decay of a dying star, or 'taste' the atmosphere and water of a planet while still a million miles away. The sixth, psychic sense was amplified, too: a gifted telepath such as Hank Silberhutte would become a thought transmitter to the stars; and as for a woman like Moreen, whose empathy with all living creatures must surely be the result of a unique mutation ...

Oh, Moreen could 'talk' to Sssss, most certainly, but all de Marigny got was a mush of mental static. He could *not* talk to the gas-being, not possibly. To the amphibian holothurians he'd met on a mainly water-world, yes, and to the pollen-gathering apoideans of a savannah planet in Aldebaran; but these had been alive as he understood and was physically aware of life. 'Fire' to him was fire to them, and likewise 'danger', 'good', 'bad', 'joy', 'flight', 'walking', 'pleasure', 'food', and 'drink'. And of course 'life' and 'death'. Most creatures have some common ground, recognize parallel links in the chain of life. But Sssss? The gaps were too great, for The Searcher, anyway.

And so de Marigny could only shake his head in defeat. 'Then you'd better translate,' he said. 'Ask him if we can help.'

She did so, at once, and de Marigny heard her thoughts go out with crystal clarity to the fleeing gas-being – and heard them answered. The mush of psychic static altered its pitch, tone, timbre, became more controlled, more purposeful. Moreen and the gas cloud Sssss conversed.

'You know,' de Marigny told her in something of awe, 'I believe that if you'd wanted to you might even have talked to Armandra's familiar winds.'

'I would not have dared to try,' she told him in an aside. 'The plateau is Armandra's domain and her winds are loyal to her. No, I didn't try to talk to them; but when she had drawn them to her, I couldn't help but overhear a little of their conversation. Just a little, for indeed they're secretive things, winds . . .'

Again de Marigny marvelled, and almost laughed. But just then –

'He wants to know if the Elder Gods sent us. The time-clock isn't entirely strange to him for he's seen one before, quite recently. It was piloted by a – I don't know,' she paused briefly, ' – by a creature, anyway.'

De Marigny was elated. 'A time-clock was here, recently? Ask him what he can tell me about Elysia. Ask him if he knows the way there.'

Moreen put his questions to the gas cloud, and after a moment's listening said: 'He doesn't really understand the concepts of "ways" or "paths". He has only his orbit and can't remember when he might ever have deviated from it.

But he does appreciate the idea of places. He knows for instance that *this* place is usually fraught with hounds.'

'But didn't he talk to this visitor of his at all? What did the pilot of this other time-clock say to him?'

Moreen tried her best, and after a moment: 'They ... they passed a little time, that's all. Their concepts, too, were different, do you see? The creature in the clock talked in terms of pressure, temperatures and radiation, some of which Sssss understood. And he in his turn spoke in expressions of gravity, velocity, density and capacities.'

Frustrated almost beyond endurance, de Marigny gritted his teeth and cursed under his breath. One might as well try to make sense of a shooting star! 'He's talked to someone, some*thing*, from Elysia – and I can't find out what passed between them!'

Moreen ignored this very untypical outburst, continued to pour urgent thoughts in the direction of the green-glowing gas cloud. 'I'm telling him who, what we are,' she explained. 'Trying to get it over to him how important he may be to us. How far we've come and how long you've been searching. It's not easy, but ... *wait!*'

'Yes?' de Marigny felt his spine tingling.

'He understands "search"!' said Moreen excitedly. 'He, too, searches. In his orbit he seeks out dead planetoids to draw in, food or fuel to power him on his way. Yes, and he asks ... he asks ... are *you* the one called The Searcher?!'

De Marigny's mind reeled. 'He's heard of me?'

'The other time-clock's pilot mentioned you, "one who searches". He said that if Sssss should meet you in his orbit, he should tell you to look inside yourself – that the answer you seek lies in your own past, and in your future, and in your dreams!'

'What? Are you telling me now that a cloud of gas understands the concept of dreaming?'

'Of course! When he cruises in the outer attraction of

great stars and pivots about them – when he has not the need to power himself but rides the forces of gravity – then he shuts down. And like all sentient beings, Sssss also dreams.'

'Look inside myself,' de Marigny repeated feverishly. 'The answer lies in my past, my future, my dreams. And Titus said much the same thing: that I should look in the land of Earth's dreams . . .'

Moreen nodded. 'Yes,' she said, 'I'm sure that's right – but not until we've done what we can for him.'

'You're sure there's nothing more he can tell us?'

Moreen was almost in tears. 'There may be, I don't know. But I do know that the hounds are hurting him, Henri. And I know he's afraid.'

Something of her horror got through to de Marigny. For all the sentience of Sssss, he still seemed little more than a green comet to the Earthman, or would if Moreen were not there to remind him otherwise. And suddenly de Marigny felt like some merciless inquisitor. 'You tell him,' he said, applying mental brakes, slowing the time-clock's forward velocity, 'that we're going to teach these Hounds of Tindalos the lesson of their lives – or their un-lives. Tell him *bon voyage*, and I hope his orbit never decays.'

As the emerald nucleus shot forward in space, so Moreen passed on de Marigny's message. And while he primed the clock's incredible weapon, so she relayed the answer of the being called Sssss. 'He says, may your search be of short duration. Also, you're to give the Elder Gods his thanks when you reach Elysia.'

The nucleus of Sssss was already thirty thousand miles ahead now, and his flaring tail rapidly drawing up alongside. With it came the hounds, their hellish, mindless bat-chitterings menacing in the sensors. Then the clock's scanners were full of them, a mighty pack of unprecedented size.

'They feed on the substance of Sssss and they spawn,'

533

Moreen sobbed. 'They devour him, his goodness, and increase themselves.'

'Well, they're about to suffer one hell of a decimation!' de Marigny was grim. 'I'll never get a better chance than this to even up a few scores. It's impossible to miss them.'

Even before he opened fire the hounds recognized him. De Marigny, and Titus Crow before him, were matters of fearful legend now: they and the time-clock had openly defied whatever laws governed the Hounds of Tindalos. Lacking true life, the hounds could hardly 'die' as such, but they could certainly be destroyed. And this coffin-shaped clock had become a destroyer with a will!

Rotating the clock on its own axis like a top, de Marigny opened up. Pencil beams of the purest white light struck forth, shredding the evil, ethereal stuff of the hounds wherever it was met. The wispy green tail of Sssss became filled with hound debris, ragged black fragments flying in all directions, upon which others of the pack fell like a great shoal of frenzied sharks! But in a very short while de Marigny saw that he'd set himself a hopeless task; there were simply too many of them.

'This is like swatting flies in a field on a summer day!' he said. 'If we were a fleet of a hundred clocks, then we might make a dent in them. But we're not.'

'But we're going to try anyway?' Moreen was anxious. 'We won't leave Sssss to be devoured?'

Still firing, he answered, 'There has to be a better way than this. These hounds have broken the rules, left their own environment and come through into space.' He narrowed his eyes, opened his scanners on the distant Red Medusa Nebula. 'And maybe – just maybe – that's where they've made a very grave error of judgment!'

'Henri?'

'Time's their element, isn't it? And back there near the Red Medusa, there are places where time itself is frozen. According to a certain theory, anyway. Well, such theories rarely apply to the time-clock, but as for the hounds ... ? It's worth a try, anyway.'

He stopped firing, deliberately sent the clock tumbling end over end, so that it must seem completely out of control, a simulated malfunction. This proved no discomfort at all to the clock's passengers: their space-time machine simply compensated, and it was as if space turned while the clock stood still.

The hounds closest to the clock had been fleeing in disarray, but now they paused, gathered in chittering clouds, began to fly in ever decreasing circles toward a common centre which was the time-clock. The rest of the vast pack did likewise.

'Henri, they're coming!' cried Moreen. 'What are you doing? Have you forgotten that they can break through the clock's angles?'

'I know it,' he answered, 'and so do they. I'm far more important to them than poor old Sssss there, Moreen. They're Cthulhu's scavengers, remember? What a great prize we'd make, eh?'

Believing the clock crippled, the hounds closed in. Now de Marigny could sense their psychic feelers groping for the clock, soul-sucking tendrils of mental energy; and now, too, their chittering was a frenzy of lust and monstrous anticipation. And only at the last moment – when it seemed the closest of the nightmare things must surely fall upon, fall *into* the clock – only then did de Marigny accelerate away from them. Not far, a short spurt, and then a pause as he let the clock tumble once more and waited for them to catch up. So he played them, the entire pack, like some vast and monstrous fish on a line.

And yes, they were hooked!

Sssss was free of them now, powering himself on and on along his orbit, his distance increasing by leaps and bounds. They could never catch him now, not in three-dimensional space. But in fact they had lost all interest in Sssss. De

Marigny and whoever journeyed with him, they were the new targets; the travellers, and the time-clock itself.

Now the gas-being was little more than a mote speeding away into far infinities, a green speck, gone! And now, too late, the hounds felt the irresistible attraction of de Marigny's trap: one of those greatest of black holes where it circled the Red Medusa. For he was leading them straight into its heart! Deeper still de Marigny drove, and ever faster, until even the time-clock's near-impervious fabric began to strain under the forces working upon it. And only then did The Searcher break the time-barrier and leap forward into a future where the hole was long extinct.

He did it only just 'in time'; for at this range, so close to the black hole, even time itself was beginning to bend and lose its shape. But too late for the hounds, far too late. Matter could not escape the maw of that Great Omnivore; space was warped inwards; the ethereal stuff of the hounds was flimsy as cobweb, no match at all for this vast insensate monster. Down they fell, ever faster, toward a point where time for them would freeze. And them with it.

Very few of them escaped to limp back to the corkscrew towers of dead and spectral Tindalos . . .

Moreen picked up all of these mental pictures from de Marigny's mind and shuddered. 'Horrible,' she said. 'A horrible fate, even for such as them.'

'Moreen,' The Searcher answered, 'sometimes I think you're just too good to be true!' But he hugged her anyway.

And then he set course for Earth . . .

1
Ulthar and Atal

'If only,' thought de Marigny, as the time-clock winged him back through time and space to the 20th Century Earth of his past: if only Elysia were as easy to discover and enter into as the dreamlands of Earth. For certainly in their diverse ways both places were parallel worlds of wonder; oh yes, and be sure that there were places in the dreamlands gorgeous enough to rival anything in Elysia.

Except ... except that not *all* things were wonderful there. No, for the lands of Earth's dreams were also of necessity the lands of her blackest nightmares.

'Tell me again of the Motherworld's dreamlands,' begged Moreen, as her man, The Searcher, began to recognize familiar constellations and knew now that he was not far from home – or at least, not far from the world which had once been his home. 'Please, Henri, tell me more of these places I have never dreamed of.'

It was true, for while she was of Earth stock Moreen had been born and raised in a moon of Borea; she had never once visited the human dreamlands of her birthright but only the subconscious, haunted dreams of her native Numinos. By no means an expert dreamer himself (and this despite the fact that he and Titus Crow had been honoured and feted there, until indeed they had become one with the stuff of dreamland's legends itself), stumblingly at first and then with more assurance, de Marigny had related yet again his earlier adventures in the strange dimension of Earth's dreams. He told of how he had gone there to rescue Crow and the girl-goddess Tiania, trapped in abysses of trauma; and how with the help of certain inhabitants of the dreamlands he had succeeded; and then how the three of them together had gone on to triumph over an insidious incursion of Cthulhu and the Great Old Ones into the subconscious worlds of mankind's innermost dreams. And when all of this was not enough for Moreen, then de Marigny went on to tell of places he knew there in that imagined yet real otherworld, and of places he'd only heard of and never (or at best only rarely) seen; places he had dreamed of long ago, which had faded now as all dreamstuff does in the cold morning light of the waking world.

He spoke of monstrous Kadath where it aches in the Cold Waste, forbidden to all men ever since the immemorial dreaming of certain hideous dreams there; and of the no less ominous icy desert Plateau of Leng, where horrible stone villages squatted about central balefires which flared continuously, while Leng's *denizens* danced grotesquely in flickering shadows to the rattle of strange bone instruments and the droning whine of cursed flutes. And seeing how Moreen shuddered at the tone his voice had taken and crept closer to him, he at once turned his attention to healthier regions of the dreamlands.

He spoke of the resplendent city of Celephais in the valley of Ooth-Nargai beyond the Tanarian Hills, whose myriad glittering minarets lie mirrored in the calm blue harbour; and of the galleys anchored there, with furled, multicoloured sails, beneath Mount Aran where the ginkgos sway in the breeze of the sea; and of the tinkling, bubbling Naraxa with its tiny wooden bridges, wandering its way oceanward; and of the city's onyx pavements and maze of curious streets and alleys behind mighty bronze gates. He made mention of sky-floating Serannian (which had always reminded him of Crow's description of Elysia's sky-islands) high over the Cerenerian Sea, whose foaming billows ride up buoyant as clouds into the sky where Serannian floats on their ethereal essence.

He talked of Zak with its many-templed terraces, abode

of forgotten dreams where many of his own youthful dreams and fancies lingered still, only gradually fading away; and Sona-Nyl, blessed land of fancy where men dream what they will, none of which might ever take on real material form; and the sea-spawned Basalt Pillars of the West where they rise from the furthest reaches of the Southern Sea, beyond which (so legend has it) lies a monstrous cataract where all the seas of the dreamlands pour abyssally away forever into awful inchoate voids. He mentioned Mount Ngranek's peak, and the great face graven in that mountain's gaunt side; and having spoken of Ngranek he could not help but mention the hideously thin and faceless, horned and barb-tailed bat-beings – the night-gaunts – which ever guard that mysterious mountain's elder secrets.

Then, because he believed that despite Moreen's fears she should know the worst and not go into the dreamlands a total alien and unprepared, de Marigny hurriedly went on to tell of the Peaks of Throk, those needle-like pinnacles which are the subject of many of dream's most awful fables. For these peaks, higher than any man might ever guess or believe, are known to guard the terrible valleys of the Dholes, whose shapes and outlines have often been suspected but never seen; and in one such place, the ill-omened Vale of Pnoth, there the rustling of the Dholes is ever present in utter darkness, where they infest mountainous piles of dried-out bones. For Pnoth is the ossuary into which all the ghouls of the waking and dreaming worlds alike throw the remains of their nighted feastings.

Finally, and yet more hurriedly, for by now Earth was swelling large in the time-clock's scanners, he made mention of Hlanith of the oaken wharves: Hlanith, whose sailors are more like men of the waking world than any others in the dreamlands – and ruined, fearsome Sarkomand, whose broken basalt quays and crumbling sphinxes are remnant of a time long before the years of men – and the mountain Hatheg-Kla, whose peak Barzai the Wise once climbed, never to come down again. He spoke of Nir and Istharta, and the Charnel Gardens of Zura where pleasure is unattainable; also of Oriab in the Southern Sea, and infamous Thalarion; and at the very last, for he wished to be done now, he mentioned Ulthar where no man may kill a cat.

And Ulthar he had deliberately kept to the last, for it was where their quest must start. Indeed, for of all the towns and cities and lands of dream, Ulthar was the one place which had its own Temple of the Elder Gods; and who better to talk to about Elysia than the priest of that temple, who himself aspired one day to a position there?

'And do you know him?' Moreen asked when de Marigny was done and the time-clock sailed in an orbit high above Earth's nightside. 'Is he a friend of yours, this high-priest of the temple?'

'Oh, yes,' he answered with a nod, taking her in his arms and settling down for sleep. 'I know him fairly well – or as well as any man of the waking world might be expected to know him. I've met him several times before: twice when I sought his help, and the last time at a banquet at the Inn of a Thousand Sleeping Cats, in Ulthar. But as for "friend" – I wouldn't presume. Ancient beyond words, he was around when the dreamlands were young! There's one thing I can guarantee, though, that he's pure as a pearl. As for his name: it's Atal the Ancient – Atal of Hatheg-Kla, who came down again when Barzai did not – and if there's one man in all the dreamlands who can help us, Atal's that man ...'

The first time de Marigny had used the time-clock to enter into the lands of Earth's dreams might well have been his last; he remembered that fact now as he drifted into sleep in the arms of Moreen, but this time he had resolved it would be different. The trick was this: to meld one's mind with that of the clock itself (for indeed it had a mind) as one fell asleep, and falling asleep to command the clock that it proceed into the neighbouring dreamlands. That way a man might take the clock with him into dreams, not merely use it as a gateway into those subconscious regions. That had been his mistake last time: to use the clock as a gateway, leaving it in orbit while he literally became stranded in darkling dreams! After that ... but that's a tale already told.

This time he made no such mistake. His will, slipping ever deeper into sleep, clung tenaciously to the time-clock, and even more especially to Moreen; so that all three of them, man, girl and machine, entered the dreamlands as a single unit. Physically, of course, they remained in orbit, all three; but psychically they dreamed, the time-clock too. What's more, de Marigny's dreaming was accurate to a fault: the clock materialized in Ulthar beyond the River Skai, in the courtyard of the Inn of a Thousand Sleeping Cats.

There the lovers 'awakened' in each other's arms, rose up and yawned, stretched, stepped out through the clock's frontal panel into Ulthar's evening. De Marigny was not sure what welcome he might expect, or even if he'd be remembered or welcomed at all; for surely his coming again would only serve as a vivid reminder of the Bad Days, when all the dreamlands had been in a turmoil of terror. But the scanners told him that the courtyard of the inn was set with tables, and that the evening was filled with the scents of flowers in full bloom, and that already people were arriving and seating themselves outdoors for an evening meal. What they could not tell him was that the tables had been set *since* the arrival of the clock, while he and Moreen had lain 'asleep', and that the meal in preparation, like the last one he'd eaten here, was in his honour!

But when at last the lovers left the clock and its

541

door closed behind them, closing in the purplish glow of its extraordinary interior and leaving them in Ulthar's lanthorn-illuminated twilight ... ah, how de Marigny's 'forgotten' friends in the dreamlands crowded to him then!

Now, time is a funny business in the dreamlands; in places like Celephais or Serannian it can seem to stand quite still, so that nothing changes much. But to dreamers from the waking world who go there only rarely, it often seems that many years have passed between visits. Or perhaps it is the attitude of the dreamer himself, for it must not be forgotten that the dreamlands are themselves built of men's dreams. De Marigny's attitude – his desire – had been to enter the dreamlands 'now', not in the future or the past, and so he and Moreen had arrived at a time little changed from when he was last here. In other words, dream-time had kept pace with his waking-world time: the friends he saw now had aged a year for each of de Marigny's years – not merely an hour, and God forbid a century!

Grant Enderby was there and his strapping sons; his daughter, too, dark-eyed Litha, blushing as she thought back on earlier dreams. But she was wed now to a quarrier and had her own house close to her father's, and those had been vain dreams anyway for Henri was a man of the waking world, a tall ship passing in the night of the dreamlands. Oh, he had planned one day to build a villa here, in timeless Celephais, perhaps – what dreamer hasn't? – but these, too, had been only dreams within dreams.

Then there were dignitaries from several local districts, some of which de Marigny recognized, and the fat inn-keeper and his family – beside themselves with pride that the visitors had chosen this particular place in all the dreamlands into which to dream themselves – and finally there was the venerable Atal himself, who had been a mere boy in that immemorial year when the city's elders had passed their ordinance prohibiting the killing of cats. Atal, borne in by four young priests of the temple, reclining upon a canopied litter and dressed in his red robe of high office. His priestlings wore grey and were shave-headed, but their respect for the Master was not born of arduous ritual and service but more of love. For while he was undeniably the high priest of the temple, he was also simply Atal: which is to say that he was one of dreamland's greatest legends.

Deposited at the head of the rows of small tables – where stood a somewhat larger table – Atal's litter was tilted and part-folded to form a carved chair, where he sat beneath his gold-embroidered canopy while de Marigny and Moreen were ushered to their places of honour beside him. Then, after the briefest but warmest of greetings and introductions, a fabulous, sumptuous meal was served; and at last, when the throng began to eat and under cover of their low, excited chattering, finally de Marigny was able to talk in earnest to the high priest of Ulthar's Temple of the Elder Gods.

'I knew you were coming,' the ancient told him at once, almost breathlessly. 'You or Titus Crow or some other emissary of the waking, outer spheres. I knew it, for there have been portents aplenty! You know how the people of Nir and Ulthar fear eclipses? No? But of course not, for you are still a novice dreamer – though of course that is not said to slight you. No, for you've served the lands of your dreams well enough in your time. Anyway, this fear of eclipses all dates back to my youth and is unimportant now; but in the past month there have been two eclipses of the moon, and both of them unforeseen. Now, the orbit of dreamland's moon is at best less than entirely predictable – and never more so than recently, since the dreamlands waged a war there – but our astronomers are rarely so awry as to miss an eclipse! And as for two, that is surely unheard of! How do I read it? I'm not sure, but I know that in the Bad Days, when Cthulhu's influence was strong here, eclipses were frequent. They occurred whenever Nyarlathotep, the Great Messenger, came to spy on the dreams of men ...

'Another omen: in Serannian of the Clouds there has been a visitation, a singular thing. I have had this from Kuranes himself and know it to be true: an event has occurred there which never occurred before, and so has been the cause of much speculation. Likewise, strange thoughts have entered the dreamlands. I myself heard the merest echoes of them in dreams within dreams, and they were not the thoughts of men – but I believe they were good thoughts for all that. They came out of Elysia, I think, and fell to the ground somewhere beyond Thalarion. But who in Elysia would wish to speak to someone beyond Thalarion, de Marigny?' The ancient shook his head. 'Omens, my young friend, all of these things, and more still to come. Would you hear?'

De Marigny gazed long and wonderingly at the old man, near hypnotized by the gentle sigh and rustle of his voice. Frail and weary with years the ancient was; his face a wrinkled walnut, head sparsely crested with white hair, beard long and white and voluminous as a fall of snow; and yet the colourless eyes in that worn old face were lit in their cores with all the wisdom of the dreamlands. And so: 'Say on, sir,' said de Marigny, stirring himself up and giving the patriarch all of his attention.

Atal reached out to take his hand in a trembling, mummied paw. 'I am the priest of Their temple, as you well know, and I aspire one day to serve Them there in Elysia as I now serve Them here. In return – though of course I would not presume to bargain – it is my prayer that They shall give me back a little of my youth, so that I may enjoy more fully something of my time in Elysia, the place of the Elder Beings I serve.'

De Marigny nodded, however ruefully, and answered:

'We both aspire to great things, Atal, though I admit that at times my faith has weakened.'

Atal answered de Marigny's nod with one of his own. 'Impatience is the privilege of the young,' he said, 'while still they have the energy for it. But now is not the time for a weakened faith, of that I am sure. I *am* the priest of the temple, and I know as much as any priest of the Elder Gods knows of Elysia; except do not ask it, for even I cannot tell you the way there. What I must tell you is this: recently, though I have prayed as always, I know that my prayers have not reached Elysia. The way is barred! Prayers go unheard, unanswered, and strange thoughts no longer fall to earth beyond Thalarion; an inhuman messenger has come into Serannian, and abides there still, and no human being knows what message he brought; aye, and there have been the eclipses, and now you, The Searcher, have returned once again to dreams. Strange times, and I cannot fathom the whys and the wherefores of it all – unless, perhaps, you can enlighten me?'

De Marigny, noting that he had now acquired a dream-name – the same one by which he was known in many dozen worlds – quickly explained his purpose here in the dreamlands: the fact that while he was needed now in Elysia, which stood imperilled by an imminent eruption of the Great Old Ones, still there was no royal road to that place; for which reason Titus Crow had given him certain clues to the route he must take, clues he now pursued as best he might. Then he asked the elder to go into more detail in respect of certain of his 'portents', those singular occurrences he had mentioned:

'What of those alien thoughts,' he asked, 'which you heard in your dreams? Can you not tell me a little more? And what of this weird visitation Lord Kuranes reported from sky-floating Serannian?'

'As I have said,' Atal replied, 'the thoughts from outside were not human thoughts, but yet they were not evil or inimical to man. Indeed, they may even have had some bearing upon your quest – though I cannot swear to that. Ah, but now I see it written in your face that you will go at once into Thalarion's hinterland! So be it, but remember: that region is not much travelled. It borders on the old territories of the eidolon Lathi – lands where for long she reigned supreme – and so there may well be danger lurking there yet. However, there are others here in the dreamlands who can tell you more reliably of such things; for of late there have been such marvels and tumults and victories ... the battle of the Mad Moon ... Zura's treacheries, and the triumph of the ships of the dreamlands ... an old man is hard-pressed to stay well informed.'

De Marigny frowned to himself in the light of the lanthorns and allowed himself a few thoughtful bites of food while Atal got his breath. The Searcher knew that the temple's high priest was growing weary – he was beginning to ramble a little, so that his words no longer completely made sense – else The Searcher might also ask him about those recent 'marvels and tumults and victories', and perhaps something of the war in dreamland's moon; but he was sure there would be others he could talk to of those things, which must certainly be matters of wider report. And so it seemed to him that there remained only one more thing requiring the elder's clarification.

And as if Atal read his mind, at last that ancient had control of himself sufficient to say: 'A visitation, aye, a strange new thing come into Serannian. It is a small grey metal cube,' (and he made its shape and size with his trembling hands), 'which flew out of the sky one morning when the city was just astir, and poised itself at the mainland end of that narrow promontory whereon Curator keeps his Museum. There it hovered and spun like a top in the air, seemingly sentient, a dull leaden box containing – what? And from where?

'Ah! – but let me tell you this: the strange cube was not

featureless. No, for upon one of its six sides it bore hands, like those of a clock – even like those of your time-clock there – and aye they numbered four and moved in a manner without rhyme or reason!'

De Marigny gasped and sat up straighter, but before he could form a question:

'Wait!' said Atal. 'Let me say on. The longshoremen and sailors spied the cube there where it spun in mid-air, dully agleam, and word was sent to Kuranes who of course came at once from his ivied manor. A great dreamer, Lord Kuranes, but this was a matter beyond even his dreaming. Natheless he questioned the box in all the tongues of the dreamlands; but it answered him not, merely spinning there at Serannian's rim, where the narrow span of the causeway goes out to Curator's marvellous Museum . . .' The ancient paused.

Now de Marigny knew something of Curator and his Museum, but not a great deal; his time in Serannian had been very limited and in the main restricted to visiting Kuranes' manorhouse. He knew however that Curator was a mechanical man, or that his body at least was of shining metal, and that both he and his Museum had existed in Earth's dreamland at least as long as Serannian; but just what the robot really was, and where he came from, and why he had brought the collection which formed his Museum's exhibits here in the first place ... no one knew those things. It was sufficient that he did no harm – within certain limits, and provided the Museum and its contents were not threatened or interfered with – and certainly the place did contain many wonderful things. Kuranes was known to frequent the Museum with some regularity.

'I should not think,' he finally prompted the old man, 'that Curator would be much taken with this enigmatic visitor, spinning there in mid-air so close to his Museum!'

'On the contrary,' Atal sighed, once more taking up the

547

tale, 'For as the sun rose up and broke free of the horizon, so Curator came out and scanned the cube where it whirled; and he must have taken note of its erratic hands where they measured conjectural matters upon its sixth side; and he stared at it with his crystal eyes along the length of the bridge which connects the Museum to Serannian's rim. Then –

'A passing *weird* thing! For Curator, who has many arms, formed four of them into hands like those of the cube, all sprouting from a central place, and these he jerked and twirled in a singular fashion, duplicating to a large degree the movements of the cube's hands!'

'They talked to each other!' gasped de Marigny at once. 'Curator and this time-clock – for it can only be some sort of strange time-clock – conversed!'

'More than that,' came Atal's rustling affirmation. 'For in a little while Curator strode out along the causeway, and the leaden cube moved forward to meet him, and there in the centre of that spindly span they paused, as it were, face to face. And while longshoremen, sailors, citizens and Kuranes himself looked on, panels opened in Curator's chest to reveal a space just so big,' (again he described a small cube with his fluttering hands), 'in which without pause the enigmatic visitor located itself, ere Curator's panels closed again to fold it within his breast. And so the wonder was at an end, for without more ado Curator turned and clanked back to his Museum. And still the mystery of this meeting and its meaning remain unknown.'

'So,' said de Marigny, 'not only must I visit Thalarion's hinterland but also Serannian, to talk to Curator.'

But here Atal shook his head. 'Not possible,' he said, 'not even remotely. It is a matter of immemorial legend that no man in all the dreamlands ever spoke to Curator!'

'Never?'

'Not ever. Ask yourself these questions: does Curator

even understand the speech of men? Does he care? Is he even *aware* of any reason or purpose outside his one task of preserving and protecting his beloved Museum? But on the other hand – '

'Yes?'

'Curator has had *to do* with men – with certain men, that is. By that I mean that while he converses not, still he can make his desires known to men – especially those who would harm his Museum or attempt to disorder or even steal its exhibits!'

De Marigny frowned, tried hard to understand. 'You mean that he chastises would-be thieves?'

'He has done so, yes. And he has had occasion to merely warn others. Indeed I know of two such, er, gentlemen, cautioned by Curator, as it were – ex-waking-worlders, as it happens. And by rare coincidence, though I for one do not believe in coincidences, these same men have also ventured beyond Thalarion – ventured there and more – *and* returned unscathed! You should talk to them, Henri, before proceeding further with your quest.'

'Do you know them, these two, and where I might look for them?' The Searcher was eager.

But while they had talked something had been taking place to attract the attention of all the others at their tables: a curiosity at first, which had now grown into something so strange and wondrous rare as to be a singular occurrence in its own right. It concerned the cats of Ulthar, and it also concerned Moreen.

For during her man's conversation with the temple's high priest (and knowing the importance of their subject), Moreen, seated on Atal's left, had not interrupted but had taken the opportunity to eat; and having eaten she had then found a kitten to talk to, which had jumped into her lap from beneath the table. Now the cats of Ulthar are a special breed and have their preferences; they know good men from bad and true from false, and are mainly indifferent toward all but the warmest, purest hearts. How then Moreen's heart? For where one small kitten had coiled in her lap and purred –

– It seemed to the people gathered in the courtyard of the Inn of a Thousand Sleeping Cats that at least half and probably more than half of all the cats in Ulthar must have come to congregate here in the last half-hour, and all of them worshipping at the feet of Moreen! Of every type and size and description they were, though outside the circles of lanthorn light their colours were quite uniform; for of course it was that hour when all cats turn grey, except in the light. Kittens galore (Ulthar's cats have large litters), and huge, prowling toms, and sleek, well groomed matrons, all rubbing shoulders and straining forward; but never once a snarling or spitting, for theirs was a unity of curiosity – a group engrossment, a mass hypnotism – whose soul and centre was Moreen.

De Marigny and Atal, deep in conversation, had barely noticed the gradual encroachment and massing of the cats; but now, as all chatter died away, in the glimmer of lanthorns and perfume of Ulthar's night blossoms, and in the sudden astonished sighing of all humans who congregated there in that courtyard, they could scarce help but notice it. And more cats arriving by the minute, until the cobbles were crowded with them where they spread out in concentric circles from Moreen's feet; and the girl still petting that smallest kitten while she spoke purringly to all the cats in general. And them beginning to purr back at her, in a concerted rumbling that spoke of all the contentment in the world!

Forgetting de Marigny almost entirely, Atal took Moreen's hand and pressed it, and said: 'You must have loved cats for a very long time, my dear, and loved them well. For the cats of Ulthar are very discerning.'

'Cats?' she smiled at him. 'Is that what they're called? Oh, yes, I remember now! Cats are mythical creatures in

Numinos, only ever heard of in legends of the Mother-world, passed down from generation to generation.'

De Marigny quickly explained Moreen's origin – and the fact that Borea's moon, Numinos, had no cats, for Ithaqua had never taken any there – and Atal was rightly dumb-founded. 'And she befriends all beasts in this manner, you say? But this is an astounding thing, and as surely as all the other portents have been bad ones, this *must* be a good one! Merely to have this wonderful girl with you bodes well for your quest, Searcher.'

'Then you'll tell me where I can find these men you spoke of, who've travelled beyond Thalarion and had something of business with Curator?'

Atal nodded his old head. 'Anything you desire to know,' he said. 'Except, if I told you *all* I've heard of these two it would take all night – and half of it at least would be fabulous anyway, I'm sure – and both of us would fall asleep ere I was done. And so I'll be brief:

'They came from the waking world and were stranded here when their lives were prematurely ended in that plane. At first they seemed at odds with the lands and men and customs of Earth's dreams, they became wanderers, adventurers, great brawlers and even thieves; but because they were artful dreamers, finally the dreamlands accepted them and gave them shelter. And rightly so, as it turned out, for now it seems they're destined to grow into legends in their own right. They are questers now, agents of ever-watchful Kuranes, and their many deeds have included keep-climbing and exploring, black wizard-slaying, gaunt-riding and far-adventuring in some of dreamland's most monstrous places. Why, it was them burned down the paper city Thalarion, and almost the wicked eidolon Lathi with it! – though I'm told she's building that awful hive once more. They were dreamland's warlords in the battle of the Mad Moon; they put an end to Zura's plot to sink Serannian; for all their roguish natures, even the King of

Ilek-Vad is said to number them among his personal friends!'

'Randolph Carter?' de Marigny was impressed.

'Himself!' Atal nodded. 'And talking of King Carter, and remembering your reason for coming here at this time, his current absence is a great pity; for Randolph Carter has been to Elysia in his dreaming and might perhaps show you the way; except that he's once again gone off, exploring in undreamed of places, ever searching for your father, Etienne, his old friend from the waking world.'

Again de Marigny turned a little sour. 'It has always been the same story,' he said. 'Like father, like son. I'm what I am because of Etienne-Laurent de Marigny. His love of mysteries rubbed off on me, and now I'm a searcher, too. *The* Searcher!'

'Aye, your destiny,' Atal sighed.

It was late now and the people were coming forward in small groups, politely nodding their farewells and goodnights as they went off to their homes. The moon had risen and the lanthorns were burning low, and even the cats were stirring now and their ranks thinning as they went off to seek the shadows. For delightful as Moreen was, there were more important things for cats to be about when the moon hung full and high in the night skies of dreamland. Which was just as well; for at that juncture there came a soft flapping of wings, and down out of scented darkness fluttered a bird of Ulthar's Temple of the Elder Ones, a pink pigeon, to alight on Atal's shoulder.

A few departing cats looked back, their almond, slant-eyes yellow in the night, and two or three lean toms might just have considered the possibility of a little fun and flying feathers; but Moreen was wise to their ways now and tut-tutted, which was chastisement enough. So off they went as Atal tremblingly took the tiny cylinder from the bird's leg and unwrapped the scrap of paper tucked inside it.

'A message,' he husked, screwing up his eyes and

drawing a lanthorn closer. 'But from where, and about what?' Then –

'*Ah!*' the old man sighed as finally his eyes focussed. 'And indeed this arrives at an opportune moment. For if you really wish to meet the two men I've mentioned – the questers from the waking world – it would seem it's now or never. Here, read it for yourself, for unless I'm much mistaken it's couched in runes you'll know – English, I believe.'

De Marigny took the note, smoothed it out on the table, read its short, sharp legend.

'HELP!' it said in black, jagged lines, 'AND MAKE IT FAST – FOR TOMORROW AT FIRST LIGHT GUDGE SENDS US TO HELL!' And it bore the signatures of David Hero and Eldin the Wanderer . . .

2

Hero and Eldin

Playing *Pass The Time Before—*, David Allenby Hero, late of the waking world, where he'd been a sensitive painter of matters ethereal, and Professor Leonard E. Dingle (Psychology and Anthropology), ex-lecturer on the subconscious mind of man, had almost inevitably ended up in the doldrums of the game yet again. Hero, or more formally Hero of Dreams, as he was now known, and Eldin the Wanderer, had most recently been enumerating 'Things Ridden Upon'.

Before that they'd recalled 'Inimical Creatures, Beings or Persons Slain or Otherwise Subdued', had listed alphabetically 'Ladies Lusted After', chronologically 'Fantastic Feats', and somewhat morbidly in light of their current circumstances 'Deaths Defied'. The first of these had included a certain black wizard, species of man-eating flora and fauna, night-gaunts, dholes, zombies, termen, moon-beasts and Lengites and so on, all leading eventually to Gudge, whom they merely wished dead but who, ironically and in all likelihood, bar a large miracle, would shortly gain some notoriety in the dreamlands as *their* executioner!

The second series in *Pass the Time Before—*, 'Ladies Lusted After', had been a bad choice of subject; Eldin had led off with 'Aminza Anz', immediately breaking down in tears before the game could go any further. For Aminza, may the Lords of Dream bless her memory, had woken up on the very day she and Eldin were to have been wed, which had brought about an abrupt termination of that romance.

'Fantastic Feats' had been a good one, for both of the

554

questers were given to boasting a bit and vied with each other in respect of frequently recounted acts of heroism. What thief in all the dreamlands (for example) could match Hero's feat in 'cracking' a great keep of the First Ones? And who but that magnificent arsonist Eldin the Wanderer would ever have dreamed of burning down an entire city (the hive Thalarion) with his firestones? (Of that last: Hero was wont to point out that it had been done before by someone called Nero, a waking-worlder, he thought.) And so on. Alas, their most recent 'feat' had been to come a-spying for Kuranes in the Badlands back of Zura the land, where Gudge the pirate had discovered, recognized, captured and would now kill them.

Which had led them to 'Deaths Defied'. This list had been longest of all, involving not only all of the Creatures, Beings or Persons in the first series but sundry menaces such as: freezing in the upper atmosphere; drowning in a whirlpool; walking-the-plank two and a half miles over the Southern Sea; a moonbeast spell of petrifaction; being devoured by Oorn the Gastropod Goddess in primal Sarkomand; seduced to a soggy pulp by Lathi and romanced to rottenness by Zura of Zura; and so on, etc., *ad infinitum*. Except, quite naturally, this had only brought them to the current Death Defied, which being unavoidable couldn't be so much defied as simply waited upon; hence the game of *Pass the Time Before*—in the first place. For of course that pair of indefatigable dreamers were only passing the time before their mutual demise.

Except that demise was not upon them yet, and there were other lists to be considered, most recent of which had been 'Things Ridden Upon'. And boastful or not it seems highly unlikely that any dreamers anywhere could summon up a list of conveyances half so fabulous (and yet so thoroughly authentic) as that of Hero and Eldin. They had sailed a reed-tree raft across the blue lake beyond the Great Bleak Mountains, and down a whirlpool to a swamp beyond Thalarion. They'd ridden (flown) on a Great Tree's life-leaf from Thalarion's hinterland to the gardens of Nyrass the Mage in Theelys. They'd been transported 'magically' from Theelys to a mighty mountain keep, all in the blink of an eye. They'd been aboard Kuranes' ships of dream, Zura's ship of death, the eidolon Lathi's ship of paper. They'd been flown by night-gaunts across all the gulfs of dream, and vented in ethereal essence from Serannian's huge flotation system, and bustled on the back of a many-legged Running Thing through the Caves of Night in Pnoth and across the Stickistuff Sea. And that wasn't all, far from it:

They'd slid down a beam of light from Curator's curious eyes to a sky-ship in the aerial Bay of Serannian; and rushed up into higher space on a broken mast and a bag of air; and flown to dreamland's moon on a spiral moon-beam! Last but not least they'd been borne by Eeth, a moon-moth maid, to the feet (or roots) of a magical moontree; absorbed by him and transferred to seedlings, which had then twirled them back down to the dreamlands; and finally, as grotesque gourds, they'd fallen to earth on the banks of the Skai near Ulthar, where both had been 'reborn' full grown.

'And now,' Eldin morosely concluded, 'it seems we're to careen on these damned great crosses to dreamland's very core – perhaps to the pits of nightmare themselves!'

Hero could only nod (literally) and agree: 'Aye, this is another hell of a crucifix you've got me onto.'

'Is that a joke or an accusation?' Eldin asked suspiciously.

'*Huh!*' Hero snorted.

'I accept your apology!' said Eldin; and: 'You know, lad, there's a list far more important than all these others we've played with. One which we haven't considered at all as yet.'

'Oh?'

'Indeed! It's called "Narrow Squeaks Squeezed

Through", and it might just provide a clue as to a way out of this current mess.'

Hero carefully moved his head (about the only part of his person he *could* move) to peer at the other in the gloom of their predicament. Lashed to a great wooden cross and suspended over the rim of a pit that went down almost (but unfortunately not) without limit, the Wanderer was not a pretty sight. He never had been, but now he looked particularly ugly.

Eldin was older than Hero's maybe thirty years by at least a dozen; he had a scarred, bearded, quite unhandsome face which yet housed surprisingly clear blue eyes – for all that one of them was now black. Stocky and heavy, but somehow gangly to boot, there was something almost apish about him; yet his every move and gesture (when he was able) hinted of a sensitivity and keen intelligence behind his massive physical strength. Alas, half beaten to death by Gudge's freebooters, that giant strength wasn't much in evidence now, else Eldin's bonds were long since torn asunder. Instead the Wanderer had his time cut out simply forcing words past his broken lips; so that Hero's niggling words and manner were deliberately designed to keep him on his mettle and chipper, as it were. Eldin knew this, knew too that Hero himself had seen better nights. He gloomed back at the younger dreamer, said: 'Well, what about it? Is there a way out of this, or – ?'

'Most likely or,' Hero glumly answered, and when he laid his head back winced from the spasm of pain in the soft spot behind his left ear, where his hair was matted with clotted blood.

Hero was tall, rangily muscled and blond in dreams as he'd once been in the waking world. His eyes were blue like Eldin's, but lighter; they could redden very quickly, however, in a fury, or go a thoughtful, dangerous yellow in a tight spot. They'd been yellow a while now, though nothing had come of it. His nature in fact was usually easy-going: he loved songs a good bit and girls a great deal, but he was also wizard-master of any sword in a fight, and the knuckles of his fists were like crusty knobs of rock. He was very different from Eldin, yes, but they did have several things in common. They shared the same wanderlust, for one, and the same sometimes acid sense of humour for another. The lands of Earth's dreams occasionally make for strange travelling companions.

'Are you saying we should just hang here and wait for the new day?' Eldin seemed surprised. 'Our last day, as it may well turn out to be?'

'Hell, no!' Hero grunted. 'By all means, let's be up and on our way!' He sighed. 'Look, old lad, I don't know about you but I can't hardly move a muscle. I can blink, talk, wriggle my backside, nod my head and wag it too, but that's all. Ergo: knackered! Physically, emotionally, mentally knackered. I haven't completely given up hope, not yet, but at the same time I have to admit that I can't see much future for us. Not if I'm to be truthful about it.'

'Hmm!' said Eldin, gruffly. 'Just as I suspected: you expect me to get us out of it, right? What David Hero can get you into, Eldin the Wanderer can get you out of – just like that!'

However weakly, Hero had to grin. Now Eldin was needling him – deliberately, of course. In fact, neither one of them had been to blame for their untenable situation; their task had been impossible right from square one. And now Hero looked back on how they came to be here . . .

. . . At that same moment but many miles away (the actual distance is conjectural; spans of time and space are deceptive in the land of Earth's dreams) in the resplendent city of Celephais, King Kuranes was echoing Hero's thoughts; except that he did it out loud, for the benefit of friends and visitors from the waking world. For upon reading that brief SOS borne on the leg of a pink temple pigeon, de Marigny had said farewell to Atal, bundled Moreen into the time-clock, travelled at once to the valley of Ooth-Nargai beyond the Tanarian Hills. Since the questers Hero and Eldin were agents of Kuranes, who better to ask of their likely whereabouts – and something perhaps of this Gudge who apparently threatened their lives – than Kuranes himself?

Now, in the King's palace (in fact an ivied manor-house, the very replica of his loftier seat in Serannian), The Searcher and Moreen of Numinos sat at a great table with the king, while whiskered, liveried servants stood in attendance. In his long nightshirt and still not fully awake, Kuranes had put on square-framed spectacles, read the scrap of paper they brought him, turned pale in the steady glow of a pair of antique oil lamps.

'Gudge has them!' he'd gasped then. 'Gudge the pirate, scourge of the Southern Sea and the skies around Zura and Thalarion!'

Kuranes was slightly built but regal in his bearing, grey-bearded yet sprightly and bright-eyed, with nothing of the occasional fuzziness of natural-born dreamlanders (*Homo ephemerans*, as Eldin the Wanderer had long since dubbed the peoples of dream) about him. Quite obviously a man late of the waking world, still he was a powerful force for good in the dreamlands and a long-time enemy of all agencies of horror and nightmare. On reading the note he'd come wide awake in a moment and grasped de Marigny's arm.

'And you came here in your time-clock, that awesome vehicle and weapon I remember so well from your last visit?'

'Oh, yes,' The Searcher had nodded. 'It's out there in the gardens, where your pikemen have placed it under guard.'

'Good!' Kuranes had uttered a huge sigh of relief. 'So perhaps there's a chance for that pair of great-hearted rogues even now.' And then he'd told his visitors all he knew:

'Since the war of the Mad Moon things have been allowed to get a bit lax here in the dreamlands. Our victory was so massive, so decisive, that we've done precious little since but celebrate! A grave, grave error. Atal will have told you of the incidence of unorthodox eclipses? Just so. And did he also read an omen into your presence here at this time?'

'Expertly,' said de Marigny, 'even though Atal had not foreseen just how serious our business here.' And he'd quickly sketched in what he knew of matters: the imminent uprising of the Great Old Ones, as evidenced in the alignment or re-alignment of certain stars; his own presence as a positive necessity now in Elysia, into which place there was still no royal road; Titus Crow's hint that certain clues as to Elysia's whereabouts might be obtained in Earth's dreamlands. Finally: 'And I believe that with the help of Hero and Eldin, I may be able to narrow down my search.'

'Which makes their rescue that much more urgent, indeed entirely imperative!' said Kuranes, slamming down his palms flat upon the table. 'Once more it seems the dreamlands are at risk, and not only the dreamlands but the sanity of the entire universe! Now listen carefully:

'Some six months gone, the Southern Sea and the skies over dreamland were safe and free as never before. With Lathi and Zura defeated in the Mad Moon's war and banished out of the sane lands of dream back to their own dark demesnes – and the Lengites crushed and sorely depleted; and the surly Isharrans subdued, what few of them remained in Sarkomand and points west – honest folk were able at last to go about their businesses and pursuits as is their right, unhindered and unafraid.

'The sky-trade between Serannian, Celephais, Ilek-Vad and Ulthar prospered; sea-trade and -farings between all the ports of the Southern Sea flourished; the Isle of Oriab lost much of its previous insularity and pleasure-seekers flocked to Baharna as before, to enjoy its wonders. Merchantmen had never sailed so close to the shores of infamous Thalarion, or with such small concern past Zura the land – not with guaranteed impunity, anyway – and sightings of black Leng galleys, in both sea and sky, became so few and far between that Captains soon lost the habit of reporting them. It seemed that in the main the horned almost-humans stuck to their forbidden plateau, Lathi to Thalarion, rebuilding her twice-ruined hive, and Zura to her moon-ravaged Charnel Gardens.

'Serannian's guardian sky-armada was expensive to man and maintain; patrols were long and boring for the crews; men were better employed putting to rights the damage rained on the dreamlands in the time of the Mad Moon. All in all, the lands of Earth's dreams were peaceful and prosperous once more, and the memories of dreamlanders are extremely short. Peace, aye, but it was only the lull before the storm . . .

'And so the stage was set for mischief, which came all too quickly in the shape of Gudge and his pirates. Ships began to disappear: on the sea between Oriab and the continental dreamlands, along the coasts of Zura, Thalarion and Dylath-Leen, even in the skies. That's right: even the occasional warship, patrolling out of Serannian, disappearing without trace. And what small pockets of intelligence and information I controlled all pointed in the same direction, arrived at the same conclusion: piracy! Sea-pirates, sky-pirates, probably one and the same! But from where, and under whose black-hearted command and control?

'Oh, I had my suspicions. Zura had built herself a new sky-ship, *Shroud II*, and crewed it with zombies – a "skeleton crew" – hah! Lathi was rumoured to have repaired and fortified her previously flimsy *Chrysalis*, and brooded aboard while her ter-men and -maids fashioned a new

Thalarion of their extruded paper-paste wastes. But how could Zura be the miscreant? What use to her the spoils of piracy? Anyway, *Shroud II* was only ever spied over the Charnel Gardens sails furled, a kraken-prowed corpse of a ship and gloomy as a menhir. And as for Lathi: her wispy *Chrysalis* could scarce be considered a threat – certainly not to the practised gunners of a warship of Serannian! Cannon-shot would pass right through her, aye, but a fire-rocket would burn her to a crisp. So much we'd learned in the war of the Mad Moon.

'I increased patrols over suspect areas, issued harsh punitive instructions, incurred heavier losses. And I began to lose patience and a deal of complacency. Obviously the problem was greater than I'd suspected; nor could I retaliate until I knew my enemy and his base of operations; patently I must now employ as much cunning as that unknown enemy himself. But then, some real information at last!

'But first ... have you heard of Gytherik Imniss?' Kuranes raised a questioning eyebrow to peer keenly at de Marigny. 'No? Well, I'm not surprised; you've been away for quite some time and he's fairly new on the scene, and something of a novelty to boot. He's a lad from Nir and commands a singular power – a power over night-gaunts! In fact he's dreamland's first gaunt-master, with the freedom of all the skies of dream.'

De Marigny curled his lip in disgust and drew back aghast. 'What a menace!' he said.

'Eh?' Kuranes looked puzzled for a moment, then shook his head. 'No, no, you misunderstand: I myself conferred his freedom of the skies. What's more, his grim won medals in the battle for the Bay of Serannian!'

'Grim?'

'Collective noun for a gathering of the rubbery horrors,' Kuranes explained.

'Very appropriate, too!' said de Marigny, making no

effort to hide his astonishment. He shook his head. 'Things have really changed. I mean, am I to believe in beneficent gaunts?'

'It depends who's controlling them,' Kuranes answered. 'But you're perfectly correct: old fears and legends die hard, and gaunts have a very bad reputation. Even now there's a saying in the dreamlands: that the only good gaunt's a dead 'un! Except Gytherik's grim would seem to be the odd-grim-out, the exception that proves the rule. Anyway, back to my tale:

'I was in Serannian pondering my next move, when who should drop in on me but Gytherik and a handful of his gaunts. It was somewhat into the morning and the gaunts were looking a bit grim – if you'll excuse the pun – and not alone from the sunlight, which they don't much care for at the best of times. Two of them at least had jagged tears in their rubbery hides and limbs, which seeped a bit so that Gytherik had to tend them. Afterwards, I put them up (or down) in a dungeon for their comfort while we talked.

'It came out how he'd been to the mountain Ngranek, letting his gaunts do some socializing there; you know how night-gaunts guard or haunt the entranceways to dreamland's underworld, and how there's one such gateway under Ngranek? Yes – well, the lad's solicitous of the beasts in his charge, you see. Anyway, on his way back to the mainland, flying on the back of a huge brute of a gaunt and with the rest of the grim all about him, he spied below the lights of a merchantman out of Serannian on course for the Isle of Oriab. She was venting flotation essence and settling to the sea for the second half of her trip; Baharna, Oriab's chief port, being a pretty perpendicular place, hasn't much in the way of level mooring for sky-ships, which are obliged to use the harbour like purely mundane vessels. So there she was, this ship, settling down to the sea, when out of the sky like vultures fell three black galleys in a spiral, closing her in!

'Gytherik sent his gaunts winging down through the night to see what the matter was; and there in the darkness he saw these three black ships, showing never a light, set upon the unsuspecting merchantman and pound her to matchwood! Pirates they were, beyond a doubt, who swarmed aboard the doomed, foundering vessel in a trice, putting down all but the Captain and several paying passengers, whom they took off from the sinking ship. As for the crew of that stricken vessel: horrible! There were guttings, hangings and plank-walkings; until Gytherik, watching from on high, was sick from the vileness of it all.

'Now the gaunt-master was just one man, more properly a youth, and unarmed. Likewise his gaunts: they had only their paws to fight with and their wings with which to buffet. Nevertheless he set the grim to diving into the rigging of the black ships and doing whatever damage they could. Alas, the pirates were ready for Gytherik, for they had seen his grim flitting against the disc of the moon. Now that's a strange thing in itself – the *preparedness* of these black buccaneers for the likes of Gytherik and his gaunts – which I'll get to in a minute. Anyway, seeing what he was about, the pirates dragged out hurling devices from under tarpaulins, loading them with tangles of netting armed with razor-sharp barbed hooks! And as the grim swooped and tore at the topmost sails and rigging of the black galleys, so these weird ballistae were fired up into the night! Hooked, maimed, net-entangled, many a gaunt fell into the sea and drowned, victims of the first salvo; others were slashed by hooks, or had the membraneous webs of their wings pierced; so that Gytherik feared he'd soon lose the entire grim.

'Naturally he quickly stood off – there was little more he could do – and there under the moon and stars the pirates hailed him, calling:

'Hey, gaunt-master! You, Gytherik! Let this be a lesson! You're not alone in your freedom of the skies. Let it be known that henceforth Gudge the pirate claims sovereignty over the sea between Oriab and the mainland, also over the skies and shores and hinterlands of Zura and Thalarion!'

'And they set up a great concerted shouting: "Gudge – Gudge – Gudge the Merciless!"

'And out from his cabin on one of those barbarous black vessels came the leader of that terrible band: Gudge himself!

'It was dark, remember – the dead of night – and Gytherik wasn't able to see as well as he'd like. Also, his viewpoint was aerial: he looked down on things from on high. But still it seemed to him that these pirates were a queer bunch. There was that in their voices which he couldn't quite place: a nasal, guttural quality, if "quality" is the right word. Also, they all wore turbans or tricorns – to a man, that is – and seemed uniformly short or squat for the barrel-chested, bow-legged brigands you might expect. Still, they did carry cutlasses, and some had eye-patches, and all were attired in gaudy rags and striped pants and so on; so what else could they be but pirates?

'But if the motley crews of the black ships were a bit strange, what of their pirate chief? For in answer to the call of his bully-boys he'd fired a brand and tossed it aboard the doomed merchantman; and in the bright glare of that burning vessel, at last Gytherik should be able to get a good look at him. So thought the gaunt-master, but –

'Gudge, whoever he is, was covered head to toe, cowled too, in such voluminous, bulging, billowing robes that Gytherik caught never a glimpse of his actual form or features; and the monster might as well be dumb, too, for all he uttered by way of words or sounds where he stood on the deck of his black command vessel, adored by his terrible crew. And not once did he lift his cowled face to the skies where Gytherik flew; so that the gaunt-master supposed he'd seen and learned all that he might of these

565

pirates and their master at this time; and so, being concerned over his much-depleted grim, that handful of sorely wounded gaunts which remained to him, finally he turned away and limped for Serannian. Which was how he came to me in the morning of the next day.

'But to go back a bit: there's this matter of the pirates expecting or anticipating a gaunt-attack, and their knowing the gaunt-master's name and reputation. Now Gytherik was a veteran and hero of the wars against Zura and the Mad Moon, where he'd used his gaunts to great advantage. Aye, for then there'd been little in the way of defence against gaunt tactics. Also, he'd worked for me, right alongside Hero and Eldin; so maybe these pirates had expected *me* to send him out on patrol. If so, did that give me a clue as to who they might be? Had they perhaps experienced his sort of warfare before? Well, I have my suspicions but I'll keep them to myself for now; but be sure I'd dearly love to know who – or what – it is that keeps itself hidden in that voluminous robe and under that cowl, and sinks the fair ships of dreamland and murders their crews for no sane reason that I can see. For this is the hell of it:

'In all Gytherik told me he never mentioned seeing those dogs take any booty; but he *did* see them cutting down the bodies of those they'd hanged, and gathering the lifeless corpses of those they'd gutted!' And here Kuranes paused and shuddered, and pushed away the plate of cold meat that one of his retainers had placed before him.

'Now,' he eventually continued, 'I thanked Gytherik for his invaluable information and gave him the run of my place until his gaunts were well enough to fly; and in the course of a few days off he went again, bent on recruiting more gaunts to strengthen his grim. For there was little he could do with such a sorry bunch as he now commanded. But he swore he'd be back as soon as he'd beefed up his band a bit.

'And meanwhile ... meanwhile I'd sent out messengers into all parts of the dreamlands to find and bring back to me Hero and Eldin, my agents extraordinary!

'They were found prospecting in the Great Bleak Mountains, grimy as gargoyles and loaded down with their own weight in "simpleton's sapphires" – that is to say a great pile of blue stones, sapphires that weren't. Like "fool's gold", you know? They'd been digging them up for weeks apparently!' Kuranes grinned despite his sombre mood and shook his head. 'How does a man weigh up two such as these?' he asked of no one in particular.

'Anyway, they were penniless, lean and hungry – and completely demoralized that they'd been shovelling pretty pebbles and not fabulous gems – and so ripe for a real quest. So they shipped back to Serannian where I dined them royally for a week, promising them their own sky-yacht and a house by the harbour with a white-walled courtyard, if only – '

'If only they'd go into the badlands along the eastern coast and seek out the lair of the pirates!' de Marigny finished the tale for him.

Kuranes nodded. 'Correct. So they fitted themselves up with a fancy wardrobe: eye-patches, a moppish great wig for Hero (Eldin shaved his head shiny bald!), black leather belts and notched cutlasses, calf-boots to tuck their striped pants into and the like, and off they went one night aboard one of Serannian's galleys, all painted black for this one trip. They were dropped this side of Zura the land, where the Southern Sea meets a craggy shore, and that's the last I've heard of them – till now.'

De Marigny pursed his lips. 'And now they're captives of Gudge, doomed to die at dawn, and the night already two-thirds flown.'

'Dead men, aye,' Kuranes gloomily replied. 'Unless you can find them in time and get them out!'

'Right,' said de Marigny. 'Then here's what I'd like you

to do for me – and it must be done swiftly, so that I can be on my way in less than an hour. First – '

'We,' Moreen cut him off, sweetly but surely.

'Eh?' said de Marigny and Kuranes together.

'So that "we" can be on "our" way,' she repeated. 'You don't think I'm going to let you go off adventuring in the dreamlands on your own, do you, Henri? Oh, I know: you're "The Searcher", not I. But if I were to lose you ... should I, too, spend the rest of my life searching?' And there was that in her voice which told him there'd be little to gain from arguing ...

Hero, thinking back on precisely those things Kuranes had related to Moreen and de Marigny, had recalled one certain ludicrous aspect of his and Eldin's 'kitting-up': the choosing of their piratical wardrobes and props. 'Madness!' he sighed now, shaking his head weakly, suspended on his cross over that black pit that went down to dreamland's core.

Eldin had been quiet for some little time, lost in his own thoughts, but now he dragged his head round to peer at Hero through the gloom. 'Eh? What is?' he rumbled, his voice echoing. 'Are you finally admitting it was madness to accept this damned quest in the first place? If so I wholeheartedly agree – you should never have taken it on!'

'*We* took it on,' Hero reminded. 'I clearly recall you drooling over Kuranes' promise of a sky-yacht. "We'll sail off to Oriab," you said, "and look up Ula and Una. We'll drop anchor on some jewel isle and spend a whole month just fishing and fondling." That's what you said.'

'And you were all for lazing in the sun in your own courtyard,' Eldin countered. ' "I'll sit on the wall with a spyglass," you said, "and watch the ships rising out of Celephais to where the sea meets the sky. And I'll spy down on all the pretty girls in the gardens of the villages along the coast." That's what *you* said – lecherous little devil!'

'The specific madness I refer to,' said Hero, 'is the business of the pigeon.'

Eldin gave a groan. 'Not *that* again!'

'See,' Hero growled, 'pirates have parrots, not pigeons. And certainly not pink pigeons! That was a dead giveaway. I mean, fancy tying a damn pigeon to your shoulder, and squawking "pieces of eight" out the corner of your mouth every five minutes! Madness – not to mention messy!'

'But it came in handy in the end, you have to admit,' Eldin justified the thing. 'Before they tied us on these crosses we managed to get a note off to old Atal. By now all Ulthar will know the pickle we're in.'

'Fat lot of good that will do us,' Hero was quieter now. 'Like screaming after you fall off a mountain. Different if we had another two or three days . . .'

Eldin knew what he meant: pigeons are pretty speedy creatures, but sky-ships and rescue missions take a lot longer. 'Gytherik and his gaunts could manage it,' he said, with something of desperation beginning to show in his gruff voice.

Hero grunted. 'If we had some bacon,' he shrewdly replied, 'we could have bacon and eggs – if we had some eggs.'

'Eh?'

'It's wishful thinking, old lad,' the younger quester explained. 'Hoping that Gytherik'll be along, I mean. But you're right anyway: remote as the chance is, still it looks like the only one that's left to us . . .'

3

Zura of Zura

In fact Hero was wrong, but could hardly be expected to know it. In the night skies of dreamland, at this very moment, there was a second chance. Shaped like a coffin – but yet reminiscent of some weird grandfather clock – it moved at incredible velocity toward Zura the land, where the foetor of rotting flesh hung forever like a mouldering cerecloth over that domain of death.

And in a little while, slowing the time-clock's speed to a crawl, indeed de Marigny knew that he had crossed the borders of sanity into a region of nightmare. For there below, stretching mile on endless mile, lay that monstrous plain of leaning, mouldy menhirs known as the Charnel Gardens, a colossal graveyard where the diseased earth within each and every plot had been pushed up from below! Oh, yes, this was surely that land where graves and corpses are uniformly unquiet, but de Marigny's interest was centred rather in Zura the woman than Zura the land itself.

'And where to find her?' The Searcher wondered out loud.

'Lying in some grave,' Moreen shuddered and crept into his arms, 'with some poor corpse, if what you've said of her is true.'

'All hearsay,' answered de Marigny. 'I've told only what I've had from others. But those who've actually met her in the flesh are few and far between – who lived to tell of it, anyway. She's the sovereign of dreamland's zombies, Mistress of the Living Dead. All those who die cruel or monstrous deaths must go to Zura in the end, to do her bidding in the Charnel Gardens ...'

'Dawn is only an hour or two away,' Moreen stated the obvious.

'And Zura the land is deep and wide,' de Marigny nodded. 'I know. But Kuranes said she had a sky-ship, *Shroud II*, this awful princess. So maybe that's where we'll find her, aboard her corpse-crewed vessel. For if Hero and Eldin went missing here, in Zura the land, who better to ask of their present whereabouts than Zura the Princess, eh?'

Moreen was at the scanners, widening their scope as she scanned afar, toward Zura's heartland. And in another moment she drew breath in a sharp hiss. Then:

'Oh, yes,' she said. 'That'll be Zura's ship, all right. And very aptly named, too. Why, it's the same shape as the time-clock – except where we stand on end, *Shroud II* lies horizontal, like a great black floating coffin! There she is, moored centrally over that direful city there.'

De Marigny applied his senses to the time-clock's scanners, saw what Moreen had seen: a horizon of mega-lithic mausoleums whose gaunt grey facades reared high and formed the ramparts of the city Zura itself. 'Zura,' he nodded then. 'And you're right: that coffin-ship with its squid figurehead can only be *Shroud II*.'

Now The Searcher scanned the eastern horizon, where he fancied a faint nimbus of grey light made a wash on dreamland's rim. And:

'No more time to waste,' he said then, his voice grim and urgent. 'So ... let's see if Zura's aboard, shall we?'

Zura was indeed aboard, and in an especially black humour.

She stood frowning in the prow of her vessel, behind the blood-eyed figurehead, wide-legged and arms folded across her bosom. A princess of all she surveyed, of bones and mummies and dust, and crumbling sarcophagi.

Tall and long of leg, Zura wore a single black garment

which sufficed to cover her arms, back, belly and thighs but left the rest of her quite naked. Golden sandals accentuated the scarlet of her toenails, while wide golden bands on her wrists gave something of a balance to her slender hands and pink nails. Her lips were full and red as her painted toes – too full, perhaps, too red – and they pouted a little as her sensitive nostrils flared in the reek drifting up from the city of the dead beneath the keel of her coffin-ship. A thin film of heavily perfumed oil covered her body, giving her breasts a milky sheen where they stood proud and high and tipped with dark-brown buds.

And seen like that, at a glance – like some strange lewd statue under the moon with its yellow glimmer upon her – Zura was very beautiful, incredibly so. Yet hers was a tainted beauty, like that of the man-eating flowers of jungled Kled, whose tendrils are suckered and pollens lethal. An almost visible aura of evil seemed to surround her, issuing waves of near-tangible terror. Her huge, black, slanting eyes that shone and missed nothing, seemed imbued with the hypnotic gaze of serpents; snaky-sinuous, too, the ropes of shining black hair which fell about her alabaster shoulders.

This then was Zura of Zura, smouldering and silent, and her crew knowing enough of her moods to keep well out of her way this night; so that it might seem she was alone aboard her gaunt, leprous grey vessel. She was not alone, however, not for all the stillness and the quiet; her zombies would stand still just as long as she'd let them, and corpses are mostly silent creatures anyway, especially when their tongues have rotted to slime in their mouths ...

And: 'Damn!' said Zura of Zura. 'Damn! Damn! *Damn!*' She breathed the words into the night like four grey ghosts, fleeing from between her clenched teeth. 'Damn Gudge and his so-called "pirates", and damn the pact I made with them! They've robbed me of what was rightly mine, and nothing to be done about it.'

She thought back on the hand that fate had dealt her since the war of the Mad Moon:

First her return to Zura the land, under threat of banishment to the alien and utterly horrible – even to her – dreamlands of other worlds if ever again she should set foot outside her own boundaries. That had been disappointment enough: to see her dream within dreams of turning all the dreamlands into one gigantic nightmare of death themselves turned to dust. But then ... to discover Zura the land empty, even deathless! For Mnomquah, the lunatic god of a Mad Moon had drawn all her zombie minions up to the moon on a beam of powerful attraction, and not a single dead creature remained in all Zura the land. Even the foetor of that unthinkable place had been much reduced.

But the worm will have his way, and death conquers all in the end. A quarrier was crushed by a rock-fall in Nir, and his corpse came to Zura one night, shattered ribs and trunk and all. A pair of prospectors in the uplands, stung by a pack of six-legged spider-hounds, arrived all puffed up and bloated with poison. A great ceremonial canoe out of Parg, carrying a bride-to-be and her entourage from Parg to the isle where she'd wed her lover, struck a reef and sank. All were chewed by sharks, and swam to the shores of Zura. And close behind came the bereaved lover, who jumped from a cliff to the sea and the rocks. And so Zura was back in business again.

In a little while a boat-builder came to her, crushed between ship and wharf, and Zura commanded the building of *Shroud II*. But he was an ex-waking worlder, and his previous occupations had included mortician and coffin-maker – which perhaps accounted for the shape and style of Zura's ship. All to the good where she was concerned (the sails were of cerecloth, with ligament rigging and bones for the rungs of ladders).

And soon, once again as before, a ripe miasma of rot

hung over Zura the land, and once again the Princess Zura commanded her legions of the morbidly dead. But corpses disintegrate all too quickly, and suitable lovers are rare in the ranks of the direfully dead and last only a little while. So Zura dreamed dreams within dreams of a great disaster, which would send dreamland's peoples to her in their thousands, and a war where they would slaughter each other mindlessly – but no disaster came, and the peoples of dream war hardly at all. And so her frustration grew . . .

Then –

– Then came Gudge and his 'pirates'! Oh, that peculiar band of supposed buccaneers fooled her not at all; she knew who and what they were, if not what they were about. They'd be up to no good, be sure, but fell motives were not Zura's concern.

What they offered was this: that if Zura step aside and give them free run of the skies over Zura and lands adjacent, and if she make no report of them or their presence here – in other words, ignore them entirely and let them get on with their dubious business – then they'd send her the poor doomed remains of crews and passengers of all the vessels they intended to sack over and around Zura the land, Thalarion, and the Southern Sea. For ostensibly they were to be pirates, and where pirates sail death is a frequent occurrence and corpses very commonplace. Lathi of Thalarion had been likewise approached, though in her case (because she had no interest in cadavers) the pressure applied had been that of sheer threat undisguised: if she failed to accept the presence of the pirates or created any sort of difficulty for them, then they'd simply fire-bomb Thalarion the hive; which the eidolon Lathi knew all too well would prove a very harrowing and possibly fatal experience!

Zura had considered, and it had seemed to her that she was getting the better of the bargain; Gudge, as he called himself, had not even requested harbour or mooring for his ship in Zura (oh, yes, for there had been only one black pirate vessel in the beginning) but had settled for an extinct volcano in the mountains between Zura and Leng for his headquarters. And there, in that dead cone and in the tunnels formed of ancient lava ruins, he had made his home and garrisoned his crew.

Things had gone well at the start; Zura reaped the rewards of her passive assistance; her zombie legion grew apace. But then things started to change, however marginally at first. Numbers of zombie recruits, initially high, began to drop off; Zura complained and the pirates offered her booty rather than bodies, for which she had little use. Then, periodically, the 'extinct' volcano would throw up smoke rings in the hinterland, which might or might not be responsible for certain strange and unforeseen eclipses of the moon; also, there were at times dull rumblings underfoot – like the evenly-paced pounding of mighty hammers or subterranean engines – whose epi-centre would seem to be the root of that self-same ex-volcanic mountain. And then one day Zura's zombie spies reported that instead of one pirate ship there were now three, and that plunderings (or at least sinkings) of dream-land's innocent vessels had increased dramatically – at which Zura had flown into a raging fury!

She'd summoned Gudge to attend her in Zura the mausoleum city, but only the Captain of one of his two surplus vessels came; and when she'd put to that squat, offensive, eye-patched and tricorn-hatted – person? – cer-tain questions, then he'd only laughed unpleasantly. Where were all the freshly dead going? (Zura had wanted to know), for they certainly weren't entering Zura the land. Indeed she was lucky if she saw more than two or three corpses from each ship sacked! Did her pact with Gudge count for nothing at all, and should she now treat it with a similar lack of respect? And anyway, what was that silent, cowled, voluminously-robed creature up to in the mountains, that a dead volcano should suddenly belch itself back into life, however sporadic? Was it the pirate leader's intention to submerge the Charnel Gardens under a lava lake? These were the questions she had put to the wide-mouthed Captain-messenger.

'Cause trouble,' she'd been informed then, gutturally and with many a sneer, 'and Gudge will blow your worm-eaten shell of a ship right out of the sky, reduce your bony bully-boys to glue, put mausoleum Zura to the cannon and the torch, and spray perfumes of Kled over all Zura the land until it may never stink so badly again!' And laughing even more unpleasantly than before, Gudge's man had gone off and left her in a shocked condition bordering on trauma!

Even now she had not fully recovered, so that when the lookout attempted to croak something down to her from *Shroud*'s carrion-crow's nest she almost failed to hear or heed him. But the disturbance was such an uncommon event in itself (so few of the crew having tongues at all) that finally the lookout's harshly gabbled, clotted message got through to her:

'Something approaches from the West, O Princess.'

'Something? Something?' she hissed up at him then, half in astonishment. Had his brain rotted away entirely? 'A sky-ship, d'you mean?'

'If so, a very small one,' came the gurgled, hesitant answer. 'And no sails whatever, and fast as cannon-shot to boot!'

Snatching up a glass, Zura scanned the night sky to the west – then caught her breath as, in the next moment, the time-clock rushed in on her and slowed to a halt, hovering no more than a sword's reach beyond *Shroud*'s octopus prow. And:

'Ahoy, Zura!' came a ringing cry from the curious vessel (de Marigny's voice, amplified by the time-clock's systems).

'Permission to come aboard, if you please.'

She narrowed her slanty eyes and peered hard. 'Ahoy ... whatever! Who is it approaches Zura of Zura so bold, taking liberties with the sky-space I alone control?'

'That's not what I've heard!' de Marigny contradicted, and the time-clock rose above the rail, came forward and slowly settled to the deck. He opened the door and stepped out – alone. 'As for my name,' his voice was normal, quieter now, 'it's de Marigny – Henri-Laurent de Marigny – The Searcher to some.'

'The Searcher, you say?' and her eyebrows narrowed in a frown. 'Never heard of you!' She backed away, putting distance between herself and the time-clock, whose interior was invisible in the purple glow spilling out onto the ship's deck. This retreat was not fear on Zura's part; she merely wished to draw de Marigny forward, separate him from his vessel; and all along the ship's sides her zombie crew stealthily closed in.

De Marigny could see that worm-ravaged bunch, and certainly he could smell them, but he moved after her anyway. And shrugging, he said: 'I didn't expect you to have heard of me, but you know my surname, certainly; Etienne, my father, is a great friend of King Carter of Ilek-Vad – that is, when he's not exploring in undreamed dimensions.'

By now he'd allowed himself to be lured almost to Zura's cabin door; and there that Princess of death paused, hand on one perfectly fashioned hip, breasts brazenly jutting, her natural pout turning to a languid smile as she noticed just how handsome her visitor was, how tall and strong-seeming. 'Your father, eh?' she said, almost absent-mindedly. 'Aye, I've heard of him. A great dreamer, that one, so I'm told. Well, now ...'

Behind de Marigny but not unnoticed, Zura's zombie crew ringed the time-clock about. All held rusty cutlasses in white bone and black leather talons.

'Bold, I called you,' she said then, her low voice a sin in itself, 'and obviously brave, too, like your father – or utterly foolish. It seems the waking world breeds many brave men these days – and lots of fools, too.'

'Zura,' said de Marigny, moving closer still, 'I'm not much of a one for banter, least of all now. As for being a fool: you're probably right. And I'm searching now for two more fools – except they're very worthy ones, whose lives are in jeopardy.'

But an amorous mood was on her and she hardly heard him. Eyes slitted like a great cat's, she licked her lips and reached out to trace the strong curve of his chin, the column of his neck, the broad reach of his shoulders. Behind him, zombies closed in and placed their swords at his back, where he could feel their points just pricking him. And finally:

'Well, Searcher,' Zura sighed seductively, 'it seems you've come searching in one place too many. Anyway, what could you possibly have hoped to find here? Did no one tell you that Zura is the Land of Pleasures Unattained and Desires Unrealized – except the pleasures and desires of Zura of Zura?' And she laughed however coarsely and arched her body against his, so close that he could smell something of the reek beneath her perfume and oils.

De Marigny only smiled – even a little sardonically, perhaps – and continued to watch her keenly; which Zura noted, mistook for appreciation, and silently approved.

And while her thoughts were on other, more intimate things, still she forced herself to carry the line of the conversation, playing it like a lover's game: 'Why don't we talk some more in the privacy of my cabin?' she purred. 'And anyway, who are these men you seek, these "worthy fools" of yours?'

'Ex-waking worlders,' he answered at once, still smiling, 'and I'm told you know them well. They are called David Hero and Eldin the Wanderer.'

Zura's manner changed on the instant. She snapped erect, nostrils flaring. 'Hero? Eldin? You search for them? For what reason? Anyway, too late, for Gudge has them. Hero will go a-heroing no more, and Eldin's wandering days have meandered to a close.' Now, relaxing a little, her tone grew less sharp than sour. 'Aye, Gudge the so-called "pirate chief" – he robbed them away from me, as he'd doubtless try to rob you away, if he knew you were here.'

'Where's he taken them?' de Marigny's expression had also changed; his words were hard-edged and issued from behind teeth very nearly clenched. Suddenly taut as a bow-string, he was visibly eager – but not for anything of Zura's.

She felt spurned, drew herself once more erect, stood regal and smouldering and quite the most beautiful – the most *evilly* beautiful – creature de Marigny had ever seen. 'You can't help them!' she snapped then, her mouth writhing. 'You're only one man, so how could you? And I can't help them, not even if I would, for I've only one ship. No one can help them – so forget them!' She caught his hand, adopted a pose less seductive than threatening, said: 'And now come and make love to me – love me like you've never loved before, and like you'll never love again – or I give you to my zombies here and now! The choice is yours: you can love me alive or love me freshly dead. For that's how it will be in the end, be sure.'

'Be not so sure!' came the cry of a sweet, angry, infinitely female voice.

'*What?*' Zura's gasp was one of instant rage and astonishment combined. 'You brought – you dared to bring – another woman here? A *living* woman? In that – ?' She pointed a trembling hand at the time-clock. 'Then damn you, Searcher! Your life is forfeit, and then I'll have you anyway!' De Marigny felt the dead men behind him draw back their swords for thrusting. 'And as for your woman, hiding behind that purple haze – some slut of the waking world, no doubt – this is one dream she'll not be waking up from. Instead my zombies – '

But what her zombies would do was never learned.

Twin beams of light, pencil slim but so pure and bright that the eye could scarce discern their colour, leapt from the time-clock's dial and touched, oh so briefly, the undead corpses at de Marigny's back, where even now they would drive their swords home. And where those creaking cadavers had stood ... motes of mummy dust danced in the light of the moon; bones crumbled to chalk in mid-air and rags of clothing fluttered, suspended momentarily; and as twin cutlasses clattered to the deck, so their owners gained merciful release.

And now from the open door of the time-clock, pouring out of the throbbing purple interior, a full ship's complement of sky-sailors, bright steel flashing as they swept aside Zura's zombie crew like so much chaff blown on the wind, toppling their mouldering remains over the rails. For these were Kuranes' veterans of the bloodiest sky-battles, not to be denied by a handful of liquefying flesh and brittle bones.

It was all done in a minute, almost before the mortified (or mortifying) Doyenne of Death could draw breath. But not before she could draw her knife.

'I don't know what sort of vessel or weapon that damned coffin is – ' she hissed then, placing the cutting edge of her steel against de Marigny's neck, ' – and I shall never understand how it is bigger inside than out, but if it issues one more threat – '

Which, at that precise moment, it did. 'Put down your knife, Zura,' came that sweet, angry, amplified voice a second time; and again a pencil beam struck forth. For the merest moment the blinding ray passed between Zura's neck and shoulder, and ropes of shining black hair fell loose, smouldering; and behind her, where the beam touched wood, the timber of her cabin door turned black and issued smoke.

Zura did not fear death for he was her fondest companion, but she did fear burning, utter disintegration and unbeing. And slowly she put down her knife.

Kuranes' men were at de Marigny's side; one of them took Zura's knife and tossed it down to the deck, looked to The Searcher for instructions. 'Ready the ship for sailing,' said de Marigny; and to Zura: 'I'll ask you again, O Princess – where has Gudge got Hero and Eldin?'

By now Moreen had come from the clock. Zura saw her and sniffed haughtily, said: 'Well, at least this explains something of your reluctance. She's pretty, I'll grant you – for a live one, anyway.' And then she turned away, for Zura could not bear the sight of living beauty, not in her domain of death.

De Marigny caught her arm and turned her back to face him. 'I'll ask it just one more time, then take you back to face Kuranes' justice. The dreamlands beyond Hali are hellish, I'm told.'

Zura, pale as death, went paler still. For a moment she slumped, then tossed her head and straightened up. 'Kuranes? Why should I fear the justice of Kuranes? He gave me warning, aye, and set a certain stricture: that I should never more fare forth beyond the borders of Zura the land. Well, nor have I. How then may you illegally abduct me from my own Charnel Gardens, and Kuranes punish me? For what?'

De Marigny was growing desperate. A pale stain was spreading itself over the entire horizon, brightening, sending tenuous streamers of mauve light westward. 'Zura, it's almost dawn. They die at dawn, as I'm sure you know. Now you'll tell me where, and why, and by whose hand. If not ... then obviously you're in league with the pirates; for which, and for the loss of his finest agents and questers, Kuranes will surely punish you as no one was ever punished before.'

Zura frowned, licked her lips, narrowed her eyes. And

581

slowly she tilted her head a little to one side, nodded, as if to herself, and began to smile. Gudge and his gang owed her one, didn't they? – owed her more than one, for hadn't they also crossed her in the war of the Mad Moon? And in a battle, whichever way things went, lives were bound to be lost and Zura the land enriched. She reached a decision, said: 'If I side with you and supply the answers you seek, and if there's to be fighting – for I warn you now, Gudge has three ships and we have only *Shroud* – will you allow me the captaincy of my vessel, with these fighting men of Celephais and Serannian under my command? This way there'll be no doubt that the pirates are no friends of mine, and Kuranes can apologize if he pleases.'

De Marigny looked at the stern-faced men flanking her, tilted his chin sharply in a gesture of inquiry. 'Well?'

'She's an able Captain,' their spokesman answered. 'Indeed, I cheered her on in the Mad Moon war. And yes, if it will speed matters, we'll accept Zura's orders – lawful orders, that is – for this one night only; for it's a weird ship, this *Shroud*, and who'd know its whims better than its natural, or unnatural, mistress?'

'Zura, O Princess,' came a croak from on high, where at least one member of her crew had been overlooked. 'A ship approaches from the East – Lathi's *Chrysalis*. The grub-Queen pays you a visit!'

'Moreen,' snapped de Marigny at once. 'Into the time-clock, quickly!' But:

'Hold!' said Zura. 'I was expecting Lathi sooner or later. For you see, I'd already decided it was time we did something about Gudge, and so invited the Queen of Thalarion to come a-calling. But tonight of all nights! What a bonus – what an omen!'

The eidolon Lathi's paper ship was closer now; she gusted along at a good pace under her varnished paper sails, leprous decks sickly agleam in starlight and the glimmer of a sun not yet quite risen. And soon:

'Ahoy, Zura!' hailed a voice strange and honeyed, while *Chrysalis* came alongside and dropped anchor on Zura the land.

Zura, Moreen, de Marigny and the spokesman for Kuranes' men went to the rail and stared across at the paper ship and her mistress, the beautiful ter-Queen, Lathi of Thalarion.

Where Zura was dark and oil-gleamy, Lathi was all golden and blonde and green-eyed. Young as a girl she looked, and lovely as a rose in full bloom. Except –

She sat (or seemed to sit) upon a bench-like seat beneath a canopy of pink-hued paper; paper curtains hung behind her, extending to the sides. Attended by handmaidens – beautiful-seeming, scantily-clad girls who sprawled at her feet – she was naked from the waist up, but from there down was draped in ruffles and fluffs and piles of silky, glossy pink and purple tissues. De Marigny, who knew almost nothing about Lathi, found her astonishingly attractive; and yet, paradoxically, at the same time he felt inexplicably repulsed.

In a quiet aside to Moreen, The Searcher said: 'Something fishy about this one. Indeed, almost as fishy as Zura.'

'You're right,' she answered. 'Her handmaidens, too. Lathi *looks* real and human enough, but those handmaidens ... their nipples are painted on, Henri, unreal!'

'I've noticed,' de Marigny felt obliged to admit. 'But Lathi's not all she seems either. The word "eidolon", after all, is often used to describe a confusing image or reflection – something other than what is seen. Perhaps, under all those paper frills, there's a lot we *can't* see.'

'And a good thing too!' whispered Moreen. 'Are all dreamland's females so brazen?'

De Marigny frowned, left Moreen's question unanswered. He couldn't know it, but he had hit upon the truth: behind the curtains, hidden from view, more of Lathi's termaids were at work even now, massaging and smoothing soft oils into her monstrous lower body – which was nothing less than the vastly pulsating cylinder of a termite Queen! But if her grub-body was monstrous, what of her *appetites*? De Marigny knew nothing of them – the fact that she took her termen whole, and occasionally the men of other races – which was probably just as well; otherwise he might not have been so ready to accept the alliance which Zura even now proposed:

'Lathi,' the Princess of Death called out. 'This is The Searcher, de Marigny; you may or may not have heard of him.' And (though less enthusiastically), 'And this is his woman, Moreen. The men are Kuranes' lot, but I can't deny they're brave fighters for all that. Your ship and mine make two, and with these men and your termen to crew them – and with The Searcher's vessel, small and curious but carrying an awesome weapon – we plan to give Gudge's gang a well deserved clout. What say you? Have you had enough of Gudge and his so-called "pirates" over and around Thalarion?'

The termen Zura had mentioned were tall for dream-beings, handsome and bronzed, with a light yellowish tinge to their skins like sick gold. They were also like as peas in a pod and uniformly vacant-looking where they stood at the rail of the paper ship, their arms crossed on their deep chests. Blank-faced they stood there, dressed only in loin-cloths, like so many mental eunuchs. And if de Marigny could have seen beneath those square flaps of garments, then he would have known the real extent of their 'vacancy'. For all their robotic attitude, however, the termen were well-muscled and carried scythe-like weapons in sheaths strapped underarm. These were Lathi's 'soldiers', her workers, and if they had one purpose in life it was this: to do their Queen's bidding whatever, and protect her life with their own to the very death.

'Had enough of Gudge, did you say?' Lathi now called back, a slightly alien ring to her voice, her beautiful face clouding over. 'Too true I have, Zura of Zura! He's threatened the hive Thalarion once too often. When do we sail?'

'Immediately!' cried Zura with a throaty laugh. 'A surprise dawn attack. Haul up your anchor, Lathi, and we're off.' She fired orders at her new crew, then turned to de Marigny and Moreen. 'Quick now, and as we go I'll tell you all you want to know. Then, while you drive on ahead in that queer coffin of yours and try to rescue those great buffoons, we'll follow on behind and ready ourselves for battle!'

4

Engines of Horror!

In the heart of a certain mountain in the range behind Zura the land, foothills of a mightier, more distant escarpment, itself a stony prelude to the forbidden Plateau of Leng, a pair of haggard questers hung on their crosses over the rim of a black pit and waited for the fast approaching dawn and the death it would bring. The ex-volcano's tunnels were like six outwardly radiating spokes or ribs with Hero and Eldin at the centre; one spoke pointing to each of the four cardinal points of the compass, one pointing straight up through the mountain's peak to the skies overhead, and the last – forming the pit itself – pointing inexorably down.

The tunnels had all been lava runs in the fire-mountain's heyday, with the vertical shaft serving, of course, as the main vent. Even now that shaft (certainly its lower reaches, in the very roots of the dreamlands), while something other than volcanic, remained no jot less deadly. The tunnel to the north was more or less level, cathedral-like in its great height and width, a mile long from the centre to where it opened facing distant, ill-reputed Leng. There, at the mouth of that ancient, gigantic blowhole, that was where Gudge harboured his three black vessels and their crews.

As for the eastern, southern and western tunnels: they were narrow, low-ceilinged, in places choked with tephra and solidified lava; home to spiders and cave-lizards and other small, creeping creatures.

'The hell of it is,' said Eldin rumblingly, breaking a silence which had lasted for maybe a half-hour; during which time the pair had performed sombre inward-directed inspections of their somewhat dubious pasts, perhaps in anticipation of yet more dubious futures, 'that we still don't know what it's all about! I mean, *why* are Gudge and Co. masquerading as pirates? What evil is it they're hiding, or doing, or brewing here? Apart from the sinking of innocent ships, that is, and the eating of their crews. Oh, it has to be something big, be sure – else no rhyme or reason to all the scheming – but what?'

As the echoes of his voice died away in that grim place, Hero tried to shrug and couldn't, so simply answered: 'Beats me. Except ...'

'Yes?'

'Except I keep thinking we'll be finding out soon enough. Too soon, if you take my meaning. For it has to do, I think, with this volcano – or rather, this ex-volcano.'

Even as he spoke there came echoing up from below a dull, distant booming or pounding, as if some Colossus of inner earth had chosen that precise moment to commence banging away on demon drums. The reverberations from unguessed abysses caused the air to vibrate, brought down rills of dust and pumice from crevices and small ledges; and slowly the pounding took up a steady rhythm, like that of some huge and nameless engine throbbing away in bowels of nether earth.

'Umm!' said Eldin thoughtfully. 'I take it that's what you were talking about, eh?'

'Well it's hardly volcanic activity, now is it?' Hero returned. 'Which in turn begs the question: just what the hell *is* it? I mean, it must go down deeper than Pnoth, this great black flue, and yet something's alive down there ...'

'Like Oorn in her pit, you mean? That horrible gastropod mate of Mnomquah's, where we sealed her under Sarkomand at the end of the Mad Moon war?'

'Maybe even worse than Oorn,' replied Hero, darkly.

'Worse than Oorn?' the Wanderer grimaced. 'That's a hell of an imagination you've got there, lad! But I know what you mean: if not real life down there, pseudo-life – right?'

587

'Real, pseudo, whatever!' said Hero. 'Nasty-life, anyway. And – '

'Hold your breath!' Eldin cut him short.

Hero heeded the older dreamer's warning at once. This subterranean pounding wasn't new to them; so far they'd hung here for an afternoon and a night, and this was the third time that ominous thundering had rumbled up from below. By now they were well acquainted with what came with it. First the smell:

'*Yurghhh!*' said Eldin, screwing his eyes shut, clamping his lips together, even trying to pinch his nostrils in upon themselves against a reek that would make the Charnel Gardens smell good. And then:

'*Arghhh!*' agreed Hero, likewise suppressing his sensory tackle, as a hot, stinking black smoke ring came whooshing up from dreamland's core. It clung to the wall of the pit, that rolling ring of noxious steam and smoke and lord-knows-what, billowing over the questers, enveloping them, and hurtling on up the shaft in the mountain's heart to the skies above. Overhead the glimmer of stars fading in the coming dawn was shut out as the smoke ring eclipsed them; while down below the pounding continued its driving, maddening beat, accompanied by subterranean shuddering.

The pair opened their stinging eyes, breathed tentatively at first, then gulped with their mouths at the still foetid air, gradually relaxing the pressure on their nostrils. Eldin was first to speak. 'Lord, what I'd give right now for a clothes peg!' he moaned.

'Save your breath,' Hero gasped. 'You need it, for as we've seen before this is likely to go on for some little time.'

But the Wanderer wasn't listening; instead he was frowning down into the gulf, his chin jutting forward onto his broad chest. 'You'd think there were machines down there,' he said. 'And this the chimney of some monstrous mill, some foul factory of hell!'

'That's rather poetic,' said Hero, who had a good ear for such. But he had a fairly decent memory, too, and now his eyes narrowed. 'What's more, it's rather reminiscent of something I've heard before.'

'Oh? And what's that?' queried Eldin – but before Hero could answer: 'Watch it – here we go again!'

Another smoke ring whooshing past, grimy and slimy and yet hot as the breath of some dragon of darkness. And in its wake, as Hero coughed and spluttered and blinked his eyes open:

'Old lad, is it my – ' (cough!) ' – imagination, or is it – ' (cough!) ' – suddenly a bit lighter around here?'

'Not your imagination, no,' Eldin choked back. 'Before these damned smoke rings started up I'd been lying back my head and staring up at the stars. Of course, from down here there'll always be stars up there – even when it's daylight outside – but for a fact they've been getting dimmer this last hour. It's the dawn, that's what you're seeing: the cold light of dawn come a-creeping down this funnel and along these tunnels of rock. Can't you feel it in your bones? I can, even now: the sun, lifting his golden rim up over the edge of the dreamlands. The sun we'll likely never see again . . .'

'Whoah, there! Hang on, old lad!' Hero cried. 'What's all this then? The sun we'll likely never see again? Where's that old indefatigable Eldin gone to – the never-say-die spirit, the stiff upper lip?'

'As for that last,' said Eldin, 'it's a lip and a bit above this weak wobbly chin! Anyway, you were about to tell me what I'd reminded you of – you know, "foul factories of hell", and such?'

'Ah yes, that!' said Hero. 'It was Kuranes, I think, or maybe old King Carter himself in Ilek-Vad – can't remember for sure. It was at a banquet or some such, and I'd had a bit to drink. I was on muth-dew and you were on your back somewhere or other. But I do recall the subject.

It seems that scattered about in certain of dreamland's darker regions, there are these pits of nightmare that go down into unfathomed depths of madness. And I quote: "down there in the burrows at the bottom of these pits, engines of horror pound, where the souls of lost dreamers feed the blackest dreams of the Great Old Ones and fuel the nightmares which *They* send to plague human dreamers!'

Eldin's voice was much subdued when finally, after a short silence, he said: 'And you think this is one such pit, eh?'

Hero chewed his lip. 'Well, we'll not be the first Gudge has dropped down into darkness, will we? And knowing his lot – their feeding habits, that is – surely that would seem to constitute one hell of a waste of good meat. Unless the pit's needs are greater, more important.'

'Engines of horror, eh?' Eldin mumbled, licking lips grown suddenly dry. And: 'Oh, oh! Here comes an –'

– other smoke ring, he would have finished, except the stench and steam and smoke shut him off as the ring of foul vapour rolled over the questers and hissed up toward the new day. And with that third monstrous exhalation of unknown earth, sudden as it had started up, so the subterranean pounding faltered and shut down; and silence reigned once more in that gloomy, reeking place. But only for a little while. Then –

'You hear that?' said Hero. 'Footsteps! A good many of them, and coming this way.'

'From the north tunnel,' said Eldin. 'Aye, and growing louder by the minute. Gudge and his gang coming to send us to hell. Or to dreamland's black core, to fuel Cthulhu's machineries of nightmare!'

'Eldin, I –' Hero struggled to find words. 'I just wanted to say – I mean ...'

'Yes, yes – I know, I know,' the Wanderer's voice was gruff. 'It's all right – I forgive you.'

'What I'm trying to say is ... what?' Hero couldn't conceal the surprise in his voice. 'Forgive me? For what?'

'For all the bad turns you've done me, bad thoughts you've thought about me, bad things you've said to me. I forgive you for all of them.'

For long moments Hero was struck dumb. But then he began to grate: 'Well that's damn big of you – you blustering, beer-swilling, black-hearted, quirky old ...'

'... Including *that* one,' said Eldin, unruffled. 'And not so much of the "old", if you don't mind.' And before Hero could explode: 'Now then, d'you know any half-decent gods we might try praying to? If so trot 'em out, for it looks like that's all that's left to us now ...'

'Horned ones, aye, what else?' said Zura of Zura to Moreen and de Marigny aboard *Shroud II*. 'One of their black ships spotted Hero and Eldin wandering afoot along Zura the land's western border toward the hinterlands. They hoisted the Jolly Roger, dropped down out of the sky, picked 'em up. Now that's doubtless as the questers wished it – to get in with the pirates, find out about them, possibly arrange a bit of sabotage – but as soon as they were aboard they must have seen what they were up against. Lengites! Their squat little bodies would have given the almost-humans away: their wide shoes hiding cloven hooves, their too-wide mouths, the tricorn hats concealing their horns. But no way out of it: too many of them to fight and nowhere to flee, and the black ship already gaining altitude and heading for Gudge's volcano. A-ha! – and the horned ones playing along with the game, pretending Hero and Eldin were welcome aboard (which they were, of course, but not as pirates!) and the questers yo-ho-hoing and acting all piratical – but all of them knowing it for a sinister charade, which must come to an abrupt end as soon as they reached their destination ...

'Anyway, as fate would have it I was aboard *Shroud* that

evening and spied them a-sailing. I closed in and hailed them, and spotted that pair of great clowns on the black ship's deck. I called them by name – but the Lengites already had a good idea who they were, I'm sure. And then I demanded that they be handed over to me. Oh, yes, for I had scores to settle with those two!

'But the almost-humans wouldn't hear of it, not now that they knew for certain who their new "recruits" were; Gudge would want to see them, and he'd doubtless have plans of his own for them. And that was that. I should scarper, they said, and stop "interfering" – and never so much as a "by your leave, O Princess!" Well, I had only the crew aboard and no fighters to speak of; the Lengites held all the cards; I could only let them go.'

'Where exactly is this volcano, Gudge's hideout?' de Marigny was eager to be off, desperately afraid that he was already too late.

'Why, it's right . . . *there!*' said Zura, pointing. 'See?'

It was dawn. The sun was one third up and the dream-lands were turning golden – except Zura the land far below, which was gloomy as ever in the shade of misted, moss-grown, leaning tombstones. But far away to the north where Zura pointed, there the hazy peaks of mountains stood faintly purple over a sea of grey mist; and even now one of those peaks shot up a curling black smoke ring toward dreamland's last stars. Also, on the north-western horizon, a pale moon was suddenly blotted out by something near-invisible, some alien cloud that writhed and put out feelers to draw itself down across the sky toward that same range of mountains.

And now de Marigny began to understand. His eyes widened; he grasped Moreen's hand and hastened her toward the time-clock. Only as they entered into that weird vessel did he think to call back: 'Good luck, Zura. Give 'em hell!'

'Luck to you, Searcher,' she called back, nodding. 'And

my regards to that pair of scoundrels when you see them
– *if* you're in time!'

De Marigny simply pointed his strange vehicle at the
distant volcano and 'went there'. In a vessel like
the time-clock, that was perfectly feasible: to be able to
see your goal was to make that goal almost instantly
accessible. He got there as the third and last black smoke
ring was on its way up the mountain's ancient funnel,
came to a hovering halt directly over the crater as that
expanding vapour-ring whooshed up, briefly encompassed
the clock, headed for the sky. And he knew now for a
fact exactly what lay below, down in the dead volcano's
heart.

'The last time I was in the dreamlands,' he told Moreen,
'Titus Crow was in much the same fix as Hero and
Eldin, I fancy. He and Tiania were scheduled to suffer
Nyarlathotep's inquisition before being fed into the engines
of horror where the Great Old Ones fashion mankind's
worst nightmares. And this volcano, which it undoubtedly
once was, must now be the exhaust vent of just such
engines. Once you've seen those evil black smoke rings
you can never mistake them for anything else. Last time it
was a pit in the underworld, in a fantastic underground
cavern where few dreamers had ever ventured; this time
it's here on the surface, and so its gases must have been
disguised as the uneasy stirrings of a long-slumbering
volcano.'

'And that strange eclipse we saw?' Moreen's excitement
was growing. 'Didn't Atal also mention this Nyarlathotep,
the Great Messenger?'

De Marigny nodded. 'The massed telepathic mind of the
Great Old Ones. They're invading the dreams of men
again, in preparation for that same uprising which threatens
Elysia! Hero and Eldin are special, important dreamers;
Cthulhu will learn what he can from them, through

Nyarlathotep, before grinding them to pulp in his night-mare machines. Look!'

Enlarged by the time-clock's scanners, the lower slopes of the mountain to the west seemed suddenly enveloped by a sickly, crawling mist. Except this mist writhed and put out feelers, then drew itself into the mountain via the extinct, half-choked lava run which opened on that side. 'Nyarlathotep, in just one of his "thousand forms"!' de Marigny rasped. 'Well he hasn't come here for nothing, and so there has to be time yet.'

Then, without further pause, The Searcher dropped the time-clock vertically down the shaft, at the same time scanning the darkness below as the crusted lava walls rushed upwards at a terrific pace and dawn's natural light narrowed to a pallid circle receding high overhead . . .

'Well then, what are you waiting for?' Eldin roared up at the massed ranks of wide-mouthed faces leering down on Hero and himself. 'On you go, hack away! Or better still let me up off this cross, give me a sword and *I'll* hack away – but not at any ropes, be sure! *Ha!* Scummy sons of Leng – your fathers were spawned in moonlit mud and your mothers went on all fours! You weren't born but spawned! And when you die – which you all will, and soon if there's any justice – why, not even Zura would welcome such as you to the Charnel Gardens! What? I've seen handsomer night-gaunts!'

'Much handsomer –' agreed Hero, if a bit less boister-ously, and not a little envious of Eldin's inspired taunting, ' – and they've no faces at all!'

Their comments bothered the almost-humans not one bit, but Gudge, on the opposite side of the pit from where they were hanging, now pushed wobblingly forward. As he neared the rim, so the Lengites hastily made room. Hero and Eldin had met Gudge when the black ship brought them here in the first place. He hadn't fooled them then and made no attempt to do so now.

Robed in red silk, but loosely – for there was no longer any need to conceal himself, not down here under the volcano – Gudge was far less than human. As Eldin had once long-since pointed out: 'Whoever dreamed a thing such as that must have been a madman!' And only half-hidden behind the shuddering folds of his robes, Gudge was indeed a leprous white anomaly; vaguely toadish yet able, within limits, to contract or expand his jellyish body at will; eyeless, yet obviously very clearly sighted; with a blunt snout that sprouted a vibrating mass of short pink tentacles in twin bunches, whose purpose was purely conjectural. Or perhaps not; for certainly the thing's hood, thrown back now, was equipped with wide-spaced eye-holes. So perhaps the pink tentacles served as 'eyes' of a sort. But voiceless beyond any doubt, Gudge conversed by means of a whining ivory flute which he carried in a mushy paw. His interpreter as he played or 'spoke' was one of the Lengites, a more than usually puffy horned one whose position puffed him up more yet.

'Questers,' he translated now, while the torches of his massed brothers flared up evilly all around, ' – you, Hero of Dreams and Eldin the Wanderer – Gudge wishes you to know that you are singularly honoured. Nyarlathotep himself comes to examine you. Even the Great Messenger of *Them* Gudge is pledged to serve! How say you? Are you not overwhelmed?'

'I vomit on Nyarlathotep!' cried Eldin. 'If he smells and looks half as disgusting as Gudge, I vomit twice on him! Even Hero vomits on him, and he's not as fussy as me!'

'In short,' Hero added, 'we're not impressed.'

The cloven-hooved interpreter tootled their comments back to Gudge, whose form at once commenced a rapid shrinking and swelling and fluttering which the questers took for an expression of some fury. And before he could bring himself properly under control –

'Not impressed?' came a new voice, and all heads turned toward the mouth of the west-facing lava run, from which poured a sickly mist that lapped like sour milk and pulsed with a life of its own. The voice – a young voice, whose tones were rippling and mellow, so languorous as to be almost hypnotic – had issued from this bank of seemingly sentient mist. And as the Lengites drew back toward the east- and north-facing tunnels, so the mist began to thicken – or to be *sucked in* toward a focal point, to form –

The shape of Nyarlathotep!

Tall and slim, clad in bright cloth of gold and crowned with a luminous pschent, the human-seeming figure became more solid as the mist merged into it. He was (or appeared to be) a man with the proud face of a young Pharaoh of ancient Khem – but his eyes were those of a Dark God, full of a languid, mercilessly mordant humour.

'So, questers,' he stepped forward a pace or two, causing Gudge himself to draw back in wobbly alarm, 'you are not impressed ...' And he smiled a very awful smile. 'But you soon will be, believe me.'

For once Eldin was lost for words. Head level with the floor of that central cavern, where the crosses were roped with their tops projecting, he tried to speak but the words stuck in his throat. For there was that about the sinister newcomer, quite apart from his method of arrival, which was infinitely more frightening than Gudge and his horned ones could ever be. It was an alien something which Eldin didn't quite know how to handle.

Hero, who hadn't done so much shouting and whose spit was still comparatively fresh, stepped into the breach:

'Nyarlathotep, who or whatever you are, I don't know why you're so interested in us, but you'll get nothing out of us while we're hanging here. Have us hauled up and cut down from these crosses, and then we'll consider chatting to –'

'*Be quiet!*' the Pharaoh-figure hissed, his lacquered

eyebrows arching in a scowl. Gudge and his pirates drew back farther yet, and now Nyarlathotep approached to the very rim of the pit, from where he glared across at the two helpless dreamers. 'You dare to attempt to bargain with me? I am the very *mind* of Cthulhu! I carry the seething thoughts of Yogg-Sothoth! I speak with the tongue of Ithaqua the Wind-Walker, and thus know all the secrets of the winds that howl between the worlds! I *am* Yibb-Tstll, Atlach-Nacha, Tsathoggua the toad-thing, Nyogtha and Shudde-M'ell! My mind is *Their* mind, acrawl with *Their* thoughts. I am Nyarlathotep, the Crawling Chaos!'

Now Eldin found his voice, however croaky. 'Well said,' he nodded his approval. 'A bit theatrical, perhaps, but –'

'*Silence!*' howled Nyarlathotep. And more quietly: 'Silence, and live a little longer. Soon enough the engines of horror shall have you, and the essence of your crushed, terrified souls sent to start dreamers madly awake and raving forever – or would you go down to the pits of nightmare right now, on the instant, without more ado? For the longer you talk to me the longer you live, and when you stop –'

'Then make an end of it,' Hero blurted. 'If we're to die anyway let's have it now, rather than hang here passing the time with the source of all nightmares!'

'Make an end of it?' the Pharaoh-figure was obviously taken aback; but he smiled his monstrous smile to cover his confusion, and when he spoke again his voice was once more languid: 'Is that really your preference? But that implies a choice, and you have no choice.'

And now the questers knew the worst: that indeed there would be no resisting Nyarlathotep, for he commanded – he *was* – all the telepathic power of the Great Old Ones, who read the minds of men like men read open books. A creeping numbness settled over their brains, an iciness as of outer space invaded their staggering minds. And *knowing* he would be answered, Nyarlathotep began his inquisition:

'Dreamers, you have grown learned in the ways of the dreamlands and fast grow into legends. At least, *I* shall make legends of you – when I send you to be pulped in the grinding cogs of nightmare. But you two have talked with that old fool Atal, who in reality is no one's fool, and dined and chatted in company with triple-cursed Kuranes, even conversed with Randolph Carter himself. You are accepted in dreamland's highest echelons, and yet have plumbed the lower levels with equal flair. Lathi knows you, and Zura of Zura. Indeed it is your panache, your talent, that dooms you; too many powerful dreamers control man's subconscious mind in these times, which is not in acordance with *Their* plans. Especially not at this time. Which is why, when I am done with you, you are to be stopped . . .

'Ah! But where Kuranes and Carter and Atal have learned how to close their thoughts to me – to *us* – your minds are like open doors as yet! You may not deny me access. Now know you:

'The stars are very nearly right! The Great Old Ones are coming to claim what is rightly Theirs, in the dreamlands, the waking world, throughout all the worlds of space and time, and all the super- and sub-strata of endless dimensions. This *will* be! The multiverse *will* dissolve to chaos when Cthulhu comes. But there yet remains one great obstacle, one first and final goal which *They* must achieve: the discovery and destruction of Elysia!

'The way to Elysia, however, is a hidden way. The so-called "Elder Gods" hide there; they hide from Cthulhu's wrath, who has sworn vengeance on them that bound him in immemorial aeons. But you two – ex-mortals, men late of the waking world – perhaps you two may know something of Elysia, of the way to that place of the Elder Gods. Incredible, that perhaps you have knowledge of that which Great Cthulhu himself has not yet discovered! And yet I am reliably informed that even now One has come into the dreamlands to seek you out; aye, and he too searches for Elysia. Perhaps he has already found you, talked to you, learned from you . . . ? I, too, would learn from you – if you have anything to teach me – so now I command you: open up your minds to me, let me see all!'

Twin tendrils of mist reached out from Nyarlathotep's dark eyes, flowed writhingly through the air across the pit, fastened like lampreys to the foreheads of the questers where they fought a last desperate mental fight to keep their minds to themselves. Their brains felt like onions, being peeled layer by layer as Nyarlathotep commenced his 'examination' – but only for a moment.

All eyes were on the tableau formed by Nyarlathotep and the questers, all concentration centred there, so that none had seen the fractionally slow lowering of the time-clock down from the flue of the central vent. The first the horned ones, Gudge, Nyarlathotep, questers and all knew of it was when de Marigny's amplified voice boomed out in the confines of the cavern junction:

'Am I this "One" you seek, Nyarlathotep? If so, why not speak to me directly? For these questers know nothing of me.'

Now all eyes gazed upward; simultaneously, as the silently hovering time-clock was spied there, a concerted gasp broke out from all ranks. But de Marigny had confronted Nyarlathotep before and knew the danger; he had the advantage here and must be careful not to lose it.

'You!' the Pharaoh-figure's voice was now a croaking bass belch of sound. 'You, The Searcher, de Marigny!'

'We meet again,' said de Marigny – and he triggered the time-clock's weapon.

A pencil beam of incredible light sizzled down from the clock's dial, drove back the flickering shadows and put the torches of the petrified almost-humans to shame, cut through the tenuous tendril of mental mist stretched between Nyarlathotep and the questers. The connection was severed; but more than that, the shock of the severance was felt throughout the multiverse!

Yogg-Sothoth in his prison dimension beyond chaos reeled as his telepathic polyp mind felt that hot, cleansing breath of Eld; Cthulhu, dreaming mad dreams of universal conquest in R'lyeh, started fitfully, lashed out with terrific tentacles and crushed several aquatic shoggoth guards, who instantly re-formed and backed off; Shudde-M'ell convulsed deep under Earth's mantle, then dived down through salving lava as he felt even his mind singed by that pure, clean fire.

And Nyarlathotep, staggering back from the pit's rim, clapped his manicured hands to his head and croaked: 'Gudge, the questers – *send them to hell!*' And before de Marigny could trigger his weapon again, the Crawling Chaos dissolved into dank mist which writhed away into the crevices of the west-leading tunnel and was gone.

The horned ones were fleeing, stampeding down the north-leading tunnel toward their black ships of Leng, hastened by a salvo of fire from the time-clock; but Gudge, commanded by Nyarlathotep, was forbidden to flee. He took up a fallen sword and flopped wobblingly toward Hero and Eldin – toward the ropes which alone held their crosses in position over the pit's rim. Now that sword was lifted on high, and now it flashed down in an arc which would find both ropes at once where they were made fast to a projecting knob of lava. But –

That arc of bright steel was never completed. Caught by a pencil-beam from the time-clock in mid-sweep, Gudge's sword shivered into shards and took his arm, or whatever he had that passed for an arm, with it! A second stabbing beam struck him full-face, ate into his frantically scrabbling snout-tentacles, the leprous jelly face behind them, and finally the brain or ganglion behind the face. And voiceless though he was, still that creature uttered his first – and last

– shriek, like a jet of steam escaping under pressure, as he floundered to the edge of the pit, flopped to and fro there, toppled into nightmare. A shower of lava-dust and other cavern debris went with him, missing the dumbstruck, delirious dreamers on their crosses by inches.

Then ...

... In a very little while de Marigny had set the time-clock down close to the pit, and not long after that the dazed questers were freed and stumbling about in the purple glow of the clock's open door, flailing and stamping life back into their numb arms and legs. But when de Marigny and Moreen would have led them inside the time-clock:

'Hold!' growled Eldin, stepping back a pace. He looked at Hero and cocked a querying eyebrow. 'Out of the frying pan ... ?' he asked.

Hero shook his head, said: 'Shouldn't think so, old lad.' And to The Searcher, 'Didn't I hear a certain ex-moon-beast call you de Marigny?'

De Marigny grinned. 'You're probably thinking of my father,' he said. 'But don't worry, for I'm cut of much the same cloth as him – else I'd not be here.'

Eldin seemed somewhat mollified. Grudgingly he agreed: 'Aye, and I remember you now. A banquet in Ulthar – in your honour, too! Henri-Laurent de Marigny, and Titus Crow. It was toward the end of the Bad Days, in which you'd played quite a hand.' Then he looked again at the time-clock. 'Still, that's a damned weird threshold you're inviting us over. And I can't see how we'd manage it anyway. I mean, I'm hardly a stripling, now am I? You and the girl must be stifled in there, let alone asking two such as us in with you!'

Now de Marigny laughed out loud. 'The time-clock is bigger inside than out, Wanderer,' he said.

'Come on in,' said Moreen, 'and see for yourselves.'

And as a further inducement, de Marigny added: 'If we

hurry, we might just be in time to see those three "pirate" ships blown out of dreamland's skies by the eidolon Lathi and Zura of Zura.' Which finally did the trick; for *that* was a thought – and a promised delight – which Eldin couldn't resist for the world!

Deep down below in black bowels of earth, a horribly familiar, monstrous throbbing had started up again, like the thundering of vast subterranean hammers. And as Hero and Eldin at last accepted de Marigny's invitation and boarded the time-clock, and as that fantastic vessel lifted off and soared straight up the volcano's vent toward open skies, so, far behind, a hot black smoke ring was formed and billowed toward the surface.

It was an especially black, especially oily smoke ring: Gudge, of course, on his way to where he'd disperse in dreamland's high, clean upper atmosphere ...

5
Shrub Sapiens

As de Marigny had promised, they were in time to see Zura and Lathi's revenge on the horned ones. For as the time-clock rose up into the full dawn light, away down below on the northern slope of the volcano the three black ships of Leng were only just emerging from their vast keep and rising into the sky. Dangerously close together, they were, in a very tight formation, and it was plain that confusion reigned aboard. Each of the three captains had just one thought in mind: to get as far and as fast away as almost-humanly possible. Gudge was no more; a terrible destructive device was on the loose, one the Lengites had known before, which in Dylath-Leen and other places had spelled disaster for them; their moonbeast masters, of which Gudge had been only one, would be most unhappy about things, and someone – perhaps many someones – would be called to pay the price of failure. Horned heads would roll, wherefore ... now was definitely a good time to run for home and quietly disappear into the less hazardous (for almost-humans) encampments of mist-shrouded Leng.

So that the advent of Lathi's *Chrysalis* and Zura's *Shroud II* from behind the volcano's flanking crags came, as a complete surprise to them. The central 'pirate' got away, however, for it was shielded by the vessels to port and starboard, which took the brunt of Lathi's and Zura's vengeful salvoes. And as those two ships, crippled from the onset, put up what they could of a fight, so the one in the middle, unscathed, rose up higher into the sky and headed north for Leng. Its sails quickly filled as it found a good current of air, whereupon it sped off, leaving its comrades to their fate.

De Marigny let the survivor make a mile or two, then casually aligned the time-clock's weapon and triggered off a hastening beam. The black topsail and Jolly Roger went up in a flash of light and a puff of smoke, and The Searcher nodded and lowered his aim a little. But then, when even the slightest mental pressure would reduce the black ship to so much scorched wreckage, he hesitated.

'Well?' Eldin was on tenterhooks. 'What's holding you? You've got 'em dead!'

But de Marigny shook his head and released his mind's grasp on the trigger. 'No,' he said, 'for that's not my way.'

'You mean you're letting them go?' the Wanderer was beside himself. 'I don't believe it! Well, if you've no stomach for it, you just show *me* how it's done and step aside!'

But Hero said: 'Calm yourself, old friend. De Marigny's right – we're the good fellows, remember?'

'Eh?' Eldin rounded on him. 'Good fellows? You speak for yourself! As for me, where these damned Lengites are concerned I'm all baddie!'

'No you're not,' Hero contradicted with a shake of his head. 'And you know it. If de Marigny squeezed that trigger, it would be sheer slaughter. That sort of thing might be okay for Zura and Lathi, but not for us. Anyway, if we kill 'em all, who'll be left to spread our legend abroad, eh?'

'You mean, these buggers'll go back to Leng and say: "that Hero and Eldin, they got the best of us again", right?'

'Something like that,' Hero nodded.

'*Huh!*' Eldin scowled. And: 'You realize of course that it could easily be one of these very Lengites, one of these fine days, who sticks his sword right through your backbone – or mine?'

'Possibly,' said Hero. 'But not today, eh?'

Still furious, Eldin turned to Moreen. 'What do you say, lass? Are these two daft or not?'

'Maybe they are,' she took one of his great hands in both

of hers, 'and maybe they're not. But if the horned ones – and all other dark creatures and men – weren't here to do their bad things, would there be any point in a Hero and an Eldin, or a de Marigny? What would you *do*, Wanderer, if there was no longer anything to strive for? No more questing? No last small danger in all the dreamlands?'

'Me,' said Hero, determined to change the subject, 'I'd head straight for Serannian, take charge of the sky-yacht Kuranes owes me, crew her with a couple of likely lasses out of Baharna, and set sail for a tiny jewel island somewhere off – '

'Ah, but now you're talking!' said Eldin. 'What? Give me a sky-yacht, a tiny jewel isle and a likely lass – and you can keep the yacht and the island for yourself!'

And that was that. As the black ship limped for the grey northern horizon, the Wanderer watched it go and scowled a very little. But he made no further comment . . .

Lathi was already heading for Thalarion when de Marigny set the time-clock down on the deck of *Shroud II*. As he, Moreen and the questers stepped forth, Zura greeted them with a curt: 'Ho, Searcher and Co! Success to both sides of our venture, it appears.' Then, staring straight into de Marigny's eyes, she added: 'But it seems you came over all faint-hearted when you might have burned that third black ship to ashes. I was not so foolish.' And she inclined her head downward across the rail of her ship. On the volcano's lower slopes, the ruins of her own and Lathi's conquests lay scattered amidst sharp lava crags.

'Not faint-hearted, Zura,' growled Eldin at once, before anyone else could say a word. 'Big-hearted. Not foolish but compassionate. There's a difference such as you wouldn't understand. We're not all death's bosom-pals, you know!'

Hero scratched an ostensibly itchy nose, hiding his grin; he controlled himself and nodded, straight-faced, as Zura now turned her black-eyed gaze on him. Scowling, she acknowledged his nod anyway, said: 'All intact, I see. I'd thought by now that the horned ones might have eaten you.'

'Our hides might be a bit tough on their teeth, I fancy,' said Hero. 'Anyway, they weren't after eating us but sending us instead down that volcano's throat, fuel for Cthulhu's engines of horror. And it seems we've you to thank for telling The Searcher where to find us.'

'Oh?' she arched her eyebrows. 'Well, save your thanks, Hero of Dreams. Let's not get too friendly. De Marigny didn't leave me much choice, after all; and anyway, it wasn't your interests I was looking after.'

'Zura,' said Eldin, 'you like to play at being hard, but let's face it: you've had a soft spot for Hero here from the moment you first met him. Now deny that, if you can!'

Zura smiled sweetly, or it might seem so if they didn't know her better. But there were crimson points in her black eyes, doubtless in her black heart, too. 'I've soft spots for him, for you, for all of you live ones,' she said, her words honeyed. But then they came sharper: 'Or more correctly, soft plots! Row upon row of 'em: six foot of damp earth in my Charnel Gardens!'

Death leered out of Zura's soul at them, and as one person Moreen, The Searcher, Hero and Eldin, the entire temporary crew of *Shroud II*, stepped back a pace from her. 'What?' she laughed. 'And what good were you to me, if Gudge sent you down to the machineries of madness? And how might I use you, if the horned ones had chewed on all your tenderest bits? But this way – being foolhardy questers and all – one day you'll come to me on my terms. And with a bit of luck none too badly banged about. Aye, and then we'll talk some more of "soft spots," Eldin the Wanderer ...'

They sailed Zura's coffin-ship back to a mooring over the Charnel Gardens – one with sufficient elevation as to make

606

the stench endurable – and there left that peculiar squid-prowed vessel in charge of Kuranes' men for the nonce. But now, before returning to Serannian, there was another matter to consider: Thalarion the land bordered close to Zura the land, so close indeed that the time-clock would make very short work of the distance between. And there, somewhere in Thalarion's hinterland, Atal's 'strange thoughts' – possibly having their origin in Elysia – had fallen to earth, had even been answered!

'What do you know of the land behind Thalarion?' de Marigny asked the questers when they were once more airborne in the clock and making their leisurely way eastward.

'There's a swamp there where a whirlpool empties itself from a mighty lake in the Great Bleak Mountains,' said Eldin. 'All marsh and rot and toadstools, and creeping leafy things more animal than plant. Terrible place!' He gave a small shudder. 'Me and Hero, we were there once. But thanks, no, we'd prefer not to go back.'

Moreen turned to Hero. 'But is there nothing pleasant or welcoming or friendly in Thalarion's hinterland? You see' (she began to explain something of their quest), 'we're looking for someone or thing – for an intelligent being, anyway – who receives thoughts from the waking world, maybe even from Elysia. Some unknown one who talks with his mind to someone else far, far away in another world.'

'Talks with his mind, you say?' Hero raised a speculative eyebrow, glanced at Eldin.

'Er, and would this telepathic someone be sort of big and green and lumberlike?' asked the Wanderer.

De Marigny shook his head. 'We've no idea,' he said. Then he frowned. 'Did you say "lumberlike"? And do you know someone who's that way – as you've described, I mean?'

'Fact is,' said Hero, 'we do! And that's not all, for – ' he paused. De Marigny had shown the questers how to tune in to the clock's scanners, and now Hero said: 'But look! There's Lathi's *Chrysalis* dead ahead. Can we hover a bit while I ask a question or three? It all has bearing, I assure you.'

De Marigny hovered the time-clock over Lathi's paper vessel, while Hero called out: 'Lathi, it's Hero here.'

'*And* Eldin,' sang out the Wanderer, glowering at Hero. 'Nice job you did back there on that black Leng "pirate".'

Lathi under her canopy was utterly beautiful – the visible parts, at least. She turned her face indolently up toward the hovering time-clock, said: 'Hero, is that really you in there, who sang me to sleep with your beautiful songs in Thalarion the hive? And you, Eldin, who contrived to burn Thalarion to the ground while that sweet-tongued rogue sang? Then stay safe where you are and come not aboard *Chrysalis*. I have neither forgotten nor forgiven. If we were allies once ... well, that is over now. And where you two are concerned, my termen have standing orders. Now you are intruders, trespassers over Thalarion the land. Be gone from here.'

'Not so fast, Lathi,' growled Eldin. 'And stop making us out as the villains of the piece. Believe me, we've no great wish to stay in Thalarion. But first tell us this: how fares the Tree?'

'The Tree? The Great Tree? Him? What would I know of him, great shambling forest that he is? My termen are forbidden to go near him! He has roots under Thalarion the new hive, in which he holds firestones, great flints he'd strike if I stole so much as a leaf from him! Aye,' she sighed, 'and his the sweetest, most succulent leaves in all the dreamlands.' Then her voice hardened: 'And who to blame but you, Wanderer, who taught him these ... these *pyrotechnics* in the first place?'

'*Hah!*' Eldin was delighted. 'Is that so? Well, good for

608

him!' he said. 'You threatened him with fire, now he threatens you!'

And Hero added: 'We're on our way to see him right now, Lathi, and doubtless he'll tell us whether you've been giving him a bad time or not. And if you have, be sure it's not just his firestones you'll need to worry about. And if you thought my cradle-songs were sweet, just wait till you hear my warsongs!'

That was that; the time-clock fared north-east; de Marigny turned over in his head all he'd heard. And in a little while he asked: 'Are you saying you're taking us to see a tree?'

'A Great Tree,' Eldin corrected him.

'And as I was about to tell you,' said Hero, 'he has kin in Elysia.'

De Marigny's heart gave a great leap. 'Titus Crow has told me of Elysia's Great Tree!' he exclaimed. 'In the Gardens of Nymarrah: a tree to make a redwood seem the merest sapling!'

'That's our boy,' Eldin nodded. 'Or his cousin, anyway. And by the time we're over that range of hills there, we should be able to see him ...'

Eldin was right. Just across the hills north-east of Thalarion, a prairie rolled to the horizon. Broken only by receding lines of foothills that would rise ultimately to Leng, the plain was lush, golden and green; and standing there majestically, more than a third of a mile high, the biggest tree de Marigny and Moreen had ever seen.

Superficially, and apart from his massive height and girth, *the* Tree was pretty much like any other; but on closer inspection, magnified in the clock's scanners, de Marigny saw that there were several anomalies. The leaves of the giant, huge to match his other dimensions, were soft-edged and lined with a 'fur' of sensitive cilia. Tough, slender tendrils hung down to festoon the shaded area between the lower branches and the earth; tendrils full of a slow, sentient motion, seeking out dry, dead leaves and carefully removing them, casting them aside. A haze of pollens (though no flowers were visible) hung suspended everywhere, dust-motes in the sunlight, giving the Tree a shimmer almost like that of a mirage. But he was no mirage. And then there was that wide ashen swath – the Tree's 'track', the way he had come, inch by gradual inch, since all those years ago when first he took root here – leading off to the north, where the earth was no longer green but dry and crumbly. For Great Trees need a lot of nourishment.

Not knowing how the Tree would react to the time-clock, de Marigny carefully set his strange craft down just outside the three-hundred-foot radius of his branches. There The Searcher, Moreen, and their passengers disembarked; but while the three men approached with some caution, Moreen at once ran through the calf-length grass and into the Tree's shade. In Numinos all creatures had loved Moreen; she had even charmed Ithaqua the Wind-Walker – to an extent. She was the veriest child of Nature and loved all Nature's creatures. But an intelligent, indeed telepathic, Tree? – she could scarcely control her excitement.

Small roots underfoot felt her weight, her motion; the under-leaves 'smelled' or 'tasted' her texture, translated these impressions, recognized her type; the Tree felt her excitement, her wonder, and knew she was a friend. Instantly long, supple tendrils uncoiled from on high, looped down, caught her up. She was lifted effortlessly, borne aloft like a tiny child in the arms of a giant. A soughing – no, a vast *sighing* – filled the Tree's branches.

'Moreen!' Alarmed, de Marigny started forward.

'Easy, Searcher!' cautioned Eldin. 'Moreen's safer with the Tree than she'd be with ... why, with Hero here!'

'Oaf!' said Hero. 'But he's probably right: the Tree's the very gentlest soul in all the dreamlands.'

Now the three were in the Tree's shade; cool tendrils

touched them, tasted, quivered; there was an almost magical dusk all around, where the Tree's pollens were honeysuckle sweet.

'Tree,' said Hero, 'it's Hero – '

' – *and* Eldin!' (from the Wanderer.)

' – and we've brought these friends to talk to you.'

'Hero?' answered a throbbing yet ethereal voice from nowhere – from everywhere – as tendrils fell faster and touched all three. 'Eldin! Both of you, yes, and one other; but not a permanent dreamer, this one. No, a *real* man – and a girl, too – from the waking world!'

Moreen was nowhere to be seen, but her glad cry fell from high, high overhead even as the Tree's strong lifting tendrils grasped the three men: 'Henri! Oh, let him bring you up! This place is wonderful! Come see!'

But they were already on their way, wound up like bobbins on threads and passed higher and higher into the Tree's heart. Breathlessly they were whirled aloft, then suspended motionless for a moment until they got their breath back, finally deposited light as feathers in the crotch of great branches a thousand feet above the ground. And: '*Shrub sapiens,*' gasped Eldin. 'Boisterous, isn't he? For such a big 'un!'

But the Tree only chuckled in their minds. 'Hero and Eldin,' he said again. 'My very dearest friends! And de Marigny and Moreen. Well, well! Visitors again, after all this time. Men to talk to – and a real girl!'

'You've heard of us then?' said de Marigny. 'Of she and I?'

Transmitted to de Marigny's mind by touch, coming to him through leaves and cilia and tendrils, there was mental affirmation as the Tree said: 'Oh, I've heard of you, Searcher. Indeed, I've been expecting you!'

De Marigny couldn't contain himself. 'So Atal's alien thoughts from outside did come from Elysia after all,' he burst out. 'And they concerned me?'

611

The Tree read his meaning clearly. 'You and your young woman, yes, and the time-clock, too,' he answered. But now de Marigny detected a certain reluctance – a note of sadness in the Tree's touch – and his heart sank.

'There's nothing you can tell us, is there?' he said. 'If you know I'm The Searcher, then you know what I seek. And your sadness can only mean that you either can't or won't help me.'

'I can't, and I can,' said the Tree. 'I *can't* tell you how to get to Elysia, no – but I *can* help. That is, I can narrow down your search a little.'

'Tree,' Moreen cut in, 'I don't quite understand. If someone – that other Great Tree, maybe? – spoke to you from Elysia, and if you in turn talked to him ... I mean, he *must* have known where you were, and vice-versa.'

The Tree followed her meaning and his leaves trembled a little as he considered how best to explain. 'A thought is a thought, child,' he said. 'I read yours by touching you. If I couldn't touch you I couldn't talk to you. But I am more attuned to the thoughts of one of my own race. He found me, yes, though not without difficulty, and once the connection was made I could talk back. But as to his location and how one might go there ...' (a mental shrug).

'Another dead end,' de Marigny's shoulders slumped. But then he lifted his head and gritted his teeth, still unwilling to accept defeat or even consider it. 'A dead end, yes – but there's something very wrong here. I mean, I know there's no royal road into Elysia – that one makes one's own way there or not at all – but is there any sense in their taunting me? The Elder Gods, I mean? I'm given clues that lead nowhere!' He turned a troubled face to Moreen. 'No man knows Titus Crow like I do, and yet even he ...' He shook his head. 'Something's *wrong*! Titus and Armandra both, they say find Sssss and he may have something for you. We save Sssss from the Hounds of Tindalos, and he's been told to direct us to Earth's dreamlands – *told* to do that by the weird pilot of some other time-clock from Elysia. In the dreamlands we go to see Atal, the very priest of the Temple of the Elder Gods – but even he has been shut out. "Ah! – but maybe Hero and Eldin can help us," he says. So we save the questers from Gudge – '

'Narrowly!' put in Eldin.

' – and in return they bring us to see the Tree. Now the Tree can actually *talk* to his cousin in Elysia, but he can't tell us the way there, and so – '

'Wait!' said the Tree. 'I *could* talk to him – when he sought me out. And perhaps I could have sought *him* out, given time. But not any more. I tried following his thoughts – their essence – back to their source. Not because I wanted to learn his or any other's secrets, simply because I was lonely. But out there in the voids, in the star spaces between the worlds, the thought-trail petered out. And he has not come again. No royal road, you say? No road at all, not now! I'm sorry ...'

'What about Serannian?' said Moreen. She took de Marigny's hand. 'There's still Curator, in his Museum.'

'Curator?' said Hero, Eldin and the Tree all together, and with almost the same speculative edge to their voices.

'But that's it!' said the Tree, getting in first. 'That's the message Elysia's Tree gave me before he ... closed down. "Tell them to speak to Curator," he said, "in Serannian." '

'Speak to Curator?' Eldin grunted. '*Huh!*'

'What the Wanderer means is no one ever spoke to him,' Hero explained. 'He has a keen mind and he's a nice mover – and his line in weaponry is at least as good, maybe better, than yours, Henri – but where speaking's concerned he's a dummy. Why, I strongly suspect that most of the time he doesn't even know people are there at all!'

'Except when they maybe, er, annoy him,' Eldin added with some feeling, at the same time looking away.

'Moreen might be able to speak to him,' said de Marigny.

She looked doubtful. 'I can talk to all creatures of Nature,' she said. 'Of if they can't talk, at least I can understand them. But a metal man? I'm not sure.'

'Anyway,' de Marigny was determined, 'we have to try. Tree, I'm sorry but I can't stay – not even for a little while.'

'He's right,' said Hero. 'Kuranes will be anxious, waiting for our report – and there are all those lads to be picked up off Zura's coffin-ship, and – '

' – And my mission's more important than all of that,' de Marigny cut in. 'It's not just for myself and Moreen any more. It's for everything. I *have* to get to Elysia!'

'That's good enough for me,' said Hero.

'And me,' agreed Eldin. 'Let's go!'

'Your visit was welcome anyway,' said the Tree. 'I'll always remember you, Searcher, Moreen. And if you should ever be in Earth's dreamlands again ...'

'We'll always come to see you,' Moreen promised, ' – when and if we can.'

They didn't prolong it. Farewells were short. As quickly as he could which was very quickly indeed, de Marigny picked up Kuranes' men from the deck of *Shroud II* and left Zura to brood alone over her Charnel Gardens. Before noon they were all back in Serannian ...

Kuranes met them on Serannian's sky-floating rim, the wharves not far from where the Museum jutted on its vertiginous promontory. And no need to inquire after Kuranes' pleasure at the sight of his men, the questers alive and well, and Moreen and de Marigny as they trooped from the clock; his absolute joy and relief were visible in every word and gesture. As to his gratitude to de Marigny, that was beyond words; but desperately eager though The Searcher was, still the Lord of Ooth-Nargai calmed him and led him and his party to a wharfside tavern where a meal was quickly ordered and almost as quickly made ready. Famished, Hero and Eldin fell at once to their food and drink, but de Marigny was scarcely interested in eating. Instead, and assisted by Moreen, he took the opportunity to tell Kuranes all that he had not yet grasped of his mission, also all that had happened through the previous night and morning.

When he was done Kuranes nodded. 'Pirates they weren't,' he said, 'not in the true sense of the word. Their vile *acts* of piracy were a simple ploy to keep honest men and ships – maybe even explorers and settlers – away from Zura's hinterland; away from that old volcano, which will doubtless be used as a fortress by the Cthulhu spawn when finally they force themselves upon the dreamlands ... If it were allowed to go that far! But that must never be. So, when Admiral Limnar Dass gets back with my armada from the moon, then I'll – '

'Eh?' de Marigny looked puzzled. 'But you told us your ships were plentiful – and it was crewmen you were short of. You said you'd disbanded them all or something, that they'd be better employed repairing dreamland's moon-ravaged cities ...'

'Ah!' Kuranes looked confused, caught out. 'Well, yes, that's what I *said*,' he agreed, 'but not quite the whole truth. In fact, something of a large distortion. You see, if you'd been taken by Gudge and his lot, and if they'd questioned you – perhaps forcefully – about dreamland's defences ...'

'You didn't want us telling them that your ships were engaged in mopping-up operations on the moon, eh?'

'Something like that,' mumbled Kuranes. 'Not a mopping-up operation, exactly. Just a show of force, to let the moonbeasts know we can get at them any time we choose, if they ever decide to go against us in the future.'

'I see,' said de Marigny. 'And while the bulk of your fleet is there, doing whatever it's doing, at least one moonbeast, Gudge, has been here, preparing a stronghold for the Great Old Ones. Well, that's at an end now, anyway.'

'It will be,' Kuranes agreed, 'when Admiral Dass gets back and I have him bomb that shaft and block it forever! Until then ... well, what has all of this shown us, if not how badly you're needed in Elysia, eh?'

'How's that?' de Marigny raised his eyebrows.

'Cthulhu has always been a great influence in men's dreams,' Kuranes stated the obvious. 'Indeed, he's responsible for most of what's nightmarish in them! But not since the Bad Days has he made so bold, attempting to influence the dreamlands – and through them the thinking of men in the waking world – so greatly. In the affair of the Mad Moon, and now in this. The uprising, certainly an attempt at an uprising, must be very close now. He prepares the way for himself in space and time, and in all the parallel worlds. The Crawling Chaos is abroad, the stars are very nearly right, and strange times have come again ...'

'Kuranes,' said de Marigny, 'you can help me. No one knows Curator and his Museum better than you. I need to see him, somehow talk to him.'

Kuranes' turn to raise his eyebrows. 'The grey metal box?' he guessed. 'Did Atal tell you about that? A box with hands like those on your time-clock?'

'It is a time-clock of sorts,' de Marigny nodded. 'I'm sure of it. For some strange reason of their own, the Elder Gods have chosen to lead me a mazy chase into Elysia. Maybe I have to work for what I want – work hard for it – and even though I'm needed there, still they're making me earn my right of passage. Maybe it's that ... and maybe it's something else. I don't know. But I've been told to speak to Curator.'

'Nice trick if you can turn it,' said Kuranes – and he saw de Marigny's face fall. 'It would be no good my holding out false hopes,' he said. 'It's just that I don't know anyone who ever spoke to Curator – and got an answer! What's

616

more, since the advent of the cube, now locked in his chest, he hasn't even been seen. Who can say where he is? He may or may not be somewhere in the Museum. But where? I don't know where he goes. Nor why. Nor how. Sometimes he's not seen for months at a time.'

'Will you come to the Museum with us anyway?' Moreen begged.

'Of course I will, child,' said Kuranes at once. 'But it seems only fair to warn you: if Curator is not there – if we can't find him – then there's no help for it.'

When Kuranes, The Searcher and Moreen left the tavern, Hero and Eldin were hard at it, while the astonished proprietor brought them plate after plate and flagon after flagon . . .

6

Curator and the Dream-clock

At the sea-wall, where the time-clock stood under guard of half-a-dozen pikemen, Kuranes pointed across the harbour to where a great stone circular structure stood on a promontory at the eastern extreme of the sky-island. Beneath the three-tier building the rock of Serannian was a comparatively thin crust less than fifty feet in depth, and beneath that – nothing. 'The Museum,' he informed. 'Only one way in and out: along that narrow causeway over the neck of the promontory – unless you're a bird, that is! Thieves think twice and then some more, before tackling the Museum. And then, when they've seen Curator, they don't even think about it any more. Most thieves, anyway . . .' And he glanced back the way they'd come and smiled a little. 'Hero and Eldin tried it on once – twice in fact – since when they've given Curator and his Museum a wide berth.'

He led the way round the harbour to the causeway, paused before venturing out over that narrow span. 'No place for vertigo sufferers, this,' he commented. 'You've heads for heights, have you?' And as Moreen and de Marigny nodded in unison he led on.

The causeway was low-walled, perhaps thirty yards long, cobbled. Since there was room for only two abreast, the trio had to cross single-file in order to leave the way free for sightseers leaving the Museum. Looking down over the wall as they went, de Marigny and Moreen were able to gaze almost straight down into uncounted fathoms of air – the 'deeps' of the Cerenerian – at all the towns and rivers, shores and oceans of dream, which sprawled in fantastic vistas to all horizons. Far off they could even see Celephais, clearly landmarked where Mount Aran's permanently snow-capped peak stood proud of the gentling Tanarians.

They entered the Museum through a tall stone archway to find themselves in a three-storeyed building whose sealed windows were of unbreakable crystal. Ventilation was through the archway, which had no door, and also through a square aperture in the ocean-facing curve of the wall which was big as a large window but placed much higher. The first and second floors of the Museum contained only those items with which ordinary museums commonly concern themselves; as David Hero had once commented: 'mummies and bones and books', and suchlike. The ground floor, however, was where the Museum's true valuables were housed – of which the quantity and quality were utterly beyond belief.

For here were all sorts of treasures: jewels and precious stones, golden figurines, ivory statuettes, jade miniatures, priceless antiques and bric-a-brac from lands and times forgotten in the mists of ancient dreams, objets d'art which could only have been conceived in the fertile dreams of very special artists and sculptors. In its entirety, the place would be ransom for fifty worlds!

'Curator's collection,' said Kuranes, drawing back de Marigny and Moreen's minds from rapt contemplation, 'of which he's extremely jealous. Oh, yes, for each item has its place – and pity the man who'd try to change it! Myself, I find the upper floors even more awesome.'

The Searcher knew what he meant. He'd seen shrunken heads from immemorial Kled up there; and shrivelled mummies from a caverned mountain in primal Sarkomand; and stone-flowers from some eastern desert at the very edge of dreams, which must be kept bone dry, for a single drop of water would rot them in an instant; and books whose pages glowed with runes written (so Kuranes had it) by mages in antique Theem'hdra at the very dawn of time. And so:

'It is a very wonderful place,' de Marigny agreed, his hushed voice echoing in the now almost entirely vacated Museum, 'and we've seen wonders galore here.'

And reading his mind, Moreen added: 'But nowhere Curator.'

Kuranes sighed. 'I told you, warned you. No man can ever guarantee or govern Curator's comings and goings.'

They left the Museum empty of human life, walked back across the causeway. There, along the curve of the sea wall close to the time-clock, a pair of sated questers leaned, propped up by the wall, gazed out over folded arms at the merchantmen and other vessels riding at anchor on a bank of rose-tinted cloud. Hero looked up as Kuranes and his visitors from the waking world approached. 'No luck?' He read the answer in their faces.

Now Eldin straightened up, patted his belly, uttered a gentle, happy belch. And: 'Ah, well,' the older quester rumbled. 'I'd hoped it wouldn't come to this, but plainly there's little else for it.' Swaying like a sailor – or perhaps swaggering like a pirate – he passed the three by and headed for the Museum. Curious, they turned to watch him as his pace picked up and he determinedly strode toward the causeway over the promontory. And now Hero ambled up and joined them.

'See,' the younger quester explained, 'Curator has a thing about us – especially about Eldin. Damn me, but that old metal man doesn't trust the Wanderer a bit! It has to do with a couple of big rubies we once almost, er, borrowed from the Museum – almost. Curator took umbrage, of course, and stopped us, since when we've steered clear. But now it seems we can use this, er, *aversion* of his to your advantage. Except Curator-taunting's a dodgy business at best – which is why we tossed for it.' He handed de Marigny an antique, much-rubbed triangular golden tond, upon which – on both face and obverse – the same bearded, long-forgotten face remained faintly impressed.

De Marigny stared at the coin in his hand, stared harder, and:

'A double-header!' The Searcher exclaimed. 'You tricked him into it!'

Hero looked at de Marigny and narrowed his eyes a little – but only for a moment. Then he smiled and said: 'When you know Eldin and me better, you'll know there's no such thing as cheating or trickery between us. A bit of one-upmanship, maybe, that's all. The gamble was Eldin's suggestion, not mine. The coin's his, too. Oh, and incidentally – he's the one who won!'

De Marigny's embarrassment knew no bounds, but before he could say anything to perhaps make it worse –

'Ahoy there in the Museum!' called Eldin, his great hands cupped to his mouth. Passers-by paused in small groups to stare at him, and seagulls on the wall flapped aloft noisily, shocked by his shouting. 'Ahoy old klanker! Come out, come out wherever you are! An old friend's here to see you, and perhaps sample some of your valuables. And if he *doesn't* see you, he'll *certainly* sample them!'

Hero grinned as he and the other three moved closer to where Eldin stood at the mainland end of the causeway. 'He's just getting warmed up,' he stated. 'He can taunt a lot better than that, believe me.'

'Well then, you metal mute, what's it to be?' roared Eldin. He swaggered forward a few paces onto the walled bridge, cautiously began to cross. But for all his bellowing, his eyes were fixed firmly on the Museum's archway entrance at the other end of the causeway. 'Ho, tin-ribs!' he shouted. 'The Wanderer's back and lusting for loot! So where's the rusty pile of rubble who runs this ruin, eh? Come out, you cowardly can of nuts and bolts!'

Eldin was a third of the way across now and beginning to think that perhaps Curator really was absent. Hand in hand with that thought had come another: if Curator *really*

621

wasn't here, what was there to stop him from implementing his threat? Say one small pigeon's egg-sized ruby? Why, he could be in and out of the Museum's ground floor quick as thought, and not even Hero would guess what he'd done – not until they were well away from here, anyway. Eldin's eyes gleamed. On wealth like that, why, they could live like lords for years!

Now Eldin could have stamped up and down the causeway and bellowed for a month to no avail. Likewise his taunting: it would not have turned the trick. Curator was not attuned to stamping, bellowing or taunting. But he *was* attuned – sensitive to an infinite degree – to all thoughts of thievery, malicious damage, or other fell intent where the Museum was concerned. Such thoughts or intentions would have to be investigated and dealt with no matter what the source, but when that source happened also to be Eldin the Wanderer ...

'Oh-oh!' gasped Hero. 'Do you see what I see?'

Kuranes, de Marigny and Moreen, they all saw. But not Eldin, for he was facing in the wrong direction. In the middle of the causeway he now crept like a cat (remarkable, for one his size and shape), and his bluster had fallen to little more than a whisper: 'Curator? Oh, Curator! Eldin's here to purloin a pearl, or burgle a bauble, or filch a figurine. Or maybe simply rip off a ruby, eh?'

'Eldin!' Hero called out, trying to stay calm. 'I think – '

'*Quiet!*' the Wanderer hissed without turning round. '*Shh!* – I'm concentrating.' Two-thirds of the way across, he could almost taste success.

But at the landward end of the causeway, behind and below him, Curator 'tasted' something else entirely: he tasted the essence of a thief, the scent of a scoundrel, the suspicious spoor of Eldin the Wanderer. And that was a scent he knew all too well.

Dry-mouthed, Kuranes, The Searcher and Moreen could only look on as Curator emerged more fully from *under* the causeway; but Hero was already running forward. 'Eldin, you idiot! You've succeeded, man – only too well! Look behind you!'

Curator was a vaguely manlike thing; tall and spiky yet somehow lumpy looking, with many spindly arms, a metallic sheen, and faceted, glittering crystal eyes that missed nothing. He came up from beneath the causeway like some strange steel spider, making scarcely a sound as he swung his thin legs up over the wall and drew himself erect on the cobbles of the narrow bridge. At which point, hair bristling on the back of his neck, Eldin slowly turned and saw him.

'B'god!' said Eldin, trying to smile and gulp at the same time. 'If it isn't my old pal the estimable Curator!'

Curator's eyes, a glittering icy blue one moment, turned scarlet in the next. At the same time Hero hurled himself at the metal man's back and grabbed hold of the blunt projection which was his head. Which action doubtless saved the Wanderer's life. For as Hero yanked at Curator's head, twin beams of red death lanced out of his eyes, missed Eldin by a fraction and blackened a patch of stonework on the archway behind him. 'He was only joking, you metal monster!' Hero roared, still trying to pull Curator's head off.

'Curator!' Kuranes was shouting. 'Curator, you're making a dreadful mistake.' But Eldin, who knew he wasn't, had already darted inside the Museum and disappeared from view. Now Curator turned his attention on Hero, for after the Museum and its contents, his next priority was himself.

De Marigny yelled, 'Moreen, the clock!' and raced for his time machine. If he could put the time-clock between Curator and the questers, then they would stand something of a chance. The girl, on the other hand – who had no fear of creatures no matter how weird or monstrous – ran the other way, onto the causeway where even now Curator was

623

hauling Hero off his back and holding him at arm's length. There was a split-second of near-instantaneous and yet minute scrutiny, and then Curator pivoted and swung Hero out over the wall. Hero's legs hit the wall and hooked there – clung for dear life – as Curator released him!

Moreen was almost upon the metal man but Curator hadn't seen her yet. Instead his head bent forward and his crystal eyes lit on Hero's legs, bent at the knees over the top of the wall. A metal hand reached out, grasped one ankle, straightened the leg. Another arm stretched its hand toward the other ankle, and –

Moreen was there. Without pause she got between Curator and Hero, reached over the wall and grabbed at one of the quester's flailing arms. And half-turning to Curator she cried: 'How dare you? How *dare* you?! Who are you to murder men for the sake of your stupid Museum? Now you fetch Hero up at once!'

Kuranes arrived puffing and panting. He leaned over the wall and caught at Hero's other hand, began hauling him up. Together, he and Moreen finally dragged the whey-faced quester back to safety – of a sort. But still Curator had not quite released him. Nor had he forgotten Eldin.

Seeing Hero in deadly danger, the Wanderer had come charging from the Museum, fists up, adopting a classic boxing stance. Curator saw him, relinquished his hold on Hero (however reluctantly), stepped clankingly, threateningly, toward Eldin. At which point de Marigny set the time-clock down on the causeway between the two.

Curator saw the time-clock; his scarlet eyes slowly cooled to a still-dangerous orange, burned a fierce yellow for a moment, finally turned blue. They glittered like chips of ice as he took one clanking pace, then another, toward the clock. And inside the time-clock, suddenly de Marigny knew what he must do. Hadn't Atal told him that Curator 'talked' to the grey metal cube by imitating the movements of its four hands – a robotic semaphore? Well, now he must use the time-clock to 'talk' to Curator in the same manner. But how? The time-clock hid many secrets in its intricate being, and this was one of them. Titus Crow had often hinted that the device was half-animate, semi-sentient; but that it should also have this power of mechanical speech ... And yet why not? Didn't computers 'talk' to each other in the waking world? And why shouldn't time-clocks? Even Crow had never known the real significance of those four, often wildly vacillating hands: the time-clock, calculating, thinking, 'talking' to itself?

De Marigny knew how to use the clock's scanners, its sensors, its voice-amplification and weapon systems. He could drive it through time and space and places between the two. The 'buttons' and 'switches' and 'triggers' were all in his mind. In the clock's mind. In *their* minds, his and the clock's, when their minds were one. He closed his eyes now and felt for those familiar instruments, controls, and found them. And: *I have to talk to Curator*, he told the clock. *Through you. Please, help me talk to Curator.*

In the waking world it might not have worked, but in dreams things are often simpler. This time it was simple: de Marigny felt a door open in his mind, or rather a door *between* his mind and the clock's, and knew he'd found the space-time machine's 'communicator'. And now he could talk to Curator.

Outside on the causeway, Curator came closer still; his crystal eyes seemed full of strange inquiry; he 'stared' expectantly at the hands on the time-clock's dial. And de Marigny didn't keep him waiting.

The change come over the metal man was at once apparent to Kuranes, Moreen and Hero; the change, too, in the time-clock. Its hands, never less than erratic in their movements, now seemed to lose every last vestige of normalcy; they moved insanely, coordination all awry. Or all *together*, coordinated as never before. Not in de Marigny's experience, anyway. And:

'Look!' whispered Kuranes. 'Curator makes hands like those of the time-clock. See, they converse!'

Four of Curator's spindle arms had swivelled round to the front of his canister body. Now they clicked into a central position, retracted or extended themselves into appropriate lengths, commenced to whirl and twitch and jerk in keeping, in rhythm – and yes, in conversation with de Marigny.

'I am The Searcher,' said de Marigny. 'I think you've heard of me.'

'Indeed. I've heard of many things. Of you and Moreen, of the time-clock through which you talk to me, and of Elysia which you would discover. I have heard of a primal land at the dawn of time, and a white wizard named Exior K'mool. I have heard of Lith where the lava lakes boil, while Ardatha Ell sits in his floating manse and measures the pulse of a dying sun which would yet be born again. And I have heard, from many quarters, of a rising up of evil powers, one which threatens the fabric of the multiverse itself.'

'Then you can surely help me,' said de Marigny. 'Can we talk somewhere, in privacy, in ... comfort?'

'I am comfortable anywhere,' Curator answered, 'but I am most at ease beneath Serannian, clinging to the sky-suspended stone, with all the dreamlands spread below. I perceive, however, that this would never do for you; are you not comfortable in the time-clock?'

'Yes, but – '

' – But you are a human being, and need familiar surroundings, accustomed atmospheres, personal privacies. Well, I understand that. I, too, am a private being. Shall we enter the Museum? But first, there are certain annoyances I must deal with – two of them. One of which hides behind your time-clock even now ...'

De Marigny was quick off the mark with: 'Curator, you must not harm the questers!'

' "Must not?" ' Curator seemed surprised. ' "Harm?" I know the meaning of such words, but fail to see their application here. You have not understood: I merely protect the Museum, in which are stored fragments of the strangest, greatest, most fabulous dreams that men ever dreamed! For here are dreams untold, forgotten by their dreamers when they awoke; and here are nightmares, safely stored, whose release would drive men mad. There are dreams of empire here, and dreams quite beyond avarice – except – '

'Yes?'

'While *I* know the meaning of that last, and while I am sure that *you* know it, still there are two here who do not. Nor could they ever perceive the consequences of interfering with this Museum which I protect, and *from* which I must protect the lands of Earth dreams. But you say I must not harm them? Nor would I – but *they* do not know that! So step aside and let me deal with them my way. First him who cowers behind you.'

On Curator's word that he would do the questers no harm, de Marigny lifted the time-clock skyward and revealed Eldin who again raised his great hands. 'Come on then, Curator! Just you and me – man to man,' he cried, ' – or whatever!'

Curator's eyes glowed scarlet. Twin beams reached out faster than thought, ignored Eldin's fists, cut through his clothes here and there without so much as scorching a single hair beneath them. And without pause the beam relocated, slicing at this and that, reducing the Wanderer's clothing to ribbons. As fast as Eldin could move his hands, clutching at his rags, so the beams sought other targets. His pockets were sliced, releasing a fistful of large, glittering jewels to fall to the causeway's cobbles – following which Curator went to work with a vengeance!

In mere moments Eldin was almost naked, holding scraps of rag to himself to cover more than his embarrassment.

And when all of the Wanderer's bluster had been quite literally cut out of – or off of – him, then Curator turned his attention to Hero.

Kuranes and Moreen at once stepped aside; Eldin had not been hurt – except for his pride, possibly – and therefore Hero should also be safe. As for Hero's feelings:

When first the metal man had 'attacked' Eldin he'd been thoroughly alarmed; but the Wanderer's punishment had seemed only just, so that soon Hero had started to grin, then laugh. But now:

Now Curator's eyes were silver, them and the beams that issued from them. Hero felt those beams tugging at him, held up his hands as if to ward Curator off. 'Now hang fire, tin-shins!' he cried. 'I mean, what did I do?'

But the silver beams had fastened on Hero now, floating him off the cobbles and suspending him in mid-air. Curator inclined his gaze upward, lifting Hero swiftly into the sky over Serannian. The metal man's head tilted back farther yet, until he looked straight up – at which point the beams swiftly extended themselves and rocketed Hero into the clouds overhead and out of sight. Then the beams cut out, were instantly withdrawn. All human viewers of that act held their breath – until Hero came tearing through the clouds, plummeting back into view. And then the beams reached out again, unerringly, to catch and lower him to the wharfside. Breathless and dizzy, Hero staggered and fell on his backside as Curator released him.

And without pause the Museum's keeper again turned, lifted Eldin from the causeway in a like manner, dumped him beside his friend. Now golden beams lanced forth from eyes suddenly yellow. It was that bright yellow with which wasps are banded, and the beams likewise appeared to have the sting of those unpleasant insects. Yelping, leaping, howling whenever the stinging beams struck them – with Eldin doubly tormented where he clutched his rags to cover himself – the two tumbled in the direction of Serannian's mazy alleys where they quickly disappeared from view.

'Harm them?' said Curator again, clanking to where his almost-stolen jewels lay on the cobbles and collecting them up. 'A very little, maybe. If only I could be sure I had deterred them, that would suffice. But where that pair are concerned . . .' And very humanly, he let the sentence hang. And having retrieved all of the gems, he went on into the Museum.

De Marigny followed in the time-clock, and behind him Moreen. As for Kuranes: he went off after the questers. He owed them a small sky-boat – to say nothing of a telling-off – and since they'd soon be a laughing-stock in Serannian (and therefore ripe for many a brawl), it might be best to 'banish' them from the sky-island, for a little while anyway.

In the Museum, Moreen entered the time-clock and de Marigny showed her his discovery: the clock's 'communicator'. Now Curator's 'conversation' reached her also.

'You seek Elysia,' the metal man said. 'Well, it is my understanding that I was made there. I was given form in Elysia, and life here. But I can't tell you how to get there. I know nothing of Elysia, except that the way is long and hard. However, your coming here was anticipated. Before you someone – something – also came into Earth's dreamland to see Curator.'

'The grey metal cube,' said de Marigny. 'Some kind of time-clock. It brought you instructions for me, from Elysia.'

'Say on,' said Curator, impressed. 'Perhaps the dream-clock is not required. Perhaps you already possess the necessary information.'

'Dream-clock?'

'Of course. The grey metal cube is a dream-clock – a monitor working in the subconscious levels of intelligence. No previous need for such a device in Earth's dreams, for I was here. But on this occasion the cube came as a messenger.'

De Marigny frowned, said: 'Titus Crow told me to look in my own dreams, and to carry my search into the past – rather, my past. He mentioned a wizard, just as you have mentioned a wizard: Exior K'mool. The sentient gas Sssss told me much the same things. Well, I've tracked down all possible leads here in the dreamlands, so now it seems the final answer must lie in the remote past. With Exior K'mool in Theem'hdra.'

'Good!' said Curator.

'But the past is more than four billion years vast!' said de Marigny. 'Where in the past – *when* – am I to seek for Theem'hdra? And where *in* Theem'hdra will I find Exior K'mool?'

'Ah!' said Curator. 'But these are questions you must ask of the dream-clock. For he alone has the answers, which were given to him in Elysia.'

Curator's chest opened; panels of shining metal slid back, telescoped, revealed a space. And snug in that cavity, there the grey metal cube rested – but for only a moment longer. Then –

The dream-clock slid from Curator's keeping, hovered free, spun like some strange metal dervish for a few seconds until it located and recognized the time-clock, then commenced to 'talk' in its own voice, the exotic articulations of its four hands. De Marigny 'heard' the opening details of the dream-clock's message, ensured that the clock was recording the spatial-temporal co-ordinates which constituted that singular monologue, then returned his attention to Curator:

'The dream-clock's information means nothing to me personally,' he said. 'I would need the mind of a computer. But the time-clock understands and records all. It is the location of Exior K'mool in primal Theem'hdra, yes. That's my next port of call, and I have you to thank for it, Curator.'

'You owe me nothing,' said Curator. 'But you owe your race, the race of Man, everything. You deserted that race once for a dream, and now you return *to* a dream. And in you, germinating, lie the seeds of that race's continuation. The stars are very nearly right, Searcher, and you still have far to go. You seek a source and the clock now has the route, knows the destination. Waste no more time, but use it!'

The dream-clock's hands had steadied to a less erratic rhythm; it whirled for a brief moment, stopped abruptly and slid home into Curator's chest. The panels closed it in.

'Then it's time to say farewell,' said de Marigny.

'Indeed,' said Curator. 'As for the dream-clock: for the moment he stays here with me, perhaps forever, or for as long as we have. Only if you are successful will he ever return to Elysia. Until then, all Elysia's expatriate children must remain in exile.'

'Why do you say that?' de Marigny asked. 'What do you mean?'

'I have already overstepped myself,' said Curator. He began to turn away. 'Farewell, and good fortune ...' He clanked away into dream's oldest, rarest memories.

De Marigny and Moreen watched him go. Then The Searcher said to the time-clock: 'Very well, you have the co-ordinates. Now take us to Exior K'mool. Take us to Theem'hdra, the primal land at the dawn of time.'

Which without more ado the clock set out to do ...

1

Exior K'mool

Theem'hdra ...

There had been other 'primal' lands: Hyborea and
Hyperborea, Mu, Uthmal, Atlantis and many others; but
in Theem'hdra lay the first, the original Age of Man. It *was*
Pangaea, but not the Pangaea of modern geographers and
geologists and theorists. How long ago exactly is of little
concern here; suffice it to say that if the 'popular' Pangaea
was last week, then Theem'hdra was probably months
ago. Certainly it was an Age of Man which predated the
Age of Reptiles, and was dust when they were in their
ascendancy. But civilizations wax and wane, they always
have and always will, and some are lost forever.

Theem'hdra, whereon a primal Nature experimented
and created and did myriad strange and nightmarish things.
For Nature herself was in her youth, and where men were
concerned ... she had not yet decided which talents men
should have and which should be forbidden, discontinued.

In some men, and in certain women, too, the wild
workings of capricious Nature wrought weird wonders,
giving them senses and powers additional to the usual five.
Often these powers were carried down through many
generations; aye, and occasionally such a man would mate
with just such a woman and then, eventually, through
genealogical patterns and permutations long forgotten to
20th Century scientists, along would come the seventh son
of a seventh son, or the ninth daughter of a ninth daughter
– and what then?

Mylakhrion the Immortal, who had been less than
immortal after all, was the greatest of all Theem'hdra's
wizards; and after him, arguably, his far removed

descendant, Teh Atht of Klühn. Next would probably be Mylakhrion's one-time apprentice and heir to many of his thaumaturgies, Exior K'mool. And Exior would not be the first magician whose experiments had led him into dire straits ...

Mylakhrion had been dead for one hundred and twenty years, victim of his own magic. Long before that, Exior's first master, Phaithor Ull, had rendered himself as green dust in an ill-conceived conjuration. And where Umhammer Kark's vast manse had once sprawled its terraces, walls and pavilions on Mount Gatch by the River Luhr, overlooking the Steppes of Hrossa, a great bottomless pit now opened, issuing hissing clouds of mordant yellow steam. Wizards all, and all gone the way of wizards. Who lives by the wand ...

And now:

'My turn,' gloomed Exior K'mool to himself, where he prowled and fretted in his walled palace in the heart of ruined Humquass, once-proud warrior city. Lamias flaunted their buttocks at him as he passed, and succubi rubbed him with their breasts, eager to balm him; but Exior said only. 'Bah!' and brushed them aside, or sent them on meaningless errands to keep them from annoying and pestering him. Did not the idiot creatures know that his doom would be theirs also? And could they not see how close that doom was now?

Exior's hair was short-cropped and grey – as grey as it had turned on the day he first looked in Mylakhrion's great runebook, one hundred and seventy-three years earlier – and his mien, as might well be imagined, was that of an old man heavy-burdened with wisdom and knowledge and some sin; for it's a hard business being a wizard and remaining free of sin. And yet his long slender back was only slightly bent and his limbs still surprisingly spry. Aye, and his yellow eyes undimmed by his nearly two centuries of rune-unriddling, and his mind a crystal, where every thought came sharp as a needle. And for this not entirely misleading simulacrum of vitality he could thank long-gone Mylakhrion, whose fountain of youth and elixir of longevity and wrinkle-reducing unguents had kept the years in large part at bay. Alas that he must also 'thank' that elder mage for his current fix, which in all likelihood were his last.

Exior's palace had a high-walled courtyard before and high-walled gardens behind; in Humquass' heyday, the palace had been the city's tallest edifice, its towers even higher than the king's own palace. Now it was not only the tallest but the *only* building, chiefly because Humquass was no more. But the palace, like Exior himself, had survived wars and famines and all the onslaughts and ravages of nature; aye, and it would survive for many a century yet – or should.

It should, for from its foundations up the place was saturated with magical protections: spells against decay and natural disaster, against insect, fungus and human invasion, against the spells of other sorcerers, but mainly against the incursion of that which even now frothed and seethed on the other side of the walls, seeking a way in. A legacy of Exior's search for immortality. Like Mylakhrion before him, he had sought everlasting life until finally he'd attracted imminent death.

'Exior, Exior!' croaked a black, fanged, half-man, half-insect thing where it scuttled about his feet as he walked in the gardens. 'A doom is upon you, Exior! A great doom is come upon Exior the Mage!'

'Hush!' he scowled, kicking half-heartedly at the creature and missing. He stooped and found a pebble, hurled it at the scurrying, hybrid monstrosity. 'Away with you! And what are you for a familiar anyway? Be sure that if that slime out there gets me, then that it will surely get you also! Bah! I'd find a better familiar among the cockroaches in my kitchen!'

'But you *did* find me there,' croaked that unforgiving creature, ' – half of me, anyway – and welded me to Loxzor of the Hrossaks. I, the Loxzor part, was also a magician, Exior – or had you forgotten?'

In fact Exior had forgotten; but now he shook a fist at the thing, yelled: 'How could I forget, with your infernal crowing to remind me day and night? 'Twas your own fault, Hrossak – sending your morbid magics against me. Be thankful I didn't give you the habits and lower half of a dung-beetle – and then make you keeper of the palace privy! Indeed, I still might!'

As the Loxzor-thing hastily withdrew, Exior climbed a ladder beside the wall and carefully looked over.

In his life Exior had seen, had even created, shuddersome things; but nothing he had seen or made or imagined was more noxious, poisonous, mordant or morbid than the frothing slime that lapped all about his palace walls and closed them in. At present the walls and his spells combined to hold the stuff at bay, but for how much longer? In extent the slime covered and roiled over all of olden Humquass' ruins, and lay deep as a thick mist all about. But never before a mist like this.

It was mainly yellow, but where it swirled it was bile-green, or in other places red like bad blood in pus. It was a gas or at worst a liquid, but now and then it would thicken up and throw out tendrils or tentacles like a living thing. And indeed Exior knew that it *was* a living thing – and the worst possible sort.

Even now, as he stared at the heaving, sickly mass, so it sensed him and threw up groping green arms. But Exior had spelled a dome of power over the palace, enclosing the entire structure, grounds and all. Now tentacles of slime slapped against that invisible wall mere inches from his face, so that he drew himself back and quickly descended the ladder into the gardens. But not before he'd seen the crumbling and steaming of the walls where the stuff's acid nature was eating into them.

'Shewstone!' muttered Exior then, under his breath. And, stumbling toward the main building: 'Last chance ... shewstone ... no spells can help me now ... but if I can find just *one* possible future for myself ... and then somehow contrive to *go* there ... *Hah!* ... Hopeless ... Not even Mylakhrion could control time!'

Outside, were it not for the slime, the season would be autumn. In Exior's courtyard, however, it was spring; he controlled the seasons within his own boundaries; but even so, still black clouds were building, and he felt in his bones the nip of winter. The winter of his years, perhaps? His days? His ... hours? Was that all he had left, who so recently sought immortality, hours?

Grinding his teeth with anxiety, Exior entered his basalt palace, followed the corkscrew stairs of a tower where they wound inexorably upward, finally came to that place which had been his room of repose and was, more recently, his workshop. Here he had worked unceasingly to discover a way to nullify the ever-encroaching slime sea, to no avail. For here, scattered about, were the many appurtenances of his art, all sorts and species of occult apparatus.

Here were the misshapen skulls of an ancient order of sub-man, and the teratologically fabulous remains of things which had never been men; bottles of multi-hued liquids, some bubbling and others quiescent; flutes made of the hollow bones of *pteranodon primus*, capable of notes which would transmute silver into gold and vice-versa; shelf upon shelf of books in black leather and umber skins, at least one of which was tattooed!

Here too were miniature worlds and moons in their orbits, all hanging from the tracked ceiling on mobile ropes of jewelled cowries; and here pentacles of power adorned the mosaic walls and floor, glittering with the fire of gem-chips, from which they were constructed. Sigil-inscribed scrolls of vellum were littered everywhere; but alone in the comparatively tidy centre of the room, there was Exior's showpiece: a great ball of clouded crystal upon its stand of carved chrysolite.

Kicking aside the disordered clutter and muttering, 'Useless, all useless!' he approached the shewstone, seated himself upon a simple cane chair, made passes to command a preview of possible futures. This was not the first time he had scried upon the future (hardly that, for his greatest art lay in oneiromancy: reading the future in dreams, in which he'd excelled even as an apprentice) but it was certainly the first time he'd achieved such dreary results.

He was shown a future where the slime lapped over the palace, devouring it, and himself with it. He saw a time when Humquass was a scar on the land, like a great sore in earth's healthy flesh. He scried upon a stone raised by some thoughtful soul in a shrine built centrally in the blight, which read:

> 'Here lies Exior K'mool, or
> would if alien energies had
> not eaten him entirely away.
> Here his shade abides, anyhow.'

But nowhere, for all his desperate passes, could he find a possible future where Exior K'mool lived. A fact he could scarce credit, for his dreams had foretold otherwise: namely that there *was* a future for him. Indeed he had *seen* himself, in recurrent dreams, dwelling in a manse whose base was a bowl that floated on a lake of lava. And he had known the world or lake where the manse drifted on liquid fire as 'Lith', and he had lived there a while with the white wizard Ardatha Ell, of whom he'd heard nothing except in his dreams. But where was this future, and where Lith? The shewstone displayed nought but dooms! All very disheartening.

Exior sighed and let the crystal grow opaque, turned to

637

his runebook and thumbed disconsolately through its pages. Runes and spells and cantrips galore here, but none to help him escape the slime, not permanently, not in this world or time. The stuff's nature was such as could not *be* avoided, it would pursue him to the end. His end.

And full of despair, at last his eyes lighted upon a spell only three-quarters conceived, borrowed from a fragment Mylakhrion had left behind when long ago he took himself off to his last refuge, the lonely isle of Tharamoon in the north.

At first, staring at the uncompleted page, Exior saw little; but then his eyes widened, his mind began to spark; and finally he read avidly, devouring the rune almost in a glance. A spell to call up the dead, but without necromancy proper. If he could complete the rune, perhaps he could call up some wizard ancestor to his aid. There must surely have been magic in his ancestry, else he himself were not gifted. And what if he erred in completing the thing, and what if it came to nought? Well, and what had he to lose anyway? But if he were to succeed – if indeed he could find and call up some mage ancestor centuries dead – well, even at worst two heads are better than one. And certainly better than none!

He set to work at once.

Using other runebooks, lesser works, slowly he put the finishing touches to the invocation. No time to check his work however, for day crept toward evening, and a grim foreboding told him that the palace walls and his slime-excluding spell could not last out the night. And so, with stylus that shook even as his hand shook, he set down the last glyph and sat back to cast worried, anxious eyes over the completed rune.

Outside the light was beginning to fail. Exior called for Loxzor – ex-cockroach, ex-Hrossak, ex-wizard – and commanded: 'Look upon this rune. What think you? Will it work?'

Loxzor scuttled, drew himself up to Exior's table on chitin legs, glared at the freshly pigmented page with many-faceted eyes. 'Bah!' he harshly clacked. And maliciously: 'What do I know of magic – I'm a cockroach!'

'You refuse to help me?'

'Help yourself, wizard. Your hour is at hand!'

'Beastly creature!' Exior cried. 'Go then, and suffer the slime when it whelms this place! *Begone!*' And he chased Loxhor from the chamber. Then –

– Then it was time to test out the spell. The last rune of Exior K'mool ...

Far removed from his own era – if he could any longer be said to have one representative or contemporary time – The Searcher hovered the time-clock high over Exior's palace and looked down through the scanners and sensors on the scene below. Beside him, Moreen snuggled close and said: 'Henri, I know we've left Earth's dreamlands far behind – or before us – and that this is the waking world in a time when the Motherworld was in her prime, but looking down there, on that ...'

'I know,' he answered, grimly. 'You'd swear we were still dreaming, eh? Nightmaring, anyway. It seems Exior K'mool's got himself in deep waters. Also, if that dome of force is anything to go by, he's a wizard of some note.'

To merely human eyes Exior's dome would be invisible, but the clock's sensors and scanners showed it as a pale, vibrating hemisphere, with Exior's palace locked inside like a scene viewed through blue smoke or heat-haze. The scanners also showed the slime, and de Marigny's immediate revulsion told him something of its nature. 'It seems we're to be used yet again,' he commented wryly.

'Used?'

He nodded. 'We were used to rescue Sssss from the Hounds of Tindalos, likewise Hero and Eldin from Gudge, or more properly Nyarlathotep – and now – '

'Exior K'mool from that ... that filthy stuff? Or is it in fact a filthy thing? I can't tell, but I know it's nothing of nature. Not as I know nature.'

'It's both,' said de Marigny. 'It's a slime, but it gets its form, its purpose, its motive for being from a source which is far worse. Do you know what this stuff is? I do, for I've met it before – or will meet it, in the distant future. In ancient Khem it took, *will* take, the form of a proud young Pharaoh. But by then it will have a thousand other forms, too. Here in the primal land, it too is primal; Cthulhu uses crude means to achieve his ends; no need for sophistication in a mainly unsophisticated age.'

'Nyarlathotep!' the girl shuddered. 'Again?'

'I'm sure of it,' de Marigny nodded again. 'The Crawling Chaos – but formless in this age. A mass, crawling, chaotic. A primal force in a primal land. It's an age of magic and monsters, remember? And certainly this stuff is monstrous. It's the morbid mind-juice of the Cthulhu Cycle Deities, telepathy bordering on teleportation; it's something the Great Old Ones have sent to exact a revenge, or collect a debt. It seems Exior has had business with Cthulhu, which is the same as making a deal with the devil!'

'It's eating at those walls,' said Moreen, 'and it seems to me that Exior's dome grows thinner, weaker, with each passing moment. 'Can we get inside?'

'I think so. The time-clock ignores most barriers. It was designed to breach the greatest of them all: time and space and all the planes and angles between and beyond. We'll soon see ...'

He located K'mool in his tower workshop, slipped the clock sideways through space-time, emerged in a shimmer of air *within* that marvellous room – where a moment before the wizard had spoken his rune and completed the intricate attendant passes. And:

'By all the Lords of Darkness!' Exior gasped, his jaw falling open. He stumbled back from the time-clock where it hovered inches over the mosaic floor, tripped, flopped backward into his cane chair. 'I called upon a dead ancestor and got him – coffin and all!'

But as de Matigny set the clock down, and he and Moreen stepped out of the open door in a wash of purple, pulsing light: 'Two ancestors!' Exior croaked. 'And solider far than any ghosts I ever say before!'

None of which made any sense to the time-travellers, for it was spoken in an alien – a primal – tongue. 'We'll have to speak to him through the clock,' said de Marigny, turning as if to re-enter the time-clock. But –

'Wait!' Exior cried, this time in English. 'No need for any interpreter. I, Exior K'mool, am a master of runes – and what are languages if not runes expressed as words? Magic or mundane, all is one to me; I understand tongues indeed, I've fathomed yours from the merest sentence.'

'Amazing!' said Moreen, round-eyed. She approached the wizard and he made a bow. 'You heard a few words and learned a language! But you must be the greatest linguist of all time.'

'So I pride myself,' said Exior. 'It is a measure of my magic – with the help of some skill – all of which is in the blood *you* passed down to me, O mother of all my ancestors.'

Moreen laughed, shook her head. 'But I'm not your ancestor,' she protested. 'I won't even be born for millions of years yet – and when I am born, it won't be on this world! We're from the future, Exior, far in the future.'

The wizard was astounded. 'It's true I was less than one hundred per cent sure of the rune,' he gasped. 'But to have got it totally reversed is ... are you saying I've called up *future* dead? Not my ancestors but my descendants? *Hah!* So these lamias and succubi had their uses after all!'

'Ah, that's the other let-down, I'm afraid – ' said de

Marigny, ' – depending on your point of view, of course. We're not dead, Exior, and we're not your descendants. I'm Henri-Laurent de Marigny, called The Searcher, and this is Moreen of Numinos.'

Exior peered at him (very closely, de Marigny thought), then at Moreen. And finally, slowly the wizard shook his head. 'No,' he said, ' – oh, I grant you all else you've said – but not the matter of your lineage. Man, look at you – then look at me. And you tell me I am not your ancestor? In this I am surely not mistaken; apart from our ages, we are like as petals of the same flower, or eyeteeth of the same dog! At least I *cannot* be mistaken when I name you for a magician. In this, and in the matter of your calling, I am surely correct; indeed, for you came in answer to my summons, my rune. Alas, I was in haste with the thing; instead of getting someone out of the past, I got you out of the future.'

Moreen was both embarrassed and sorry for him. 'No, Exior,' she said, softly. 'We aren't here to answer your call or spell or rune. We were looking for you anyway.'

'And through you,' de Marigny added, 'hopefully, we may yet find Elysia.'

'Too much, too much!' Exior cried. He threw up his hands, collapsed again in his cane chair, let his arms and his head flop. 'I have been under great stress,' he mumbled. 'The filth closing in ... and no escape, no refuge ... You come from the future, you say? And what good is that to me? I have no future ...' But then he looked up, narrowed his eyes. 'Unless – '

'Why don't we trade?' de Marigny suggested. 'I can take you out of this, wherever you want to go. In return, perhaps you can tell me about Elysia. I have to find Elysia.'

Exior seemed to ignore him. Eyes gleaming, filled with a strange excitement, he leaped up. 'From the future! But how *far* in the future?'

'Millions of years,' said Moreen, backing away.

'Eons,' said de Marigny.

'Yes, yes – you said that before!' Exior danced feverishly. 'But I scarce heard you – I'm under such pressure, you see? Millions of years, you said, eons. And I scanned mere thousands! I have searched for a future for myself, to no avail. And yet in my dreams, which are oneiromantic, I have *seen* a future: in distant Lith, where I dwelled with Ardatha Ell in his manse, floating on a lake of lava.'

De Marigny's turn to be excited. Goose-flesh crept on his back, set the small hairs erect on the nape of his neck. Curator had mentioned this same Ardatha Ell, these same lava lakes of Lith – and then had gone on to remark how he'd said too much! And the name itself, 'Ardatha Ell', was an echo from something Titus Crow had once told him of Elysia: that he'd met a white wizard there from doomed Pu-Tha – Ardatha Ell, of course! One and the same! So if any man might know where Elysia could be found, surely that man *must* be Ardatha Ell.

'I could take you there,' he told Exior, 'if I knew the way. To Ardatha Ell's house – or manse – in Lith.'

Exior wasn't listening, or barely. Instead he stood before his shewstone, making weird, rapid passes with his hands while the crystal ball as quickly flickered from scene to scene. 'Millions of years,' he muttered to himself. 'Many millions of years. Very well, now I cast my net wide as I can, and – '

Moreen and de Marigny moved to flank him where he stood before the crystal on its pedestal.

' – There!' said Exior K'mool.

In the shewstone, two men sat at an ornate table before a curving window of some glass-like material. Beyond the window, distorted by its propeties, yellow and crimson flames leaped like a scene from hell; but the men at the table showed no discomfort, carried on with their game.

643

De Marigny saw that it was chess. One of them was clearly Exior K'mool himself, unchanged, the same man as stood here now. The other was tall, incredibly so. Eight feet, de Marigny reckoned him, standing; slender as a reed in his robes of fiery mesh-of-bronze; zombie-like in aspect, this man – if he *was* a man! For his hands each had six digits, with thumbs inside and out, and his features were sharp as blades. He could be none other than Ardatha Ell; little wonder Titus Crow had recalled him so vividly.

'There!' said Exior again. 'See?' And at that precise moment there sounded a low rumble – like a wall collapsing!

Moreen looked up anxiously, hurried out onto a balcony, came back pale and breathless. 'The slime has forced an entry. It's pouring in through a breach in the wall!'

'Exior,' said de Marigny sharply, 'where is this Lith?'

'Watch!' the wizard answered. He made more passes in the air, his practiced fingers building skeins impossible to follow. The picture in the shewstone blurred; the scene switched to outside; de Marigny seemed to look down on the manse where it floated on a turgid, red and black, fire-streaked lake of lava.

The place was like two disproportionate hemispheres, with the small one on top like the dome of some observatory. A central pole or axis looked as if it went right through the structure, forming a single antenna on top and (de Marigny supposed) a sort of keel below, giving the manse its lava-worthiness. There would be a heavy blob of material at the sunken end, keeping the place from capsizing.

'Fine,' he said. 'Now I know what Ardatha Ell's manse looks like, but I still don't know where it is. Can you back off some more? If that's a planet I need to know where in space I can find it.' He stepped to the time-clock, leaned head and shoulders inside, made mental adjustments. 'There,' he said, returning to the display, 'now the clock will record this, trace the co-ordinates. But not until we can see that entire world against a background of stars. After that it should be a simple – '

The palace trembled violently, causing the three to stumble. For a moment the scene in the shewstone convulsed, then steadied, as Exior regained control. More yet the picture retracted: it showed not a lake but a veritable sea of lava now, where the floating manse was the merest speck of white in a crusted cauldron of slowly, oh so slowly congealing rock.

Moreen rushed to the head of the stairs, cried: 'Oh, no! The stuff's in the palace – it's coming up the stairs!'

'Moreen, get in the clock!' de Marigny yelled. And to the wizard: 'More yet, Exior – let's see this Lith from space.'

The scene in the crystal drew away; the lava sea became an angry sore on a mighty black disk that floated free in the velvet void; stars showed beyond its rim. 'There,' said Exior K'mool. 'There – a dying sun!'

'More yet,' de Marigny repeated, his voice hoarse.

Something gurgled at the head of the stairs and the tower rocked again. Moreen gave a little shriek, ran to the time-clock, entered into the purple glow beyond its door. Exior sweated, struggled, his eyes stood out in his head. His passes were weird and wonderful: his hands described figures at least as complicated as those of the hands of the clock. De Marigny was struck with the similarity. Magic, or a primal science?

Living slime came slopping through cowrie curtains!

And at that precise moment the scene in the shewstone retreated suddenly and violently. Lith jerked away from the viewers, grew tiny against the vast backdrop of space, became a smouldering smudge of light in a great wheel of stars whose brilliance quickly drowned it. And –

'Andromeda!' de Marigny gasped. And without pause: 'Exior, that's all we needed. Quick, into the clock!'

The tower was sinking down into its own foundations, melting like a sandcastle. Its master stumbled, staggered; the scene in the crystal ball blinked out. 'All done, all gone,' moaned Exior. 'The end of all this. My runebooks, instruments, shewstone – '

The slime was on the move. De Marigny grabbed the wizard, half-pushed, half-dragged him toward the clock. The slime rose up in a stinking great flap of filth like a wave, and –

A pencil-slim beam of purest light lanced out from the time-clock, played on the slime – *and halted its progress not at all!*

De Marigny jammed Exior in through the purple-pulsing door, quickly followed him inside. 'Moreen,' he croaked, 'the weapon isn't working! Here, let me try.'

'Not working?' said Exior. 'A weapon? Of course it's not. Hurtful mechanical magics are forbidden in my palace. So I spelled it when Black Yoppaloth of the Yhemnis sent a squad of onyx automatons against me. They had quicksilver blood and glass scythes for arms, and – '

De Marigny frantically commanded the clock forward in time – and it stood stock still! 'But this is only hurtful to us!' he yelled. 'Now the time-clock is stuck!'

'My protective runes at work!' cried Exior. 'A rune against abduction, which – '

'Man, your runes are going to *kill* us!' de Marigny grated through clenched teeth.

The slime slopped across the mosaic floor, reared before the clock.

'We entered,' shrilled Moreen, clutching at both men, 'and so should be able to leave.'

Exior shook himself free of her hand. 'You entered because I called you,' he insisted. 'Such a fuss! – *there!*' and he made a simple downward-sweeping pass.

The slime hurled tentacles to encircle the clock – but too late by a single instant of time. Side-stepping through space-time, the clock disappeared, re-appeared a mile high over the crumbling, slime-reduced pile which was once Exior's palace. Tapering tentacles of filth lashed skyward after the clock failed, fell seething back to earth ...

2

Ardatha Ell's Vigil

De Marigny sighed, allowed himself to slump for a moment. 'That's the closest I ever want to come,' he said. 'That Cthulhu mind-stuff – Nyarlathotep, sentient slime, call it what you will – could have entered the clock as easily as the Hounds of Tindalos themselves. But now,' he straightened up, ' – now let's get out of here.'

'Wait!' something clacked harshly where it scuttled about their feet. 'And what of me?'

De Marigny saw the thing, gave a violent start. 'What in the name of all the hells – ?'

'This is Loxzor,' said Moreen. 'He got in while you and Exior were busy.' She looked reproachfully at the wizard. 'And Loxzor's not quite what he seems to be, either. Like Exior, he's something of a linguist – yes, and he's been telling me a few things.'

Exior hastily offered his version, and added: 'But since he's here anyway ... I suppose we could always take him back to his steppes? If you feel inclined.'

De Marigny flew the time-clock south-west at Exior's direction, brought it to rest on a hill crested with a bleak stone shell. 'My castle,' clacked Loxzor, 'fallen into ruins through these fifteen years of hybridism.' He scuttled out of the door as soon as de Marigny opened it for him, crying: 'Ruined, aye, all ruined – thanks to Exior K'mool!'

'No,' Exior shook his head, 'thanks to your own dark inclinations, Loxzor. However, since I'll no more be here to suffer you as a neighbour, I'll now unspell you.' He pointed a bony finger, uttered a word. It had a strange sound, that word, impossible to remember or repeat, except for Exior. Green lightning lashed from his finger, set the hideous roach-man leaping and shrieking where it covered him in a mesh of emerald fire. There came a puff of smoke, and when it cleared –

Loxzor of the Hrossaks stood there, a whole man again. A pallid, yellowy bronze in his dark cloak and cowl, he stood hunched, scowling. At his feet a cockroach scurried. He spied it, said '*Hah*!' – crushed it with his naked foot.

'And there stands Loxzor,' said Exior in disgust. 'He shared that poor creature's body many a year, and now pulps the life out of it without a moment's thought. Well, farewell, Hrossak mage – but one last piece of advice. 'Ware wizards whose powers are greater than your own, eh, Loxzor?'

Loxzor stared stonily, eyes yellow and unforgiving. The three turned away from him, entered the clock. As the door closed on them, Moreen queried: 'But what's he doing now?'

Exior, during their brief flight to Hrossa, had explored something of the clock's workings; his wizard's mind had quickly discovered the use of most of its 'accessories'. On entering the clock this second time, he had followed Moreen's lead in tuning himself to the scanners. De Marigny, taking the actual controls (as it were), was startled yet again when Exior answered Moreen's query with a cry of warning:

'Hurry, Searcher!' hissed the wizard. 'That's a "follow-him" spell he's weaving! See, he makes his wicked passes, points in the direction of my late palace in Humquass – and now he points directly at us!'

De Marigny saw – saw, too, the thin trail of noxious yellow vapour, like the trail of a meteorite, on the horizon, speeding toward them – and gave the clock its instructions. Wisps of slime, made aerial and lightning-swift by Loxzor's spell, arced down toward the clock ... but the clock was no longer there.

'I think,' said de Marigny with feeling, piloting the clock into the future, 'that if that was Theem'hdra, then I've had all I want of it!'

'What of Loxzor?' asked Moreen.

'Eh?' said Exior. 'But surely you heard me warn him, child? Never a mind so contrary, so warped, as Loxzor's. And never a man so doomed.'

'Oh?' said de Marigny.

Exior nodded. 'The mind-slime has lost us, but Loxzor's spell calls for a victim. Such black magic as he used carried its own retribution. The slime now follows him . . .'

'And no escape?' Moreen was full of pity.

'None,' Exior shook his head. 'It will follow him to the end and take him, just as it would have taken me but for your intervention.'

There was a long silence, then Moreen said: 'I sensed him as a cruel creature, but still he was a man. It seems a monstrous way for a man to die.'

To put the matter in its correct perspective, and also to clear the air, de Marigny said, 'As Exior points out, Loxzor brought it on himself. The best thing to do is forget him. After all, he's already a million years dead.'

And that was that . . .

'How did you get in that mess?' de Marigny asked Exior when they were well underway.

'It's a long story,' said Exior.

'Tell me anyway.'

Exior shrugged. 'As a boy,' he began, 'I was apprenticed under Phaithor Ull. In his dotage, Phaithor sought immortality – we all do – and made himself the subject of several thaumaturgies. One morning when I went to wake him, he was a heaping of green dust on his bed, all spread out in the shape of a man. His rings were in the 'hand' formed of the dust, as was his wand. It, too, fell into dust the moment I took it up.

'Later I served Mylakhrion, however briefly. To test my worthiness, he sent me on a quest. I was to find and return to him a long-lost runebook. I succeeded – barely! My reward: Mylakhrion gave me his palace, made me mage to Morgath the then King of Humquass. And off *he* went to seek immortality! Strange how men want to live forever, eh?'

De Marigny smiled, however wryly, and nodded. 'Some men seek to slow time down, yes,' he said. 'Others speed it up!'

'Eh? Oh, yes! Your time-clock, of course. Very droll! But to continue:

'Eventually I, too, began to feel the weight of my years. Humquass was forsaken, except for me. The city fell into decay. Years went fleeting. Naturally – and unnaturally – I too sought immortality. I went to Tharamoon hoping to find Mylakhrion. His potions and ointments and fountain of vitality had held the years back a little, but not entirely. Perhaps by now he'd discovered the secret, maybe he'd even share it with me. So I thought. But in Tharamoon, when I found Mylakhrion's tower, it too was a ruin. Mylakhrion's bones lay broken at its base.

'I searched the place top to bottom, brought back with me all I could of his paraphernalia: books and cyphers, powders, elixirs, unguents and the likes. And I read Mylakhrion's works most carefully. His diary, too ...

'He had fallen foul of Cthulhu, who sleeps and dreams and makes men mad. Do you know of Cthulhu?'

'Too much!' de Marigny frowned.

'To know his name is too much!' said Exior. 'Mylakhrion had promised to do Cthulhu's bidding in return for immortality. But when that most monstrous of the Great Old Ones ordered that which might free the prisoned demons of his evil order ... Mylakhrion refused! For which Cthulhu killed him. Mylakhrion had broken the pact – Cthulhu broke Mylakhrion.'

De Marigny nodded. 'That's a familiar pattern,' he said. 'And you fell for it too, eh?'

Exior hung his head. 'Indeed. Foolish old Exior K'mool, who thought himself mightier than Mylakhrion. I made the same pact, for I was sure I could defend myself against Cthulhu's wrath. As you have seen, there was no defence – except this. Flight into the future.'

Something bothered de Marigny. 'But you had made a form of agreement, a contract with Cthulhu. And did you get your immortality? It seems unlikely, for if we hadn't come along in the time-clock you'd be dead. If you can die you're hardly immortal.'

Exior looked up and slowly smiled. A wondering smile, very peculiar. 'But I am not dead,' he pointed out. There was something about his voice . . .

De Marigny said: 'Tell me, just exactly what did Cthulhu tell you about immortality? How were you to make yourself immortal?'

Exior shrugged. 'All a trick!' he snorted. 'The only way I could become immortal was in my children's children. Which is the same for all men, for all creatures, even for the simple flowers of the field. A blade of wheat grows, sheds its seed, dies – and is reborn from its seed. And a man? This was the immortality for which Cthulhu drove so hard a bargain. A man's natural right!'

Moreen had overheard all. 'Then perhaps you've succeeded after all,' she said. 'Or if not immortality, something close to it.'

They looked at her. 'He's right, you know,' she said to de Marigny. 'About how you both look alike. Like two petals of the same flower . . .'

'Ridiculous!' said de Marigny. 'There are eons between us.'

She smiled. 'Then that really would be immortality, wouldn't it?'

De Marigny shook his head, said: 'But – '

' – We *think* we went back into time of our own accord,' she cut him off, determined to make her point, 'but what if he really *did* call us back – to save him? Perhaps Cthulhu didn't cheat him after all, the secret did lie in his children's children. He was saved, made "immortal", by his own descendent – by you, Henri.'

'Her reasoning is sound,' said Exior. 'And with luck, I shall yet make myself truly immortal. You seek Elysia, correct? Yes, and so do I – now! Why, Elysia *is* immortality!'

'That's playing with words,' de Marigny protested – but he remembered that Titus Crow had told him to look in his past. Not *the* past but *his* past. And wasn't there something else Crow had said to him long ago: about a spark in de Marigny carried down all the ages, which would flare up again one day in Elysia?

'We can put the girl's theory to the test,' Exior cut in on his thoughts. 'Wizards often run in unbroken lines of descent. You are a wizard, even though you deny it. Oh, you haven't discovered your full potential yet, but it's there. The proof is this: your father would have been another.'

'My father?' de Marigny almost laughed out loud. 'My father was a 20th Century jazz buff who lived in New Orleans! He – ' But here the smile died on The Searcher's lips and his jaw dropped. For Etienne-Laurent de Marigny had also been New Orleans' premier mystic and occultist – and even now he was a prominent figure in the land of Earth's dreams. In short, a magician. In his lifetime and after it. A wizard!

Wide-eyed, de Marigny gazed at Exior K'mool.

And Exior gazed at him.

And the time-clock sped into the future . . .

'Time travel takes time.' De Marigny grinned and did it again: 'An amazingly accurate alliteration.'

'What's that?' Moreen had been half asleep.

'Nothing,' said de Marigny. 'Sorry I woke you. I was just thinking out loud. About time travel. It takes time.'

Exior approached, his face animated, excited in the clock's soft purple glow. 'Yes, it does,' he agreed, 'if you only use this wonderful device as a conveyance. And of course you must, for the time-clock is vital to you. It has to go where you go.'

'Just what are you getting at?' de Marigny raised an eyebrow. 'And you really shouldn't go wandering about in here on your own. The clock's a death-trap for the unwary. You could end up almost anywhen.'

'Precisely my point. You use it as a conveyance, but it could be used as a gateway!'

De Marigny nodded. 'We know that. Titus Crow has used it that way. As for myself: I don't know how to. I've never had to or even wanted to. In any case, if I did use the clock that way, what if I couldn't find my way back again?'

'Exactly!' Exior answered. 'You depend upon the clock – but I don't. The only place *I* want to be is Ardatha Ell's manse in Lith. And right now I'm wasting time getting there.'

'What?' de Marigny had suddenly realized what Exior was saying. 'Exior, you're out of your mind! I've piloted this ship for more than six years now, and I still don't know half of all there is to know about it. And you're telling me that after a few short hours of travel in the clock you plan to use it as a gateway?'

'Henri,' said Exior patiently, 'I unriddle runes, languages, systems. My mind is built that way. Yours, too, but undeveloped as yet. The time-clock's systems are intricate, yes, but not unfathomable. Your friend Titus Crow has done it, and I'm going to do it too – now.'

'Now?' Moreen gasped.

'I only came back to say goodbye – for now. For of course, I'll see you both again in the lava-floating manse on Lith.'

'But ... right now?' de Marigny still couldn't accept it. 'I mean – how?'

Exior smiled, meshed his mind deeper with the clock, deeper than de Marigny had ever dared to go. 'Like this,' he said. His form wavered, broke down into bright points of light, blinked out.

And de Marigny and Moreen stood alone ...

Exior and Ardatha Ell met over the lava lakes. Below, no manse was anywhere visible. Exior, now an extension of the time-clock, slowed himself down, cruised into the future rather than rocketed. His speed was now only a little faster than true time itself. 'No manse,' he said to the other, deeming introductions unnecessary.

'Indeed,' said Ardatha. 'I had assumed it was your place.'

'And I thought it was yours!'

'No matter, we'll build one.' Ardatha used cohesive magic to draw together a great mass of heat-resistant matter, which formed like a scab on the bubbling lake below. Exior pictured the manse as he had seen it in his shewstone, formed it in two hemispheres, welded them together. The work took moments, but it drained both of them.

'Let's get inside,' said Exior, breaking his connection with the clock and slowing all the way down to normal time. And within the lava-floating manse, after briefly resting, they each constructed rooms to their own tastes. Later still:

'It seems we've known each other for some time,' said Exior, where they sat sipping conjured essence in a room with tinted portals.

'Because we knew it would be, it feels like it has always been,' replied Ardatha Ell. 'In fact, when I explored a little of Lith's future, from Elysia, I was surprised to find your manse – er, this place – floating here. I had intended to come anyway, you see, as an agent for Kthanid. It seems that Lith, in some manner yet unknown to me, will soon become vastly important.'

'Oh? Could that be, I wonder, because the son of my most remote sons, Henri-Laurent de Marigny, called The Searcher, and Moreen are even now en-route here?'

'Ah!' Ardatha was pleased. 'So they've fathomed all clues, overcome all obstacles, have they? Kthanid foresaw it, of course – or at least, that was one of the futures he foresaw. But so many possible futures! Kthanid is incredible! Such computations! Such permutations! But he chose the best future he could, then set about to make it work out that way.'

This conveyed a great deal to Exior's wizard's mind. He drew much more from Ardatha's words than any ordinary man might ever comprehend. 'In my shewstone,' he said after a while, 'I saw that we played a game. It was strange to me. Obviously it had not been invented in my time, though it reminded me of trothy, which is also played on a board.'

'That must have been chess,' Ardatha beamed. 'A favourite of mine!' He conjured a board and pieces. 'Here, let me explain the rules ...'

They played, and at the same time and for long hours amused themselves with certain matters of cryptical conjecture – hypothetical problems of interest only to magicians – and yet still found time and space to carry on a more nearly normal conversation:

'Your purpose in coming here?' Ardatha eventually asked. 'Apart from carrying out a temporal necessity, of course. That is to say, having seen yourself here – and while obviously you obeyed the omen and came here – was that the only reason?' Wizards seldom have only one motive for their actions.

'I seek immortality,' Exior explained. 'I have done so for years. When de Marigny mentioned his goal, Elysia, I saw the answer at once. For as I said to him: Elysia *is*

656

immortality! And so, since this manse, Lith, and you yourself formed a focal point, a way-station along de Marigny's route ...'

'Hmm!' Ardatha mused. 'And how will you complete the final stage? From here to Elysia, I mean, when the time comes?'

'In the time-clock, with The Searcher and his woman. Won't you join us? Since you already have a place in Elysia, and Lith being such a boring place and all ...'

'I think not,' answered Ardatha Ell. 'You see, I don't know how long I may be called upon to stay here – or even *why* I'm here – except that it was Kthanid's wish that I should come. Also, I rode a Great Thought to this place. My shell – my flesh-and-blood body, that is – is still in Elysia. And so when I return it shall be a simple matter of instantaneous transfer. However, I thank you for your – ' He paused abruptly, came stiffly erect in his chair.

'Is there something?' Exior enquired.

Ardatha unfolded his tall, spindly frame, stood up. 'A messenger enters my sky-sphere in Elysia,' he said, his eyes far away. 'I had expected some such. A message from Kthanid. Come, you shall see.'

He quickly loped to his room and Exior followed on behind. There they seated themselves before Ardatha's shewstone, in which a picture had already formed. A Dchi-chi stood at the threshold of Ardatha Ell's inner sanctum in his sky-floating sphere high over Elysia. Ardatha himself – or his body – lay suspended on a gravitic bed of air in the centre of the room. All was silent until the Elysian wizard's Lith facet made a six-fingered pass, and then the scene came alive with conversation:

'I beg to differ,' came a voice from some mechanical source, but clearly Ardatha's voice, or a good imitation. 'The lesser part, surely? For his recumbent shell here is only the flesh of Ardatha Ell. The mind – which is greater by far, which is more truly *me* – that is in Exior K'mool's manse in Andromeda.' And so the conversation continued, as we have previously seen, while in Lith Exior and Ardatha looked on. Until finally the Dchi-chi passed his message.

In Lith Ardatha absorbed that message, reeled for a moment, then frowned mightily. And from the shewstone he heard himself say: 'There, all done. Aye, and this is an important task Kthanid has set me. You should have said so before now, little bird, instead of posing and parroting.'

There followed the matter of the Dchi-chi's exit from Ardatha's sphere – his hasty, somewhat fearful exit – after which, chuckling good-naturedly, the wizards in Lith returned to their game of chess.

And in a little while: 'What was Kthanid's message?' Exior asked.

'It contained the reason for my being here,' Ardatha answered. 'Which is this: that I keep a vigil.' He won the game in three moves, produced a wand which elongated into a rod six feet long, stuck its ferrule in the floor and bent his ear to the silver handle. He seemed to listen to something for a moment, straightened up, smiled grimly. 'A vigil, aye,' he repeated.

And then he explained in greater detail ...

In Elysia all was ready, all preparations made. Kthanid – *only* Kthanid – had retained a measure of surveillance on the outside multiverse, and now even he was 'blind' to occurrences beyond Elysia's boundaries. Nothing physical or mental departed from or entered into Elysia. No Great Thoughts went out, no travellers returned; no telepathic transmissions were sent or received; no time-clocks plied the limitless oceans of time and space. Elysia lay silent, hidden, secret, more mythical than ever before ...

And yet, because Kthanid himself was of the flesh and the mind of the Great Old Ones, he was not entirely closed off, not totally insulated from their activity. In his own incredible dreams he heard echoes from outside. The massed mind of the Great Old Ones – their use of telepathy, their 'Great Messenger', Nyarlathotep, which carried their thoughts between them in their various prison environs – would occasionally impinge upon Kthanid's mind; and then, in snatches however brief, he would learn what they were about.

When de Marigny and Moreen had left Borea in the time-clock – and when Ithaqua had tormented certain minds to extract information from them, which was then passed on to the rest of the Great Old Ones, particularly Cthulhu – Kthanid had known it. He had known, too, of the loss of countless Tind'losi Hounds in a black hole, and of the saving of Sssss. From Earth's dreamlands, echoes had reached him of damage inflicted on Cthulhu's plans to further his infiltration of Man's subconscious mind, and one shriek of mental fury and frustration had signalled a strike against Nyarlathotep 'himself'.

Most of which had been anticipated ...

And between times:

In the Vale of Dreams the gigantic N'hlathi had emerged from their immemorial burrows to graze on the seeds of great poppies, and even now a team of Dchi-chis attempted communication with them. Even more ominous, the N'hlathi were seen to be harvesting poppy seed, storing the great green beads in their burrows. And those burrows themselves were now seen for what they really were; for when the seals on the N'hlathi doors had sprung and the doors had opened, then those massive cylinders – the 'burrows' themselves – had slowly unscrewed from the basalt cliffs. More than mere hibernation cells, those cylinders: thirty feet in diameter and sixty feet long, of a white metal unknown even to Elysia's science, they had commenced to give off certain hyper-radiations – the self-same energies which powered Elysia's time-clocks! The burrows of the N'hlathi *were* time-clocks – which they now provisioned as for flight!

As for the pattern those doors had duplicated, the great whorl of Andromeda and the emergence of certain stars of ill-omen there:

Now indeed those stars were very nearly right; in fact, only one more was needed to complete the pattern. Its location was well known to Kthanid, its condition, too. For this was a dying star, but a star with a difference. It was the second of twins, the first of which had already self-destructed, and it harboured in its core the seed of universal chaos.

The name of this star?

It was Lith, of course. Lith, where even now Ardatha Ell kept vigil, monitoring the fatal foetal pulse of that which might well signal a new beginning – or a monstrous end . . .

3

The Stars are Right!

When de Marigny slipped the time-clock sideways in space-time and entered their manse in Lith, Exior K'mool and Ardatha Ell were waiting for him. Nor did they fail to note the wisps of greenish mist, materializing into a thin, vapid slime that clung in a sticky layer to the windows of the upper dome, which he brought with him out of the past. The manse was rune-protected, however, and constructed of near-impervious materials, so that they were mainly unconcerned. But Exior sniffed and commented:

'So Loxzor's follow-me spell was effective after all, at least in part. A little of Cthulhu's mind-slime managed to follow the time-clock, and so has found me again. Much weakened now, I note. Why, I could banish it with a simple "get-thee-gone".'

'Let it be,' said Ardatha Ell. 'It changes nothing – indeed, we may even benefit ...'

De Marigny and Moreen emerged cautiously from the clock, found the wizards waiting. The final stages of their trip had not been uneventful: Tind'losi Hounds had chased them for seven million years, ignoring the time-clock's weapon in a manner de Marigny had never seen before, in a suicidal way that had puzzled and worried and wearied him. They had lost countless thousands tracking him, and had only given up the chase when he reverted to three-dimensioned space over Lith.

But now the time-travellers squared up, nodded their tired acknowledgment to Exior, gazed up in awe at Ardatha Ell.

'Crow's friend,' that towering, slender, powerful person nodded, returning de Marigny's gaze; but though he spoke

661

to them, Moreen and her Earthman noted that his lips moved never a fraction. 'De Marigny The Searcher – and Moreen, whose innocence and beauty shall surely whelm all Elysia. Eventually . . . ' And still his lips hadn't moved.

Moreen blushed and smiled at his compliment, but de Marigny frowned. 'Eventually?' he repeated the wizard's word. 'Soon, we had hoped.'

Ardatha inclined his sharp-featured head. 'Well, it's true that the futures are narrowing down,' he said, 'but until a thing is we can never be entirely certain that it will be. Only the past is fixed, and even that is not entirely immutable.'

'*Ahem!*' said Exior. 'Best remember, Ardatha, that their ways with words are not our ways. Their thoughts run straighter courses than ours.'

He was right in more ways than one; by now de Marigny's thoughts were more than ever one-tracked. 'Ardatha,' he pressed, 'you know why we're here. You yourself hail from Elysia. If anyone can help us get there – '

' – Wait!' said Ardatha, holding up a six-fingered hand. 'Waste no more words, Searcher, the matter is out of my hands – and out of yours – now. Now we can only wait.'

'Wait?' de Marigny cast a puzzled glance at Moreen, who was equally mystified. 'Wait here, on Lith? But wait for what?'

'For whatever will be,' the wizard answered. Bending his ear to his silver-handled sensor, he listened patiently for a moment or two to the strengthening pulse in Lith's core. 'Aye, for what will surely be,' he repeated. 'One thing I *can* tell you, Searcher,' and he straightened up. 'It won't be a long wait. No, not long at all.' And more than that he would not, must not, say . . .

De Marigny slept and dreamed.

In weed-festooned, submarine R'lyeh, Cthulhu's groping

face-tentacles reached for and almost found him before he fled screaming into time. Bat-winged, like flapping black rags of evil, the Hounds of Tindalos awaited him there, came winging out from the corkscrew towers of Tindalos itself at de Marigny's approach. To escape them he transferred from time to space, found himself on the shore of a vilely lapping lake somewhere in the Hyades. Turning his gaze from the waters of that lake to the sky, he saw the black stars burning and knew at once where he was. Along the shoreline, coming his way, a Thing in yellow flopped, and in the waters something monstrous floundered! De Marigny wrenched himself free of the place, where even now the Lake of Hali's waters broke in a lashing of loathsome tentacles. Hastur wallowed in The Searcher's wake ... And now de Marigny wandered in unknown space and time, lost and alone in some weird parallel dimension. But alone for a moment only. For now, surging out of nameless vacuum, came a frothing, liquescent, blasphemous shapelessness that masked its true horror behind a congeries of iridescent globes and bubbles – the primal jelly seething forever 'beyond the nethermost angles' – Yog-Sothoth, the Lurker at the Threshold!

De Marigny screamed again as the thing covered him, folding him into its mass –

– And found himself like a child in Moreen's arms, awake, hugged safe to her bosom.

'Henri! Henri!' she rocked him. 'What was it? A dream?'

He shuddered, sat up on his bed in the room Ardatha and Exior had made for them. 'A ... a dream? A nightmare!' He hugged her, forced himself to stop trembling. 'Just a nightmare. Yes, that's all it was ...' But in his mind he could still hear the thin chittering of the Hounds, the black gurgling of Hali, and frothing and seething of Yog-Sothoth, and the – laughter? – of Cthulhu in his watery sepulchre; all of these sounds, withdrawing now as he came more fully awake.

'I came to wake you,' Moreen said, 'and found you

shouting and tossing. Henri, Ardatha wants you. He says it's nearly time.'

De Marigny got up at once, followed her a little unsteadily into the communal room. Ardatha Ell was there, his ear pressed to the silver handle of his elongated wand. Exior was also present, but he stood much closer to the time-clock. Both magicians were plainly excited, agitated.

'Ardatha,' de Marigny began, 'Moreen tells me that you –'

'Yes, yes,' said the wizard, cutting him short. And: 'Sit, please sit, both of you. Now, I have a tale to tell – which in itself contains something of an explanation, if you can unriddle it – but just so much time in which to tell it. The stars are coming right, de Marigny – do you know what that means?'

De Marigny drew a sharp breath, let it out more slowly. 'Yes,' he said, 'only too well.'

'They are coming right ... now,' Ardatha nodded, 'at any moment. We shall have –' he snapped his fingers, ' – *that* much warning!'

De Marigny looked blank, shook his head. 'I –'

'This star, Lith itself, is the final one in the pattern,' Ardatha said. 'And Lith is about to nova, perhaps supernova!' Even as he spoke the manse rocked, and beyond the tinted windows geysers of molten rock vented fire and steam at a madly boiling sky of smoke and bilious gases. As the floor tilted back to a level keel, de Marigny jumped to his feet, grasped Moreen's hand and headed for the clock.

'Wait!' cried Ardatha Ell, his mouth a thin, hard and immobile slit in his face. 'You may *not* run from this, Searcher – not if you want to enter Elysia!'

De Marigny paused, turned and stared hard at the tall magician. 'I don't run for my own sake, Ardatha Ell. You'd better get that fact fixed firmly in your head. And you'd better talk fast too, while I'm still here to hear you. I don't know about you and Exior, but if this dead sun is about to explode, Moreen and I – '

'It is the *way* to Elysia!' again Ardatha cut him off.

De Marigny opened the clock's door and purple light streamed out.

'Go on then, flee!' Ardatha Ell shouted from a closed mouth. 'Time yet for you to get away, Searcher. Run – and lose everything!'

'Hear him out,' croaked Exior K'mool. 'At least hear him out, son of my sons. You cannot imagine how much depends upon it.'

De Marigny held Moreen close. The interior of the clock was but a step away. 'Go on then,' he said. 'We're listening.'

Ardatha sighed, put his ear back to the sensor for a moment, again straightened up. The manse rocked again, but less violently. Ardatha waited for the disturbance to cease before beginning. Then –

'Once long ago, where now the Milky Way sprawls its myriad stars against the sky, there was nothing. And there, to that vacuous region, came Azathoth.

'Born in billions of tons of cosmic dust, in matter forged by gravity, in the slow seepage of massively heavy metals toward a universal centre, he *was* a Nuclear Chaos. And the report of his coming went out to the farthest stars, so that even now its echoes have not died away! But while Azathoth was of Nature, a true power without sentience, still he spawned others which *had* sentience: he was not only, in a sense, the Father of all "life" as we know it, but also of certain thermal, rather thermo-nuclear beings.' Ardatha paused, shrugged, continued:

'I will not go into nuclear genealogy here; your scientists will one day fathom it in their own way, define it in their own terms – if they tread warily. But just as there may be intelligence in air, and in water, in earth and even in space, so may there be intelligence in fire. Alas, but nuclear fire transmutes all things: metal into liquid or gas or other metals, life into death, time into space and vice versa. Its massive release warps space-time itself. Yes, and it transmuted the thermal beings, too. They themselves were changed by their own chaos of energy. Sanity into madness! They became as mad and ungovernable as the unthinking Father who spawned them. Mercifully their insanity is self-destructive: they are born mad, and on the instant annihilate themselves – and, unfortunately, all who stand near. Which is the reason why even the Beings of the Cthulhu Cycle fear them . . .

'So, what shall we call such creatures, who, when they are "summoned" or born, can turn worlds to cinders and rekindle dying suns to nuclear furnaces? In eons past they were named the Azathi – Children of Azathoth. Now, I have said that they die in the instant of their birth, which is self-evident. But if they can be kept – or keep themselves – in a prolonged or extended foetal condition, then their excess 'madness', their energy, may be drawn off and used. Unwittingly, men have been doing this since the construction of the first atomic pile; though of course theirs is only a synthetic form of the actual Azathoth life-force itself, without the sentience of the Azathi. But not only men have used – are using – this awesome power!

'Long ages past Cthulhu saw a use for such primal forces. He calculated the angles between the Nggr, the Hnng and the Nng, fathomed the warp-energy required to release him and his brethren and their allies from their prisons. Then he searched far and wide in time and space, seeking to learn that precise place and moment when the stars would be *almost* right, when with a little assistance the space-time matrix might be caused to warp sufficiently to break his bonds. And he saw that eventually, in Andromeda, just such an almost-perfect pattern would form itself. A vast equation, complete but for two missing qualities or quantities – forces which Cthulhu himself must insert into the equation. The Azathi, of course!

'Cthulhu knew that at least three of Azathoth's primal children had controlled or contained themselves. Oh, they were mad – but not so mad as to will themselves to annihilation. He searched the void for them, at last found two. We shall call them Azatha and Azathe, and they were all the Lord of R'lyeh required to put his eon-formed plan into being, to set ticking his unthinkable cosmic time-bomb! As for Azathu, the third of Azathoth's primal children: he could not be found, perhaps he had after all become unstable, detonated in some remote region.

'But Azatha and Azathe remained, out there in the deepest, darkest reaches, forging ever outward in abysses beyond man's wildest reckoning. And Cthulhu reached out after them – sent his Great Messenger, Nyarlathotep, to parley with them – and made a pact. It was this: that they return, locate themselves in the hearts of certain suns, remain dormant down all the eons and wait on his instructions. Then, at a time of his choosing, he would awaken them, let them be fulfilled, give them glory and life-everlasting, free them of their elemental madness! His reward? – the very multiverse would see how great are the works of Cthulhu, who causes stars to blaze up at his coming!

'Since then . . . the stars have wheeled in their inexorable courses, the pattern has formed, the time is nigh. A little while ago a star exploded, became a super-nova on Andromeda's far flank. That was Azatha. And in the heart of Lith, at this very moment . . .'

De Marigny, despite his urge to get away, had been fascinated by Ardatha Ell's story. Now he completed the wizard's tale: 'Azathe?'

Ardatha nodded. 'And the pattern will be complete. All chains broken, all "spells" unspelled. The Great Old Ones will be free.'

Moreen spoke up: 'But how can that possibly help us? We seek Elysia, from which place Henri hopes to fight the Great Old Ones, assist in their destruction.'

'Wait!' Ardatha commanded. He listened yet again to his wand and his eyes grew huge. 'Soon now!' he hissed. 'Very soon!'

'Exior,' said de Marigny, his voice tense, 'get in the clock. You, too, Moreen.'

Outside, beyond the windows, the lava lake had grown calm. It was an utterly unnatural calm, producing a leaden oppressiveness that came right through the walls of the manse to those within. The lava swirled slowly, sluggishly, red-veined under a crumbling crust of black rock and ash; the smoke- and gas-clouds churned low overhead; in the distance, lightning raced in weird patterns along the underside of the clouds, springing sporadically to strike the sullenly shuddering surface.

'Well,' said de Marigny, one foot on the clock's threshold. 'Is there an answer to Moreen's question? How *can* the death, or rebirth, of this star help us?'

Ardatha smiled, a strange cold smile. 'You have seen how Cthulhu is a great magician, a fabulous mathematician. Aye, but he is not the only one. The N'hlathi knew Cthulhu's purpose at once, and they fashioned a reminder and a warning in the Vale of Dreams in Elysia. Kthanid is of the very flesh of Cthulhu; when he knew what Cthulhu would do, he set about to maintain a balance. You ask "where is Elysia?" Elysia is where Kthanid and his elder-council desire it to be. When Lith evaporates, space-time will warp and thrust *in the direction* of Elysia, and your time-clock will be propelled through that warp, that fracture, *into* Elysia. Don't fight it, de Marigny. Don't try to fly out of it or avoid it. Do nothing! All has been calculated.'

De Marigny knew he must enter the clock, but there was still so much he didn't understand. 'But how do you know all of these things?' he asked. 'How can you be sure?'

Ardatha raised an eyebrow. 'And am I not a magician in my own right? Some of it I have fathomed, unriddled. And some I have had from Cthulhu himself. For have I not eavesdropped on his communications with Azathe? This was Kthanid's reason for sending me here, so that he might know the precise moment when – ' He paused, came instantly alert as never before.

Ardatha's wand began to tremble. The tremors rapidly spread themselves to the entire manse; it shuddered, rocked, was shaken as in the fist of some inconceivable colossus.

'Ardatha!' de Marigny cried out loud over the groaning and grinding of the manse. 'Quick, man – get in the clock!'

'I don't need your time-clock, Searcher,' said the wizard. 'But you do. You need it right now. Good luck, Henri!' He snatched up his wand – which at once retracted to its normal size – saluted the time-clock with a strange gesture, disappeared like a light switched off!

Moreen and Exior dragged de Marigny into the time-clock. And after that –

Lith was no more!

The time-clock was very nearly impervious to all forces and pressures. It had survived, even escaped from, the lure of black holes; it had breached all known temporal and spatial barriers; it had journeyed in weird intermediate, even subconscious dimensions. But even so, it had never before encountered *forces* like those which worked on it now. Ardatha Ell had warned de Marigny not to resist; now, even if he would resist, he could not. Time did not allow. The time-clock itself did not allow. Its controls no longer worked. It was a twig whirled along a gutter in a cloudburst, a canoe caught in the maelstrom.

Light and heat and radiation – even a little matter – exploded outward in such a holocaust of released ENERGY that the clock was simply carried along on its shock wave. For those within – because they were enclosed in an area which was timeless, and yet, paradoxically everywhere and when – it was acceleration without gravity, without the fatal increase in mass which Earthly physics would otherwise demand. But it was more than that. Space-time's fabric was wrenched by Azathe's rebirth and instant death; it was torn, finally ripped asunder. All dimensions of the continuum became one in a crazy mingling, became a new *state*. Barriers Man's science had not even guessed at went crashing, and crashing through the chaos of their collapse came the time-clock.

And it came –

– Into Elysia!

Elysia, yes, but no longer that magical place as described by Titus Crow. De Marigny saw this as soon as the whirling of his psyche settled and his mundane senses regained control. For this was Elysia with all of the magic removed.

Rain lashed the time-clock where it sped of its own accord high above a land grey and sodden. Black clouds scudded in boiling banks, turning the rays of a synthetic sun to the merest glimmer. The sky-islands and palaces floated on air as before, but no transports came and went, no iridescent dragons sped on bone and leather wings through the lowering skies. The aerial roadways of the cities carried no traffic; the streets below shone dully, empty of life; there did not appear to be *any* life in all Elysia.

But then the scanners told de Marigny how he erred, the scanners and Moreen and Exior's combined cry of warning. There *was* life here, behind him, even now bloating monstrous in the wake of the clock!

The blow fell on de Marigny like a crashing, crushing weight. He saw, and was shattered by the sight. For in one soul-destroying moment he saw exactly how, exactly why, the clock's scanners and sensors were now full of the sight and sound and presence of these things: *the massed hordes of the Cthulhu Cycle – including and led by Cthulhu himself!*

It was as simple as this: they had followed him through

670

the breach! He who had sought only to assist Elysia, had doomed her! Cthulhu was free, he was here, and The Searcher had *led* him here!

It was all so obvious, so very obvious. Everything de Marigny had done since Titus Crow rode his Great Thought to him in Borea might have been designed to draw Cthulhu's attention. Ithaqua the Wind-Walker had doubtless known de Marigny was seeking Elysia; Nyarlathotep, in both his primal and current forms, he too had known; the Hounds of Tindalos had known; and because all of them reported directly to Cthulhu, so too the Lord of R'lyeh. And where better to strike their first blow against universal sanity than Elysia? And how better to get there than by following de Marigny, whose place in Elysia was assured?

'I've betrayed you!' de Marigny cried then in his agony, through clenched teeth. 'All of you ... all Elysia!'

'Oh, Henri, Henri!' Moreen clung to him sobbing.

'*No!*' he put her gently aside. 'I came here to fight, and I can *still* fight!' With his mind he reached out for the time-clock's weapons.

'They won't work for you, Henri,' Exior K'mool shook his head. 'See, the clock has a mind of its own now. It flees before this hideous army. And they follow on, determined to hound us down, and whoever awaits us at the end of our journey.'

Exior was right: the clock's weapons would not fire, the space-time machine refused to respond to de Marigny's touch. And faster than its unimaginable pursuers – answering some unknown, unheard summons – it sped on across Elysia, across the once-Frozen Sea, where now the ice bucked and heaved and waterspouts gouted skyward, toward its goal, the Icelands, where dwelled Kthanid in the heart of Elysia's mightiest glacier. The Hall of Crystal and Pearl: de Marigny saw it again in his mind's eye as once he had seen it in a prophetic dream, that throneroom of

Kthanid, spokesman of the Elder Gods themselves. And how would that mighty beneficent Kraken greet him now, he wondered, whose ambition had brought ruin on all Elysia?

The time-clock dipped low and skimmed across ice-cliffs, plunged toward an entrance carved from the permafrost of a vast cavern. But even upon entering the complex of caves and corridors that led to Kthanid's sanctum sanctorum, the clock was slowing down, its scanners dimming, sensors blanking out. The controls were totally dead now, and darkness closing in fast.

'Henri?' In the deepening gloom, still Moreen clung to The Searcher.

'Elysia's finished,' de Marigny felt drained, his voice was cracked. 'Even the time-clocks are running down. This place must be their final refuge – the refuge of Elysia's peoples, I mean, and of their leaders. If Cthulhu can find them here he can find them anywhere, so why run any farther? This is the end of the line ...' Even as he spoke the clock came to a halt; its door swung open and its now feeble purple glow pulsed out; the three gazed upon the interior of the vast Hall of Crystal and Pearl.

Exior K'mool was first to step out. The clock had come to rest deep inside the enormous clamber, close to the curtained alcove where sat Kthanid's throne. The curtains were drawn now and the throne itself invisible, but still Exior felt the awesome atmosphere of the place, knew that he stood at a crossroads of destiny. The shimmering curtains went up, up and up, to the massively carved arch which formed the alcove's façade. And wizard that he was, master of wonders, still Exior went down on his knees before those curtains and bowed his head. 'The place of the Eminence!' he whispered.

De Marigny and Moreen followed him, flanked him, gazed with him as he lifted his head. And as at a signal the curtains swept open!

De Marigny might have expected several things revealed when the curtains swept aside. He might even have guessed correctly, if he'd guessed at all. But in fact it had happened too quickly; his mind had not yet adjusted to his whereabouts: the fact that, however disastrously, he finally stood in Elysia; and so the physical presence of what – of *who* he saw there at the head of the great steps behind the curtains, before the throne and beside the onyx table with its huge crimson cushion and shewstone big as a boulder, was simply staggering.

'*Henri!*' Titus Crow's face had been drawn, haggard – but it lit up like the sun at the sight of The Searcher. 'Henri – you made it – but of course I knew you would. You had to!'

'Titus!' de Marigny tried to say, except nothing came out. On his second attempt he managed a croak, but recognizable anyway. 'Titus . . .'

It shuddered out of him, that word, that name – and in it was contained all the agony of his soul. He swayed, might have fallen. Crow started forward, paused, spoke quickly, forcefully: 'Henri, I know how you feel. Like the greatest traitor who ever lived, like Judas himself. I know, because that's how I've been feeling. Forget it. You're no Judas. You're Elysia's greatest hero!'

'What?' de Marigny's brow furrowed; he knew he was hearing things.

'What?' Moreen was equally confused. 'A hero?'

But Exior K'mool only smiled.

'No time for long explanations, Henri, Moreen,' said Crow. 'You know what's followed you, who's on his way here – to the Hall of Crystal and Pearl – even now. Come up here, quickly! You too, Exior.'

They climbed the steps, de Marigny falteringly, assisted by Moreen and Exior. 'They say a picture's worth a thousand words,' said Crow. 'So look at this – for I've lots to say to you and no time to say it all.'

He touched the great crystal – and milky clouds at once parted.

They gazed upon Elysia. Upon an Elysia falling into ruins!

The drenched, leaden skies had been empty before, but now they were full of death. The Hounds of Tindalos were everywhere, chittering round and about the aerial palaces, the tall buildings, even the lower structures. They were like a cloud of lice around host beasts: the Beings at the head of that monstrous airborne procession. Cthulhu was there, no longer dreaming but awake, crimson-eyed, evil beyond imagination. Flanking him, on his right, Yog-Sothoth seethed behind his shielding globes, unglimpsed except in the iridescent mucous froth which dripped from him like pus; and to Cthulhu's left, there strode the bloated figure of Ithaqua the Wind-Walker, snatched here in an instant from Borea, beast-god of the frozen winds that howl forever between the worlds. And these were but a few . . .

They did not fly but seemed half-supported – suspended on the unbreakable strands of Atlach-Nacha's webs, which even now the spider-thing wove fast as the eye could follow across Elysia's drab skies. Yibb-Tstll was there, and Bugg-Shash, both of them close behind their cousin and master Yog-Sothoth; and Tsathoggua the toad crept apace with Cthulhu's shadow. Hastur, eternal rival of the dread Lord of R'lyeh, kept his distance from the main body of the procession, but still he was present, equally keen for revenge. Dagon cruised amid the icebergs of the now melting Frozen Sea, shattering ice floes as he came, and with him Mother Hydra and certain chosen members of the Deep Ones.

Shoggoths surged across the earth like formless towers of filth, while beneath it ran the steaming tunnels of Shudde-M'ell and his burrowers. And all of them converging on the Icelands, closing with the great glacier which housed Kthanid's immemorial palace.

And wherever they moved, each and every one of them brought destruction: sky-islands plummeted and cities went up in gouts of fire; aerial roadways were sliced through, sent crashing, and once golden forests roared into infernos. The waters of a blue, tropical ocean turned black in moments, and mountains long quiescent cracked open and spewed fire, smoke and stinking tephra . . .

'Hero?' said de Marigny dully, flinching from these scenes of destruction. 'I can write my name on . . . on *that*, and you call me a hero?'

Crow grasped his arm, said: 'Let me show you something else, my friend.' Again he touched the shewstone, his hand erasing the scenes of destruction and replacing them.

In the miles-long corridor of clocks, the last of Elysia's exotically diverse peoples and denizens filed into the remaining handful of time-clocks, which then blinked out of existence on this plane. In the Vale of Dreams the last N'hlathi centipede crawled into his life-support cannister, his own time-clock, and was gone from Elysia. With him, as with the rest of his race, he carried life-sustaining – life-assuring seeds of the great poppy, to sow in fresh, far distant fields. High over Elysia, where even now the Tind'losi Hounds streamed ravenously, the silver-sphere manse of Ardatha Ell – in which he had first come to Elysia – slowly faded to insubstantiality, seemed to disappear in drifting wraiths of coloured light. And in the Gardens of Nymarrah, there about the titan wine-glass shape of a Great Tree, a squadron of time-clocks hovered like bees, all perfectly synchronized. In another moment they, too, were gone – and the Great Tree with them. Only the mighty hole which an instant earlier had housed the Tree's taproot remained to show where he had stood.

'He would have been satisfied if we'd taken only his life-leaf,' said Titus Crow. 'Kthanid insisted we take the whole tree.'

'But ... where to?' de Marigny's mind was still reeling.

'Watch!' said Crow. He put his shoulder to the crystal, and as the three got out of the way toppled it from the table. It jarred, rang hollowly when it hit the floor, but it didn't break. Then it rolled ponderously across the floor of the dais, clanged down the steps and across the massively paved hall toward the several entranceways. There it finally came to rest, spun sluggishly for a moment and was still.

'Come on,' said Crow. He led the way down the steps to the time-clock. 'We're very nearly finished here,' he said, putting his hands on the clock's panelling. Then he smiled wryly, added, 'A million memories here, Henri.'

De Marigny couldn't believe it. He began to doubt Crow's sanity – maybe even his own. For in the midst of all this, Crow seemed completely calm, unpanicked. 'You're thinking of using the time-clock?' The Searcher said. 'But its controls have failed, energy all drained off.'

And Crow's smile was as wide as de Marigny had ever seen it. Incredibly, he suddenly seemed younger than ever! 'What, the old clock finished?' And slowly he shook his head. 'Oh, no, Henri. Even now he leeches warp-energy from Elysia's heart. See?' And sure enough, the familiar purple pulse was building in power, the enigmatic light from within streaming out as of old.

'But where can we go?' De Marigny grasped Crow's shoulders. 'Where? They followed me here – they can follow us anywhere!'

'They?' Crow's eyes narrowed. 'Ah, yes!'

It was then that the centuried odour of deep water hit them. That and the alien stench of things no ordered universe should ever contain. And into the vast hall, squeezing his bulk in under the arch of the main entranceway, came Cthulhu, the Lord of R'lyeh – now destroyer of Elysia. Behind him and from all quarters crowded the rest.

And there across the floor of the Great Hall of Crystal and Pearl, four human beings gazed into the very eyes of hell itself.

The tableau held, for a moment. Then –

Cthulhu's *mind* reached out, spoke three words, and in so doing paid humankind its greatest ever tribute:

CROW! that awesome, threatening thought rumbled like thunder in their minds. *AND DE MARIGNY!*

The tide of uttermost horror swayed forward – and Titus Crow, a man, held up a hand to stop it. For one and all they remembered, respected him, even though they would now, in the next moment, destroy him.

'Cthulhu!' he called across the sweep of the floor, his voice strong, unwavering. 'You came for Kthanid and the Elder Council and found only me. But Kthanid left you a message. It is written in his great crystal there.' And he pointed.

As the nightmare horde turned to observe the new scene now framed in the shewstone, so Crow whispered to his friends: 'Now, into the clock!'

Moreen and Exior obeyed at once, but de Marigny must see this out. He stood shoulder to shoulder with Titus Crow, and:

MESSAGE? WHAT MESSAGE? Cthulhu gazed rapaciously into the sphere. *I SEE ONLY ... CHAOS!*

'That's right!' Crow yelled, and his laughter rolled out to fill the Hall of Crystal and Pearl. 'It's the legend you brought with you when first you came, Cthulhu – don't you remember? You spoke a word, a Name, and worlds burst into flame. The crazed children of Azathoth destroyed themselves at your command, to light your coming. Isn't that how the story goes? And now you've used two more of these bereft nuclear beings to blast your path into Elysia. Aye, but there's one here who *knows* what you've done. One who doesn't fear you, who fears nothing. One who was satisfied simply to exist and serve, who now

677

is satisfied to sacrifice himself in the name of Sanity! Now *I* speak a word, a Name ... Can you not guess it, Cthulhu?'

The Lord of R'lyeh's octopus eyes bulged hideously, focussed on Kthanid's crystal, where a seething holocaust raged. And so intense his gaze that the shewstone shattered, spilled cold white liquid fire across the paved floor. As if in answer to which –

The floor bucked, heaved – crashed upward and open! Elysia reeled!

NAME? WHAT NAME?

The hell-horde could not be contained; they surged forward.

Crow balanced himself on the tilting, grinding floor, shoved de Marigny toward the clock. And:

'*Azathu!*' he cried. '*Azathu*, who has powered Elysia from the beginning – who was sane and sedated, kept that way by Kthanid – and who now takes his revenge, for his poor demented brothers' sake!'

NO! Cthulhu's mental croak of denial followed Crow even inside the time-clock. *NO, NO, NO!*

'Damn you, *yes*!' answered Titus Crow and de Marigny together. And together they piloted the clock a billion miles distant ...

The scanners showed the rest: an area of space-time warped and torn beyond recognition. A supernova to end *all* supernovas, one whose energy could not be contained in this continuum, and so flowed through into another. It brought into being the mightiest black hole ever to exist, which *itself* swallowed up the nuclear holocaust that made it. All that had been Elysia – and all it contained at the end – was sucked into the funnel of that hole and passed into the far, fabulous legend of The Beginning.

And as far as Crow and de Marigny had shifted the clock, still the waves of that massive disruption reached to them. The time-clock tumbled end over end in deepest night, slowly righted itself, warped back into normal space and time. Stars twinkled afar.

'What ... what the *hell* ... was that?' de Marigny finally found strength to ask.

Crow's voice was tiny as he answered. 'Creation, Henri. That was Creation ...'

Epilogue

After some little time, de Marigny said: 'Three questions, Titus – to which you'd better have the answers. Because if someone doesn't tell me the whys and wherefores of it, then I'll surely go out of my mind. I mean, I realize that I was used, that I was made a focus for *Their* attentions, some sort of decoy – and of course I knew that Cthulhu intended to take his revenge on Elysia, and that like me he therefore sought to discover its whereabouts – but *how* did he do it? How did he follow me through, him and all the rest? That's my first question.'

'Cthulhu knew all the angles,' Crow answered at once. 'I mean that literally, not in any sort of slang context. He had had billions of years to calculate the vectors. But it must be done in one fell swoop: all of the greater Beings of the Cthulhu Cycle brought through the gates at the same time.'

'Gates?'

'Yog-Sothoth's department,' said Crow with a nod. 'Yog-Sothoth knew the gates, he *was* the gates. The stars were coming right – made to come right by Cthulhu – when all restrictions would be lifted. Then for a period the Great Old Ones would be able to move at will through the space-time continuum, go wherever they wished to go. It was like that at the beginning – though by the time you have all your answers, "the beginning" as a phrase probably won't make a lot of sense any more. Didn't they come "seeping down from the stars ... not *in* the spaces we know but *between* them"? And don't we use our time-clocks to achieve the same sort of travel? Anyway, Yog-Sothoth, coexistent with all time and conterminous in all space, would be the guide, would show them the gates.

First they must strike at Elysia, remove all opposition. But in fact Elysia would be the only real opposition. As for the rest . . . a walkover.

'You were a decoy of a sort, yes. They knew you were coming through. It wasn't that you were cleverer than them, simply that in the end you would have Elysia's assistance. In the end you would be *directed*. And so they focussed on you. Oh, if they could they would kill you en route, certainly, for you were a great danger to them. You must be, for why else would Kthanid want you in Elysia? They would kill you in Borea, in the dreamlands, in Theem'hdra, wherever – if they could. In which case Kthanid would have relied on Ardatha Ell. That was Ardatha's other reason for being in Lith: to act as the lure if you . . . if you didn't make it. But the laws of probability said you *would* make it, and of course you did.

'So, when the stars came right – with Lith's termination – when space-time was warped and the gates were opened . . .'

Still de Marigny didn't understand. 'But they all came through together, physically en masse! Teleportation?'

'No,' Crow shook his leonine head, 'though certainly you can be forgiven for that wrong conclusion. It *looks* like teleportation, but it's a world apart. Even Kthanid can't teleport, and neither can Ardatha Ell. Riding their Great Thoughts is about as close as they can come. Likewise Cthulhu, except he uses Nyarlathotep.'

De Marigny nodded. 'I see. They were all in telepathic contact with one another at the moment the barriers went down.'

'Of course. When Lith blew and warped space-time, Cthulhu guided the Great Old Ones along the Vectors and Yog-Sohoth was there – as he is "everywhere" – to bring them through the gates. From there they could go anywhere they wanted to, but this was their main chance. *You* were going to Elysia. So they followed you.'

681

'That's my second question,' said de Marigny. 'Why Elysia? Couldn't I have been caused to guide them elsewhere? I sought for a dream only to see it shattered, to watch it turn into a nightmare ...'

For a moment a shadow passed over Crow's face. 'No,' he said then, 'it could only be Elysia. The destruction of Elysia was Cthulhu's greatest ambition. And after Elysia ... there'd be nothing left to stand in his way. It *had* to be Elysia, surely you can see that? Would you have had him start with the Earth and "clear it off"? Or with Borea? Or any of the civilized worlds and races you've visited?'

'No,' de Marigny shook his head, 'of course not. But that leads to my third question. I can't believe that we've finally destroyed them. Cthulhu and the Great Old Ones were, they are, and they always shall be. That's the way I'll always think of them. But if not dead, where?'

'Cthulhu, dead?' Crow shook his head. 'Oh, no, not dead, Henri, but only dreaming! Their misguided followers, some of their inexperienced progeny, their lesser minions – these can be destroyed. But not the Great Old Ones themselves. They're beyond death. Truly immortal. Their bodies regenerate, reform, renew themselves. But their minds, their memories, they *can* be damaged, erased! That was why they feared the Azathi: not for their destructiveness but their contamination, their contagion! And they were right to fear them, for now they have scars – mental scars, gaps, erasures – which will be a long time in the healing, Henri. Even billions of years ...'

Exior K'mool touched de Marigny's elbow. 'Do you recall, son of my most distant sons, what Ardatha Ell said of Kthanid: that he, too, was a miraculous mathematician? Cthulhu wasn't alone in his knowledge of the angles. No, and Yog-Sothoth didn't know *all* the gates. That final "gate" – the great black hole – that was the Completely Unknown ...'

De Marigny's mind suddenly reeled, somersaulted. He

looked at Exior and Crow and his jaw fell open. 'Dreaming but not dead,' he whispered. 'And that great black hole, a monstrous gateway into the past. *Into their own past!*'

Crow smiled.

'Titus,' said de Marigny, his mouth dry as dust, 'tell me, just exactly *where is* Kthanid? Where is he, and where the others of the Elder Council right now? Where – or when?'

'Ah!' said Crow. 'But that's your fourth question, my friend. And I won't answer it for I know you've already worked it out for yourself.'

De Marigny felt dizzy, feverish with the one gigantic notion spinning like a top in his head. 'Time is relative,' he whispered, more to himself than to the others. 'If anyone knows that, I do. In "the beginning" Cthulhu and the Great Old Ones "rose up against the Elder Gods and committed a crime so heinous ..." '

'Like ... the destruction of Elysia?' said Crow.

'... But the Elder Gods pursued them to punish them. And back there in the dim mists of time ... back there ... memories mostly erased ... they only remember their hatred of the Elder Gods and Elysia ... and ... and ... damn! *The whole thing is a cycle!*'

Crow clasped him by the shoulders. 'But haven't we always known that, Henri? Of course we have – it's the Cthulhu Cycle ...'

A long time later:

De Marigny came out of his mental torpor. He was still a little feverish, but Moreen was there to hold and kiss him. 'Where are we going?' he asked, when he was able.

'There's a world in Arcturus which is a jewel,' said Crow. 'Elysia's peoples are there right now. Tiania, too. They're building new lives for themselves, and for us.'

'But it isn't Elysia,' de Marigny's voice was flat, without flavour.

'It can be, my friend,' said Crow, helping him to his feet,

683

'it can be. In any case, I'm going there because my woman is there – but we don't have to stay. Elysia? I loved Elysia, Henri – but look out there.'

In the scanners, all the stars of space receded to infinity in all directions. 'Done, Henri,' said Titus Crow, 'a chapter closed. Or perhaps a new one started? And as I believe I've said to you before – '

'Wait,' said de Marigny, no longer The Searcher. His smile was still wan, but at least there was feeling in it now. 'Let me say it this time,' he said. 'Damn it all, it has to be my turn *this* time:

'Worlds without end, Titus – worlds without end!'